No. 1.   32 Pages.   Price One Penny.

THE SLAPCRASH BOYS.

The Liveliest of School Stories.

"DID YOU EVER SEE THE LIKES O' THAT, ANYWHERES?"

THE SLAPCRASH BOYS.

The Liveliest of School Stories.

"WAIT UNTIL I AM SETTLED INTO IT," DICK COCKLES SAID.

No. 1.　　　　　　　　　　　　　　　　　　　Price One Penny.

THE SLAPCRASH BOYS.

The Liveliest of School Stories.

CHAPTER I.

THE PLAYGROUND OF SLAPCRASH SCHOOL—A NEW ARRIVAL—WHAT IS THE MYSTERY?—A DARK CHALLENGE AND VALIANT BEARING OF DICK COCKLES.

"As I live," said Dick Cockles, "if there isn't another lamb brought here to be slaughtered."

Dick Cockles was one of the pupils under the care of a Mr. Benjamin Slapcrash, a pedagogue with peculiar ideas, as you shall presently see, who lived in the old cathedral town of Smockley.

The above remark was made from the summit of a wall of the limited playground, from where Dick had a view of the High-street and the front door of Slapcrash Academy.

Dick had been hoisted up to his elevated position by Tom Biron, the strongest boy in the school, who, however, did not attempt to continue to support him, and had no intention of easing him down.

"What sort of fellow is he?" asked Tom.

"I'll tell you in a minute," replied Dick, hurriedly, as he began to slip down. "Here! catch hold of me some of you—Oh!"

He came down and alighted on the ground in the form of the capital letter L, and the shock of his fall deprived him for a few moments of the power of speech.

The interval was made use of by a tall, lanky boy of fifteen, who struck a tragic attitude, and elevating his right arm, exclaimed: "Mark how he fell—an' it were ever thus. Say that the gifted Dickey, whose father is thane of a thriving pork and sausage business, should in the chances of life be hurled from a balloon, he would fall upon that part of his anatomy nature intended him to sit upon."

"Oh! you dry up," grunted Dick, who had got his breath again, and rose up stiffly from the ground. "Whatever happens you must cut in with your gibberish."

"Well, what's the fellow like?" asked Tom, impatiently; "does he look as if he had any go in him? Could he take a licking from Slapcrash without winking?"

"He's a good-looking chap," said Dick, "and solemn-looking, and— Here he is."

There were about a dozen lads in the playground, comprising the whole school, and every eye was turned upon a man and a boy who entered the playground from the school.

The man was tall, raw-boned, hard-featured, and with a dry smile, without which his face was never seen.

It was put on record by Jem Stager that the smile was "a thing he slept in," but this cannot, without further evidence, be accepted as a fact.

Anyhow, there the smile remained during his waking hours, and the curious part of it was that nobody, not even a stranger, ever for a moment accepted it as indicative of inward joy or mirth.

It was the smile of a stone figure.

We have no desire to be unjust to Mr. Benjamin Slapcrash. He was one of the old school, who believed in the rod and Spartan treatment.

"The harder the boy-life the better the man will be," was his motto.

How it acted on his pupils we shall soon see.

The boy with him was about the age and height of Jem Stager, and although not spare in form, he had a look which suggested that a great deal of his young life had been spent at his mother's apron string.

He need not be the worse for that, provided his mother did not coddle him like a baby, but he seemed to be rather shy, without being stupidly bashful, and he stood quietly by the side of the schoolmaster as he introduced him.

"Boys," said Benjamin Slapcrash, "I have the pleasure of introducing to you another companion, Warren Fane. Biron, you can tell him the rules of the house. They are very simple."

Without anything more in the way of introductory ceremony, Benjamin Slapcrash retreated, and Warren Fane was left to the tender mercies of his new friends.

As usual, they crowded round him, and Tom Biron, on behalf of the whole school, shook him by the hand.

Then Dick Cockles came to the front.

"I say, Fane," he said, standing with his legs wide apart, and his hands in his pockets, "what crib have you come from?"

"Excuse me," replied Fane, in a soft, melodious voice, "but I do not quite understand you."

"Well, what school did you patronise before this one?" asked Dick.

"I have never been anywhere," replied Fane.

"Jiminy!" exclaimed Dick, with a low whistle; "he's just out of the nursery."

"I will ask you not to be impertinent," said Fane, serenely. "If you are I shall pull your ears."

"You pull my ears," exclaimed Dick, looking around him in amazement. "Here, do you know who I am?"

"It does not matter who you are," returned Fane. "I do not intend to put up with insolence."

"Perhaps I can ask you a question?"

"Oh! yes, there is no harm in that. I am not bound to answer, of course."

"Most boys do," said Dick.

"I know very little of boys," was the answer.

Dick appeared to be getting nonplussed, but as he was the accepted cross-examiner of new pupils he felt bound to go on.

"You've got a father, haven't you?" he said.

"I don't know," replied Fane.

Dick lifted up his left leg and scratched it, to ease his perturbed mind.

"Mother alive?" he asked.

"I don't know," Fane replied.

"Brother and sisters? I know you've got some," Dick said, desperately.

"If I have I have not seen them," Fane rejoined.

"But you know whether you have any or not?"

"No, I do not, I assure you."

"Where have you been living?" asked Dick, his hair upright with disappointment. "Come, you can tell me that."

"No, I cannot," answered Fane.

"Why not?"

"Because I do not choose to do so."

"So you won't tell us anything about yourself?" said Dick, like a learned counsel addressing a contumacious witness.

"Certainly not," replied Fane. "You shall know just as much about me as you can find out, and no more."

"That won't do, Fane," Biron struck in; "you mustn't treat us like that."

"I don't feel that I am at liberty to talk about myself," replied Fane, "and if you do not like it, I must put up with the consequences."

"You will be sent to Coventry," threatened Dick Cockles.

"Your life," said Jem Stager, with a portentous wave of his arm, "will be a curse. You will be as one out in the wilderness. The crows will come and pick your bones."

"Oh! cut that short," interrupted Tom Biron, impatiently, "and finish him off by handing him over to Dickey's father to make into sausages."

"I wish you would leave the sausage shop alone," said Dick, with an injured air; "you fellows never refuse to peck into them when I get a pound or two from home, I notice."

"The sausage, deepest of human mysteries," interpolated Jem Stager, "is not to be despised after the Spartan fare of this blessed crib, but at the same time, Dick, you must admit it is natural, when bits of tobacco pipe and fragments of leather are seen lurking within the recesses of the skins, for some of us to try and find out what we are eating."

"All right," exclaimed the exasperated Dick Cockles; "the next lot that comes I'll eat myself. Now Fane—"

But Warren Fane had walked away with Tom Biron by his side, and it was apparent that the latter was expostulating with the new pupil on the position he had taken up.

"I wonder why he should be so close," said Dick, after a stare at the pair.

"Something disgraceful in the family," replied a piping voice close to his ear.

"Oh! you are sure to arrive at something complimentary," said Dick, facing round; "it wouldn't be Sam Fusby if there was anything kind in the notion."

Sam Fusby was a boy who might have been sixteen by his height, but who had the general physique of one three years younger.

In addition to a spare and rather ill-shapen frame, he had a mean face, with a pair of restless eyes, that were for the most part employed in furtive glances or looking on the ground.

Sam Fusby had never been known to look anyone straight in the face.

"People don't conceal things they are proud of," Fusby retorted.

"In that case," said Dick, "we ought to take the trouble to hide you. Hullo! what's that?"

A shrill whistle in the street outside was heard, followed by a rough voice bawling out a sort of challenge.

"Now then, you Slapcrash duffers, ain't any of you coming out to be licked?"

"That's Jerry Bott, the sweep," said Dick; "hoist me up, some of you. I'll take the cheek out of him."

"Roll over and smash him," returned Jem Stager, as he gave Dick the required leg-up.

"Steady!" said Dick, as his head got level with the top of the wall; "don't hoist me up too high. They may have half a brick ready for us."

With the discretion that is admitted to be essential to true valour, Dick slowly got his eyes into a position to see into the street below.

There he beheld a pugnacious-looking young sweep, accompanied by half-a-dozen hobbledehoy roughs, all on the grin.

Seeing that none of them bore a brick or stone for hurling purposes, Dick boldly pulled himself up and leant his arms on the wall.

"What do you cads want?" he asked.

"Come out and fight," replied Jerry Bott, ferociously.

"Yes, come out and fight," chorussed the others.

"You know we can't," returned Dick, "and that's why you are whistling and howling here. Come over into this ground and we will make mincemeat of you."

"Say sausage meat," hinted Jem Stager.

"I wish you would be quiet," pleaded Dick, "and don't keep wriggling so or you will let me down. Now, Bott, are you coming over?"

"Come out here, you lot of worms," returned the sweep. "Yah! there isn't an ounce of fight in the whole school."

"All right!" said Dick, "you can talk now —now—Jem—oh!"

Dick was down again in the old position, shaken as before, and very wrathful.

Jem and the other boys were inconsistent enough to laugh.

"Just like you," said Dick, when he was able to speak, "and only listen to that lot outside. It's the laugh there that riles me."

"Swee-up!" yelled Jerry Bott.

"Cock-a-doodle-do!" crowed one of his companions.

These derisive sounds were followed by a smart shower of pebbles and street refuse thrown over the wall.

Then the shuffling of several feet revealed that the derisive callers were going away.

"That Jerry Bott has been cheeky for a long time," said Dick, as he got up and dusted his nether garments, "and somebody will have to take it out of him."

"That somebody won't be you," returned Jem Stager.

"I don't know so much."

"He's a head taller than you."

"What's a head against pluck and science?" demanded Dick, as he went through a variety of contortions supposed by him to be illustrative of the high art of pugilism.

"When you meet him," said Jem Stager, impressively, "let your watchword be a prompt retreat. Don't flutter your banners in the breeze before such a foe."

Dick opened his mouth to make a reply, indicative of his contempt for any foes, but at that moment the school-bell rang.

The dinner hour was over, and the boys were called to resume the duties necessary for their after-life welfare, but just then decidedly distasteful and emphatically a bore.

———

CHAPTER II.

NIGHT IN THE SCHOOL—NO HAMPER, BUT CURRENT COIN FORTHCOMING—A VOLUNTEER FOR A PERILOUS TASK—GREAT WAS THE FALL THEREOF—WHERE IS DICK COCKLES?

NIGHT had come, and the boys were upstairs, where they all slept in one large dormitory. Mr. Benjamin Slapcrash was known to be away on his usual evening visit to the White Hart, where he discussed stout and bitter and politics, and Mrs. Slapcrash, a lady of chronic delicate constitution, was supposed to be in bed with the toothache.

None of the boys had undressed, as yet, although their candle had been taken away by the cook, but darkness had no terrors for them.

It was, in fact, not dark, for they had the blind up and the window open.

There was also a full moon in the summer sky.

The window looked upon the garden, which adjoined the playground, and admission to the street was to be gained through a wooden door in the high wall.

This door was always kept locked, but the

lock was of that class which a skewer skilfully applied would open, and every boy of Slapcrash School knew the trick of it.

Warren Fane sat on the side of his bed slowly unlacing his boots. Among the other boys there was inactivity and a constrained silence.

It was broken by Dick Cockles.

"It's the usual thing, you know, Fane," he said.

"What is the usual thing?" Warren asked.

"Everybody brings a hamper with him, and there's a general blow out on the first night of his arrival," replied Dick.

"I did not know it," said Fane, quietly, "but, of course, if I had heard of it you should have had a big hamper."

"That's well spoken," said Dick, "but words are poor wittles, as my father's head shopman says."

"Verbal utterances are not akin to sausages, pork or beef," murmured Jem Stager, dreamily. "My goodness, what is a poor supper of limited bread and cheese to a hungry growing boy?"

"If there is any money to be had," hinted Dick, "somebody could go out and get something."

"Oh! if money will do," returned Warren Fane, "I am ready to put down half-a-sovereign."

"Well said, Warren," clamoured the boys, in an undertone, and their boots were beaten softly on the floor by way of approval.

"Stop that row," said Tom Biron, "or we shall have Mrs. Slapcrash here to see who is in bed and who out of it."

"I'm ready to go," remarked Dick, "if you will lower me in a sheet—half way, say. It's too far to drop with half-a-pint of Slapcrash's table beer inside me. I don't know what it is made of, but it always makes a balloon of me."

"There's the money," said Warren Fane, "and you can do as you like with it."

"Here's the sheet," observed Jem Stager, whipping the top one off his bed. "Biron will help me to lower you, Dick."

"Very well," replied Dick, "only mind how you do it. If I'm dropped to-night I feel that I shall go off with a bang."

The sheet was lowered out of the window, Jem Stager holding one end and Tom Biron the other.

They made a sort of hammock of it, into which Dick Cockles got with great care.

"Wait until I am settled into it," he said, as he grasped the sheet in his arms and drew it close to him; "and when I say 'all right,' one of you let go. I shall then drop gently to the ground."

Nothing could be nicer or more complete than these arrangements, and the lowering began.

As Dick was rather solidly made, great care had to be exercised, and they let him down inch by inch.

When Dick had got about a foot down, Fusby, who stood behind the rest, suddenly broke the thrilling silence with which the lowering operation was being watched.

"Somebody's coming upstairs," he whispered, "and it's a woman's footstep."

"Here, Dick," said Jem Stager, "you must come back."

But letting him down and hauling him up were two different things.

When, as had happened on rare occasions before, one of the boys had gone into the town at night, on returning he usually made use of a short ladder that was kept in the garden.

The schoolmaster rarely went into the garden at all, and Mrs. Slapcrash only walked there when the weather was very fine.

Everything favoured these late excursions, and there was only the off-chance of being discovered by somebody in the house.

That discovery was now impending.

Somebody was really coming upstairs.

"You must drop down, Dick, and hide somewhere for a few moments," gasped Jem, after two or three frantic efforts to get the solid youth back again. "Now, Biron, quick!"

"I'm not ready—easy, will you," muttered Dick, struggling; "bother it—oh!"

A hand was on the bedroom door, and Jem let go.

Down went Dick, and the smack of his fall was heard in the room like the application of the flat side of a cleaver to a round of beef.

Dick did not groan or cry out, simply because he could not.

It was his third heavy fall that day, and it fairly staggered him inside and out.

The other boys dived into bed, as Jem Stager would have said, all accoutred as they were, and the door of the room was opened a few inches.

"What is that noise you are making?" asked a weak voice, the property of Mrs. Slapcrash.

Nobody answered, and Jem Stager got up a gentle snore.

"Oh! you are not asleep, I know," said Mrs. Slapcrash, "and I could prove it if it were proper for me to come in. You had better be quiet, you wicked boys—Mr. Slapcrash will be home directly."

As before, there was no answer, and Jem did another snore, which seemed to excite the risible faculties of the rest, for sundry half-smothered gurgling sounds and chuckles were heard under cover of the bedclothes.

"How dare you laugh at me?" asked Mrs. Slapcrash, angrily; "first you wake me up by rattling your boots on the floor, and then, when I come up to beg of you to be quiet, you laugh at me. I shall tell Mr. Slapcrash of it as soon as he returns."

Having uttered this threat, no idle one, the irate lady closed the door with a sharp jerk, and beat a retreat.

One of the boys' heads emerged from the bedclothes, and after listening for a few moments, Jem Stager whispered—

"She's gone."

"I told you boys not to make such a row," said Tom Biron; "sleeping right under us she was bound to hear it."

"Oh! it doesn't matter," returned a boy named Dan Mittens; "if we are not being licked for one thing we are for another. It's the old game."

"The good old ancient order of things," murmured Jem Stager, as he slowly slipped off the bed; "now let us see what has become of Dick."

He went to the window and looked out, when he saw Dick in a kneeling position, carefully feeling the parts of his anatomical structure likely to be injured by the fall.

"Are you hurt, old man?" he softly whispered.

Dick looked up, and the moonlight falling on his interesting countenance revealed the fact that it was suffused with dire exasperation.

"That's a nice question, ain't it?" he grunted. "I don't believe I've got a whole bone in my body."

"Oh! come, old man, it's not so bad as that."

"Anyhow, I'm broke somewhere, and I feel as if I'd been sitting on something red hot."

"Swift reaction always follows a blow, hence the pain," said Jem. "For full particulars run your eye over Joyce's scientific dialogues."

"I'd like to run my fist over your nose," grunted Dick; "what did you let go for?"

"Mrs. Slapcrash came up to know why we were making such a row," replied Jem.

Dick muttered something and got upon his feet.

Then he again felt that part of his body which had come into collision with Mother Earth.

"If I haven't broken any bones," he said, "I'm one big bruise. I shall have an extra bit of the tuck-out over this job."

"You shall have what you like," said Jem, soothingly, "only get along and fetch the prog."

Dick limped off towards the garden gate, stopping every few yards to re-examine himself, evidently not sure that he was in a whole condition, but he got to the gate at last, and in a few seconds had it open.

The boys saw him cautiously put his head out and look up and down the street.

Then he went through and pulled the door softly behind him.

"He's not hurt," said Jem Stager, as he turned back into the room, "and that's put my mind at ease. I was afraid he had met with a serious accident or was killed outright."

"It isn't far to fall," sneered Sam Fusby.

"It is too far for you, I should say," replied Tom Biron, "as we have never been able to get you to risk the job."

"I don't think it right," said Sam Fusby, sullenly.

"No, everything is wrong with you," replied Tom Biron, "and that is why you are always right with Slapcrash; but remember this—if you peach on to-night's business I will give you such a hiding as you never had before."

"It doesn't follow because things are found out that I peach," grumbled Sam.

"No, it's difficult to really get at what you do," said Tom Biron, "but Mr. Slapcrash somehow gets to know a lot of things which can only be told him by one of ourselves. If he hears of this I shall reckon it's you, and act accordingly."

Sam Fusby muttered something between his teeth, and laid down on his bed. Warren Fane, who was lying at full length outside the bedclothes, with his arms above his head, asked—

"What's the punishment if we are found out?"

"A licking all round," Tom Biron answered.

"I hope he won't attempt to lick me," said Warren.

"But he will. He licks us all."

"I don't think I could stan ! it."

"Ah!" returned Tom Biron, drily, "that is because you don't know the man you have to deal with. If he makes up his mind to give you a licking, you will get it as sure as the sun will shine somewhere to-morrow."

"We shall see," observed Warren, quietly.

"Slapcrash believes a licking is a good thing for a boy," Tom Biron went on. "I don't say that he means to be cruel, or enjoys it as some schoolmasters do, but it is part of his teaching creed."

"Tell him about Will Staunton," interposed Jem Stager; "give him an outline of that short but striking drama."

"Perhaps it won't interest you, Fane?" Biron said.

"Oh! yes, it will!" observed Warren; "all this sort of thing is fresh to me. It is a new life revealed. Go on."

"Will Staunton," began Tom Biron, "was a tall fellow, almost a man in looks though a boy in years, when he came here last November. He had a way of carrying himself high—a sort of touch-me-if-you-dare style—and when we first talked to him of getting a licking he said he would not take one."

"He even said he would kill Slapcrash if he touched him," interposed Jem Stager.

"That was a bit of bounce," continued Tom Biron, "although he really thought that he could hold his own in a row with Slapcrash. Well, the next day he did something, I forget what it was—"

"Whistled in school hours," observed Sam Fusby.

"Oh! of course you know," retorted Tom Biron. "Yes, he was softly whistling while he was looking over his lessons, and Slapcrash, hearing the sound, looked round the room for the culprit."

"At first he thought it was me," interrupted Jem Stager.

"Hold your row, will you?" said Tom Biron. "Anyway, he did not lick you, but seeing that Will's mouth was screwed up he came softly round, got behind him, and laid the cane across his back as hard as he could."

"Which is about as hard as any man can do it," remarked Dan Mittens, with a sympathetic wriggle.

"I sat facing Will," Tom Biron went on, "and I saw the fury leap into his eyes as the cane fell. 'Don't do that again,' he said, wheeling sharply round. Slapcrash seized hold of his collar, and then the struggle began."

"Ye gods! and a Titanic struggle it was," Jem Stager interposed.

"Will was as strong a fellow of his years as I ever knew," continued Tom Biron, after a minute's pause, "but he was a child in the hands of Slapcrash. The man must have muscles of steel. He turned him this way and that, and he beat Will as if he had been a sack of sawdust, until I saw the perspiration of terror break out all over the poor boy's face. He asked for mercy and then the caning came to an end."

"He was broken, I suppose?" said Warren Fane.

"Completely," replied Tom Biron, "and although he did not shed a tear, I could see that he suffered tortures for hours afterwards."

"What did his friends say to it?" asked Warren Fane.

"We don't make complaints to our friends," replied Biron, drily.

"No, I suppose not," returned Warren, quietly. "But what became of Staunton?"

"He went away that night and has never been heard of since."

Although the end of the story was nothing new to the boys, the hushed silence in the room showed that it was not yet deprived of it startling effect.

To Warren Fane it seemed to come like a galvanic shock.

"Not heard of since?" he slowly said, breaking the silence.

"No," returned Tom Biron; "he got out of that window when we were asleep, and went away. I think his pride was hurt more than his body, and after being so severely beaten he was ashamed to look us in the face again."

"Poor fellow," observed Warren; "wasn't there any disturbance about it?"

"Oh! yes," said Biron. "His friends came —father, mother, and an uncle. Slapcrash told his own story, and I believe it was fairly truthful. We were not called upon to make any statement, but I heard his father say that Will had always been a dogged, determined boy. They went away, and we never heard any more of him or them, but I've always had an idea that Will will turn up again one day."

The end of the narrative was followed by some desultory talk about canings in general, and two or three of the boys dwelt with some force on their own particular experiences in this matter.

Presently a church clock near struck the hour of ten.

JERRY BOTT GETTING READY TO SMASH A SLAPCRASHER.

"Dick ought to be back," said Jem Stager.

He again went to the window and looked out, but there were no signs of their companion nor of any living thing except an old tom cat on the prowl.

"What a stupid chump he is," muttered Jem Stager.

"Perhaps he's been taken bad," suggested Sam Fusby.

"You might be taken bad with slipper fever," returned Jem, "if you don't keep quiet."

"You talk enough for two," observed Fusby, defiantly. "You slipper me and I'll make an awful row."

"All right, my tulip," retorted Jem, "in the sweet by-and-bye I'll wait upon you. There is a tide in the affairs of boys that, taken at

Jerry Bott after the smashing.

the flood, leads on to lickings. I wonder what's become of Dick?"

And they all wondered in vain.

The time crawled slowly, never so slowly before to some of the boys, and another hour passed by.

The church clock struck eleven.

"Here's a go," said Tom Biron. "Dick's got into some mess or other."

"I'm so glad," chuckled Fusby; "he's a little beast."

Jem Stager rose up in his wrath and walked over to the side of Sam Fusby's bed.

"What did you say?" he asked.

"You touch me," returned Fusby, sullenly, "and I'll yell murder."

Jem Stager was in the humour to risk that much, and he made a grab at Fusby, who rolled across the bed and fell on to the floor.

"Let him alone," said Tom Biron, testily;

"settle with him to-morrow, for I hear Slapcrash at the door."

In Smockley the inns closed at eleven, and Mr. Benjamin Slapcrash had, by the force of the laws of his country, been driven out with other mild bacchanalians from the White Hart.

He was a moderate man, never returning home in a state that confounds one end of the latchkey with the other, but little as was the noise he made, Tom's quick ear heard him.

The schoolmaster, after lingering below to secure the front door and look to the fastenings of the windows, came slowly upstairs.

The boys, awake and watchful, listened to his heavy footstep with a sensation akin to that Jack of the Beanstalk must have felt when he heard the step of the giant on the stairs.

The fact is, they were all a little unstrung.

Dick's long absence, and the eagerness with which they had looked and hoped for his coming, had not been without its due effect on their nerves.

CHAPTER III.

MR. SLAPCRASH MAKES A PROMISE—DICK IN THE TOWN—A SOOTY ENCOUNTER, WITH AN AWKWARD TERMINATION.

THE boys could hear the movements of the schoolmaster with terrible distinctness in the silence of the night.

As he opened the door of his bedroom they heard the querulous voice of his wife, and although they could not catch exactly what she said, the boys knew that she had at once laid her complaint against them before her lord and master.

If any doubts were entertained on this score they were speedily dispelled by the door of the bedroom below being opened again, and the voice of Benjamin Slapcrash, announcing his intention of going upstairs, was heard.

"I'll see if they are asleep yet," he said, "and if they are not—"

No more was heard, but he came up softly, having changed his boots for slippers.

The boys, still in their day clothes, had no resource but to get into bed again, just as they were, and chance what followed.

Jem Stager saw the light under the door, and got ready to perpetrate his unrivalled snore, although he had little hope of deceiving the astute schoolmaster.

The door of the room was thrown open and Mr. Slapcrash entered.

He held in his hand a paraffin lamp, which he raised above his head, and quietly scanned the beds one after the other.

"I see," he said, in a cold, hard tone, "none of you are undressed. This is a wilful and deliberate infringement of my rules. To-morrow we will confer on the subject."

He walked out, closing the door behind him, and in the frozen stillness of the room they could hear his soft footfall as he descended.

"He didn't miss Dick, that is some relief," said Jem Stager. "But what a warm day it will be to-morrow!"

"We shall see what Fane will do," observed Tom Biron, "for a licking all round there is sure to be."

"Hush! I hear a voice," whispered Jem. "It is our own Dick, the joy of my heart."

It was Dick, and he was below the window, making efforts to get the ladder up.

But the task was too much for him. He appeared to be very weak, quite worn out, in fact.

"Somebody must come and help me," he whispered, hoarsely.

Dan Mittens was a breakneck sort of lad, and he volunteered to drop to the ground and give Dick the assistance he stood in need of.

He could come back by the ladder, as Dick would, so he swung himself out of the window, and went down with a rush.

Dick would have fallen on the flat of his back, but Dan, cat-like, lit upon his feet.

"What's up, old chap?" he said; "you look pretty well done for."

"Wait till I get into the room," replied Dick.

They put the ladder close to the window, and Dick went slowly up, Dan following. Then Tom Biron ran a piece of cord round the top stave of the ladder and lowered it.

As soon as it touched the ground he let go one end of the cord and drew it in.

All this was done in a few moments, and without making any sound likely to raise an alarm.

Having closed the window he said—

"Get out our bit of candle, Jem, and let us have the feed—I am beastly hungry."

"You can't have any feed," said Dick.

"Why not?"

"Because there's nothing to eat!"

A chilly silence rested for a moment on the whole room. It was broken by Warren Fane.

"Did you lose the money?" he asked; "if you did it is of no consequence—you can have some more to-morrow."

"I did not lose it," replied Dick, miserably; "I spent it all in jam tarts, and sausage rolls, and other stuff."

"Then sat down and ate them," interposed Sam Fusby.

"I'll punch your head to-morrow for that," said Dick; "eat 'em—no— I was coming back as quick as I could when I ran against that beast, Jerry Bott. I shouldn't have got so near, but he'd washed his face, and I didn't know him until he spoke."

"Of course he recognised you?" observed Jem.

"He did," said Dick, seriously; "and before I knew what he was up to he had me by the collar.

"'Hullo, young 'un!' he says; 'where do you think you are going at this time of night?'

"'Never you mind,' said I; 'you leave go of me.'

"'What are them packages?' he asks.

"'Boots to mend,' says I.

"I was just going to give him a shinner, although I would rather have had an up and down fist fight with him," continued Dick, "when up came three or four of his pals, and they all wanted to know what was the matter. Jerry Bott tells them, and they all laughed."

"They took the tarts, of course?" asked Jem, who wanted to get at the vital part of the story.

"Wait a moment," returned Dick. "It was in Mulberry-street where he spotted me—close to those old empty cellars—and I'm blessed if they didn't all set on me and run me down there—and they took me—"

"Took you!" echoed Tom.

"Dragged me, as good as gagged and bound, to a cellar at the far end, where they pushed me in and shut the door. Jerry Bott struck a light, and then I saw that it was a place they were in the habit of using."

"Regularly furnished, I suppose?" observed Sam Fusby, sarcastically; "what sort of curtains had they to the windows—chintz or lace?"

"Perhaps you don't believe what I am telling you?" said Dick.

"No, I don't," replied Sam.

"Ah! We will talk that over to-morrow," rejoined Dick.

"Don't heed him," observed Biron, "but

get along—it's no use keeping us awake all night when there's nothing to eat."

"They had straw in the place," said Dick, "several stools, a table, two old candlesticks, and an egg chest, which Jerry Bott said was his seat. He also said he was the captain of the Brothers of Blood, the Gory Avenger of Smockley, and he told me straight that if ever I put the coppers on his trail that I should die as sure as eggs is eggs."

"Nice boy, this Jerry Bott," observed Warren Fane, drily.

"He's close on a man in years, I believe," said Tom Biron, "although he calls himself a boy. Get along, Dick."

"After they had all sworn to have my life if I betrayed them," Dick resumed, "they laid hold of the tarts and things and ate all they could, saying they were the spoils of war and the avengers' due. Then when they could not eat any more they gave me my share."

"I thought as much," interposed Sam Fusby, "blessed if I didn't."

"My share," resumed Dick, sternly and emphatically, "was two sausage rolls, three jam tarts, and a beef pie."

"You did not do so badly then," Tom rather grievously observed.

"Wait till I've done," said Dick. "The sausage rolls they rubbed all over my head and into my eyes and ears, the jam tarts they put into my pockets and squashed, and then they took off my boots, put bits of the beef pie into them, and pulled them on again.

"'You will find it better than cork socks,' said that beast, Jerry Bott, and I've got it there now. I've also got no end of crumbs down my back, and am all over a beastly mess of jam tart and sausage roll."

Dick paused, uttering a deep sigh.

His gloomy narrative had had a chilling and an exasperating effect upon the listeners, for Jerry Bott was their hated foe, and of late had pursued a victorious course, riding rough-shod over them.

"When they had done all that," Dick continued, "they brought out knotted handkerchiefs and bits of rope likewise knotted, and told me that it was a rule of the Brothers of Blood to larrup all intruders out of the town, and to kill 'em if they offered any resistance."

"My eye!" exclaimed Dan Mittens, "you have had a night of it."

"I sha'n't forget it," returned Dick, "until I stand straddle-legged over the cold corpse of Jerry Bott, and afterwards I'll burn him in a bag of his own soot. Wait! Where was I?"

"They were going to escort you out of the town," observed Jem Stager, putting the case as mildly as he could.

"Oh! yes," said Dick, "they did escort me. They chivied me right away to Barker's mill, where they told me to go home by the marshes and the dykes, and that if I tried to get back by the road I should find them waiting for me. So you may guess what a high time of it I've had. But here I am at last."

"Poor old Dick," observed Tom Biron; "but never mind, we'll wait on these Brothers of Blood."

"I hope so," Dick returned, with a moan; "but we won't talk any more about it to-night, as I am pretty well done up, and shall be glad to get to sleep."

As this was a general desire, nobody demurred, and five minutes afterwards the boys had lost all their cares in sound repose.

CHAPTER IV.

MR. BENJAMIN SLAPCRASH SHOWS HOW HE KEEPS HIS WORD—TOM BIRON IS SENT INTO THE TOWN AND ENCOUNTERS A SWORN FOE.

MOST of the boys slept until the warning morning bell aroused them from sleep.

Then they opened their eyes together, as if moved by clockwork, and simultaneously the same thought flashed through the brains of the majority—

"This is going to be a very warm day."

In the excitement of the previous night, being fairly worn out, Dick Cockles had gone to bed all jammy and sausaged as he was, and the result was appalling.

His interesting countenance had left records on the pillow-case that only the most energetic washing would be able to get out.

"Well, I'm blessed," he said, as he sat up and looked at it; "couldn't any of you fellows give me a hint to wash before I went to sleep?"

"We did not think of it," replied Dan Mittens.

"I shall have a nice time of it," groaned Dick.

They rolled out of bed, and, in accordance with their Spartan training, put on their trousers and slippers and went downstairs to wash.

Provision for morning ablutions was made in an outhouse adjoining the kitchen, where there was a tap, sundry metal basins, and two endless towels on rollers.

"This is a nice arrangement," said Warren Fane, looking round him in disgust.

"Only temporary," observed Dick Cockles, buoyantly; "old Slapcrash is going to invest fifty pounds in china chamber sets."

"Is he?" said a deep and dreaded voice, as Slapcrash appeared in the doorway.

He had a cane in his hand, and his eye betrayed the dismal fact that he meant business.

It was decidedly artful of him to come down and catch the boys so lightly attired, and after a few words about their evil sitting-up propensities, he proceeded to "turn on the torture," as Jem Stager expressed it.

He went all round, beginning with Dick Cockles and finishing with Sam Fusby, who w s the only boy who howled.

And he not only howled, but begged for mercy.

One boy was not touched.

And that one was Warren Fane.

Mr. Benjamin Slapcrash went up to him, and their eyes met with a steady stare.

"Fane," said the schoolmaster, "you are new to the rules, and I attach no importance to your share of last night's doings, but in future I shall hold you responsible."

Warren Fane made no answer, but he smiled slightly as Mr. Benjamin Slapcrash, a little tired with his early morning exercise, hurried away.

"This world's turned upside down," said Jem Stager, who was rubbing his thighs to ease his anguish. "Slapcrash has positively let Warren Fane off. He never did such a thing before."

"'Twas just as well he did," observed Warren.

"What would you have done?" asked Tom Biron.

"I don't know," was the quiet reply; "but it might have been something to be remembered."

"Oh! that's bragging," observed Sam Fusby.

"I have not bragged," replied Warren Fane, "that's not in my line."

"Put his head under the tap," said Dick Cockles.

"You do it," retorted Fusby.

Dick went for him at once, and they closed.

Fusby was the stronger and taller boy, but he lacked the grit that fully utilises strength and height to the utmost.

Dick got his head in the sink, and was going to turn on the tap when another bell rang.

"Breakfast in ten minutes," cried Jem. "Drop that, Dick."

A scampering ensued, and after a hasty wash the boys scuttled upstairs. They were finishing their toilets as the bell rang again.

After that they had two minutes' grace, and the boys who came late were locked out.

That was one way of teaching them punctuality.

Two-thirds of the boots put under the table that morning were either imperfectly laced or not done up at all.

The dining-room of Slapcr sh School was a dingy apartment, with no more furniture in it than was absolutely necessary.

By way of pictures, two maps, prodigiously fly-spotted, hung upon the walls. The one window was at the top end of the room, where Mr. Slapcrash sat mute for the most part, and in the matter of countenance was as inscrutable as the Sphinx.

Weak tea and thick bread and butter, the bread decidedly and unduly predominating, was the fare, but poor as it was all did justice to it.

People young or old who go to bed hungry are usually ready for breakfast in the morning.

Twenty minutes was allowed for the meal, and after that there was an hour in the playground if fine, as it happened to be on this occasion.

While the boys were making the most of this relaxation the cry of "swee-up" was heard outside.

No notice was taken of it, so it was followed by jeering laughter and an inquiry if "they had any tarts to throw away."

"Let him go on," said Dick Cockles. "I shall take that Brother of Blood in hand before long, and then I will put a colour about his eyes that won't wash out for a week."

This terrible threat was not received with any signs of alarm. On the contrary, most of the boys laughed.

Warren Fane asked Tom Biron why this recalcitrant sweep selected the school as his pet aversion.

"He's the bully of the town," Tom replied. "Boys, big and little, go about in terror of him. He's cock of the walk at present."

"Have you ever had a turn-up with him?" Warren asked.

"Nothing worth speaking of," Biron

answered; "he has always such a rowdy crew with him that the prospect of a fair fight isn't good enough."

"I can't use my fists worth speaking of," said Warren; "but I should like to learn."

"To go for the sweep," returned Tom, laughing.

"Yes, that's the idea."

"I can box a bit. Come to this corner, out of sight of the windows of the house, and I will teach you the rudiments of the noble art."

Tom Biron was really a very fair boxer, and Warren showed himself an apt pupil. After a quarter of an hour's exercise the former said—

"You will pick it up in no time. What you want to do is to guard your face and ribs and keep your head up. Never strike out wildly, but wait until you see an opening—then let go."

"Where did you learn?" asked Warren.

"Not far from here," replied Tom, laughing; "I will show you the crib one of these days."

The boys did not get on very well that morning.

Dick Cockles opened school by taking another thrashing for having eaten tarts in bed, which he certainly had not been guilty of.

This was especially hard when his sufferings of the previous night are borne in mind.

All went wrong, and the Spartan business proceeded merrily until the cane, on being applied to the back of Dan Mittens, showed signs of splitting.

Mr. Slapcrash went to his private cupboard and saw that his stock had run out.

"Biron," he said, "go and get me a dozen at the barber's. You know the sort to pick—not too thick—pliable."

Biron had been sent on that errand before, and he was not averse to it, as it gave him an opportunity of roaming about the town for half-an-hour or so.

Leaving the school, envied by the majority, he got out of the grounds with all speed, and ran to a quiet spot where there was a bit of the old city wall left.

There he intended to remain awhile and enjoy the sunshine, but fate threw him into the hands of the common enemy.

As he turned the corner he came upon a group of hulking fellows playing pitch and toss—Jerry Bott and some of his particular friends.

Retreat, without running away and showing the white feather, was out of the question, and that kind of thing was not at all in Tom Biron's line.

So he put his hands into his pockets and began to whistle, intending to saunter by.

But Jerry Bott had already seen him, and stopped his gambling with an evil glint in his eye.

"Hullo! you Slapcrasher," he said, "wot do you mean by coming and interrupting us? Can't you let us play our game without interfering?"

"I have not interfered with you," replied Tom, very pale and quiet.

The loss of colour was not due to fear, but to a determination to stand his ground if he had to fight the lot.

"Punch him, Jerry," said one of his companions.

"I'm going to," replied the sweep, ferociously.

Tom began to back towards the wall, but one of the young ruffians got behind him and knocked his hat off.

This notable feat was hailed with derisive cheers.

"Go at him, Jerry," roared another.

"Ain't I going to do so?" replied Jerry, advancing with his left arm bent, ready to parry a blow.

Tom put his hands up, and quietly stood on the defensive.

Somehow Jerry Bott did not quite like the look of him, and he did not enter the fray with the ardour his companions desired.

"Let out, Jerry—there's no fight in him," roared two or three.

"You leave me alone," replied Jerry; "if I don't know what to do you can't tell me."

With a reputation to keep up, Jerry Bott was bound to fight, win or lose, and after two or three feints he aimed a blow at Biron which was easily parried.

The next moment he received a lunge in the chest which sent him staggering back.

"Why do you let him knock you about?" demanded one of the spectators.

They expected great things of Jerry, and he had no right, according to their notion, to make a waiting business of it.

This question exasperated the sweep, and he rushed in for a close.

But Tom Biron was too wary for that game, and, slipping aside, he allowed Jerry to dash himself against the wall with a violence that shook a little cloud of soot out of him.

Jerry was completely staggered for the moment, and fell on his side, his fall being hailed with shouts of surprise by his companions.

"Don't let the Slapcrasher bounce him," roared one of the foremost.

"He isn't bounced yet," replied another; "he's up again.   Go it, Jerry."

Jerry tried to go it, and rushed in like a young bull.

But Tom now felt that he had his opponent in hand, so he first of all gave Jerry a smack on the nose that raised a million fiery stars and a dozen Catherine wheels before his eyes, then he hit him in the ribs, and followed this up with an upper cut that laid the great Jerry on his back upon the ground, breathless and defeated.

With a yell the little band of ruffians bore down upon Tom, but he charged at them, hitting out right and left, and having bowled over three of the foremost he got clear away.

Some of the most daring rushed after him, but when he suddenly wheeled round and addled the little brains possessed by the foremost with a terrific blow between the eyes, they prudently pulled up, and Tom got away as fast as he could.

It was the only thing to be done with such heavy odds against him.

The dismayed ruffians went back to Jerry Bott, who was standing up with his back bent and one of his hands gingerly feeling his nose.

"Lord! what a smash it was!" he groaned.

"Is he a hard hitter?" asked one of his friends, named Mike Buttons.

"He must have had a knuckleduster on," groaned Jerry.

"His knuckles seem to be good dusters, anyway," Mike rejoined.

"Who are you cheeking on?" roared Jerry.

"You," replied Mike.

An hour before he would not have cheeked Jerry if anyone had offered him a five pound note.   But now he felt safe.

A defeated gladiator soon finds out that there is a difference in the feelings of those who used to believe him invincible.

Jerry looked at him with all the ferocity left in his body, but it had been pretty well knocked out of him, and Mike only laughed.

The others then took to chuckling.

"You are a lot of worms," said Jerry, "to stand by and see me knocked about with a knuckleduster."

"There wasn't no knuckleduster," replied Mike.

"There was."

"There wasn't."

"Here, wot's the row now?" demanded a stentorian voice.

The young roughs looked up and beheld a thick-set adult sweep, with his sweeping machine on his shoulder.

This sooty gentleman was Abe Bott, the acknowledged father of Jerry.

"Wot's the row, I say?" he demanded. "And what are you holding your nose for, Jerry?"

"He's been licked by a Slapcrasher," replied Mike.

"You tell me that," said Abe Bott, "and I'll ram my machine down your throat."

"But he has been licked," insisted Mike. "The Slapcrasher did just what he liked with him."

A chorus of affirmation broke from those who had witnessed the brief but telling fight.

Abe Bott dropped his machine from his shoulder, and put it against the old wall.

"Jerry Bott," he said, "just fix your eye on your father."

Jerry did his best to obey, but it was a shifty eye, and the sooty brow of his parent became clouded.

"To think that I should live to see the day," he continued, "when you have been licked by one of them bread-and-butter chaps!"

"He had a knuckleduster," moaned Jerry.

"He hadn't," cried Mike.

And the other fellows, like the rest of the world, gloating over a fallen hero, supported Mike.

"Knuckleduster or no knuckleduster, Jerry," said Abe, "you had no right to let him lick you. How is it that I am champion sweep of Smockley?"

Nobody answered this question, and Abe proceeded to give them a little needful enlightenment on this point.

"Because I don't allow no other sweep to do business in this town," replied Abe. "A man who wants to sweep chimneys here has to fight his way right up to every one of 'em. So I make myself champion, and there ain't a sweep in the whole country that I couldn't whip into a wisp o' straw."

"That's quite true, Mister Bott," returned Mike; "nobody durst come a-sweeping nigh you."

"Licked by a Slapcrasher," continued Abe, sweating with indignation. "You—my Jerry —the son your mother brought into the world one night when there were two chimneys afire, and one of 'em the doctor's who wouldn't

"STOP, YOU LITTLE BEGGAR!" CRIED JERRY BOTT, "OR IT WILL BE THE WORSE FOR YOU."

come till he see it put out. Jerry, I'm a broken-'arted man."

He leaned against the wall and passed his hand across his eyes, evidently deeply affected.

Jerry continued to staunch the blood flowing from his nose, with a dogged expression on his face.

"Perhaps you wouldn't be champion," he said, "if t'other sweeps came round you with knuckledusters."

Abe laid hold of his machine and aimed a blow at him, which Jerry, from long experience, was able to dodge.

"You talk to me, you reptile," replied Bott, "and I'll take you home and choke ye in a bushel o' soot. Licked by a Slapcrasher, a

Jerry Bott comes to a sudden stop.

boy who goes to school and wears white collars. I'm done at last, I am. I don't care for anything more in this world. I wish I wasn't champion sweep, I do."

He was indeed much overcome, and after another brush at his eyes he hoisted the machine upon his shoulders and looked wildly around him.

"Go, somebody, and get a light weight sweep and send him into Smockley. Now's his time to open business and throw me out of every chimney in the place. Why, you sarpent, what do you mean by being my son?"

Jerry made no answer.

Perhaps he did not feel that he was wholly accountable for being the child of his parent, but he did not dare to say so much to his irate father.

"You mind this," said Abe, wagging a fore-finger at the wretched Jerry, "you've got to lick that Slapcrasher—all the Slapcrashers if it comes to that—and I'll take old Slapcrash on if he don't like it. He's a stiff 'un, but I think I've got his weight to a ounce, and I shall know how to walk round him. Come here, Jerry."

Jerry did not immediately advance.

He was not sure as to the intentions of his grief-stricken parent.

"You needn't be afraid," continued the champion sweep, speaking in a quieter tone. "I ain't going to clout you. I'm thinking, Jerry, that you must ha' been out o' training or this would not ha' come about."

Jerry saw that his father was softening, and drew up to his side.

Abe took hold of his arm and felt his muscles. Then he ran his hand over the calves of his legs.

"As I was afraid, Jerry," he said, "you are out of training. Been making too free with the wittles and not doing no exercise. I'll take you in hand for a fortnight, and then if there's a Slapcrasher to be found who can stand up to you for two minutes, dashed if I don't climb up a crooked flue, stick myself fast, and put an end to my miserable existence."

He was going away when another thought occurred to him.

Addressing Jerry's grinning followers, he said, in a warning tone—

"And don't none of you go a bellowing this knuckleduster business about the town or I'll let you know what the inside of a soot bag is like. Hear me, do you?"

They heard him, as their frightened faces showed, and shouldering his machine, with a grim smile on his sooty countenance, the elder Bott walked away.

CHAPTER V.

DICK COCKLES AND JERRY BOTT HAVE A MEETING—A WILD FLIGHT, WITH AN UNEXPECTED TERMINATION THERETO.

A TRULY brave boy is seldom or never a braggart. If he talks about anything he has done it is in a quiet, modest way, undervaluing his deeds.

Tom Biron went back to the school looking none the worse for his encounter with Jerry Bott. By the time he had been to the barber's and bought the canes he was perfectly cool.

The appearance of the fresh instruments of

torture was hailed with anything but exuberant delight, and the movements of Mr. Slapcrash while selecting one for immediate use were watched in a furtive manner by those keenly interested.

"I say, Tom," whispered Dick Cockles, "you have got some stingers this time."

"The worst I could pick," replied Tom; "but I was in a hurry. I went round the city wall and met Jerry Bott."

"Did you have a fight with him?"

In his eagerness Dick spoke a little too loud, and the quick ears of the schoolmaster heard him, but he was not able to detect who it was.

"Silence!" he cried, smiting his desk with the cane.

"Silence it is and hard-a-starboard," muttered Dan Mittens.

Whatever atom of humour there might be in this remark sufficed to make the boy next to him laugh.

He was an undersized lad, with a swarthy face, to whom we have not yet introduced the reader.

It was suggested and believed that he had nigger blood in his veins, which he denied; but nigger blood or not, he had a lot of pluck, and was generally willing to settle any question by combat if the size of his opponent permitted.

He bore the rather extraordinary name of Selah Finch, and Selah, of course, had been promptly turned into Sarah. Therefore was he addressed as Sarah on all occasions that permitted it.

"Finch!" exclaimed Mr. Slapcrash, "what are you laughing at?"

"Nothing, sir."

"Finch, what you say is false on the face of it," exclaimed Mr. Slapcrash. "Come here."

Finch arose from his seat, went there, and took the expected licking with fortitude.

"How's the new cane, Sarah?" asked Dan Mittens.

"Quite up to the usual mark," Selah Finch replied, "and a trifle over."

This made Dan laugh, and, he also being detected, in his turn he was called up to estimate the merits of the new purchase.

He was able to endorse Selah Finch's opinion of it.

Tom Biron had no opportunity to tell the story of his fight with Jerry Bott during school hours, but it was soon known that a meeting had taken place, and the youngsters were burning to hear about it.

Never did the dismissal, "Twelve o'clock,

boys," sound more musical in their ears, and right glad were all that nobody had to stay in to do penance for their geographical, or arithmetical, or any other sins.

Tom got into a corner out of sight of the house, and his companions clustered around him.

"There isn't much to tell," he said. "I met Jerry and we had a bit of a slog, but I can't say it came to a finish. His gang was there, and I had to run. But I can tell you one thing, you need not be particularly afraid of Jerry Bott. If you meet him alone, stand up to him, any of you—he's got a white feather in his tail."

"I always thought so," replied Dick Cockles; "by Jingo, I shall be glad to catch him alone!"

"Don't make so cocksure about what you will do," returned Tom, quietly.

"Cockles-sure, you mean," suggested Jem Stager.

"Don't my name please you?" asked Dick.

"No, it doesn't," returned Jem; "by having such a name, your offence, like that of Hamlet's uncle, is rank—it ought to have been Mussels, Shrimps, Winkles, anything but Cockles. What does your father mean by having such a name?"

"Oh! Jem, you're a—you're a—" Dick began, but, being at a loss to find a fitting epithet to bestow upon his dramatic friend, he finished off rather tamely with, "you're anything but what you ought to be."

The laugh went against him both ways, and digging his hands deep down into his trouser-pockets he sauntered off, feebly whistling.

The other boys dispersed, to amuse themselves in various ways, and Tom Biron and Warren Fane, arm in arm, strolled up and down.

"Tell me all about it," said Warren.

"About what?" asked Tom.

"The fight."

"I've told all that is worth telling—it was a good start, but, as I have said, I can't say there was an end. I did not finish him."

"I want to have a go at this Bott myself," said Warren, with sparkling eyes. "I hate these bullying blackguards, who make themselves a terror to boys smaller than themselves."

"All in good time," replied Tom; "you must get a little more muscle on you first. I have a pair of dumb-bells in my box, and you must work at them every morning for a bit.

Why, here's Slapcrash! What's the row now?"

The schoolmaster entered the playground with a telegram in his hand.

"Boys," he said, "attention all!"

But little need was there for this command. Every game had stopped—every eye was on him.

"Boys," he continued, "I regret to say that there will be no school this afternoon."

The regret in the boys' faces was shown by suppressed grins of delight. Dick Cockles was obliged to grunt or he must have laughed outright with joy.

"I have received a telegram," pursued Mr. Slapcrash, "informing me that my brother-in-law is very ill and is not expected to recover. He is a rich man compared to me—one whom we have always deeply respected—and it is imperative that I should go to him immediately."

A cheer in recognition of the unexpected holiday was out of the question, but Dick Cockles felt that something ought to be said in honour of it. Accordingly he burst out with—

"We hope, sir, that he will leave you some of his property."

The eye of Mr. Slapcrash lighted upon the unhappy boy with marked severity.

"If you think, Cockles," he observed, "that in going to him I am moved by any such sordid consideration you are wrong, besides which the thought is unworthy of the meanest mind and is an insult to me."

Immediate collapse of Dick Cockles.

"The sad tidings," pursued Mr. Slapcrash, "has naturally had a disturbing effect upon the nerves of Mrs. Slapcrash, and the noise you would be sure to make in my absence would naturally have an injurious effect upon her. I think, therefore, that you may spend the afternoon in the fields, but you are not to go beyond the canal bridge, and I forbid you to play near the water. If any boy comes back with wet clothes he will be sent to bed without tea or supper. I shall leave instructions to that effect."

General murmurs, intending to imply that they would rather perish by inches than go outside the place specified or risk their precious young lives by disporting themselves within measurable distance of the canal.

"You understand me," said Mr. Slapcrash. "Now get an early dinner and take yourselves off."

They marched into the house, sober and grave as judges in the bud.

The eye of Mr. Slapcrash was on them, one and all, and an unseemly smile would have ensured the smiler an afternoon alone in the schoolroom.

Mr. Slapcrash knew them, and they knew him, so both played their parts to perfection.

Surely there never was a more decorous meal partaken of in an educational establishment for young gentlemen!

So silent were they that they might have been so many ghosts of departed pupils, eating shadowy food, but for an occasional feeble rattle of a knife or fork.

After it was over the boys arose, and Mr. Slapcrash favoured them with a few parting words.

"I believe," he said, "that some of the town boys have recently exhibited animosity towards you. The ignorant mind has a born antipathy to respectability, but respectability must ignore all vulgar animosity and avoid fighting. Again I hope you understand."

More murmurs, expressive of an iron resolve to be indifferent to all that was vulgar, in word or deed!

"Now go," said Mr. Slapcrash.

They went out actually on tiptoe, thereby showing a regard for the nerves of Mrs. Slapcrash not often exhibited by them.

Once clear of the house they lost no time in getting away from the town, and they did not stop until they reached a stile that led into the fields.

"A blessing on the nerves of Mrs. Slapcrash," said Jem Stager, standing on the second rail of the stile and extending his hands towards the school, "may she live long and—"

But his blessing was cut short by his losing his balance and rolling over on the other side.

The boys scrambled after him, laughing, and away they went.

At first they kept together, but the principle of natural selection soon led them to separate and go in different directions.

Tom Biron, Warren Fane, and Jem Stager made for a copse reputed to be the lair of foxes, with the hope of unearthing one of these highly-scented animals; while Dick and Dan Mittens decided that they would just go and look at the canal.

Now it so happened that Jerry Bott had, in obedience to the instructions of his parent, already entered into training, and he was doing a stiff bit of walking up and down the towing-path that afternoon.

He was accompanied by some of his usual companions, who, notwithstanding the damaged faith in their accepted leader, were interested in the training business.

Dan and Dick came upon them suddenly, as they jumped through a gap in the hedge on to the towing-path, and were immediately espied.

"Slapcrashers!" roared Mike Buttons, one of the party, "and little 'uns."

That was enough, and with a rush the sweep and his crew were upon the two boys.

Unfortunately, or fortunately it may be, Dan bolted up the towing-path, while Dick dashed back into the fields.

Jerry Bott, still rankling under the defeat of the morning, went for Dick, he being the smaller of the two, while his companions made after Dan.

But Dan was a smart runner and outpaced them easily, so they soon gave up the chase and returned on the trail of Jerry Bott, hoping to share with him in the joy of safely maltreating one small boy.

By that time Jerry and Dick were some distance across the field.

Dick, forgetful of the assurance of Tom Biron that Jerry Bott only wanted to be boldly faced, was flying for his life, and Jerry, with dogged fury, was pounding after him, gaining at every stride.

"Stop, you little beggar," he cried, "or it will be the worse for you."

Dick meant to keep on, but he suddenly stopped against his will by tripping over a stone he failed to see in his path.

He went down as if he had been shot, and Jerry, who was now close upon him, had no time to avoid going over him.

He stumbled against Dick's body and pitched forward with great violence, falling at full length, and sliding a foot or two along the ground.

Dick was up again like a sprite, and espying Tom Biron and Warren Fane in the distance, ran off towards them.

The companions of Jerry Bott also perceiving the hero of the fight by the city wall, prudently pulled up and raised the fallen Jerry. He was so utterly flabbergasted —no other word will describe his state of mind and body—by his fall, that for a few moments he could do nothing but open and shut his mouth and roll his eyes.

He did not even seem to know where he was.

"You came a cropper," said Mike Buttons.

This needless piece of information caused Jerry to turn his eyes towards him, and after an effort he spoke.

"You are a nice lot," he said, "to leave me to run him down alone."

"We tacked after the other cove first," replied Mike.

"You tacked," sneered Jerry; "that's all you can do. Tacked, did you, you duffers!"

"Don't you jaw me!" said Mike, ferociously, raising his arm.

"What are you going to do?" asked Jerry. "Can't you see I am lame?"

"Then keep civil," grunted Mike.

Jerry was lame—there was no shamming now. He had taken the skin off both knees, and a small circular bit off the tip of his nose. He had split the knees of his trousers also.

"Just help me, some of you," he said, miserably; "I think I had better go and lie down a bit."

Mike Buttons laughed derisively.

"What's there to laugh at?" demanded Jerry.

"It don't take much to settle you," returned Mike.

"I'm out o' training, ain't I?" demanded Jerry.

Again Mike laughed—short and dry.

"Any excuse is better nor none," he said. "Oh! my—out of training! Ha—ha!"

CHAPTER VI

THE CHAMPION SWEEP GETS ANOTHER STAGGERER—HIS GRIEF AND HIS WRATH— HE HAS AN INTERVIEW WITH TOM BIRON.

ABE BOTT was a very regular liver. Every morning he swept all the chimneys he had to sweep, and every afternoon and evening he spent the proceeds in getting drunk.

He was so regular in his habits that the sight of him, after three o'clock in the afternoon, sober and in his right mind, was an amazing spectacle to the inhabitants of Smockley.

On this especial day he began his gin crawl, as usual, at the Bell and Tun, where he met a navvy with whom he fraternised and drank.

The talk was all about feats of strength, and their respective fistic abilities.

Abe said he could lift a form in the tap-room with one hand, and hold it out at arm's length.

The navvy said he could not—if he died for it.

Abe thereupon took up the form in one hand, shot it out at arm's length, and dropped it upon the navvy's toes.

Being accused of having finished the feat in this way "on puppos," Abe denied it, and the navvy emphasised his declaration by dealing the sweep what is known among such people as a "smash on the jaw," the champion being unduly and violently doubled up in the fireplace.

He did not rise as promptly as a champion ought to have done under the circumstances. Indeed, if it had been an encounter in the pugilistic ring, he would have been a long way behind time.

And when he did begin to rise he only sat up.

"Look here," he said, "I don't stand that sort of thing."

"Sit it then," replied the navvy, "which is what you are doing of."

"I'd have it out with you," continued Abe, "if I hadn't got my boy in training for a fight, and I'm bound to see how he's getting on. I've sent him down to the canal to do a ten mile stretch up and down the towpath."

"Well, I'll go with you," said the navvy. "If you don't want to fight I don't. I ain't a quarrelsome man, so if you stand another drink before we start we'll consider it's over."

"That's a fair and friendly offer," returned Abe.

He got up with alacrity and held out his hand. The navvy grasped it.

"We'll have two drinks," he said.

Abe was not prepared for this burst of friendship, and his eyes gleamed, as if he would have dissented if he had not been in such a hurry to see how Jerry was getting on.

They had their two drinks, one after the other, and sallied forth. A walk of about half a mile brought them to the canal.

Abe Bott looked up the towing-path, but no Jerry was to be seen.

He had been cramming the navvy on the way with stories of the doings of his wonderful son, how he had licked all the Slapcrash boys one after the other, and was now training to take them on two and three at a time, according to size.

"He's going in for it as if it was for the championship of England," he said.

"Now, what's the meaning of this?" exclaimed Abe; "he ain't here."

"Perhaps he's training up in the moon," suggested the navvy, sarcastically.

Abe did not reply, but he went through the act of swallowing something like a very disagreeable pill.

"I'm that boy's father," he said, "and he's got to do what I tells him, or I'm down on him."

"There's some boys coming along the field," said the navvy, peering through the fence.

Abe stooped down and saw his son, his only son, being led along by his companions, and a horrible thought entered his head. Had he been fighting again, and got another licking?

With parental wrath in his eye he made for the gap in the fence and faced his offspring.

"Now then," he said, "what's the move this time?"

"Had a fall," replied Jerry, sulkily.

"A fall—where?"

"He's been chucked over by another Slapcrasher—a little 'un," replied Mike Buttons, that ready young spokesman.

A laugh fell upon the ear of Abe Bott. It came from the rear, and he knew it was the navvy who sent it forth.

"Jerry," said Abe, in a tone of anguish, "ain't there to be no end of this loss of character? Don't you know whose son you are?"

"You says you are my father, and I believe you," replied Jerry.

"Then why don't you keep up the character of your father?" asked Abe, mournfully. "Come, did he do it?"

"I runned arter him, he fell down, and I went over him."

"I thought he regler threw you," put in Mike Buttons, relentlessly.

Abe Bott aimed a blow at him, which he expertly avoided. Then the grief of the champion sweep died away, and wrath took its place.

"I shall kill somebody afore I've done," he said. "I can't stand it. These things upset me."

"Like the upset in the Bell and Tun," remarked the navvy.

Ignoring this unnecessary interruption, Abe Bott went on.

"I'm going to end it somehow, and it must be done in the regular way. Where are the Slapcrashers?"

"There's four of 'em at the end of the field," said Mike Buttons.

The champion looked in the direction Mike

pointed, and saw four boys together, evidently watching his party.

"All of you stop here a minute," he said, "and I'll go and have a word with them."

He strode off, looking very much like a ferocious bull on the rampage, making for the four boys.

If he expected them to run away he was disappointed. They did not budge an inch.

He came up to them as if he meant to walk over them, and pulled up within a foot of Tom Biron, who was foremost.

"Now, you Slapcrashers!" he said.

"What do you want?" asked Tom.

"That 'ere boy o' mine," said Abe. "You don't treat him fair."

"I don't treat him at all," replied Tom.

"You do—you know he's a-training, so as to be a match for you, and you want to hustle and bustle him out of it."

"Pardon me," returned Tom, "but I have not been within a hundred yards of him this afternoon, although I had a meeting with him this morning."

"So you are the chap as hit him below the belt, are you?" said Abe, eyeing him critically; "all I can say is it was lucky for you I wasn't there."

"I daresay you would have joined the young blackguards and helped them to mob me," retorted Tom, quietly.

"What are you saying?"

"What I mean."

"Fix your eye on me, you Slapcrasher," said the sooty champion. "Now, have you got it there?"

"Yes," said Tom, "both of them."

"All right, then. Do I look like a man who goes agin his word?"

"I would rather not say what you look like."

"Perhaps you are afeard to."

"Indeed I am not. I'll say it if you like."

The champion of the chimney business looked at him with a decided squint, so great was his wrath.

"You are a cheeky youngster," he said, "but I think it can be taken out of you, and my Jerry shall do it."

"When?" asked Tom.

"Within a fortnight," Abe answered.

"Will he take it out of me instead?" asked Warren Fane.

Abe turned towards him, and saw that he was a slimmer and altogether a more desirable opponent than Tom Biron.

"I should think he could settle you in about two minutes," he replied.

"He shall try," said Warren. "When is the next half-holiday, Tom?"

"We have one in ten days," replied Tom.

"Will ten days be enough to get your redoubtable son in trim?" asked Warren of Abe Bott.

"In five if you like," replied the champion sweep.

Tom said something in an undertone Abe Bott did not hear, but he caught the reply.

"I insist upon it," Warren said; "you must not treat me as a child."

To this Tom replied—

"Very well, just as you like, old fellow—I like your pluck."

"You know the gravel pits?" said Tom to Bott.

"I should think I do," replied the champion sweep.

"Meet me there in ten days' time, at three o'clock," continued Tom, "and bring a few friends, but not a mob. I only want what is fair."

"And I want no more," observed Abe Bott; "it shall be straight business, man to man—I mean boy to boy—and he who gets licked shall take his licking and go away."

"I'll see to that," said a voice behind him.

It was the navvy, whose interest in the affair had brought him to the spot.

"I don't see as you've any call to come," retorted Abe.

"Maybe not," was the curt reply, "but I'm coming. Excuse me, young gentleman, but I'll see you treated fair—my name is Dossy Dodge, and I'm a straight 'un."

"That I can believe," said Tom, looking at him critically; "so it is settled—time and place, and all that—good day, gentlemen. Now, boys, we'll get along."

They were all laughing, and in the highest spirits.

The offer of Dossy Dodge was a very acceptable one, as they had felt at first that Abe Bott was not entirely to be trusted.

"You've got a way of cutting into things," said the champion sweep, as he walked away with his companion.

"I'm there or anywhere when I fancy I can be useful," Dossy Dodge replied.

"But—this is a boys' affair, and you are not wanted."

"Anyhow I'm coming, I say. You are going on one side, I on t'other, and there's an end of it."

THEY WENT HOME TWO BY TWO, TO HIDE FROM THE NATIVES THE WORK OF THE ENEMY.

Nothing more passed between them, and they returned to Jerry, who was sitting on the bank rubbing his knees.

"Get up," his father said, "and move along, will you?"

"I can hardly walk," pleaded Jerry.

"Hop then," said his father, ferociously; "people like us don't take no notice of little knocks. You ain't got any bones broke, have you?"

"I don't think so, father."

"Then walk, and smart about it, too. Go home, for me and Mister Dodge have got to go and have another friendly drink together."

"Not to-day, thanky," returned Dossy Dodge; "we'll leave that until after the fight,

Billy Pink under the tap.

and then we'll let it slide still if you've a mind to."

The champion sweep took his son by the arm and jerked him to his feet.

"Step out," he said; "we ain't good enough company for some people, and had better get along."

The young roughs went away in a body, and Dossy Dodge set out across the fields.

He was bent on seeing Tom Biron again, and having a word or two with him.

After a long stroll he saw him in the distance with Warren Fane, to whom he was giving a sparring lesson.

He got up pretty close to the pair without being seen, and stood there for a few minutes watching them.

"A lively pair of lads," he said, "and too good to be bashed about by Bott's lot. I'll see nothing unfair is done, or Abe Bott had better look out for himself. He wants that champion rubbish taken out of him, and perhaps I may find a sweep who can do it."

He walked slowly on, and the boys perceiving him, stopped their work and came forward.

Tom in a few words thanked him for espousing their cause, and asked him if there really was any need for him to waste his time about it.

"I'll tell you what it is, gentlemen," replied Dodge; "in dealing with Abe Bott you can't do better than see that everything is square. Win fair or foul is his motto, so I mean to be on the spot when the fight comes off, and if there's anything unfair why Abe will go to grass."

The quiet determination in his eye showed that he meant business.

"This young gentleman," he continued, pointing to Warren, "doesn't want pluck, I can see, but Jerry Bott is heavy, and he's older than he pretends to be. He'll try to rush in and bounce him."

"I hope to be ready to stop him," said Warren, with a smile.

At this moment Dan Mittens suddenly broke through a fence hard by.

"Come this way—quick!" he cried. "Jem Stager is up a tree, really up a tree, and the roughs are stoning him. They vow they'll have his life as soon as they get him down."

CHAPTER VII.

ANOTHER BRUSH WITH THE ROUGHS—STRANGE BEHAVIOUR OF MRS. SLAPCRASH—DICK COCKLES IS ENTRUSTED WITH ANOTHER MISSION.

"YOU need not come," said Tom Biron to the navvy; "we can settle these fellows without help."

"I'll just look on if you don't mind," replied Dossy Dodge.

Time pressed, so they hurried off, Dan Mittens leading the way back to a copse on the opposite side of the field.

They were guided to the exact spot by the shouting of voices, worthy of Indians triumphing over a foe.

"To the right," cried Dan.

So they bore away to the right and came upon Mike Buttons and the rest of the roughs lately in attendance upon Jerry Bott, all hard at work stoning Jem, who was fairly up a tree, near the top of a well-grown ash, and in imminent danger of receiving serious injury.

It was no child's play, for his foes were old hands at stone-throwing, and but for the sheltering branches Jem would soon have been brought down.

As it was he had received a cut on the head, from which the blood flowed freely, and his right hand had a big bruise on the back of it.

"Come down!" roared Mike. "Yah! you coward—afraid to fight!"

He had barely uttered these words when he found himself seized by the collar and swung round.

Facing him was Tom Biron. Around the leading Slapcrasher two or three of Mike's companions lay on the ground, and Warren Fane and Dan Mittens were sparring merrily with the others.

Mike had more real courage than Jerry Bott, and he stood his ground for a few moments.

Then he went to grass with a pair of promising black eyes, and a sensation of having been in collision with a windmill.

"Hold off!" he gasped. "I'm done—I give in."

"You curs!" hissed Tom. "If it wasn't disgraceful to do so, I would kick you like footballs all the way home. Get up and run for it."

They all ran off as soon as they had a chance, and Dossy, with his hands deep in the pockets of his corduroys, smiled seraphically.

"I like that," he said; "two to one they were, but bolted. Still, it isn't all over, gentlemen. That gang will fight foul if they can't do it fair, and you will have to keep your eyes about you."

Tom thanked him for the caution, and then they parted finally for that day.

Dossy Dodge filled his pipe and went away smoking, as if he enjoyed the fun, and Tom looked to the wounds of Jem Stager.

He had come down from the tree the moment his friends appeared, and was ready to join in the fight, but it was all over before he touched ground.

"By my faith," he observed, "but the scurvy knaves assailed me unfairly. My noble friends, you are indeed welcome!"

"It's a good job that stone didn't hit you an inch higher," said Tom; "if it had you would now be minus an eye, Jem."

They went to a spring, where Tom washed the wound and tied a handkerchief across Jem's face to stop the bleeding.

Thus adorned, Jem looked like one of those eastern women who hide the lower part of their faces from base man.

An arrangement had been made for the boys to collect at the stile near the town at half-past five, so as to return home decorously.

But when they got together they found that a decorous procession was out of the question.

Dick Cockles when he fell had also split the knees of his trousers, and Jem Stager looked as if he had been in the wars.

Another lad, named Adam Gander, known out of school hours as Goosey Gander, had managed to fairly smash his stiff billy-cock hat; and Sam Fusby, to the great joy of everybody, had torn his nether garments in the rear in such a fashion that for decency's sake he would have to go home sideways, with his back to the wall.

In addition there were others suffering from minor calamities, and the majority were dusty about the clothes and grimy as to their faces.

"We had better get back at once," said Tom Biron. "And Sam Fusby ought to have a cab."

"Who's to pay for it?" asked Sam.

"You, I suppose," returned Tom.

"I haven't any money," muttered Sam, sulkily.

"You never spend any," returned Dick, "and I know you have some. I shook your box the other day, and distinctly heard a rattling of tin."

"You let my box alone, will you?" said Sam Fusby, furiously.

"The miser hoards his gold," exclaimed Jem Stager, as he took the handkerchief from his face. "He sells his soul for filthy lucre."

"My father don't allow me much," said Sam.

"Much or little," interposed Tom Biron, "is no matter to us, for we don't want it. You had better get along home. Who'll go with him?"

"I will," said Dick Cockles.

"Yes, and tell everybody we meet what's happened," replied Sam. "No, thank you, I will go alone."

He set off sideways, like a crab, followed by derisive cheers from some of the youngsters, which he replied to with sundry motions of the hands and fingers, expressive of contempt.

When he had turned the corner, Jem Stager and Dick Cockles followed on. So they proceeded, two by two, Tom and Warren bringing up the rear.

They had not got far to go, and hoped to get home without raising any commotion in Smockley.

A baker's boy, however, discovered Sam Fusby's condition, and began to make boisterous fun of him, but Jem Stager put an end to his humorous outburst.

He took hold of that young baker and turned him over—basket, loaves, and all—into the middle of the road, which was none too clean.

"Now understand this, doughey," he said; "no Slapcrasher can be insulted with impunity."

Leaving the young purveyor of bread to dismally reflect on the state of his cottage and tin loaves, Jem hurried on.

"It wasn't for Sam's sake I did it," he said to Dick, "but for the good name of the Slapcrashers. We are bound to defend all who walk beneath our banner."

"I wish you would teach me the trick of that fall," said Dick, as he stood by the school-door.

"It is done in this way," returned Jem; "you put your heel so, then get your elbow under the fellow's arm like this, and away he goes."

And away went Dick, with a bang against the door that must have been heard all over the house.

"Oh! hang it! Jem," remonstrated Dick; "draw it mild."

"You'll know how it's done now," said Jem, coolly.

"I don't want another lesson unless you practise on some other fellow," returned Dick.

The door was opened by a servant, and they entered. The moment they were under the Slapcrash roof they became changed boys.

"I say, Mary," said Jem, softly, "can you get me a little bit of sticking-plaister from somewhere?"

"Lor', Master Stager," exclaimed the girl, "what have you been a-doing?"

"Within the shadow of a wood I met my foe," replied Jem, aping a tragic attitude, but speaking low. "I sought the shelter of a friendly tree, while the base churls plied their catapult-like arms, and by dexterous aim chipped my blushing cheek. Oh! gentle maiden, I beseech thee put balm upon my wounds!"

"Mrs. Slapcrash is coming," whispered Dick.

"I'll put the plaister outside the school-room door," said Mary; "I have some in my box."

"Not a bad sort of girl," observed Dick, as they entered the temple of learning and sat down by one of the desks.

"A ministering angel," replied Jem, with a knightly air; "by the love I bear her I will break a lance with any belted knight who declares her otherwise."

The only person likely to do so was Sam Fusby, and he was upstairs changing his trousers, so the challenge passed unheeded.

In a few minutes the boys were all ready and waiting for the tea-bell to ring.

"It must be past time," said Dick. "I feel as if I could eat a sack of sawdust."

"Suppose we cast lots?" suggested Selah Finch.

"What for?" asked Dick.

"To see who shall be killed to satisfy the appetite of the rest," replied Selah.

"I always said you were a cannibal in disguise," observed Sam Fusby, who had rejoined his companions.

Selah turned quickly upon him.

"Say that again," he cried.

"Sha'n't!" returned Sam.

"You dare not. Bah! you are a coward!"

The tea-bell rang at that moment, and the cannibal question was laid aside for the present, but Sam had quite a gift of saying disagreeable things and repeating them. A repetition of his insinuation was thereupon to be expected.

To the surprise of the boys Mrs. Slapcrash was at the table, and she seemed to be in a remarkably good state of health, with her spirits approaching to buoyancy.

She was good-tempered, talked to the boys, and even joked.

They were so staggered by her bearing—for she was usually, in schoolboy vernacular, "down upon them"—that they almost forgot to laugh in due season, but on the whole acquitted themselves very well.

"You may disport yourselves in the play-ground until half-past eight," she said. "I am going out this evening, and I am sure I can trust you to behave yourselves like young gentlemen."

She rose, smiled in a genial manner, and left the room, skipping like a sportive young maiden as she passed through the doorway.

"My eye!" exclaimed Jem Stager, "I was

never so licked in all my life! What does it mean?"

"Never mind the meaning of it," said Warren Fane; "we have got the evening to ourselves, and I'll tell you what I will do. I will shell out another half-sovereign, and we will have a feast in the playground."

"We will disport ourselves in the shade of —of the surrounding houses," observed Jem Stager. "Come, let us away—to the open air, let us away!"

"Go out quietly," suggested Tom Biron, "or Mrs. Slapcrash may change her mind and stop at home."

The bare idea of such a calamity reduced them to a frozen state of demeanour, and they went forth in the most gentlemanly manner, orderly to the border of melancholy.

"I'll watch and see when she goes," said Dick Cockles. "I can see the hall-door through the passage window."

In a few minutes he announced the good tidings.

"Gone!" he whispered, from his watching-post.

The banging of the front door—that door always banged with the least inducement to do so—confirmed what he said. The place was left to them—freedom was theirs.

Mary did not count. She was a good-tempered, heavy sort of country girl, who would rather die at the stake than tell tales about the boys. Her heart, as Jem used to say, was "planted in a bosom filled with the tenderest emotions for the opposite sex, size and age no consideration."

Having given Mrs. Slapcrash half-an-hour's grace, Tom Biron opened the gate that led into Mr. Slapcrash's private garden by simply shaking the door.

All the locks attached to the place had been reduced to abject submission by a long course of maltreatment.

"I had better go for the grub," Tom said.

"Do let me go," pleaded Dick Cockles. "I made such a beastly mess of the last job that I want to put it right."

He was so eager to perform the duty that it was not in the heart of Tom to refuse, so he replied—

"Well, cut along, and be quick about it."

"Here's the money," said Warren Fane.

He spun a coin in the air, and Dick caught it as it fell.

The outer door was soon opened, and after a look up and down, to see if Mrs. Slapcrash was in sight, Dick sped upon his errand.

CHAPTER VIII.

DICK MEETS WITH A BITTER ENEMY—A BLACK BUSINESS—DOSSY DODGE PROVES HIMSELF TO BE THE RIGHT MAN AT THE RIGHT TIME.

DICK was bound for a tuck-shop on the other side of the small town, where there was a variety of good things to choose from.

It was much patronised by boys of the better class, because they could not only get fair value for their money, but everything was good and clean.

To get at it he would have to pass through two or three streets, or make a circuit of the old city wall.

He chose the latter way, as it offered less chance of being seen by anyone who might report his absence from school to Mr. or Mrs. Slapcrash.

Again his evil star was in the ascendant. If any horoscope-caster had gone into the matter of his birth he would have written down something like this:

"Born under Mars when Saturn was in the ascendant—general life turbulent—a bad hand at doing the right thing at the proper time— haunted by enemies—unfortunate in war— should avoid combats and all civic commotions."

He had just passed the spot where Tom Biron fought Jerry Bott when he saw a man leaning against one of the giant elm trees.

He was a man likely to attract attention anywhere, for he was a big-boned fellow, of sinister appearance—a heavy-looking ruffian, not entirely unconnected with the chimney-sweeping business—in short, Abe Bott.

The champion sweep was in a gloomy state of mind. Things had gone wrong with him lately.

Jerry was a source of grief and trouble to him, and Dossy Dodge, by the force of fistic argument and sarcastic treatment, had that day curdled the little milk of human kindness in his composition.

It is needless to say that he knew Dick, and knew him as a Slapcrasher.

On beholding the chubby person of the boy his ferocious instincts came to the front, and stepping forth, he barred the way, holding a soot-bag in his hand.

"Jest stop a minute, will you?" he said.

Dick stopped, because he had not the strength to do anything else.

"Where are you going?" demanded Bott.

"Only into the town," replied Dick, in the hollowest of hollow voices.

"You are out without leave," said Bott.

Dick could not deny it, and he watched for the assault he knew, in his heart, would surely come.

"Disobedient boys," observed the champion sweep, with the air of a great moralist, "are like vipers to their friends and parents—they bring trouble and sorrow wherever they go—they cast a shadder on their homes, and they drives their fathers to drink."

"My father don't drink," said Dick, hoping to show by this correction that he was not quite so bad as he was supposed to be.

"Then he oughter," Abe Bott returned, savagely, going on another tack. "I hates them sneaks who turn up their noses at a man because he takes a drop o' beer. They are down on men who does, and as a man I feels it my duty to be down on them and all as they have in the way of offsprings."

He stopped, took breath, and firmly grasped the end of the soot-bag.

"Now I'm going to act like a father to you," he went on; "it's my duty so for to do—take that."

That was a bang on the side of the head with the bag, and Dick, half-blinded by the cloud of soot that came from it, staggered against a tree.

"Let me alone, will you?" he cried, "or I'll call for the police."

"Call away," said Abe; "they don't come here at this time o' day—and why don't you get along?"

He assisted Dick to "get along" by giving him several heavy blows with the bag, smothering him from head to foot with the black dust in its folds.

Having started on the job he rapidly warmed to it, and was proceeding to further assault Dick when a guardian angel appeared on the scene.

This was Dossy Dodge.

How he came there is of no moment, but there he was, and he fell upon the merciless Bott like an avalanche.

The first sign of his presence Bott received was a blow on the side of the head that raised five hundred electric lights before his eyes.

The next was a kick, justly and honestly delivered on that portion of the person where it can be lawfully bestowed upon a knave by a truly indignant man.

It was so good a kick that the champion sweep felt himself rise a few inches with it.

The third indication of the presence of Dossy Dodge was a blow on the other side of the head, that sent the chimney-cleaner to the ground in a heap.

"Now get up," said Dossy Dodge, "and let's have it out like men."

"I ain't a going to get up," gasped Abe Bott; "why should I?"

"Because you've got to fight."

"I ain't a fighting-man."

"Oh! yes, you are, when the game is a safe 'un. Get up."

Dossy stood over him with his fists clenched, evidently in the humour for real business.

"Would you hit a man on the ground?" asked Abe, in a loud voice.

"No, nor a man who runs," replied Dodge; "you can get up and bolt if you like."

Abe Bott needed no further offer of clemency.

He got up with all speed, and ran away at a rate that was marvellous when his size and weight were considered.

Dossy Dodge gave vent to the low chuckle he usually indulged in when thoroughly amused. Then he turned to Dick Cockles.

That unfortunate boy presented a truly pitiable figure of woe. He was engaged in scooping the soot out of his eyes, and in so doing was rubbing it well into his skin.

Dick looked like a young sweep who had dressed for a holiday and had forgotten to wash himself.

"Well! you are in a mess, young 'un!" said Dossy Dodge, in a commiserating tone.

"Thank you for coming to take my part," replied Dick; "the beastly cur!"

"He's all that; but, I say, you must have a wash before you go home."

"Where?" asked Dick, miserably.

"There's no place that I knows on," replied Dodge, "unless it's the parish pump, and that being in the middle of High-street, won't quite do."

"I can go home and wash," said Dick. "Mr. and Mrs. Slapcrash are out. But I've got to buy some things first."

"What things!"

"Tarts and lollipops. We are going to have a feed in the playground."

"I'll get 'em for you," said Dossy; "give me the money and tell me what you want, then go back."

Dick thanked him and brought out the half-sovereign.

Dossy Dodge eyed the coin as if it had been a dear friend on whom he had not set eyes for some time past.

"Three dozen jam tarts, three dozen

sausage rolls," said Dick, "a shilling's worth of cakes, and the rest in hardbake and mixed sweets."

"All right," replied Dossy Dodge, pocketing the money; "get along and I'll soon be back."

"Come to the garden gate," said Dick; "we shall look out for you there."

They parted, and Dick, now able to see about him with tolerable distinctness, started on the return journey.

He kept his eyes ahead to see if anyone was coming, and after two or three false alarms, that each time sent him behind a tree to hide, he turned the corner and disappeared.

Dossy Dodge took out the coin and turned it over and over in his hand.

"Oh! you beauty!" he mused; "I don't think I've ever set eyes on such a nice half-sovereign before. I've been out of work three weeks, and—"

He stopped and looked about him with a face that was white with the struggle that was going on within him.

He had been on short commons lately, and that coin would buy him food for a week. What a temptation for a man in his position!

"I dare say the young 'uns won't miss it much," he muttered, passing his hand across his brow. "Ten shillings isn't a fortune to them, and it's life to me. Oh! dear, why didn't he say he couldn't trust me with it? I shouldn't have thought much on it."

He thrust his hand deep down into his trousers-pocket, and with a set face hurried away.

In joyous anticipation of the coming treat the boys romped about the playground, suspecting no evil.

The minutes flew by rapidly until somebody heard the garden gate close.

Then the intervening door opened, and Dick stood before them.

Nobody knew him.

"Why, here's a sweep!" said Selah.

"No, it ain't," replied Dick; "it's me."

They knew his voice, if not his recently-maltreated person, and overwhelmed with surprise they gathered round him.

"What have you done now?" asked Tom Biron.

"Met Bott," replied Dick, sententiously.

"The old man?"

"Yes; I went round by the city wall."

"The wall on which lies a curse," observed Jem Stager, theatrically.

"Dry up," said Dan Mittens; "let us hear what's been done."

"I met Bott," continued Dick, "and he banged me about with a soot-bag."

"And so you came back again," said Tom Biron, cheerfully. "Quite right. Give me the half-sov. and I will go for the tommy."

"I haven't got it," returned Dick.

A burst of dismay rent the air.

"Are Bott took it away from you?" asked Tom. "If so it is robbery, and we must lock him up."

"No, I gave it to Dossy Dodge," replied Dick.

Another shout was heard—this time it was one of surprise.

"He came up," continued Dick, "took my part, and gave Abe Bott the biggest licking you ever saw in three seconds."

"And then you gave him our money?" said Sam Fusby.

Dick aimed a blow at him which missed, and nearly fell upon his nose.

"Your money, you aggravating beast!" he observed; "what have you to do with it?"

"Dossy deserved it," said Warren Fane, quietly; "and for my part he would be welcome to twice as much. You did quite right, Dick."

"But I did not give it to him," Dick answered; "he offered to get the tarts, as I was not fit to go through the town, so I gave him the money, and he's gone."

"Gone for good," sneered Sam Fusby.

"No, he ain't," roared Dick; "he's an honest man."

This opinion did not meet with general endorsement. The boys' experience of the people of the town, which it must be confessed was limited, led them to think otherwise.

A short silence ensued.

"Well, the money is gone," said Tom Biron, "and there's an end of it. I am sorry I did not go myself."

"Here's another coin," observed Warren Fane.

"A boy made of money!" cried Jem Stager; "what ho! there, welcome to the golden stranger!"

"Put back your tin, Warren," said Tom Biron, "as we are not going to bleed you in that way. We will give Dossy half-an-hour's grace, and if he don't turn up with the grub we will do without it."

"But I insist," replied Warren.

"Insist in half-an-hour's time then," said Tom Biron.

THE SLAPCRASH BOYS.

The Liveliest of School Stories.

"IF I DID MY DUTY," SAID MR. BEANS "I SHOULD SEND YOU TO PRISON."

No. 2.   Price One Penny.

Play was not resumed. Under the circumstances it was not to be expected.

In the first place, Dick had to remove the signs of his recent encounter, and that was no easy task. He did not lack friendly assistance.

They took his upper garments off, and while Jem Stager knocked the soot out of them against the garden-wall, Tom and Warren led Dick into the washing-room.

The friendly Mary, on hearing of the affair, brought an extra bit of soap, and Dick was put under the tap.

"Shut your eyes and keep still," cried Tom, "and we will soon have it off you."

They rubbed and scrubbed for some time before their object was effected, and even then

Modified punishment.

there was a light shading of soot in the few crevices and hollows of the face of the unfortunate Dick.

"It will all wear off in a day or two," said Tom, cheerfully.

"I'm blessed if I don't feel as if I had been scrubbed with a scrubbing-brush," observed Dick, as he put on his coat and waistcoat.

"Has Dossy come with the things?"

"Not yet," replied Sam Fusby; "nor likely to."

"Oh! you miserable duffer!" said Dick. "Do you think everybody is as mean as yourself? Here, you fellows, just listen to me. If Dossy doesn't come back I vote we make a raid on Sam's money-box."

"You touch it if you dare," cried Fusby, white with affright.

"Look at him," said Dick, scornfully; "and yet he said to-day that he had no money."

The detected humbug put his hands into his pockets and tried to whistle, but it was the feeblest performance ever heard.

"Dossy Dodge won't come back," he cried, as he scampered away.

The others were far from willing to endorse this opinion, but in their heart of hearts they feared the worst.

Dodge was, in the true sense, a stranger to them. Until recently they had never set eyes on him, and the only recommendation he brought with him was a promise to stand by one of them in a fight.

That spoke well for his manhood, but was no guarantee of his honesty.

They had taken no note of the time when Dick returned, and they had to guess when the half-hour was up.

As a matter of course they were in too much of a hurry about it, and when twenty minutes had expired they began to talk of an hour having elapsed.

"Done!" said Tom Biron, aside to Warren Fane.

"I am afraid so," was the reply; "but I was never more deceived in my life if it is so. I thought his face was honest."

"Half a sovereign is a great temptation to such a man," Tom said.

"Hurrah!" cried Dick Cockles, "there is a knock at the gate."

Immediately everybody who had said hard things veered round to praise Dossy Dodge, and Sam Fusby cried out, "Three cheers for the navvy!"

"Dry up, you sneak!" said Dick.

He ran off to the gate and saw before him, not the expected Dodge, but a boy from the post-office.

"A telegram for Mrs. Slapcrash," he said.

"Oh! blow your telegram!" replied Dick, sharply.

"And blow you!" returned the boy.

Dick, in anything but his best humour, forthwith reckoned that boy his foe, and went for him.

The two closed and rolled over into the road, until Tom Biron lifted them up, clinging to each other like a pair of limpets, and forced them asunder.

CHAPTER IX.

A MILD MAN IS SCRATCHED AND SHOWS THE
TARTAR UNDERNEATH—TIMES ARE VERY HARD
FOR DICK COCKLES.

"DON'T be a fool, Dick," Tom said ; "the boy
has done nothing to you."

" He told me to be blowed," replied Dick.

The boy, who was picking up his cap from
the pavement, howled out—

" You told me to be blowed first."

" What if I did?" demanded Dick; "who
are you that you are not to be blowed?"

" Get in with you," said Tom, laughing.
" Go to the front door, my boy, and give the
telegram to the servant."

" I shall catch him out one day," replied the
boy, ferociously, "and then I will give him a
licking."

" Yah!" said Dick.

" Booh!" bellowed the boy.

So ended this fearful encounter. Dick was
pushed back into the garden, and the boy
went to the front door to deliver the telegram.

Two minutes later there was another tap at
the gate.

" Dodge this time!" cried Dick.

He would go to the gate again, where he
saw a solemn-looking man dressed in black.

" Can you tell me if this is the servants'
entrance to the bishop's palace?" he inquired.

" Do I look like a bishop?" asked Dick,
venomously sarcastic.

" Don't be rude, boy. Answer my
question."

" No, this isn't the bishop's palace, but we
think it ought to be."

The stranger looked at him pityingly and
passed on.

" The next person who comes to that gate,"
said Dick, " had better be Dodge, or it will be
the worse for him."

" Oh! you will do a lot," remarked Sam
Fusby, sneeringly.

" Wait and see," said Dick.

He went into an outhouse, and after some
rummaging routed out an old door-mat, which
he brought into the light of day.

" This is for the next wrong-comer," he
observed.

" I tell you again," ventured Tom Biron,
" not to make a fool of yourself."

" Can't I make a fool of myself if I like?"
asked Dick.

" Oh! certainly; it's natural," replied Tom.

Tom was amused at the state of exasperation
into which Dick had been worked by untoward
events.

Although another stranger could not
reasonably be expected, they resolved, in case
one did come, to let him do as he pleased and
take the consequences.

Dick took up a position near the gate, with
the door-mat in his hand. Dogged resolution was in his eye, a hard smile about his
lips.

Within a few feet of him stood Sam Fusby,
sceptical of Dick having the courage to carry
out his threat if he had the chance of doing
so.

But it was a day of moving events, and
sure enough within five minutes there was
another knock at the gate.

Dick opened the door with his left hand,
holding the old mat in his right. It was not
Dossy Dodge—they had almost ceased to hope
for him now—but a tall, quiet-looking man,
wearing spectacles.

" I wish to know," he said, " if this is—"

Dick did not hesitate a moment, but with
frenzied force raised the mat and hurled it at
the head of the stranger. It struck him full
in the face, knocked off his hat and spectacles,
and sent him staggering back into the street.

If the gentleman thus unwarrantably
assaulted by Dick Cockles was of mild appearance, he soon showed that he was a person not
to be trifled with.

Discomposed for a moment by the sudden
removal of his hat and spectacles, he rapidly
recovered himself, and seized Dick by the
collar of his coat.

At the same time one of the Smockley police
appeared upon the scene.

It was just like Dick's luck that this officer
should be within hail and a witness of the
assault. The man was ready to do his duty.

" Shall I lock him up, sir?" he asked.

" One moment," said the stranger. "I am
peculiarly situated. The fact is, I have been
engaged by Mr. Slapcrash to take charge of
his school for a time, and this boy, if I am not
much mistaken, is one of the pupils."

" Oh! yes," replied the officer, with a curious
twinkle in his eye; "he's one of them."

The announcement made by the stranger
had a freezing effect upon Dick. The other
boys, who had been standing quietly inside the
gate, exchanged glances of amazement, and
awaited the issue of Dick's unfortunate
rashness.

" My name," continued the stranger, " is

Beans—B. Rord Beans, M.A., F.R.O.I. Probably I am not entirely a stranger to you."

The officer was obliged to confess that he had never heard of him before, and Mr. Beans appeared to be disappointed.

"If I did my duty," he said, turning to Dick, "I should send you to prison, but I think a modified punishment will suffice. Policeman, I thank you for the offer of your services, but will not avail myself of them."

Still holding Dick by the collar—and Dick felt that his grasp was a pretty firm one—he passed through the gateway into the garden, closing the door behind him.

Looking round he said, quietly—

"This is not your playground, is it, boys?"

Tom Biron admitted that it was not.

"Then you have no right to be here," said Mr. Beans, "and I will trouble you to retire to your proper place."

They lost no time in clearing out, for Mr. Beans had a way with him that admitted of no parleying.

"Is Mrs. Slapcrash at home?" he asked.

On being informed of that lady's absence he said it did not matter. Opening the back door he entered the house, taking Dick with him.

For a few moments the boys did nothing but look at each other. The silence was disturbed by Jem Stager.

"Well, this is a start!" he observed.

"What an odd-looking fellow!" said Dan Mittens.

"Odd or not," replied Warren Fane, "we've got a man who knows what he means. Eccentric I should say."

"B. Rord Beans, he said his name was," said Jem, reflectively. "Broad Beans, of course."

"Very broad Beans, I should say," returned Tom Biron; "be quiet there! Somebody, I fancy, is knocking at the gate."

It was so—somebody was gently tapping at the door where Dick had recently distinguished himself.

"Dossy Dodge this time," said Jem Stager.

"Perhaps," replied Selah Finch, grimly.

"Well! somebody had better see who it is," said Tom Biron, "and that somebody had better be me."

All there felt he was running a risk in returning to the garden, but naturally enough they let him go. This time it was Dossy Dodge.

The navvy had resisted all temptation, and been true to his trust.

"Here's the things," he said, handing in several well-filled paper bags. "I've been a long time, but—but—"

Tom understood him.

"Stop here a minute," he whispered. "I've something to say to you before you go."

Tom hurried back to the boys, and having laid the eatables in a heap on the kitchen window-sill, he addressed them, speaking low—

"Dodge has been a long time," he said, "because he's been tempted to take the money. I can see it. He looks clemmed, as they say up North, which means half-starved. Let us have a whip round for him. If any of you have any coppers just put them into my cap."

Unfortunately it was hard times with most of them, but some were gathered together, and Tom Biron had a shilling which he dropped in.

Warren Fane wrapped something in a piece of paper and quietly put it into the cap.

"You have given nothing!" said Tom Biron to Fusby.

"I haven't any money," snivelled Sam.

"You are a mean little beggar," returned Tom.

He emptied the money out of the cap into his hand, and seeing the paper Warren Fane had put in, he exclaimed—

"What's this?"

"It's all right," replied Warren; "give it to him, and say that it is from one who will never miss it."

Tom looked at him curiously, but he said no more just then, and went back to Dodge.

"Here's a trifle got together for your trouble," he said, "and in that paper there is something from one who gives it to you freely."

Dodge, a little bit overcome, unfolded the paper and brought a sovereign to light.

"Why—why—" he began, but he could say no more.

"It's all right," said Tom, hurriedly, "but I can't stop now. No thanks—the coin doesn't come from me. We shall see you another day."

Then he closed the door and rejoined his friends.

Meanwhile Dick had, under compulsion, shown Mr. B. Rord Beans where the schoolroom was, and the future usher of Slapcrash School bade him sit in a corner.

He next got a sheet of cartridge-paper out of the cupboard, and carefully constructed one of those conical caps with which the masters of old-fashioned schools loved to adorn the heads of their backward pupils.

"What is your name?" he asked.

"Richard Cockles, sir," replied Dick.

"Cockles is a good name," returned the usher, "for it is one not likely to be forgotten. You will wear this cap for three days, and do not let me see you without it. You are to remain here until you go to bed."

Left to himself, Dick had a very mournful time of it for the first quarter of an hour.

He was so impressed by the manner of the singular-looking Mr. Beans that at first he was afraid to move. But by-and-bye he got up and stretched his legs.

Finding this act did not bring Mr. Beans back like an avenging spirit, he cautiously started across the room on tip-toe.

He reached the window safely, and breathing hard with excitement, sat down, so as to see without being seen. And what he saw was hard to bear.

They were all busy with the good things Dossy Dodge had brought, and Dick had good reason to repent of his rashness.

"If I had only waited," he thought; "and I am so jolly hungry."

Hungry or not, he was a prisoner until it was time to go to bed.

How wearily the time passed. The only relief he had was listening to the varied sounds in the house as darkness came on.

First he heard the boys come in and go to supper—the supper which they did not want and he longed for so bitterly.

Then he heard the front door open and shut, and Mrs. Slapcrash talking to Mr. Beans in rather a patronising manner in the hall.

After a short delay the boys went to bed, and still Dick was left lonely and sad in the dark room.

"That blessed Beans has forgotten me," thought Dick. "I shall be found cold and stiff on the floor in the morning, and I hope they will hang him for murder!"

But Mr. Beans had not forgotten him. Half-an-hour after the usual time for the boys to retire his footsteps were heard upon the stairs, and he came into the school-room with a candle in his hand.

"Put that cap on the desk," he said, "and come with me, Cockles. I will see you to bed."

Dick removed the cap and meekly followed him—hungry and heartsore.

"He's worse than Slapcrash," thought Dick. "I think I shall run away to sea."

"Show me where you sleep," said Mr. Beans, when they reached the upper landing.

Dick showed him the room and they entered it. The boys were all still; apparently sleeping peacefully.

"Just like 'em," thought Dick, bitterly; "full as aldermen, and not thinking a moment of my empty stomach."

"Undress," said Mr. Beans. "I will wait until you are in bed."

Dick hastily pulled off his clothes, and was instructed in the art of folding them up.

"Clothes well taken care of," said Mr. Beans, "last twice as long as the clothes of careless people."

At last Dick was in bed, and Mr. Beans, after surveying the room through his spectacles, retired.

Dick put his head under the clothes and gave vent to a groan. Then he popped his head out again and listened.

Mr. Beans was closing a door below, evidently that of his own bedroom.

"The beast!" exclaimed Dick, half aloud.

"Who are you abusing now?" asked a quiet voice from the next bed.

It was Jem Stager, who had been awake the whole time. All the boys were, in fact, awake.

"A nice time of it I've had," grunted Dick, "shut up in that beastly school-room, with nothing to eat."

"There is a bagful of something under your bed," replied Jem.

"You don't say so?" responded Dick, briskly.

Several of the boys began to talk, but Tom Biron told them to be quiet.

"We've had all we want," he said, "and Dick's got what he's been groaning for, so go to sleep."

A bagful of good things, more than he could reasonably expect, had been saved for him, and Dick pegged away like a sportsman returned from a day's hunting.

It was rather a mixed feast, but Dick took everything as it came and cleared the bag.

"I feel better now," he murmured.

The only answer he got was a genuine snore from Jem Stager, and feeling rather heavy about the eyelids after his gastronomical exertions, Dick soon fell asleep also.

CHAPTER X.

A PRESENT FOR TOM BIRON—MR. BEANS TAKES THE SCHOOL IN HAND — SYMPTOMS OF REBELLION.

MR. SLAPCRASH was not coming back for a week, and before breakfast time the following morning all the boys knew the reason why.

Mary learnt the fact from her mistress and confided it to Jem Stager—after that it became, as a matter of course, public property.

The rich relative was dead, and Mr. Slapcrash was not coming back until after the funeral and the will had been read.

Hope was in the heart of Mrs. Slapcrash, for the relative just before he departed had said to her husband, "I have not forgotten you, Benjamin," which was, to say the least, encouraging.

A parcel arrived for Warren Fane the morning after the feast, which he opened in the playground. It contained a letter, which he put into his pocket, a gold watch and chain, and a purse quite bulky with money.

It made the mouths of the boys water, and the eyes of most of them stood out like those of a lobster after a short residence in the cooking copper.

Sam Fusby fairly gasped with envy.

"You've got a lot of money there," he said; "your people must be rich."

"Never mind my people," said Warren, quietly; "somebody sends me money. What do you think of this watch, Tom?"

"English lever," replied Tom, putting it to his ear; "first-class workmanship."

"Glad you like it," said Warren; "it's for you!"

"Me?" exclaimed Tom.

"Yes," Warren answered; "I wrote for it—not a word, old fellow."

Tom hardly knew what to say. When a person is truly pleased and grateful words do not come so glibly as they might do, and Tom best expressed his feelings by grasping Warren's hand and holding it tight for a few moments.

It is not to be supposed that all the boys could look on the gift without envy, but only one showed it, and that was Sam Fusby.

When Warren and Tom had sauntered off together, Fusby said—

"Toadying seems to be well paid for!"

"What do you mean by that?" demanded Jem Stager.

"What I say," replied Sam; "I always thought Fane belonged to rich people, but I wasn't going to hang about him for all that."

"Of course not," observed Dick Cockles, sarcastically; "you never hang about anybody when they've got anything good going. But you just go and tell Tom what you've told us."

"I should be a fool if I did," sneered Sam.

"You are a fool always," retorted Dick.

Then there were more ructions, interrupted by the ringing of the school-bell.

Mr. B. Rord Beans was in his place, or rather Mr. Slapcrash's place, and Jem Stager, as he looked at him—tall and inclined to be bald—reckoned him up as something out of the common.

"Just look at his bumps," he whispered to Dan Mittens, as he slipped into his seat; "his head is like a magnified tomato!"

Before the usual routine had proceeded half-an-hour the usher let the boys fully into the secret of the sort of man he was.

Mr. Slapcrash was, as Jem Stager remarked, "very small potatoes beside him."

"Boys," he said, by way of an opening address, "you come to school to learn, and you've got to learn. If you don't learn I shall make you."

"Sultry weather, with heavy showers advancing," muttered Jem Stager.

Poor Dick, whose conical cap had been subjected to many critical comments, was not allowed to sit in his usual seat, but was desired to dispose of himself on a box in a corner.

There he gave up his time to his books, and made gigantic efforts to get them by rote. He was not particularly successful, for the anxiety to acquire something acted as a deterrent and resulted in failure.

Mr. Beans did not hesitate to utilise the cane.

"I am personally averse to using it," he said, "but I am instructed to do so, and I must not forget my duty."

The majority of the boys got a taste of it before the morning was over, but it was observed that Warren Fane, although behind with his lessons, escaped as before.

Mr. Beans simply remonstrated with him.

"You really must try to do better, Fane," he said; "it is essential to your future welfare."

"Can't make it out," muttered Jem Stager; "there's a reason for it, or he would have been licked like the rest of us."

Three days passed over the heads of the

boys, and it was about as rough a time as they had ever known.

For a man averse to the use of the cane, Mr. B. Rord Beans plied it pretty freely, and even Tom Biron got a dose. But it was never so much as wagged at Warren Fane.

Dick Cockles was relieved of his cap, and matters were going on as well as could be expected, when a very disagreeable thing happened.

Warren Fane and Tom Biron spent a lot of their time together, having in view the coming encounter with Jerry Bott.

Neither of the sweeps had shown up since the meeting in the fields, and what they were doing the boys did not know. For the most part they did not care.

The weather was now very hot, about as hot as it ever is in England, and Smockley, lying low, got the full benefit of the sun.

The boys played about in their shirtsleeves, and their coats were hung in a passage they had to pass through on their way to the school-room.

On the day when Mr. Slapcrash was expected back they had their usual noon-day diversion, and in due time were summoned to their really arduous school duties, the weather considered.

The boys hastily put on their coats, and in a body ascended the stairs. Half-way up Warren Fane hastily tried his pockets.

"Odd," he said.

"What's odd?" asked Tom.

"My purse," replied Warren. "I thought I had it with me, but I must have left it in the bedroom."

"When did you see it last?"

"This morning when I was dressing. I took it out for a moment and put it on my bed."

"Do you remember putting it back into your pocket?"

"Can't say I do exactly, but I am almost sure I did."

"How much is there in it?"

"Between ten and eleven pounds."

"By Jove! that's serious."

They had no time to discuss the matter then, nor during school hours, but as soon as they got out again Warren slipped up to the dormitory and searched for the lost purse.

Tom mooned about the playground until he came down.

"Found it?" he asked.

"Not a sign of it," replied Warren, "but I don't want to make a fuss—I have only to write to get some more."

"Have you got a banking account?" asked Tom.

"No—but something quite as good. I don't think we will say anything about this affair."

"Warren—we must. If it has only been mislaid it must be searched for and found. If anybody has taken it we ought to try and find the thief."

"Goodness only knows what I did with it," said Fane. "I think I took it up from the bed and put it into my pocket; but there was the usual morning scramble, and I am not sure."

"Mary has always been looked upon as honest," observed Tom, thoughtfully; "but ten pounds—in gold—I don't know what to think."

"We won't think about it," answered Warren Fane, cheerfully; "perhaps the purse will turn up."

Mr. Slapcrash came home that evening. The station was on the other side of the town, but not more than a mile away, and he usually walked.

On this occasion he came home in an open fly, looking radiant. Mrs. Slapcrash received him in the hall, and the meeting was an affecting one.

It was not generally supposed that their married life was perfect, an occasional "rumpus" between them having been noticed by the boys, but no lovers ever met with greater warmth.

"My dearest Benjamin!"

"My darling wife!"

Jem Stager, from the passage, witnessed the meeting, and drew his own conclusions.

"He's got a lot of money left him," he said; "behold how the wicked thrive."

The main body of the boys did not see Mr. Slapcrash until the following morning, and then not until school began.

Mr. B. Rord Beans presided at the breakfast table, and for his use a second desk had been placed in the school-room.

"Slapcrash means to keep in harness, then," said Dan Mittens, discontentedly; "I was in hopes he intended to give it up."

"What!" interposed Jem, "and hand it over to Beans—the gods forbid!"

With two iron hands over them the boys were kept well at work, or, as they put it, "their noses were held to the grindstone," but Mr. Beans as a champion thrasher was deposed. He was going to perform on Sam Fusby when Mr. Slapcrash interfered.

JIM STAGER AS CHIEF EXAMINER

"Excuse me," he said. "I will do that. Kindly report the boys who are disobedient."

"Very good, sir," replied Mr. Beans, but he did not quite like it.

And that was very strange when we take into account his aversion to the cane.

"I can see one thing which will happen shortly," observed Tom Biron to Warren when school was over.

"What is that?" asked Warren.

"Those two will come to loggerheads before long, and then we shall get some fun out of Slapcrash versus Beans."

"But Beans can be sent about his business."

"Not a bit of it. Mary says he is engaged for six months. Oh! we have good times coming! Hallo! what's this?"

Punishment indeed.

They were crossing the playground, and Tom Biron's foot kicked a small, dark object with a rim of steel, lying on the ground.

It was Warren Fane's purse—empty.

CHAPTER XI.

TOM AND WARREN MAKE A STRANGE DISCOVERY —JEM STAGER PLAYS THE SCHOOLMASTER, WITH DOUBTFUL RESULTS.

THE two boys looked at each other, quite taken aback by this discovery. Tom appeared to be overcome, but at length he said—

"It was not merely mislaid, old fellow. What a miserable business!"

Again there was silence, and as some of the

other boys came near, Tom hurriedly picked up the purse.

"Don't say anything now," observed Warren, hastily; "let us think it over."

The same thought was in the minds of both —Mary must be the thief.

The fact of the purse being in the playground—it had evidently been tossed there during school hours—pointed to her as being the culprit.

"The act of a fool," observed Tom, suddenly; "as if its being found here would implicate any of us."

"Perhaps she simply thought of getting rid of it," returned Warren.

"Of all people in the world, Warren, I should not have suspected her."

"She seemed to me, Tom, to be a good sort of girl."

"The only creature in the house we cared for—rough and kind-hearted. Ah! Warren, she must have been terribly tempted."

"It is my fault," observed Warren, "leaving the purse about. Nobody has a right to place temptation in the way of another. I had better have given it to the girl."

"Come in," said Tom, "and see if we can get a chance to talk to her."

The opportunity they sought was not always to be obtained, for Mrs. Slapcrash devoted most of the little energy she possessed to following the girl about and keeping her going.

Idleness in a servant Mrs. Slapcrash considered an unpardonable sin.

But the legacy had worked a change in that lady as well as in her husband. It had gilded her whole nature, and made her feel that she was a woman of position in the world.

Thereupon she deemed it *infra dig.* to dance attendance on Mary any more, and Mary, it may be said, did her work very much better without her.

The two friends were favoured by circumstances, and found the girl busy dusting the hall.

Her usual appearance was that of a ruddy-faced rustic, with most enviable health, and the average mental capacity of her class. The ordinary expression of her face was stolid.

Now, however, she looked troubled, and there was a tinge of paleness under the sunburn of her skin.

As the boys approached her she turned her

back to them, and proceeded with her work in feverish haste.

"Mary," said Tom.

"Yes, Master Biron," replied the girl.

"Something has been lost—do you know anything about it?"

The girl faced about, flushed and angry.

"What should I know about it, Master Biron?" she demanded.

"I only asked you a question," returned Tom, quietly. "You need not take it up so hotly."

"I don't like it, Master Biron," said Mary, bursting into tears. "It isn't right. If I found anything I should give it to missus."

"Come away," whispered Warren Fane. "I can't stand tears from anyone, much less a woman."

It seemed to be a very sad affair. Everything pointed to Mary's guilt, but the evidence against her was mainly circumstantial.

"Not a word, Tom, to anybody," said Warren. "Let it go until something else turns up, then if it looks black against the girl it will be our duty to speak out."

So the matter rested for awhile. But it was a secret that lay heavy on the hearts of both the boys.

Warren Fane did not care for the loss of his money. It was, in fact, of no moment to him, as you will see by-and-bye, but he felt the whole trouble was something for which he was personally responsible.

He reproached himself again and again for being the means of injuring the simple Mary.

How gladly would he have gone up to her and said, "Keep it, Mary, but never do that sort of thing again." Only he could not see his way clear to do it.

The girl might deny it, and there was, after all, nothing to bring home positive guilt to her.

"Better let it alone," he finally decided, and Tom agreed with him.

Presently there were signs that the prophecy concerning the possible rupture between Mr. Slapcrash and his assistant might be fulfilled.

The principal of the establishment continued to monopolise the corporeal punishment, and Mr. B. Rord Beans manifestly did not like it.

While watching the sometimes deserved lickings bestowed upon the boys, he looked very much like a Peri shut out of Paradise.

Jem Stager compared him to "a muzzled pauper at a feast," but Jem was always great at simile and metaphor.

It was Dick Cockles who was undergoing the familiar ordeal when the signs of rupture came.

In the course of a geographical inquiry, in which all the boys were called on to take part, Cockles said that Mexico was in Africa, then he shifted it to the north of Europe, and finally declared that it was a Mahomedan state in the south of Asia.

This was too strong even from the heir of "The Sausage Emporium," and he was called out to have his mental faculties stimulated by physical application.

On his way to the open space in front of Mr. Slapcrash's desk, which was the recognised place of execution, he had to pass Mr. B. Rord Beans, who rapped Dick's head with his knuckles.

It was a pretty stiff rap, as raps go, and Dick's head being as hard as an ivory ball, gave out a ringing reply. Another time he would have taken it with philosophical indifference.

Now he chose to howl, or rather to give vent to a series of sharp barks, peculiarly hideous to the ear.

"Cockles, be quiet," said Mr. Slapcrash, sternly. Turning to the usher, he added— "Mr. Beans, you forgot yourself."

"Pardon me," returned Mr. Beans, with a slight curling of his lip. "How?"

"You administered chastisement, sir, and that is reserved for me."

"Naturally, Mr. Slapcrash, you would reserve it, and it appears to me to be the only part of a schoolmaster's duty you can creditably perform."

Then they glared at each other, and the eyes of Mr. Beans shone through his spectacles like bits of red-hot iron, but no more words passed between them then.

"The gauntlet has been thrown down," muttered Jem Stager.; "will it be taken up?"

Dick was the greatest sufferer right through, but that was his luck. He got an extra rap with the knuckles because Mr. Beans could not resist temptation, and Mr. Slapcrash gave him an extra dose of cane to show that he, and he alone, had a right to do that sort of thing.

"I am sure I shall run away to sea," muttered Dick, as he resumed his seat.

"A nice sailor you would make," whispered Selah Finch; "why, you'd roll about the deck like a wooden ball in a rocking cradle."

To this Dick made no reply. Neither

mentally nor physically was he fit for a contest with his fellow scholar.

Night came, and the boys were in bed. With the exception of Tom Biron and Warren Fane all in the big dormitory were asleep.

Neither of the friends could lose themselves in the sweet oblivion of slumber, for their minds were busy with that miserable business of the stolen money.

The blind was drawn up, or rather it had never been drawn down, and the moon sent its rays half way across the chamber.

The outlines of the beds and sleeping boys, for the most part, were clearly visible.

Suddenly the stillness of the place was broken by a rustling sound near the door.

"Who's there?" asked Tom.

He and Warren Fane sat up simultaneously, and saw that it was Sam Fusby out of bed putting on his clothes.

"What are you doing, Fusby?" asked Tom.

No answer, but Sam buttoned his braces and moved towards the door.

"You had better answer, you cub," said Tom, angrily.

As before there was no reply. Then Tom got out of bed sharp, and Warren Fane followed his example.

"Don't be in too much of a hurry, Tom," the latter observed. "I think I know the reason of his silence."

Sam had opened the door quietly, and stood for a moment like one listening.

Warren Fane glided up close behind him, with Tom in attendance.

Sam showed no signs of being conscious of their presence.

"You understand now?" whispered Warren.

"Not quite," replied Tom.

"He's asleep!" said Warren.

"A somnambulist!" exclaimed Tom. "I never heard of his being one before."

"And perhaps never will again," replied Warren; "extraordinary mental activity will bring on an attack of it—once in a lifetime only, it may be. He is going ahead—let us follow him."

"Hadn't we better wake him?"

"No, that would be dangerous. We can see that he doesn't get into mischief."

Sam went forward with a curious gliding motion, very unlike his everyday walk, and having reached the head of the stairs he paused.

In the gloom Warren and Tom could only faintly see him, and altogether it was rather a ghostly business. Tom was no coward, but he could not help shivering.

Downstairs went Sam, with no sound save the faint rustling given out by his clothes. Steadily the others kept upon his trail.

He made his way to the school-room, and, opening the door, a flood of moonlight pouring through the windows made the place look as bright as if illuminated by two or three good lamps.

Sam Fusby entered the room and walked straight to the desk usually occupied by Mr. Slapcrash.

It was of the old-fashioned type, plain and strong, standing on legs about three inches in length.

This left a space underneath, where dust and all sorts of odds and ends accumulated until the holidays came round, when the desk was shifted and the rubbish removed.

Down by the desk Sam knelt, and putting his hand under it, groped about slowly and carefully.

"What is he doing?" asked Tom.

"I can only guess," was Warren's soft reply.

They were close behind Sam now, indifferent to the fact that they had only their night garments on, so completely were they absorbed in the movements of the sleep-walker.

After a while Sam brought out a packet and laid it on one of the boys' desks near the window. It was a paper packet tied with a piece of string.

With great care he untied it and disclosed some gold coins and loose silver.

"My money!" said Warren Fane, between his teeth.

"Sam the thief!" muttered Tom. "I thought mean things of him, but never that. Shall we wake him?"

"No," said Warren. "I will tell you of a better plan than that by-and-bye."

Sam, after apparently gloating over the money, did the parcel up again and replaced it. Then he rose and walked with slow and ghostly step from the room.

As he passed the watching boys they saw that his eyes were open, but in them was the strange lifeless look that is seen in those of persons under mesmeric influence.

Fusby went upstairs, and Warren drew out the parcel he had hidden.

"I think, Tom," he said, "that I may lawfully call this mine."

"Assuredly," replied Tom.

" That is all right then. Now we will go to bed again."

" What will you do?"

" Nothing to-night, but to-morrow I may have a word or two to say to Sam Fusby. Poor Mary, how unjust we have been to her."

" But she knows nothing about it," said Tom.

" Well, I shall ease my mind by giving her a tip," returned Warren.

" And I shall ease my body by going to bed," remarked Tom, as they went quietly upstairs.

Sam Fusby was in his bed and calmly sleeping. In a few minutes Tom and Warren were also in the land of dreams.

Another derangement of the school routine took place on the morrow.

Mr. Slapcrash had some legal business to transact in connection with the property he had inherited, and Mr. B. Rord Beans was left in charge of the school.

This was known to the boys before the day's work began, and the morning being wet, they went straight from the breakfast-room to the " Star Chamber," as Jem Stager sometimes called it—the seat of Slapcrash learning.

Having half-an-hour to themselves, and knowing that any great noise would bring Mr. Beans up to make inquiries, the boys were rather puzzled to know what to do with the time.

" We won't waste it," said Jem Stager. " I'll give some of the backward beggars a brush up."

He jumped into Mr. Slapcrash's seat, and taking up the cane from the corner, tapped the desk smartly with it.

" First duffer," he said.

" That's Sam Fusby," replied Dick Cockles.

" I'm not playing," returned Sam.

He was sitting near the window close to the desk, with his hands in his pockets and his eyes moving to and fro, but mainly resting on the spot where he supposed the stolen money was lying.

" Needn't play unless you like," said Jem; " next duffer."

" Selah Finch," replied Dick.

" Not me," returned Selah, contemptuously, " with you in the house."

" Toss for it," said Tom Biron.

Dick borrowed a penny of Warren Fane and tossed.

Of course he lost, and had to accept the position of second duffer in the school.

" Stand there," observed Jem, imitating the voice of Mr. B. Rord Beans; " now compose yourself, and listen to me. Who was the first schoolboy, and what is the date when he got his first licking?"

Dick offered no answer.

" Come—come," continued Jem, tapping the desk with his cane; " don't puzzle over a simple question like that."

" You can't answer it yourself," replied Dick.

" That's impertinent," returned Jem; " here, where's that cap?"

It was in the cupboard behind the desk, and having got it out he put it on Dick's head.

" Harmonious headgear," Jem observed; " now let us proceed with the examination. If you can't answer that question I will ask you something else. Who originated toffee? Who created hardbake? What was the idea of the man who made the first three-cornered tart, and what becomes of the jam that ought to be inside them?"

Again Dick was silent.

Jem Stager got the cane ready.

" As sure as my name is Broad Beans," he said, " I'll give you beans if you don't answer me."

Dick fell upon his knees.

" Oh! Mr. Beans—don't," he cried; " if you hit me I'll tell my mother."

" I don't care who you tell," returned Jem, " so long as it isn't Slapcrash. He'd put a curb on me, and I run a risk in hiding you, but—"

Jem stopped, and a sort of image-like expression came into his face.

Dick got hastily up from his knees and made towards the chimney, as if he thought of going up it. The other boys looked round, following Jem's eyes, and an icy stillness fell upon them all.

Standing at the door was Mr. B. Rord Beans, looking on at the interesting little game.

" So," he said, breaking the silence, " this is how you amuse yourselves in the absence of your teachers."

Jem lost no time in dropping the cane, and if he could have dropped through the floor he would have done so.

But, alas! there was no getting there. He had to stand his ground and take the consequences of playing the pedagogue.

CHAPTER XII.

MR. BEANS IS NOT TO BE TRIFLED WITH.

MR. BEANS walked across the school-room and occupied the seat vacated by Jem Stager.

"You need not remove that cap, Cockles," he observed; "come here."

He took up the cane, gave it a swish or two, and looked like business.

"Excuse me, sir," said Dick, "but Mr. Slapcrash said you wasn't to do it."

A look of general amazement at Dick's daring was observed in the room. He was coming out as he had never done before.

"I can settle that question with Mr. Slapcrash myself," replied Mr. Beans.

Then he gave Dick his dose, a double one, and Dick bore it with Spartan fortitude.

After him came Jem Stager's turn, and when it was all over Mr. Beans took breath. Then, pointing to the door, he said—

"Go to bed, both of you, and stop there during the day."

This amazing sentence caused quite a commotion in the room. The like of it had never been heard before.

Go to bed! Pass the day, the long day, between the sheets! Why, it was the most horrible thing ever heard of.

Once more Dick came to the front.

"Can't we have another licking instead, sir?" he asked, faintly.

"I don't know what you mean by licking," replied Mr. Beans; "I said go to bed."

There was no escape from it, and they went sadly out, conscious of being in a ridiculous and painful position.

"You will undress yourselves," cried Mr. Beans, as they passed through the door.

Slowly and sadly they crawled upstairs, and encountered Mary on the landing.

"Finished our room?" asked Dick, gloomily.

"Half-an-hour ago," the girl replied.

"That's all right," observed Dick. "I hope you have made my bed well, as I've got to stop in it until to-morrow morning."

"Goodness gracious!" exclaimed Mary; "what are you took with?"

"He's been took with an overdose of beans," replied Jem, gravely.

"They does sometimes give people the colic," observed Mary, as she wended her way downstairs quietly.

"Things have come to a crisis at last," said Dick, as he sat down on his bed and began to unlace his boots. "I'm off as soon as I can see a chance of stowing myself away on board some ship."

"Try one of the coal barges that come up the canal with coals and go back with red sand," returned Jem; "if you crawled into the hold you could get well covered up when they are loading."

"You always cut in with a beastly joke," observed Dick; "look here, and here, and here. Isn't that enough to make anybody mizzle?"

He had got some of his clothes off, and turned himself this way and that, exhibiting on his legs and back various records of the cane.

"Bad," returned Jem, "but not bad enough to lead me to make a fool of myself. Believe me, we shall be level with Beans before we've done."

They got into bed without delay, expecting an early visit from the usher, but he did not come near them.

He knew he would be obeyed.

"How beastly cold bed is in the day-time," said Dick.

"Makes one think of sheets of putty," replied Jem.

Leaving them to their irksome confinement, we will go below and put on record the final scene of what may be called "The Slapcrash Purse Trick."

School was over, the rain had stopped, and the boys were dismissed. The morning had been rather a trying one for the majority, and they were glad to get out of the room.

But one lingered. It was Sam Fusby, who was some time in putting his books and things away, so long indeed that Mr. Beans left him at it.

When the usher was gone Sam went to the door, closed it softly, and walked to the desk under which he had deposited his ill-gotten gains.

Unconscious of the surprise in store for him, he knelt down and groped about. Nothing like the packet he sought could, of course, be found.

He felt underneath, with a cold sensation creeping over him, drawing out all sorts of rubbish, such as bits of paper, fag ends of pencils, but nothing else.

"Has somebody stolen it?" he asked himself. Then in his heart there arose a strange unreasoning anger against the thief.

Sam felt bitterly annoyed, and he could have killed whoever had robbed him of his spoil. But he found it hard to believe that the packet was really gone.

Lying at full length upon the floor, he tried to pierce the gloom under the desk, and succeeded in assuring himself that the packet was not there.

"I've been robbed!" he gasped.

"Who has robbed you?" asked a quiet voice behind him.

He looked round and saw Warren Fane, the last person on earth he at that moment wished to see.

"Fusby," continued Warren, "I have come here especially to talk to you."

"Have you?" returned Sam, sulkily, sitting up. "Well, what do you want?"

"I know what you have been trying to find there," said Warren.

Sam turned ghastly pale, and it is no figure of speech to say that his eyes stood fairly out of his head.

"You are looking for the money you robbed me of," continued Warren; "but you will not find it, for I have it myself."

Sam thought he saw a loophole for escape, and stood upon the defensive.

"I have not got your money," he said, "and I never had it."

"Won't do," replied Warren, shaking his head. "I saw you put it there, so did Tom Biron."

"You couldn't have done that," said Sam, eagerly, "for you were in the playground."

"And yet you did not steal it?"

Sam saw the mistake he had made and hung his head.

"When did you take my purse?" continued Warren, after a painful pause. "Tell me the whole truth."

Sam fell upon his knees.

"Oh! forgive me—forgive me!" he cried, holding up his clasped hands. "Don't let it be known at home that I am a thief. Don't—don't!"

"I won't harm you in any way," said Warren Fane, "if you will tell me the whole truth, and promise never to do such a thing again. Get up—don't kneel to me."

There was a strange and wondrous dignity in Warren's manner, quite beyond his years. Sam sat on a form and laid his head upon the desk sobbing.

"Now," continued Warren, "the whole truth, and nothing but the truth."

"I took it out of your coat-pocket as it hung in the passage," replied Sam. "I—I—didn't mean to do it."

"Are you sure of that?" Warren inquired.

Sam writhed like one in physical pain, and gave no answer to the question.

"The whole truth, Sam, out with it," said Warren, impressively.

"I longed for it from the moment I saw it," replied Sam, slowly. "It seemed so much money, and they send me so little from home."

"You are fond of money, Sam?"

"Ye—es."

"Well, there is no harm in that, but don't make it your idol, or it will bring you to grief some day. Now, your promise."

"I will never do such a thing again," said Sam, earnestly; "indeed I won't."

"Very well. Then let it pass," returned Warren. "I blame myself a little for being so thoughtless in displaying my money, and so careless in not keeping it in a place of safety. Only Tom Biron and myself share this dreadful secret with you. You may trust us never to speak of it again. We will try to forget it also."

Sam was quite overcome.

In one way he felt the blow of forgiveness as much as the shame of discovery. The noble generosity of Warren Fane hit him home.

Although not among the most sensitive of boys, he could feel acutely anything that concerned himself, and the pain he now felt was almost unbearable.

"I will leave you now," said Warren Fane, "and you may trust me to take no more notice of the matter."

We may here say, once for all, that he and Tom Biron kept to the agreement, and such high-born generosity, such noble conduct, could not do less than bear fruit, even in the rather sterile soil of which Sam's nature was composed.

CHAPTER XIII.

A VISIT TO A PROFESSOR—JERRY BOTT GETS FIXED—GRIEF AND RAGE OF THE CHAMPION SWEEP.

IN the course of the day Tom and Warren were talking of the coming fight, and Tom, among other things, observed—

"I've taught you all I know, and you have it at your fingers' ends, but a lesson or two from someone better qualified would not be amiss."

"And who is that somebody?"

"That you shall know to-night. I think of going out for an hour."

AT SOME DISTANCE APART THE COMBATANTS GOT READY.

"Leave that to me," said Warren. "I fancy I can get leave for both of us."

"If you can," replied Tom, grimly, "I look upon you as a magician."

"Put me down as a prophet," returned Warren. "I say that I shall not be refused."

He proved to be a true prophet—Mrs. Slapcrash, who was applied to in the absence of her estimable husband, making no demur.

Warren, to show how easy a task it was to obtain leave, asked her when Tom was near.

"You must be back by half-past ten," she said.

"Not a word about where we are going," observed the amazed Tom, when they had left her; "what does it mean?"

Warren Fane only smiled.

Even-handed justice.

"You shall know some day," he replied.

Tom asked no more. He knew there must be some good reason for Warren's reticence, or he would have been confided in, so he was silent.

Eight o'clock was being announced by the cathedral clock as the boys walked through the town, where the slow business movements of the day were being succeeded by the semi-liveliness of the evening.

Half the shops were closed, and the rest were in the course of being shut up for the night.

The assistants, anxious to get away from confinement, were as busy as bees rolling out stuff from the windows, pulling down iron shutters, or putting up old-fashioned ones. Their activity was something to wonder at.

"We are going down a street near where Bott lives," said Tom, "but I don't think we need be in fear on that account."

"I am not afraid," replied Warren, smiling.

They passed Dossy Dodge, who was walking slowly down the street smoking, with his hands in his pockets. He took one of them out to touch his cap, but he made no attempt to stop the boys.

As soon as they had passed him he, however, wheeled round and followed. True as a guardian angel was Dossy Dodge, and although Tom and Warren did not know it, he was on their track all the night until they were safely back in the school.

"Here we are," said Tom, turning into a main street; "I am going to introduce you to Ned Eade, a retired professor of fisticuffs."

"What! *the* Ned Eade?" exclaimed Warren.

"Yes—what do you know of him?"

"Oh! I have read a lot about him—what a manly fellow he was, and all that sort of thing."

The retired prize-fighter lived half-way down the street, and he was standing at the door—a quiet-looking man, between fifty and sixty, with an expression of countenance inclined to be sad.

There was nothing of the rough or black-guard in the old gladiator.

"Good-evening, sir," he said to Tom.

"Good-evening," responded Tom. "I have brought a friend who wants a lesson from you."

"Happy to do what I can for the gentleman," Ned replied.

They entered the house, and Eade opened the door of the front room. The only furniture consisted of half-a-dozen plain windsor chairs. On the walls were a few sporting prints, and half-a-dozen sets of boxing-gloves were hanging together over the mantelpiece.

One solitary gas jet near the gloves was used to illuminate the room, and this Eade lighted.

"Close the door and bolt it, Mr. Biron," he said. "When my neighbours know there's any pounding going on they drop in to enjoy the fun, but when I gets young gentlemen like you it's better to be by ourselves."

The boys thanked him for his discretion, and taking one of the seats the noted prize-fighter said—

"Put on the gloves and have a bout together. Let me see what sort of ground I've got to work upon."

After five minutes' sparring between them he got up and felt Warren's arms.

"Good stuff here," he said, "only it wants to be cultivated. At present you would have to hit twice to knock down the monument."

"The monument he's got to knock down is Jerry Bott," replied Tom, laughing.

"Is that so?" said Eade.

They told him about the challenge and its acceptance, the old prize-fighter listening with a face that might be called lugubrious.

"Young Bott's a thick 'un," he said, "and if he only had as much heart as he's got muscle he would be what he tries to make out he is—boy-champion of Smockley. Unless you can give him something he doesn't bargain for early in the fight he will make a bundle of straw of you."

"My friend will take some licking," observed Tom.

"All the pluck in the world won't put a man on his feet if he's knocked clean out of time," returned Ned Eade, sententiously; "however, I don't want to dishearten you."

"You will not do that," replied Warren, composedly.

"I like that," said Eade; "a stout heart is one of the best seconds in a fight. Now have a turn with me, young gentleman, and don't be afraid of hitting out. Smash at me as if I had killed some of your relations."

The old prize-fighter slipped on a pair of gloves, and Warren, as he was told to do, went for him. He lashed out furiously, but the blows were quietly warded off, Eade watching every motion he made.

"Not a bad attack," he said; "now look out for yourself. I am not going to hurt you."

Warren defended himself pretty well, but, of course, the professor did almost as he liked with him. He, however, honestly expressed approval of Warren's performance.

"You have a quick eye," he said, "and a smart delivery; you also keep your temper. Boxing is not taught for people to batter their friends about, but to defend themselves. Another turn and then we will finish for to-night."

It was soon over, and after a few verbal directions had been given, the boys took their departure.

"Really a decent fellow," said Warren, as they sauntered up the street.

"A very good specimen of his class," replied Tom. "I say, look! there is Jerry Bott."

The young sweep was on the opposite side of the road, hurrying off like one who had to keep an appointment.

He did not see either of the Slapcrash boys, and in an instant an idea flashed upon Tom Biron.

"He is going to the cellars in Mulberry-street," he said; "if so we will have a lark with him."

They were standing close to an ironmonger's shop, into which Tom, after asking Warren to watch which way Jerry Bott went, entered. In five minutes he was out again.

"He is gone down that street," observed Warren, pointing to one twenty yards off.

"Mulberry-street," replied Tom, in high glee; "it's all right."

They strolled on and came to the street which Dick Cockles had such good reason to remember, and were just in time to see Jerry join a knot of boys, who all dived down to the disused cellars.

"We will give them a minute or two," said Tom, "and then follow."

"What are you going to do?" Warren asked; "we shall never be able to tackle that lot if they turn upon us."

"You come with me," answered Tom, "and say nothing."

Warren was game for anything, and after a short wait Tom led the way into the cellars. It looked very dark when they got there, but after a few moments they could see a faint gleam of light ahead.

"The Brothers of Blood are illuminating their council chamber," said Tom.

He walked forward slowly, not knowing what obstacles might be in his way. Happily he found none.

They reached the cellar door and found that the faint streak of light came through the keyhole. Inside the Brothers of Blood were talking and laughing in their rough fashion.

"Stand here," whispered Tom, "and give me these one by one."

He put into Warren's hand half-a-dozen long screws, and went to work with a good strong gimlet.

He had obtained it, with the screws and a screwdriver, at the ironmonger's shop, for Mr. Slapcrash.

It was a rash proceeding, but he expected some money from home on the morrow, which would enable him to pay for the goods.

Swiftly and silently he went on with his work, while the unsuspecting Brothers of Blood enjoyed themselves in their council chamber. Tom Biron judged that they were boxing and skylarking with each other.

At last his work was done, and the gory band were prisoners to a man—or boy.

"Now," said Tom, "we will go home, trusting that they will pass a pleasant night."

It wanted yet half-an-hour or more to the time they were expected back, so they strolled about the town.

It was quiet enough—most cathedral towns are after dark. There is at least an outward appearance of sobriety and order, whatever there may be behind the scenes.

After awhile they came to a public-house, where somebody inside was talking very loudly. They had no difficulty in recognising the voice of the champion sweep.

"Let us hear what he has to say," said Tom Biron.

They stopped outside the door, and heard Abe Bott, who was in the bar, holding forth in this style—

"Stuck-up boys have got to have their stuck-uppishness taken out of 'em, and there's two or three starchy ones in that Slapcrash lot who will have to lie low. My Jerry is going to do it for 'em."

"What do you think of that, Warren?" asked Tom.

"I think that Jerry may possibly fail," replied Warren.

Then they sauntered on, and after an uneventful stroll got back to the school.

We will keep with Abe Bott for a brief spell, and not recounting what happened during the rest of the evening at the public-house, come to the time when it closed.

One of the last to leave was the champion sweep, who lingered long enough to be duly hustled by the potman. He had announced "Time's up, gentlemen," half-a-dozen times before he resorted to an application of physical force.

Abe Bott finding himself in the street, and his late companions being indisposed for any more of his society, rolled homeward with the air of a man who was ready to meet any foe.

Mrs. Bott was sitting up for him with a nightcap on.

She was a little waspish sort of woman, whose life would never have been all honey, but under the circumstances was naturally all vinegar.

Abe spent most of the money he earned, and the poor wretched little woman had to work hard to keep the home together. All the thanks she got were in the form of bad words

and occasional blows, and between her husband and family she had a very fine time of it.

"You are late, Abe," she said.

"Wot of that?" he demanded.

"I only said so, Abe."

"Then don't say it. Wot time did Jerry come home?"

"He ain't home yet, Abe."

The champion sweep was so astonished that he sat down at once, and did so without considering whether or not there was a chair behind him.

As ill-luck would have it there was not a seat within a foot of him, and he went to the floor heavily.

Being a solid man, he fairly made the house shake, and the shock to his system, combined with surprise, rendered him speechless.

Quite a minute elapsed before he could vent his feelings in words. Then, having stripped his language of the inevitable garnishing, we may briefly record his utterances as follows—

"Not come home yet, when I told him to be in by ten o'clock? I'll skin him!"

But we all know that the hare has to be caught before it can be cooked, and Jerry was not there for the skinning, so his father decided to wait up for him.

Having dismissed his wife to bed by asking her "Wot she was sitting there for staring like a howl," he filled and lighted his pipe, and watched for Jerry's return.

Bott watched until he fell asleep, and he slept until daylight came. He awoke shivering, and having, after some mental exertion, recalled the events of the previous night, he went upstairs to see if Jerry had come in and stolen softly to bed.

But the usual sleeping-place of Jerry was empty. Abe Bott did not utter more than a few words.

"Poaching when he's in training. I'll break his neck."

But he had to wait until the neck was in his grasp, and official duties which he could not neglect called him abroad, as they embraced sweeping the kitchen chimney of a minor canon and two flues at the White Hart Hotel.

Shouldering his machine and soot-bag, he went forth into the grey light of the deserted streets, with the fires of parental wrath burning in his bosom.

"I'll make an end on him!" he muttered.

Being out of sorts he rather bungled his work that morning, and was longer over it than usual. He was a good way from champion form.

Having finished with the minor canon's chimney, he turned again into the streets, and the public-houses being by that time open, he had a morning refresher in the form of a pint of purl.

While drinking it an ostler came in, literally laughing all over his face.

"Blest if ever I came near such a lark!" he said.

"Wot lark?" demanded Abe Bott, who was not in the humour to enjoy a jest, and resented anyone else relishing such a thing.

"There's a lot of boys screwed up in one of the cellars in Mulberry-street," the man replied; "old Tom Adams heard 'em howling in the night, and thought it was cats. He went down just now with his dog to settle two or three of 'em. They are getting the screws out, and the police are there to see who it is."

Abe did not wait to hear another word, but, asking permission to leave his machine and bag, he finished his purl at one gulp and hurried off.

Boys screwed up in a cellar in Mulberry-street! He knew very well who those boys were, and had a good idea as to who had done the screwing-up business.

Sick with the angry bitterness he felt, he arrived at the cellar just in time to see a number of laughing people descending, and with them he hurried into the gloomy depths below.

He was soon near the cellar-door, where an old man with a terrier dog beside him was at work with a screwdriver, a policeman providing him light with one of the official lanterns.

"There! that's the last!" observed the old man.

"Come out of it—you there!" said the policeman.

They came out, Jerry foremost, a limp lot of young roughs, scared half out of their wits by their incarceration, which had appeared to them longer than it really was.

Abe Bott collared his son with no gentle hand.

"Come here, you riptile!" he said. "Blarmed if I don't think you are playing a cross against your father with them Slap-crashers!"

"I'll take the names of this lot before they go," interrupted the officer.

This was done, accompanied by a running fire of jocular comment from the laughing spectators, and then they were allowed to leave.

Abe never let go of his son, but when the ceremony of name-taking was over he dragged him out of the cellar into the light of day.

"Oh! don't, father!" pleaded Jerry. "I'm almost dead, I am."

"You will be right down dead and done for," his father said, "if you go agin me this way. Come along home and tell me all about it, you young wampire. Licked by one Slapcrasher, tripped up by another, and now screwed up all night in a cellar. It's enough to make me get a barrel of soot and stand it on my head until I'm choked right off! Come home, you—you—kangaroo—come home!"

———

CHAPTER XIV.

MEETING IN THE GRAVEL PIT—THE FIGHT.

MONDAY was fine, and nothing had transpired to keep the boys from the appointed meeting in the gravel-pit.

With the exception of Sam Fusby and two others, who rather funked the affair, thinking it might end in a general row, all the Slap-crash boys were there, and they were first in the field.

Warren Fane looked pale, but there was a determined expression in his handsome face which showed that he had come there to do his best to win.

He had, indeed, resolved that while he could stand upon his feet he would never give in to that unmitigated young blackguard, Jerry Bott.

Warren stood a little apart from the rest with Tom Biron, and the others were silent, or speaking to each other in whispers.

"Don't forget Ned Eade's instructions," said Tom; "hit hard and straight, and don't let him get hold of you for a throw."

"I will do my best," replied Warren.

Dossy Dodge at that moment lounged into the pit. He came up and touched his cap to the boys, and they returned his salute.

"Abe Bott is priming his cub with drink," he said. "That will give him pluck for a time, but it isn't the sort of thing to last. I am sure, sir, you will knock him into smithereens."

"I will try to beat him," Warren returned.

"Here they come," cried Dick Cockles.

Abe and his son, attended by some of the

usual set of young roughs, now entered the pit, and Abe was talking loudly to his son.

"Don't kill him outright," he said, "for that would be boy-slaughter, and them magistrates might call it murder, for they are allers agin poor honest folks. Just larrup him so that they've got to carry him home."

"Big bluster ain't so good as hard knocks," observed Dossy Dodge.

There were no preliminaries, for the usual courtesies of combat would have been thrown away on Abe Bott and his companions.

At some distance apart the two antagonists got ready for the fight.

Warren Fane took off his coat and waistcoat, folding them up carefully and laying them on the ground as coolly as if preparing for bed.

Jerry Bott dragged off his upper garments and dashed them to the ground with a lot of show and swagger. He also rolled up his sleeves, as if he meant to kill somebody right away.

Then they advanced—Jerry attended by his father and Mike Buttons, while Warren Fane was looked after by Tom Biron and Dossy Dodge.

The rest kept at a moderately respectful distance.

"Now the point of this fight—" began Abe Bott, when Dossy Dodge interrupted him.

"The point of it," he said, "is that you've got to say nothing, but pick up your cub when he's knocked down."

"Oh! indeed," replied Abe Bott, with an evil glint in his eyes.

Abe said no more, and Dossy Dodge, content with having cut short the eloquence of the champion sweep, drew a little aside with Tom Biron.

Abe Bott and Mike prudently did the same, and the two combatants stood face to face. The contrast between them was very marked.

Warren Fane, slim-built, refined in face, and undoubtedly in his boyhood.

Jerry Bott, unwashed, brutal in face, strong in build, and almost a man.

The hearts of the young Slapcrashers went pit-a-pat. They feared that Warren would have but a poor chance with such an antagonist.

Tom Biron was not exactly funking, but he was anxious. If Jerry Bott once got hold of his friend he might gain an easy victory.

Dossy Dodge was as cool as a cucumber.

"It ain't so one-sided as it looks," he said, softly, to Tom.

The boys put up their hands, and took a steady look at each other. It was particularly steady on the part of Warren, but Jerry's eyes were inclined to be shifty.

Suddenly Jerry made a rush for a close, but Warren was too quick for him. He stepped lightly aside, and dealt the young sweep a blow on the side of the head that made him stagger. He followed it up with another blow, a shade lower, that sent Jerry to grass.

Roars of delight from the Slapcrashers.

Abe Bott lugged his son to his feet, and said something in a savage undertone to him.

Jerry promptly came forward again, and before Warren could so much as guess what was coming, the young sweep had closed with him.

It was a cowardly way of fighting, but it was useless to object. Tom Biron, with a quivering lip, looked on the struggle for a fall.

Abe Bott was delighted.

"Give him a downer, Jerry!" he cried.

But Warren was not so easily thrown. He was nimble on his feet, and struggled to hold his own.

"That's a mistake," muttered Tom; "he should get down without winding himself."

In this form of encounter Warren was no match for his foe, especially as Jerry had been primed with drink by his father. The fall soon came, and Warren was undermost.

"That's a beauty!" roared Abe Bott, as his son got up and swaggered back to what may be called his corner, where he sat down upon the knee of his delighted father.

Tom Biron and Dodge went to Warren's assistance, but he told them he was all right, and got upon his feet.

"Why did you let him do that?" asked Tom, in a low tone.

"He came upon me too quick," replied Warren, faintly.

"How do you feel, sir?" asked Dodge.

"A bit shaken," replied Warren, "but no real harm done."

"Poor Warren!" said Dick Cockles; "I wouldn't have had that fall for—for—"

"All the sausages in the kingdom," observed Jem Stager, gloomily. "By my halidame, but the knave had him there!"

"Time!" roared Abe Bott.

"Don't be in a hurry," Dodge replied. "Now, sir, are you ready?"

"Quite," replied Warren, as he stood up.

Jerry, cheered by his supporters, advanced with a confident swagger, and was going to make another rush, but before he could do so he received a smart smack on the nose.

The blow made him blink, water rushed into his eyes, and he stepped back. It was a dangerous movement, and Warren was upon him.

Half-a-dozen blows were rained upon Jerry's head and body, and to escape punishment he deliberately dropped to the ground.

More cheers from the Slapcrashers, and a muttered " You cur!" from the lips of Dossy Dodge.

Tom Biron's face beamed as he gave his chum a rub down, and the next call of " Time " came from their side.

" Now then, hurry up," cried Dossy Dodge.

" Don't be afeared," replied Abe Bott; " we are a-coming."

Jerry advanced with a ferocious expression of face, but instead of rushing he stood on the defensive. Warren, steady and cool, but suffering from his fall more than he cared to show, was in no hurry.

Both were quiet for awhile, and then Jerry made another rush, this time with his head down.

Warren dealt him several stingers upon his thick head, but Jerry was not to be denied. The young sweep's powerful arms were round Warren's legs, and once more he was thrown heavily.

" All over," shouted Abe Bott.

" Not yet," replied Warren Fane, springing up lightly.

Jerry was still near, and tried to close again, but, quick as lightning, Warren hit him twice in the face, then on the chest, and finally on the ear.

Jerry was staggered by this onslaught from a foe he considered he had defeated, and he fell like a coward.

" It will soon be all over," observed Dossy Dodge.

Jerry was not prompt to the call of time, and one of his eyes was almost closed. His mouth, never a pretty one, was now decidedly an ugly object.

As soon as they got within distance Warren was at work again and struck Jerry on the chest.

" Foul!" cried Abe Bott.

" I'll foul you if you are not quiet," replied Dossy Dodge. " Go in and win, sir; he'll soon have had enough."

Warren was now excited, and his spirit flashed out of his eyes like sparks of fire. Two rounds were fought in a give-and-take

fashion, and he received several heavy blows, but kept his feet.

At this juncture Abe Bott gave his son something out of a bottle, and Dossy Dodge cried " Shame!" but the champion sweep only answered him with a derisive gesture.

Jerry now came forward as ferocious as a wild boar.

" Keep cool," said Tom to Warren.

Warren steadied himself, and then the final round of this memorable fight took place.

It opened with an exchange of blows, one of which nearly knocked Warren down. Then Jerry tried the old game of closing, and received a terrific uppercut under the chin, delivered with wonderful force by Warren.

It fairly lifted his head up, and as he uttered a howl Warren went for him. From that moment Warren seemed to do just what he liked with his burly foe. He literally walked round him, staggering him with blows all over the face and body.

Jerry tried to ward them off, tossing his arms up and down. Failing, he tried to run, and then it was all over with him.

Collecting his whole strength, Warren dealt him a blow that knocked the burly young ruffian to the ground as if he had been shot.

The fight was over. Jerry either could not or would not rise, and his father raved at him in vain.

Thrice was " Time " called and there was no response. Then up went the Slapcrash caps and hats into the air.

Abe Bott turned fiercely towards them, and was about to rush into their midst, when Dossy Dodge put himself in the way.

" None o' that," he said; " I'm here," and Abe Bott stopped short. " I knew that would be his game," continued Dossy Dodge. " Can I help you, sir?"

" If you please," replied Warren, faintly; " and, Tom, let us get away from here."

" What's the matter, old fellow?" asked Tom, in alarm.

" I feel as if I'm going to faint," replied Warren. " I am not used to this sort of thing. Don't let that blackguard see what the fight has cost me."

Tom took his arm, and they hurried out of the pit as fast as Warren's condition would permit.

As soon as they were out of sight of the dismayed friends of the defeated Jerry, Warren said he would like to sit down.

" I think I have got a rib broken," he said;

THE SMOCKLEY AVALANCHE, THE SCENE OF THE GREAT CATASTROPHE.

"it was when he threw me first. But don't be alarmed, I am better now."

"Talk of pluck," observed Dossy Dodge, quite overcome with admiration. "Ah! now I understand the feelings of officers when they lead their men right up to the canon's mouth."

The Slapcrash boys had gathered round, quiet as mice. Their feeling towards Warren might be called reverence.

In a few moments Warren said he would go on, and in a body they walked slowly towards the town.

Ere they had gone far they heard loud noises in the pit, followed by a dismal howling. Abe Bott was chastising Jerry for having suffered defeat.

The ruins.

CHAPTER XV.

WARREN FANE AFTER THE FIGHT—LEAVE TO GO INTO THE TOWN—SUCH A GETTING DOWN-STAIRS AS NEVER WAS SEEN.

IT was about a week after the fight between Warren Fane and Jerry Bott, and the evening hour. Scene, the private sitting-room of Mr. Slapcrash.

On a sofa, by a window overlooking the playground, lay the victor of that never-to-be-forgotten fight, looking out in excellent spirits.

By his side sat Tom Biron, and outside, leaning one arm upon the window-sill, stood Jem Stager.

"And they have neither of them asked what has been the matter with you?" observed Tom.

"Not so much as hinted at it," replied Warren. "I did not expect they would. The doctor knows, of course, and he was kind enough to say the fracture of the rib was a minor one, but it has been painful enough to earn the name of major."

"You are better now?"

"Oh! yes, immensely. I am to go out to-morrow, but I must be careful for a week or two."

"By my sword of steel," exclaimed Jem Stager, "but it was a knightly victory! The son of the arch-sweep, thy foe, has not been lurking round our castle since the hour of his fall."

"I meant to win or get killed outright," said Warren. "By-the-way, is it known in the town that I received an injury?"

"Only to Dossy Dodge," Tom Biron replied, "and he loves us too well to give the smutty Bott the joy of knowing how you have suffered. Of course we have not sung songs about it, and you may rely upon Mr. and Mrs. Slapcrash not talking about one of their pupils fighting with a sweep."

"Especially since they inherited the family estate," said Jem Stager, "and eat periwinkles off plates of gold. Mrs. Slapcrash now takes in two Society papers and talks scandal. Ah! 'tis a parlous state of things. What say you, Dick?"

"Nothing to you," replied Dick Cockles, who at that moment presented his rubicund countenance at the window. "I came to ask Warren how he was."

"Better," returned Warren; "almost well."

"Thanks to our kindly care," observed Jem Stager, softly.

"You've got a lot of kindly care in you," said Dick, disgusted; "all you think of is getting up a joke at the expense of somebody, while other people get licked for it."

"What's the matter now?" asked Tom Biron.

"Oh! nothing," replied Dick, with an injured air; "but when a fellow shoots a pea out of a catapult and hits the hat of a tutor, he ought to see first that another fellow isn't close by to get the blame."

"By the honoured name I bear," observed Jem Stager, "the pea was aimed at thee in jest, and at a part of thy noble frame on which no hat was ever hung. Tempted by the preternatural tightness of thy garment, I hurled the little pellet, to my shame, with faulty aim."

"It made his hat ring like a basin," said Dick, relapsing into a grin, "and he turned round and looked at me with eyes like bassinets—"

"Like what?" asked Jem.

"Well, basse—something," replied Dick; "we were reading about it the other day in class. Fascinates things when it looks hard at 'em."

"Hear it, ye gods!" observed Jem Stager, in a tone of unadulterated horror; "this boy, the pride of the unrivalled mystery-producer, calls a basilisk a bassinet. Away with him to the scaffold—hang him by one leg from the battlements—let him writhe in chains—of sausages—"

"Oh! drop it, Jem," said Tom, laughing; "Warren can't stand it yet—he has to be kept quiet. By-the-way, it just occurs to me that I never paid for those screws and the screw-driver wherewith I imprisoned the Brothers of Blood all night in the cellar. I suppose I can get leave to go out for an hour."

"I, too, have business of importance within the precincts of the town," observed Jem, reflectively. "I lack ammunition for my catapult."

The door of the room opened at this moment, and Mr. and Mrs. Slapcrash came in.

They appeared to be in a good-humoured frame of mind, and with a kind word checked Jem and Dick, who were on the point of skedaddling—sharp.

"You do quite right in endeavouring to relieve the solitude of your sick friend and fellow pupil," Mr. Slapcrash said. "I trust, Fane, you are better. The doctor gives a good account of you."

"I am better, thank you," Warren replied, "but there is one thing I should like, and that is some fruit."

"You shall have it at once," said Mrs. Slapcrash. "I am going into the town—"

"Indeed," interposed Warren, "I should not think of troubling you. Biron will go, and if he is accompanied by two or three others he will not be molested by the roughs."

Tom was about to declare that he did not care a straw for all the roughs in the neighbourhood, when he caught Warren's eye.

It flashed upon him then that the object of his friend was to save him and the others the bother of asking for leave.

"You are prudent, Fane," said Mr. Slapcrash, "and there is security in numbers, of course. Biron, you had better go at once, and take some of the quieter boys with you."

The quieter boys with whom Tom left the house were Jem Stager, Dick Cockles, and Dan Mittens, and they went forth in high spirits.

Nothing had been seen of Jerry Bott since the fight in the sand-pit. He and his followers had alike made themselves conspicuous by their absence. But it was hardly likely that the boys would be able to walk through the town without seeing some of them.

Tom Biron called at the ironmonger's and paid for the things he had for Mr. Slapcrash, and then he proposed to go and see Ned Eade, who had not as yet received a record of the fight.

Smockley is a town where there is a considerable difference in the level of the streets, and in some cases it is so steep that foot-passengers make use of a flight of stone steps built between the houses.

The boys were now in Barton-street, which is on the high level, and below was Pilby-street, which was reached by one of the flights of steps aforesaid.

It was down these steps they meant to go, but on nearing them they became aware of the presence of Jerry Bott and Mike Buttons.

They were lying curled up on a sort of coster's barrow, in which Abe Bott used to bring home the soot he obtained from the country or distant places.

It was, in one sense, a most unfortunate meeting.

In the first place the Slapcrashers, elated by unwonted liberty, were ripe for mischief—Jem Stager particularly so—and the sweep's barrow and flight of steps as a combination offered them a means for the indulgence of their animal spirits.

The first thing Jem did was to stop and dig Jerry in the ribs.

"Wake up," he said; "what do you mean by making a four-post bed of your father's barrow?"

Jerry opened his eyes and glared at him.

"You let me and my father alone," he replied, sullenly.

"Where is your father?" asked Jem.

"In Pilby-street if you want him," growled Jerry.

"He wants you, he longs for you, he thirsts for his only son!" said Jem.

"Well, let him thirst, or burst, or do what he likes," returned Jerry.

"Unfilial wretch—ingrate!" cried Jem; "go to your parent and ask his pardon. Lay hold, Dan—away with you!"

Neither Tom nor Dick knew or guessed what was about to be done. As for Mike Buttons, he was lying lazily on his back, indifferent to what was going on.

Both the young roughs had been drinking. But when the barrow began to move Mike sat up with a jerk and bawled out—

"What are you doing? Clear out, you whelps!"

"Down with it, Dan," said Jem.

It was done in a moment.

Tom Biron had no time to interfere, which he probably would have done had he known what was in Jem's mind, and the barrow was swung round and shot down the flight of steps into Pilby-street.

By good luck nobody was coming up, and the terrified occupants of the vehicle made no effort to jump out.

With a crash the whole concern descended into the street below, pitched on the fore part, and turning right over, buried Jerry and Mike under it.

"I say, Jem," said Tom Biron, "what have you done now?"

"Shaken the rest of the soot out of that scurvy knave," replied Jem Stager, easily.

"I must go down and see what mischief has been done," observed Tom.

"Better all go!" said the others.

By this time there was no small commotion in the street below.

As a rule it was one of the quietest parts of the town, many of the houses being occupied by that deserving class, clerks with limited pay, and small tradesmen, to whom position was no great object.

There was a baker, a grocer, a bird-fancier, a jobbing tailor, and a barber. Hearing the unearthly rattle of the barrow, they all left their domiciles in hot haste to see what had happened.

Others came out—men, women, and children —some thinking that an earthquake had occurred, a few opining that dynamiters had been at work, and one dear old girl fully believing that the end of the world had come.

Abe Bott, who had been having a "quiet glass" in a beer-shop, rushed out too, and as soon as his fatherly eye beheld the barrow, with a pair of ill-shod feet sticking out from under it, his astute mind realised at least half the fact.

"My Jerry and the Slapcrashers!" he roared out. He rushed forward, turned over the barrow, and picked up his promising son.

Jerry gave no sign of life, but his father knew that beyond a shaking he had received no material hurt.

People lying stiffly in the arms of those who pick them up after a fall have no bones broken.

Mike Buttons was left to take care of himself, and he rose to his feet and stared wildly about him.

"Jerry," said Abe, making the most of the situation, "speak to your dad."

Jerry opened one eye and coughed.

"Who done it?" asked Abe.

"Wot's the good of my saying?" gasped Jerry. "You knows."

"I does," replied Abe, looking around at the wondering spectators, "and I says that it's now come to a case of public inquiry, with Government inspectors and other coves as knows how to get at the bottom o' things."

"Your son seems to ha' got at the bottom," remarked the baker, who had a faint sense of humour in him.

"Jokes, Mister Doughey," replied Abe, severely, "are out of place when boys is crashed, and bashed, and smashed. Hallo! here's the party as did it."

Tom Biron stood near, and as Abe pointed a finger in his direction every eye was turned upon him.

"Pardon me," replied Tom, "I have not interfered with your son."

"Who ha' done it, then?" demanded Abe.

"Find out!" replied Tom. "It was a wild, foolish trick, but I don't sympathise with you, because you are a bully."

"Hear—hear!" cried the tailor, a little man, weighing something under eight stone.

"What do you mean by your 'hear—hear,' Mister Cabbage?" demanded Abe.

"What I says," replied the tailor. "You are a bully, and he's a bully. Now then, old sooty head, make what you can of that!"

"If anybody will hold my mortially wounded boy," said Abe, "I'll take the nonsense out of goosey snip."

"Lay him down," suggested the baker; "a little wallowing in the dirt won't hurt him."

"I'll be blessed if you ain't a nice lot!" said Abe, swelling with disgust; "if I'd ha' known the sort of persons there was in this place I'd ha' never come to live among you."

"You don't want an Act of Parliament to go away again," remarked the tailor.

"No," said Abe, "and Acts of Parliament won't make me go away. Now, Jerry, are you a coming round?"

"I'm a gettin' better, father," replied Jerry, making the most of his shattered condition.

"Gettin' better!" observed Abe. "What do you mean by 'lowing yourself to be thrown down a flight of steps? If I was chucked off a steeple I'd git up and larf at the low people as served me such a mean trick. Stand up, will you?"

A jerk of unnecessary violence planted Jerry on his feet, and Abe Bott proceeded to take possession of his barrow.

Mike Buttons being in his road, he thrust him out of the way without the slightest ceremony, and laid hold of the handles.

"Git on it, Jerry," he said, "and I'll wheel you home. Maybe I'll take you to the dean or the bishop, to hear what they thinks of it, but anyhow I'll bring the marauder who did this scurvy trick to shame. This sort of thing goes on for a time, but there comes an end to it at last. Get aboard, Jerry!"

With every show of intense suffering, Jerry crawled on to the barrow, and Abe started on his homeward journey.

A derisive cheer from the spectators penetrated his sooty clothing and reached his very heart.

"Look here," he said, "if anybody in this street gits his chimbley afire, don't send for me. I wouldn't come for untold gold, all put up in bags like real suverins at the bank. Now, Jerry, if you means to balance the barrer, get more forrard, or it may be you'll turn over in the road again."

Burning with just indignation he moved on, followed by a score of idle little boys, who, with the joy of their race in cheap exhibitions, were bent on seeing him home.

More derisive cheers pursued him up the street, and even after he had turned the corner.

"All right," he muttered; "the Slapcrashers are on the top now, but wait until I get one of 'em in a quiet corner. Get a little more forrard, Jerry. Ain't you got no respect for your father, or do you want to wear him out with the job of wheeling you home?"

CHAPTER XVI.

ABE BOTT INVOKES THE LAW ON HIS SIDE.

MR. SLAPCRASH no longer took his meals with the boys—that duty was deputed to Mr. B. Rord Beans.

On the second morning following Jerry Bott's aerial flight down the steps the principal of the school and his wife sat at breakfast enjoying a variety of good things, which their recently-acquired money enabled them to obtain.

To them entered Mary all in a fluster, red and white by turns, and evidently, in a metaphorical sense, standing upon her head.

"Oh! if you please, sir, and ma'am," she gasped, "here's the supperintender of the police in the hall, and he wants to see master pertic'ler."

"What's the matter now? I wonder what they have been doing?" muttered Mr. Slapcrash. "Show him into the parents' reception room, and tell him I will be there immediately."

"Who are they?" asked Mrs. Slapcrash, sweetly.

"Isn't that a donkey's question?" asked Mr. Slapcrash, glaring at her.

"You ought to know!" she retorted.

Mr. Slapcrash angrily pushed his plate away and left the room.

The apartment in which he usually received parents was on the other side of the hall, and here all the arts and sciences had been gathered together for their edification.

There was a pair of globes, a worn-out old piano, several maps, a box of mathematical instruments, an easel with a half-finished picture upon it, and sundry other articles calculated to impress the parental mind.

The inspector was studying the unfinished picture with a dubious expression of face when the schoolmaster entered the room.

He was a portly, well-made man, with a very pronounced official manner, but gracious withal.

The inspector and Mr. Slapcrash were old friends, as they frequently spent an evening together at the White Hart Hotel.

"How are you?" he asked. "I have come over with this thing myself." He held up a slip of paper. "It's a summons taken out by Abe Bott, the sweep, against two of your boys, for violent assault upon his son."

"Who are the boys?" asked Mr. Slapcrash.

"Biron and Cockles."

"I'll have them in and hear what they have to say."

He rang the bell for Mary, and she was despatched with a message for the boys. In a few minutes they were in the room.

"Leave them to me, Mr. Slapcrash," said the inspector. "Now, young gentlemen, I've a summons for both of you"—Dick Cockles turned pale—"to attend the police-court"—

Dick staggered a bit—" from Abe Bott. You know what it is about, don't you?"

"About that barrow business, I suppose," said Tom, gravely.

",That's it!" returned the inspector; "now tell me all about it—how much you didn't do."

Tom told him he did not touch the barrow, but would rather not say who did.

"It's all right," said the inspector, complacently. "What I want is to settle Bott. He's a troublesome fellow, and he won't get too much favour in court."

Tom then told him all, and the inspector listened with a quiet, satisfied smile on his face.

"That will do," he said; "the summons is returnable at twelve to-day. You must appear, and I should like to have the other two young gentlemen in my room until they are wanted."

"What are you going to do?" asked Mr. Slapcrash.

"Come to the court and see," replied the inspector. "You understand these gentlemen are not to be punished."

"Very good," said Mr. Slapcrash, with a grim smile; "but it might have been otherwise if I had found them out."

The inspector then went away, and Jem Stager and Dan Mittens were apprised by Mr. Slapcrash of the need of their appearance at the police-court.

As the reason for their attendance had been withheld by the inspector, they were imbued with the belief that Tom and Dick would be examined and the case dismissed. Then they would have to go into the dock and suffer.

This did not tend to the fixing of their minds upon their books that morning.

"I hope they will fine us," said Jem Stager, dolorously, "then Slapcrash will pay and put it down in the bill, but should we be sent to prison—"

He could not pursue the subject further. The termination of their little adventure threatened to be too fiercely dramatic even for him.

"You won't fatten on skilly," observed Selah Finch, a little later on.

"I'll skilly you if you don't hold your tongue," growled Dan Mittens.

Neither of the expectant sufferers was able to get through a single lesson in a satisfactory manner, but Mr. Slapcrash was very merciful to them.

He probably understood the mental disturbance with which they were afflicted.

The whole school, in fact, showed that the educational air was disturbed, and in all the history of the Slapcrashers there had assuredly been no day like it before recorded.

One good thing came out of it, from a boy's point of view. To attend the court with punctuality it was necessary to close the work of the morning half-an-hour before the usual time.

It was announced by Mr. Slapcrash about eleven o'clock, and that made matters worse. A terrible demoralisation of the pupils ensued.

Blunders right and left took place. It was like a game of cross-questions and crooked answers, until even the patience of Mr. Slapcrash, very great that morning, was nearly exhausted.

Selah Finch was the last straw that broke the camel's back, and the back he broke belonged to Mr. B. Rord Beans.

The usher had suffered terribly. Not only did he feel the pangs of Tantalus through being shut out from the Paradise of thrashing, but he saw so many good opportunities wasted—literally thrown away—by the legitimate operator that his heart fairly ached.

He had a cane down by his desk—it had been there from the first, and had long lain idle.

Fully a score of times that morning did he grasp it with itching fingers, but could not quite summon courage enough to use it.

At last Selah Finch came up to be examined in arithmetic, in which he was ordinarily very smart. He was, in fact, just then being coached to make a sort of show-pupil before friends and visitors on breaking-up day.

Now, however, he exhibited an exasperating ignorance of the most ordinary calculations, and Mr. B. Rord Beans, almost beside himself, brought out his cane and stood erect.

"Now," he said, "answer me. If—"

"I really don't know anything about it this morning, sir," interposed Selah, "and it is no use asking me."

This was very bold, but it was nothing but the truth.

"I must see if I cannot extract an answer from you," replied Mr. B. Rord Beans.

Cane in hand, he was about to go on with the question, when the eyes of Mr. Slapcrash fell upon him.

"Mr. Beans," he said, "you are forgetting yourself again."

"Mr. Slapcrash," replied the tutor, "I do not forget myself. This boy deserves a thrashing, and I must administer one."

"If Finch is to be flogged," retorted Mr. Slapcrash, descending from his perch, cane in hand, "that duty devolves upon me."

"I cannot admit that much," replied Beans.

"Sir!"

"Sir to you."

Then the master and tutor faced each other, and a dead silence fell upon the school.

CHAPTER XVII.

THE STRUGGLE IN THE SCHOOL—AWAY TO THE COURT—EVIDENCE FOR THE PROSECUTION.

IN one way the two men were suggestive of two gladiators in the arena preparing for a struggle.

Mr. Slapcrash, it was known, was a very muscular man, but the tutor was as one untried—a sort of dark horse, who might do a great deal or nothing. Nobody knew what he was capable of.

"Mr. Beans," said Mr. Slapcrash, "will you have the goodness to resume your seat?"

"I shall do nothing of the sort," replied the tutor, "until I have corrected the pupil entrusted to my care."

"Mr. Beans, consider yourself dismissed from this school."

"I was engaged for six months, and for that period I shall remain."

Mr. Slapcrash took a deep breath, and went on, after a struggle with his pecuniary leanings—

"You shall have your six months' pay, but you will leave my house this day—this very hour."

"I shall do no such thing," replied Beans. "It would prejudice my future career. Here I remain, and let me tell you this, sir—if I am not allowed to cane an obstinate boy neither shall you."

A glow of joy went through the whole school. The boys, one and all, saw a joyous time ahead.

Mr. Slapcrash now lost control of himself, and being unable to put his wrath into words, pointed to the door.

Mr. B. Rord Beans smiled contemptuously, but did not budge an inch.

Then Mr. Slapcrash did a very rash thing. He put a hand on the coat-collar of the tutor with the intention of ejecting him.

The next moment he received a blow in the eye that sent him staggering back. It was a good hearty smack straight from the shoulder, like a brisk application of the flat side of a chopper to a round of beef.

The first blow was followed by a wild sort of upper-cut and a fine display of sparring on the part of the tutor.

Mr. Slapcrash did not return the blows, but he backed to the door with his hand to his eye.

"Mr. Beans," he said, "this matter must be settled legally. Boys, the school is dismissed."

Mr. Beans subsided into an attitude of contemptuous indifference, and with one hand on his hip and the other in his trousers-pocket he watched the boys file out.

As soon as all were gone Mr. Slapcrash, quivering with rage from head to foot, advanced a step or two nearer to his assistant.

"Mr. Beans," he said.

"Sir, to you," replied the tutor.

"You shall repent your dastardly work as sure as you are a living man."

Mr. Beans snapped his fingers derisively, and whistled two bars of "Rule Britannia" a note and a half flat.

Nothing more was said, and Mr. Slapcrash, retaining what dignity he could, strutted from the room.

The moment he was gone Mr. Beans struck an attitude copied from the statue of Ajax defying the lightning, and laughed hoarsely.

"'Tis done," he said; "the blow for liberty has been struck. Beans, you are a man."

Meanwhile Mr. Slapcrash had precipitated himself into the presence of his wife, burning with the tidings of the tutor's rebellion, and she, seeing his swollen eye, precipitated herself upon his bosom.

"Benjamin," she cried, "what is it?—speak."

"That villain, Beans," replied Mr. Slapcrash, "has struck me before the whole school."

"What!" shrieked Mrs. Slapcrash, really concerned.

"I will tell you all by-and-bye," observed Mr. Slapcrash; "but now I fear I have no time to spare, as I have to be at the police-court in a quarter of an hour. Get some warm water and bathe my bruises, also that old green shade your mother used to wear, to put over my eye."

Mrs. Slapcrash hastened to obey, and murmuring all sorts of things she would like

THE SLAPCRASH BOYS.

The Liveliest of School Stories.

LIKE TWO GLADIATORS THEY STOOD BEFORE EACH OTHER.

No. 3.   Price One Penny.

to do to the pugilistic Beans, soon had her husband fixed up well enough to attend the court.

The green shade, being a large one, acted as a very fair screen to the bruised optic, and if it did not improve Slapcrash's limited stock of beauty, it took away the utter degradation attending the possession of a black eye.

The superintendent called at ten minutes to twelve, and took Jem Stager and Dan Mittens away with him.

Mr. Slapcrash, Tom, and Dick followed a minute later, Tom having had a few hasty words with Warren Fane to explain matters.

The rest of the boys were told they could attend the court if they liked, and of this permission they all availed themselves.

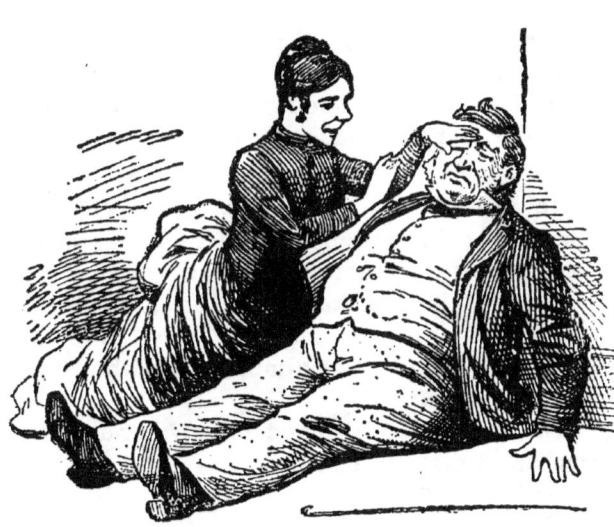

Tending the wounded.

Mr. B. Rord Beans invited himself, and Mrs. Slapcrash being promised a seat at the solicitors' table by the obliging inspector, she went also.

Thus the whole establishment—excepting Mary, who wanted badly to be there, and Warren Fane, not yet able to indulge in any excitement—attended the court to hear the case or take a share in it.

The people of the town showed up in force. Everybody who could leave their work, or had no work to do, put in an appearance, and the place was full.

It was an impressive scene.

There was a chief magistrate—the Mayor of Smockley—on the bench, and all the officials were in their places.

Abe Bott and Jerry stood near the witness-

box, ready to get up and give annihilating testimony against their foes. Jerry had been prepared for his public appearance as a witness by his father.

He had his head tied up and his arm was in a sling. Acting also in accordance with instructions from his astute parent, he put on a sort of collapsed air, as if he had been utterly smashed, or nearly so.

As a matter of fact he had by good fortune received no injury at all. The hardest knocks fell to the lot of Mike Buttons, who did not appear as a complainant.

Tom and Dick were not put into the dock. The inspector whispered a few words to the magistrate, and they were told to sit down in front of it.

"If I was them and them was me," said Abe Bott, "things would be different."

"Silence!" cried the usher.

"Who is the complainant in this case?" asked the chief magistrate.

"Here he is, your washup," replied Abe Bott. "Now, Jerry."

It was a beautiful sight to see the fatherly care with which he assisted Jerry into the witness-box.

"Bear up, my boy," he said; "it's an orgeal for you, but you've got to go through with it as a public duty."

"If you are not quiet," the magistrate observed, "you will be removed from the court. Are you a witness in this case?"

"I am, my lord—your washup," replied Abe.

"Then I think you had better retire."

Abe was not prepared for this, and there was a troubled look on his sooty face as he replied—

"I goes freely, my lord, if you wish it, but my boy is bad and may miss his father."

"You will have to leave the court," was the calm reply.

Abe left, and Jerry was called upon to tell his tale. In brief it was this—

He was sitting in the barrow waiting for his father when Tom Biron and Dick Cockles came up, and the former, without a word, struck him in the face. Then, before he could recover himself, they laid hold of the barrow and ran it down the steps.

Having told his tale he was allowed to go without being cross-examined, much to his relief, and he fairly skipped out of the witness-box.

This activity, being compared to the way he was helped in by his father, excited the derision of the spectators, and a titter ran round the court.

Enter Abe Bott.

He came into the court like a man who had a lot of truth to tell, and meant to out with it all if he were led the next moment to the scaffold for it.

Abe's story naturally differed from that of his son.

"I was not on the barrer, my lord—your washup," he said, "but I was at the bottom of the steps and see it all done. It was a mercy I wasn't killed myself."

"Could you not have stopped the barrow in its descent?" asked the magistrate.

"My lord," expostulated Abe Bott, "it came down like a cattlerack driven forward by an earthquake."

"Well, you saw it done. What next?"

"I heard the prisoner at the bar—that one," pointing at Tom, "holler out, 'I hope as your neck is broke, as that is what I have been laying myself out to do for a long time.'"

"You swear to that?"

Abe Bott looked at him before he answered.

"I want the book I kissed just now," he said, "and you'll see how I'll swear to it."

"There is no need to go through the form again," the magistrate replied; "you have sworn, and that is enough."

"I may say, my lord," observed Abe, "that I don't bear no malice to the prisoners at the bar, but simply come forrard as a protector of the public, to stop the lives of innocent people being put in peril."

"You can stand down," was all the magistrate said.

Abe Bott, with a satisfied smile upon his face, left the box, and sat down beside Jerry on a seat in the rear.

"We've done 'em, Jerry," he murmured; "six months at least."

CHAPTER XVIII.

EVIDENCE FOR THE DEFENCE—IS THIS LAW?

THEN up rose the inspector and addressed the court.

"Your worship," he said, "I have, at the desire of Mr. Slapcrash, who only wants the truth to come out and justice to be done, investigated this case, and will now with your leave call his witnesses."

"I hope you are not counsel for the defence," observed the magistrate, smiling; "that would be outside your office."

"No, your worship," the inspector replied; "I simply wish to show what really happened, and for the right parties to have the blame, if blame is to be attached to anybody."

Abe Bott sat quite still, with his ears pricked up to catch every word. He began to wonder if there was any hitch in the case, and if so, what it was.

No time was lost in enlightening him as to the nature of the defence.

Enter the witness-box Jem Stager, feeling very much like a strong-nerved actor appearing in public for the first time.

"Witness for the defence, your worship," said the inspector.

Mr. Slapcrash's one available eye was fixed upon Jem with a look of keen interest. He had never before seen his dramatic pupil in his real character.

The fact was, Jem did not bestow a thought upon the presence of the schoolmaster, but kept his mind on his being in the witness-box, and he meant to make the most of the position.

He told his story simply and clearly, restraining himself by a violent effort from interjecting any embellishment. "By my halidame," he checked twice upon his lips, and the longing to speak of Jerry Bott as "a scurvy knave" was almost irresistible, but he let it slide.

The magistrate listened closely, and when Jem had finished he asked—

"What induced you to do such a thing?"

"It was done almost without a thought, sir," replied Jem, "and Jerry Bott is always playing tricks upon us. He never loses a chance of annoying or beating the smaller boys of the school."

"Is that so?" asked the magistrate.

Abe Bott rose up inflated with indignant denial, but the inspector was too quick for him.

"The boy Bott is a pest in the town," he replied.

"Well—" exclaimed Abe, and then he was cut short by a cry of silence from the indignant usher of the court.

Mr. B. Rord Beans had taken a seat beside Bott, and the champion sweep, not having any knowledge of the usher, sought to make a friend of him.

"Them Slapcrashers," he said, in an undertone, "boys, master, usher, and all, are a low lot—"

"Excuse me," interposed Mr. Beans, "but

I think you are an unmitigated blackguard. I am the second master of the school."

Abe leaned back and stared at him indignantly, but Mr. Beans was occupied in listening to Dan Mittens, who was in the witness-box.

The champion sweep measured the usher all over, and came to the conclusion that he could double him up in something under two minutes.

"Which I will do," he muttered, "if ever I gits him in a quiet corner. An unmiti—miti—something blackguard! Hang his cheek!"

Dan was rather nervous, but on the whole he acquitted himself very well. Whenever the truth is told a witness does not as a rule quite lose his head.

He confirmed what Jem Stager had said, and nobody cross-examined him. When he stepped down the magistrate bade the two sweeps stand up.

"Come forward!" he said, as they showed a desire to tarry a little in the background, "and let me ask you both whether you still adhere to the evidence you gave a quarter-of-an-hour ago?"

Jerry made no attempt to reply, but his father, after going through the action of swallowing something that stuck in his throat, rose to the occasion, and treated the court to a burst of eloquence.

"My lord—your washup," he blurted out, "I've been a master sweep in this town for siveral years, and I've got a character for honesty and strict attention to business that's kep out all others from coming into the same line and cutting down the prices. I'm alser the father of a family, and I've brought 'em up to regler habits, even 'lowing two of the young un's to go to Sunday-school, therefore I ask you, my lord and washup, if you think I'm a born liar?"

"The case is dismissed," replied the chief magistrate, sternly, "and I think, Bott, you may congratulate yourself if you are not prosecuted for perjury. Leave the court and amend your general conduct, or you may find yourself in trouble ere long."

Abe stared hard at the magistrate, breathing like a slow-working model of a grampus, and when the last telling words had been spoken he turned slowly round and addressed the body of the court.

"And this is law," he commenced.

"Outside, please," interrupted the inspector.

"What do you hang about for?" Abe demanded of his flabbergasted son; "ain't you satisfied with coming here and trying to swear your father into a prison? Come here, you boa-constrictor. If his washup knowed what it was to have a son like you he'd be sorry for me."

Railing the hapless Jerry in this way, Abe was hustled out of court, and a number of people, grinning in a most inhuman manner over the confession of the sweep, followed.

In the open air Abe felt more free, and he was going to address the little crowd when his eye lighted on Dossy Dodge.

"Go home, you cur," said the navvy, "and if what you've got to-day ain't enough, there's something in store for you to-morrow."

"And what may you have in store for me, Mister Dodge?" asked Abe, with dry politeness. "Let me say that there's the law in case of 'sault and battery."

"A cousin of mine is coming to open a sweep's business here," replied Dodge.

Abe turned so white that the change was clearly observable through the soot on his countenance. Some of the bystanders around laughed.

"All right," observed Bott, huskily; "let him come, but he's got to work his way as I've done, to git the bishop to stand by him through thick and thin. Now, Jerry, ain't you been here long enough—ain't you got the least bit of feelin' for your father?"

As Abe and Jerry went up the street Mr. Slapcrash and the boys came out of the court.

Close behind them was Mr. B. Rord Beans, and there was a twinkle in the eye of the usher, as if he were on mischief bent.

"I think, Mr. Slapcrash," he said, "that we may congratulate ourselves on the issue of this case. The high tone of your admirable academy has been in no way destroyed or marred."

He finished up by laying his hand in a familiar manner on the schoolmaster's shoulder, and afterwards slipping that hand through his arm.

"Sir!" cried Mr. Slapcrash, "how dare you?"

"All right," replied Mr. Beans, "don't make a row in the street, unless you want your reputation to go to smash."

"But this liberty—taking my arm, I—"

"Mr. Slapcrash," observed Mr. B. Rord Beans, "I've got your arm and I mean to keep it until we get home. I can hold on pretty tight."

Mr. Slapcrash had to submit, for a fight between master and usher in the street would have been something terrible. So home they went together, with the boys as appreciative spectators behind them.

"I knew we should have a rare treat out of Beans," said Tom; "he's a Tartar."

"He has the spirit of an ancient jester," replied Jem Stager, "only my Lord Slapcrash doth not fully enjoy the antics of the fool."

There was a side-door to the school, by which the boys entered. Mr. B. Rord Beans ought to have accompanied them, but he still clung to his superior, who went to the front one.

Mr. Slapcrash knocked violently, in his wrath, and Mary was there almost as quick as a released jack-in-the-box. The two men entered the hall together.

"Now, sir," said Mr. Slapcrash, putting his umbrella into the stand, "may I ask you one question?"

"Two or three if you desire to do so," politely responded Mr. Beans.

"Will you tell me the meaning of your insolent conduct to-day?" demanded Mr. Slapcrash.

"We quarrelled this morning," replied Mr. Beans, smiling, "hence that eye of yours. Possibly you may have meditated seeking legal assistance to avenge it. I made up my mind to stultify all such proceedings. We have sauntered home together, arm in arm, in sight of all Smockley. Now what will you do?"

"Sir, you are a low, cunning villain."

"Pooh—bosh—nonsense!"

And Mr. Beans, snapping his fingers in derision, skipped gaily upstairs to his room.

CHAPTER XIX.

WARREN FANE ON THE ROAD TO CONVALESCENCE—DICK COCKLES GETS A NEW SORT OF STAGGERER.

WARREN FANE was in the playground that evening, and his appearance was hailed with joy. There was not one dissentient voice in giving him welcome—not even the voice of Sam Fusby.

Sam was a changed boy, and no longer made himself disagreeable upon every possible occasion. He was subdued, and in a measure broken, by the noble treatment he had experienced from Warren Fane.

Forgiven and forgotten, or as good as forgotten, was the petty crime of Sam, and through it his eyes had been opened to his faults, which he now strove to amend. He was one of the first Warren spoke to.

"How are you, Sam?" he said, holding out his hand.

Sam took it, and looked into Warren's face with eyes that were a little misty, beside a quivering lip.

"I am very glad you are about again," Sam replied.

"I am sure you are," Warren returned; "you are a good fellow, Sam, although you seem to be only just now waking up to the knowledge of yourself."

Dick Cockles had noticed the change in Sam Fusby, but could not quite make it out; indeed, it may as well be said at once that he never did fully understand it. Dick, as a thinker, was not at the top of the tree. As Jem Stager once said—

"Dick's got his mind filled with good things, but he doesn't keep them in order, and when he wants something he doesn't know where to lay hold of it."

He was one of the spectators of Warren's treatment of Sam. There was no mistake about the warmth of it. It was just as if they were close friends. A very strange thing when Sam's previous record is considered.

Warren had stood high from the moment he first entered the school, but Sam had always been looked upon as a sneak, and justly so.

It was but too true that he had been a fetcher and carrier of things to the schoolmaster, but now that was all over. Since the time when Warren forgave him for the wrong he had done Sam became another boy.

No more tales were told by him, and if Mr. Slapcrash did not wonder why his spy had ceased to bring him information, it was because his mind was too full of his recently-acquired property.

However, it is with Dick we have to do—Dick, who was so puzzled by what he had witnessed.

Suddenly he called to mind that Sam had ceased to jeer at him, or to put in disparaging words when they were not wanted—in short, to do anything like the Sam of old.

Dick felt he must find out the reason for this great change, or give up all chance of inheriting the sausage business. In other words—die.

As soon as he could get near Sam without seeming to make a rush at him, he went to work.

"I say, Sam," he said.

"What do you want, Dick?" asked Sam.

"Nothing particular, but how are you?"

Sam coloured.

"There is very little the matter with me," he replied.

"There used to be a lot the matter with you," Dick answered; "but such a change in a fellow I never came across before."

Sam looked at him, smiling, but a little mournfully.

"I am changed, Dick," he said, "and I suppose you don't know the reason why?"

"Not me," replied Dick, digging his hands into his pockets; "it's precious little I do know at any time, and the change in you is a nut too hard for me to crack."

"I can't tell you what has done it," said Sam, "unless you like to put it down to Warren Fane."

"Did he do it?"

"Yes."

"Then all I've got to say is that he's a wonderful fellow."

Dick began to whistle, and Sam was silent for a minute or two. Presently he spoke again.

"Dick," he said.

"What now?" asked Dick.

"Do you remember when I first came to school?"

"Am I likely to forget it, or anybody who was here?"

"Why do you remember it?" asked Sam.

"Because you came without a hamper or a bag of toffy, or any blessed thing which goes by the name of 'usual,'" returned Dick.

"Just so," said Sam; "now I want to make amends for it. I wish to stand a feed."

Dick stopped whistling, and the expression on his intellectual countenance could not have been improved had he been hoisted up by a ton of powder and after a lengthened sojourn among the stars come down unhurt.

"You!" he exclaimed; "stand a feed?"

"Just so," replied Sam.

"After being more than a year at school and never spending a copper?"

"I've said it, and I mean it."

Dick looked around him, wondering if he were dreaming, or chaos had come.

"I don't know what to say to you, Sam," he observed, "I don't, indeed."

"If you think the fellows would not mind it," returned Sam, hesitatingly, "I should like to spend a sovereign."

Dick put his hand to his head. This totally incomprehensible change was really too much for him.

"Sam," he said, "have you really got a sovereign."

"Two," replied Sam.

Then did Dick breathe short, as a beggar might do when he suddenly finds that he has been unconsciously travelling with a millionaire.

"You've got all that?" he murmured.

Sam nodded.

"And you won't go back on what you've said?"

Sam nodded again.

"Hand out that sovereign," said Dick, "and leave the arrangement of the job to me."

"You won't make a mess of it this time?" said Sam, dubiously.

"Me make a mess of it!" exclaimed Dick. "Did I ever make a mess of anything?"

"To that," replied a voice behind him, "all good men and true will answer—that you make a mess of everything."

It was Jem Stager, and upon him Dick turned an indignant eye.

"I shouldn't make a mess of anything," he retorted, "if it was left alone by you."

"Oh! friend of my youth," said Jem, laying a hand on each of his shoulders, "and coming companion of my riper years, if we only understood each other how happy we should be! What's the row?"

"The row is," replied Dick, "that Sam wants to plank down a sovereign for a feed."

Jem Stager in his turn got a staggerer. He was not by any means prepared for this announcement, or for anything approaching it, and there was a truly dramatic expression upon his countenance as he stared at Sam Fusby.

"It's a lark, I suppose," he said.

"Not a bit of it," replied Sam. "I mean it."

He put out his hand, and in the palm of it was a bright golden coin, with the unmistakable stamp of the Royal Mint upon it.

Then both Jem and Dick spoke together like a stage-chorus, and all they said was—

"Well! I'm blessed!"

CHAPTER XX.

DICK DOES ONE PART OF A GOOD PIECE OF BUSINESS ALL RIGHT, BUT IN THE END THE USUAL HITCH COMES IN.

DICK COCKLES was finally entrusted with the funds for the feast provided by Sam Fusby, so when night had come he was lowered out of the window with a sheet in the old style, and sped away on his errand.

The shop where the supplies were usually obtained did not close until ten o'clock, and as the boys went to bed at nine there was ample time.

By half-past nine Dick was back, laden with enough tarts and buns to make the whole school bilious for a week.

It will be remembered by the majority of our readers that the way in and out chosen by the boys was through the garden gate, which could be opened on the inside, and if left ajar the return was easy. But if closed a friend on the other side was necessary to obtain admission.

Dick's bad luck never wholly deserted him. In his absence the garden-gate got closed, and there he was, laden with all the good things, unable to obtain admission. He tried the door with his knee, kicked it gently with his toe, but it stood fast.

"Another blessed mess!" he muttered, with a sensation of his hair rising.

He turned his despairing eyes up the street, and to his terror saw the front door of the schoolhouse open.

Flight was impossible, laden as he was, and he stood up straight against the wall, holding the bag of eatables so as to form a sort of screen—a very poor one at the best.

It was Mr. B. Rord Beans who came out. He stood on the doorstep with a defiant air of independence, and lighted a cigar, deliberately blowing some of the smoke into the house through the open door. Then he sauntered a little way up the street away from Dick. Here was Dick's chance. He could go in by the front door, and, if he were careful, get upstairs without being observed.

It was his only chance, and, as rapidly and lightly as he could, he made his way into the hall. The usher did not observe him. Mr. B. Rord Beans was wrapped in the contemplation of the spirit of manly defiance he was exhibiting. He had entered on a course of war-like conduct in the house of Slapcrash, and up to the present had been victor.

He had also partaken of a full bottle of Guinness's a few minutes before he came out, and the heavy liquid had stimulated him to a very high pitch.

The cigar he was smoking was a good old Smockley twopenny, originally designed by the maker to be recognised as a full-flavoured article, and really strong enough to curl the hair of an ordinary smoker.

Dick got into the hall, but he got no further for awhile, for, as he entered, the voice of Mrs. Slapcrash was heard upon the stairs calling for Mary.

Not wishing to be seen by either, Dick stepped into a big cupboard, where odds and ends were kept, and, being rather tired of the parcels, he quietly put them on the floor.

Mrs. Slapcrash only wanted a little hot water, presumably for refreshment purposes, and when Mary had supplied it all was quiet again.

To make sure that the coast was clear, Dick stole softly from his hiding-place, leaving the parcels for the moment behind him.

There was not a sound in the house, but Dick, whose powers of imagination were very great, fancied he heard whispering on the landing above, and he crept to the foot of the stairs to listen.

The next moment Mr. B. Rord Beans re-entered the hall. He had come up the street smoking, until suddenly he discovered that the cigar was a little too much for him.

Hastily tossing it aside he came in, and as he made for the stairs Dick had no resource but to fly.

Dick got as far as the first landing and stopped. Mr. Beans had stopped too, at the bottom stair, on which he was sitting and groaning.

"He's taken ill," thought Dick, "and I can't help him."

"Oh! why did I?" moaned the usher, "not being used to it, and such a beastly strong thing, too. I don't believe it was tobacco at all!"

A brisk footstep was heard in the street, and then the voice of Mr. Slapcrash.

"Hallo!" he exclaimed, "the front door open, and the place in darkness. What does this mean?"

Nobody answered him. Mr. Beans subsided into silence, and Dick stood as still as a mouse when a cat is near its hole.

Mr. Slapcrash came in, closed the door with a bang, and groping his way in the dark, proceeded across the hall with the intention of ascending the stairs.

The usher, being in a dogged mood, neither moved nor spoke, and Mr. Slapcrash fell over him, with a result startling to both.

The schoolmaster was alarmed to find himself in contact with a man who might be a burglar or worse, and Mr. B. Rord Beans had

MR. AND MRS. SLAPCRASH GET A NIGHT ALARM.

his head knocked against the stairs, the blow producing brilliant pyrotechnic effects.

Mr. Slapcrash got up and in terror ran to the front door calling for the police, whilst Mr. Beans, reviving from his temporary confusion, made his way noiselessly upstairs.

Dick had no chance but to go before him, and thought it prudent to retire to the dormitory. There he found all awake and expecting him.

Tom Biron and Jem Stager sat by the open window watching for his arrival by the garden door, and his appearance at the other end of the room had a most startling effect.

In the first place, the boys hearing the door open thought it was Mr. Slapcrash, and there

Poor Dick Cockles!—At it again.

was a general rush for the beds. Then Dick's voice was heard saying—"It's only me," and so far they were reassured.

"But how came you that way?" asked Tom Biron.

"I'll tell you in a minute," Dick replied. "I fancy we shall have somebody up here directly."

"But let us know where the grub is!" said Jem Stager.

"Oh! that's all right," replied Dick, with assumed carelessness.

"Gone wrong again!" groaned Jem; "was there ever such a parlous son of a sausage-maker?"

"Be quiet," whispered Tom Biron.

He closed the window, and they all got into bed, many of them only half undressed.

Then the voice of Mr. Slapcrash and heavy footfalls were heard upon the stairs.

"I saw the fellows rush upstairs," Mr. Slapcrash was saying. "There's three at least. Have you got your truncheon ready?"

"All right, sir," was the reply.

The boys lay still and heard Mr. Slapcrash, with his official attendant, go from room to room below, and presently they began the ascent to the topmost part of the house.

The rooms opposite were looked into, and then they came to the dormitory. Mr. Slapcrash opened the door, and the light of a bull's-eye lantern flashed from end to end.

"Nobody here but the boys, sir," said the officer.

"It is very odd," replied Mr. Slapcrash. "They must have eluded us somehow. The only room we have not examined is that occupied by a person I employ as usher, and we need not examine that."

The room in question was next to the dormitory, and Mr. Beans, like the boys, was listening to the movements of Mr. Slapcrash and the officer. He now popped his head out of the door and asked who was there.

"It is only me," said Mr. Slapcrash, severely; "we have reason to think that there are thieves in the house. You need not disturb yourself."

"Indeed!" retorted Mr. Beans, "it is *you* who disturb me. But that is nothing. Mr. Slapcrash, you ought really to come home sober."

Having fired this shot, which fairly staggered the object aimed at, Mr. Beans closed his door, and, by audibly locking it, announced that he had nothing more to say to anybody that night.

"Well, I never!" gasped Mr. Slapcrash. "Officer, you heard that?"

"I did, sir," replied the officer, in a tone of voice which showed that he heeded also.

"You understand that abominable insinuation? Do I look as if I had been drinking?"

"There's a kind of skeered look about you, and you are rumpled a bit."

This cautious reply, while it left Mr. Slapcrash's sobriety an open question, had an exasperating effect upon the schoolmaster.

"Scared," he replied. "I am not frightened, but naturally my dress is a bit disordered by my struggle with the burglars."

"I'd like to see 'em," chuckled the officer.

"Constable," observed Mr. Slapcrash, with dignity, "it was my intention to give you a shilling for your trouble, but by your levity you have forfeited it."

"I don't know what my levity may be, not being an eddicated man," replied the officer, "but it's like your cheek to come home, tumble over the mat, and take me off my beat to tramp all round the house. I shall report the job."

With this declaration the officer marched off, and Mr. Slapcrash, hissing like a tea-urn, followed him below.

There was the sound of the front door closing, the pushing home of the bolts, and the return of Mr. Slapcrash to his room. Then all was still.

—————

CHAPTER XXI.

A DESCENT ON A FORAGING EXPEDITION—THE ALARM — DICK IN FOR IT — MR. B. RORD BEANS THE DEFENDER.

"Now, Dick," said Tom Biron, "you can tell us how you came to make a mess of it this time."

"I haven't exactly made a mess of it," replied Dick, in an injured tone. "I've got the tommy in the house."

"Tell us all about it."

Dick told his story, and by way of accompaniment there was a running comment of groans, chuckles, and occasional sarcastic remarks.

"It might have been worse," said Jem Stager, when Dick had concluded his yarn, "but you are a messer—so mixed in all you do. I suppose it arises from being born in the sausage business. That is an awfully mixed affair."

"Perhaps you would have done no better," growled Dick.

"Stop that wrangling," Tom observed. "Dick had better go down and get the things."

"If he goes alone," replied Jem Stager, "he will make a mess of it."

"I'll go with him," replied Tom, "and you can come too, Jem. Be quick!"

Tom opened the door and listened.

"It is dark," Tom said; "but we ought to know our way."

They went out and with great care descended the stairs.

As they passed the door of Mr. Slapcrash's room they heard the murmur of voices, and were thus made aware of the schoolmaster's wakefulness.

They were all very careful, but Dick, who

was the last of the trio, had only got about half way down the flight of stairs when he slipped and fell upon his back.

"Oh!" he gasped.

Everybody knows that when one falls on the edge of a stair a little skin-scraping is sure to follow. Dick being like the others, only imperfectly dressed, fairly rasped himself, and the exclamation was excusable.

"You miserable duffer!" whispered Jem.

They got into the hall, where the gloom was partly dispelled by a lamp outside shining through a small window over the door. Tom went to the cupboard and opened it.

"How many parcels?" he asked.

"Five," groaned Dick.

"Hush!" whispered Jem; "they are moving upstairs."

The boys stood still, and the voice of Mrs. Slapcrash floated to their attentive ears.

"Benjamin, if you are a man, go down and see what it is."

"I'm—a—a—going," replied the school master; "give me time to—o—o put—on—s —omething."

"You have enough on," said Mrs. Slapcrash; "take the poker, and I will follow you."

"Here's a go," muttered Tom, savagely; "get into the cupboard."

He pushed Dick in first, Jem next, and then followed.

Before he could close the door Mr. Slapcrash was heard descending the stairs.

"If any person is skulking about these premises," he cried, "I will punish him with the utmost rigour of the law."

"Don't talk but go at 'em," said Mrs. Slapcrash, impatiently.

Her voice sounded immediately behind him, and she was evidently following her spouse.

Tom dare not close the door. Any movement on his part might draw attention to the hiding-place. They had to take their chance of being discovered.

Mr. Slapcrash did not observe the half-open door, but crossed the hall and made his way towards the kitchen.

Mrs. Slapcrash followed, and Tom had a tolerably clear view of that lady in *déshabille*.

"Catch hold of some of these parcels, Jem," said Tom, as soon as Darby and Joan had disappeared. "Dick, you let them alone. How many have you, Jem?"

"Two."

"I have the other three. Come along."

As Dick had been the first to go into the cupboard he was necessarily the last out, and being still a little lame from his fall he was not quite so quick as his companions.

They were half-way up the stairs, and Dick had but just begun the ascent, when Mr. Slapcrash was heard returning.

Dick was horribly scared, and his legs became as limp as bits of rope. He could hardly get along at all.

The consequence was that when Tom and Jem had got safe back to the dormitory, Dick was still two stairs short of the first landing.

Mr. Slapcrash carried a light, and as it cast a glare up the stairs his wife espied the frightened Dick.

"It's one of the boys," she said.

In a moment Mr. Slapcrash was himself again. Only a boy. That was enough. With an elastic step he bounded up the stairs, and although Dick put on a spurt he had only reached the upper landing when he was overtaken.

"Stop!" Mr. Slapcrash cried.

Dick stopped, and from sheer exhaustion and terror fell upon his hands and knees.

Mr. Slapcrash espied an old walking-stick lying on a sideboard, and rapidly exchanging the poker for it he fell upon Dick.

He gave him three or four tremendous cuts, and would have given him more, but the click of a lock was heard and a ghostly figure appeared upon the landing.

It was Mr. B. Rord Beans in his nightshirt.

"What fiend's work is this?" he asked.

"Return to your room, sir," replied Mr. Slapcrash.

"I will not be a silent witness to these scenes," observed Mr. Beans, dramatically. "Apparently it is not enough that you beat the boys like—like—doormats during the day, but now you must drag them out of their beds at night and knock them about like—like skittles!"

"You misunderstand the whole affair, sir," retorted Mr. Slapcrash, haughtily.

"Give him a thrashing, Benjamin," cried Mrs. Slapcrash from below.

"Madam," replied Mr. Beans, "I trust you will have the decency to retire to your room. I am not apparelled for ladies' society."

"Go to your bed, Cockles," said Mr. Slapcrash, chokingly. "I will call you to account to-morrow. Mr. Beans, this must come to an end."

"I intend it should," replied Beans, "for I mean to communicate with the parent of this much injured boy. I believe that gentleman to be an influential member of the sausage trade, and if he does his duty as a man he will put you through one of his machines."

Mr. Slapcrash tried to say something biting in reply, but he was unable to put it together, and, shaking his fist at the usher, he beat a retreat.

Mr. Beans retired to his chamber and shut the door with a bang that shook the house.

Dick Cockles, very sore, but not so sore as he might have been but for the intervention of Mr. Beans, lost no time in getting into the dormitory, where he was expected with some anxiety.

"I'm bound to run away," he said, as he lay down on the side of the bed; "life on a cannibal island would be better than this, for they would put a fellow out of his misery at once."

"Did you get it hot?" asked Jem.

"I call that a fool's question!" replied the exasperated Dick; "does Slapcrash ever lay it on cold?"

"Well! jump into bed and sit up," returned Jem; "I am about to pass round the provender."

"I can only sit sideways," groaned Dick; "no matter what is going on I'm always in a miserable state of bruises."

"You shall have an extra tart," observed Jem; "hallo! what's this?—a cucumber! How came you to think of buying that, Dick?"

"I thought some fellow would like it," groaned Dick.

Nobody wanted any cucumber but the purchaser, and Jem Stager hit the mark when he said that Dick, when buying it, had thought of himself first and the others afterwards.

So Dick had the cucumber all to himself, and he ate the lot.

It was a terribly rash thing to do, but it was Dick's way to do a thing first and consider afterwards.

The feast on the whole was a great success, and Sam Fusby, complimented on his liberality, felt that glow of satisfaction which invariably accompanies good and generous actions.

For the first time in his life he understood how much better it is to be host than guest, and how sweet are the fruits of generosity.

Possibly a supper of tarts is not the best thing in the world to partake of, but healthy boys make light of such things. It is when an injudicious addition is made that suffering may follow.

The boys had been asleep about an hour

when a dismal groaning awoke them one by one.

The first to open his eyes was Jem Stager, and he thought that something heavy was being drawn up and down the landing.

Then Dan Mittens was aroused, and others speedily followed, until all were awake.

"What's that row?" asked Tom Biron.

"It's something outside," replied Jem.

"No, it's me," groaned Dick; "I'm taken bad."

"What's the matter with you?" asked Warren Fane.

"I don't know," replied Dick; "but I've got a feeling as if I was going to blow up, like a powder magazine."

"Verily," said Jem Stager, "the cucumber hath laid hold of him."

"Oh! no—it isn't that," groaned Dick; "it's cramp. I got a cold in my legs when I went downstairs, and it's gone up—oh—oh!"

Dick was rolling about his bed in the most awful manner, and going a little too far on one side he fell out and came to the floor with a heavy bang.

"I never saw such a fellow," said Tom Biron. "What are you doing now?"

"I'm going. It's all over with me!" gasped Dick.

"Get up."

"I can't."

Jem Stager got out of bed to give him a hand.

"Let me help you, Dick," he said; "try to stand up."

Dick made no answer beyond giving a faint gasp or two and convulsively twitching his legs.

"He's really bad," cried Jem, in alarm; "come here some of you fellows."

"I'll get a light," said Tom Biron. "Stop a moment!"

All the boys were out of bed now, standing around terrified, for it seemed as if it was all over with Dick.

"Let us lay him on the bed," continued Tom Biron; "catch hold of the candle, Mittens."

In lifting Dick it was seen that he was quite stiff, like a pantaloon when he has been mal-treated by the clown.

"Dick, how do you feel?" asked Tom.

A sharp jerk of the body was all the reply that came from Dick.

"He is very ill," observed Tom, "and some-body ought to go for a doctor. Rub him hard while I wake up Mr. Slapcrash."

CHAPTER XXII.

DICK'S SEVERE ILLNESS — MR. SLAPCRASH TROUBLED—AN UNEXPECTED OUTCRY.

TOM took upon himself the task of rousing Mr. Slapcrash, and hastily putting on a few clothes, he hurried downstairs and knocked at the door of the schoolmaster's bedroom.

A grunt within was the only reply, and he had to knock again. This time the voice of Mrs. Slapcrash was heard, tartly inquiring—

"Who's there?"

"It is I—Biron," Tom replied. "Poor Cockles is taken ill. We think he is dying."

"Benjamin, get up," said Mrs. Slapcrash; "that little villain Cockles is bad."

Mr. Slapcrash was not aroused without some vigorous shaking and possibly a dig or two in the ribs from his spouse, but after a short delay he appeared at the door in his trousers and shirt, with a candle in his hand.

"Cockles ill? What is the matter with him?" he asked.

"I don't know," Tom replied; "but he is quite stiff, and is getting cold."

This was alarming news, and Mr. Slapcrash, with a guilty remembrance of the violent punishment he had inflicted on the boy, hurried upstairs.

Tom followed, and on reaching the dormitory they found that Mr. Beans had been aroused also. He was bending over Dick with quite a fatherly air, and seemed to be much upset.

"Another victim," he wailed, as Mr. Slapcrash appeared; "whatever the world may think of it, it's murder."

"Let me come," said Mr. Slapcrash, savagely.

"Ah! come," replied Mr. Beans, "and look at your work. This boy is suffering from internal injuries."

Mr. Slapcrash made no reply, but he shook visibly as he stooped down to look at Dick, who was quite still, although Tom thought he was breathing a little easier.

"Biron," said the schoolmaster, "will you run for Dr. Jones? I am afraid Cockles has taken a chill."

"A chill!" echoed Mr. Beans, scornfully; "rather a warm one, if I am any judge of a brutal beating."

Again Mr. Slapcrash offered no reply. He was not going to give the usher another advantage by wrangling with him before the boys.

Dr. Jones was not long in coming.

Tom had taken good care to arouse him, by pulling his night-bell nearly out of its socket, and a brief description of Dick's state had assured his coming with all speed.

He was a stout, bustling little man, kind-hearted in the main, and rather a good friend to boys generally, having seven of his own, all of lively disposition.

"Ha, h'm!" he observed, as he came into the room. "What's this? Please get away from the bed—he wants all the air he can have."

The quick eyes of the doctor had been roaming about while speaking, and he detected some pastry crumbs upon the floor. A quiet smile spread over his face.

He bent over Dick and put his ear to the boy's mouth. Then he felt his pulse and raised one of his eyelids.

"Can he be put into a separate room?" the doctor asked.

"Mine is at his service," replied Mr. Beans, briskly; "I am only too glad to be of help to the little victim."

Mr. Slapcrash was silent once again, and the doctor and usher carried Dick into the next room. Mr. Beans proceeded to complete his toilet, expressing his intention to sit up with the patient.

"Perhaps it will not be necessary," Dr. Jones said.

Mr. Slapcrash stood in the doorway looking gloomily on while restoratives were administered to Dick. After having had a small draught forced down his throat, he opened his eyes and stared hard at the doctor.

"It wasn't the cucumber," he groaned.

His speech was hard to understand, and Mr. Slapcrash did not catch what he said, but the doctor did. Holding up his finger he observed—

"You must not talk, my boy. It is not good for you. All you want now is to keep quiet."

"What is the matter with him?" asked Mr. Slapcrash.

"A shock to the system," put in Mr. Beans.

"Undoubtedly a shock of some sort," observed the doctor; "and his whole system has been temporarily in a state of collapse. But he has got over the worst of it. I will leave these draughts for him—let him have one every two hours, and if he has no relapse do not send for me, as I will give him a look in in the morning."

"I will watch over him like a father," murmured Mr. Beans.

His manner was rather strange, for the Guinness's stout still lingered in his veins, but the doctor did not seem to notice it, and after a few more words to Dick he left, Mr. Slapcrash accompanying him downstairs.

In the hall the schoolmaster asked if there was any real danger in Dick's case.

"Not imminent," the doctor replied; "but he has had a shock—ahem!—undoubtedly."

"What do shocks come from?" asked Mr. Slapcrash, faintly.

"Oh! all sorts of things," was the consoling reply. "Fright, fear, sudden and unexpected blows. It is difficult to say what they come from, unless the patient is willing and able to tell you. I will talk with young Cockles in the morning and get at the truth."

Then the doctor went away, and Mr. Slapcrash, with the feeling of being on the verge of a catastrophe of some sort, retired to bed.

Well might he murmur—"What a night I'm having!" as he entered his chamber, but he was glad to find that Mrs. Slapcrash, untroubled by Dick's illness, had gone to sleep.

The boys soon fell asleep also. Somehow they had arrived at the conclusion that Dick's illness had nothing serious about it, and Dick himself was again in the land of dreams.

Mr. B. Rord Beans, seated on a common cane chair, was also in a somnolent state, but he could not be considered to be sleeping comfortably.

He swayed to and fro, until he woke up with a jerk. Then he would stare at the candle burning by the bedside. Next his eyes would find out Dick, and a sweet smile would spread over his face as he realised the situation.

"I have got Slapcrash's nose on the grindstone now," he murmured, as he settled again in his chair.

So he passed the night in dozing, rocking, and soliloquising, until daylight came.

All the time Dick slept on, and Nature's sweet restorer helped materially to digest the dangerous quantity of cucumber he had partaken of. When he awoke in the morning, aroused by the call-bell rung by Mary, he was almost himself again.

Not so Mr. Beans. The sort of sleep he had been able to get had been very little good to him, and the double stout had played sad havoc with his liver.

He had a washed-out appearance, and in the matter of temper he was at his worst. But still he kept up the appearance of being kind to Dick.

"How are you, my dear boy?" he asked.

Dick replied he thought he was quite well.

"Oh! no, not quite well," said Mr. Beans, gently; "a long way from that. You have had a shock—a tremendous shock—and I hope Mr. Slapcrash is sorry for it."

"I don't think he is," replied Dick.

"Not he," observed Mr. Beans, mournfully; "he is a wicked man."

Dick could not confide in Mr. Beans about the cucumber. He did not pursue the subject as the boys were hurrying downstairs to their ablutions, and he was listening to the sound they made, with a longing to get up.

CHAPTER XXIII.

DICK AS A MALINGERER—A HOLIDAY OUT—UP A LADDER AND DOWN AGAIN—A WEAPON OF SPITE.

MR. SLAPCRASH and his wife held a consultation over their breakfast, and it was of a nature to lead to important changes in the lives of many who figure in our story.

Not to make any mystery about it, we may at once state that Mr. Slapcrash contemplated giving up his school.

"With the money we have," he observed to his wife, "and the price we can get for the goodwill of the school, we could buy an annuity that would keep us comfortably."

"But why give up?" Mrs. Slapcrash inquired; "the school is paying."

"It may pay now, but it won't for long," replied Mr. Slapcrash. "That fellow Beans will pull it to pieces."

"I will pull him to pieces," replied Mrs. Slapcrash, instinctively crooking her fingers, "if he gives us much more trouble."

"A fight between him and me was bad enough," observed Mr. Slapcrash, grimly, "but—"

He stopped short, as he could not summon words that would adequately describe such an encounter as was contemplated in his mind, and breakfast being over he arose from the table.

We have given this much of their conversation, as it bears upon coming events, that will not fail to prove interesting to the reader.

Meanwhile let us see how it fared with Dick. The doctor came about eleven o'clock, and by that time all effects of the cucumber had disappeared, but Dick was not going to get well all at once.

He had partly dressed himself, but he lay on the bed very limp, and as the doctor felt his pulse he reduced his breathing to a series of short gasps, and rolled his eyes as if in great pain.

Dick was, in fact, distinctly malingering.

Dr. Jones looked at him with a sidelong glance, that took in Dick's dramatic efforts and clearly appreciated them. The doctor put his hands to his mouth to hide a smile.

"Do you think you could walk—you would be all the better for a little fresh air?" he inquired.

"I could try," replied Dick, faintly.

"A short walk in the country," continued the worthy doctor, "with a companion to help you in case you should be faint. How about that?"

"I should like it, sir," replied Dick; "it might do me good. Jem Stager could go with me."

"I will see Mr. Slapcrash," said the doctor, rising. "You had better have something light for dinner—a pudding or custard, and then go for your walk. But let me tell you, young gentleman, you have had a narrow escape."

"Have I, sir?" exclaimed Dick, startled.

"You have," replied the doctor, with a grave face but twinkling eyes. "By some means or the other you have got something into your gastronomical organs that threatened to produce syncope. Perhaps you know what it was, and in future will avoid eating it so late at night again. Good-morning."

The doctor left him and went down to Mr. Slapcrash, who had come out of the school-room to receive his report. The doctor's face was very grave.

"The boy is better," he said, "but he ought to have all the fresh air he can get. With a companion he could take a stroll."

"He shall have as many as he likes," replied Mr. Slapcrash, eagerly.

The relief he felt was immense.

"That I leave to you," returned the doctor, putting on his gloves. "He talks a great deal about Stager, and that boy had better go with him."

Mr. Slapcrash was quite agreeable. He also promised that Dick should have a rice pudding for dinner, and, what is more, Dick in due time got it.

Dick ate the lot, and had but one fault to

THE MAN WAS NOW WELL UP THE LADDER.

find with it. Its dimensions were not in proportion to his appetite.

He had barely finished his pudding, really the best thing he could have had, and quite sufficient after his overnight gastronomical performances, when Jem Stager came bounding into the room.

"I say, Dick," he said, "isn't it jolly—how do you feel? All the other fellows are waxy over our getting a holiday. What's been the matter with you?"

"The doctor says that I have had an internal geographical derangement that nearly brought on a hencoop," replied Dick.

"Oh! come—stow it," said Jem, "don't take to joking about it."

"*I'm fairly drenched,*" *growled Dick Cockles.*

"It's a fact," replied Dick, earnestly, "and he told me if ever I caught it again I should not get over it."

"Well, by the seven Knights of the Crescent," observed Jem, "it matters little what was the matter with you so that the worst is over, and you and I have got half a day in the fields. Let us away."

Dick got up and groaned.

"I'll try to walk," he said, "but you must help me downstairs."

"All serene," replied Jem, taking his arm; "but I say, old fellow, don't overdo it."

"Perhaps you don't think I've been bad at all," retorted Dick, suddenly bristling.

"Oh! yes," returned Jem, "you looked bad enough—a flabby cod-fish would be a pleasant picture compared to you last night. But soften your groans and then on we go."

Dick gave up groaning altogether, but the way he crawled down the stairs was a caution. Nor did he show any signs of activity until they were well out of sight of the house—then he suddenly became quite well.

"The doctor said that the fresh air would do me good," he observed, with a grin, "and he was right."

"Look out!" said Jem, quickly, "here's Slapcrash."

Dick was limp again in a moment, and his face became as long as a fiddle.

Jem burst into a roar of laughter.

"Oh! what a sell," he cried.

"Just like you, Jem," said Dick, with an injured air. "How should I know you were gammoning. You made me feel real bad, I can tell you."

"It was wrong," returned Jem; "I might have brought on another hencoop. Ha—ha—ha!"

Dick declined to laugh with him, and for a moment looked rather sulky, but he soon recovered his normal serenity.

"What shall we do?" he asked.

"We must take what turns up," replied Jem.

They went away into the country, keeping to the high road, and for a long time found nothing to do—in other words, they discovered no chance of exercising their mischievous propensities.

At length they came upon an old-fashioned thatched cottage, standing alone, with a ladder reared against the roof.

"Stop a minute," said Jem; "we will go up there, Dick. Ever been on a roof?"

"Never," replied Dick; "isn't it dangerous?"

"Not a bit," said Jem.

Jem went to the front door and knocked, intending to ask for a drink of water if anybody appeared.

There was no answer.

A second knock was likewise unattended to, and then Jem slowly strolled round the house, keeping a sharp look-out for any person or dog that might chance to be about. But he found nothing, and came back to Dick.

"It's all right," he said; "nobody's at home. We may go up."

But Dick hesitated a little.

"You know, Jem," he said, "that I always get into such a horrible mess when I do anything of this sort."

"Oh! fudge," replied Jem, impatiently; "let's have a view of the surrounding country—it must be lovely."

Dick, thus urged, cautiously went up the ladder, and Jem followed. The pair got astride the roof, and had really a comfortable seat.

Dick began to feel ashamed of his fears.

"What a long way we can see," he said.

"Yes," replied Jem; "there's the old town, and that square building to the right is the schoolhouse—there's the sandpit where Fane fought Jerry Bott—there's—why, there's a lot of fellows coming down the road. As I carry knightly arms, it's the boys. Slapcrash must have given them all a holiday. Hurrah!"

"I say," whispered Dick, clutching his arm, "there's a man in the garden."

So there was—a sturdy man of agricultural appearance and rather a vicious expression of countenance. He had a stick in his hand, and he came slowly to the foot of the ladder, his eyes on the boys and their eyes on him.

"Hullo!" he cried.

"How do you do, sir?" replied Jem, politely.

"What are you doing up there?" demanded the man.

"Contemplating the beauties of nature," replied Jem.

"I'll contemplate you if you don't come down," the man replied.

"Perhaps you will contemplate us with that stick if we do," observed Jem. "If you will kindly retire to the end of the garden we will descend and leave your domain."

Dick said not a word. He felt that he was in for it again, and whatever blows might be about he was sure he would get his full share of it.

"I tell you to come down," shouted the man; "if you don't I'll come up, and then it will be the worse for you."

Jem saw that he must gain time and hold the enemy at bay until reinforcements arrived.

A glance up the road showed him that it was indeed the Slapcrash boys, coming along in twos and threes. By some means the holiday given to Jem and Dick had been extended to them.

"We are coming," said Jem; "but make allowance for our being slow and not at all used to this work. Now, Dick, don't keep the gentleman waiting. Go down and let him see what a nice boy you are."

"Yes," retorted Dick, "and while he is icking me you will get clean away."

"By the Slapcrash brotherhood," returned Jem, "I will stand by you and share what good things may be afloat—go on."

"Are you coming?" roared the man.

"Anon, sir, anon," cried Jem.

He wanted yet a little more time. Jem could see that Tom Biron, Warren Fane, and several others were sauntering down the road, but they were still too far off to be of service in case of a rumpus.

The man below was not disposed to wait. Grunting furiously, and breathing fire as he came, he began the ascent. All compromise was therefore at an end, and it was a case of open war.

"Keep back," shouted Jem, "or I will pull down a chimney-pot and hurl it at you."

"I'll chimney-pot you," was all the man said.

Dick at this moment tried to shift his position, and in so doing overbalanced himself.

"Help, Jem!" he cried.

But Jem, although he made a clutch at his jacket, failed to save him, and away went Dick down the other side of the roof with a rush.

He disappeared like a ball going over a precipice, and the next moment there was a splash.

"Water-butt," thought Jem. "Poor old Dick! it was ever thus."

But his interest in Dick was naturally deadened by his own peril.

The man was coming up rather warily, but evidently bent on mischief, and Jem tried one of the chimney-pots. It was far too well fixed for him to move it, and the man laughed grimly.

"That's no use, young gentleman," he said; "you had better come down."

"I'm going," replied Jem.

The roof in the rear hung low, and the drop from it was by no means dangerous—he could slide down, and if nothing serious had happened to Dick, they could clear off before the man could descend the ladder and intercept them.

Jem was quick to decide on a course of action, and had resolution to carry it out.

Kissing his hand to the man, now well up the ladder, by way of adieu, he launched himself from the top of the roof—tobogganed himself down it—and dropped easily to the ground, close to the water-butt.

As he landed in the garden Dick came into view, and for the life of him Jem could not help laughing.

A more woebegone picture than Dick presented he had never seen. Jem leaned against the butt for a moment, quite limp with laughter.

"Just like you," grunted Dick. "Help me out, can't you? I'm drenched, for the butt's half full of water."

Jem saw that fooling about would not do. The man would soon be down, and the escape of the pair would become more than problematical.

He looked at the water-butt, and saw there was only one way of getting Dick out in a hurry. It must be overturned.

There was some old iron bars and hooping lying about, and Jem picked up one of the former.

"Look out, Dick," he cried.

"What are you going to do?" asked Dick, in alarm.

"No time to jaw," was the answer.

Jem thrust the bar under the water-butt, and exerting all his youthful strength, prised it up.

Over it went with a crash that burst the rotten iron hoops around it, and a flood of water spread abroad.

Dick lay gasping among the wreck of staves and hoops, from which Jem hauled him.

"Quick! collect your wits," said Jem.

The man came round the house to the right with a run, and Jem, dragging Dick along with him, bore off to the left.

Dick was too much staggered by recent events to quite understand what he was doing, and he was almost a dead weight for Jem to drag along.

They must have fallen into the hands of the enemy but for the remnants of the shattered water-butt.

The man in pursuit tripped over them, and fell with sufficient force to prevent him rising for a moment or two.

Thus was grace obtained, and Jem got Dick round the side of the house, where he gave him a hearty shake, and quickly told him he would be left if he did not "wake up."

This aroused Dick a little, and he broke into a feeble trot, his boots, full of water, giving out that peculiar sodden sound one always hears in like circumstances.

They were on the high road when their pursuer again hove in sight, and he was now in a frame of mind bordering on the murderous.

"If I don't kill both of you I'll be hanged," he roared.

"Now, Dick, for your valuable existence, run!" cried Jem.

Dick's run was a very poor performance, and he would have fallen into the hands of the foe but for the timely arrival of assistance.

As the pursuer bounded out of the garden gate he saw half-a-dozen other boys bearing down at a trot. In his wrath he was still prudent, and was not prepared to face the advancing host.

"I'll take stock of 'em," he said, "and find out who they are."

Then another thought came into his head, prompted by the spiteful mood he was in.

"I'll throw a brick into the thick of 'em," he muttered, "and chance what follows."

Dick and Jem meanwhile had met their friends, and the former was quite overcome with joy at the sight of them. He tumbled into the arms of Dan Mittens, who was one of the foremost, and grasped him round the neck.

"Here, get away," said Dan; "what a beastly mess you are in—sopping."

With a jerk he dislodged Dick, and Tom Biron took the boy by the arm.

"What have you been doing to him, Jem?" he asked. "After last night's illness this may kill him."

"It was a pure accident," replied Jem, dismally; "there was no occasion for him to get into the water-butt if he had only been careful. But you know him—always finding something."

They gathered round Dick, surveying the wretched figure he cut, and hardly knowing whether to be sorry for him or to laugh.

Two-thirds of the school had come up by this time, and the knot of boys formed a fair mark for the man behind the hedge with half a brick in his hand.

Watching his opportunity, he waited until no eye was turned in his direction, and then he hurled it with all his force into the thick of the little gathering.

CHAPTER XXIV.

WHO DID IT?—SCHOOLBOY REVENGE—MR. B. RORD BEANS AND ABE BOTT HAVE A MEETING.

IT was Dan Mittens who received the missile thrown, and it caught him fairly on the back of the head. He went down as if he had been shot.

"Goodness!" cried Jem Stager, "what now?"

"Look to him!" shouted Tom Biron. "I'll see who did that cowardly thing."

Nobody had seen the hand that dealt the cowardly blow, and Tom really thought it was one of the Botts who had been guilty of it.

Judging the direction from which it came, he ran at the fence, jumped it like a deer, and dropped into the garden beyond.

Not upon his feet, however, but upon the edge of an empty barrow, which he overturned, and shot head foremost into a double row of scarlet-runners, through which he broke like a cannon-ball, afterwards striking the top of a low brick wall, and landing at last full length upon the ground beyond.

This gave the author of the cowardly deed time to get away, and when Tom—somewhat shaken by his fall—got up again he was gone.

Behind the garden there was a wood, and this gave the fellow an opportunity to beat a safe retreat. His guilt could therefore only be surmised.

Tom was followed into the garden by several other Slapcrashers, but they came through the gate, and only arrived in time to see Tom dusting his clothes and looking savagely about him.

"Who did it?" cried Selah Finch.

"Somebody who has got clear away," returned Tom. "Is Dan much hurt?"

"He seems a bit stupid," replied Finch, "but he says it isn't much."

Tom strode back to have a look at him, and found Dan sitting by the roadside looking very pale. Jem Stager was staunching the blood from a wound that bled pretty freely.

Warren Fane was tearing up his handkerchief so as to make a bandage of it.

"There's nothing to make a fuss about," observed Dan, looking up; "but I should like to know who did it. Was it Jerry Bott?"

"The same thought occurred to me," replied Tom; "but whoever did it has got away."

"It was the fellow who lives in the house," said Jem Stager. "He was wild because Dick and I got upon the roof."

Dick, who had been trotting up and down for the last few seconds to dry his clothes, gave a confirmatory opinion.

"He was awfully riled," he corroborated, "and looked murder at us. He meant to kill me, I am sure."

"Let our watchword be 'vengeance,'" said Jem Stager. "It is our duty to lay waste the lands of the villain."

"On my word he deserves it," observed Warren Fane.

"Go to work, boys," cried Tom Biron.

It was not often he counselled anything of this sort, but the attack had been so cowardly that he had no thought of mercy.

Dan Mittens looked very bad, and his white face touched the hearts of those who looked at him.

The boys were roused, and all but Jem and Dick rushed into the garden on mischief bent.

Jem remained behind to attend to Dan, and Dick kept up his trotting to and fro, for drying purposes.

As it happened there were several garden tools lying about—a spade, a prong, a hoe, and a rake. These were utilised for destructive purposes, and in a short space of time the place, in a garden sense, was a howling wilderness.

"So far the matter is squared," said Tom. "Now, boys, let us see how Dan is, and then we'll get away."

Dan said he was all right, but he looked all wrong, and the bandage Jem had put about his head had a wounded-warrior effect rather horrible to look upon.

And when he walked away with the rest he soon began to reel. He would have fallen but for the watchful Tom, who took him by the arm.

"You ought to go somewhere," he said, "and lie down a bit."

"Nonsense," replied Dan; "you want to make a baby of me. I shall be all right in a minute."

"Blows on the back of the head are nasty things," said Tom, uneasily; "but I am glad you bled freely—that will help to ward off some of the ill effects of it."

Dan laughed, and vowed he felt quite well.

"But I'll tell you what you may do," he continued; "when we get away from here you may find me a place where I can sit down a bit while you fellows go off and enjoy yourselves—I won't spoil your half-holiday."

"By-the-way," asked Jem Stager, "how did you get it?"

"Slapcrash said he had important business calling him from home," replied Tom. "Mary says that Mrs. Slapcrash told her he was going to sell the school."

"Sell the school!" said Dick, opening his eyes; "sell a lot of boys?"

"The good-will, you duffer," replied Tom; "we can stay or not, as we please. I daresay some of us will leave if the new man isn't of the right stamp."

"That would mean a break-up," remarked Jem.

Somehow the news was not relished

Personally Mr. Slapcrash was welcome to go away and do what he pleased. He had never won the hearts of the boys, and they had united against him, which made the bond closer among themselves.

It was the prospect of being separated from their chums they did not like.

"But if he sells he can't give up at once," observed Finch.

"Perhaps nothing will come of it," replied Tom.

They were moving on while talking, and had soon put the better part of a mile between them and the thatch cottage.

Coming to four cross-roads, with an enormous wide-spreading elm growing in the centre, they stopped. Here was a place where Dan could rest in safety.

"Somebody had better stay with you," said Tom.

"I won't have anyone," replied Dan; "a nice lively game it would be watching me."

A smart argument ensued. Dan was firm, and the boys were equally determined not to leave him alone.

The friendly wordy warfare was waxing warm when Mr. B. Rord Beans hove in sight. He was coming along with the manly stride which had distinguished him since he had made himself antagonistic to the schoolmaster, and he did not see the boys, being occupied with his thoughts, until he was close upon them.

"Boys," he said, looking at Dan Mittens, "what is the matter?"

They told him that somebody had thrown a brick at them from behind a hedge, but did not, of course, enter into the previous adventures of Dick Cockles and Jem Stager.

"And who was the nefarious person?" asked Mr. B. Rord Beans.

"That we don't know for certain," Warren Fane replied.

Mr. Beans was willing to stay with Dan when he heard of the discussion. He had come out to find a quiet place in which to read, and the elm tree was just the spot he wanted.

The roots afforded a dry seat, if not a luxurious one. So the boys went away, and the usher remained behind with Dan.

They sat down, and the usher took out a book, which he did not make any attempt to read, but with a pencil figured out something on the cover.

"No," he said, half aloud, "it can't be done. I'm out of it."

Dan wondered what he was out of, but we need not make any mystery of it to the reader.

Mr. Beans had also heard that the school was to be disposed of, and he was trying to work out the ways and means of getting it into his own hands. But he could not do it.

His own private property was limited to what he carried in his pocket, and all the possible sums he might borrow of friends and relations would not be half enough for the purpose.

He was interrupted in his pecuniary meditations by the noise of some light vehicle approaching, and presently he beheld Abe Bott, accompanied by his son, returning from a sooty excursion into the country.

It had been a heavy job for them, and there were five sacks, filled with soot, upon the barrow.

Abe Bott was never at any time in a very pleasant humour, and that day he happened to be worse than usual. Ill luck had thrown him upon two teetotal houses in one day, and the utter lack of beer had embittered him.

Espying Mr. Beans, he called to mind the scene in the court and the vow he had made on that occasion. That was to take the first opportunity to see who was the best man—he or Beans.

The usher, of course, was unconscious of the mental vow, and saw no danger in the approach of the sweep. He only looked upon him as an unpleasant addition to the landscape.

Abe Bott brought his barrow to a standstill in front of Mr. Beans, and told Jerry to keep an eye on it. Then he advanced nearer to the usher.

"You stand up," he said, ferociously, "and let us settle that question atween us!"

"I am not aware that I have any question with you," replied Mr. Beans, haughtily.

"So you shows the white feather, do you?" said Abe Bott. "Then there's only one thing left for me to do."

He went back to the barrow and took the smallest bag in his arms, returning shortly to the usher, who wondered what on earth it all meant.

He was not long kept in doubt, for Bott, with a dexterity acquired by many years' practice, tilted the sack so as to get hold of the two bottom ends, and in a twinkling shot the soot over Mr. Beans.

Dan, at the last moment, suspected what was coming, and shifted his ground, so that beyond being enveloped in some of the cloud he was none the worse. Not so the staggered usher.

The volume of soot was fairly emptied over him, and smothered him from head to foot. In a moment he was transformed from a respectable tutor to a sweep in an extra good suit of clothes.

"There!" said Bott, "that's how I settle with all cowards. Jerry, we will purceed homeward."

He had tucked the sack under his arm, and was turning round, when Mr. Beans rose up in his wrath, and, half-blinded as he was, went for Bott.

The usher had no science, but he possessed some latent muscular power which anger developed to the full, and the blow he gave Abe Bott on the side of the head would have staggered most men.

Abe went down with a crash and lay there, bent on his usual tactics—to argue the matter out now that he had got into real warfare.

"Here," he cried, "who are you hittin' on? Do you call that fair fighting? Jerry, stand by your father, as a son ought to do."

But Jerry, terrified by the awful figure Mr. Beans in his fury presented, had bolted off as fast as his legs could carry him, leaving his noble father to the mercy of the foe.

"Don't hit a man on the ground," cried Abe Bott.

Mr. Beans offered no reply. Lifting a sack off the barrow, he turned it mouth downwards, and emptied it over Abe's head.

That the champion sweep did not mind. He was accustomed to soot, and it was not so heavy as blows.

So he lay still, and Mr. Beans, having emptied the whole of the sacks over Bott, so as to make him look like a mound of soot with two legs sticking out of it, overturned the barrow into a ditch and returned to Dan Mittens.

"If you are not ashamed of the appearance I present," he said, "we will seek a more retired spot."

Dan did not wish to remain. Whatever he might think of Mr. Beans in his then condition as a walking companion, he felt it was dangerous to remain there alone and risk the anger of the fallen sweep.

So they went off together, Mr. Beans leaving a trail of soot on the ground to mark the road he took.

A few minutes after they were gone Abe Bott rose, like the proverbial phœnix from its ashes, and clearing his nostrils with a grampus-like puff, looked about him.

"Well!" he muttered, "this is a game! Who did it? Not that lanky chap alone—Jerry must have turned agin his father! I'll be the death of him afore I'm done. To go a throwing over his father, and to help a lowborn usher chap to bury him in soot! A man would have to look far and wide to find another son like him. What was it the chap said in the play? 'The boy as raises his hand agin a parient will—will—' What was it? But it don't matter. If Jerry never had a real warming afore he'll have one to-night when I get home."

Soliloquising thus, he dragged his barrow out of the ditch, and, putting the empty sacks upon it, wheeled it slowly off, his watchful eyes roaming here and there in dread of a return of the foe.

Whether Abe Bott believed Jerry had a hand in his downfall or not matters very little. He had accustomed himself to argue out his defeats in this way and to act accordingly. Poor Jerry!

CHAPTER XXV.

MRS. SLAPCRASH MEANS TO KEEP HER BIRTHDAY, AND DICK ASSISTS AT A PREMATURE PYROTECHNIC DISPLAY IN CONNECTION THEREWITH.

MR. BEANS and Dan were the last home that night. It was twilight when they entered by the back way.

The usher had removed some of the effects of his encounter with Abe Bott, so that he did not excite any great amount of attention as he passed through the streets.

Dan, too, had recovered in a measure from the blow he had received, and was able to show up at supper without the bandage about his head.

Mr. Beans, having changed his clothes, presided, and although not a word was said about the sooty encounter, he could see that every boy at the table had learnt the particulars thereof, and he felt like a warrior knight who had returned victorious to his castle.

While they were at supper Mr. Slapcrash's voice was heard in the hall. He was speaking in a loud voice to somebody who came in with him.

"Put down the box carefully, my man," he said.

DICK HAD NEVER BEEN SO ASTONISHED IN HIS LIFE.

"All right, sir," replied a gruff voice.

After this there was the sound of a box being deposited on the floor, and the banging of the front door. Then the dulcet tones of Mrs. Slapcrash reached the ears of the boys, who were as silent as so many lay figures.

Mr. and Mrs. Slapcrash met outside the door of the dining-room.

"Benjamin, my love," she said, "welcome!"

"Safely returned!" replied Mr. Slapcrash, as if he had been to the North Pole and back, "and I've got a lovely box of fireworks. To-morrow we will illumine the heavens in honour of your birthday."

Then there was the sound of a chaste salute, and they moved away.

Fireworks!

Real table-turning.

The boys looked at each other with joyous eyes. Here indeed was an unexpected treat. Even Mr. Beans appeared to like the prospect, and he gave the boys a short discourse on pyrotechnic displays.

"The Chinese," he said, "are masters of the art. They fill the air with fantastic figures of fire, and they can produce a class of harmless inodorous firework to be used within the home. We have not yet reached that pitch of excellence, and indoor exhibitions in this country are practically unknown."

Poor Mr. Beans! He little thought how circumstances were working towards a display in that very house.

All boys are curious, but Dick Cockles was one of the most curious of them. He felt that he could not go to bed without seeing the outside of that box at least. With his soul unsatisfied in this respect he would never sleep.

What was in his heart he told no one, but when supper was over, and the boys retired for a few minutes to the schoolroom ere proceeding to rest, he lingered behind.

Mr. Beans went to find Mr. Slapcrash, to report to him the conduct of Abe Bott, and also to make the most of his victory over the sooty champion, with the idea of impressing the schoolmaster with his fighting powers.

Dick had, therefore, a grand opportunity to gratify the longings of his heart, and, as he was descending the stairs, Mary appeared with an old-fashioned candlestick and tallow candle in her hand.

The latter had not been snuffed lately, and had a top to its wick like a small mushroom.

"Mary!" whispered Dick.

"Yes, Master Cockles," replied the civil Mary.

"Show me a light for a moment, I want to look at this box."

"What box?"

"That one."

Dick pointed to it—a rough sort of box, without any cord round it. The fireworks had evidently been simply laid in for transport home.

Mary was quite willing to show Dick a light, and as the lid was unfastened Dick raised it. The cat at that moment came up, and they all looked in together.

"Oh! my," exclaimed Mary, "what are them beautiful things?"

"Fireworks," replied Dick, with a learned air; "pyrectic things, as we call them. There's rockets without the sticks—there they are in the corner, Mary—and crackers, and Roman candles, and bombs—that's a bomb—"

"If you will kindly help me to carry the box upstairs, Mr. Beans, I shall be obliged."

It was the voice of Mr. Slapcrash that fell upon their startled ears. Mary gave the candle a jerk that shook off the mushroom-like top as Dick hastily closed the lid and from sheer limpness of limb sat down upon it.

There was no way of retreat, for the schoolmaster and usher were coming down the stairs.

"Cockles," said Mr. Slapcrash, as he reached the hall and saw Dick seated on the box, "what are you doing there?"

"Nothing, sir," replied Dick, feebly. "I was only—"

Then he felt himself rising, and the next moment chaos had come without a doubt.

Dick, as far as he could make out, turned about nine somersaults, and then came down flat on his stomach—the table came down upon him, and then Mary on the top of the table.

Mr. Beans and Mr. Slapcrash both went down like soldiers before a withering fire, and the cat was sent half-way up the stairs, with all its hair standing out like wire.

Bombs, rockets, crackers, and a pound of powder for use in an old brass cannon in the possession of Mr. Slapcrash, went off together, or with separate reports, that shook the house and raised a series of wild screams from Mrs. Slapcrash above.

The boys, truly alarmed, came hurrying down, but had to beat a retreat owing to the fumes that rolled up the stairs.

"It's the fireworks!" cried Tom Biron. "Open the windows there."

In a few seconds the schoolroom windows were thrown open, and Dan Mittens, in his hurry, knocked out a pane of glass, thereby giving further ventilation.

Tom and Warren ran upstairs, and also opened the windows there, through which the smoke poured in thick volumes.

To the presence of mind of the two friends the prostrate party in the hall probably owed their lives. But for the quick uprush of smoke they had a fair chance of being smothered.

Mrs. Slapcrash had given herself up for lost, and fainted away.

In a quiet town like Smockley the explosive sounds could not fail to attract attention, and a cry of fire was raised by a passer-by.

Then somebody else dashed off for the Smockley fire-engine, and before Mr. Slapcrash had recovered from the staggering results of the explosion there was a mob around his door.

On getting up he saw Mary seated on the overturned table, and Dick lying under it, therefore it needed no professor of second sight to lay the sin of explosion to Dick's charge.

"You villain!" said Mr. Slapcrash, hoarsely. "It was an evil hour when you entered my house."

Dick did not answer him, and if he had been able to do so he would not have been heard, for a dozen people outside began to rattle sticks upon the front door, while another tugged away at the bell and nearly pulled it off the wire.

"Confound it!" muttered Mr. Slapcrash; "the town will be in an uproar."

By that time the smoke was fairly out of the hall, but it still poured from the windows above, and excited the gathering crowd to a pitch of frenzy.

"The place is afire—all the boys will be burnt in their beds! Hurrah! here's the engine—and here's the fire escape!"

As these two valuable adjuncts to modern civilisation rattled up, Mr. Slapcrash opened the front door, intending to assure everybody that there was no real danger.

He meant also to make a speech, telling and impressive, and had got as far as—"My fellow citizens," when he was bowled over by the mob of people, who rushed into his house like a flood from a burst reservoir.

Now Dick had just regained sufficient consciousness to form a dim idea of what had happened, and he was wriggling out from under the table when the mob rushed in.

Fortunately it was a small mob, or the Slapcrash house would have been torn to pieces by kind friends anxious to save the furniture from the flames.

The table under which Dick lay barred their way, and, not seeing it, the foremost came down heavily, and other eager helpers proceeded to pile themselves on the top of it, to the number of a dozen or so.

It was a mercy that both Mary and Dick were not killed outright, but some people have charmed lives, and they were among the number.

The arrival of two Smockley policemen helped to restore order, and the firemen, having learnt that their services were not required, assisted the officers in clearing the hall.

Perhaps a little unnecessary violence was used, for the "chucking out" was smartly done, and anathemas on the house of Slapcrash resounded in the street.

———

CHAPTER XXVI.

THE COMING CHANGE—A LETTER FROM BUMBLE TOWN—MR. BEANS ARRIVES AT AN IMPORTANT DECISION.

INSIDE explanations were offered and beer distributed to officials. Dick was ordered to bed, with a promise of being "talked to" in the morning, and Mary got a month's warning on the spot.

Mrs. Slapcrash, having recovered from her

fainting fit, played mistress in the hall, and helped to pour out the beer with a grace peculiarly her own; while Mr. B. Rord Beans, who had been doubled up in a corner of the hall during the greater part of the turmoil, manfully helped to drink it.

He made rather too free with it, and Mrs. Slapcrash, with a forced smile, ventured to remonstrate with him.

"This is very heady beer, Mr. Beans," she said; "I should advise you to be moderate with it."

"I could drink a barrel of it," replied Mr. Beans, "and then dance a jig in a six-inch square."

It was not only the beer, but the events of the day that helped to make the great mind of the usher inordinately active.

The encounter with Abe Bott began it, the explosion advanced it, now the beer was putting a final coat of grease to his mental wheels, and the machine was going apace.

As for the police and firemen, they were in no hurry to go while there was beer about, and Mr. Slapcrash, in a moment of rash hospitality, had bidden them not to spare it. So there they were—a jovial party.

"After all," said Mr. Beans, "no great harm is done. Boys will be boys—eh! Slapcrash?"

And he winked at Slapcrash in a manner that inferred they had been precocious boys in their time.

Mr. Slapcrash tried to look dignified, and over Mrs. Slapcrash there came a coating of ice.

"It's long ago," mused Mr. Beans; "but we were boys once—both of us—I'll take a little more beer"—he helped himself—"long —ago—heigho!"

Here he raised his glass and looked solemnly around.

"It's hard to part with youth," he continued; "but youth will not stop with us. Well, we have some consolation in thoughts of the past, Slapcrash, eh! my boy? You remember the old days, don't you?"

"I do not remember you as a boy," replied Mr. Slapcrash, stiffly.

"I remember the time!" said Mr. B. Rord Beans. Then he burst into song—

"*When we were boys, merry, merry boys,*
When we were boys together."

He finished off by slapping Mr. Slapcrash on the back and digging him in the ribs, a proceeding that excited the schoolmaster to a state of blind fury. But he dare not resent it.

"Don't be afraid of the beer," pursued the usher, addressing the official company. "Slapcrash had a nine-gallon cask in on Tuesday, and there is sure to be a thunderstorm on Saturday, so we had better drink the generous liquor before it is spoilt. Here, get some chairs, and we'll gather round and make a jolly night of it."

"Mr. Beans," said Mrs. Slapcrash, "you forget yourself!"

"Maybe—maybe," he replied, "but I'll never forget thee, thou pearl of Smockley. Good old town, Smockley, only I wish I had never come to it. I gave up a high-class Government appointment to help this old snob "—pointing to Slapcrash—"with his school, and now that he has got all he can out of me, robbed the bee of its honey, he wants me to leave his establishment. But I never will. I'm here for life, and the man who tries to turn me out dies. Come on, the lot of you."

Men in the condition of Mr. Beans are subject to varying moods, and one of those changes had taken place in the usher.

He had cast aside the pacific for the pugilistic, and was ready for a general fight. Then it was that one of the police stepped in as peace-maker.

"Sir! don't you put yourself out about fighting to-night," the officer said, "but let it bide till to-morrow, and then take us on one by one in a six-foot ring. You are the man to do it."

"I am," said Mr. Beans, proudly, "but as there's such a lot of you, hadn't I better begin to-night?"

"No—no!" returned the officer, soothingly; "you go to bed and get a bit o' sleep. Then you will be up to the mark. Shall I show you a light?"

"A little more beer first," said Mr. Beans.

"The can is empty," replied Mrs. Slapcrash.

"Ah! is the fountain of hilarity stopped?" exclaimed Mr. Beans. "Then all is gloom! Some boy has put a cork in the pipe and checked the flow. Boys do such things— Slapcrash did it when a boy—I saw him do it, but I never peached. Good-night, thou radiant Peri of Smockley!"—to Mrs. Slapcrash, who was too much flattered to be very angry with him. "Adieu, old chum!"—to Slapcrash—"you are not a bad sort of fellow, but as a boy you were dull as ditch-water, and time has only made an unmitigated ass of you. Good-night, gentlemen all!"

Mr. Beans left them with a dignified air, that would have been very impressive if he had not lifted his legs quite so high or so stiffly, but that is a little peculiarity of gentlemen who are elevated, and wish it to be known that they can walk as well as any other man—and better.

The soothing officer followed Beans upstairs, showing a light with his lantern, but it was some time before he could get him fairly into bed.

At first the usher declined to undress.

"I'd rather go for a walk," he said, "and contemplate the beauties of Nature."

"It's rather too dark for that," replied the officer.

"Well, then! let us go to the White Hart and play skittles," observed Mr. Beans. "I played a game once and broke a window with the ball. They made me pay for it. It was unmanly and unfair."

"So it was," replied the officer, "and I'll talk to 'em about it."

After a time he succeeded in getting Mr. Beans into bed, and by surreptitiously slipping his clothes under it, prevented his resuming them that night at least.

As he left the room Mr. Beans once more burst into song—

"*Strew them, oh! there, on bed of rushes,*
And here we'll stay till morning blushes."

He chanted this again and again, his voice slowly dying away, and at last he slept—and snored.

Happily for the peace of Mr. and Mrs. Slapcrash, they were troubled no more by the tutor that night.

After a final glass of beer the officials went away, but not before Mr. Slapcrash had desired to see the two policemen in the morning.

Out of the night's doings he meant to manufacture a means of getting rid of Mr. Beans.

"I can do it," he said to Mrs. Slapcrash when they were alone. "He has committed himself, and has been seen the worse for liquor by those men. He must go."

"Is it absolutely necessary that he should leave us?" Mrs. Slapcrash asked.

Mr. Slapcrash stared.

"What do you mean by that?" he asked, roughly. "You don't want the fellow to stop, do you?"

"He can be very agreeable if he likes," returned Mrs. Slapcrash.

"Just like all women!" retorted the schoolmaster. "Any fool's compliment will go down. He called you the Peri of Putney, or something of that sort, and now of course he's a dear man!"

"Don't be jealous, Benjamin!"

"Jealous be hanged! especially of such a fellow as that! Besides, there is this fact, Mrs. Slapcrash—you are no longer young—"

He stopped suddenly. The eye of his spouse was on him, and what an eye—a living gimlet!

"We will talk the matter over in the morning," he said, and Mrs. Slapcrash let the matter slide.

Early next day Mr. Slapcrash began the work of ousting his foe.

Having desired Mr. Beans to take entire charge of the school during the first portion of the studies, he went forth and sought the officers who had been in attendance the previous evening.

The interview was a very satisfactory one to him, and he returned home in the highest spirits.

"I shall be free of the villain in twenty-four hours," he kept saying to himself.

As he neared his house he became conscious of sounds inside that were strongly suggestive of the roaring of a distant sea agitated by a storm.

He knew that sound well, having heard it many times before. It was indicative of the boys being left in the schoolroom by themselves, and high jinks were in progress.

Mr. Slapcrash had no need to knock, for the door was ajar. Pushing it open he entered, and found Mary sweeping the hall.

"Where's your missus?" he asked, sharply.

"She's gone a-marketing, sir," replied Mary. "It's Irish stew day, sir."

"Ah! yes, so it is," continued Mr. Slapcrash. "Where's Mr. Beans?"

He had to raise his voice so as to make himself clearly heard, for the roaring above was something overwhelming.

"He went out a minute ago, sir," replied Mary. "He said he was going to put his watch right by the clock at the White Hart."

At another time Mr. Slapcrash would have been indignant, but now he appeared to be pleased.

"Go up to those boys, Mary," he bawled, "and tell them I've returned. I'll be back in a minute."

He bounded off, and the road to the White

Hart being short and familiar, he was there in about a minute.

Entering the hotel bar, which was a very snug retreat, he came upon Mr. Beans drinking with a rough but very honest-looking fellow, who is known to the reader as Dossy Dodge.

The usher was holding his hand, and the clinking of two glasses fell upon the ears of Mr. Slapcrash.

"While I live," said Mr. Beans, thickly, "I shall 'spect you as the friend of those boys. To me they are shons, and I'm more than a father to 'em. Slapcrash is a beast."

"Mr. Beans!" said Mr. Slapcrash, in a loud voice.

The usher started, and tilting his glass so as to empty two-thirds of its contents over his boots, he turned in the direction of the speaker.

"I left you in charge of my school," continued Mr. Slapcrash. "Is this the way you fulfil your duties?"

"I've got one duty to perform," replied Mr. Beans, putting the glass down, "and that is to pulverise you."

"Don't do anything of that sort, sir," observed Dossy Dodge, getting in front of him, "or you will be in the wrong."

"Shall I?" said Mr. Beans, staring at him with advancing vacancy in his eye.

"In course you will," replied Dossy Dodge.

"This conduct," observed Mr. Slapcrash, speaking loudly, so that the people in the hotel might hear him, "is but a following up of your disgraceful exhibition last night. I have two police officers ready to swear that you were intoxicated in my house, and one of them put you to bed."

"A policeman put me to bed?" exclaimed Mr. Beans, indignantly. "What next? I've seen one put you to bed, and Mrs. Slapcrash, too—both the worse for drink. Slapcrash, I'm disgusted with you!"

Mr. Slapcrash was flabbergasted. The barefaced assertions of Mr. Beans rather winded him, but after a short pause he returned to the fray.

"I shall take steps to ensure your leaving my house to-day," he said. "If you remove your things quietly, well and good; if you do not, force will be employed."

"I would not stay in your house another week for a million a minute," returned Mr. Beans; "but, of course, I shall expect my money in place of notice."

"I will pay you to the end of the month," replied Mr. Slapcrash.

"Do it at once, then," observed Mr. Beans, "and then this worthy gentleman "—pointing to Dossy Dodge—"shall bring away my box."

Mr. Slapcrash was only too glad to find the usher in such a pliable mood, and he was also sorry for having wasted half-a-sovereign that morning in tipping the two policemen.

He wished to get rid of Mr. Beans without consulting Mrs. Slapcrash, who was veering round in a most objectionable way in the direction of the usher.

So the barmaid was asked for pen and ink, and Mr. Slapcrash wrote a cheque. Since he had been in possession of a fortune he always carried his cheque-book in his pocket, and never lost an opportunity of producing it.

The pecuniary part of the business being finished, Mr. Beans carefully folded the cheque and put it into his pocket.

"I suppose you think you have got rid of me?" he observed.

"I hope so," replied Mr. Slapcrash; "if you make any further disturbance at my house I shall know how to deal with you."

Mr. B. Rord Beans snapped his fingers— once, twice, thrice.

"I shall bring you down to the dust." he cried. "I shall henceforward make that the great purpose of my life. Beware!"

"Oh! bosh," returned Mr. Slapcrash.

"Wait and see," hissed Mr. Beans. "I have not left Smockley yet. When I do go I may elope with somebody."

There was a deadly meaning in this threat that turned Mr. Slapcrash cold.

Of course it was absurd of him to be jealous of such a man as Mr. Beans—and Mrs. Slapcrash a decidedly waning beauty, too—but it made him feel chilly.

"All I've got to say is," he replied, with an assumption of disdain he did not feel, "that if you annoy me in any way I shall appeal to the law."

Mr. Beans laughed loudly and derisively.

"Go your way, old Slapcrash," he observed; "the war has only just begun. Another small quantity of this liquid, miss, with a bit of lemon. A ditto repeato won't hurt me this morning, as I am taking a holiday."

Mr. Slapcrash returned home, and found the storm in the schoolroom had subsided a bit, but the surf was still beating rather heavily on the shore. He met Dossy Dodge coming downstairs with the tutor's box, Mary following behind.

" I trust you've got all the fellow's things," said Mr. Slapcrash, haughtily.

" If I haven't I can come back for what's left," replied Dodge, quietly. " There seems to be a nice pair of you."

Mr. Slapcrash ascended to the schoolroom, and halted at the door to listen a bit before going in, but he could make out nothing personal or particular.

The boys seemed to be all talking and laughing together. Then he entered, and found the whole place in confusion.

Dick Cockles was doing a bit of ventriloquism, or what he called ventriloquism, and had his head up the chimney, so as to hold proper converse with an imaginary individual near the chimney-pot.

Sam Fusby and Selah Finch played the part of audience.

Jem Stager was riding a form horse fashion, jerking it about and offering his kingdom for another steed, which he certainly wanted if he meant to get anywhere, while the others were amusing themselves in various ways.

Warren Fane alone was quiet, and he was seated at the schoolmaster's desk writing a letter.

" Boys!" cried Mr. Slapcrash, in a voice of thunder.

In a moment a change came over the spirit of the scene.

Dick Cockles was so startled that in withdrawing his head from the chimney he knocked it against the side, and so shook a liberal amount of soot over his interesting countenance.

The spectacle he presented was of a nature to try the risible muscles of his friends, and in spite of the awful presence of the schoolmaster they burst into roars of laughter.

Warren Fane went on writing his letter, heedless of all things around him.

Mr. Slapcrash did not argue the sooty matter with Dick, but settled it there and then by boxing his ears and sending him back to his seat with a peal of jangling bells ringing in his ears.

On the rest there fell silence.

Mr. Slapcrash walked up to his desk and tapped upon it with his fingers. If any other boy of that school had been usurping his place he would have dragged him violently out, and chastised him with due or undue severity.

Warren Fane looked up quietly.

" Oh! I beg your pardon," he said ; " I did not know you had returned. Excuse me while I direct this letter."

He glanced over it, put it into an envelope, directed it, and dropped it into his pocket. Then he descended from his perch and walked unconcernedly to his seat.

All this was done, not in an impudent fashion, but in the unconscious way of one who had the right to do as he did, and had been accustomed to that sort of thing all his life.

" I'm blessed !" whispered Dick, as he smeared his face with his jacket-sleeve and made it hideous with well-rubbed-in soot, " if I can understand Fane."

" Or why Slapcrash doesn't say anything to him," muttered Jem Stager. " If it had been either of us who had dared take possession of his stronghold he would have hurled us from the battlements. By my faith, it is a parlous mystery."

Shortly afterwards Mr. Slapcrash announced the retirement of Mr. Beans from the post of usher, and the news fell upon the boys in the form of evil tidings.

" The fountain of fun is cut short," observed Tom Biron, when school was over and they were discussing the usher's departure in the playground. " I thought he would have kept the game alive a little longer."

" Take him for all in all," returned Jem Stager, " we shall ne'er look upon his like again."

Then sadly they talked of the man who they believed had departed from them for ever. But it was not so. Mr. B. Rord Beans had come to Smockley, and he meant to stop there for some time.

He lived only for vengeance now, and how he consummated that vengeance is matter for future chapters of this particularly veracious story.

CHAPTER XXVII.

A SLAPCRASH PURCHASER—DICK COCKLES AND JEM STAGER GET INTO A MILKY WAY—MR. BEANS' TO THE FORE.

WE must now pass over a week, leaving untold much that would have been interesting or amusing, perhaps both. But time presses, and we must get on with the more important matters connected with Slapcrash School.

The advertisement put in by the schoolmaster had borne fruit, but not exactly of the nature he expected.

No tender to purchase the school outright had come of it, but an offer had been made which Mr. Slapcrash was inclined to accept.

THE SLAPCRASH BOYS.

The Liveliest of School Stories.

"DID YOU EVER SEE THE LIKES O' THAT, ANYWHERES?"

No. 4.   Price One Penny.

Perhaps the shorter and clearer way of putting it before the reader will be to give the letter containing the offer verbatim—

"*Bumbletown, Sept. 10th, 18—.*

"DEAR SIR,—*I understand from your advertisement that you wish to dispose of your school, but I fear you will not find a ready purchaser. However, I make you an offer. I will come and work it for you, bring additional pupils, and give you a handsome share of the profits. I have been a schoolmaster in this town for many years, and can give you the highest references. Unfortunately an epidemic has been raging here, and most of the parents have taken their children home. I*

"*Come on, the pair of you.*"

know not when I may be able to gather them together again, so I think I had better leave the place altogether. Pray send an early answer.—Yours very faithfully,

"FOSSIL BONE, F.A.S., M.O.B.P.S.

"P.S.—*Among the pupils I shall bring with me will be the son of an eminent mandarin named Ching Ching. Young Ching is a gifted boy, and will do credit to Slapcrash Academy. I shall also bring my own bootboy, having a very excellent one.*"

This proposal pleased both Mr. and Mrs. Slapcrash. To be able to enjoy the profits or part of the profits of the school without the bother of it was a very alluring idea.

"If he is an honest man," said Mr. Slapcrash, "I shall accept his offer. Next half-

holiday I will go over to Bumbletown and quietly make inquiries."

"Meanwhile," returned Mrs. Slapcrash, "write and say you will think of his offer. By-the-way, I met Mr. Beans to-day."

"Oh! hang Beans!" replied Mr. Slapcrash, testily.

"What has the poor man done now?" asked Mrs. Slapcrash.

"I decline to talk about him," replied Mr. Slapcrash, banging the table violently. "The very name of the fellow is offensive."

"Oh! very well," retorted Mrs. Slapcrash, "then we won't talk about him. Only I shall think it right to be civil to him when we meet."

The eyes of Mr. Slapcrash flashed thunderbolts, but as his wife took no further notice of him he said no more. Beans had better beware, however, or bloodshed would come of his folly.

"Perhaps he's been telling her again that she's the Peri of Paddington," muttered the schoolmaster. "If he goes on with that sort of thing I shall one day ask him to have a drink and poison him."

Mr. Slapcrash's journey to Bumbletown was of course known in due time to the boys, and the prospect was delightful to them. They could enjoy their half-holiday with absolute freedom, and without any fear of tumbling across him.

Mary as usual told them of it, and at the same time imparted the good tidings that the month's notice had been withdrawn by her mistress.

"Because she wouldn't get another like you for double the money," said Dick Cockles, who was always deep in Mary's confidence.

Dan Mittens felt no ill effects from the half-brick beyond the temporary pain, and as matters were supposed to be squared with the owner of the house, nothing more was said about it.

But the affair was not at an end. A game of hare and hounds was suggested on their holiday, and Dick and Jem being drawn for the hares, they started off, each supplied with a bag of paper by way of scent.

Having given them a good long law, the rest went in pursuit, the way taken by the quarry leading up the road past the thatch cottage.

A mournful-looking woman with a child in her arms was standing by the gate, and a man with a worn face was digging up the ground immediately behind her.

There was something in the look of the pair that induced Warren Fane to stop, and Tom Biron pulled up also. The rest kept on in pursuit of the hares.

"Pardon me," said Warren, "but do you live here?"

"Yes, young gentleman," the woman replied, "and a nice living it will be now the garden's spoilt. We were in the fields at work little more'n a week ago, and a man was mending the roof, when some boys came along, and having beaten him insensible, chopped our garden up."

"I should like to see that man," replied Warren.

"And there's the water-butt, too—that's bust," said the man, stopping and leaning on his spade. "Maybe you know the boys who did it?"

"I do," replied Warren, frankly, "and I can tell you all that happened. If you don't mind I will square the garden job, and then you can buy your vegetables."

He told them exactly what had occurred, and finished off by slipping some money into the woman's hand.

"That will put you right," Warren said. "Good-bye."

After Warren and Tom had run off, the woman looked at the money left in her hand.

"Oh! my," she exclaimed, "he couldn't have meant it."

"How much?" asked the man, peering into her hand. "Why, it's five fardens."

"Suvrins you means," replied the woman.

"Suvrins!" the man gasped.

"Yes! and he's a prince of a boy, whoever he is. Why, the whole stuff wasn't worth more'n a pound, besides, the taturs isn't hurt, and—"

She could say no more, but kissed her baby, and said the little one should have a grand Sunday rig out to wear for the sweet gentleman's sake.

Meanwhile Tom and Warren had gone in pursuit of the rest, and after a considerable time overtook them close to the railway-station, where they had come to a dead-stop.

The scent had been very good up to this spot, but it died away suddenly, and none was to be found.

The boys crossed the line, went all round the station, and had a peep into the goods-yard.

"The scent's given out," said Tom, "and they are hiding somewhere. Let us have a look in the railway trucks."

They went down to a siding for that purpose, but the station-master came out and stopped them.

"I can't have you young gentlemen hanging round here," he said; "there are two expresses due—one down and the other up—and some of you will be killed."

So they had to clear out, and after looking about for a while, they went off, accepting the situation. The hares had evaded the hounds, and the day's run was over.

Had it occurred to them to look into some large empty milk-churns on the platform they would have discovered the missing game.

Dick and Jem having arrived on the platform and found nobody there, the latter, in one of his wild freaks, suggested getting into the churns.

"Can we get out again?" asked Dick.

"Of course we can," replied Jem, confidently; "be smart. I can see some of the fellows coming along the meadows."

With the aid of a porter's truck they got into the milk-churns, and although they were of a good size and constructed to hold many barn-gallons, the twain found them a pretty tight fit, Dick especially so.

With the lids sufficiently open to give them air, they kept close for awhile, and heard the boys discussing their whereabouts.

Dick would gladly have spoken, but as Jem did not and he always followed his friend's example, he bore his tight-fitting lot with the resolution of a martyr.

"Only I wish I hadn't got into the blessed thing," thought Dick.

After the hounds went away a man's voice was heard on the platform asking if there was time to get the churns across the line before the express came through.

"Plenty," the station-master was heard to say. "Here, lend a hand."

"Oh! murder," thought Dick, "in for it again. Just like Jem, getting a fellow into a mess."

On the platform were four men—the station-master, two porters, and a thick-set man, to judge by his dress not entirely unconnected with the agricultural interest.

The last-named laid hold of one of the churns and gave it a shake.

"Hullo!" he said, "there's summat inside."

"It's me," replied Jem Stager, popping up his head.

Dick, hearing his friend's voice, likewise emerged from his place of concealment.

The four spectators stared for a moment, then three of them began to grin. The farmer remained as stolid as ever—that is, as stolid as a man can be.

He did not see any joke in boys getting into his churns with dirty boots, and giving his man an extra job of cleaning.

"Did you ever see the like o' that anywhere?" he asked.

"Can't say I ever did," replied the station-master. "Boys, what are you doing there?"

"If you will help us out," replied Jem Stager, "we will tell you the pitiful story. It is one of the greatest mysteries of modern times."

"I'll mystery you," returned the farmer, tilting over the churns and shooting forth the occupants in a most unceremonious fashion.

As they scrambled up he laid violent hands on them.

"Come on, the pair of you," he said; "if there's a law in the land I'll give you six months for this."

"Hear my story," cried Jem, wriggling like an eel.

"Lay hold o' that chap," said the farmer, letting Dick go; "I've got a job here with this one."

But the station-master did not feel called upon to obey. He was not a policeman, and the farmer was never a man to give a tip, even at Christmas-time, so help was denied him.

Jem was not by any means easy to hold, as he had elevated the art of wriggling to a science, and by expert movements he gave the hand of the farmer a twist or two that threatened to dislocate it.

"Keep still, you little beast!" he hissed.

"All right," replied Jem, as he jerked himself forward and got free.

The farmer made a grab at him, but he was already down on the line.

"Come along, Dick," cried Jem.

"Stop, you boys," shrieked the station-master; "the up and down express together!"

But Jem was not coming back, and Dick followed. The two trains were seen approaching at the top of their speed.

"They will never clear the line!" gasped the station-master, and he shut his eyes.

The two trains thundered through, raising a cloud of dust, and whirling straws and odd bits of paper high in the air. Whirr—boom—rattle—and then the hoarse rush began to soften down.

The station-master opened his eyes and looked along the line for pieces of the boys. But there were no Slapcrash fragments about—nothing but portions of the farmer's hat, which had tumbled off and got under the wheels of the train.

It had been a very close shave for Dick, and but for Jem the train on the up-side bid fair to make what his father called "ready-made meat" of him.

Dragging the bewildered Dick with him, Jem skedaddled through the booking-office, and then they lost no time in putting two or three hundred yards between them and the station.

"I hope you will be more careful next time, Dick," Jem said. "Never get into a milk-churn again."

"I don't know what I wanted to do it for this time," moaned Dick. "What an awful tight fit it was."

"Never mind, now; but we must go and ask the fellows why they did not find us."

The day's sport was over. We may safely leave all explanations to Jem, and come to the time of Mr. Slapcrash's return.

He had found everything satisfactory with regard to Mr. Fossil Bone, insomuch that he called upon him and settled the whole business.

"I have also," he said, "seen the engaging young mandarin who is to embellish our establishment. He has all the composure of a true Celestial, and will give a tone to Slapcrash School it has not had before."

And never, in all his life, did Mr. Slapcrash make a remark with so much true prophecy in it. Young Ching was just the boy to give tone to any place, but whether it was the tone the schoolmaster wanted time alone will tell.

END OF PART I.

PART II.

—••—

CHAPTER I.

THE NEW ORDER OF THINGS AT SLAPCRASH—
MR. FOSSIL BONE AS RULER.

"GENTLEMEN, this is Young Ching."

The son of the world-renowned Ching Ching stood for a moment in the doorway of the schoolroom, looking carelessly about him, as if to see what sort of place and people he was to become associated with.

The audacity of his early boyhood, which some people called "cheek," had developed into a quiet confidence, totally devoid of impertinence.

After all, it was simply a matter of nerve, and no reasonable person would dream for a moment of calling it impudence.

His introducer was Mr. Fossil Bone, a small gentleman, with a learned-looking head and bright eyes, that twinkled behind a pair of nipper spectacles. He was now the head and active working partner of Slapcrash School.

After a moment's pause Young Ching entered the room, and Tom Biron and Warren Fane simultaneously rose to greet him.

In a moment each was yielding to the other, but Biron promptly said—

"It is your place, Warren; bid him welcome."

Warren made no further fuss about it, but, advancing, held out his hand to Young Ching.

"We are glad to have you among us. Your name, at least, is familiar to us all."

"Thanks," replied Young Ching. Then, turning to Mr. Fossil Bone, he said, "I missed the first train, sir. The cord came off Billy's box, and then the bottom came out as we were refixing it. Billy's things were all over the place."

"You did quite right to remain," said Mr. Fossil Bone. "Pink is a good boy, but he has no head. It was kind of you to stay and look after him. Did you find your old home all right?"

"Not so much as a window cracked!" replied Young Ching. "Everybody respects my father too much to injure anything belonging to him."

"Perhaps they fear him, too!" said Mr Fossil Bone, with a faint smile. "You will sit here, next to Fane."

Mr. Bone had only been at the head of the school for two days, but he was already popular with the boys.

He was firm in his mode of treatment, but he was kind, and the half-dozen boys he brought with him, of whom more anon, all spoke well of him.

Young Ching settled into his place, and for a few moments every eye was on him.

There he sat, with his historic name, Celestial attire, and developing pigtail, worn in honour of his sire, a good specimen of boyish shrewdness, pluck, and muscular development.

It needed not a second glance to find out that he inherited some of the wiry strength of his immortal sire, and was, in a pugilistic sense, not to be trifled with.

Even Dick Cockles recognised it, and whispered to Jem Stager—

"I shouldn't care to have a turn-up with him!"

"It would soon be a turn-down with you, by the Knights of the Round Table!" returned Jem.

"Then you don't think I could fight him?" said Dick, roused to anger by his suggested speedy defeat.

"Oh! yes," replied Jem, curtly, "if his hands and feet were tied and he went to sleep."

"Anyhow," said Dick, "I'll have a go at him!"

"Don't be a fool!"

"I am no more a fool than you are!"

Dick was annoyed, and, as usual, the more Jem tried to make him accept good advice, the more dogged he became.

"I shall have a turn at him!" he said, and, accordingly, he wrote the following challenge on his slate—

"It is usual for strangers to have a mill when they come here, and you've got to fight me."

He passed the slate down to Young Ching, who read the portentous words with an unmoved face, and promptly wrote beneath an acceptance, in two words—

"All serene!"

The slate was passed back to Dick, and meanwhile, having cooled down, he was beginning to ask himself if he had not been in too much of a hurry.

Young Ching's cool reply convinced him that he had.

But there was no going back now. He—the challenger—would have to go on and take a licking or give one.

Dick was getting a tolerably clear idea which it would be.

Young Ching did not plunge into his studies with any great ardour, but he went quietly to work, and, with occasional conversational relaxations with those near him, got through the morning.

Mr. Fossil Bone had a good way of handling the boys, and when he got hold of a dunce he made no great fuss over his ignorance; as for the cane, it was never brought out or referred to.

Odd as it may seem to some people of the old school, the boys got on much better without it.

Dick's rash challenge becoming public school property, some curiosity was felt as to the issue of it.

Selah Finch sat next to one of the new boys—Charley Green—and from him he gathered an idea of the probable issue of a fight between the pair.

"Young Ching won't hurt him much," he said; "he will simply dust the playground with him."

Between Tom Bixon and Warren Fane, the accepted leaders of the school, a few words passed.

"I think," said Tom, "that we ought not to allow the fight to take place."

"Leave Cockles to Young Ching," Warren returned.

"Cockles will be half-murdered."

"We shall see."

School over, Young Ching lingered behind the rest, and was the last out of the room.

Before going he had a short conversation with Mr. Fossil Bone, and this delayed him a few minutes.

Then he sauntered downstairs into the hall, and was looking about him when he suddenly remembered Dick's challenge, which he had entirely forgotten.

"Bother the fellow!" he muttered; "why did he want to make a fool of himself?"

Guessing the way out to the playground, he soon showed himself there, the boys being much exercised as to his late appearance.

Dick Cockles was getting ready for the fight on the blind side of the house, where there were no windows to overlook the movements of the boys.

Young Ching sauntered up, with his hands in his pockets, and looked at Dick, who was rolling up his shirt-sleeves.

The rest of the boys had gathered round with expectant faces.

"Well! what are you going to do?" asked Young Ching.

"You will see," replied Dick, with forced ferocity; "perhaps you don't want to fight?"

"No, I don't," replied Young Ching.

"Then you must take the coward's blow."

Young Ching leant against the garden wall and laughed softly.

"And what would you expect in return?" he asked.

"Oh! don't come that bounce over me."

"Look here, young—what's your name?"

"Cockles—Dick Cockles."

"Well, Dick, we can settle this matter without fighting," said Young Ching; "I have not come here to bounce and brag and make myself cock of the walk, but to be chummy with you all round. I've heard something about you Slapcrashers and the town roughs here, and what fighting I've got to do must be for and not against you."

"You are afraid," said Dick.

Young Ching laughed again.

"No, I am not," he said, "unless it is afraid of giving you more than you are able to bear. Come, Cockles, you are a plucky fellow, but you can't fight."

"Not fight!" exclaimed Dick, amazed.

"No—not better than a rabbit," returned Young Ching; "I can see that, and I should be a duffer if I laid hands on you. But to ease your mind we will have a friendly wrestle if you like, just to show you what chance you'd have."

"We'll begin with that," said Dick.

Young Ching, without removing a garment, closed with Dick, and the next moment lifted him like a baby and laid him gently and quietly on the ground.

"I hope I haven't hurt you?" he observed.

A roar of laughter, in which Dick joined, echoed round the playground.

Warren Fane came up to Young Ching and clapped him on the back.

"You are a proper chum," he said. "Shake hands, you two."

Dick did so, looking a little sheepish; but,

after a short struggle with himself, his good nature prevailed.

"I was an ass to think of fighting," he muttered; "it was Jem's chaff that led me to do it."

"Verily, thou art a recreant knight!" replied Jem; "but you mean well. It is no fault of yours that sausages and feats of prowess do not go together."

"That's right," said Dick; "rail at my father's sausage-shop again."

"I should like to make a selection of its famed mysteries," replied Jem. "Put on your coat, Dick. The war is over, and all you have to do now is to go into hospital for repairs."

Another laugh followed, Dick joining, as before, and so things became pleasant all round. It was better than fighting, especially as it would have been such a one-sided affair.

Nobody thought the worse of Dick, for nothing in this world could ever have made a pugilist of him, and all his failures were so many little humorous episodes to laugh at.

"By-the-way," said Tom Biron, "you were saying something about Billy's box—who is Billy?"

"As good a fellow as ever lived," replied Young Ching, "although he will have to black our boots. We have been chums ever since we could toddle about together. Billy's friends are poor, and he has to work; out of love for me—it's a fact, I assure you—he has chosen to follow me here."

There was some curiosity to see the world-renowned Billy, and ere long it was gratified. Billy came into the playground to find a broom, revealing a short, thick-set form, and a round, good-natured, simple face.

"Here, come and make yourself known," said Young Ching. "Gentlemen Slap-crashers—my old friend and companion in many a little rumpus—Billy Pink."

Billy's face brightened up until it looked like a harvest-moon, and a broad grin widened his mouth as he was thus introduced.

"Billy is a poor talker," continued Young Ching, "but he is a grand worker and sound here," smiting Billy on the breast; "give him a good word, plenty of food, and an occasional glimpse of geese on a common, and he'll ask no more—eh, Billy?"

Billy grinned again, and then went in search of the broom, which was lying on the other side of the playground.

"Seems to be a bit of a fool," said Dick Cockles.

"Oh! yes, a bit of one," replied Young Ching, "but we are all that, more or less, you know. Anyway, I hope you'll all be kind to Billy."

CHAPTER II.

THE CULTIVATION OF ATHLETICS—BILLY TAKES TO ROWING, WITH THE VIEW OF BECOMING AMATEUR CHAMPION OF SMOCKLEY — WAR UPON THE WATER.

"IT is Young Ching's coolness I like," observed Warren Fane.

"Only a fellow truly plucky would have refused to fight Dick Cockles," returned Tom Biron; "he knew it was a one-sided affair, and on his side generously abstained from giving poor old Dick a licking."

They were walking arm-in-arm down South-street, on their way for an evening stroll by the canal.

With the coming of Mr. Fossil Bone there was a change of treatment, that the boys found very much to their taste—lots of liberty, and an encouragement of all athletic pursuits.

The evening being fine, the boys were allowed to go out until dusk, and were scattered all over the place in search of congenial amusement.

Warren and Tom were going to do a little boating on the canal, and they were discussing Young Ching, after he had been five days at Slapcrash School.

"I asked him about his father," said Warren, "and he told me that he had not heard from him since he went away, but he was sure he was all right. 'What's the good of my bothering?' he said; 'dad is the sort to be in and out of adventures all his life. If danger doesn't come to him he will go to danger. He likes it. An easy-going life would soon kill him.'"

"I like a fellow who believes in his governor," returned Tom. "But look here! What's this?"

At the bottom of South-street there was an old house which for many years had been without an occupant.

It was said to be in Chancery, and, as there was no board up and nobody knew who owned it, it was naturally supposed that a tenant was not wanted.

The house was a big, shambling place, with high-peaked gables and large chimneys, all with a shaky appearance, brought on by old

YOUNG CHING SHOWS THE STUFF HE IS MADE OF.

age, and a sort of touch-me-down-I-come look, which ought to have acted as a warning to any sensible man not to attempt to reside under that roof.

But a tenant had taken possession of it, and was at that moment superintending the fixing of a long board underneath the first-floor windows.

On that board, with much flourishing around it, was the following inscription—

MR. B. RORD BEANS, M.A., F.R.O.I.
Select Academy for High-Class Pupils.
Instruction by Certificated Masters in all the Educational Branches,
Including the Arts and Sciences,
Navigation, etc.

Not an ounce of pluck in him.

Mr. Beans himself, tall and raw-boned, was standing with his hat on the back of his head in the road, directing the men who were at work, in the tones of a pompous commander-in-chief giving orders to his soldiers.

He did not see Warren or Tom, as his back was towards them.

"Higher up that end," said Mr. Beans; "the board must be level. Everything connected with this establishment must be harmonious and true."

"I don't know what sort of heye you've got, mister," replied one of the men; "but if we puts the board where you wants it people will think it's had a drop o' beer."

"Which we ain't had on this job," hinted the other man.

"Elevate the end as I desire," said Mr.

Beans, loftily; "it is my board, my house, and my high-class educational academy."

"All right, mister," replied the first of the men who had spoken. "Shove the nails in, Dan—he's responsible."

Warren and Tom walked on laughing, leaving the men busy fixing the board awry, and Mr. Beans looking on with chilling hauteur.

"It's a rum go," said Tom, "and Beans will give us some fun. I wonder what sort of academy he will get together in that musty old den?"

"None at all, I should say," replied Warren.

They turned down a narrow way that led to what was called the dock, and there they found half-a-dozen boats waiting for hire.

These were the property of Ned Eade. He had invested the little money he had in boats, to give himself some employment, and to make a living.

Ned was cleaning out a skiff as the boys appeared, and, looking up, touched his forehead.

"Nice evening, gentlemen," he said.

"Prime, Ned," replied Tom. "Any of our fellows gone out?"

"Two of 'em," replied Ned, "in a punt—Mister Stager and the fat little chap. They talked of going up the branch that leads to the Manor, which is nigh choked up, and never was intended for more'n one boat."

"Oh! let them go where they like," said Tom, carelessly.

"I only mentioned it," returned Ned, "because the branch is narrow, and a place where few people go. And I saw Jerry Bott, with some of his gang, going along in that direction. Nothing would please them more than to have a game with a couple of young 'uns."

"We will go and look after them," said Tom.

Choosing a light boat, Tom took the sculls, and Warren sat in the stern. Ned pushed them off, and with a strong stroke Tom started up the canal.

The branch, as it was called, was about a mile out of the town. It was a narrow cutting, made long ago for the benefit of a big house called the Manor, once the residence of a county magnate, but now empty, and pretty well in ruins.

The branch had fallen into disuse also, and its narrow way was only navigable to those who enjoyed what is called pottering about in a boat. Fair rowing was out of the question.

Halfway between the canal and the ruined Manor the narrow waterway was spanned by a wooden rustic bridge, which was kept in repair, for a public footpath ran over it.

After entering the branch this bridge was visible to Warren Fane, who saw in a moment that some lively work was going forward.

On the bridge were several of the town roughs engaged in pelting two lads in a boat below, while on the bank stood Jerry Bott engaged in the same cowardly amusement.

The two in the boat were Dick Cockles and Jem Stager.

Dick was sitting down, holding his head between his arms, and Jem was standing up with an oar in his hands, striking at the blackguards on the bridge.

"Pull, Tom," said Warren; "we are wanted."

"The water is choked with weeds," replied Tom, "I can't get along."

"They will be half-murdered," said Warren.

Tom looked round, and, seeing what was going on, pulled for the bank. They sprang out, and were making towards the rustic bridge to assist their friends when help came from another quarter.

From out some bushes by the side of the canal there sprang Young Ching.

No longer cool and collected, but with a fury that was like the rush of a cyclone, he sprang upon Jerry Bott, seized him by the throat, and hurled him into the water.

Then with a couple of bounds Young Ching was on the bridge, wrestling with Mike Buttons, who alone of all the party stood his ground. The rest bolted at the first sight of coming help.

Mike was a strong lad, also he was heavy, and the struggle between him and Young Ching was like that between a half-grown bull and a young tiger.

In a few moments they fell, Mike underneath, his head striking the bridge and making him see dynamite stars.

"I give in," he gasped.

Young Ching rose up, and, finding no more foes to conquer, his fury died away in a moment.

With his hands in his pockets he sauntered back to the bank, where Warren and Tom were helping Dick out of the boat.

He had received a nasty blow from a stone, and the wound was bleeding rather freely.

Jerry Bott stood up to his waist in water, looking on with a terrified face.

"Come ashore, you cur," said Young Ching, "and take a licking."

"Do you think I want to be small-ganged?" asked Jerry. "A nice thing for a whole lot of you to set on a fellow!"

"Don't talk to the brute," said Tom Biron. "Jem, punt your boat back to the canal. Dick had better walk a bit."

Then they all moved towards the main channel, Young Ching coming last, softly whistling a tune.

Mike Buttons got up and came down from the bridge, rubbing his back, to ease sundry aches and pains he was troubled with just there.

"Ain't you coming out?" he asked Jerry.

"Wait till they are furder away," replied Jerry.

"You ain't got a ounce of pluck in you," said Mike. "I wonder who that little devil is. They are getting some rum 'uns at Slapcrash. He chucked you into the water as if you had been a bag of soot."

"And what did he do to you?" asked Jerry, as he slowly waded out.

"Put me on my back a buster," replied Mike; "for his size he's a gummer."

"Gummer or not," said Jerry, "I'll be even with him one day."

"You!" sneered Mike.

"Yes, somehow; them Slapcrashers ain't going to have it all their own way, but I shall have to do it alone. Nobody ever stands by me."

"I'll clout your head if you say that."

"All right, I've done," said Jerry; "you needn't put yourself out."

"Yah! you duffer!" cried Mike, as he walked on ahead. "Oh! my back! It was a buster, and no mistake! Blow them Slapcrashers, old and new!"

Meanwhile the Slapcrashers had got back to the canal, Dick suffering with some stoicism from the blow he had received.

It was on the side of his head, where there was a bump like half an egg.

Young Ching gathered some particular sort of weeds from the hedge-side, crushed them to a pulp in his hands, and then applied them poultice-fashion to the injured part.

"How's that?" he asked.

"Cool and comfortable," replied Dick. "Where did you learn that trick?"

"From Billy, whose father showed him," replied Young Ching.

He got into the boat with Jem and Dick, and Warren and Tom having got into their boat, they went up the canal in company. Dick, reclining in the stern, played the invalid with good effect.

"I feel glad that I didn't fight you the other day," he said to Young Ching; "lor'! how you went for those fellows!"

"My father always told me to fight as little as possible," returned Young Ching, "but, if I went in for it at all, to do it well. Those fellows are all curs."

"They came upon us without warning," said Jem Stager. "The first hint we had of their being near was a stone as big as my fist that whizzed by within an inch of my nose. Dick found the second."

"I always get hold of hot things!" groaned Dick.

They had a very pleasant row, without being further interfered with, and as the evening was closing in they returned home.

On the landing-stage was Dan Mittens, who seemed to be out of breath.

"Come on," he said, breathlessly. "I've been waiting for you. There's such a lark in South-street."

"What is it?" asked Tom.

"Broad Beans," replied Dan, with a grin; "don't stop or you'll lose the fun."

CHAPTER III.

MR. B. RORD BEANS AS A PUBLIC SPEAKER— MR. SLAPCRASH AS A PRIVATE GENTLEMAN.

DAN MITTENS led the way, keeping silent as to what was going on, with the evident idea that anything he might say would only spoil the treat in store.

As soon as they got into South-street the boys espied a crowd assembled round the house of Mr. B. Rord Beans, whilst Mr. Beans was leaning out of the first-floor window, engaged in delivering a public address.

Whatever he was saying, it was sufficient to elicit frequent cheers, and when the crowd roared the late usher of Slapcrash folded his arms like Napoleon at St. Helena, gloomy and meditative, until he could be heard again.

Close behind him was an elderly woman, sufficiently like him to be recognised as his mother. She had a curious faded, musty look, and wore an old poke-bonnet tilted over her eyes.

Every few moments she touched her son upon the shoulder and addressed a few words to him, but he took no notice of her whatever.

As the boys came up a burst of cheering was dying away. They squeezed their way to a good place in front, where they could see and hear plainly.

Silence came, and Mr. Beans spoke again.

One thing was clear, and that was—however close Mr. Beans had been in the matter of beer for the workmen who had fixed his board, he had not forgotten himself.

His eyes were heavy, and his hat, like the board with its glowing inscription, was awry. The worthy usher had evidently gone wrong.

"Gentlemen," he said, extending his right arm, "I have said enough to let you know the wrongs I've endured, and I ask the men of Smockley is there to be punishment for the offenders? Will you stand by me in my efforts to avenge myself?"

Jeering cries of "We will—we will!" answered him, and when they died away Mrs. Beans was heard speaking.

"Oh! do come away, Rordy," she said; "everybody is looking at you."

"It is my intention," observed Mr. Beans, ignoring the appeal, "to open this palatial academy with a ball!—I shall also give a tea-party to five hundred aged and infirm women —the same quantity of men going down the hill of life will get beer and tobacco—money is no object to me—mother, will you let me alone?"

His companion had given him rather a sharp poke in the ribs—being led to do it probably by the reference to money. She had the appearance of an old woman who looked after the pence, and declined to allow the pounds to take care of themselves.

"You do go on so, Rordy," she said; "come downstairs and have a cup of tea."

"Tea be bothered!" he replied; "get me a bottle of dry champagne—bin forty-two—for I've got a lot to say to these people. Friends — fellow - countrymen — patriots — men of Smockley, I—"

Here his speech was suddenly cut short, and he disappeared as if he had been drawn back with a strong hand.

The window was closed with enough violence to shake out a pane of glass, and the fun was all over.

Not another sound was heard from within, and the crowd, after lingering a bit, began to break up slowly.

"Nice sort of fellow, that," observed Young Ching, as he sauntered up the street, people turning to look at him curiously as he went along.

"Beans hasn't done with Smockley yet," said Tom Biron, laughing.

Tom told Young Ching about his having been usher at the school—a torment to Mr. Slapcrash, and a source of amusement to the boys—also of his sudden departure.

"Something ought to be made out of him," replied Young Ching.

"I wonder what sort of school he will get together?" mused Dick Cockles.

"You might go over to him," suggested Jem Stager, "and make yourself into a nucleus."

"Into a what?" cried Dick.

"A nucleus."

"I don't know what that is, but it sounds shell-fishy, and it's like your cheek, Jem."

"Nucleus," explained Jem, "is the central part of anybody."

"As if I didn't know that!" replied Dick, angrily. "What do you take me for?"

"A very good chum," said Jem, taking his arm, "but not even distantly related to Solomon."

As they turned into High-street they met a young gentleman coming along with his cap very much on the back of his head and his hands in his pockets, and there was a general happy-go-lucky appearance about him that was rather taking.

This was Charley Green, one of the boys who came with Mr. Fossil Bone.

"Hallo! Young Ching," he said, "I've been looking everywhere for you. Where have you been?"

"I went to have a glance at the old house I spotted from the railway," replied Young Ching, "and met these fellows up the canal."

"Are you romantic?" asked Jem Stager; "and do you like ruined halls, and knights, and squires, and dames?"

Young Ching looked at him with a curious twinkling in his eyes.

"Not overmuch," he replied. "I went to look at the old place—well, never mind what for."

"Billy's been at it again," said Charley, after a moment's pause.

"What's he done now?" asked Young Ching.

"Fallen downstairs with a tin of paraffin-oil. Of course he knocked the cork out, and equally of course he let every drop run away. There is such a beastly smell all over the house. We shall get bread and cheese and paraffin for supper to-night."

"Poor Billy!" said Young Ching, serenely; "he's never yet wandered up or downstairs many times without falling."

"Hallo!" exclaimed Jem Stager, "here's Slapcrash and his wife coming up the street. Oh! my, talk of a duke and duchess!—not in it with them, dear boys, not in it!"

Mr. Slapcrash and his wife were indeed a sight.

It was time for the closing of shops, and just the hour when everybody is turning out for an evening stroll if it is fine.

It was fine that night, and the streets were getting lively.

Mr. Slapcrash was dressed, as slangy people would say, up to the nines. He wore a tall hat, frock-coat, light-coloured trousers, and patent-leather boots; he likewise had a flower in his buttonhole.

Mrs. Slapcrash was also a thing of beauty, if not a joy for ever. In the matter of bonnet and bustle, or "improver," as they lightly call it nowadays, she left nothing to be desired.

They were coming up the street like people who were independent and lived on private property. There was a how-do-you-like-this-style-of-thing? air about them.

The boys stood in a group quietly watching them, Warren Fane with a contemptuous gleam in his eyes, not often seen there.

Mr. Slapcrash, as he approached, hailed the boys patronisingly—

"Ah! boys—how-de-do—fine evening—enjoying a stroll, eh?"

They gave him no answer, but raised their caps to Mrs. Slapcrash, who bowed with a grace that gave her back the appearance of having a hinge in the middle.

"Mrs. S. is not so bad, although she is a fool," observed Tom Biron, as they disappeared, "but I never could quite stand Slapcrash."

"You do not know how to manage him," replied Warren Fane, with a quiet smile.

"I wish I possessed your secret," observed Tom; "he always seems afraid of you."

"I think I can guess why Warren Fane gets on so well with Slapcrash," remarked Young Ching.

"Not you," replied Tom.

Young Ching beckoned Warren aside and whispered a few words in his ear.

Warren's face flushed and he laughed in rather a forced manner.

"Not far out, perhaps," he replied, "but you will say nothing."

"Never fear," answered Young Ching.

There had from the first been a secret about Warren Fane. Always exempt from school punishment when it was rife under Mr. Slapcrash, it had given rise to all sorts of surmises, but none knew why he should be treated differently from the rest, not even Tom Biron.

And now Young Ching had got at the truth somehow.

Tom was puzzled, but be sure that his growing admiration for the son of the unrivalled Ching Ching was in no sense diminished. Quite the contrary.

They had another half-hour's liberty, and devoted it to strolling up and down the main street, which was the favourite promenade.

Young Ching excited attention wherever he went, but was apparently unconscious of it. He walked between Tom and Warren, quite as much at home as if he had lived in the place for years.

They pointed out to him several people he ought to know, amongst others Dossy Dodge —the kind-hearted navvy—who had seen fair play in the fight between Warren Fane and Jerry Bott.

By his appearance it was pretty well certain that he was in work again, and had no need of help in any way. He gave them a quiet "good-evening" as he passed.

At the top of the street they came upon Jerry's father, Abe Bott, the self-styled champion sweep of Smockley.

The cowardly ruffian was, as usual, the worse for drink, and was holding forth to two or three of his friends, who gauged their admiration of him by the amount of liquor they drank at his expense.

With boys Abe generally felt pretty safe, and espying our friends, he must needs have a few words with them.

"Hallo! you Slapcrashers," he said, "who let you out of your monkey-den?"

"Shut up, cur!" replied Tom Biron.

"Lor' sakes," retorted Abe, "you must be Earl Smockley, and who's that young chap off the tea-chest, with a pigtail like a sprouting broccaler?"

Young Ching happened to be near him, and Abe put out his hand to grasp the sacred emblem of the boy's birth, but ere he could touch it he got a back-handed smack on the nose that made him blink again.

"You spiteful little beast," he said, clapping his hand to the smitten organ, "what's that for?"

"For your impudence," replied Young Ching. "Don't you try that sort of nonsense with me."

"If there wasn't such a lot of you," said Abe, "I'd make you smart for it."

"Oh! go ahead," retorted Warren Fane; "he's about your size."

"Seen Dossy Dodge lately?" asked Jem Stager.

"Or Mr. Beans?" queried Dick Cockles.

"Your cub has had a dipping in the canal to-night," observed Tom Biron, "and this gentleman off the tea-chest did it."

"Not he," replied Abe Bott, glaring from one to the other with his sooty eyes. "All Slapcrashers are born liars."

"Say that again," returned Tom Biron, "and we'll carry you down to the dock and give you a dip."

"And I'll have the law on you for it," replied Abe. "Here's a policeman coming, and if you go on annoying me I'll charge you."

There was indeed a policeman sauntering up the street, with the slow, majestic step of his fraternity, but the boys made no effort to go away.

They continued to chaff the sweep until he turned on his heel and, vowing vengeance, rushed down a side street.

As they went back to school, laughing over the scene, Young Ching was told a great deal about Abe Bott he had never heard before.

"I shall make a mark of that fellow," he said. "Black as he is, all his tail feathers are white."

On their way down the street they picked up several of the other boys, and, as it was now growing dusk, they went home in a body to supper.

The door was opened by Billy Pink, who smelt like a dealer in paraffin-oil, but was smiling from ear to ear.

"Well, Billy," said Young Ching, "have you got over your misfortune? Seen Mr. Fossil Bone?"

"Yes," replied Billy, "and he told me not to do it again."

"Which you won't—until next time!" said Young Ching. "What a blessed smell! It's enough to poison a Tartar!"

CHAPTER IV.

MR. SLAPCRASH THINKS THE WORLD TURNED UPSIDE DOWN — YOUNG CHING BEGINS TO WORK ON ABE BOTT.

MR. SLAPCRASH had taken up his abode in a small private house in North-street, and it was his intention to occasionally pay a visit to the school and take part in the educational duties by way of recreation.

But Mr. Fossil Bone, knowing his man, did not intend to let him interfere, and the agreement signed between them was very binding.

Fossil Bone was to have the whole school under his care, and Slapcrash was to take half the profits when all expenses were paid.

A breach in the agreement on either side would make it null and void.

Fossil bone was not married, but he had a housekeeper—a grim-looking old woman named Grumps.

She was short in her speech, stiff in her manner, and her face and name were against her, but a kinder-hearted old woman never existed.

A remarkable trait in her character was her faith in Billy Pink.

"One day," she had said again and again, "that boy will make a name. He's got genius!"

And not all the blunders and messes Billy was guilty of shook her conviction in the least.

The way he mixed up boots was frightful, and the boys always had to sort them over when Billy had polished them and ranged them in the hall.

As for the boots of Fossil Bone and Mrs. Grumps, they were seldom put outside their bedroom doors in their proper order.

Sometimes Billy would give his master two right-footed boots, then two lefts, and occasionally one belonging to Mrs. Grumps —a cloth-topped article with side-springs.

As for Mrs. Grumps, she got all sorts of boots and shoes mixed with her own—Fossil Bone's, the boys', Mary's, and once a short Wellington and a slipper did duty as a pair.

The short Wellington boot Billy found in a cupboard, but to whom it belonged nobody knew—the fellow one was not forthcoming— nevertheless Billy cleaned it and put it outside Mrs. Grumps' bedroom door.

Some people may think Billy was a joker, but he was nothing of the sort. He was a steady-going, serious boy, willing to work in his own way, and devoted to Young Ching— that was all.

The morning following the adventure on the canal Mr. Slapcrash appeared at the door of the school, and knocked and rang with no gentle hand.

Every day he got bigger and bigger in his own estimation. He had been swelling like the frog in the fable, and an accident was bound to happen to him ere long.

Mrs. Grumps opened the door.

She had on a coarse apron, her cap was on one side, and fragments of pastry were on her fingers.

"Well! what do you want?" she asked, curtly.

Mr. Slapcrash stared.

"Perhaps you don't know who I am?" he replied.

"Oh! yes I do," returned Mrs. Grumps; "you're old Slapcrash. What do you want?"

"I've come to see how the school is getting on," he answered, faintly.

"It's getting on better without than with you," said Mrs. Grumps. "Go up and look at it, but wipe your boots on the mat, for I've got enough cleaning to do without your bringing a lot of dirt into the house."

Was it a dream?

Could it be that he, Benjamin Slapcrash, the real owner of the school, had been thus spoken to by a venomous-looking old woman?

He wiped his boots mechanically on the mat, and went upstairs with an unsteady gait.

Opening the familiar door of the school-room he entered and found the boys fairly busy with their work.

A few were talking to each other in an undertone, and Sam Fusby was visibly eating something—a protruding left cheek was indisputable evidence against him—while Mr. Fossil Bone was kindly guiding Dick Cockles through the mazes of arithmetic.

Could this be the old place, without a sullen face in it, and not a trace of tears anywhere —no cane in sight? Mr. Slapcrash thought he must be dreaming.

Mr. Fossil Bone looked up and gave him "good-morning."

"I thought I would drop in and lend a hand," said Mr. Slapcrash. "Can't quite give up the business—must do a casual bit now and then to keep myself from rusting."

Mr. Fossil Bone laid aside the book he had in his hand.

"Cockles," he said, "sit down. Mr. Slapcrash, will you come out of the room a moment with me?"

Mr. Slapcrash said he should be delighted, but his face was that of a man who was politely desired to come and be kicked.

The two men went out, the boys exchanging glances of exultation. They knew what it meant.

CHAIRING A SOOTY MEMBER—RUNNING HIM DOWN TO THE CANAL.

The interview between the old and new masters was very brief.

"You will please go home and read your copy of our agreement," said Mr. Bone, as they descended the stairs, "of which you have committed a breach. Don't make another mistake."

"I thought you would be glad of a little help," replied Slapcrash, dismally.

"At present I can get on very well by myself, thank you," was the reply. "Our views are different as to the treatment of boys. Glad to see you at any other time. Good-morning!"

He opened the door, and Mr. Slapcrash, looking very much like a collapsed balloon, tottered up the street.

"Where's the manliness of this place?" Abe asked.

"Done—regular done," he muttered; "but I'll get the upper hand of him yet."

As he turned the corner of South-street another staggerer was in store for him. There was Mrs. Slapcrash, talking to Mr. B. Rord Beans.

They separated the moment they saw him, and Mr. Beans, with a knightly flourish of his hat, departed.

"Talking to that fellow again?" hissed Slapcrash. "What does he call you now, the Peri of Peterborough?"

"He says I'm the Sylph of Smockley," she replied.

"I'll make a sylph of him," retorted Mr. Slapcrash; "blood will come of this."

"Fiddlesticks!" said Mrs. Slapcrash, as she walked homeward.

Mr. Slapcrash went into the country to work off the morning's excitement and collect his faculties.

.   .   .   .

There was another individual with a troubled mind that day, which was Abe Bott, the champion sweep.

A rival chimney-sweep had appeared in Smockley, but Abe had not yet seen him. Two sweeps in that place were too much, and one of them would have to go—Abe meant it to be the stranger.

When Abe was troubled he took to drink as a consoler. He drank whether he was troubled or not, but when disturbed he laid in an extra cargo.

All the afternoon he had been hard at it, and when evening came he was seen staggering down the main street, pausing now and then to cast a few defiant words into the air.

Young Ching, Tom Biron, Dick Cockles, and Jem Stager were coming along together, wending their way to a tuck-shop, when they espied him.

He did not see them as he went rolling by, and at the suggestion of Young Ching they turned and followed him.

Arriving at the White Hart, he went down the yard to the tap. There they refused to serve him, and in a moment he came out again with sullen fires in his eyes.

The boys had followed him to the tap, and although they stood within a few yards of him, he neither saw nor recognised them.

Suddenly he made up his mind to go to sleep somewhere. In the yard of the White Hart there were sundry vehicles for hire—flys, dog-carts, and waggonettes.

In one particular shed was an old sedan-chair, a curiosity of the place and a relic of its earlier days.

Visitors to Smockley always came to see this old chair as one of the sights. It was in a good state of preservation.

Abe Bott, after a look round, got into that chair, and sinking into a corner he went to sleep immediately.

"Now, boys," said Young Ching, "let's trot him out and give Smockley a treat."

It was a daring suggestion, and they hesitated for a moment, but no more.

"Lay hold," continued Young Ching, "and let us get it out as quickly as we can—there's nobody about."

Grasping a pole each, the boys trotted out of the yard and across the road with their burden.

It being the parson's dinner-hour in the Close, they got right through with the sleeping sweep, and no man hindered them.

An old verger, taking his evening walk near the cloisters, saw them, but he only stared as if some spectre of the past was stalking by.

The shaking of the sedan-chair had a rousing effect on Abe Bott, and on reaching South-street he woke up.

"What now!" he roared, as the chair lurched over to an angle of forty-five. "Is it an airthquake?"

Then it rolled back the other way, and boyish laughter was heard outside.

Abe thrust his head through the open window.

"I'm blessed," he said, "if it isn't Young Pigtail. Here, you stop this, or I'll be the death of every Slapcrasher! What do you mean by drugging a 'spectable tradesman and then making a hexibition of him?"

Abe was too well accustomed to waking up and finding himself in strange places to be particularly staggered by his present position.

But the old sedan-chair rocked in an alarming manner, and the street was getting lively with people wanting to know what was the matter.

"Run him down to the canal and pitch him in," said Dossy Dodge, who suddenly appeared on the scene.

"I can't go any further," gasped Dick Cockles.

"Here comes the policeman!" cried somebody from behind.

Young Ching, who had done his best to make Abe's journey an uncomfortable one, looked back and saw the familiar helmet at the top of the street.

"Time to go, boys," he said, and with a bang that shook Abe like a fall from a housetop, the sedan-chair was thrown down and left in the middle of the street.

The four boys vanished sprite fashion, and a crowd gathered round the wreck, but nobody offered to help the occupant within.

Recovering from the shock, Abe got upon the seat and surveyed the crowd through the top of the chair with a ferocious countenance.

"Got up a new sort of chimney-pot, Abe?" said Dossy Dodge. "Why don't you rattle your broom and cry 'swee—up'?"

"I want to know where the manliness of this place is, to let a 'spectable tradesman be served in this way. Ain't any of you got any feelings?" yelled Abe.

"Come out of that chair," retorted Dodge; "a bloomin' nice mess you've made of it altogether!"

"I'll come out when I like, and not afore," replied Abe. "I've been brought here from —from—somewhere, and I ought to be took back again by rights."

CHAPTER V.

MARKET - DAY AT SMOCKLEY — YOUNG CHING ASSISTS THE VENDORS IN MANY WAYS—MR. SLAPCRASH IS DRIVEN TO VIOLENCE.

"Now then, what's this?" asked a police-officer, pushing his way through the crowd. "Drunk again, and up to your tricks, Abe Bott?"

"There's no tricks in me, sir," returned Abe, hoarsely. "I'm a wictim of the Slapcrashers, specially the new one with the pigtail."

At this moment the proprietor of the White Hart appeared on the scene, furious.

"Lock that man up!" he said. "He did this to spite me, because I wouldn't let him have anything to drink."

"Here, that's a bit too strong!" replied Abe, crawling out of the door opened by the policeman. "I was brought here by some Slapcrash boys, and there's a score of people see it done."

But nobody said a word. Abe was not a popular man.

"What!" he cried. "Ain't none of you going to speak?"

"Come on!" said the officer. "We have had enough of your performances. I shall run you in!"

"Run me in?" gasped Abe. "Could I get inside that chair and carry myself?"

"I don't know," replied the officer; "you are always up to some fool's game."

"Lock him up!" cried a chorus of cheerful voices.

Dossy Dodge and three other men volunteered to carry the chair back, and the procession up the street was a very striking one.

Abe Bott, in the grasp of the officer, headed it, and the chair following close behind, the natural inference was that Abe Bott had stolen it.

The report soon took the form of his having purloined it to make firewood of, and Smockley being fond of its old sedan-chair, public indignation swelled at an alarming pace.

Before Abe got to the station there were cries to settle him, and bits of vegetables and sticks began to fly about.

"Here, run me in quick," said Abe, alarmed, "or I'm a dead man."

And right down glad he was when they got him inside the station and closed the door against the noisy congregation of the Smockley people.

"It's all them Slapcrashers," said Abe, sinking down on the prisoners' form, "and Jerry may have had a hand in it; he ain't a natural boy, and I'm a father to be pitied. I hope you'll 'low somebody to bail me out."

"You look as if you want to be baled out badly," retorted the inspector, sternly. "I suppose you've got half a barrel of beer inside you."

But Abe did not see the official joke, although the reserve men laughed at it, as in duty bound.

"I ought to be bailed like any other 'spectable tradesman. Send for my missus, she'll do it," was all Abe replied.

The police would not go for Mrs. Bott, and Abe, being unable to name anybody else who would bail him, had to pass the night in a cell.

After indulging in vows of vengeance on "Young Pigtail" for an hour or so, he fell asleep, and snored until he was wanted in the morning.

The next day was Saturday—market-day—and Smockley came out in its best.

The shops were dressed for the occasion, while farmers and agricultural characters poured in from all quarters. Cattle, sheep, pigs, and other live stock were driven along, and the streets resounded with their various vocal performances, melodious and otherwise.

It was a joyous day at Slapcrash School, for books were put aside, and Mr. Fossil Bone gave them a holiday.

In the old days it had been a holiday, too, but the boys used to be kept in the playground, where their young lives were made miserable by the sounds of life without, while they were shut up like prisoners in the Bastile.

Now Saturday was to be a day of bliss to them, and breakfast being over, they were dismissed by Mr. Fossil Bone with a few kindly words.

"Don't you get into mischief!" he said; "enjoy yourselves by observing the ways of man and beast—the knowledge you will obtain may be useful to you in after life."

Warren Fane and Tom Biron were going for a drive, the first they had had together. Warren had hired a dog-cart at the White Hart, and most of the boys went to see the start.

Young Ching watched Warren take the reins and get into his seat, with a critical air.

"He can drive," he said. "He's been used to it."

"There isn't much in driving," observed Dick Cockles, disparagingly; "all you've got to do is to sit still and pull the reins, according to which side you want to go."

"I daresay you are a good whip," returned Young Ching.

"I can handle the ribbons a bit," replied Dick, calmly, "and when my money comes next week I will take you for a drive."

"So you shall," returned Young Ching.

"There they go!" cried Jem Stager.

With an easy air Warren drove out of the yard, and away the dog-cart went up the street at a smart pace. Tom Biron looked back and waved his hand to the group of boys, who for the most part were a little envious.

"I mean to have a drive next week," repeated Dick.

"The dog-cart holds four," observed Jem Stager, "and thou shalt have a goodly company—even Dan Mittens, Young Ching, and myself."

"Consider it settled," replied Dick, carelessly.

Poor boy! It was his fate to find pit-falls at times—on other occasions he made them for himself. Not having the power of diving into the future, he could not foresee what would follow his first attempt at handling the "ribbons."

A number of schoolboys about the streets on market-day is not, perhaps, an unmixed blessing. Boys will be boys!

"*And talk and whack 'em as you will,*
They will be up to mischief still."

Smockley found it out that day—the first market-day, in fact, on which the Slapcrashers had enjoyed full liberty.

"Let's go and see what they've done to that fellow Bott," said Young Ching.

"Hear—hear," replied Jem Stager. "Perhaps they have boiled the parlous knave in oil."

With half-a-dozen followers at his heels, Young Ching, his hands tucked carelessly into his trousers-pockets, sauntered off to the police-station.

There, as elsewhere, they had made preparations for a busy day, the weekly conviviality generally leading to two or three agricultural fights, and it was the practice of the Smockley police to lock all pugilistic parties up with the least possible delay.

A stolid policeman, of heavy proportions, stood at the door of the station, and as he saw Young Ching approach a gentle smile widened his mouth to about five inches.

"Morning, sergeant!" said Young Ching.

The man was a full private, and this sudden rise in his position was very flattering.

"Morning, sir!" he said.

"How did the sweep get on?"

"We kep' him all night, after which, as Mr. Biffins said the chair warn't much damaged, and he didn't wish to go furder with it, we just bundled Abe out neck-and-crop."

"You did your duty nobly," said Young Ching, with the gracious air of a general addressing one of the ranks. "Farewell, sergeant, for the present."

"He's a cool un," thought the officer. "I wonder whether that sergeant business was really meant, or if it was only cheek?"

As he could not settle the question we shall not attempt to do so, but leave it to the reader to determine.

The vegetable and meat-market of Smockley was an open one, and thither, at the suggestion of Jem Stager, the boys wended their way.

They had to pass through the High-street, where preparations for a vast business, when the cattle dealing was over, were apparent.

In some of the shops the windows were raised, exposing window-boards laden with eatables; others had trays and boxes outside, filled with wares; and the doors of the tailors and bootmakers were almost blocked with cheap specimens of their respective works.

Young Ching said a few words to his chums, and they went through the street in such a quiet and orderly manner that it was in its way quite as attractive as a noisy demonstration.

It is true they lingered here and there to look at the shop-windows, especially the open ones, and if they made a remark it was a complimentary one on either the goods displayed or the owner thereof.

"Those Slapcrashers are a nice lot of boys and very well-behaved," more than one tradesman said as they passed by.

The street was very quiet at the time. All the cattle had passed through, and the farmer visitors were busy in the market.

There was no business doing just then, and the tradesmen were within their shops.

But when the boys had gone along matters became a little more lively.

A grocer came out to have a look at his display of cheese, and was astonished to find a Cheddar labelled "Cheap—Two pounds ten!"

He stared at the ticket like a man in a dream, and then had a look at his eggs and butter.

The eggs were labelled "Spring Chickens, two-and-six each!" and the butter bore the startling inscription—"Best Oil for Carriage Lamps."

Suddenly his brain was illuminated.

"Some mischief-maker has changed the tickets," he muttered.

Next door to his shop was a tailor's, and in the doorway were two dummies of boys in washing-suits.

On the breast of one was a ticket announcing "Fish is cheap to-day!" On the other was a placard declaring that "Bank's Clothing Establishment is the best in Smockley!"

Bank's was a rival establishment lower down.

In five minutes all the tradesmen up and down the street were outside their shops looking at the work which had been done, as they said, "by malignant spirits."

Such an exchanging of tickets as never was, went on between them for about twenty minutes, accompanied by threats of what would be done to the offenders if they were caught.

An easy-chair worth two pounds was ticketed "fourpence-halfpenny," a cooking stove at the ironmonger's was offered at sixpence, with a reduction made on taking a quantity, fowls at a penny each, apples two-and-six a pound, sacks of seeds at the corn merchant's were apparently to be sold at two-three-farthings a yard, and so on, right up the street.

The trail of the serpent was upon them all, and deep and bitter, if not loud, were the execrations of the tradesmen as they righted the wrong done to them.

Meanwhile the boys had got into the market-place, where the first thing they saw was Billy Pink with a huge basket on each arm, following Mrs. Grumps, who was bargaining with the stall-keepers for sundry articles of consumption.

Billy was not carrying the baskets quite as straight as he might have done, and every few steps he tilted something out, which some kindly passer-by picked up and replaced for him.

" Hullo ! Billy," said Young Ching, digging him in the back; " foraging ?"

Billy grinned, and tilted up the left-hand basket, when out rolled an egg, which of course could not be picked up.

" That's the fourth," he observed; " they are awful things to carry."

At this moment Mrs. Grumps turned round.

" William," she said, then catching sight of the egg she threw up her hands and exclaimed—" What—another! Well! for a boy with your gifts you do tumble things about terribly."

" They roll out, ma'am," replied Billy.

" Bless your heart, boy! of course they do. Eggs are round—there's no square ones about. Hold the basket straight and come along."

Billy and the housekeeper proceeded on their way, and the boys stood watching them as they went down the street.

Occasionally Billy looked back to grin, and when he did so he tilted one of the baskets and shot out something.

Finally he got a little out of the track, and fell upon a huge wooden tray filled with onions for sale.

Then ensued ructions. The stall-keeper pounced upon Billy, and Mrs. Grumps came to the rescue.

A lot of language, not entirely complimentary, ensued, and after that the onions were picked up, many unnecessary volunteers assisting.

Anon Billy and the housekeeper disappeared, and for the time the boys saw them no more.

Somehow by this time a breath of suspicion had been wafted from the High-street to the Market-place.

As Young Ching, cool and easy, sauntered along with his followers, an extra watchfulness was observable on the part of the stall-keepers.

If one was asked the price of a fowl the answer was, " Git away with you," and the simple transaction of purchasing a penny-worth of apples was carried on with all the care, on the part of the stall-keeper, of a man dealing with a treacherous foe.

" It's very slow here," Young Ching presently observed; " let us go to the Cattle Market."

The shortest way was through High-street, but it was deemed advisable to make a circuit, and this led them by narrow ways into North-street.

There, to their great joy, they found a little drama of domestic interest going on.

Standing with his back against a barrow-load of vegetables was Mr. B. Rord Beans. On his face was a contemptuous sneer, and his air was quietly defiant.

Facing him was Mr. Slapcrash in a boiling rage, evidently without command of himself.

The owner of the barrow, an old Irish-woman, with the native love of a row warming her heart, was watching the pair with touching interest.

A few spectators were looking on, but at present there was no crowd.

" Here's a game!" said Jem Stager. " Now's the day and now's the hour which will test the Slapcrash power. He ought to fight now or never. Come on, boys!"

CHAPTER VI.

THE BATTLE OF SLAPCRASH—A VISIT TO THE MANOR—DOWN BELOW—DICK COCKLES HAS A STRANGE EXPERIENCE.

" STEADY there," said Young Ching; " go quietly or you may spoil the fun."

So they crept towards the barrow, and the fun, as they chose to call it, soon began in earnest.

" I say, sir," said Mr. Slapcrash, violently, " that you are a pitiful dastard."

" And I say," replied Mr. Beans, coolly, " that you are a miserable fool."

" I deny it. I am as happy as you are. I—"

Mr. Beans laughed derisively, and his opponent became red-hot with rage.

" I have requested you," he said, " not to annoy Mrs. Slapcrash with your attentions."

" I do not annoy her," replied Mr. Beans; " she is pleased with them. She seeks them. She beholds in me a man of many graces. She—"

He was cut short by Mr. Slapcrash going for him.

The late usher of Slapcrash School was first driven against the barrow, when over went the show, and Mr. Beans was mixed up with other vegetables.

The old Irishwoman, who was standing between the shafts complacently listening to the quarrel, was also taken at a disadvantage, and thrown down on her back.

Her squalling was of the strength and hideousness only to be got from women of her class.

Mr. Slapcrash fell upon the handle of the barrow and lay across it, a bit staggered by the success of his onslaught.

Young Ching laid hold of one of the Slapcrash legs, and said, quietly—

"Now, boys, let us have a rally. Don't let the vegetables lie idle."

A "rally" on the stage is the pelting that ends up a scene in a pantomime, and as the boys began a fair imitation of that lively work, Young Ching tilted Mr. Slapcrash over on to Mr. Beans, just as that gentleman was rising, on pugilistic thoughts intent.

A very lively scene followed.

Mr. Slapcrash and Mr. Beans fought on the ground, one with the fury of jealousy, the other with the frenzy of fully-aroused anger.

The old woman continued on her back squalling her loudest, while the boys utilised the vegetables by "rallying" with a spirit and energy rarely equalled and never surpassed.

People began to gather, and soon took up the parable of pelting—first the two struggling men, then each other.

A watchful Smockley policeman loomed in the distance, and Young Ching espying him, quickly gave a hint to his friends.

"'Ware helmets!" he said.

Slipping his hands into his pockets and bidding the others "keep cool," he sauntered up the street, with a somewhat heated following of friends.

"Make haste," he said to the policeman; "it's a case of wholesale murder. Two are dead already. Shall I go to the station for assistance?"

"Yes!—do! Quick—run!" replied the officer.

Young Ching broke into a gliding trot, and with his friends disappeared round the corner.

The officer, loosening his truncheon, bore down upon the scene of deadly warfare.

But it was coming to an end before he was half-way there. Somebody saw him and the "rally" terminated.

The energetic hurlers of vegetables, with an eye to possible damages, disappeared; and Mr. Beans, having tilted Mr. Slapcrash over on his back, got up and walked off, dis--hevelled but dignified.

Only the Irishwoman and Mr. Slapcrash were left, and a very wordy warfare commenced, the chief number of shots and the heaviest being fired by the lady.

It would be interesting, perhaps, to record all she said, but space fails us, and one choice piece must content.

"It's your mother, ye leather-headed spalpeen," she said, "as sent into the worreld a fayend to take away the manes of a poor craythur's living, and she with seven childer and a husband who's given to gitting all the dhrink he can git and more if there's the money to pay for it. It's every hair of your head and whiskers I'll have off if you don't pay for my vigitables."

Mr. Slapcrash could not deny his responsibility.

Undoubtedly the riot originated in the forward movement he had made on Mr. Beans, and in the end he had to pay.

The day all round was what might be termed an eye-opener for Smockley.

What the Slapcrashers used to be in the minds of those quiet people was quite bad enough, but developments had taken place.

Instinctively their accusative powers turned to and dwelt upon Young Ching. The first opinion—that he was a nice, quiet, foreign boy—died away, and another took its place.

"We shall have to put a stop to his goings on," they said.

Neither Young Ching nor his chums turned up again that day in Smockley. At dinner time they came home with lamb-like faces, and after dinner they betook themselves into the country.

The watchful eyes of newly-created foes were exercised in vain.

And whither went Young Ching and his party?

To the old deserted Manor House, locked up many years before, and closed against the public still.

The heavy doors would not stir, and all the windows below were covered outside with huge wooden shutters, warped here and there, and easily to be broken open if anyone had attempted it.

"We must get in," said Young Ching, "but not that way. People passing would notice and somebody would be sent to examine the place. We must have a secret way in and out."

Nothing could be more delightful. The only thing to do was to find that secret way.

Young Ching had his father's spirit, and he was not easily beaten.

They went twice round the house without

A PRETTY DISH OF VEGETABLES.—SLAPCRASH VERSUS BEANS.

finding any means of entrance, but the third search revealed a circular stone, which, on being raised, disclosed a "shoot" into the cellars below.

"That's the ticket," said Young Ching. "All we've got to do is to drop down. I wonder how far it is?"

He took up a stone and dropped it in, listening closely.

"About ten feet," he continued. "A mere nothing. Now, who goes first?"

"But how are we to get out again?" asked Jem Stager.

"Go inside and see," replied Young Ching. "You lead the way."

Young Ching slipped through the opening,

Mr. Slapcrash left so settle.

held to the sides for a moment, and then let go.

They heard him pitch lightly below, and then his voice came up to them.

"It's all right," he said; "good soft ground—feels like rotten straw. Come on."

Jem Stager went next, then Dan Mittens, after him Dick Cockles, who, of course, fell upon his back, and then the rest, among whom were Selah Finch and Charley Green.

There was a chain fixed to the stone slab, and by its aid they drew the stone into its place, when they found themselves in what appeared to be pitchy darkness.

"Hallo!" said Jem, "I didn't reckon on this."

"I did," replied Young Ching, quietly. "But I have a box of matches, and we will soon find a door."

"Suppose it's bolted the other side of us?" suggested Dan Mittens.

"Ugh!" said Dick Cockles, shuddering, "don't think of it."

Whether Young Ching had overlooked this possibility was not clear. Anyhow, he made no remark about it, but having lighted a match he held it above his head and looked round.

On the right he saw a door. It was closed and covered all over with cobwebs.

This did not look promising, and the conviction that it was bolted flashed upon him.

"Keep still a moment," he said, as he glided over to the door.

Young Ching tried it and it was fast.

He pressed with all his might, but found no sign of yielding, and the others by this time began to guess what was the matter.

"The door won't open," said Jem Stager.

His voice was just a little shaky, but he was evidently trying not to show that he was troubled.

"No, it will not open," returned Young Ching, composedly; "but don't get flurried. I have brought you here, and I will get you out somehow."

"Can't you climb the chain and push the stone up again?" suggested Dick Cockles.

"Hanging to the chain at the same time, I suppose?" replied Young Ching, drily; "that would be a feat. Stand where you are. I am going to work my way round, to see if there is another door."

They stood still in the almost absolute darkness, listening to Young Ching as he slowly felt his way round the vault.

It was of considerable extent, about thirty feet square, all under the garden of the house. The door was the means of getting into the house, and the only one.

No sign of any other way could Young Ching find.

"Well, boys," he said, cheerfully, "this promises to be a real adventure. One after your own heart—eh! Jem?"

Jem Stager did not answer so readily as he was wont to do, and when he spoke it was in a restrained manner.

"It's an adventure, certainly," he replied; "but suppose we can't get out or make anybody hear? People don't come near the Manor, as they say it's haunted."

"Haunted by your grandmother," returned Young Ching.

"Oh! that's all right, of course, although I

do not quite agree with you," observed Jem; "but this ghost belief is against us."

"Nothing is against anyone so much as want of pluck," replied Young Ching; "not that I think it is the case with you. Let us try the door again. Some of you come and help me."

They all went, aided by another match he lighted, and as many as could get in a line put their hands against the door.

"All together!" said Young Ching; "nothing like making one push of it."

They settled into their places, Dick Cockles being one of the foremost ones.

Ever energetic, ever wanting to be to the fore, he was bent on doing his full share of pushing.

"Now, then, are you all ready?"

"Yes."

"Push!"

They did so with all their might, but the door stood as fast as a rock.

"Again! All together!"

"Murder! Help!"

CHAPTER VII.

THE END OF THE CELLAR ADVENTURE — ARRANGEMENTS FOR A GREAT BANQUET— DICK COCKLES TURNS DRIVER WITH START- LING RESULTS.

IT was Dick Cockles' voice that filled the vault with startling force.

Selah Finch and Charley Green started to run, without seeing where they ran, and cannoned against each other with a force that bowled both over.

Jem Stager and Dan Mittens staggered back from the door.

Young Ching stood his ground.

"Help! Murder!"

Dick screamed again, with double force, and Young Ching, groping about, laid hold of him by the jacket.

"Here, what's the matter with you?" he cried.

"My arm," gasped Dick; "something's got hold of it."

"Nonsense!" replied Young Ching; "come back will you!"

"I can't," gasped Dick. "Oh! murder!"

Young Ching gave him a bit of a tug, and by the resistance he met with it appeared as if somebody was indeed holding Dick to the door.

Putting a little steam on, Young Ching jerked him back, and Dick being suddenly released, the pair staggered and rolled on the floor together.

"What was it?"

This was the question that flashed through the minds of all, and for a few moments something akin to terror kept them in wild commotion.

"Stand still and be silent," said Young Ching. "It isn't a lion or tiger, anyway."

"Oh! but it must be a horrible thing!" groaned Dick.

"What did it feel like?" asked Young Ching.

"Something soft closing round my arm."

"Well, being soft, there nothing to howl about. Wait a moment while I get a light."

"It was a ghost!"

"Don't be a fool, Dick. There are no such things as ghosts."

He struck a match and stepped up to the door.

The next moment it was blown out, and they were again in darkness.

For a time there was a panic among the boys, then was heard the voice of Young Ching.

"Don't be scared—it's nothing! I'll get another light."

"But who blew the last match out?" asked Jem Stager, with a quaver in his voice.

"Don't know. Find out in a minute," was the cool reply.

Another match was struck, and Young Ching, holding it above his head, stooped down and looked at the door. The next moment he burst into a roar of laughter.

It was the first time the boys had heard him laugh heartily. He did not often indulge in such outbursts, but it was all the more lively for its rarity.

"Ha-ha-ha-ha!"

It rattled like the tapping of a drum round and round the cellar, and it had almost as much effect on the listeners as the sudden putting out of the light.

"Oh! what a game!" he said. "Ha-ha! Dick's done it."

"Done what?" asked Dick, with his hair lifting.

"Why, found out a rotten panel in the door, and made a hole in it!"

Such indeed was the case, and the boys, relieved beyond description, all laughed until their sides ached, mainly because in the rotten panel they saw a means of getting out of their trouble.

So it proved. The door was divided into six panels of wood, with iron bands as a framework, and one of them, for some reason, had rotted until it was mere touchwood. Probably it was of different material from the rest.

Anyway, Dick's arm had gone right through it, making a hole that was nearly round, and he felt as if something had clasped him just below the elbow.

Hence his shrieks of " Help! Murder !"

Young Ching got Jem Stager to hold a lighted match, and in a very short time he had kicked the rotten panel clean out. Then he crept through, and with other matches lighted the boys as they followed him.

The way to the upper part of the house was easy. A flight of stone steps led to an unfastened door, and that opened into a passage. The passage led into the hall.

Not one of the boys there had ever before so truly felt the beauty of daylight, and they clustered together in the hall with hearts almost too full to speak.

" What a glorious old place !" said Jem Stager, breaking the silence; " a genuine banqueting hall."

So it was.

It lacked some of the accustomed fittings, but there were pictures in the panels, old arms hung about, a complete suit of chain-armour stood erect on a dummy figure, and there was an old oak banqueting-table, with three or four seats alongside it.

" A famous place for a spread," said Dan Mittens.

" A midnight one," added Jem, enthusiastically, " with a fire burning on the hearth and the red light glowing on the walls as we quaff each other."

" Look here, boys !" said Young Ching. " We will have a spread of that sort if you are game to come. I'll provide the feast. What do you say ?"

" Glorious !"

" Splendid !"

" The best thing going !" they cried in chorus, and with a " Consider it done " from Young Ching they started up a broad staircase to ramble about the house.

For the present we will only say that it was a ghostly old place, full of odd corners and dark cupboards.

After an hour's rambling about they made their way downstairs to the hall again, and Jem Stager scrutinised the suit of chain-armour.

" Looks rather small, doesn't it ?" he said.

" I believe I could get into it and walk about with it on."

" Leave things alone !" observed Young Ching. " It's getting time to go, so let us search for a way out."

They found an old postern door at the end of the house. In the lock was a key, which they eventually succeeded in turning.

" With a little oil," said Young Ching, " the lock will work A1."

They had a look outside, and noticed that they were not likely to be observed.

Right opposite the door was a tangled shrubbery, through which they could creep to one of the garden paths, and thence to the canal bridge where the struggle with Jerry Bott had taken place.

Young Ching locked the postern door and put the key into his pocket. Then they made their way to the canal and so into the town.

In South-street they were overtaken by Warren Fane and Tom Biron returning from their drive. Warren pulled up the horse with a skilful hand, and asked if they had had a pleasant day.

" So—so," replied Young Ching. " We have begun to wake up Smockley. By-and-bye there will be some life in the place."

They told them of the Slapcrash and Beans affair, at which both Warren and Tom laughed, and Young Ching's opinion that Slapcrash was a " duffer " met with general endorsement.

Then Warren drove on, and Dick Cockles became horsily critical.

" That's not much of a nag," he said ; " got no go in it."

Young Ching looked at him with a humorous expression in his eye.

" The horse," he observed, " knows he has his master driving him, and tries no tricks."

" It won't do for me," replied Dick. " There's a place at the top of the town more in my line—what's the name of the owner ?"

" Masker's," said Jem, " and he's got a name for letting out queer horseflesh."

" The one I mean," returned Dick, " is a tall, good-looking horse, easy to handle by one who knows how to do it."

And Dick bent his legs in a horsey manner, to show that he was the sort of party to handle that horse.

So he went on the road to his fate, and no voice was lifted up in warning, simply because everybody knew it would be a waste of breath.

The High-street was now filled with people, and business was brisk. The murmur of voices, with sharp cries from the butchers of "Buy—buy!" filled the air.

Young Ching was for going "in the middle of the street," and in that way he and his followers passed through.

Many a watchful eye was on them, but nobody had time to utter a word, so unmolesting and unmolested they wended their way homeward.

Billy Pink opened the door, and gratified them by revealing the fact that he and Mary between them had set the kitchen chimney on fire. They were frying some bacon and eggs for tea, and Billy had been entrusted with the care of the frying-pan for two minutes.

Of course he upset it, and there was a conflagration.

"Two sweeps came," he said, "one a little man and the other a big one. The little sweep knocked the big sweep off the doorstep, and came in and put the chimbley out. He said his name was Dodge, and he'd got a cousin who was known to the boys."

"Hurrah!" cried Jem Stager; "the champion of old is beaten by a true knight of the soot-bag. Exit Abe Bott amid the execrations of the multitude!"

And so it was. Abe Bott was deposed, never to rise to the proud position of champion sweep of Smockley again.

Saturday night was "tub" night for the boys, and after the usual scrubbing and larking among themselves they went to bed and slept the sound sleep that comes of a clear conscience and a day well spent.

Monday came and with it a parcel for Dick Cockles.

Several pounds of prime family sausages, made by his father, were inside, with a dozen veal-and-ham pies, also a letter from his mother with some money enclosed in it.

Dick showed the money to his chums, but he read the letter alone, and was much affected by it.

His mother, of whom Dick, like an honest lad, was very fond, rejoiced to hear—as she did from Dick himself—that he was getting on so well with his learning, and she recommended him to spend his money in scientific books, as his father for some reason wanted to make a philosopher of him.

"I wonder what a philosopher is," thought Dick. "Anyhow, there's lots of time before I go into that business, and the scientific books can wait."

In the evening he went up to Masker's and engaged the high-stepping horse for Wednes-

day afternoon, paying down half the charge in the form of deposit-money.

Then he told Dan Mittens, Jem Stager, and Young Ching what he had done.

"We will have such a drive as never was," he said.

With the exception of Young Ching there were misgivings.

Dick knew he had never driven before, and was not by any means sure of the way he would come out of his first attempt at playing Jehu.

Dan Mittens and Jem Stager were dubious, but they resolved to risk it, especially as Young Ching seemed to think it all right. They inferred as much by his silence.

The time passed and Wednesday afternoon came—a half-holiday for all, and soon after dinner the quartette stole away to Masker's.

This man was a livery-stable keeper who had the character of being a downright thief in horse-dealing.

He had the horse and dog-cart ready for them, and a more ill-visaged looking brute than that horse never stood between a pair of shafts.

"I never lets my lots out unless the parties are responsible for damages. Not that there's any fear," said Masker, "but poor men like me have to be on the safe side."

"Of course I am responsible," replied Dick, with glowing airiness. "All gentlemen are."

"The safest part of this trap," said Young Ching to Dan Mittens, "is behind."

And behind they got, while Jem, with a presentiment that he was going to the scaffold or something akin to it, took his seat beside Dick.

A beery-looking ostler led the high-stepper into the street and turned its head countrywards, but the moment he let go it faced about, and with the action of a galvanised camel bore towards the town.

Dick pulled first one rein and then the other, but the high-stepper treated him with the utmost contempt.

"Whoa! you beast, come back!" cried Dick.

"Go through the town," observed Jem Stager, "and out the other side."

Dick, with his eyes half out of his head, sat well forward, holding the reins as if they had been red-hot wires, and required gingerly handling.

Young Ching and Dan Mittens stood up behind, watching the issue of what promised to be a very lively business.

Arriving at where there were four cross roads, the high-stepper wanted to turn to the left, but their way lay right ahead.

Dick tugged hard at the right rein, and a dancing performance began.

"Give him a touch of the whip," suggested Jem Stager.

Dick took it out of the socket and just laid t across the haunches of the brute, when the high-stepper broke into a gallop.

Dick pulled with all his might, but the beast had a mouth of iron, and the harder he pulled the faster it galloped.

"Don't flurry yourself," observed Young Ching. "Let him once get into the country and we'll sail clear away. He will soon tire of this game."

"I can't hold him a bit," gasped Dick. "Oh! my poor mother!—I wish I had bought the books—I'll be killed!"

"Hadn't we better jump?" asked Dan Mittens, who felt white if he did not look so.

"No," replied Young Ching; "that is the worst thing you can do."

Just as there seemed to be a fair prospect of their getting into the country, Jerry Bott came out of a street ahead of them.

He was half-way across the road when he saw the dog-cart coming, and with a yell that was worthy of a savage he threw up his arms.

The high-stepper swung sharp round and threw Jem Stager into the road upon his back, then with a crash the fiery steed went through the window of an eating-house.

It was a large plate-glass front, and there were a lot of good things exhibited in the window, among which the high-stepper fell.

Dick, who had been glued to his seat with terror, felt something like the lash of a whip —it was a piece of the shattering glass—across his face, and was reeling out of his seat when Young Ching grasped him by the collar and dragged him over the back.

It was all the work of a moment for the trio behind to tumble into the road, while the horse, paralysed and terror-stricken, lay quiescent, half in and half out of the shop, with the ruins he had made scattered around him.

———

CHAPTER VIII.

YOUNG CHING DOES DICK A GOOD TURN—MR. SLAPCRASH GOES IN FOR ALDERMAN.

IT is hardly worth while dwelling on the scene that followed. The row, of course, was tremendous.

The police were soon in attendance, while a little host of volunteers cut the harness, backed the dog-cart, and helped the high-stepper out of the fix he was in.

Marvellous to relate, the noble steed had come out of the business with nothing more than half-a-dozen minor cuts and scratches, and on being got into the roadway he began to caper about and kick again.

Young Ching, meanwhile, had whispered to Dick—"You get along home. I'll see that the horse is sent back."

Dick hurried off, glad to get away, but he must have been miserable. His nose was cut across the bridge, and to stop the bleeding he rolled up his handkerchief and made a bandage of it.

When he got back to the schoolhouse he saw Mary standing on the doorstep.

"Lor' a mercy, Master Cockles!" she said; "what now?"

"Don't ask me," groaned Dick; "let me come in, and bring some hot water and sticking plaister to the lavatory."

While Mary was attending to his wounds the three companions of his drive returned.

Jem Stager looked as if he had been shaken up in a bag, and Dan Mittens had the appearance of one awakened from an ugly dream.

Young Ching was softly whistling.

"What have you done with the horse?" groaned Dick.

"The police have got the whole turn out," replied Young Ching; "it's all right. You can easily square the job—a hundred pounds will do it."

"A hundred pounds?" cried Dick, aghast.

"Twenty years' pocket-money," observed Young Ching, coolly; "they will take it as it comes in—they must."

"I hope this will be a warning to you, Dick," said Jem Stager, giving his back a rub. "You are always saying you can do all sorts of things, but you are a duffer!"

"I don't deny it," replied Dick, "but a hundred pounds— Thank you, Mary, I think that will do."

There appeared to be nobody but themselves and Mary at home.

Billy Pink, left to his own devices, had trotted off to the fields, with the hope of finding some of his favourite geese, and Mr. Fossil Bone had gone away by rail to see a friend.

For those who had been in the dog-cart it was a dismal time that ensued, and three of the boys roamed about the playground, not caring to go out.

Young Ching, however, on the principle of taking the bull by the horns, went off to see Masker.

What took place between them they kept to themselves, but it is certain that " Young Pigtail " got the upper hand of the livery-stable keeper, and big damages for the injury to the high-stepper were not asked for.

From there he went to the eating-house, and had a talk with the proprietor, who calmed down after a little outburst.

The result of these two interviews was that not a word of the accident came to the ears of Mr. Fossil Bone.

He did not associate with anybody in Smockley, and between him and Mr. Slapcrash there was a marked coolness.

The only fear was that he might read about it in the local paper.

When the boys were all back—and they returned well primed with the particulars of the accident—Young Ching had a chat with Warren Fane and Tom Biron.

"All I want," he said to Warren Fane, "is the tin until my dad returns. He won't be long now. It was all my fault, for I ought to have stopped him, but I did not look for such a precious smash."

"You can have as much as you like," replied Warren Fane. "I will write to-night for what you want."

So Young Ching took the payment upon himself, but Dick knew nothing about it until a week later.

It had been seven days of torture to him, and every knock at the door made his heart leap into his mouth.

Then Young Ching took pity on him.

"It's all right, Dick," he said; "the damages are paid for."

"Who paid them?" asked Dick, hardly believing him.

"The town of Smockley," replied Young Ching. "In recognition of your skill as a whip they got up a subscription for you."

"I knew you were joking," said Dick, wearily.

"On my word it's all paid," replied Young Ching. "Look—here are the receipts exonerating you from all further claims."

Dick took the two pieces of paper handed to him, one a receipt for two pounds from Masker, the other an acknowledgment of receiving ten pounds from the proprietor of the eating-house.

"You've done this," said Dick, quite overcome, "and I don't know what to say. I'll pay you back. I'll give you all my pocket-money. I—"

"Dry up, Dick," replied Young Ching; "not another word about it. If you offer me your pocket tin I'll give you a good licking."

And so the subject dropped.

Mr. Slapcrash had been seen very little since the affair of the barrow, but he was soon to the fore again, as he put up for alderman for the ward of St. Mary's.

There was opposition, of course, and the boys took a strong interest in it.

They got hold of a lot of the enemy's bills, and pasted them all over the front door of Mr. Slapcrash's private residence.

Young Ching made the paste, and he put a lot of alum in it, which made the bills stick —what is more, he put them on four deep.

It was done after dark and during an absence without leave.

Mr. Slapcrash had a man washing those bills off half the morning, but when another day arrived the light revealed that the enemy had been at work again.

Not only was there a fresh supply of bills all along the brickwork on either side, but the front door had been painted a light blue, which was the enemy's colour.

Then did Mr. Slapcrash go forth to meet his rival and reproach him. After a short war of words, fisticuffs commenced and Mr. Slapcrash went home with a black eye.

The two parties then summoned each other, and Mr. Slapcrash showed his eye to the magistrate, while his opponent exhibited a swollen nose.

Both summonses were dismissed.

On the way out of court Mr. Slapcrash was interviewed by a disinterested party, who had seen Young Ching and Jem Stager doing the bill-sticking.

Boiling with fury, Mr. Slapcrash went off to the school and asked for an interview with Mr. Fossil Bone, who listened quietly to his story.

"I really wonder at you, Mr. Slapcrash," he said. "Not content with libelling the boys all over the town, you now come to me with a cock-and-bull story about two of the best lads in the school. If you do not restrain your animosity I shall bring an action for damages against you."

Mr. Slapcrash left the house "seeing red." The state of his mind was murderous, and it was not softened when he found out that the

THE SLAPCRASH BOYS.

The Liveliest of School Stories.

WITH A CRASH THE FIERY STEED WENT THROUGH THE WINDOW OF AN EATING-HOUSE.

No. 5.   Price One Penny.

ward of St. Mary's had elected his opponent by five to one.

"I'll be even with that Young Ching," he said to his wife. "Until that boy came I was a respected man. I—I—"

"Oh! nonsense!" replied Mrs. Slapcrash; "shame on you! If you attempt to chastise him he will be the victor."

Mr. Slapcrash said no more, but all his malevolence was aroused, and he determined upon having his revenge.

Meanwhile Mr. Beans had made an advance as a schoolmaster. He had got one pupil.

Who the boy was or where he came from nobody knew.

He was about fourteen, tall for his age, with

"Lor' a mercy, Master Cockles, what's up now?"

rather a soft expression. The Slapcrashers christened him Duffy.

He was never seen out alone. Mr. B. Rord Beans was always with him, and they were about the town at all hours.

Duffy appeared to be a haughty boy, and probably instructed by Mr. Beans, he stared at the Slapcrashers whenever he met them, with a very aggravating sneer upon his face.

That sort of thing was not to be borne, and Dick Cockles was the first to resent the insult put upon the Slapcrashers.

He wrote a challenge to Duffy to meet him down by the canal and have "tots up," which means, in other words, a fight.

Mr. Beans enclosed the letter to Mr. Fossil Bone inside one of his own, asking "why his high-class academy should be outraged by such low blackguardism?"

Mr. Fossil Bone gave Dick the two letters without a word, and left him to infer what was expected of him.

CHAPTER IX.

MR. B. RORD BEANS IS LURED FROM HIS HOME — A GREAT VICTORY — TWENTY POUNDS REWARD.

"OUR difficulty," said Dick Cockles, "is to get at Duffy. Beans is always with him."

"Give Billy Pink a letter," suggested Young Ching. "I'll bet that he delivers it. Billy, as Mrs. Grumps says, has genius, peculiar perhaps, but of great service to him."

The fact is there was a very strong desire on the part of the Slapcrashers to witness an encounter between Dick and Duffy.

In the opinion of the best judges of the school they were about evenly matched, and a fight between them would be sure to bring out some novel results.

But there was no getting at Duffy.

Even Billy Pink, with his gifts, could not do it.

He hung about the establishment of Mr. Beans until he saw Duffy at the first-floor window, when he beckoned him, and Duffy opened the window.

"What do you want?" he asked, in a deep voice, very startling coming from a boy.

"I've got a letter for you," replied Billy. "It's a invitation to a picnic. Dick Cockles wants to give you toko."

Billy picked up a stone and was folding the second challenge round it, when the door opened and Mr. Beans descended upon him.

Most boys would have got out of the way, but Billy was not brisk, and he was captured by the enemy.

"Vile boy!" said Mr. Beans, "what is this?"

He wrenched the letter from Billy's hand, but Billy gave him a kick on the shins that made him hop round about, with his eyes tightly screwed up, before he could speak.

Billy, when speech was restored to Mr. Beans, had got away, and was off home to report his failure.

"Never mind," said Young Ching; "that Duffy's got to be interviewed, and if nobody else can do it I will."

And when Young Ching set his brains to work he generally carried out his project. In this case he brought off a fight of the most novel description.

The very next day Mr. Beans received a

letter which he read with a glow of joy, that was like the application to his back of a sponge filled with warm water. Here it is verbatim—

"DEAR SIR,—*I am desired by Lady Far-thingale to ask you to call and see her as soon as you can. She has five sons in need of educa-tion, and, having heard of your promising academy, thinks it the very place for them. Will Tuesday evening suit you? If so, come.*—Yours truly,* "TOM FUSTIBUS, *Secretary.*

"P.S.—*If you have a housekeeper, Lady Farthingale would like to see her. The resi-dence of her ladyship is the large white house which stands on the Coldham-road, near the second mile-stone.*"

"Mother," said Mr. B. Rord Beans, "our fortune's made. We will go and see Lady Farthingale."

Shortly after six o'clock they started, leaving Duffy alone in the house.

The head of the house of Beans had not been gone a quarter-of-an-hour when there came a knock at the door.

Duffy, already weary of complete solitude, promptly opened it.

Young Ching stood in the doorway.

"How are you?" he said, cheerily.

"Here, you let me alone!" replied Duffy, putting his arm up horizontally, level with his eyes.

"All right," returned Young Ching; "I won't interfere with you, but a friend of mine particularly wants to see you."

Then Dick Cockles showed himself, and in his company were sundry boys, to the number of half-a-dozen, among whom were Charley Green, Dan Mittens, Jem Stager, and Billy Pink.

They all entered the house, and Duffy back-ing, the door was closed.

"Now the question is," said Young Ching, "where can the fight come off?"

He opened a door on the right, and beyond it was a room furnished for the reception of visitors. The furniture was rather poor, but there were a lot of cheap glass nick-nacks about, arranged with an eye to effect.

"Go in, you two," continued Young Ching, "and see who is the best man!"

He took hold of Duffy's arm and conducted him in. Dick Cockles, burning to distin-guish himself, quickly followed.

"We are not going to interfere," said Young Ching; "settle it between you."

He closed the door, shutting himself and companions in the passage.

"No talking," Young Ching whispered; "let us hear what is going on inside."

They all stood still, and in a few moments the voice of Dick reached them—

"Come on, you Duffer, and take a licking."

A moment's pause, and then the voice of Duffy—

"You let me alone—I'll kill you if you don't!"

A rushing sound followed, with a stamping of feet, the overturning of furniture, a crash of glass, and then a rattle of fire-irons.

The latter sound went on for quite a minute, accompanied with sundry gasps and cries, such as "How's that?" "Another for you!" "Give in, won't you?"

Some were spoken in the shrill tones of Dick, the others in the deep voice of Duffy.

There was some little excitement in the passage, and after a bit of scuffling Jem Stager got his eye to the keyhole.

Young Ching leant easily against the wall, cracking nuts, as if unconscious of anything extra going on.

"They are getting up," said Jem. "I think Duffy has had enough of it. No he hasn't; he's going for Dick again."

"Here, let me come!" said Dan Mittens.

"In a few minutes," replied Jem. "Houp la! there goes the table with wax fruit under glass on it. Great is the smash thereof! Duffy's got Dick down! Over he goes! Hurrah for the sausage hero! Down comes the what-not! Dick's under the china! Good! Blow for blow! Poor Dick's eye! Duffy's got a winder! It's all over!"

Jem Stager threw open the door and they all entered the room, Billy Pink, unobservant of a footstool, falling over it a purler, that knocked all the enjoyment out of him.

"What a fellow you are," said Young Ching, lifting him up by the waistband of his trousers.

"Had enough?" he asked Duffy.

"Yes, I have," replied Duffy, in sepulchral tones.

"Then you give in?"

"Of course I do."

Jem Stager gave Dick a smack on the back that set him coughing.

"It were well done, and it were done quickly, thou valiant knight," he said.

"Than-nk you," replied Dick; "but go easy with that slapping."

"Can we do anything for you?" asked Young Ching, addressing Duffy.

"No!" was the sulky reply.

"Cold water, sponge, or poultice?"

"I only want to be left alone."

"Very well," said Young Ching; "as everybody seems satisfied we will go."

"Let's have a look over the den," suggested Jem Stager.

"No," replied Young Ching, firmly; "we did not come here for that. We wanted a fight between Duffy and Dick, and it has come off. Let's go to the Manor House and arrange about the midnight feast. I've got a bottle of oil to ease the locks."

They then went away, and Smockley remained in ignorance of the fearful fray that had taken place in its midst until the following morning, when a bill appeared headed—

£20 REWARD!

It went on to state that a band of ruffians had forced their way into the High Art Academy of B. Rord Beans, Esquire, and after maltreating one of the pupils left in charge, had deliberately broken up the furniture and destroyed a valuable collection of bric-a-brac.

The above reward was to be paid to any person on conviction of the offenders.

Billy, Pink, being out on an errand, saw a printer's boy distributing these bills, and having got hold of one, he returned with all speed to the school, entirely forgetting the errand he had been sent upon.

Tom Biron happened to be downstairs looking for a book that Mr. Fossil Bone wanted, and Billy gave him the bill.

Tom read it through, with a face inclined to be grave.

"You are all in a nice mess," he said.

"Will they send Young Ching to prison?" Billy asked, in quavering tones.

"Can't say," replied Tom; "but it's a nice affair certainly."

Of course he had heard of the fight, and laughed over it. The bare fact of Dick having come off best in any encounter was enough to excite his risible faculties.

But this bill, with the offer of a reward, was the other side of the medal.

Having found the book, he went upstairs and handed it to Mr. Fossil Bone, then he quietly passed the bill to Warren Fane.

"Read that," he said, "and hand it round."

Warren Fane read it, and looked at Tom for his cue. Seeing he was very grave, he became grave also.

The bill went round, carrying gravity with it, and at last reached Dick, who, on perusing it, felt his valiant spirit sink slowly into his boots.

"What will they do?" he asked Young Ching.

"Nothing to anybody but you," was the reply. "Couldn't you lick the fellow without making a smash of the whole place?"

"I didn't mean it," groaned Dick. "We did it between us."

"It's serious business," observed Young Ching.

So all thought, and by the time school was over Billy Pink was waiting for the boys, brimful of further intelligence.

He had been sent out a second time on the errand—a simple one, to get a pair of staylaces for Mrs. Grumps—and was wise enough to attend to that first.

Then he went down South-street to have a look at the house of Mr. Beans, and there saw matter for further reporting.

On the way back he lost the staylaces, and by that means astonished Mrs. Grumps, who wondered how a boy of his genius could do such a thing.

Despatched a third time, he got what was wanted, and returning safe with the small parcel, was in the playground ready to impart the gloomy tidings.

"There's two policemen," he said, "examining the door to see where we broke in, which we didn't do, and Mr. Beans was pointing to some marks on it, which he said were made with a burglar's jemima."

"Jemmy," corrected Young Ching. Turning to Dick—"Beans seems to be making it hot for you. I think you ought to be got away from the country before the warrant is out."

"I shall never be a philosopher now," groaned Dick. "What will my father and mother think? But I don't care. I'll go to prison, and never peach."

"Not if they put you on the rack?" asked Jem Stager.

"No."

"Or give you a taste of the thumbscrew and bootjack?"

"I'll die, and not say a word."

Then he got sundry smacks on the back, which made him cough as before, and he was called a jolly good fellow, which almost reconciled him to his impending fate.

134   THE SLAPCRASH BOYS.

Whatever tale Duffy may have told Mr. Beans, the proprietor of the High Art Academy made no direct attack upon the Slapcrashers.

He had good reason to go for somebody, for he had been made a victim of by some practical joker.

There was no such person as Lady Farthingale, with five boys. The occupant of the White House was a drunken squire of the old school, deep in debt, and having his place in a state of siege.

A number of bailiffs were hovering about, trying by all sorts of devices to get into the place.

B. Rord Beans had been taken by the squire to be a bailiff, and his mother as one in disguise, so when they presented themselves at the door and rang the bell a bucket of soapy-water was emptied over them from a window above.

On stepping back to remonstrate, Mr. Beans saw a double-barrelled gun presented at him.

"Be off!" roared a dreadful voice, "or I will give you a charge of sparrow-shot."

Astonished at his reception, Mr. Beans retreated with his mother, and made inquiries of a man who was seated by the road-side eating cold bacon and bread.

This man was a real bailiff, and he put the mind of Mr. Beans at rest about Lady Farthingale and her sons.

"There ain't no such party round here," he said, "and you have been sold."

"The fiend who did it will die!" replied Mr. Beans, tragically. "Mother, let us go back to our High Art Academy, and take steps to bring the perpetrators to justice."

The steps he took are already known, but the bill brought forth no good fruit, except to fasten the crime upon an innocent man, Abe Bott to wit.

The burly sweep was going down the hill rapidly.

Deposed from his proud position of champion sweep by a man half his size, all who used to tremble before him suddenly became very brave.

They worried and harassed Abe until he was pretty nigh frantic.

Then it got about that he was the party who would bring the reward to somebody, and he was candidly told that he was the man.

Walking past the gate of the Close one evening, two days later, he saw Mr. Beans and his one pupil standing in the shadow of it.

Mr. Beans was instructing his pupil in the beauties of architecture, as illustrated by the fine old gateway.

In a quiet corner, a few yards away, Jerry Bott and some of his choice companions were playing pitch and toss.

Abe was in the mood for mischief, and stealing up to the boys, he whispered, hoarsely—

"Stop that game, and go for Beans. He says you've robbed his house. Bonnet him!"

Mr. Beans was busy with his explanation.

"Observe," he said, "the graceful unity of the entire arch, the tall, slender columns, the inward easy turn, the—"

Bang!

As if the whole arch had collapsed and fallen upon his hat. The crash was deafening and bewildering.

He felt that necessary article of attire come down over his eyes, then the brim was torn away and fell upon his neck.

Another crash and a roar from Duffy.

He, too, had been bonneted.

Mr. Beans faced about, and with a violent effort got his hat up, so that he could see again.

Then he beheld Abe Bott urging on the crew behind him to further violence.

"Give it to 'em," he was saying. "What! are you afraid of one man and a boy?"

"You take the man, father," replied Jerry, "and we'll tackle the boy."

"Off, ruffians!" yelled Mr. Beans, shrinking back.

The violent nature of the unexpected interruption to his lecture had unnerved him.

Shrinking back was a fatal step, as it gave courage to Abe Bott.

"All right, Jerry," he cried; "I'm at him!"

He got ready for a rush, and was about to start when there stepped in between him and his prey a slight, boyish form.

It was Young Ching.

"You beggarly lot of cowards!" he said. "Come on—I'll give you something!"

To some people the idea of such a boy interfering would have been absurd, but his dauntless bearing, evident pluck, and the knowledge of his activity and strength were all in his favour.

Jerry Bott shrank back, and his companions, having no real interest in the matter, made no step forward.

Abe Bott turned to look at them, and Young

Ching dealt him a blow on the side of the head that made it rattle like an imperfect iron saucepan.

"Good!" cried Mr. Beans. "Charge!"

Mr. Beans uttered the familiar war cry without any intention of doing anything.

As for Duffy, he seemed to have been scared out of his senses, but Abe Bott never stood a blow like a man, and he began to turn tail.

"Jerry!" he roared, "are you going to stand by and see your father murdered?"

"No, I ain't," replied Jerry; "I'm going home. Here comes the perlice!"

There was no police, but young Jerry wanted to get away, and evaporated with his cowardly following, while Abe Bott ran across the street and disappeared down a narrow passage.

Mr. Beans seized Young Ching by the hand.

"Though a member of my foe's household," he said, "I am grateful. This night will never be forgotten."

"Don't mention it," replied Young Ching. "Excuse me, but I've got an appointment. I am going down South-street. Can I see you home?"

"Well," returned Mr. Beans, "it would be as well, perhaps."

Duffy stared from one to the other in a bewildered manner, but he followed Young Ching without a word.

On reaching the door of the High Art Academy the son and heir of the Immortal One wished them a hurried good-night and skedaddled off.

Then Duffy found his voice—deeper than ever.

"Why," he said, "that's the pigtail chap who brought the fellow to fight me."

"You think so," replied Mr. Beans, "but you are in error. He may bear some slight resemblance to the malefactor, but so true a friend would never bring ruin on the house of your principal. Go in—your bread and cheese awaits you. I would walk awhile and meditate."

Duffy was not quite satisfied.

Although Young Ching had come to the rescue, it did not entirely atone for that bit of work the other night.

In the eyes of the one pupil of the High Art Academy the invasion of the Slapcrashers, followed up by the maltreatment of his own person, was a crime more infamous than ordinary burglary.

"Are there two pigtailers here?" he asked himself, and went indoors dismally brooding.

CHAPTER X.

DICK COCKLES ONCE MORE MADE EASY—YOUNG CHING MAKES ARRANGEMENTS FOR HIS MIDNIGHT FEAST — DETONATORS, BOOTS, AND EGGS.

THE result of Mr. Beans' meditation was that he felt he must, at any cost, make a friend of Young Ching. Possibly by skilful manœuvring he might get him as a pupil. Then, indeed, the High Art Academy might be considered to be looking up.

"With him to harass the foe," thought Mr. Beans, "I should have nothing to fear."

The Smockley weekly paper came out the next day, and in it was the following paragraph—

"GALLANT RESCUE.—Our respected citizen Mr. B. Rord Beans, proprietor of the High Art Academy in South-street, was last night assailed by a number of ruffians, with whom this city is unhappily infested. Luckily aid was near in the person of the son of the Mandarin Ching Ching, who beat the assailants off with a spirit and vigour rarely equalled and assuredly never surpassed. The origin of the rescue no doubt lies in the admiration the intelligent young foreigner feels for the learned proprietor of the academy. It is a pity he is a pupil elsewhere. A teacher and pupil of their excellence working together would bring about some startling educational results."

A copy of the paper, addressed to "The Young Mandarin Ching Ching," was left at Slapcrash School, and Young Ching found the paragraph marked and read it.

"Bother his impudence!" he said.

He knew that Mr. Beans had put the paragraph into the paper, although he did not know that it had to be paid for.

Young Ching did not feel at all complimented by it, but he had no time to attend to it then, having several irons in the fire.

The chief one was the proposed night feast at the Manor House.

All the boys knew of it by this time, and it was generally considered a daring thing to do.

Billy Pink was to be of the party, as he had become a general favourite, and Young Ching would have asked Mary also, if there had been "any other lady to meet her," as he gallantly said.

Tom Biron and Warren Fane talked it over between themselves.

"If there isn't a mess made of it," said the former, "it will be all right, but—"

"Well, let the 'but' take care of itself," interrupted Warren Fane, laughing.

Although Young Ching had borrowed money of Warren Fane to settle for the damage arising out of the driving feat of Dick Cockles, he had a weekly allowance coming to him that amply sufficed for his needs.

As he said, he meant the feast to be a really good one.

No odd bits of tart and cake in bed, but a banquet; and what is more, he intended to make all the preparations himself.

Therefore was he busy, and several evenings in succession were spent by him alone down at the Manor House.

"Are you not afraid of being in that ghostly old place all by yourself?" Dick Cockles asked Young Ching one evening, as he was setting out.

"Not exactly!" replied Young Ching, hesitating.

"Not exactly!" repeated Dick, looking at him curiously. "Have you seen or heard anything?"

"Not much," returned Young Ching, in the same constrained manner.

"You have seen a ghost!" said Dick.

"Never mind what I've seen," replied Young Ching, hastening away.

The curiosity of Dick was aroused, but he was not able to get anything out of his keen companion, so he did what a good many grown-up people would have done under the circumstances, he created a yarn out of his inner consciousness.

First he got hold of Sam Fusby and Selah Finch.

"I'll tell you fellows something," he said, "if you won't say anything about it."

Of course they promised, meaning to keep their word, and Dick, with a face that looked cold, softly whispered—

"Young Ching has seen a ghost!"

"Where?" they asked, breathlessly.

"At the old Manor House."

"Then it won't do to go there at night."

"Oh! it will be right enough," said Dick, digging his hands into his trousers-pockets, and trying to look as if he had rather a liking for ghosts than otherwise. "We shall be all together, you know."

This was the general feeling in the matter when the story got well about.

Dick told his secret to half the boys, and the rest soon heard of it.

Warren Fane and Tom Biron professed to be much concerned, but they laughed at the notion when alone.

"There are no such things as ghosts," said Tom.

"If there are they would not trouble Young Ching," responded Warren.

Ghost or no ghost, Young Ching did not leave off visiting the Manor House.

He spent all the evenings that week in the grim old deserted place, generally returning soon after dusk, in a grave and silent mood, so much at variance with his usual elastic spirits that the ghost story became an accepted fact.

Saturday evening Young Ching came home early, and had a long consultation with Jem Stager, the two walking solemnly up and down the playground with many watchful eyes upon them.

"He's seen another ghost," said Dick Cockles, and he and two or three near him shivered in their boots.

"I wish I was not going," observed Selah Finch.

"We must go," replied Dick. "What's one ghost amongst the lot of us?"

Dossy Dodge came to the gate that night, and received instructions from Young Ching to be early in attendance on Monday evening, to carry to the Manor House sundry parcels and packages which had been ordered at certain shops.

"You can get them there without being seen, I hope," said Young Ching.

"Trust me, sir," replied Dossy Dodge; "it's easy enough."

After he was gone Young Ching went into the house and routed out Billy Pink, who was cleaning forks in the pantry, bending the tines in the operation, and otherwise maltreating the plated property of Mr. Fossil Bone.

"I've arranged for you and Dick Cockles to come on Monday night together," he said; "it won't do for us all to go in a body, in case we tumble across any curious person, say a policeman."

"All right, Ching," replied Billy; "it will be a glorious night, won't it? But, I say, what's this I've heard about a ghost?"

Young Ching looked at him anxiously, and seemed to be struggling against an impulse to speak out, but, as with Dick Cockles, he was vague in his reply.

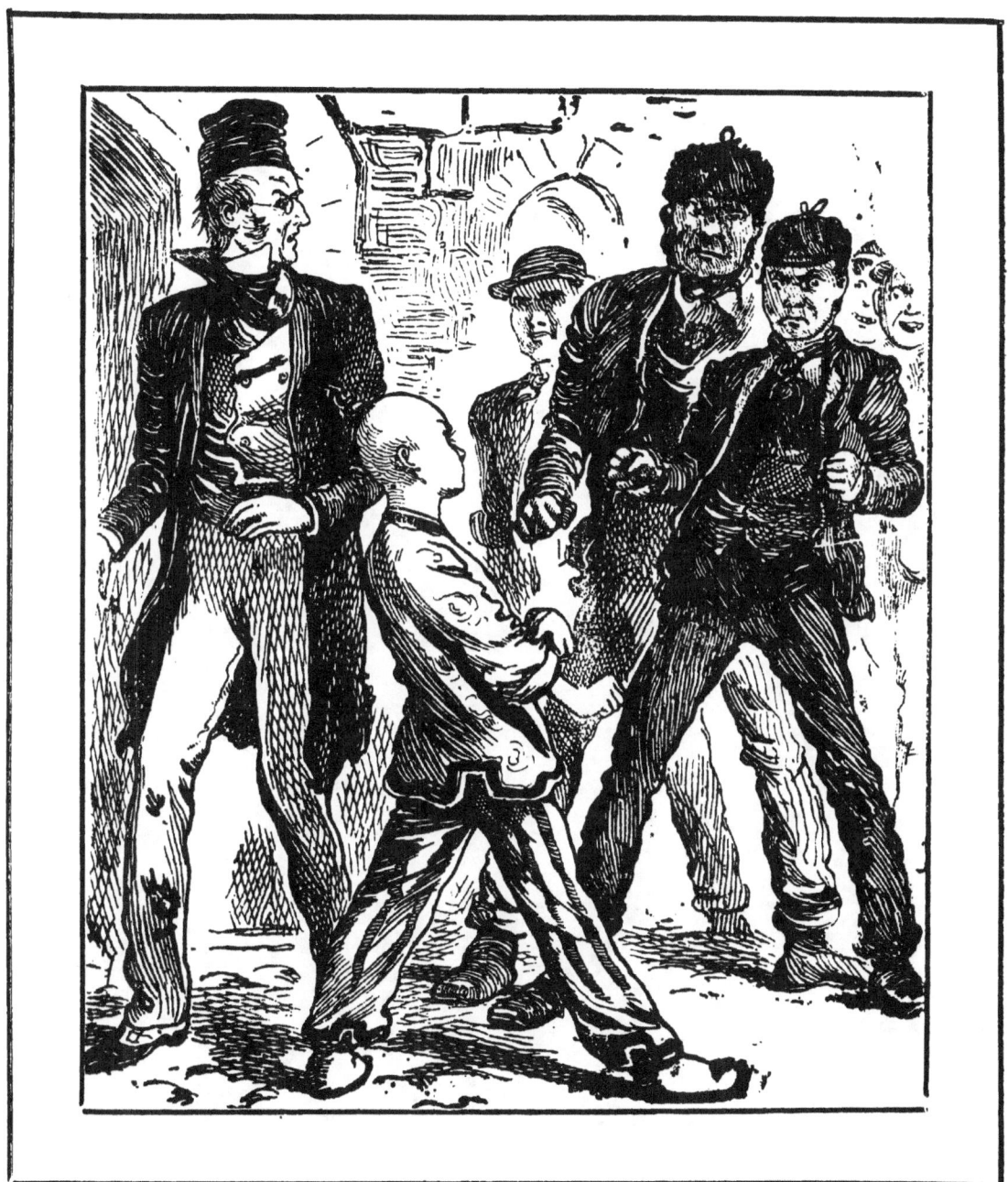

"YOU BEGGARLY LOT OF COWARDS," YOUNG CHING CRIED, "COME ON!"

"Oh! bother ghosts, Billy!" he said; "there's only one sort of ghost that might scare you, and that's the ghost of a goose."

"I'd give that a walloping!" replied Billy, with a grin, and he was so tickled with the idea that he leant his whole weight on a fork and fairly broke it in two.

"You've done it now," said Young Ching.

"That's the second this week," replied Billy, ruefully. "The last one I had on a plate when I fell over the mat, the plate smashed and the fork stuck in my waistcoat—I broke it just like this."

"What did Mrs. Grumps say? Put it down to your gifted nature?"

"No," said Billy; "I put the bits on her

Young Ching escorts the victims home.

chair—then she sat down on them and thought she'd done it."

The face of Billy, as he made this confession, was a study.

Young Ching looked at him gravely, shaking his head slowly.

"Oh! Billy—Billy," he said, "what do you expect will become of you if you go on in this way?"

"I ain't worse than others," replied Billy.

"Well, I don't know," observed Young Ching. "You are going out to-night, I think?"

"I have to call at the cobbler's for Mrs. Grumps' boots," replied Billy.

"Then here are some little pills to put on Slapcrash's doorstep," said Young Ching, handing him about thirty small round pellets.

"What are they for?" asked Billy.

"Only to surprise him when he gets home from the White Hart," replied Young Ching.

"I'm going now," said Billy, taking the plate-basket on his arm.

He went out of the pantry, and barely had he got outside when he dropped one of the pellets, trod upon it, and off it went with a bang.

Down went Billy with the plate-basket, creating a clatter that could be heard halfway down the street.

Mary came running out of the kitchen, and Mrs. Grumps, with a lamp in her hand, appeared at the head of the stairs.

"What's happened?" she asked.

"I've dropped the plate-basket, ma'am," replied Billy.

"I'll come down and help you pick the things up," said Mrs. Grumps. "What a boy you are!"

Young Ching backed into a dark corner as Mary and the housekeeper came to Billy's assistance.

By that time Billy had, of course, dropped the detonators all over the place.

Then ensued a lively scene.

As soon as Mary and Mrs. Grumps got among them the banging commenced.

They skipped about, uttering—"Oh—oh!" hopping here and there, and dropping upon the explosive pills with wonderful accuracy, until half-a-score of them had gone off.

By that time Mary, scared half out of her wits, was down among the forks in a sitting position, and Mrs. Grumps had got into a chair, with her feet drawn up and her face as white as a sheet.

"What's come to the place?" she asked. "Is it alive with fiery bombs?"

"I don't know, ma'am," replied Billy; "it is a curious thing." He made a step, and—bang! "Oh! lor'! I never!"—bang!— "It's horrible! fearful!"—bang! bang!

And then Billy, not a little alarmed himself, fell over Mary, and the confusion was complete.

In the midst of it appeared Young Ching, overwhelmed with surprise.

"Oh! please do help us!" cried Mrs. Grumps. "The place is full of fiery bombs! We shall be blown to bits!"

"I will pick up the plate first," said Young Ching.

Stooping down he began his work, passing the flat of his hand over the floor, and so feeling for and securing the detonators. Swiftly he got hold of most of those left, and the forks too.

Placing the latter in the basket, and holding the former in his left hand, he first lifted Billy up and then Mary.

"The danger is over, whatever it was," he said, and Mrs. Grumps in a gingerly manner put her feet upon the floor.

Bang!

"Oh! mussy!" she exclaimed, and Mary, with a scream, fled into the kitchen.

"It certainly is a most mysterious thing," said Young Ching. "Take away the plate, Billy."

Billy retreated on tiptoe, and all went well with him until he was half-a-dozen steps away. Then he got upon a detonator that had rolled the farthest.

Bang!

Billy did not fall that time, but he turned up the plate-basket like an umbrella over his head, and down rained a shower of forks.

"The place is bewitched," said Mrs. Grumps. "William, have you been a studyin' chemistry?"

"No, ma'am," replied Billy, rubbing his cranium where the points of some of the forks had made an impression.

"Then it's a mystery of mysteries," continued Mrs. Grumps.

After a short delay, occupied by Billy and Young Ching in picking up the forks for a second time, she got off the chair again, and succeeded in getting to the stairs without treading on a "fiery bomb."

"I must get Mr. Bone to look into this," she said. "If it isn't witchcraft there never was such a thing."

She went upstairs, and Young Ching carefully felt all over the floor, until he reckoned he had got all the explosives that were left.

"I'll take what remains of the pills to Slapcrash, Billy," he said, "or we shall have you blowing up a bishop. Wait outside a moment, and I'll go to the cobbler with you."

Billy more than cheerfully consented, and five minutes later the old friends were on the way to Mr. Slapcrash's residence.

There Young Ching duly peppered the doorstep with the remainder of the detonators, adding a few more he had in his pocket, and then he went on to the cobbler's with Billy.

It was Saturday night, and the streets were very lively—so lively, indeed, that the boys were tempted to linger.

Billy had got Mrs. Grumps' boots under his arm, and with his hands in his pocket sauntered up the High-street.

The tradesmen were doing a brisk business, and outside one of the butter shops there was a long wooden box of French eggs, ticketed "Quite fresh—sixteen for a shilling."

"We only got twelve for a shilling in the market to-day," said Billy, stooping to look at them.

At that moment a passer-by brushed against Billy and nearly upset him.

Throwing out his arm to restore his equilibrium, he dropped the parcel of boots into the egg-box with considerable smashing results.

"Look out for your eggs, mister!" roared somebody in the middle of the street.

Young Ching knew the voice and dashed at the speaker, Jerry Bott.

Before the young rough could get out of the way he had received a blow that sent him over upon his back, and he began to yell "Murder!"

There was a rush in his direction, and Young Ching, satisfied with what he had done, sauntered slowly down the street, looking for Billy, who had disappeared.

Getting out of the High-street, he came to some private houses, and there all was comparatively dark.

Very few people were about, and nobody took any notice of him until he was passing a deep doorway, from out of which emerged Billy Pink.

"Let's go home," he said. "Don't touch me, I'm in such an awful mess."

"What's the matter with you?" asked Young Ching.

"When you rushed at that chap," said Billy, "I was so startled that I fell among the eggs. I'm in a blessed state of yolk—"

"So are the boots," observed Young Ching.

"The boots!" exclaimed Billy. "I'm blessed if I didn't forget them. I left 'em in the box, and Mrs. Grumps' name is on the lining."

"In that case," said Young Ching, with emphasis, "you have more than done it."

"How's that?" asked Billy.

"They will send the police to lock her up for wilful damage," replied Young Ching. "I don't know that they won't come and drag her out of bed at midnight."

Billy leant against the wall of a house and gasped.

"Poor old girl!" he whispered, "and so kind to me, too."

"Perhaps I can save her," said Young Ching. "Wait here for me."

He was off in a moment, and at a swift trot made his way back to the butterman's shop.

Billy's descent among the eggs had been discovered by that time, and the butterman, surrounded by a number of people, was just fishing the parcel of boots out of the yolky wreck.

"All I want to know is," he said, "who's done this? I'd give him a month for it."

"What's in that parcel?" asked a man.

Here Young Ching stepped forward.

"I think," he said, "you had better mind how you handle it."

"What for?" asked the butterman, eyeing him suspiciously.

"It may be a packet of dynamite," replied Young Ching, "for the man who put it in the box said it would blow up Smockley when it went off."

"Oh! lor'," gasped the butterman, as he dropped it from his hand.

Young Ching caught it as it fell.

"I'll take it down to the canal and throw it in," he said.

They made no effort to stop him, and off he bounded with the dangerous parcel, leaving the bystanders to go about with all sorts of yarns, which finally assumed the form of one thrilling narrative.

And that was—an attempt had been made to blow up the bishop and his palace, and three men were already in custody.

To return to Young Ching.

He gave Billy the boots, and they got home with all speed, entering by the back-door, Young Ching showing a laudable desire to escape observation.

Billy had two hours' scraping and cleaning in the privacy of the pantry, and succeeded in removing the greater part of the damaging eggy evidence against him.

By that time the hour for all to be in bed had arrived, and Billy got between the sheets, only to dream that he was in a country where the streets were paved with eggs four feet deep, all with thin shells and big yellow yolks, mixed with detonating pills.

CHAPTER XI.

THE START FOR THE MANOR—BILLY AND DICK COCKLES APPROPRIATELY GO TOGETHER—THE GHOST.

"I WISH you fellows to understand that you are about to do a risky thing," said Tom Biron, "but I don't want to stop you. I shall make one myself, so will Fane, but you will have to be cautious."

The school for the day was over, tea had been partaken of, and they were all in the playground, as far as they could get away from the house, to escape the chance of being overheard.

Young Ching was standing beside Tom Biron, looking as if he had nothing particular to do with it, and was not at all concerned.

"You see," continued Tom, "the utmost caution will be necessary. First we have to get out of the house, then through the streets, and so on to the Manor House. Luckily it will be dark, as the moon is on the wane, and does not rise until one o'clock."

"I don't see why the moon doesn't come up regularly like the sun," grumbled Dick Cockles.

"Perhaps if you had mentioned it," suggested Charley Greene, "it would have got up an hour or two earlier to oblige you."

The boys were all in a state of feverish excitement.

The charm of novelty, combined with risk, was before them, but many things were in their favour.

Mr. Fossil Bone believed in the boys, and either could not or would not think ill of them.

It was quite useless for persons to lodge complaints against any of his pupils without they possessed absolute proofs of guilt.

Mr. Slapcrash had failed to do so, and sundry tradesmen had failed likewise.

Duffy, who perhaps was not quite such a fool as he looked, had written an anonymous letter and put it in the post without a stamp.

Mr. Bone paid the twopence charged on it, read a long list of atrocities laid to the charge of his lambs, then burnt the missive and said nothing about it.

"Anonymous writers are liars," he said. "It is a cowardly way of assailing anyone."

And he was undoubtedly right. The behind-your-back scribbling fraternity are the meanest of their kind.

The boys did not go out on the eventful evening, but sauntered about the playground doing nothing, talking in whispers of the coming affair.

By two and two they were to get away about half-past eleven, and Billy Pink and Dick Cockles were to be the starters.

"They had better go first," said Young Ching, "as they may not get there so easily as some of us."

The usual supper that night was scarcely tasted, but acting on the advice of the giver of the feast, a lot of bread and cheese was surreptitiously pocketed, so as to give rise to no suspicions.

Mr. Fossil Bone presided, and saw nothing unusual—he never did—and at the usual hour the whole house was apparently at rest.

At eleven o'clock the preparations for departure began.

Billy Pink had placed a ladder against the dormitory window, and the first to descend was Dick Cockles.

The pair made their way through the garden and out by the gate into the deserted street.

"You know your way, I suppose?" said Billy.

"Every inch of the ground," replied Dick, "and I shall take you a short cut."

As they were about to start, Young Ching appeared alone.

"I am going on first," he said. "As the giver of the feast I ought to be there to receive you."

He was gone like a shadow, and Billy Pink, as they walked along, waxed warm in praise of his old friend.

"Whatever he does," he said, "is sure to be done right. There never was such a fellow as Young Ching."

"He's a puzzler," replied Dick, rather vaguely.

In pairs the boys got away, and no Smockley eye saw them go.

The very last to set out were Tom Biron and Warren Fane.

It was a dark night, but not a pitch black one, so they easily found their way down to the canal, and then on to the path that led to the old Manor House.

Ahead they saw a light, which they rightly judged to come from the open postern door.

"That's not being cautious!" said Tom.

"It will only give rise to a ghost yarn," replied Warren.

They hurried up and made their way to the hall.

There they found the table covered with good things, eatable and drinkable. The greater part of the boys were also there.

But there were absentees—Dick Cockles, Billy Pink, and Young Ching.

"It's odd," said Jem Stager. "Billy and Dick can be accounted for, but where is our host?"

"Gone to look after the other two, perhaps," suggested Tom.

At that moment the pattering of feet was heard outside, and Billy and Dick appeared.

Their clothes were covered with mud, and they were quite out of breath.

"Thank goodness!" said Dick. "We've got here at last."

"Whence this mudsomeness?" asked Jem Stager, eyeing the pair, as the others did, with curious eyes.

"I took a short cut," replied Dick, "and forgot the ditches. We've been in eleven of 'em."

"Twelve," said Billy, rubbing his legs together. "I counted 'em."

"Well!" observed Jem, "it is Dick's fate to get into messes and out of 'em. What's the time?"

"Three minutes to twelve," replied Warren Fane, looking at his watch.

"Young Ching ought to be here," said Tom Biron.

"Especially as he came on first," observed Jem Stager.

Jem was uneasy, and so they were all. That Young Ching had been there was clear from the fact that the door was found open and the table arranged. What could his absence mean?

They all thought of the ghost stories that had been told, but no one liked to start the subject.

"He'll be here in a minute," said Dan Mittens, hopefully.

And then a silence settled upon them.

There certainly was an uncanny look about the unexplained absence of Young Ching.

Jem Stager sauntered over to the suit of armour which he had noticed before, and gradually the others gathered behind him.

"I wonder what the person who wore it would think of us if he saw us here?" he whispered.

"But he can't see us!" replied Dick.

"I don't know that."

They raised their eyes to the suit of armour, made centuries ago for some son and heir, the pride of a great family.

The boy was gone—the way of all flesh— the armour remained, a mute witness of the glories of the past.

"Hark!" cried Tom Biron, "the city clocks are striking twelve!"

The sound of half-a-dozen recorders of time floated through the open door, the deep tones of the cathedral clock being heard above the rest.

Instinctively the eyes of every boy were turned towards the door, as if they expected some spectre of the past to walk in.

But no ghost appeared.

The clocks ceased to strike, the slowest of all, the cathedral clock, finishing its two last strokes alone.

Eleven—TWELVE!

"Ha-ha!"

The boys all started, and several made for the door, but stopped half-way.

"Who-o-o-o laughed?" asked Jem Stager.

"Ha-ha!"

It was a weird, wild laugh, that echoed strangely about the neglected hall, and it came from the suit of armour.

"Ha-ha-ha!"

A look of ghastly terror was on the face of half the boys at least, and their alarm was increased by the figure slowly raising its right arm and pointing at Dick Cockles.

"You are not afraid of ghosts," said a hollow voice within the helmet.

"Ow—oh!—oh!—ow—ow!" roared Dick.

Then the figure raised both its arms, whipped off the helmet, and disclosed the head and face of—Young Ching.

"Welcome, my noble friends!" he said; "a right royal welcome to our lordly halls!"

They all laughed, some of them a little hysterically perhaps, but the musical clatter of their voices echoed all over the place.

"Close your door," cried Young Ching, leaping down with a clatter upon the floor. "Thanks, friend Mittens. What, Jem! still feel a little white?"

"It was a licker," replied Jem, slowly. "I never dreamt of it, but you have managed it well. It was a—a—pleasant surprise."

"Glad you liked it," said Young Ching, with a humorous twinkle in his eye. "I was beginning to think that some of you took it rather seriously. It cost me many an hour to oil this old suit and get it into working order, but it fits easily now, and I'll sup in it with your leave."

With Tom Biron on his right and Warren on his left, he took his seat at the head of the table.

From some of the upper rooms he had rummaged out a few time-worn and moth-eaten chairs, but they were tolerably sound still.

"It was the best joke ever carried out by a Slapcrasher," said Tom Biron, and so they all said.

What a feast it was!

A very liberal board was spread—tarts, sandwiches, veal-and-ham pies, beef pasties, and other toothsome things—with some really good British wine to wash them down.

How they ate and drank, and toasted Young Ching and then each other! How they laughed at ghosts, now that the fear of them was no longer in their hearts!

It is a pity we cannot dwell upon the scene, but this is a story with a lot of movement in it, and we must get to other things.

No interruption took place.

The Manor House was out of the way of the ordinary police-patrol, and nobody had visited it at night for years.

What if any wandering keeper or poacher saw a light or heard sounds in the old place? At the most it would only give rise to another of those fabulous ghost stories that are told by the fireside and believed in by some people.

It was half-past one when Young Ching arose from his seat.

"Gentlemen," he said, "it is time we returned, or there will be leaden eyes in the schoolroom. I hope you have all enjoyed yourselves."

"We have, thanks, old fellow!" replied Warren Fane, smacking him on the back, and the others echoed his reply.

"Then get along home," said Young Ching, "two by two. Billy and Dick go first. The moon is up, and you need not get into more than five ditches this time."

"I won't get into any sort of mess," replied Dick, bravely. "As for ghosts—I never believed in them—quite."

"Away," said Young Ching. "Jem, most valiant of squires, help me off with my armour, and put it carefully away; it may serve us a good turn another day."

Dick and Billy started off, and Tom Biron went out to see that they took the right direction.

Dick's head would never allow him to become a toper. The currant wine had got into it, and he was disposed to be frisky.

But Billy Pink was the boy to keep him straight, if anybody could do it.

"You come along quietly," he said; "or do you want to get Young Ching into a row?"

"All my time is taken up with getting myself out of rows," replied Dick, with some truth. "You let me alone—I know my way back as well as you do."

CHAPTER XII.

DICK'S MIDNIGHT OUTING IS ACCOUNTED FOR—
WARREN FANE'S VISITOR — MR. SLAPCRASH
AGAIN SUFFERS.

AND so it proved.

They got home safely, after having dodged one policeman in South-street, and entered by the old garden gate.

Billy had left the back door ajar for himself, and as he slept on the ground floor, that was the right way to enter.

Not so the boys, who had to get in by the window of their dormitory, assisted by the ladder that had been used oft-times before.

"Good-night, Billy," said Dick, grasping his hand. "We are friends for life, ain't we?"

"Of course we are," replied Billy; "but don't you jaw so much just now. Do you want to get Young Ching into a mess?"

"It is always Young Ching with you," retorted Dick. "Don't you ever think of yourself in the matter?"

"I don't know that I ever do," replied Billy Pink, after a moment's reflection.

"Oh! faithful Billy," murmured Dick, "your friendship is a pearl worth seeking. Good-night, dear old pal, good-night!"

"Good-night."

"Another grasp of the hand, Billy."

It was given.

"Friends for life!"

"Of course."

"All serene. Once more, good-night."

Billy glided into the house, and Dick picked up the ladder, which was lying near the wall of the house.

He was in a meditative mood, and did not give so much heed to what he was doing as he ought to have done.

He raised the ladder and put it against a window—the wrong one, of course.

Slowly he mounted the ladder, still meditating, then he reached the window, tried it, and found it fast.

"Here's a go," he muttered. "But perhaps it only sticks."

He was about to try it again, when the click of the inside fastening being drawn back was heard.

Then Dick wanted to go down in a hurry, but he could not, for his legs would not move.

The sash was shot up, and a night-capped head appeared.

It was the property of the intelligent and appreciative Mrs. Grumps.

The waning moon shone on Dick's intel-

lectual face, so distorted by terror that she did not know it.

"Help! Murder! Thieves!" she cried, and then struck wildly at him with her clenched fist.

Dick made no effort to dodge the blow, but received it on the crown of his hat.

Then his legs gave way, and down he rolled head over heels to the ground.

The squeaky voice of the good old housekeeper could be heard half over Smockley, and it fell upon the ears of the policemen whose duty it is to act as nocturnal guards to the city.

Immediately they were on the alert, and hastened in the direction they thought the sound came from, but they all thought wrong.

Smockley was blessed with police of peculiar mental endowments. They were gifted with lots of manly strength and energy, but their mental capacity was of thimble measurement. Whenever they did the right thing it was by accident.

On that night, when the voice of Mrs. Grumps came from the west, they bore to a man eastwards, and rummaged among a lot of deserted side streets, in the vain hope of finding the squealer.

Meanwhile the Slapcrash boys, homeward bound, had heard it too.

Young Ching, Tom Biron, and Warren Fane formed the rear of the party.

"What's that?" asked Tom, pulling up.

"It comes from the direction of the school," replied Young Ching, coolly. "I'll go bail that Billy, or Dick, or both have done something."

They broke into a trot, and rapidly overhauling the other boys, gathered them up as they went along, and so in a body they arrived at the side gate of Slapcrash School.

The voice of Mrs. Grumps had ceased, but there were murmurs in the lower part of the house.

"Come in quickly," said Tom Biron.

They passed like spectres through the garden, and saw that the kitchen window was made transparent by a light within.

The ladder lay on the ground just as it had fallen with Dick, and the window of Mrs. Grumps' room was still open.

Young Ching grasped the situation in a moment.

"Dick went to the wrong window!" he said. "Lose no time. Slip up into the dormitory, and I'll just see what's happened."

The ladder was quickly put into position,

WITH A QUICK MOVEMENT THE FIGURE RAISED ITS ARM.

and the boys went up like harlequins, one after the other.

They occupied two adjoining rooms now, owing to their increase in numbers; and in less than a minute all but Young Ching were pulling off their clothes with lightning speed.

"Nobody's been here," said Biron. "Now, boys, between the sheets, and get ready to be sound asleep."

They needed no second injunction, and at a pace never known before they undressed and tumbled into bed.

A minute or so later Young Ching came leisurely up the ladder and stepped lightly into the room.

"It's all right," he said. "Dick's in such a

The way Dick returns home.

muddled state that he can't explain anything, so they are explaining things for him."

"Who are they?" asked Warren Fane.

"Mrs. Grumps and old Fossil Bone," replied Young Ching. "Mrs. Grumps thinks that Dick has been dragged out of bed, or dreamed of burglars, but Fossil Bone says the 'unfortunate boy walks in his sleep.'"

The ladder was lowered again, the window closed, and Young Ching was soon in bed.

Very little comment on the events of the evening was indulged in. Silence, under the circumstances, was considered most prudent.

Presently voices were heard on the stairs, and Mr. Fossil Bone appeared, leading Dick by the arm.

"You have had a merciful escape, my dear boy," he said, in a low tone, "and it is a law

of somnambulism, I believe, that a good fright is a certain cure. You may safely go to bed again now. Are you sure you have no bones broken?"

"I've got several big bumps, sir," replied Dick, with a groan.

"Bumps are painful, but seldom fatal," observed Mr. Fossil Bone. "What a fortunate thing it is you did not disturb your companions. Get into bed, blow out the candle, and go to sleep."

He was gone, and Dick, left to himself, sat down stiffly on the side of his bed.

Prudence, as before, kept the boys quiet.

Dick looked about him like one in a dream.

"I suppose I have been out to-night," he said, half-aloud, "but I'm blowed if I know how they could have all got back again."

"Get into bed," growled Jem Stager. "As usual, you have made a hash of it."

"Then it is all real," sighed Dick. "I'm satisfied, but lor', what a twister I came down. So would anyone else after seeing how she looked in her night-cap."

"Tell us about it to-morrow, Dick," observed Warren Fane, sleepily; "so long as we are all home and are not bowled out we need not trouble."

A sense of security coming on the top of the fatigue engendered by their excursion soon sent all to sleep, and for the rest of the night peace reigned.

Early in the morning Dick told his tale, and was complimented in a sarcastic manner. At breakfast, however, he got the best of it.

Mrs. Grumps, in the full belief that somnambulism was weakening to the constitution, had provided him with a very unusual rasher and egg, which he ate with exceeding gusto.

Jem Stager, who sat next to him, got the aroma for his share, and was disgusted beyond measure.

"Verily, Dick," he said, "but thou art a scurvy knave. All honest men blush as they think of the way thou seekest the fleshpots of Egypt."

"All right," replied Dick, with a grin; "it's a lovely rasher, and the egg isn't a day old yet."

In the middle of the morning studies in the schoolroom an interruption took place which put some of the boys in a flutter.

A knock was heard at the door, and Mr. Fossil Bone cried out—"Come in."

Then entered Billy Pink, and with the remembrance of his training in the old village school he held out his right arm and waited for permission to speak.

"What is it, William?" asked Mr. Bone.

"A visitor for Master Warren Fane," replied Billy; "a lady."

Warren turned pale and rose hurriedly from his seat. The visit was evidently as unexpected to him as to the others.

"You can go down, Fane," said Mr. Fossil Bone.

Warren disappeared, and a buzz of conjecture went round.

Was it his mother, aunt, or sister?

Jem Stager was inclined to think that it was a princess, who, having fallen in love with him, had called to say that she would wait for him a few years, until he was old enough to be made a husband of.

But this idea was rather scouted by the less romantic portion of the boys.

Warren was absent from the school quite half-an-hour, and when he returned his face wore a troubled look.

But he said nothing about his visitor, nor did he refer to her until long afterwards.

Meanwhile curiosity was very strong, and after school quite an avalanche of boys descended on Billy Pink, who was engaged just then in putting an outhouse in order, or what he called order, eventually producing a state of chaos which only a boy of his great intellect could have successfully accomplished.

Young Ching was not of that party.

He was one of the few who showed no curiosity on the subject.

As Dick Cockles said, he behaved exactly as if he knew all about it, and meant to keep his knowledge to himself.

"How are you, Billy?" said Jem Stager, the leader of the inquiring party.

"Well, I'm middling," replied Billy; "as well as can be expected after last night. I don't think I'm the chap for dissipation, for I couldn't eat half a breakfast this morning."

"That's bad," said Jem, meditatively. "Had a visitor, haven't you, Billy?"

"No," Billy answered, round-eyed.

"Well, Warren Fane has."

"Oh! yes, he has."

"What was he like?"

"It was a she," replied Billy; "a female she, a lady she."

"Of course," returned Jem, lightly; "quite young and pretty?"

Billy shook his head.

"I don't know that," he said. "She wore a veil—a thick one."

"What was she like—generally?" inquired Jem. "Did she seem poor, or rich, or look vicious, or ill, or strong, or weak?"

"She looked," said Billy, "like a downright lady, and when she took off her glove to find a bit of money for me she'd reg'lar blinding jewels on her fingers. They sparkled like—like—well, ten times better than Mrs. Grumps' best silver teapot."

"Oh!" observed Jem. "Did she speak?"

"Rather," replied Billy, "and her voice was just like music. She said I was a good boy, and gave me half a suvrin."

"Didn't you feel bad when you took it?" asked Dick Cockles.

"Bad. Why?" returned Billy.

"Because I've never been called good without feeling like a fool."

"Perhaps you feel like that without the compliment," suggested Jem Stager, and Dick's little eyes glared at him banefully for quite two seconds.

They had got out of Billy all he could tell, and it was not satisfying.

The mystery which had attached to Warren Fane from the first hour he appeared at the school was broadened and deepened by the arrival of that lady visitor.

"Why can't he trust us?" sighed Dan Mittens.

"Because he knows that you would all keep his secret," replied Jem Stager, sarcastically.

Well! things were so, and they had to make the best of them. From Warren Fane there came not a word to lighten the burden of their curiosity.

Two or three evenings later Young Ching was in high spirits. By post from India he received a letter containing information about his father.

As it was in the handwriting of one, Eddard Cutten, a gentleman not entirely unknown to our readers, we give it word for word—

"DEAR YOUNG MR. CHING CHING,—I am desired by your respecktid father to tell you that he will shortly be comin home, when he hopes to pay a visit to Smockley, prire to a enterin on serus life in London. We have had good times, and all been happy together, which it is too long to put in a letter. So no more from yours respeckfully,

"EDDARD CUTTEN.

"P.S.—Sammy sends his love, and William. Both are hearty, and Sammy says I'm to put *in 'eber de same and more so,' which I done rather than have my head punched, as he threatened for to do."*

"I reckon," mused Young Ching, "that about two days of the governor and his pals will be as much as Smockley will stand. But I'm awfully pleased to hear they are all right."

He was naturally elated, and when he turned out of the school with a few of his select chums for the evening stroll he could hardly contain himself.

"I feel I've got to do something to-night or bust," he said.

He had not long to wait.

As Young Ching and his friends turned into North-street they came in view of Mr. Slapcrash strolling up and down. He was waiting for Mrs. Slapcrash, who was doing a bit of shopping.

Mr. Slapcrash had his back to the boys, and was slowly moving along with a majestic stride, intended to impress beholders, of whom, however, there were very few.

"Had his back starched!" suggested Jem Stager.

"I'll take it out of him!" yelled Young Ching.

And before they could so much as guess at his intention he had charged like a young bull upon the retired schoolmaster.

Bending his head down, he butted that unsuspecting gentleman in the small of the back, with a violence that not only deprived him of the power of speech, but sent him sliding down the pavement for a yard or two.

He would have gone farther but for a piece of orange-peel, which gave an additional impetus to his left foot, and up he went—to come down again, of course.

His fall was of the nature to check an immediate tendency to rise, and he lay there gazing with blinking eyes at the fleecy clouds overhead, wondering what had happened.

Young Ching, it may be said, did not expect such extreme results from his escapade.

He meant to astonish Mr. Slapcrash, and argue the matter with him afterwards. But when he saw and heard that gentleman fall, he felt that for once in his life he had overstepped the limits of legitimate fun.

"He's broken something," said Jem Stager. "I heard it crack—like bones."

"Let us go and see what the time is by the cathedral clock," observed Young Ching, and away they went in a body.

There was nobody handy to give Mr. Slapcrash assistance, and it so happened that ere he could get up his beloved wife appeared in the doorway of a shop close by.

As soon as her eyes fell upon the prostrate form of her better half she hastened towards him, exclaiming—

"Benjamin! Benjamin! get up, do. What will people think of you?"

He struggled into a sitting position, staring at her with an owlish expression of face.

"What have you been drinking?" she asked, sharply.

"Me! nothing," he replied. "But have you seen a battering ram go down the street?"

"Don't talk stuff!"

"It was a bull then. I was butted in the back."

"Bosh! nonsense! Go home and have a nap, and a bottle of soda-water will do you good."

Mr. Slapcrash's face flushed, and his eyes got a touch of the basilisk tint.

"Woman!" he said, "what do you mean?"

"Oh! you know," was the reply.

Mr. Slapcrash arose quickly, with indignant fires burning in his bosom. A terrible domestic drama was about to take place in public, but it was happily averted, for at that moment Abe Bott arrived on the scene.

He came out of a narrow passage on tiptoe, and crossed the road, after a quick glance up the street to see if the boys were really gone.

"Excuse me, marm," he said, "but it warn't liquor."

Mrs. Slapcrash looked down upon him with chilling hauteur.

"Go away, fellow," she observed.

"D'rectly," replied Abe; "but I see 'em do it. Them Slapcrashers—axing pardon for taking your name in vain, sir, but it's by that name they are beknown—come on you, led by young pigtail, and bounced you. I see 'em."

"I'm glad it's no worse," said Mrs. Slapcrash, sweetly, "but really—"

"Woman!" replied Mr. Slapcrash, "be quiet. I've borne too much already—the hour of retribution has arrived."

"Poof!" said Mrs. Slapcrash, derisively.

"Bott," observed Mr. Slapcrash, "follow me. Let me see if the evidence you are able to give will suffice to convict the offenders."

He turned away, and the same instant his hat was tilted over his eyes. Mrs. Slapcrash, in playful contempt, had performed the trick with her parasol.

A smothered exclamation escaped Mr. Slapcrash, and with all the speed he could muster he hurried along, to confer in some quiet spot with the leading witness against the authors of the dastardly outrage.

CHAPTER XIII.

ONE PUPIL—MANY RIGS.

THE High Art Academy of Mr. B. Rord Beans, M.A., F.R.O.I., remained *in statu quo.*

One pupil only had he got, and no others came to keep poor Duffy company.

But Mr. B. Rord Beans was a man of many resources, and not easily disheartened. He always spoke of his pupils, and ere long began to resort to expedients to show that Duffy was not only one boy but many.

With the aid of different apparel he made his one boy look like several boys.

Sometimes Duffy was taken out in a tall hat and jacket, at another time in a fur cap, tied well over his ears, and an ulster.

Blue spectacles also lent their aid to deception, and a pair of cork-soled boots, worn now and then, made Duffy of a different height.

Some people penetrated these disguises, others did not, and many declined to bother their minds at all about it.

The Slapcrashers "twigged," of course. Duffy was Duffy to them in whatever guise he appeared.

"I pity the poor little beggar," said Dick Cockles, "and wonder he stands it."

One day Duffy was found alone in the Close by Young Ching. It was a very quiet spot, of which there were several in the enclosure.

As a fact it may be stated that there were corners in the Close where a dead man could have lain a week without being found.

Duffy was wearing his fur cap, ulster, and cork-soled boots.

"Hullo!" said Young Ching, "how came you here?"

Duffy rubbed his nose with the back of his hand, and looked askance at his interlocutor.

"You let me alone," he said.

"Of course I will," replied Young Ching.

He was feeling in his pockets for something, which he secured and brought out in his closed hand.

"Your name is Duffy, isn't it?" he asked.

"No, it isn't," was the reply.

"What is it, then?"

No answer.

"Come, none of that," continued Young Ching; "out with it."

"I've got lots of names," replied Duffy; "it's according to the dress I'm wearing."

As he made this confession the semblance of a grin appeared on Duffy's face, but it quickly died away.

"What's your name now?" asked Young Ching.

"The Honourable Julius McGrath," Duffy replied.

Young Ching eyed him with a peculiar smile for fully half a minute. Then he repeated, slowly—

"The — Honourable — Julius — McGrath. Don't you feel small over such a piece of humbug?"

"It don't matter to me," Duffy replied.

"You don't mind who you are?" said Young Ching, quickly.

"Not a bit," replied Duffy.

"Then let me make you into Professor Buffalo, the renowned Queen's Jester," said Young Ching.

He opened his hand and exhibited two small tubes of water-colour—one red and the other white.

He had only just purchased them for Dick Cockles, who had promised to sing "Hot Codlins" (in character) in the schoolroom after supper.

Young Ching had volunteered to paint Dick's face, but it now occurred to him that a portion of the colour might be used on Duffy.

"Will it hurt me?" asked the one High Art pupil.

"Oh! no," replied Young Ching; "it will beautify and disguise you as Beans never disguised you yet. It is the same colouring used by ladies when they go to Court, and imparts a brilliancy to the complexion and creates a charm in the countenance of the wearer to which the radiance of the sun is very small beer."

But Duffy was not quite convinced. He had no great faith in Young Ching.

"I do wish you would let me alone," he said, feebly.

"But I can't," replied Young Ching, "and if I did so other people would be at you. You are the sort of boy who can't hope to be let alone. Stand still!"

Duffy, with his eyes shut, leant back against the wall, and Young Ching, having squeezed a portion of each colour into the palm of his left hand, set to work.

Using his forefinger as a brush, he rapidly

and skilfully made the face of the helpless Duffy fit for any clown in a circus, finishing him off with black from a third tube he brought out of his pocket.

"It doesn't hurt you, does it?" he asked.

"It's awfully sticky," Duffy replied.

"So are all cosmetics used by the rich," observed Young Ching. "What an improvement, to be sure!"

"I hope it is," said Duffy, drearily. "What do I look like?"

"The King of Sheba in mufti!" replied Young Ching. "Now get along and go out at the North Gate."

"But that isn't my nearest way home," pleaded Duffy.

"Why should you go the nearest way home?" asked Young Ching. "Show yourself round the town. I'll bet you cause a bit of a sensation."

"I feel as if I had been gummed all over the face," moaned Duffy. "You wouldn't like me to do it to you."

"That's another thing," observed Young Ching. "Don't rub it or it will get into the skin and never come off."

Duffy, walking as some boys do when they are cold, with his arms out in a milkpail-carrying style, shuffled down a passage into the cloisters.

Young Ching kept a few paces in the rear of him, to stop all possible attempts to take a short cut home.

In the cloisters there was one of the canons meditating.

He was a deep-thinking man, and a firm believer in ghosts and uncanny things generally.

Hearing the shuffle of Duffy's feet he looked up, and the hideous spectacle that unfortunate boy presented fairly staggered him.

Clasping one of the stone columns, he watched Duffy go slowly by, and the moment he was past he bolted for dear life.

"Duffy will do," murmured Young Ching.

The North Gate was reached, and as Duffy was going out a doctor's boy happened to be coming in. He had a basket full of physic bottles on his arm, and he was whistling cheerily.

Suddenly his whistling stopped, and down went the basket with a bang that settled half the physic.

"Here!—hi!—who-o-o-o are you?" he gasped.

"Run!" cried Young Ching; "he's mad!"

The doctor's boy revolved on his right leg, nearly fell over, recovered himself, and levanted.

"You get along home as quick as you can," said Young Ching to Duffy; "he's gone for the police."

"Let 'em come," replied Duffy; "I don't care."

Duffy went slowly up the street, and ere he had gone far the sensation began.

In daylight people are not particularly afraid of unusual sights, and Duffy, notwithstanding his hideousness, terrified no other person.

"Who is it?" asked a man in a white hat.

He followed Duffy into the High-street, so did others, and then a real crowd began to muster.

Dejected, miserable, indifferent to public curiosity, Duffy slowly pursued his weary way.

Nobody got in front of him, but the boys ran by his side, and the men, with a sprinkling of women, formed a tail in the rear.

Cries of wonderment were heard, questions were asked which nobody could answer, but Duffy still trudged on.

Cabs and carts stopped, their drivers bawled out queries to each other, but the mystery of the strange figure was a mystery still.

Suddenly Mr. B. Rord Beans was seen approaching.

He, too, was attracted by the crowd, and was hurrying up to get his share of cheap excitement.

Just then some of the boys were getting bold, and the ancient order of pelting was beginning.

Half an apple, not gathered the day before, smote Duffy on the side of his head, and a good solid turnip hit him in the back.

He wheeled round.

"You let me alone!" he said.

Mr. Beans was close behind, staring at him like a man in a dream.

He recognised the fur cap, the ulster, and the cork boots; but who was this ghastly creature wearing them? Then Duffy's familiar request to be left alone fell upon his ear.

"It is Duffy!" he gasped.

Seizing him by the arm he turned him round and gazed upon the ghastly face skill and paint had made.

"Degenerate boy!" he said; "what is the meaning of this unseemly jest?"

"It's the High Art kid," observed somebody in the crowd, and a burst of laughter followed.

Mr. Beans, who had partaken of a refresher or two in the course of the day, gazed about him with noble scorn.

"That this miserable youth," he said, "is one of my pupils I do not deny. But the dishonour of one is not to be cast upon the whole. For the sake of others, whose welfare is my daily hope and nightly dream, the offender shall be expelled from my High Art Academy, where competent masters are engaged for all the sciences, and the terms can be had on application to the principal, B. Rord Beans, Esq., M.A., F.R.O.I."

"Take him home and wash him," suggested the man with the white hat.

"But for the social gulf between us," replied Mr. Beans, "I would wash you."

"Oh! don't let that disturb you," returned the man in the white hat. "I'm not proud. Come outside the town and I'll have a round or two with you."

Mr. Beans threw up his head in scorn, but doing it a little too emphatically, his hat tumbled off. Stooping to recover it, he fell upon and flattened it.

Ignoring the unseemly laughter following this feat, he rose and proceeded to brush his hat with the calmness of a superior mind in the presence of the vulgar and ignorant.

The hat, however, had "been there" before. It was not the first time that its crown had been knocked in, and it refused to stand up any more.

At last Mr. Beans put it on as it was, took Duffy by the arm, and turned homeward.

The police being conspicuous by their absence, the crowd was at full liberty to enjoy itself, which it proceeded to do.

Heralds, in the shape of boys, now ran before, to announce the coming of tutor and pupil, while other boys aimed all sorts of things at the damaged hat worn by Mr. Beans.

Careless men, reckless of High Art feelings, dug him in the back with sticks and umbrellas, but haughtily indifferent to all, he strode on until he came to a spot where some brewer's men were lowering casks down a cellar.

Mr. Beans did not see the rope or heed the warning cry, so over he tripped, and like a flash of light disappeared down the cellar, taking the unhappy Duffy with him.

CHAPTER XIV.

MR. BEANS MAKES THE MOST OF A PAINFUL SITUATION—YOUNG CHING MAKES THE MOST OF MR. BEANS — HIS MOTHER COMES OUT STRONG.

WHEN Mr. B. Rord Beans disappeared down the cellar the mirth of the crowd suddenly ceased. The general opinion was that the fun had ended in a calamity.

The brewer's men were the first to do anything of a practical nature, but what they did was not much. They walked to the edge of the cellar and looked down.

Then, in a moment, they saw that nothing serious had happened.

The descent was not a sheer one, but was relieved by a sliding plank, down which Mr. Beans and his pupil had shot with considerable velocity, and they now lay among the sawdust.

Mr. Beans was not, of course, benefited by the fall. It increased the effects of the "refreshers" he had partaken of, and further fuddled his learned mind.

Duffy, beyond having his eyes, nose, and mouth filled with sawdust, had come off without material harm.

Mr. Beans was in the cellar, and there for the time he intended to stay.

Having got himself up, and assisted Duffy to his feet, he bade his one pupil take a seat on an empty beer-barrel.

"For myself," he said, "I will not depart until a physician comes and examines my injuries. Pitfalls must not be left open in the street for unwary travellers. I have the law on my side."

The innkeeper, hearing of the accident, came down by the steps inside, and, in tones of sincere sympathy, asked Mr. Beans if he were hurt.

"I have not a whole bone in my body," was the prompt reply. "Call in the nearest physician."

The crowd outside were hustling each other to get a peep of the scene below, and at that moment an over-eager errand-boy was pushed forward and tobogganed down the plank into the cellar.

"I say, you are not all wanted down here," roared the publican. "Get away, the lot of you!"

A policeman now came up, and the public were cleared off the footpath.

Then Mr. Beans, on having refreshment

YOUNG CHING CHARGED LIKE A BULL AT THE RETIRING SCHOOLMASTER.

suggested to him, said he would make an effort to get his broken bones upstairs.

He succeeded so well that soon he subsided into a seat in the back parlour, with Duffy beside him.

"I think," he said, "that brandy for internal bruises is good for adults, and to boys lemonade is a restorative."

Leaving the landlord to act upon these suggestions, we will return to Young Ching, who was back at school, varying his afternoon studies by enjoyable reflections on the lovely figure Duffy had presented.

He did not say anything about it just then, however, nor would he have done so but for Billy Pink, who had been "erranding" about

"*What have you been drinking?*" *she asked.*

the town, and had picked up a version of the fall down the cellar.

It was the sort of thing that generally gets about on these occasions, and was to the effect that Mr. B. Rord Beans had broken his neck, literally smashed Duffy, and the pair were now lying at the public-house awaiting a coroner's inquest.

It would be absurd to say that Young Ching was not affected by the dismal news, but his anxiety was not of the nature warranted by the gravity of the report.

"Let's go out and see what old Beans has been up to," he said to Jem Stager.

With Jem of course Dick must go, and likewise Dan Mittens and two or three more.

Fortune favoured them, for ere they had gone far they espied Mr. Beans homeward bound.

It was the hour when Smockley was at its quietest. The workpeople had not brushed themselves up after the day's work, and the tradesmen were seated in their back parlours resting or making up their accounts.

Mr. Beans had, therefore, the street almost to himself, and he was making the most of the liberty of the subject by tacking about in a very suspicious manner.

Walking a few yards behind him was Duffy, washed and in his right mind, looking as if he had all the cares of the world on his young shoulders.

As soon as he espied the Slapcrashers he put up his arm and said—

"Come, you let me alone for once, will you?"

"We are not going to interfere with you, Duffy," replied Young Ching; "it's Beans we intend to operate upon."

"You may do what you like with him," observed Duffy, generously.

Young Ching was in no hurry. He wanted first of all to see what Beans would do himself. Indeed, there was quite sufficient amusement in the movements of that mistaken professor of High Art Education.

The landlord had been too liberal with his refreshers, and Mr. Beans was in a state unworthy of his great aspirations.

"What I want to know is," he observed, as he stopped and addressed a long-disused public pump, "when am I going to be recognised as a man of ghentiun—I mean, genus—geni-us, that's the word?"

Without waiting for an answer he passed on, and tripping over a rough bit of pavement, offered it an ample apology, following it up with a "Don't mention it—I beg of you —it was my fault."

Then he came suddenly upon a barrow, standing by the kerb side, and stopped to regard it with a gentle smile upon his face.

The barrow belonged to a gardener, who had gone into one of the numerous beershops with a friend to "have a pint," as they neatly put it.

Mr. B. Rord Beans looked a second time at the barrow. Then he sat down in it and went straight off to sleep.

"Now, boys," said Young Ching, "let us take him home."

He laid hold of the barrow, wheeled it with wondrous ease, and away they went.

Duffy fell into the train, and in a miserable way seemed to be enjoying the affair.

A few straggling wayfarers also looked on

themselves as a valuable addition to the procession, and a joyous party went off down South-street.

Before they had gone far Mr. B. Rord Beans woke up, and without any preliminary humming or hawing, as ordinary people are wont to indulge in, began to sing—

" *I kno—o—ow a mai—ai—den fair;*
   Ta—a—ke care!
She ca—a—a—an bo—o—oth false and
   fri—fri—fri—endly be;
Be—e—e—e—ware—e—e!"

The broken nature of his singing was the outcome of the jolting of the barrow. It gave a sweet tremulousness to his voice that was absolutely thrilling.

It had such an effect on one old man who had joined the throng that he was obliged to stop. His legs were affected with a sympathetic trembling.

"By the love of the knights!" said Jem Stager, "but he is a troubadour! Hark! he sings again!"

Mr. Beans could sing no more. He opened his mouth, it is true, but his voice suddenly deserted him, and all that came forth was a curious little squeak, such as one gets from a cheap indiarubber figure.

He was going to sleep again, when Young Ching tilted the barrow up and nearly threw him out of the top end.

"Go easy," he said, "if I do travel third-class. Tell me when we get to Banbury-junction."

"Lay hold, Jem!" said Young Ching. "Take a turn. He's heavy!"

Jem, nothing loth, laid hold, and away they went again right merrily, until one side of the barrow collided against a letter-box and nearly upset it.

"These air-brakes," said Mr. Beans, staring around, "are too sudden. Will you boys reshume your seats?"

"All right," observed Jem; "train going on. Dick, take a turn."

"No," interposed Young Ching, "Dick will only upset him. I'm ready again."

They were not far now from the High Art Academy, towards which Duffy had run without being observed by anybody but Young Ching.

He guessed why he had gone before, and kept an eye open for possibilities.

He ran the barrow down to the house, and was about to tilt Mr. Beans upon the door-step, when the door opened and a remarkably active old woman popped out.

She had a heavy gingham in her hand, and, wielding it like an expert swordsman, she gave Dick Cockles a blow that laid him on the flat of his back, then knocked off Dan Mitten's hat, and finally, with a back-handed sweep, caught Jem Stager a terrific smack just below the belt, which took all his breath away.

"I'll kill the lot of you villains," she said, "if you don't let my son alone."

It is needless to say that there was a general clearing away from this very expert old wielder of a heavy umbrella, and Dick was quick enough up to escape a second blow aimed at him.

Mrs. Beans, having no other foes to strike, took hold of the coat-collar of her son, jerked him out of the barrow, hustled him inside, and closed the door.

He was so staggered by her prompt treatment that he knew nothing of what had been done until he awoke and found himself seated in a chair, with his mother standing before him.

"Rordy," she said, "there must be an end to this."

"The end is not far off," he replied, huskily; "the baker told me to-day we can't have any more fancy bread, but must go on to plain household seconds unless we pay his bill."

"Rordy, you ought to give up the High Art School. My sixty pounds a year won't keep a house like this."

"Look here, mother, it only wants time to take hold. Already I am talked about—"

"Goodness! you are," said his mother, fervently.

"Genius," replied Mr. B. Rord Beans, gloomily, "has always uphill work. No matter —my time will come. Ha—ha! Ho—ho!"

"Rordy," said Mrs. Beans, severely, "if you go on that way again I'll box your ears."

"All right, mother," he replied, humbly, "I'm done. I forgot to say that the milkman has struck. He says we had better go to the pump for credit, and I told him it was only a step to go. Then he became low and abusive. But, as before observed, a time—"

"Rordy!"

"Mother, I'm mum. Where is Duffy?"

"Having his supper in the kitchen."

"I will join him there. A humble face and a clear conscience will carry a man over heaps of stones. The High Art Academy will triumph yet."

CHAPTER XV.

MR. SLAPCRASH COMES TO THE ACADEMY WITH A COCK-AND-BULL STORY—HE GOES AWAY IN AN ORNAMENTAL CONDITION.

IT was a wet evening, and the boys were confined to the schoolroom, where they first got through the lessons for the morrow, and then gathered round a fire which Mrs. Grumps sent Billy up to lay and light, because it was rather chilly.

Billy did his work very well, barring his tripping up with the coalscuttle and scattering the contents about the floor. The labour of picking up the coal was considerable, but he accomplished it at last, and having in a fit of absence of mind wiped his fingers on his face, he sat down on one of the lockers.

"That's the last job to-day," he observed, "and I'm not sorry."

"You don't like work, I suppose?" said Dick Cockles.

"Well, I don't know about liking it. I'm not afraid of it, because I've got to do it or get the sack, and then I should never see Young Ching."

"Don't you think you could live without him?" asked Dick.

Billy's face suddenly became very grave.

"Live without him?" he repeated. "I hope I shall never have to try."

"What are you talking about there?" asked Young Ching. "I heard my name mentioned."

"Billy says he wants to live without you," replied Dick.

"What's that?" asked Billy, rising with bristling hair.

"Oh! I was only joking," said Dick. "Don't be a fool, Billy."

"Where's Mr. Bones?" asked Young Ching.

"Gone to a meeting of the British Assassination," replied Billy.

"Gone where?" exclaimed Dick, aghast.

"He means Association," observed Young Ching; "and Mrs. Grumps, what is she doing?"

"She's out somewhere," replied Billy; "she told Mary she would be back at nine o'clock."

"Then we have the house to ourselves," said Young Ching; "not that it matters. Fossil Bone treats us well, and my motto is to give him as little trouble as possible."

"Hear—hear!" observed Dick.

"I like that from you," cried Jem Stager; "he spends half his life hammering ideas into you, and then they don't get there."

"To hear you talk, anybody might think I was a fool," exclaimed Dick, indignantly.

"Which of course you are not," observed Young Ching, soothingly.

"Dick's no fool," said Jem; "he's made of the right sort of stuff, but it isn't mixed properly. He is like some sausages—"

"Oh! let him alone," interpolated Young Ching, giving Jem a dig in the ribs. "Now, boys, what shall we do to pass a quiet evening pleasantly?"

"Let me play something," said Dick. "The Corsican Brothers—I'll be a brother."

"You be the ghost," replied Jem, "for then you will have nothing to say. Now hark ye, my brethren, the play's the thing. If we move the desks up to the top end of the room and pile them together we can make a gallery. That will do for the audience, and Mr. Richard Cocklesonia will begin with the dagger scene from Macbeth. Hi! there—the dagger—bl-o-o-d!"

"Oh! dry up, Jem!" interrupted Tom Biron; "we can't have a play, for none of you know your parts."

"Then what shall we do?" asked Young Ching.

Rat—tat—rat—tat—tat—tat!

"Hallo!" exclaimed Billy Pink, "somebody's at the door. I wonder if Mary will answer it."

He sat on the locker quite at his ease, and the boys, all suddenly silent, listened intently.

"I don't think Mary means to go," said Billy, still without moving.

"In that case," suggested Warren Fane, "don't you think you had better see who it is?"

"Perhaps I had," Billy replied, rising slowly.

Rat—tat—tat!

"Somebody in a hurry," observed Billy, as he opened the door and proceeded leisurely down the stairs.

When about half-way his foot slipped and down he went with a rush into the hall.

"Are you hurt, Billy?" asked Young Ching, over the balustrade.

"I'm done for!" gasped Billy. "Give my love to mother and my sisters. I leave all my bit o' property to you, Ching. Oh—oh!"

Rat—tat—bang!

"I'll come and open the door for you," said Young Ching, as he glided down the stairs with an agile step worthy of his father.

He opened the front door just as the person outside was making another angry grab at the knocker, and the consequence was that the person in question having nothing to grab, he fell forward upon his hands.

Rising up, he disclosed the face of Mr. Slapcrash.

"Mr. Bone in?" he asked, savagely.

"Not at present," replied Young Ching.

"I'll come in and wait for him," said Mr. Slapcrash, with a baneful glare at the imperturbable youngster.

"I would rather you did not," replied Young Ching.

"I shall put a stop to this insolence—one day," retorted Mr. Slapcrash, pushing into the hall. "I know my way and will wait here."

He walked towards the visitors' room, which was just at the bottom of the stairs. Billy still lay at full length upon the mat, and Mr. Slapcrash, unfortunately, did not see him.

The result was that he tripped over Billy, and projected himself with such violence against the door that he may be said to have opened it with his head.

"What new fiend's trick is this?" he asked, wildly. "Boy! I bid you beware!"

"I have done nothing," replied Young Ching, "but I should say that you have about killed Billy Pink! How are you, Billy?"

"Crushed to atoms!" moaned Billy.

Mr. Slapcrash, having had some experience of injured boys, went into the room and closed the door with a bang.

"I wonder what he's come about?" mused Young Ching. "Get up, Billy!"

"I can't—I'm dead!"

"No, you are not. You were never in better fettle in your life."

"If you think so," said Billy, getting up without any visible painful effort, "I suppose I'm not hurt!"

By this time there was a little crowd of eager boys on the top of the stairs, all wanting to know what had brought Mr. Slapcrash to the house, for it was known that Mr. Fossil Bone had as good as forbidden him to come.

"Complaints, of course," observed Jem Stager.

"Here, you boys, get back," said Young Ching. "I'll find out what it is. No row there. Billy!"

"Yes—I'm here," replied Billy.

"Come to me," said Young Ching; "I've a message for Mr. Slapcrash."

Billy came to him, and they whispered together for a few moments.

"Now mind what I say," continued Young Ching. "Don't make a hash of it."

Billy nodded his head, went downstairs, and entered the room where the retired schoolmaster was sitting.

"Do you want to see Mr. Bone?" Billy inquired.

"Of course I do," replied Mr. Slapcrash. "What do you think I am here for?"

"Will you please send word what is required?" said Billy.

"Oh! this is unbearable," replied Mr. Slapcrash, "but I must submit, I suppose. Tell him that I am about to institute a prosecution against a boy named Ching, for violence and attempted robbery in the open street. I have a witness who saw him make an effort to pick my pocket."

Billy was too much aghast to offer any reply, nor had he any need to do so.

He was drawn back by a hand laid upon his shoulder, and Young Ching took his place.

"Go and ask the other fellows to come down," he whispered. "They are all on the top of the stairs."

Mr. Slapcrash rose from his seat with a heavy frown upon his face.

"Get out of my way, boy," he said. "I can see that you have been set on to annoy me. Mr. Bone shall repent of this."

"Mr. Bone knows nothing of it," replied Young Ching, "and you had better remain where you are."

Mr. Slapcrash had to do so, for at that moment the whole of the boys crowded into the room, Tom Biron and Warren Fane foremost.

"I sent for you all," said Young Ching, "to hear an accusation which has been made against me. Mr. Slapcrash, speak up."

"I have nothing to say here," replied Mr. Slapcrash.

"Oh! yes, you have!" retorted Young Ching. "Mr. Bone is not at home, nor will he be for the next two hours, and Billy Pink will be sure to forget your message. You had better give it to me."

"I decline to do so," persisted Mr. Slapcrash, with a slight quiver in his voice.

"I will give it for you, then," said Young Ching. "What do you think he accuses me of?"

"Oh! anything and everything," replied Warren Fane.

"He says I tried to pick his pocket in the street," continued Young Ching, speaking with great deliberation, "and he has a witness to prove it."

"I can only go by what my witness says," observed Mr. Slapcrash. "Will you allow me to pass?"

"Who is your witness?" asked Tom Biron, standing in front of the ex-schoolmaster.

"A poor but very respectable man named Bott," was the reply.

"Mr. Slapcrash," said Tom, "don't you feel ashamed of yourself? You know that fellow to be a blackguard."

Young Ching at this moment backed to the side of Jem Stager, to whom he whispered a few words, and Jem disappeared.

"I know nothing whatever against Bott," replied Mr. Slapcrash. "Will you boys stand aside and let me pass?"

But they all resolutely barred his way, and he made no effort to break through them. Boys though they were, he knew some of them were pretty tough customers to deal with.

"Mr. Slapcrash," said Tom, "here, in the presence of the whole school, I proclaim you to be a scoundrel. You know that no attempt was made to pick your pocket, and you have leagued yourself with a foul-mouthed blackguard to ruin the good name of as fine a fellow as ever lived."

"Hear—hear!" cried Dick Cockles, and the cry was taken up all round.

"Now, sir," continued Tom, "I think you may go. You understand what we think of you? Get out of the house. As soon as Mr. Bones returns he shall be made acquainted with all that has taken place here to-night."

"Let me get at him," cried Billy Pink, suddenly waking up from a sort of trance. "Young Ching a thief did he say? I'll murder him!"

Billy made a plunge forward, but Warren Fane laughingly held him back. Then did Dick Cockles show the stuff he was made of.

"I'll have a go at old Slapcrash," he said, "single-handed."

Jem Stager at this moment reappeared with a paper-bag full of something soft. He had borrowed some flour from Mary.

"Gentlemen," said Young Ching, "I think Mr. Slapcrash may go."

"He sha'n't," roared Billy, "until I've had a go at him. Let me do it. Young Ching a thief!"

But Warren Fane held him tight, and as Mr. Slapcrash, with his hat on his head, advanced warily and with watchful eyes, the greater part of the boys backed into the hall.

Mr. Slapcrash seemed anxious to get away, but his manly pride would not permit him to hurry.

Quite leisurely he sauntered down to the door, and he was turning the handle when Young Ching jumped up behind and bonneted him.

He turned savagely, and then Jem Stager, previously instructed, hit the false accuser of Young Ching full in the face with the bag of flour.

"Open the door there," cried Tom Biron.

Somebody opened it, and in a moment Mr. Slapcrash, wildly blundering about, was shot forward into the street, and the door closed behind him.

CHAPTER XVI.

MR. SLAPCRASH GOES DEEPER AND DEEPER STILL—BILLY ON THE STAIRS—"RULE BRITANNIA" IN BED.

MR. SLAPCRASH walked away from the schoolhouse door with such feelings raging in his breast as he had never known before.

The conviction that he had got what he deserved did not lessen his misery, and his boiling passion, impotent in one direction, turned to another.

He could not, at present, injure the boys, but he could vent his fury on Abe Bott, who had been the indirect means of heaping up mortification upon him.

The unlucky star of the ex-champion sweep had prompted him to wait in the street for Mr. Slapcrash, and ask him how he had succeeded. It also led Abe to hide in a doorway near the White Hart, and to pop out suddenly upon his co-conspirator.

Mr. Slapcrash started back a step, and then in a wild way he hit out straight from the shoulder.

The blow went home, smiting Abe Bott fairly between the eyes, and causing him to fall against the wall of the White Hart with considerable violence.

Now Abe, although an arrant cur, would fight if he thought he was sure of victory, so he went for Mr. Slapcrash, and in the result fairly tumbled him over upon his back in the road.

A disinterested bystander raised an alarm, and a small crowd quickly collected.

Abe, having got his man down, meant to keep him there if he could, and hammered away until he was dragged off.

Then up rose the retired schoolmaster, and exhibited the strangest countenance lately seen in Smockley.

Flour, dirt, and the " Badminton " Abe had drawn from his nose, made him more than hideous.

For all that he was recognised.

" Lock the blackguard up, Mr. Slapcrash," suggested one of the bystanders; " it will do him good."

" Lock me up?" bawled Abe; " why he hit me first."

It was the truth, and not to be denied. The cup of humiliation was full.

Mr. Slapcrash, who aspired to be considered a gentleman, had fought a sweep in the streets like a common ruffian.

" Let me retire," he said, huskily. " I am not very well."

The crowd parted, and he passed through the opening made with his head down, to all appearance a broken man.

The people spread out, and Abe Bott went swaggering up the street as if he had won another Waterloo, but victory had not softened him towards his recent foe.

" Confound him," he muttered. " What did he hit me for? I'll make him smart for it."

That night when Mr. Fossil Bone returned he was told that Young Ching desired to see him. He readily granted him an interview, and was told the story of the evening's doings.

" I am sorry you did not let Mr. Slapcrash go away quietly," said Mr. Fossil Bone, uneasily.

" I felt, sir, that I couldn't," replied Young Ching.

" Well! do you wish anything more to be done?" asked Mr. Bone.

" I think," said Young Ching, after a moment's reflection, " that I would rather leave it until my father comes home."

" He will settle it," said Mr. Bone, with a quiet smile. " Anything more?"

" No! sir."

" Then good night."

It was close upon bedtime, so close that the boys were going upstairs, Billy Pink leading the way, with two huge dip candles, six to the pound, and leaving a clear trail of dropped fat behind him.

" What's Mr. Bone going to do?" asked Billy, eagerly.

" Nothing!" replied Young Ching.

A chorus of disappointed " Oh's!" led off by Billy, followed this announcement.

" He is going to leave him to my father," added Young Ching.

" That will do," said Billy, with a beaming face, as he turned the two candles nearly over.

" What are you doing?" asked Tom Biron. " Look at the grease spots on the stairs."

" Did I do 'em?" exclaimed Billy.

" Certainly you did."

" Blessed if I should have known it if you hadn't told me."

Then Billy, for some reason which he was never able to explain, dropped the left-hand light, candlestick and all. It fell upon its head, and the wick was of course squashed right into the tallow.

It took a few seconds to put the wick right, and as that was the one for Charley Green, who was " boss " of the second dormitory, he took it and with his following disappeared.

Tom Biron received the second candle, and stood at the door of the room as the other boys filed in.

Billy waited until they were all in, and then gave them a general " good-night," which was heartily responded to.

" Shall I light you down, Billy?" inquired Tom Biron.

" Me! No, I should think not," Billy answered. " I am not afraid of the dark."

" But you might fall."

" Me! Come, that is a good 'un."

Tom went into the dormitory, and had barely closed the door when a noise like the shooting of a hundredweight of coals was heard.

" Save us all!" exclaimed Jem; " what's that?"

" Billy," replied Young Ching, sententiously.

" He's a dead 'un," observed Dick.

" Not he," replied Young Ching.

Tom threw open the door, and all the boys became silent and listened intently.

The voice of Mrs. Grumps was heard below.

" Oh! you unfortunate boy, what's happened to you now?"

" I think, mum," gasped Billy, " that I've fallen down some of the stairs."

" Some," exclaimed Mrs. Grumps; " all, I should say. It sounded to me as if a big mountain had been shot down by a cattleput. Can't you get up?"

" I don't think so," groaned Billy.

" Surely you've no bones broken?"

THE SLAPCRASH BOYS.

The Liveliest of School Stories.

BEFORE THEY HAD GONE FAR MR. B. BORD BEANS WOKE UP AND BEGAN TO SING.

No. 6.

Price One Penny.

"No, mum, but I've split my—"

"Never mind," hastily interposed Mrs. Grumps; "here's a bit o' liquorice, which is soothing after shocks. I'll leave the light until you have got downstairs."

"Shall I go backwards, mum?"

"Oh no. What a thoughtful boy you are! I will retire to my room."

"It's all over," said Jem Stager, making a squeaking noise like Punch, and there was a general laugh as Tom closed the door.

"Billy's got one gift," he said; "he knows how to keep the right side of Mrs. Grumps."

Soon after the boys were in bed, Jem Stager, who was revolving some highly

"There must be an end to this, Rordy."

dramatic incidents in his romantic mind, heard a curious kind of buzzing near him.

"What on earth is it?" he asked himself.

It was not a bluebottle, or a bee, or a hornet, as far as he knew. When insects buzz they move about, and this sound was certainly stationary.

After carefully focussing it in his mind, he came to the conclusion that it arose from Dick Cockles' bed.

Leaning over, and listening closer still, he ascertained that the sound came from the middle of the bed, and from under the clothes. Slipping quietly out of his own bed, Jem felt about Dick's pillow, and discovered that his head was not there.

Dick and the sound were under the clothes together.

Jem was now in a position to leisurely analyse the humming or whatever it was, and putting his ear to the counterpane, he made out a tune that suggested "Rule Britannia," with the jumps.

It was being played by Dick on the humble instrument to be made out of a comb and piece of paper.

"I'll cut that short!" muttered Jem, and, laying hold of the clothes, he whisked them off as the cloth is removed from the Vanishing Lady.

"Oh-oh! who's that?" gasped Dick.

"What are you doing?" demanded Jem, "buzzing like a bee in a sausage-skin. Hang it all, Dick, you shouldn't!"

"What's the row there?" asked two or three sleepy voices.

"Nothing much," replied Jem.

"I was only getting up something to please my brothers and sisters when I go home at Christmas," pleaded Dick.

"If that sort of thing pleases them," grunted Jem, "they must be like the many edibles your father purveys—a little soft. Here, catch hold of the clothes, will you?"

"You are not going always to have your own way," retorted Dick, as he rolled himself up in the disordered bedclothes; "who are you, I should like to know? Was your father a Baron of Beef? or was he—"

"Quiet, there!" said Tom Biron. "Drop it, Dick."

"All right, if you wish it," replied Dick, in an injured tone. "There, now I've laid on my comb and broken it. All I have to say is—"

"Look here!" exclaimed half-a-dozen exasperated voices; "we've had enough of it, Dick."

"So have I," said Dick; "can't a fellow play on a comb—"

"No, he can't," interposed Jem.

"But I say he can."

"If you are not quiet, Dick," observed Tom Biron, "I will come and spank you."

Dick grunted out something not clearly understood, and with his usual rapid return to serenity settled down and went to sleep.

CHAPTER XVII.

A RAID UPON A DUMMY—THE INTRUDER ON THE HIGH ART DOORSTEP—THE CRIME AND THE REPENTANCE.

"I THINK," said Young Ching, "that such things are a public nuisance, standing in the doorway in that stiff attitude, and staring everybody out of countenance with their goggle eyes."

He was standing on one side of the High-street, looking across at a tailor's shop on the other.

By the door stood two of those agonising dummies which, in the opinion of purveyors of cheap clothing, set off their wares.

By what mental process they arrive at this conclusion we are unable to say, but certainly those worthy tradesmen are not governed by high art rules.

Young Ching had often noticed these dummies, and having a constitutional objection to anything wooden or inane, he had learnt to think of them as a public nuisance.

"I think we could get away with one if we were smart," he said.

It was the twilight hour.

A lovely calm rested on the city of Smockley. Its streets were almost deserted, the last rays of sun rested on the Cathedral spire, and under the eaves of time-worn towers the wild pigeon cooed in peace.

The bishop and canons were dining, while the tradesmen were washing and brushing-up preparatory to spending the evening at the White Hart.

All things favoured a raid upon the dummies.

Young Ching's companions were Dick Cockles, Jem Stager, and Dan Mittens. These four had settled down into a close companionship, and generally shared the perils of their doings abroad.

"If you take one, Ching," said Dick Cockles, "I could collar the other."

"And be collared in your turn," remarked Jem Stager; "no, Dick, be content to act as one to cover the raid."

"Now, boys!" said Young Ching, after a glance up and down the street, "this is the time, if ever. There's nobody about. Come on."

"Forward to the war!" said Jem Stager, in a whisper.

Young Ching crossed the road, the others followed him, and after another quick glance round, the young heathen boldly took up one of the goggle-eyed dummies and marched off with it.

But unluckily for the success of the raid the tailor was on the watch.

He saw Young Ching standing on the opposite side of the road, and suspecting evil intentions, he lay close behind a pile of over-coats in the window and kept his eyes upon him.

It was the same tailor who on a previous occasion had had one of these dummies labelled with a fishmonger's placard of the most incongruous nature, and popular report pointed to Young Ching as the offender.

The tailor was therefore prepared for some trick, but not for anything of the magnitude perpetrated.

Steal one of his dummies!

It was as if somebody had boldly walked into the bishop's palace and run off with his mitre.

The breath of the little tailor—and he had none too much of it—was fairly taken away.

He bounded into the street, and at that moment a policeman most opportunely came round an adjacent corner.

"Quick!" gasped the tailor; "look there."

The policeman looked, and saw Young Ching gliding like a first-rate skater down the street, with his companions ramping along behind him.

"One of my dummies," gasped the tailor, "the best of the pair."

"Right you are," said the officer, tightening his belt. "I'm after him."

He was a true Smockley policeman—agricultural by birth, and extra heavy footed by cultivation. He had two eyes in his head, but he knew better than to wear them out by keeping them too much on active service.

"Preserve your eyesight," was the motto of the Smockley police, and, therefore, as a body they never saw anything unless it was within an inch of their noses, and not always then.

Now, right in the path of this worthy official there was a small object, to wit, the skin of a banana, and although he had the whole pavement to tread upon, he must needs put his foot upon it.

Then did he, with an activity not all his own, fly up into the air and fall to the ground with a force which, if what philosophers say about vibration is true, must have given a minute shock to some New Zealander on the other side of the earth.

The tailor fell over him, and for at least half a minute they were both in a mental state bordering on chaos.

When they came round the boys had disappeared, and the direction they had taken was very uncertain, but the tailor was in a position to swear to their identity, at least to one of them, and he determined to go at once to Slapcrash School.

The police-officer readily accompanied him, or went as readily as his aching bones would permit, and their knock at the door was responded to by Billy Pink.

That astute boy saw at once that something was wrong, and he laid himself out as defender of the school.

"Ain't you come to the wrong house?" he asked, before they had time to speak.

"This is Slapcrash Academy, isn't it?" asked the tailor, severely; "we want to see Mr. Bone—the new proprietor."

"Gone away, and won't be back for a month," replied Billy.

"Boy," said the police-officer, "play no tricks with us."

"Oh! git along with you, bothering here," replied Billy; "who are you—chief commoner of the police?"

"We'll come in and wait," said the tailor.

"No you won't," replied Billy, barring the way. "Mary, bring a mop."

"What's the matter there?" inquired Mrs. Grumps, from above.

"Two burglars, ma'am," replied Billy.

Mrs. Grumps uttered a short "oh," and came hurrying downstairs at a rate of speed highly creditable to one of her years.

"Now, what do you fellars want?" she asked, glaring at them in a way that put all created basilisks into the shade.

"Let me explain, ma'am," said the tailor, breathlessly.

"Well, do it on the doorstep," replied Mrs. Grumps; "you haven't any right here."

The two men backed into the street, the policeman trying to look as if he had no fear of Mrs. Grumps, but had retired out of courtesy to one of the fair sex.

The tailor explained, and Mrs. Grumps listened to him with her head on one side, like a judge anxious to get all the facts of the case.

When he had finished she looked at him for one moment, with an eye that was like the point of a bit of red-hot wire.

"Is that all?" she asked.

"All!" exclaimed the tailor, aghast; "isn't it enough? Them there dummies cost—"

"Shut the door, Billy," said Mrs. Grumps.

The door was banged to, and the tailor, after a wild stare at the knocker, turned to the policeman and said—

"What's to be done now?"

"Summons," was the prompt reply.

"But my dummy! I couldn't sleep to-night if I thought it was lost. I gave—"

"We will go and look for it," said the officer.

Together they roamed up and down several streets, but saw nothing of the marauders or their prey. The only Slapcrash boy they came across was Sam Fusby, who was hurrying back to the school with a bag of tarts in his hand.

"Can you swear to him?" asked the officer.

The tailor shook his head.

So Sam went on in peace, and the White Hart being handy, the pair turned in for a light refresher before parting.

That night, about ten o'clock, Mr. B. Rord Beans might have been seen slowly wending his way home down South-street.

Domestic matters were coming to a crisis, and unless a sudden rush of pupils took place, the High Art Academy was doomed.

He had been drowning his apprehensions with potations, that might check reflections for a time, but would make matters worse in the long run.

His gait was unsteady, and he wore his hat very much on one side, while his hands were planted on his hips.

Occasionally he stopped to talk to inanimate objects, as he was wont to do on these occasions.

Pulling up by an iron post, he laid his hand affectionately on the top of it.

"Never mind, ole friend," he said, "things won't always be so bad. Why heed the low-born butcher who asks you if joints grow on apple-trees? Laugh at the man who declines to let you have a new hat when he has hundreds in the shop rotting, yes, rotting for want of customers. As for the low-born grocer, let him go on sanding his sugar, for as there is a moon—by-the-way, is there a moon?"

He stopped and lifted his eyes to the sky. There was no moon, and he smiled drily.

"As there wash no moon," he said, "as there wash—what in the name of goodness am I talking about—can't talk to you any longer, you are a fool."

Leaving the post to bear this bitter reflection on its intellect as best it could, he tacked across the street and addressed half-a-dozen words to a barber's pole.

Getting no answer, he tacked again, and in due time reached the doorway of the High Art Academy.

It was a deep doorway, but not particularly dark, for a lamp on the opposite side of the road threw some light into it.

Standing on the step close against the door was the figure of a boy.

A glance sufficed for even the imperfect vision of Mr. B. Rord Beans to recognise that it was not Duffy, and the probability of its being a Slapcrasher up to some trick flashed upon his mind.

"Now, young man," he said, getting ready to deal the intruder an open-hander as he descended, "perhaps you will come out of there."

No answer was vouchsafed to him, and the figure never stirred.

"I have to warn you," continued Mr. B. Rord Beans, with dignified deliberation, "that I am not a man to be trifled with, nor is this the class of establishment on which low-born tricks can be played with impunity. Are you coming out?"

No answer and not a movement. Mr. Beans saw the open eyes fixed upon him with impudent disdain. This was very hard for him to bear.

"Deeply as I should regret to have recourse to violence," he said, "I must, in defence of my position as a purveyor of High Art Education, subject you to a thrashing if you do not come off my doorstep."

Those impudent eyes never blinked, and the attitude of the intruder was that of dogged defiance.

Now, we all know that a man who drinks is subject, under provocation, and sometimes without provocation, to sudden fits of passion, therefore it is no marvel that one now took possession of Mr. B. Rord Beans.

He had found his doorstep invaded by one who, palpably, had no right there. A polite request to come off that doorstep had been met with impudent defiance. What else but violence was left?

In a transport of fury Mr. Beans dragged the offender into the street, and dealt him two violent blows, one on the ribs and the other on the side of the head.

The latter knocked off his cap, and left exposed a head of curly hair.

Not a cry did the receiver of the blows utter, and when Mr. Beans let go, the intruder fell to the ground straight and stiff.

This rather alarmed Mr. B. Rord Beans, who was expecting the boy to make an attempt to kick his shins and run away.

A sudden alarm sprang into his heart.

"Come," he said, "don't sham. Get up. I haven't hurt you much."

But no sign of life was visible in that outstretched form.

Mr. Beans was now horribly frightened and half-sobered. Kneeling down, he put his hand upon the heart of his victim, but could find no signs of a beating pulse.

A touch on the face showed that it was cold and clammy.

"I've done it!" gasped Mr. Beans. "I'm a murderer."

He rose up, staggered to the door, and fell against it.

The noise he made brought his mother to the door. She opened it with a jerk, and he rolled in.

"Rordy," she said, angrily, "what did I tell you when you went out to-night?"

"Oh! my dear mother," he replied, hoarsely, "I've done it! I've killed a boy."

He looked so terrified, and spoke so earnestly, that his mother saw something more than an extra glass of grog was agitating him.

She closed the door, and led him into the sitting-room, where he sank into a chair and covered his face with his hands.

"Tell me what you've done," said his mother, gently.

She was a quaint figure of a woman, but there was a pathos in the tender way she spoke to him in the hour of serious trouble.

He was her son, and she loved him with all his faults.

"Come, Rordy, tell me all about it."

"He was standing on the doorstep," replied Mr. B. Rord Beans, shaking all over, "and wouldn't come off when I asked him, so I hit him hard, and killed him. If I hadn't been, you know how, I should not have done it."

"Drink! Rordy, drink!" wailed his mother. "I said it would be your ruin."

"If I get out of this mess I will never touch it again," said Mr. Beans.

"Where's—the—the—boy?" asked his mother.

"Lying outside. Oh! it's horrible!" moaned Mr. Beans. "Can't we bury him in the back yard, and say nothing about it?"

The answer to the query was interrupted by a sharp double rap at the door.

"What's that?" exclaimed Mrs. Beans.

"The police for me," replied her son, wildly.

"Hush! Rordy," she returned, "you must hide. Go into the coal cellar, and I'll say you haven't come home. Your mother will save you."

Mr. Beans, in a most pitiable state of fear, staggered out of the room and sought the coal cellar, where he shut himself in.

Another sharp knock summoned his mother to the door.

With a trembling hand she opened the door, and on the doorstep a policeman stood revealed. He held in his arms what looked like the body of a boy.

"Is Mr. Beans in?" he asked.

The poor old woman tried to answer in the negative, but her voice failed her, and with a sob she sank into a sitting position on the floor.

At that moment Duffy appeared at the foot of the stairs in an exceedingly short night-shirt.

"I can tell you all about it, Mister Policeman," he said; "I saw it done."

CHAPTER XVIII.

THE END OF THE DUMMY BUSINESS—A MYSTERIOUS STRANGER—DANGER SHADOWS WARREN FANE.

As Duffy spoke, a wild cry was heard behind, and Mr. B. Rord Beans reappeared from the coal cellar, which, by-the-way, was only a big cupboard at the top of the kitchen stairs.

Brief as the time was that he had spent there, he had made the most of it by first falling on his hands and knees, and then covering his face with his dirty palms.

"Heed not that boy," he said; "if he says I killed him he lies."

They all stared at the horrible figure before them, but happily recognised the great High Art proprietor under the coal-dust.

"Killed him! Who?" asked the policeman.

"Why, that hapless boy," replied Mr. Beans.

"Bless your innercent 'art, sir," said the policeman, "it's only a tailor's dummy. It was stole to-day from the High-street, and finding it close to your house, I thought you could give information—"

Mr. Beans leant against the wall, quite overcome with the reaction.

He saw it all, and the relief was immense. But—another thought—what of the ridicule? Perchance this astute officer had marked his terror and understood it. His silence must be purchased.

"I don't know anything about the figure," he said, faintly; "somebody must have thrown it down outside."

"If you please," said Duffy, "I—"

"Silence!" cried Mr. Beans, aiming an open-handed blow at him. "Go to bed—you know nothing about it."

"I saw that Young Ch—" Duffy went on, and then Mr. Beans gave him a dig on the side of his head that effectually cut his story short and sent him back to bed.

"Mother," said Mr. Beans, "give this trusty officer a shilling. He deserves it for the care he shows in looking after the property of the ratepayers."

Mrs. Beans did not readily produce the coin, but after some fumbling in her pocket she found a sixpence, a threepenny-bit, and a penny.

With this the officer took his departure, and so ends the night's adventure.

The next day Mr. B. Rord Beans, accompanied by his mother, called upon the leading temperance man of Smockley and signed the pledge.

How he kept it time will tell.

There was a row about the dummy, of course. The tailor was not satisfied with its state when it was brought back to him, and he wrote to Mr. Fossil Bone a long account of its abduction.

Mr. Bone wrote back to ask for confirmatory evidence, the word of one man, as he truly remarked, not being considered sufficient in a court of law.

To this the tailor wrote a very offensive letter, asking if Mr. Bone thought he did not tell the truth, only he put it in a stronger and more vulgar way.

That letter was burnt, and there was an end to the matter so far as Mr. Fossil Bone was concerned.

The tailor, however, was not appeased, and he adopted the wild course of calling after the boys—"Who stole the dummy?"

Jerry Bott and his father took it up, and perhaps it would have become popular had it not been suddenly checked.

Dossy Dodge's cousin, who was doing the greater part of the Smockley chimney-sweeping, gave Abe a hint, and he stopped, while Tom Biron took the trouble to hunt up Jerry near his house, and gave him a thrashing before a lot of his companions, who were deterred from interfering by a wholesome remembrance of Tom's early prowess.

There was one other person who would not let the subject rest, and that was Duffy.

The fact was he had got it into his head that he had seen Young Ching bring the dummy down after dark and place it on the doorstep of the High Art Academy, and he wanted to tell about it.

Mr. Beans, for divers reasons, declined to listen to him, and Duffy was obliged to go outside for a confidant.

With his usual good luck he met Billy Pink in the street, and made him the recipient of his story.

"I was looking out of the window," he said, "it's all I've got to do, for Mr. Beans never gives me my lessons, when I saw him come running down with it."

"You were dreaming," said Billy.

"No I wasn't."

"But I say you was—dreaming and snoring —and don't you go talking about it, or it will be the worse for you."

Whether Duffy talked to others or not is of no moment, it sufficed for Young Ching that he had talked of it at all, and he wanted to teach him that a still tongue makes a wise head.

The nights were now drawing in fast, and the boys were not allowed out after dark. Possibly two or three, with the connivance of Billy, did go out by the back way, but what they did generally matters little. There was no great harm in it.

One evening Tom Biron wanted a few things from the shops, and obtained leave of absence for an hour from Mr. Fossil Bone.

It was dark when Billy Pink let him out by the front door, and a drizzly rain was falling.

"Hadn't you better have a rumerelly?" asked Billy.

"Never carry such things," replied Tom, turning up his coat-collar.

He stepped into the street, and Billy descended the steps to look after him admiringly, for Billy believed in Tom, when a man pushed rudely against him.

"Here, what are you doing?" demanded Billy. "Do you know who I am?"

The man muttered something and hurried after Tom, whom he soon overtook and stopped.

Billy saw it was a stranger, and he thought the man was a foreigner, for he had long hair and wore a slouch hat.

Tom answered some questions put to him, and went on. The stranger followed him again.

"That's rum," thought Billy; "I hope he isn't up to any mischief. If any harm comes to Tom Biron let that foreign party look out. 'Billy Pink, the Avenger!' what a title for a story! Billy Pink in penny numbers! wouldn't it sell—oh! my."

Wrapped in dreams of possible future literary greatness, Billy wended his way to the kitchen, where he found Mary darning a stocking by the fire.

"Have you done your knives, Billy?" she asked.

"I've had a go at 'em. Two more out of the handles," he replied.

"How's that?" asked Mary.

"I don't know," replied Billy, adding, with a chuckle, "wouldn't it be better to ask the knives?"

"Now, Billy, if you are rude," said Mary, "I shall box your ears."

"If you do I'll kiss yer!" returned Billy, defiantly.

"Do what?" exclaimed Mary, aghast.

"Kiss yer—twice," replied Billy; "come and box away."

"And what do you think my Willie would say to that, young imperence?"

"Your Willie! who's he?"

"The young man I keeps company with."

"Oh! him!" exclaimed Billy. "I saw him the last time he came, and if I couldn't knock his two goggle-eyes into one in half a minute I'd go out and drown myself in a bucket!"

Mary looked at Billy in astonishment. When he first came to Slapcrash School he was a simple boy. Now he was developing.

Further conversation was checked by the ringing of Mrs. Grumps' bell, and Mary, putting down her knitting, went to see what was wanted.

In less than an hour Biron came back.

Billy let him in, and noticed that he was strangely quiet, and looked rather pale.

"Hullo!" he said, "you've had a scare. Did that foreign party give it to you?"

"What foreign party?" asked Tom.

"I see him following you," returned Billy.

"Billy," said Tom, "I should feel obliged if you would not talk nonsense."

"But I see him," urged Billy.

"If you did, don't talk about it," replied Tom, gruffly, as he hung up his coat.

YOUNG CHING AND HIS CHUMS HAVE SOME FUN WITH A DUMMY.

He went upstairs to the school-room, where he found Young Ching engaged in pouring out a thrilling narrative for the benefit of the other boys.

Like father like son. The blood of the yarn-spinner was in him.

"Sit down, and don't talk, Tom," said Dick Cockles; "we've come to an interesting part."

Tom sat quietly till the story ended. The finish was a regular sell, and with laughter the circle broke up and scattered about the room.

Tom beckoned Warren Fane to his side, and they sat down together.

"Warren," he said, "I wish you would tell me a little about yourself?"

"*Have I killed him?*" exclaimed Mr. Beans.

"I am not permitted to tell much," replied Warren. "I promised I would not."

"I will only ask you one question. Have you any reason to suppose your life is in danger?"

Warren paused, and when the answer came it fell slowly from his lips—

"It—might—be."

"I ask you because I met a fellow who asked me some very strange questions."

"What were they?"

"He wanted to know if there was anyone in the school who seemed to be a little above the rest."

"And you told him there was no one?"

"No, Warren, I could not, for I think you are in some way a cut above us."

"Tom, have I ever hinted at such a thing?"

"No, dear boy, but we have eyes. There's something about you that tells me, as it told Young Ching, that you are above Slapcrash rank."

Warren Fane sat for a moment with his eyes down, wrapped in deep thought. At last he looked up, and said, with a sigh—

"I would tell you all if I could, but I cannot."

"Do you fear anybody?" asked Tom.

"In a way, yes."

"In what way?"

"I believe my death would please some people."

It was Tom's turn to be uneasy now, and he looked at his friend with apprehension in his eyes.

"Warren," he said, "the man who bothered me with questions to-night had assassin written on his face. Had you not better speak to Mr. Bone?"

"What could he do?" said Warren.

"Put the police on his track."

"The Smockley police! Oh! Tom, what an idea. Let us go out and find some Old Mother Goose to protect me."

He laughed, but it was in a constrained way. Tom sat gloomily tapping the desk with his fingers.

"Anyway," he said, "you've got to be protected. You are not to go out alone."

"I've no wish to do so after what you have said," was the reply.

"Shall we take Young Ching into our confidence?"

"I think so. His eyes are as sharp as a needle. But I don't want to get any of you fellows into trouble."

"My dear chum," replied Tom, affectionately, "what would you think of us, what should we think of ourselves, if we let you run all sorts of risks alone? We will have a talk with Young Ching by-and-bye."

This talk they had, and it was agreed that whenever Warren Fane went out, one or both of his two trustworthy friends should accompany him.

CHAPTER XIX.

DUFFY IN A NEW CHARACTER—HE HAS HAD ENOUGH OF IT—A VISIT TO THE MANOR HOUSE—A NOVEL ADVERTISEMENT.

MR. B. RORD BEANS was not the man to hide his teetotal light under a bushel. Having signed the pledge, he was resolved that

Smockley should hear of it, to the profit of everybody, including himself, he trusted.

Accordingly he hired the Assembly Room, and issued placards announcing a lecture on the "Destructive Effects of Alcohol." Admission, adults a shilling a head, children half price.

The attempt to reform Smockley was only partially successful—in a pecuniary sense it was an utter failure.

Only five persons attended, and one of them got in without paying, on the plea that he was the editor of an influential London paper.

This man proved to be intoxicated, and he cut short the lecture, got up with elaborate care, by mounting upon the platform and offering to fight Mr. B. Rord Beans for a new hat.

Mr. Beans did not decline, but simply backed off the platform and got out of the place.

The London editor, if indeed he was one, offered to fight everybody else, and they cleared out also.

This was the first and last Assembly Room lecture delivered by the reformed proprietor of the High Art Academy.

A few days afterwards the school had a half-holiday, Tom Biron and Warren Fane taking advantage of it to go by rail to an uncle of Tom's who lived fifteen miles off.

Young Ching had his chosen chums with him. He and Jem Stager, Dick Cockles, and Dan Mittens were now inseparable.

They were bound for the Manor House, and Billy Pink had promised to come as soon as Mrs. Grumps had settled down for her afternoon nap.

As the four first-named neared the bottom of South-street they saw ahead of them the familiar figure of Duffy.

He was wearing his usual attire, and slouching along in his accustomed dejected way.

Young Ching went up and gave him a gentle dig in the back.

"What cheer, Duffy!" he cried.

"I wish you would let me alone," replied Duffy, his arm going up as if worked by spasmodic machinery.

"That's what we are always doing," said Young Ching. "Where are you going?"

"I don't know," whined Duffy.

"Come! none of your cheek."

"It's true; I don't know, and I don't care.

Would you if you were in my place? I can' stand much more of this High Art game."

And as Duffy, in the most dolorous tones, made this declaration, he feebly clenched his hands and ground his teeth.

Young Ching looked at him comically, and then turning to his friends winked at them.

Taking Duffy's arm, he walked on a little way with him.

"What's up now?" he asked; "anything fresh?"

"Rather!" replied Duffy; "Tommy's short. There's hardly anything to eat, and the old woman gets most of it. Then Beans is always preaching to me."

"Preaching to you?"

"Yes—on what he calls the evils of intemperance. He never comes home now without getting me into a corner, when he goes at me, waving his arms, spouting about his former sins, how glad he is that he is so much better now, calls on me to repent, and every time he finishes he makes me sign a paper which he calls the pledge. I can't stand it. I wish somebody would knock him on the head!"

"Oh! don't wish that!" said Young Ching, soothingly; "you're hungry, and that makes you feel it worse than you would do. Come in here."

It was a small confectioner's shop at the bottom of the street into which he led the too willing Duffy, and there he bid him regale himself.

"Don't eat too much new pastry," he said, "but go in for a foundation of stale buns. You want it."

The boys all had something to eat at the confectioner's shop, and Duffy indulged in such a feast as probably he had never known before.

His eyes brightened, his form distended, a grin dawned upon his face, and when he could eat no more he laughed.

The others laughed also, and Duffy warmed to them.

"You are splendid fellows," he said. "I wish I was at your school, but it can't be yet. Beans has got a contract to keep me for a year."

"You trot along," said Young Ching to Jem Stager. "Take Duffy with you to the old house, and I'll come on in half-an-hour."

"Why this mystery? Whither goest thou?" asked Jem Stager.

"Anon, old friend, anon," replied Young Ching.

The trio went forward, taking the replete and temporarily happy Duffy with them. Wonders had been worked in the High Art victim by layers of tarts and buns.

"I do feel so happy," he said again and again.

They took him to the Manor House, and Jem Stager having opened the side door, he was shown all the glories of the place.

Jem Stager was in his element—as guide of the place he had no equal in the school—and he took Duffy up to the roof, through the rooms, and into the cellars, in something under an hour, fairly freezing the blood of the High Art pupil with horrors of the past.

"You seem to know all about the place," said Duffy, as they finally turned up in the banquet hall.

It was on Dick Cockles' lips to say "he makes it all up," when he caught Jem's eye and became dumb.

Duffy was beginning to think that there was something in life after all, and just as Jem was going to give him another dose about the banquet hall, Young Ching and Billy Pink appeared.

"All's ready," said the former; "we've got the donkey and the board."

Nobody there had heard of a donkey or a board before, but all except Duffy kept silent. The Slapcrashers saw that something was afloat.

"What donkey and board?" asked Duffy.

"Come," said Young Ching, "don't back out. You promised to do it."

"Do what?"

"To advertise the High Art Academy. I've got that board Beans had hung outside the barber's shop—"

"I don't remember it," said Duffy.

"Never mind, I've got it," said Young Ching, "and let that suffice. All you've got to do is to ride the donkey and carry the board through the town."

"I think I should like to ride the donkey," said Duffy, rather helplessly, "but the board—"

"Duffy," said Young Ching, sternly, "who is your real friend?"

"Does Beans blow you out with buns?" asked Jem Stager, now understanding, and taking up the cue.

"Or show you over Manor Houses," observed Dick Cockles, "and tell you a lot of li—"

"Dick!"

"All right, Jem, I forgot."

"I don't quite understand what you want me to do," said Duffy, "but I daresay it's some lark. You boys are all larks, and I wish I was, too. Anyway, I'll do what you want, and Beans be bothered."

"Bravo, Duffy!" cried Dan Mittens, smiting him on the back, and bringing on a violent fit of coughing.

Leaving them to carry out Young Ching's idea, we will now go into the town and see what Mr. B. Rord Beans is doing.

The Assembly Room lecture having failed, he decided upon trying his teetotal luck in the open air.

Accordingly that afternoon, with a kitchen chair in his hand, he wended his way to the centre of the town and took up a position in the middle of the road.

Now, when a man stands on a chair planted on the highway he won't be there long before he gets a few people about him, especially if he be a man so well-known as Mr. B. Rord Beans.

The little crowd soon gathered, and he plunged into the task of reforming the beer and spirit drinkers of Smockley at once.

With deep regret be it announced that his earnest efforts were not received in the proper spirit.

He spoke of his evil past, and the memory of it set them grinning; he dilated on the advantages he derived from the sober present, and they roared aloud.

"Men of Smockley," he cried, "will you mock the man who gives his life for your benefit?"

"Tip us a tanner for a drop o' beer," said a gruff voice; "that will be better."

Mr. Beans opened his mouth for a scathing reply, but it remained open without a word coming forth.

For from his elevated position he could see over the heads of the unregenerate people he addressed, and coming down the street he beheld a terrible sight.

It was Duffy on a donkey, riding along grandly, and carrying a board, on which the words "High Art" were distinctly visible.

Following the donkey was Young Ching acting as driver, and in the rear were the other Slapcrashers, all enjoying themselves amazingly.

Mr. B. Rord Beans forgot his temperance

lecture, and muttering something about being wanted at home, he took the chair on his arm and disappeared down a bye-street.

Without a refresher he could not stand the inevitable chaff that was awaiting him.

Ere he had gone far he heard a mighty roar of laughter, and knew that the crowd he had gathered together had espied Duffy.

"Bloodshed will come of this," he muttered. "Duffy must be a fool. Well, if he wasn't I shouldn't have had him. Hear them! What a row!"

It was as he suspected.

Duffy was the Smockley sensation of the hour and was rather proud of it.

Young Ching, while looking after the donkey, took good care that nobody should interfere with Duffy, and when a hobblede-hoy tried to push him off he gave him a rap over the head that stopped his joking for half-an-hour.

They paraded the whole length of High-street amid such roars and cheers as had not been heard for many a day.

Observant people noticed that the letters on the board had been cut out from some bill and pasted thereon, and they rightly put it all on to Young Ching, or "Young Pigtail," as the irreverent called him.

One policeman they met with seemed disposed to interfere, but the crowd crying out—"Let 'im alone, he's doing no harm," caused him to stop.

After all Duffy was doing nothing but ride a donkey and advertise that great modern Educational Institution, the High Art Academy.

At length Duffy began to show signs of fatigue.

He was not a very strong boy, and Young Ching turned the donkey and its rider into South-street.

It was a stray one Young Ching and Billy Pink had picked up, and it was not indisposed to return to the fields where they had found it.

Possibly Young Ching had marked the stray creature before, but it does not necessarily follow that it was so.

He had the gift of quickly utilising all things that came to hand.

Poor Duffy! He was getting very tired of his ride, and dismal reflections of possible punishment from the hands of Mr. Beans, or his mother, uprose before him.

Mrs. Beans, for an aged one, was a hard hitter.

Her open-handers, as Duffy very well knew, were things to be held in remembrance.

"I think I would like to get off now," he said.

"Nonsense!" replied Young Ching; "ride home now you have come so far."

Duffy yielded with a sigh, and Young Ching stimulated the donkey with a final whack.

"Hold on!" cried Young Ching.

"All ri-i-i-ght," replied Duffy.

The donkey increased its pace and got a little way ahead. Then Jem Stager cried "Whoa!" and it kicked up its heels.

Duffy dropped the board and lay full length upon its back.

Mr. Beans was on his doorstep watching for the return of Duffy. Hatless he rushed into the street and barred the donkey's path.

"Degenerate boy!" he began, impressively. "I tell—"

The donkey whipped round and let out its heels like a flash of lightning. Duffy fell to the ground and Mr. B. Rord Beans reeled back.

"I've been struck in a vital part," he gasped; "I'm a dead man!"

CHAPTER XX.

THE BEGINNING OF WINTER—MR. BEANS TURNS UP THE PLEDGE AND GOES IN FOR THE OLD, OLD GAME.

THE assurance that the kick from the donkey did not kill Mr. B. Rord Beans will no doubt be received with subdued joy by the reader.

The total extinction of the High Art school-master by such inferior means would have been little short of a public calamity.

But if it did not kill it scotched him a bit. In other words, it laid him up for a day or two, and his anxious mother had a high old time of it.

As for Duffy, he was very little the worse for his day's outing—better, perhaps, for he developed a rising spirit, and rather staggered Mrs. Beans, when she threatened to box his ears, by declaring that if she did he would have "the law on her at the police-court before the magistrates."

Leaving the little household to get along as well as it can, we must attend to the Slap-crashers.

Several days went by without anything of importance happening.

Billy Pink fell downstairs with Mrs

Grumps' supper tray, it is true, but as that estimable lady traced the calamity to abnormal activity—one of his gifts—we cannot say anything reproachful concerning it.

One morning Warren Fane went out before breakfast alone.

Without being a gloomy fellow he was certainly thoughtful, and he was fond of an occasional stroll in the cloisters of the Cathedral.

He did not say he was going, but Young Ching, hearing a few minutes afterwards from Billy Pink that he was gone, and the direction he had taken, immediately followed him.

As he turned into the cloisters Young Ching saw him walking slowly along, and close behind him was a swarthy foreigner.

The man, who answered Tom Biron's description of the stranger who had accosted him, had his right hand in his pocket, and Young Ching at once guessed that he had a weapon there.

Immediately he hurried forward, and his footsteps being heard on the pavement the foreigner turned.

At the same moment Warren Fane looked round.

The instant he saw the stranger he turned a little pale, but clenching his fist he sprang towards him.

The man did not wait for the blow, but with a swift movement sprang aside and disappeared through one of the cloister doors.

"Who is that fellow?" asked Young Ching.

"I cannot tell you," replied Warren Fane; "at least, I must not."

"He meant mischief, I should say."

"Yes, he did, and your coming has probably saved my life."

"I don't want any credit for that," said Young Ching.

Warren Fane slipped his hand through Young Ching's arm, and together they sauntered out by the main gate.

"Believe me," observed Warren Fane, "I shall not forget this. Don't say anything to Tom about it."

"Why did you come out alone?" asked Young Ching, reproachfully.

"I thought I was certainly safe at this hour in the morning," Warren answered.

Young Ching kept this little secret, but he pondered over what he had seen, and became very close in his watchfulness over Warren.

We must pass over two or three weeks as lightly as possible. Of course, there were

incidents in the boyish life of the Slap-crashers worth recording, but more moving things demand our attention.

Mr. Slapcrash went away for a "holiday," just to let that little affair between him and Abe Bott die out in the public mind.

The latter named gentleman was going down hill rapidly. If Dossy Dodge's cousin could be got the people did not want Abe, and his chimney sweeping business hardly found him in pocket money.

His precious son had become a complete loafer, and half the boys in Smockley could lick him now.

He seldom showed himself when the Slap-crashers were abroad.

Matters were in this state when November came to an end and December began.

It opened badly, from some people's point of view, with frost and snow.

At Smockley it always snowed if it snowed anywhere, and the downfall lay thick upon the streets.

To the boys this was a grand treat.

Snowballing became popular, and Billy Pink never went on an errand without returning with a glowing face and at least one ear bunged up.

If sent for anything breakable he invariably brought it back in pieces, which gave Mrs. Grumps food for reflection.

Mr. B. Rord Beans was now virtually in a state of siege.

Tradesmen, with the hopeless idea of getting their accounts paid, knocked at his door, and were answered by Mrs. Beans through the keyhole.

"Mr. Beans will call round and pay."

That was the invariable answer.

Mr. Beans neither paid nor called round, and the exasperated tradesmen came again and again and bawled out all sorts of offensive things in the middle of the street.

He was asked why he did not pay, and who was he to go running into people's debt and then shut himself up like Lord Cockbob in a castle.

To all this the inhabitants of the High Art Academy offered no reply.

Occasionally Duffy appeared at an upper window and made signs which nobody could understand. He was called upon to open the window and speak up, but he never did it, and the unhappy tradesmen went home savage and mystified.

About this time Mr. B. Rord Beans, M.A., F.R.O.I., broke the pledge.

Nay, he smashed it.

Early one wintry afternoon—it was a half-holiday with the Slapcrashers—he appeared in the High-street with his pledge-card in his hand, and publicly trampled on it.

He even danced upon it for a few brief moments, and gave the Smockleyites a taste of the dervish business.

"Teetotalism," he said, "has been the ruin of me. I spurn it. I rise," he added, with a curious kind of metaphor, "like a pho—e—pho—e—what is it?—phœnix from the ashes of cold water, and if any temperance preacher will oblige me by coming here for a few moments, I will publicly kick him!"

The temperance preacher not showing up he had another dance upon his pledge-card, and with his hat at a wonderful angle he strode off down South-street.

Some boys followed him—boys generally go in for all gratis public exhibitions—keeping close to his heels, and offering criticisms on his appearance and High Art life.

About the middle of the street he changed his mind, and decided to go in an opposite direction.

He turned so suddenly that he came into contact with sundry boys trotting close to his heels.

Beans fell over a doctor's boy and a youth apprenticed to a grocer, whilst a boy without boots rolled under him.

Then somebody began to snowball Beans, and before he could get up he had received two in the right ear and one on the nape of the neck.

Rising, he wildly chased the offenders until he again fell over the doctor's boy, who was picking up his scattered physic, and the uproar was now so great that one of the Smockley police heard it.

Peeping round the corner, and seeing it was only boys, he bore down upon the scene, and Mr. B. Rord Beans, M.A., F.R.O.I., was spared further insult.

"Hadn't you better go home, sir?" suggested the officer.

"Home!" exclaimed Mr. Beans, glaring at him ferociously; "where is my home?"

"At the 'Igh Art Academy."

"He calls that a home!" exclaimed Mr. Beans. "Ha—ha!"

His laugh was hardly a thing of this world, it was so loud and fierce. The officer, taken by surprise, was so startled that he nearly collapsed.

Mr. Beans stalked away and turned into the Close.

Nobody followed him for the moment, and the officer cleared off.

But Mr. Beans had been observed by Young Ching and several of his select chums, and they ran to a gate near the school, with the object of intercepting Mr. Beans and having a little fun with him.

CHAPTER XXI.

MR. BEANS GETS A FINAL DOSE OF TEMPERANCE—STRANGE WEATHER.

THE boys got to the gate, but could see nothing of Mr. Beans.

"Why, where's he gone?" asked Dick Cockles.

"Out again, I suppose," replied Young Ching.

They ran to the South-street entrance, but gained no tidings of him, and as there had been hardly time for him to get clear away they concluded he was still in the Close.

After a long search among its nooks and crannies, they found him in an old doorway, standing upright fast asleep.

Half-a-dozen well-directed snowballs roused him from his slumber, and as he opened his eyes the youngsters cleared out of sight.

Mr. B. Rord Beans looked at the patches of snow upon his waistcoat, rubbed the side of his head where one from Young Ching had smitten him, and glanced up at the clouds.

"My eye," he said, "it is a heavy fall. I think I'd better get home."

He started off, and the boys went cautiously upon his trail, now and then sending a snowball with well-directed aim into his back.

Every time he was hit he muttered—

"'Bout the heaviest fall I ever knew. Flakes weigh half a pound at least."

In all probability his disordered mind mixed up snow with hail, but so it was.

He took his theory of a heavy fall with him, went to bed, and slept upon it.

That night one of the climatic changes peculiar to our country set in.

A rapid thaw melted the snow, and in forty-eight hours it entirely disappeared.

Then came an east wind that dried the streets, and in another forty-eight hours the

DUFFY ADVERTISES THE HIGH-ART ACADEMY.

previously slushy roadway became alive with gritty dust, whirling hither and thither.

Smockley tradesmen objected to dust. They paid rates, and they expected it to be laid.

We may here remark that Smockley was proud of the way its municipal affairs were managed.

The streets were kept in perfect order, and were as clean as streets could be made.

Therefore, when the dust began to fly, the authorities sent out their one water-cart, with its usual driver, who was an hilarious old party, his theory being, "Water for the streets and beer for the man."

Accordingly, having filled his cart at the

"I'm a dead man!" gasped Mr. Beans.

public pump, he proceeded to fill himself at the public-house, leaving his vehicle standing near at hand.

Just then Mr. B. Rord Beans came along.

He had repented of his folly, and was once more a shining light of temperance, in this manner exhibiting nothing uncommon among some of the fraternity.

A good many people spend a lot of time in taking the pledge and breaking it again.

Once more he was upon the war-trail as a temperance lecturer.

Seeing the water-cart, he beheld in it a capital subject for illustration, and taking up a position behind it, he began to address the empty air, and then to speak to a few men and boys who had gathered near.

We pass over his early ravings, and come to the one great point he made that day.

Tapping the water-cart, he said—

"Behold here the liquid that man should love. It is invigorating, refreshing, and—"

He stopped short with a yell, for at that moment the water began to spout out with the copiousness for which the Smockley cart was famous.

Wheeling round, Mr. Beans beheld Young Ching, who had been sent there by some evil genius to torment him.

The son of the Immortal One had mounted the cart and pulled the string.

"Fiend, avaunt!" cried Mr. Beans.

"I thought you were fond of it," said Young Ching, lightly dropping to the ground.

Mr. Beans, in a sort of helpless fury, shook his fist at him.

"If I thought it would avail to pursue you," he yelled, "I would do it, but you are a Will-o'-the-wisp, an electric eel, a—a—blessed if I know what you are not. But beware!—it may be my turn one day!"

"Go home and change your breeches," cried one of the delighted audience.

"He hasn't got any more," remarked another.

Mr. Beans glared around him with ineffable scorn.

"And it is for these worms that I have laboured," he observed. "Enough! I wash my hands of you—die, drunken and unregenerate brutes!"

Then he strode away, and the water-cart man coming out, the vehicle was put to its proper use.

Young Ching had come out by special permission during the half-hour now allowed for play in the morning, as a break to the labour of hard study.

Mr. Fossil Bone believed in everything in its place—play at one time, work at another—and thus showed himself to be a sensible as well as kind-hearted man.

Young Ching had received a telegram that morning informing him that his father might be expected almost any time at Smockley, and he was going down to the station to learn about the trains when he met Mr. Beans lecturing, and acting on one of those impulses that boys are subject to, he damped the ardour of the renowned teetotaler.

Jem Stager and Dick Cockles accompanied him, and they were all in the highest spirits.

Restraining themselves with marvellous

moral force, they did not interfere with anything else or anybody, but went straight to the station.

A moment after a train came in, and Mr. Slapcrash alighted. He glanced at Young Ching, who stepped in front of him and said—

"Stop a moment, Mr. Slapcrash."

"Out of my way, boy," replied the retired schoolmaster.

"I only want to say this," observed Young Ching, "that my father is coming here, and he will call you to account for the false accusation you made against me."

"I don't care a hang for your father," replied Mr. Slapcrash, as he walked away, looking very white.

"We will see about that," retorted Young Ching; "now let us have a look at the time table."

Having looked over it, and taken down the time of the trains due that day, the boys ran back to school, getting there as the bell calling them back to work ceased ringing.

All that day the Smockley water-cart worked hard, drenching the roadway and giving the pavement a fair share of water. Then, in the afternoon, it rained a little, and at night, to make matters pleasant, a hard frost set in.

To these delightful climatic changes are we subject, and Smockley, when darkness set in, became rather lively.

Only champion skaters could hope to keep their feet on the slippery footpaths, and the well-kept roads were almost as bad.

Duffy, sent by Mrs. Beans to purchase three red herrings for supper, got half-way to the shop, falling every few yards, and then went back.

"There aren't any red herrings," he said; "they are all sold."

"That's a falsehood," replied Mrs. Beans. "You are a wicked boy. Rordy, go and get them yourself."

Rordy, who was sitting moodily before the fire, went as far as the doorstep. From thence he shot with inconceivable velocity into the roadway, and lay there for awhile, wondering in a feeble way how he could have been projected so far.

He also went back without the herrings, and the evening meal was poorer than usual.

Billy Pink had to fetch home some crockery Mrs. Grumps had purchased early in the day, and he returned with the report that he had left it up the street in pieces.

"The roads are all ice," he told Mrs. Grumps, "and millions of people are lying about on their backs, calling for help."

Mrs. Grumps, in a measure, verified this assertion.

She went to the landing window and saw a Smockley policeman lying in the road, trying to get out his truncheon as a means of self-defence, being under the impression that some marauding villain had tripped him up.

There was no doubt about the ice—the whole street gleamed with it.

"William," said Mrs. Grumps, "you are a remarkable boy—any other person would have broken his bones instead of the crockery."

All youthful Smockley was out that night, making slides of abnormal length upon the pavement, falling heavily, and otherwise enjoying themselves, as boys will do when they get a chance.

Snow began to fall again about eight o'clock, and every step was a snare to the foot-passenger.

Of such a night a poet of great power but imperfect education once wrote—

"First it rained, then it blew,
Next it frizzed, and then it snew,
Then there came a shower of rain,
After that it frizzed again."

It is needless to say that some of the Slap-crashers were out.

The back door offered them facilities for getting through the garden into the street, and along the front of the house they made two perfect slides, one each way.

Warren Fane, Tom Biron, and two or three others were getting their skates ready, hoping to have a turn in the flooded marshes on the morrow, but all the rest were busy outside.

Billy Pink joined them, and with the aid of Dick Cockles, succeeded in throwing nearly everybody down in turn, until at last they were rebelled against.

"These two must have a slide to themselves in the roadway," observed Jem Stager, "or, by the swords of the Crusaders, three-fourths of us will have to be taken to the hospital."

"Of course it's all our fault," replied Dick; "but if we fall you needn't come down on the top of us."

"Oh! never mind, let's have a slide to ourselves," returned Billy; "there will be some sense in that."

"Billy for ever," cried Young Ching.

So the two tumblers made a slide for themselves, and although it was not more than ten or twelve feet long, one or the other, and sometimes both, were down every few seconds, much wrangling ensuing between them as to who was to blame.

"I'd give in if it was my fault," said Billy; "but you can't keep your legs a bit."

"A boy without legs," replied Dick, "could slide better than you."

But, for all their wrangling, nothing serious happened. They fell, got up again, exchanged accusations, and renewed the sport.

The noise the boys made was something very unusual for quiet Smockley, and it was strange that Mr. Fossil Bone or Mrs. Grumps did not come out to see what was the matter. But they did not.

"Oh! Susannah! don't you cry for me," sang Billy; "I'm going to Ally bamer with my banjo on my—"

Flop!

Billy was down again, and Dick Cockles, being close behind him, tripped and pitched on his head, where he appeared to balance himself for a moment and then went over.

It was the champion purler of the evening.

"I hope you haven't hurt yourself?" said Billy, anxiously.

"There's a question," replied Dick, as he sat up and rubbed his head. "Did I trip you up, or did you trip me?"

"We seemed to come down together," replied Billy, mildly; "but rather than talk about it for a month I'll give in and say it was my fault."

Dick growled out something, but he soon got over the shock, and on they went again.

As for the police, they were practically in hiding, and were not disposed to risk their bones by running after boys engaged in harmless amusement.

Suddenly Jem Stager's voice was heard.

"Somebody is rambling down the street," he said; "he'll come a buster in a minute."

The boys all stopped to see the individual fall.

They could dimly see him, fifty yards away, hastily coming along, indifferent to the slippery pavement.

As he passed a lamp it was seen that he was bareheaded and strangely dressed.

"Who on earth can it be?" whispered Jem Stager; "is it a ghost?"

"No," replied Young Ching. "I rather suspect that it is my father!"

CHAPTER XXII.

FATHER AND SON—SMOCKLEY LIKES A HOLIDAY —EARLY MORNING ON THE ICE—DICK AGAIN GOING WRONG.

THERE is no doubt that Young Ching was deeply moved, but, like his father, he had the power of keeping himself cool under trying circumstances.

It was the Great Man himself coming along, indifferent to the slippery state of the Smockley streets and the frosty air.

The sliding stopped, and Billy Pink, who had just fallen down with Dick Cockles on top of him, made no attempt at the moment to rise.

He was always more or less awe-stricken in the presence of the man whose name is famous the wide world through.

They met—father and son—after a long parting, and embraced.

Few words were said at first, but that showed no lack of feeling. Chatterers and howlers keep their joys and griefs on the surface.

Then, under the lamplight, Ching Ching held his son at arms' length, and looked at him.

"You hab been a grower," he said; "de developer hab been goin' on. My sunny heir, you will be a creddle to de familer. Now interjuice me to your frens."

They crowded round, and as Young Ching named them the Great Man shook hands.

Billy Pink hung fire, standing a little to the rear, in the middle of the road.

"Do I see Billy Pinker dere?" asked Ching Ching. "Come to de fronter, my boy. How am de gooses?"

Billy came forward as directed, and the Immortal One not only shook hands with him, but patted him on the head.

He remembered Billy's love and faithfulness in all his dealings with Young Ching.

"How's Sammy?" asked Young Ching, "and why isn't he with you?"

"Coming on by next train," replied the Immortal One. "Some nefalious pusson hab purlined Eddard."

"Purloined Eddard—stolen him?"

"Seemly so, my sunny heir, but I daresay it all rightly in de end. Now I like to hab a worder wif Misser Fussey Boner if he am homer, which," he added, looking round at the boys, "do not seem to be de caser."

"Oh! yes, he's at home," answered Young

Ching; "but he's kind enough to let us play sometimes."

"Seemer so, seemer so," observed Ching Ching, with just a suspicion of dryness in his voice.

Billy Pink ran round by the back way and opened the front door.

Ching Ching and his son entered the house that way.

The other boys thought it time to go in also, and disappeared quietly through the garden gate.

Now it so happened that as Billy Pink was admitting Ching Ching into the house Mrs. Grumps was coming downstairs.

The moment she saw the Immortal One she recognised him and got into a flutter.

She was at that time five stairs from the bottom, and the flutter caused her to slip. Had it not been for the ever watchful and gallant Ching Ching she would have fallen heavily.

But he sprang forward and caught her in his arms.

She was heavy enough to have staggered most men, but the great man stood like a rock.

"Gentler, gentler, dear young lader!" he said; "like all singler pussons, you are ımpetlus."

"Oh! thank you so much," said Mrs. Grumps, panting; "but you are mistaken about me. I am a married woman."

"Neber!" exclaimed Ching Ching, holding her off at arms' length, much as he had done his son, and gazing at her with profound astonishment.

"Yes, and I'm a widder."

"It not possbile."

"Yes it is, Mister Ching Ching Mandarin," replied Mrs. Grumps, "and I've got a growed-up son somewhere. He was a trouble to me and most people who knew him, and ran away to sea."

"Affer dat," exclaimed Ching Ching, "dere is no inflamation dat will stonish me. Low me to shaker hands wif you."

The boon he named was granted, and then Ching Ching was ushered into the waiting-room by Billy.

Young Ching went upstairs to the school-room.

"You will hear how I am getting on, dad," he said, "but I don't want to listen myself, as I'm modest, and our family objects to blushing!"

"A chipper ob de ole lock," murmured Ching Ching, as his hopeful son vanished.

Mr. Fossil Bone was not long before he put in an appearance.

He had never asked Young Ching about his father, but he knew a good deal of his history, and he had looked forward to the day when they should meet.

The day—or rather night—had come, and his glowing face expressed the pleasure he felt.

The interview lasted half-an-hour, and at the end of it Young Ching was sent for.

The appearance of Mr. Fossil Bone showed that he had been deeply impressed by the Immortal One.

"I am pleased and proud," he said to the boy as he appeared, "to make the acquaintance of your naturally gifted father"—he put some emphasis on the three words. "Much that I have seen in you is now fully accounted for."

That was all he said, but was it not enough? With a final shake of the hand of the Immortal One he left the room.

Then, in a few words, did Ching Ching impart good tidings to his son.

He proposed to stay three days at Smockley, and he would have stayed longer but he was due in London.

Those three days would be a holiday for the Slapcrash boys.

This, with a few shining bits of gold stamped with the image and superscription of the Queen of Great Britain and Ireland, sent Young Ching to the supper-room with a heart as light as a feather, and it was seldom much heavier, by-the-way.

"Three days!" observed Dick Cockles; "oh! my, but what will our dads and mothers say to it?"

"They won't say much if they don't hear of it," replied Young Ching, sententiously.

Ching Ching told his son that he intended to put up at the White Hart, and he would "endebber to make it a trifler more libely dan usual."

"And you will succeed," said Young Ching.

That night when the boys went to bed the window was opened for a few minutes to listen for any signs of conviviality from the White Hart, which Young Ching said might be expected.

It was not far away, and Smockley is a quiet place; therefore it is no wonder that presently certain sounds reached their ears.

"Chorus, boys!" was heard more than once in the few minutes they listened, and it was followed by a roaring sound, which no doubt was Smockley melody.

"The law of the land will be broken to-night," said Jem Stager; "they won't be able to close at the usual hour."

The boys, however, went to bed, as they intended to be up early and wend their way to the meadows for a skate before breakfast.

As the wind was blowing, the snow would be driven off the frozen water where most exposed.

Breakfast would be ready at half-past eight, but at half-past six many boys were awake.

The majority of them had skates, and they were trooping out the back way before the lamps had been extinguished in the streets.

As a matter of fact the lamplighter was behind with his work, thanks to the condition of the streets. They saw him crawling along and dragging his ladder behind him.

Having given him a snowball or two in the the back, to rouse him to a full sense of his duty, they went on past the White Hart.

In a quarter-of-an-hour the first meadow was reached, and then they found a fine piece of ice ready swept for them by the wind.

An enterprising Smockleyite was there before them, with a chair, and two of the minor canons of the Cathedral were already performing feats of agility upon their skates.

Tom Biron, Warren Fane, and Young Ching were soon skimming to and fro like swallows. The other boys were getting ready as fast as they could.

Dick Cockles sat down upon the chair and gave his skates to the man.

"Put 'em on," he said, "and don't make any mistake about right and left."

"There ain't no right and left unless they are hackmys," replied the man.

Dick's were not acme skates, but they were pretty good ones in their way, and being duly strapped he was asked to stand up.

"I'm going to do so," he said.

Then he got up, and like a flash of light he went down on his back.

"They are not put on right!" he gasped.

"You ain't put on right!" replied the man.

Jem Stager had fixed his own, and with a smiling face he gave Dick a hand.

"Why didn't you say it was new to you?" he observed. "You have never skated before."

"That's all you know," replied Dick.

Having got upon his feet, Dick Cockles proceeded to go through the most extra-ordinary contortions, and as Selah Finch, who was also a poor hand at it, was about to start, Dick lurched against him and over they went together.

"What did you do that for?" demanded Dick.

"I like that," groaned Selah, rubbing hi elbows.

They got up again, and Selah, in a lame-duck fashion, was going off to the right, when the man with the chair bawled out—

"Keep away; there's a deep hole in the corner, and it don't bear yet."

Selah tried to turn, and he did face about, but the wind blew in that direction, and away he went, like a small yacht before a stiff breeze.

Dick Cockles, with his legs very wide apart, also started in the same direction.

Jem Stager had gone off the other way with a few more, and the Slapcrashers who had no skates had started making a slide.

Dick and Selah, therefore, in a manner of speaking, glided off to perdition unattended.

If bawling could have saved them the man with the chair would have done all that was necessary, but standing still and shouting is of very little good in the time of trouble.

Selah Finch went backwards, gathering speed as he travelled along, and by ill-fortune was taken straight to the dangerous place.

Crack!

Dick saw the ice break and Selah go into the water with a yell and a splash. Then up came his head like a cork, and his trembling hands grasped the edge of the ice.

"Help—help!" Selah shrieked.

Dick's heart turned sick within him.

The wind had now set him going merrily. He went along like an ice-boat, such as they use on the Canadian lakes.

"It's all up!" Dick gasped. "I'm done for, and just at the beginning of three days' holiday, too! Good-bye everybody!"

He was near the opening when something like a young whirlwind bore down from a side direction, and he heard a familiar voice cry out—

"You little duffer! Where are you going?"

Then he felt himself turned aside and sent spinning, apparently for half a mile or so—in reality about twenty yards.

Soon he fell, and then he saw blue lights and revolving stars in the morning sky.

All this was so confusing that he had no

sense left to note things around him until he became conscious of Jem Stager and Dan Mittens being near him.

Dan was saying—

"You thank your stars that Young Ching saved you."

"Stars!" replied Dick, feebly; "I've seen lots of 'em!"

"No doubt," observed Jem, drily.

Here a cheer was heard, and Dick, looking across the ice, saw a number of boys hastening towards the town.

"What's that?" he asked.

"Selah Finch trotting home to change," replied Dan. "Didn't you see it done?"

"I saw him go in."

"Of course you did, and were going in yourself when Young Ching rushed at you. He turned you away with one hand, and with the other laid hold of Selah Finch's collar and landed him like a big fish. Wasn't it a sight, Jem?"

"Rather," replied Jem; "but if he had stopped half a moment the ice would have given way with him. Now, Dick, here's the party with the chair. Off with your skates!"

"What for?" asked Dick.

"Because you can't skate. Go and slide."

"Are you skating-master?" demanded Dick.

"I'm your master," said Jem, grimly.

The man came up with the chair, and Dick sat down.

"I call it mean to spoil my morning," he said; "but there, take 'em off."

So Dick's skates were taken off, and in his heart he was not particularly sorry. As a slider he felt he had few equals, and what a boy shone in he ought to show to his companions.

So he went and joined the sliding party, to work confusion among the unfortunates he favoured with his presence.

Meanwhile Young Ching, having performed the feat recorded, left some of the other boys to see Selah home, and with Warren Fane and Tom Biron ran with racehorse speed round the ice.

Other people from Smockley were arriving, and among them was Mr. B. Rord Beans.

The High Art teacher had no skates, but after some little hesitation he joined the Slapcrashers who were sliding.

"Here! what now?" cried Dick. "Get off. This isn't a man's slide."

Charley Green, Sam Fusby, and others also objected to the presence of their old tutor,

but he loftily reminded them that the meadow was open to the public, and the slide thereon was public property.

As he was a slow slider it was impossible for the boys to get on with him. He did not fit in anywhere. He was like unto ten Dick Cockles rolled into one.

"Let's go and make another slide somewhere," Sam Fusby observed.

They were about making off when the striking figure of the Immortal One appeared upon the ice.

Young Ching was far away across the meadow, and his august father smilingly bade the boys good morning.

"But why not slidering?" he asked.

"Old Broad Beans came and spoiled the fun," replied Dick. "We can't slide with him."

"Den why not he go and leab you in peacers?" asked Ching Ching.

"He says he won't," chorussed the boys.

"All right," said Ching Ching. "Den I gib him an injucer to retire."

Mr. B. Rord Beans, absorbed in his exhilarating exercise, had not observed the great man's arrival, and had at that moment started off down the long slide.

He went at a snail's pace, and was promptly followed by Ching Ching, who, with the rush of a charger on the battle field, leaped upon the slide, shot down it with inconceivable velocity, and in half a second had overtaken the High Art slider.

Then was Mr. B. Rord Beans seen to fly into the air to the height of three or four feet and come down in the shape of the letter V.

He fell in a sitting position, sliding on with remarkable velocity until he came in the way of one of the minor canons engaged in cutting a figure of eight, whom he brought down on the ice with startling force.

"Dere," said Ching Ching, as he rejoined the boys, "I tink I hab injuiced Missa Broadle Beaners to be a retirer."

Indeed he had.

Mr. Beans, after exchanging a few compliments with the minor canon, slowly and painfully rose to his feet to ascertain the means whereby he had been brought to grief.

His eyes fell upon the Immortal One standing a little way off, engaged in lighting a cigarette.

"Oh! dear!" gasped Mr. Beans, "he did it. I thought it was something uncommon. The son was bad enough, but with the father

THE SON OF THE IMMORTAL ONE HAD PULLED THE STRING.

here— I'll go home and keep there till he's gone."

Which he did, giving the boys' avenger as wide a berth as possible. At a pinch Mr. B. Rord Beans could be as prudent as any man.

CHAPTER XXIII.

THE GREAT BREAKFAST AT THE INN—THE HEAD WAITER AND DICK—MORE ARRIVALS.

SMOCKLEY was alive that morning. The news had gone forth that the world-famed Ching Ching had come down to see his son, who, in his way, had made a name for himself.

Tidings of great doings at the White Hart

"Here—take 'em off!" said Dick.

on the night before—of money lavishly spent, of tradesmen amply compensated for real and supposed injuries—were spread abroad.

The tailor who had suffered in a dummy sense was one of the loudest singers of the praises of the man whom he called the Great Pekin Royal Mandarin.

Ching Ching accompanied the boys back from the meadow, and his appearance in South-street excited such a commotion as was never seen there except on very rare occasions, to wit, an election or a fire.

People came to their doors as he glided gracefully up the street with the Slapcrashers in his wake. Windows also were thrown up, and late risers put their heads out to stare at the phenomenal figure passing by.

Many of these window-gazers were women,

and some had their hair in curl-papers, a fact forgotten in the excitement of the moment, but to one and all did Ching Ching lift his eyes.

When he came to a pretty face he bowed, and this was a signal for the Smockley boys to cheer.

Young Ching, walking with Jem Stager, kept a close eye on his father, watching every movement, with the filial idea of making use of the instruction unconsciously given.

Near the top of the street Abe Bott and his son came loafing along, wondering what was up.

Suddenly Abe caught sight of a pigtail swaying pendulum-like to and fro.

"It's the China fellow—the old 'un," he said to Jerry, and they vanished up a court.

Around the door of the White Hart a little knot of people had assembled, awaiting the Great Man's return.

For the most part they were people who had partaken of his hospitality the previous night, and were not averse to a little refreshment in the morning.

Three or four of them bore marks of heavy falls on their way home the night before, which, of course, could be easily accounted for by the slippery state of the streets.

It was on arriving here that the Slapcrashers received a great surprise—it was alomst a shock.

"You break your fasters wif me, dear boys," said Ching Ching; "it am all laid outer for you."

They were soon ushered into the large dining-room on the first floor, which was generally used for public feasts and the farmers' ordinary on market days.

Here there was another shock in store for them.

There was Mr. Fossil Bone awaiting their coming.

Also Billy Pink, who had put on his Sunday suit, which was four sizes too large for him, and was, perhaps, as a work of tailoring art, the most awful thing ever made by man.

But Billy's rosy face was always pleasant to look upon, and nobody bothered themselves about his clothes.

Mrs. Grumps was likewise there, and her get-up was gorgeous. She had mounted a cap of extraordinary size, which, like Joseph's coat, was of many colours.

It was, indeed, odds on her having more colours in it than ever Joseph dreamt of.

Mr. Fossil Bone was quiet and gentlemanly, as usual.

"Finch will be here directly," said Mr. Bone. "I thought it advisable for him to have a warm bath after his ducking."

The breakfast was all ready and the urn hissing.

Ching Ching, with ineffable grace, handed Mrs. Grumps into the chair at the top of the table, and took a seat on her right. Mr. Bone took the bottom of the table.

"Now, boys," said Ching Ching, "peggy way."

The was no need for further invitation.

Three active waiters, with the head one to look on and see they did not flag, carved and served out all sorts of good things from the sideboard.

There were ham and chicken, cold beef, bacon, eggs, trout, and sundry other toothsome things not usually attainable at a boarding school.

The keen air of the morning had put an edge on appetites that were generally sharp enough, and the way the good things disappeared was a staggerer for the head waiter.

Dick Cockles especially engaged his attention, although he did not neglect Billy Pink.

In fact, he became quite anxious on their behalf.

Summoning one of the under-waiters with a crook of his finger, he bade him pass the word that the future orders of Dick and Billy had better be ignored.

"We don't want any sudden deaths here," he said. "It would be a pity to check the time of rej'icing only just commenced."

The consequence was that when Dick thought he would like just another slice of ham to fill up a corner with he could not catch a waiter's eye until he caught that of the head one.

"A little more ham, please," he said.

The head waiter was about to sternly refuse when he caught Ching Ching's eye, and at once he complied with the request in person.

Then was the corner filled up and Dick was satisfied. The head waiter felt like a man who has had to go through the disagreeable ceremony of eating his own words.

Billy Pink, happily, did not want any more.

He was in a state of repletion, and inflation also, that for the time incapacitated him from doing anything but sit still and wonder if his buttons were strong enough to stand it.

His clothes, being of extra size, saved him from a calamity.

Breakfast took a long time getting over, and afterwards they sat awhile talking in batches, Ching Ching devoting himself to the gratified Mrs. Grumps, who wished she was twenty years younger, and hadn't lost that front tooth, which gave way one day when she was cracking nuts.

Suddenly a waiter who had not been attending at the table came into the room and addressed his chief.

The words he said were few, but they put the head waiter into a flutter.

He came hurriedly down to Ching Ching and deferentially murmured something.

Ching Ching looked towards his son, who was seated on the other side of the table between Tom Biron and Warren.

"Sammy and de oders down below. Bring 'em uply," said Ching Ching.

Young Ching pushed his chair back and disappeared with sprite-like activity.

Dashing downstairs, he saw a group in the hall, with Sammy foremost, beaming like a figure of polished ebony.

"Sammy, old man, how are you?" Young Ching cried.

Then Sammy, with a loud whoop of joy, caught him in his arms and held him tight.

CHAPTER XXIV.

A SECOND BREAKFAST—AWAY TO THE TOWN—SCENE IN THE MARKET PLACE—BILL AND ABE BOTT.

"OH! Young Massa Ching," cried Sammy, "dis am a joyful meetin'."

"Let him tip me his fin," cried Bill Grunt, from the rear. "Save the boy! how he's growed. How are you, Young Ching? I'm quite well, thanky; how are you?"

Bill was evidently a little excited, and Young Ching got free of Sammy and gave him both hands to shake.

Then Eddard, standing quietly behind, in his modest, unobtrusive way, came in for a greeting.

"Well, Old Cheerful!" said Young Ching, "how are you? Tough as ever, I trust."

"Glad to see you, Master Ching," replied Eddard. "As Bill says, you've growed, but—but—totherwise I don't see no differs in you."

"And who's this? How are you, Jack?"

said Young Ching. "We are strangers in one way, but friends in another, through hearing of you from my father. And this is Posey. What a seraphic mug he's got on him—he ought to sit to a painter as the dog cherub."

This was the greeting he gave Jack Cardigan and Eddard's voluntary attendant, Posey.

Jack shook hands with him heartily, and Posey, with tongue out, a leary eye, and a wagging tail, testified to his knowing exactly what o'clock it was.

"Nice dog, Eddard." said Young Ching.

"Well," said Eddard, giving his collar a hoist up, "that's a matter of opinion. I can speak for his sticking to parties as he takes to."

"How came you to be left behind, Eddard?"

"There's the warmint as led to it."

And Eddard wheeled round to shake his fist at Jam Josser, who was standing shivering near the wall.

Of course Jam Josser had on apparel suitable to the climate. Ching Ching got it for him before they left the sea-port, and if anything was calculated to increase his villainous looks it was the hat with a gold band, the striped trousers, and the livery overcoat in which Ching Ching had arrayed him.

"Well, come along," said Young Ching, "you must tell me about it another time. There's a lot of friends upstairs, and they all know you."

He led the way, and when the party entered the room there was a scene.

The boys had left the table, and acting on one impulse, they all plunged at Sammy to shake hands with him.

After that Bill Grunt did a lot of the pump-handle business, also Jack Cardigan, likewise Eddard.

As for Posey, he made himself at home at once, and after a playful snap at the head-waiter's legs, which made that dignified individual skip a foot in the air, he got upon a chair, took half a fowl off the sideboard, and retired with it under the table.

The boys soon saw him, and down went Dick Cockles and others on their hands and knees to pat him while he polished off the fowl.

It speaks volumes for Posey that he let them pat away without so much as growling.

"So these are your friends," said Mr. Fossil Bone to Ching Ching; "the sharers of your joys, your sorrows, and your perils?"

"Dat so," replied Ching Ching. "We hab seen sumfin togedder, eh, Sammy?"

"Eber de same, and more so," returned Sammy.

"If I may put in a word," said Bill Grunt, "I'll just say this, that—"

Here he caught Eddard's eye, which was fixed upon him sarcastically.

"Hullo! Eddard," he continued; "up to it again!"

"I'm up to nothing," replied Eddard; "but up to a thing or not, you're down on me!"

"Hear—hear!" cried Ching Ching: "dat bery good for Eddard. Fren Willum, you know how to get de kindlier side ob our ole fren. No worders to-day, for all am peacers. P'raps you hab some breakfuss?"

"I could pick a bit," replied Eddard.

"Odds on that," grunted Bill. "I'd like to see the time when you couldn't!"

The waiters cleared a place like magicians—with one sweep of a wand, as it were—and the late arrivals sat down.

All this time Jam Josser had been deferentially standing near the doorway.

Ching Ching now called attention to him.

"Jamly Jossy, come forf!" he said; "let eberyone see your intelresting countlenance."

As Jam Josser came into the room the Slapcrashers burst into a roar of laughter.

Why they did so is best known to themselves, but to Jam Josser it came as a surprise.

He shrank back from it, and it hurt him more than hissing and hooting would have done.

"A nicer young man dis," said Ching Ching to Mr. Fossil Bone; "try once to pison us, besides a few oder trickers, but I make him spectable. What you tink ob dat suit? Am it a becomer?"

"Well, really," replied Mr. Fossil Bone, a little nonplussed, "I can hardly say. You see I am no judge of such things—I—"

Ching Ching laid a hand upon his shoulder and looked into his face with a smile.

"What am liberies to me?" he asked. "Do I want a serbent in uliform? Neber. But I put that cuss into dem closers. Why? Cause he not like it. Cause he got to be pulished for what he done, and it am de universal laughers dat make him feel it. Jamly Jossy, yo may be a retirer, and p'raps our kind frens who serbed us so well at de tabler will gib you sumfin to eat."

One of the waiters undertook that task, and

Jam Josser was led away, his dark eyes gleaming with malice and impotent rage.

Ching Ching, with his usual acumen, had hit upon the right way to strike home.

Jam Josser hated the garb he was put into. It outraged his feelings in every way. He felt that he was a guy, an object of derision, a mark for the finger of scornful laughter to point at.

"Now," said Ching Ching, "de atmosfear bein' clearer, let us know de reason ob your absincks, fren Eddard."

"I'll tell you how it was," replied Eddard. "When we get out of the train I see Jam Josser a sideling like to the door, and says I to myself, 'That warmint's goin' to run away.' So I pegs arter him, and Posey comes a pegging arter me, as usual."

"Faiful creeter," murmured Ching Ching.

"That's as may be, as I have said afore." returned Eddard, "but come he did. Now, Jam Josser knows a bit about London, or I'm much mistaken, for he cuts across the road like a man used to it, and strikes away east'ard. I follers, and I hollers, and when we got a bit away a policeman stops him. Then I goes up, a sort o' row ensues, and somebody in the crowd hollers out—'That's old Eddard Cutten—lock him up.'"

"Sich is popliparity," murmured Ching Ching.

"Oh! blow popularity of that sort," growled Eddard; "'specially when it leads to both of us being locked up. Posey warn't took, though somebody said he ought to be, but when he showed a tooth or two they changed their minds. Anyhow, me and that mahogany beggar were run in and put into one cell."

"Eddard," said Ching Ching, "dey shall gib you compersators for dat."

"I hope I may get it," returned Eddard, rather hopelessly. "Well, we weren't there long—about an hour and a half, I reckon—when the cell door was thrown open and a policeman says—'Come out you two,' which warn't so polite as it might have been.

"To cut the story short, Mister Cardigan and Bill was in the hoffice ready to bail us out, and who do you think brought 'em there? Why, Posey! He went back to the station and cut all kinds of capers until they follered him."

"Fren Eddard," said Ching Ching, "dere hab been timers when de attenders ob dat dogger did not excite your libely grattletude."

"That's true," replied Eddard, "and them times may come again, for it's one thing to get a chap out of a police-cell and another to be constantly chawing his wooden leg!"

The force of this observation was generally felt, and nobody demurred to it in the least.

Bill Grunt certainly asked Eddard if he'd rather have the other leg chawed, but nobody followed this line of argument up, and the matter dropped.

"All's swell dat end swell," said Ching Ching, "and when you hab refresher de inly man I tink dat we show ourselbes in de mail toroughfares ob dis anshy ole town."

"There's one party as I wants to see here," observed Bill Grunt, "and his name's Bott. I'd like to have one turn with him in a quiet corner."

"Maybe he'll obliger you," replied Ching Ching. "I alser hab an individler ob de namer ob Slapcrash to see. Mebbe I make the meeter a memolable one."

All had breakfasted now, and the travellers, after their custom, put their pipes on. Ching Ching ordered cigars for himself and the schoolmaster, but Mr. Fossil Bone did not smoke.

Pleading important business, he retired.

Mrs. Grumps was now formally introduced to the travellers, and she was most gracious. To Bill Grunt she was extra kind, at which he became alarmed, and in a hollow whisper asked Ching Ching what time he was going to "sheer off."

"It nuffin," replied Ching Ching; "she a moderly creetur—dat all."

"Then you noticed it," said Bill.

"It one ob de cusses ob being a handsome chappie," replied Ching Ching. "It your figger, fren Willum, dat bring lubly woman to your feet."

"If any other man but you had said that," returned Bill, "I should say it was gammon. But you wouldn't cut a joke at my expense."

Of course by this time it was known that the whole of the Immortal Four, as many of their admirers called them, had arrived at Smockley, and to add to the natural excitement there was the fact that it was market day.

The streets were in a condition to make things lively, so altogether there was a prospect of a joyful time.

Leading the way, Ching Ching, with his son by his side, descended the stairs—behind him came his three close friends. Following was Jack Cardigan, already chummy with

Tom Biron and Warren Fane, and then the other boys in irregular procession.

In this way they entered the street, where they found an excited host of idlers awaiting them.

People were strewing ashes before their doors, so that walking was possible, but here and there this domestic duty had been neglected.

At one of these places Eddard's wooden leg gave way, and the Old Sufferer fell sideways against a grocer's shop and broke the window.

Luckily it was only one of the old-fashioned sort, but Eddard did not want to pay for it.

The grocer, who had come out to see the party go along, had a different opinion, but nobody agreed with him.

"A few ashers," said Ching Ching, "sabe de windy. Wherefore dey not dere?"

The grocer rashly endeavoured to detain the Old Sufferer, but Eddard, although he played second fiddle sometimes, could come to the front at a pinch.

A blow in the waistcoat from his fist, and a prod from the historical wooden leg, seated the grocer in a box of Spanish onions near his door.

"All right," he gasped, "I give in."

Growling fearful threats, Eddard rolled away in the wake of his great leader, and several little boys who were about to start larking with the Old Sufferer changed their minds and cheered Sammy.

The cattle-market was visited first by the august parent of Young Ching, and the arrival of the party practically made chaos of it for the time.

Very little agricultural business is done without a drink, so when Ching Ching hailed a knot of farmers and with a comprehensive wink said—"Come and hab a lilly drinker," they advanced as one man.

Of course, only the elders of the Ching Ching party entered into this form of conviviality. The boys wandered about the market with many a wary eye upon them.

Not that they were up to mischief—of course not—but accidents will happen, and somehow a hurdle got loose and let out about a score of young pigs, which hailed the opening thus made with porcine joy as they rushed forth to freedom.

Dick Cockles was in the line they took—he naturally would not be anywhere else—and was literally borne away like a cork on the surface of a torrent for a dozen yards or so, and then cast down in the mud.

Jem Stager ran to pick him up, exclaiming in dramatic tones—

"Thus has many a slaughtered porker been avenged. The crimes of a sausage-making father have been visited on his son."

"Oh! blow you and the crimes of my father!" replied Dick; "who's got an oyster-shell or a bit of slate? I must be scraped down."

The required articles were not forthcoming, but Dan Mittens used the back of his pocket-knife, and took off the worst of the mud from Dick's nether garments.

Meanwhile Young Ching and the owner of the pigs were exchanging a few words.

"I see you jerk up the string and let 'em out," the dealer yelled.

"You don't say so," replied Young Ching.

"Yes, I do, and I'll have the law on you," observed the man. "They are all over the place, and who's to catch 'em, I'd like to know?"

"Oh! we will," clamoured half-a-dozen Slapcrashers.

"Don't let 'em, mister," cried a gruff voice, and Young Ching, turning round, saw Abe Bott standing close behind him.

He whispered half-a-dozen words to Jem Stager, who glided quietly away. Then turning to the ex-champion sweep Young Ching said—

"You must always put your word in. I've told you two or three times not to interfere with our concerns."

"I ain't interfering," said Abe Bott, "I'm only taking the part of a 'spectable tradesman, such as I am myself. There ain't no reason why you should rob him of his pigs."

The dealer was gone by this time, and with a few expert drivers was getting his lost pigs together.

"Now, look here, Bott," said Young Ching, speaking slowly, as if to gain time; "you are the sort of fellow that ought to sing small everywhere. You are a cur, a bully, a third-class rough, and— Ah! would you?"

Abe Bott aimed a blow at him, which Young Ching with a quick movement avoided. His blood was roused, and dashing in he dealt the sooty ruffian "one on the mark."

It is a spot where a stiffish blow will derange the breathing apparatus of the gentleman assaulted, and the breath of Mr. Abe Bott was fairly scattered.

Had it not been so a very thrilling scene would not have transpired in Smockley Cattle Market that day.

Abe Bott, gasping and faint, holding on to the pig pen, saw a number of people advancing, foremost among whom was the renowned Ching Ching.

Bill Grunt, engaged in rolling up his sleeves, was next, and close behind was Sammy, Eddard, and an excited following of farmers.

Abe had no breath to run, and he stood his ground because he could not help himself.

"Here's Bill," said Young Ching; "now for fun!"

"What is Bill going to do?" asked Tom Biron, who had just come up with Warren Fane.

"He's been bursting to have a go at Abe Bott," replied Young Ching, laughing. "Keep your eye on my incomparable father, and see how he will arrange the whole thing."

CHAPTER XXV.

BILL SETTLES ABE—SMOCKLEY LIVELIER THAN EVER—THE FIGHT IN THE PIG PEN.

CHING CHING had come up, and Abe Bott had gone down. That is, he had sunk into a sitting position on the ground, thereby intimating that he had no desire to fight.

"I ain't no match for you!" he said; "I niver said I was."

"Rise, fren Botter!" observed Ching Ching; "here am a floeman worfy ob your steel. Now, fren Willum, to de fore."

Bill by this time had got his sleeves halfway up his arms, and was ready for the combat. Abe Bott eyed him all over, and mentally putting him down as a "slow 'un," gathered a little heart.

"I ain't done nothing to him," he said. "Who's he?"

"You just got to get up and have one round," replied Bill. "Either that or be rolled in the mud!"

"Eber de same, and to de fore," Sammy was heard to murmur.

Eddard advanced and addressed himself to Abe.

"You'd better stand up and be knocked down and get it over," he said. "It will be the shortest way out of the job. I allus takes a short cut when I can."

"What have you got to do with it, old timber-toe?" grunted Abe.

"Here, nuffly ob dat," said Ching Ching. "Are you a fighter or not? Hard knockers or mud-larkers, which?"

"I'll have a go at him," snorted Abe, rising.

"In de absence ob a ringer," said Ching Ching, "de bess place am de piggy pen."

"Hear—hear!" cried the spectators.

It was certainly not the most desirable place for a fistic encounter, but as the market generally was in rather a dirty condition, a matter of an inch or two extra mud was hardly worth reckoning.

Bill rolled into the extemporised ring, and Bott followed.

Then Ching Ching ranged all the boys around, with himself and a fast-gathering bucolic assemblage forming the outer circle.

"You look to Botter," he said to Eddard. "Sammy, gib fren Willum a picker up when needled."

Abe Bott and Bill Grunt then began a fight which lived long in the memory of those who beheld it.

Perhaps Bill, as a fighter, lacked elasticity, and in the matter of scientific display he fell short of our chief pugilistic professors, but for all that he was a good man.

Standing in the middle of the pen, he raised one arm up to the level of his chin and drew the other back ready to strike.

There was something statuesque in his attitude, heightened by the fact that his face was entirely without expression. Abe Bott walked round Bill, who made no movement above his hips.

Abe Bott, on the other hand, showed that he knew a thing or two.

He shaped in true pugilistic fashion, and danced on his toes with elephantine lightness, watching for an opportunity to "get one in."

As a matter of fact the opportunity was there from the first, for a blow he aimed at Bill's head was not even parried.

Bill received it between his eyes without so much as blinking. Nor did it even sway his solid body, which yielded not a fraction of an inch.

Encouraged by this success, Abe tried a blow in the chest, and got home as before.

Bill's broad frame gave out a sound of a drum-like nature, but he showed no consciousness of having had anything to do with it.

Then Abe, emboldened by his good luck, rushed in for a fall.

THE SLAPCRASH BOYS.

The Liveliest of School Stories.

"HELP—HELP!" SELAH SHRIEKED

No. 7.   Price One Penny

Here was Bill's opportunity.

His arm shot forward, and his cocoa-nut-like fist struck Abe just under the chin with a force that made every spectator blink.

It was not a knock-down blow, but a knock-over one, for the ex-champion sweep was sent flying over the hurdles of the pen, and the spectators rapidly dividing to give him a clear field, he pitched backwards on his head and lay in a heap upon the muddy ground.

"Now," said Bill, gruffly, "let him come on again, and I'll knock him out of this 'ere market."

But Abe Bott could not come forward again. He was knocked clean out of time, and there

Ching-Ching applied his Celestial toe to a part of Mr. Slapcrash's anatomy.

was no shamming when he did not rise on being called upon.

"It's about done him," said an amazed drover. "I've seen some hard knocks in my time, but never one within a mile o' that one."

They called on Abe to rise, but he never stirred. Then somebody cried out—

"He's a dead 'un! and no wonder."

But Abe Bott was not dead, happily. He was simply in what a farmer—who had been to school in his boyhood and evidently made good use of his time—termed "a state of comma."

They raised him up and propped him against the pig-pen, when he half-opened his eyes.

"Parly chimbleys swep' a shilling each," he murmured; "kitchen flues one-and-six, fam'lies waited on any distance."

"You ain't in the soot business now—you've been a fighting," said a drover.

"A fightin', have I?" groaned Abe; "I feels like it. Who knocked my head off?"

"A seafarin' party," was the answer. "There he goes, with his friends."

The drover pointed in the direction of a crowd of men and boys bearing towards the town. But it was only a cloud in the misty eyes of Abe Bott.

"I can't get clear yet," he murmured, "but I swear I hit him fair."

"If his wasn't a fair hit," remarked the drover, "I never see one. Come, get on your feet and stand a drink. I'll lead you to the White Magpie."

With the man's assistance, Abe got upon his feet and stared around in a helpless manner.

"My head ain't the right way on my shoulders, is it?" he asked. "It seems to me as if I'd had it jerked backwards."

"You thank your stars it wasn't jerked off," replied the drover, as he led him away.

The farmers, as a body, went home about four o'clock on market days. A few habitual topers were all that remained until a late hour.

And these were not noisy men.

Their habit was to regale themselves, then get into their traps and allow their sagacious horses to take them home, where they generally arrived with their heels where their heads should be.

Now and then the cart or trap would turn up without the driver—Heaven forgive us for using the word—and their not over anxious friends, on searching, would find they had tumbled out, and were either sleeping by the roadside or staggering home.

On this particular market-day at least five times the usual number remained behind.

They came down in twos and threes to the White Hart, and were drawn into the long dining-room, where Ching Ching and his friends were to be found.

The Slapcrash boys, after a lively time, had gone home to tea.

Jack Cardigan and Posey had accompanied them.

That most sagacious of living dogs, Posey, had taken wonderfully to Young Ching, and Jack Cardigan, who was going home for awhile and then to sea again, talked of leaving Posey behind him.

"I won't sell him," he said to Young Ching,

"but I think he will be happier if he goes up to town with your dad."

"And Eddard," added Young Ching.

So it was arranged. Posey was to be left with the Immortal Four, and to be considered the temporary property of Young Ching.

Of the doings at the White Hart that night we can say very little.

Ching Ching, on hospitable thoughts intent, let it be known to one and all that anything and everything required in the way of refreshments was to be put down in his bill, and when all had been supplied he rose at the head of the board, and said—

"Genelmen all, I gib you a tose—'Let us be melly while we can.'"

It was received with acclamation, and then the festivity began!

The head waiter had never set eyes on such a scene before.

He had witnessed many an assemblage of farmers quietly soaking themselves and talking about turnips and top-dressing, but he was totally unprepared for the hilarity they now developed under the guidance of Ching Ching.

Toasts and sentiments followed each other in rapid succession, and then the singing began.

Ching Ching started it with one of his famous Pekin songs, with the following chorus—

> "Let us be melly while we can,
> Wif a ki—ki—ko—ko—kum,
> Ebery man a fren to man,
> Wif a kee—kee—ko—kum—rum."

It set the ball rolling, and all wanted to sing.

Nobody waited to be asked, and sometimes two, or even three, would start together, and the roaring was like that of several bulls, followed by a chorus that bore a strong resemblance to the noise made by the sea in a storm.

The head waiter was seen to join in, and old Bill Grunt was heard to give out sounds like the booming of artillery.

Sammy sat quietly, taking it as a matter of course, while Ching Ching beamed upon the company like the morning sun.

As for Eddard, he made several attempts to cut in, but had always been nipped in the bud.

At last there came a temporary lull.

It was occasioned by the arrival of a tray full of well-filled glasses, and each man was watching to see that he got one.

This was Eddard's opportunity.

Leaning back in his chair and throwing his eyes up to the ceiling he began.

The first note drew all the colour out of the head waiter's face, barring his nose, where the rosy hue was warranted to wash.

The waiter with the tray put it hastily down upon the table and looked wildly about him.

All the farmers had a galvanic shock, while Bill Grunt took up a long clay pipe and threw it at Eddard.

It caught him fairly on the bridge of the nose, and breaking into a dozen pieces, scattered right and left.

Eddard stopped.

"Who did that?" he asked.

"I did," replied Bill. "Do you think nobody here ain't got any feelings?"

"It nuff to gib eberybody eberlasting wriggles," said Sammy.

"There ain't been no objections to other parties," observed Eddard; "why, then, to me?"

"We don't object to you," replied Bill, "but to your voice."

"Dere no reaser at all why fren Eddard not sing," said Ching Ching; "but what his voicer wants is distants. Comin' trough a cubby door it sweeter 'nough."

"Same old game," replied Eddard; "but I'm not going to be put out to-night. Them as don't like my harmony can get into a cupboard and hear it that way."

"Good againer, fren Eddard," observed Ching Ching, tapping the table approvingly.

Ching Ching was evidently determined to support Eddard, and Bill Grunt yielded.

"All right," he said, "go on, but I advises everybody to take a stiff drink, or they won't be able to stand agin it."

This advice was as good as could be offered, and it was very acceptable to the hearers, so after a steady drink the company composed itself to listen.

Eddard's singing powers are known to many of our readers. They were always of a nature to act like a cry of "Fire" in a theatre and clear the house.

But now everybody stood or sat their ground.

Ching Ching, with a sweet smile on his face, beat time to Eddard's most hideous harmony, and nobody liked to quail.

But the head waiter had to grasp the sideboard to keep his feet, and the under waiters forgot their manners and sat down on the nearest chairs.

The song was—"Would you gain the tender creature?" a fine old bit of harmony such as the dandies of a hundred years ago wept over, but as rendered by Eddard it was on the borders of the unbearable.

When he finished everybody said, "Thank you." It was honest, for they were all grateful that it had come to an end.

"I ain't sung that song for twenty years," observed Eddard, complacently.

"If you don't sing it again for twenty more nobody will die o' grief," replied a farmer facing him.

Eddard made no retort, but he calculated the weight of that farmer, and mentally hoped that they would one day meet in a quiet corner.

About eleven o'clock a move was imperative, and by that time a third of the guests were asleep and the rest troubled with affected vision.

The intelligence brought by the head waiter that another rapid thaw had set in was received with contemptuous indifference, but many of them blessed the sloppy state of the streets a few minutes later, when they were tumbling about in the slush.

Ching Ching received invitations to nearly all the farms five miles around, and he was to bring Bill and Sammy, also Eddard if he wished. He was to stay at least a week, or a month if he liked.

Ching Ching, kind host to the last, assisted his bucolic friends to put on their hats and coats, and as he took the first that came to hand, things were a little mixed.

Tall men got short coats, little men long coats. All the big-headed men staggered off with undersized hats, and men with small craniums rolled away with big hats over their eyes.

Nobody complained. They were all satisfied, and more than satisfied.

The head waiter tried to put things right, but Ching Ching said—

"Letem be, fren waiter. It gib a lilly exercise on the mollow for dem to go roun and see each oder. Mebbe it will bring elemies togedder and make frens ob em. P'raps dis ebening be a oper up ob uriversal peacers in de districk."

"No doubt you are right, my lord mandarin," replied the head waiter deferentially.

Shortly after the company departed Jack Cardigan came home with Posey, and Eddard promptly asked for his bedroom candlestick.

"We have been having some fun at the school," Jack said. "Mrs. Grumps had a plum-pudding for supper, and Billy Pink fell over the mat with it. He broke the dish, but did not hurt the pudding. Mrs. Grumps said any other boy would have squashed it."

"Dear old Biller," observed Ching Ching, reflectively, "a borner gelius. He come ob a famler dat am shiner lights whereber dey go. If his fader had not been an agricultooralooral labyrer he would hab been de Sir Chief Juster ob de High Core ob Chanceitry."

At this moment a sound very much like sawing up a knotty board with a rusty saw was heard.

After a hasty glance round Ching Ching traced it to Bill Grunt, who had fallen asleep in his chair.

"Dear ole Willum," he said, "gone to de lan ob deposers. Well, it bout time all levantled in dat directer."

Turning to the waiter he went on—

"Gib me a candle and caller me earler in de morner, waity dear, for dat will be to me and seberal oder frens de gladder day ob all de glad ole year."

"I'm pleased to hear it, my lord mandarin," replied the head waiter, fervently; "but you cannot all go to bed with a single candle. Allow me to light you up, will you?"

"We will hab candles eachly," said Ching Ching. "Now, Sammy, ole man, fill your fisters wif candles. Willum, ole hoss," giving him a shake, "away to deposers, so rise and fall in de rear ob your ole leader. Two ey two. It am a stateler recession."

As indeed it was.

At the White Hart no such scene as they presented going to bed—Bill rolling heavily, Sammy a little dazed about the way he had to go, Ching Ching with the head waiter in front of him, and Jack Cardigan grinning behind, all with two candles apiece—had been seen before.

It was a striking, original, and impressive way to go to bed.

And Eddard was out of it. Just his luck.

But not Posey. He walked serenely in the rear, with that stump of a tail of his quivering with delight.

He knew where Eddard slept, and he was going to lie outside his door, so as to be the first to greet him in the morning.

CHAPTER XXVI.

MR. SLAPCRASH IS DEALT WITH—EDDARD AND
THE HEAD WAITER—MR. BEANS TRIES TO ILE
EDDARD AND FAILS.

IT was early morning, and Mr. Slapcrash was
walking abroad to get a little fresh air.

The rapid thaw had made the streets very
dirty. There was mud everywhere, and in the
less exposed places were heaps of dirty snow.

Smockley was in a dirty state.

Mr. Slapcrash had heard of the arrival of
the great Ching Ching, and he was on the
way to claim police protection. He had reason
to fear personal violence from the Immortal
One.

Although he was in a terrible state of funk,
the air of the retired schoolmaster was
dignified. He believed and trusted that the
little turn up with Abe Bott had been forgotten.

He had reached the very street wherein the
police-station was situated, when he heard a
strange voice behind him.

In one sense he knew not who it was
addressing him, but in another he had no
moral doubt as to the individuality of the
speaker.

"Stop a milute, Missa Slapcrashly."

"I decline to talk to you," replied Mr. Slapcrash, hurrying on. "I request you to leave
me alone."

The answer to this was a hand laid upon
his collar, and he was twisted round.

Face to face with the Great Man, Young
Ching, Eddard, and a little crowd of boys
and men, he felt his very life settling into his
boots.

"You cused my sunny heir ob attemp at
robbery," said Ching Ching.

"I—I have reason to believe that I was mistaken," stammered Mr. Slapcrash, "and I was
guided by the false evidence of another
person."

"I hab reasers to belieb dat you meant to
take way de chalacter ob my bonner boy,"
replied Ching Ching.

Then he twisted Mr. Slapcrash round again,
and dealt with him as he deserved, applying
the toe of his Celestial shoe with great vigour
to a part of the Slapcrash anatomy which may
be guessed at.

Mr. Slapcrash went down the street for a
distance of ten yards or so in what may be
called a series of involuntary bounds.

Then Ching Ching released Slapcrash, and,

cool as a cucumber, taking the arm of his son,
the Chinaman strolled quietly on.

This exhilarating scene was witnessed by
Jem Stager, Dan Mittens, Warren Fane, Tom
Biron, and a fair sprinkling of the Smockley
people, to all of whom it was very gratifying.

"The wretched snob deserved all he got,"
said Warren Fane.

"He did," replied Tom Biron.

A few people remained with the retired
schoolmaster, to witness the after-spasms of
suffering he endured, and they accompanied
him as he turned into a side street, with the
object of making a circuitous route homeward.

He did not go to the police-station that day
nor the next. In fact, he prudently let things
slide.

After all, he felt that he was just a little to
blame.

Ching Ching gave another breakfast that
morning, but it only included his own
particular chums, Young Ching, and his
warmer friends of the school.

Warren Fane was there, and he sat on the
right of Ching Ching, who occasionally
looked at him in an inquiring way, that
showed he was interested in him.

It was an hilarious breakfast, of course, and
all went merry as a marriage-bell, save when
Eddard choked himself with a piece of
buttered toast.

He had to adjourn to the landing, where he
was attended by Posey, who, as the Old
Sufferer choked and coughed, barked with
sympathy.

It is needless to say that Eddard came back
again and soon made up for lost time.

The head waiter, a man of serenity and
dignity by nature, seemed somehow to have
taken a dislike to Eddard.

He glared at him at all times and seasons
in a manner that was undoubtedly objectionable.

Eddard saw it, as other people did. Other
people did not object to it, but Eddard soon
had enough of it.

The Old Sufferer was taking the last piece
of toast off the plate when the head waiter
whisked it away and handed it to Dick
Cockles.

"Here, you bring that back," observed
Eddard.

The head waiter did not answer him direct.
Turning to one of his underlings he said,
loftily—

"Bring that party a 'ole plate of toast to bisself."

That party! A whole plate!

It was galling and offensive.

But Eddard bore it for a time, and when the toast came he disposed of it.

Not that he was greedy—anybody who knows him will say he is nothing of the sort—but he wasn't going to be done by a head waiter.

Breakfast over, Ching Ching, with his son, went out to do a little shopping. The company, except Eddard, also all retired, and the Old Sufferer was left alone with the head waiter.

The latter was a great man when put out, and Eddard being very small beer in his eyes, he took up a position on the hearthrug and hummed a tune.

The cold grey eye of Eddard rested on him.

It was a glittering eye, deep down in its socket—an eye that had still some of the fire of manly youth in it.

"Stop that humming!" said Eddard, suddenly.

The head waiter started, but after a moment's check he went on with the performance.

Eddard rose from his seat and rushed at the head waiter.

"Stop it, I say," he observed, in a more decided tone.

"Tumty—tum — tum — tum—tumty tum," buzzed the head waiter; "tum — tum — murder!"

There was a crash of fireirons, and the head waiter was in the fender.

He felt the heat of the fire, smelt the singeing of his black hair, and then he was drawn out of peril by the heels.

Eddard rolled him on the hearthrug at full length—an inglorious spectacle.

"Git up," said the Old Sufferer, "and I'll have a round with you."

"I am not a prizefighter," retorted the head waiter, with dignity.

"I am," replied Eddard, dancing lightly on his wooden leg and sparring with great vigour. "I've got to take my sufferings out o' somebody. Stand up!"

The head waiter declined to do so, and Eddard was proceeding to assist him, in a very unceremonious manner, when three of the under waiters rushed into the room.

Against such odds Eddard was not fool enough to contend, and with the air of a con-queror who has put off his final victory for another day, he swaggered from the room.

Having secured his hat, he went downstairs and stumped into the street. Barely had he got outside when somebody rushed at him and put a pair of long arms around his manly form.

"Old friend — brother!" yelled the embracer, who was no other than Mr. B. Rord Beans.

"Hands off!" cried Eddard; "who are you? Get out of it!"

Mr. B. Rord Beans loosened his hold and drew back. On his face was a sickly smile—in his eye a sort of leaden despair.

"You do not know me," he said, "but I know you. Your name, the name of Cutten, is famous wherever the English tongue is spoken."

"Maybe it is," replied Eddard, cautiously. "What do you want?"

"I am B. Rord Beans," was the reply; "attached to my name are the letters M.A., F.R.O.I., which indicate learning, talent, social elevation, and yet I have a bailiff in the house."

"Larning," said Eddard, "ain't enough to keep 'em out."

"I know that," replied Mr. Beans, "but learning ought to secure me friends. You are rich, you are generous, you are kind. Come to my aid. The sum due is seventeen pounds ten for rent. It is but a button from your coat."

"Whatever it is, you won't get it," retorted Eddard. "Ile to me is pison. If you've got a bailiff in the house it's your job to get him out, not mine. Good day!"

"I am friendless now," muttered Mr. B. Rord Beans, gloomily, watching the retreating form of Eddard. "I thought he was open to a bit of soap, but he is one of the cold, hard world. To bear this I must break the pledge again and take a refresher."

CHAPTER XXVII.

EDDARD PAYS A VISIT TO A PERSON IN HIGH POSITION—LAST EVENING AT SMOCKLEY—THE PARTING AT THE STATION.

CHING CHING and his son did their shopping, and were returning to the hotel with an admiring and excited crowd at their heels, when they came upon Duffy.

He was walking slowly along, with his hands in his pockets and his eyes on the ground.

"How are you, Duffy?" asked Young Ching, stopping him with a dig in the ribs.

"How would you be," replied Duffy, looking up wearily, "if you had had no breakfast? There's a bailiff in the house and Mrs. Beans is going to starve him out. She says there's nothing to eat in the place."

"Dad," observed Young Ching, "this poor lad ought to be taken in hand by some friend. I'll tell you his miserable history, as far as I know it."

"Firse," replied Ching Ching, "let him come to de hotel and hab sumfin to eat. It is not easy to modelise on a empy stomacher."

So Duffy was taken back to the hotel, where a special breakfast was ordered for him.

Probably he had never before sat down to a meal that could in any way be compared to it.

While he was disposing of it, under the hospitable direction of Young Ching, the Great Man was summoned below to receive a deputation of tradesmen.

They had come to ask him to make Smockley his home, and at the head of the deputation was the mayor of the town.

The address was a verbal one, too long to give here, but decidedly impressive.

It was pointed out to Ching Ching that Smockley, as a place of residence, was dull, and much in need of some life-inspiring presence such as he could give it.

There were several desirable family mansions to be let, one at the back of the Bishop's Palace, and the bishop himself would, no doubt, be delighted with such a neighbour.

It was also hinted that, in course of time, Ching Ching might even hope to become mayor of the place.

The Immortal One appeared to be quite overwhelmed. He shed tears of gratitude, wiping his eyes with his four-inch pocket-handkerchief, and then he shook hands with the members of the deputation one by one.

In his fervour he gave them the old grip, and it was ludicrous to see how they gasped and wriggled under it.

"Smockerly," said Ching Ching, in reply, "can nebber be my specially homer. I am a chile ob de worle, de offspring ob de universal, and my dutifulls caller me way to de mely-tropolis. Dere I hope to see you oney all some day, wif a few ryal pussons, at dinner. Mealwhile my larse momenters in dis nobly placer shall be as brilliack as possbyls. Whateber fire-workers dere am in Smockerly, let

em be sent on to Slapcrashly School, where my sunny heir will range for dem to be put to dere proppy users to-night. I arx de nobly genelmen here presen to gib orderers for whateber liquiry fluids dey like bess, from champay to ole Tommy; alser dat they will member de motter to be melly while dey can."

A murmur of gratitude arose from the deputation, and good Old Ching rang the bell.

A waiter came in, and close behind him were Bill Grunt and Sammy.

"Dese ole frens ob mine," said Ching Ching, "will act as cheerman an viser cheerman. For my own self, I muss absenter."

After a few whispered words with Bill Grunt and Sammy, he gave the members of the deputation another hand-shake, which set them all gasping like expiring codfishes, and went his way.

We may here remark that business that day at Smockley suffered from neglect.

The deputation did not leave the hotel until noon, and then it went home in cabs, singing.

Ching Ching repaired to Slapcrash School, where he got the boys together, and, with their aid, arranged an evening's entertainment.

Young Ching afterwards went with Tom Biron to buy up all the fireworks in the town, and Billy Pink was set to work sweeping a clear space in the slushy playground.

Then Ching Ching had luncheon with Mrs. Grumps and Fossil Bone, charming them by his grace of manner.

When he left, Mrs. Grumps went up to her room and burst into tears, exclaiming—

"It can niver—niver be! I'm not young enough, and I ought to have had a front tooth put in. If I was the wife of such a man I wouldn't envy the Queen of Hengland and the Hempress of all the Injies!"

Vain hope—Ching Ching had been married once, and it was a happy time enough. But to put his head into the noose again—well, it had to be thought over.

From the school Ching Ching went to the station-house, to ask if a summons had been taken out by Mr. Slapcrash. The answer of the chief officer deserves to be recorded in letters of gold, if our printer would do it without extra charge.

But he cannot or will not, so it must go down to posterity in ordinary ink.

"No, mandarin!" he said; "and if he wanted one we should not let him have it."

Having left a trifle to be consumed in

DOWN CAME THE AVALANCHE, FLOORING BILLY AND DICK.

refreshment, Ching Ching visited the National Schools, and arranged that every child should receive a new shilling, half a pound of sweets, and a toy on Christmas Eve.

Turning out of the school he ran against Abe Bott, who fled precipitately, and then Ching Ching went back to the hotel.

There he found Sammy, Eddard, and Bill Grunt sitting over the fire, Bill fast asleep, and artificially sawing wood with his nasal organ.

Having woke him up by calling " Fire " in his ear, which Bill put down to Eddard, Ching Ching proceeded to explain his future movements.

"To-mollow," he said, "we had berrer go

"*Old friend—brother !*" *yelled the embracer.*

to de mellytropolis. Dere not much in dis placer to keep us here, 'cept de Slapcrashlys, and Missa Fussy Boner say dat dey ought to be making derangements for de breaker up. What de boys do in de vacationer we will reside byer bye. Mealwhile it am de dutifulls ob Eddard, as de only pusson here wif any real mannerers, to call on de bishop."

"Do you think I'm such a fool?" asked Eddard.

"As you pleaser," replied Ching Ching. "When a pusson ob de soshal persition ob a bishop arx for a pusson to visit him, dat pusson am a ruder not to go."

"But did he ax for me?" asked Eddard, wavering.

Ching Ching gently stirred the fire and remained silent.

"In course, if he did ax for me," observed Eddard, rising and looking slowly about him, "if he did—well, there's no harm in my going."

He put on his hat and went out.

Ching Ching lit a cigarette and sat down. During Eddard's absence of twenty minutes or so very little was said, and he was not the subject of conversation.

At last Eddard came back. They heard him on the stairs snorting like a steam-engine, and on entering the room he threw his hat into a corner, reckless of the pecuniary loss that might ensue, and plumped down into the chair he had previously occupied.

"It's all right," he said; "I hopes you've enjoyed it."

Ching Ching, with raised eyebrows, looked at him inquiringly.

Bill smoked on placidly. Sammy had the face of a sphinx.

"I hopes," repeated Eddard, raising his voice, "that you enjoyed it."

Ching Ching elevated his eyebrows a little more, but said not a word.

"Anyway," continued Eddard, "it warn't all one way. I left the flunkey chap on the mat, and I don't take much 'count of the clip of the ear he gave me."

The Immortal One leant back in his chair and looked dreamily into the fire. Bill Grunt proceeded to refill his pipe, and Sammy yawned.

"I axed if the bishop was in," Eddard went on, "and the plush chap says by way of hanswer, 'You've come the wrong day for soup tickets,' which, put it as you may, was cheek."

Bill lit his pipe, Sammy closed his eyes, and Ching Ching, with airy grace, took a cinder between the tongs and lighted another cigarette.

"I don't know," resumed Eddard, " if the plush party was in the joke, but if he was he didn't get all the grin. 'What do you mean?' I says. 'If it ain't soup it's coals,' he replies, 'and there won't be no more tickets till arter Christmas.' 'Blow yours coals,' says I. 'Blankets, then,' he interrupts, 'or maybe you want a petticoat for the missus, but whatever it is you can't have it, and the next time you comes go to the back door.' Then I goes for him, and he fought like a lion, but I got him on the mat and rubbed his head hard. There I left him."

Eddard finished his narrative with some

impressive action, but nobody seemed to hear him.

Bill Grunt smoked stolidly on, Sammy dozed, and Ching Ching softly sighed, like one who thinks sadly of happy days gone by.

"Look as you like and do as you like," concluded Eddard; "you've heered me, and the joke ain't all on one side."

"Fren Willum," observed Ching Ching, "what you say to a cuppy tea?"

"The werry thing," replied Bill; "I'm a bit dry about the mouth."

"Tingle de commulicater den," continued Ching Ching.

Bill rang the bell, and the tea was ordered and partaken of.

Eddard's remarks were totally ignored, but he bore up against it as he did against other unfeeling acts. As for arguing, he was beginning to see that it was a waste of breath.

That night the Slapcrash boys had a grand time of it.

The fireworks they obtained were not the very best, and if exhibited at the Crystal Palace would not have staggered more than half the visitors, but they were fairly good.

In one sense it was a good thing that the rockets were second class, for Dick Cockles had his hat knocked off with one that rushed straight across the playground, finally going through the kitchen window and bringing down half-a-dozen dish-covers hung upon the wall.

Billy Pink, too, got his head singed by the red fire, which did not burn so briskly as it ought to have done, and as he was blowing it the stuff suddenly flared up and did him some damage, but nothing serious.

The town boys gathered outside and cheered, and crackers and squibs were thrown over to them, so that they had a little fun on their own account.

Then Sam Fusby, who had become a very quiet boy, brought out a brass cannon he had hoarded up for many a day, and it was loaded with powder by Dick Cockles, who wanted to hear a good report, so he rammed the powder well home.

And a good report there was.

It made the windows in the street rattle, and Dick Cockles was seen to fall.

They picked him up, and he gaspingly said that he had received his death-blow through the waistcoat, but he was not so much hurt, although the cannon had burst, and only small fragments of it were ever seen again.

A glorious evening, followed with a feast in bed, the like of which for variety and quantity had never been seen there before.

More festivity at the White Hart, too. A night that kept the waiters going, and made the landlord thank his stars that he had made the acquaintance of Ching Ching.

Eddard, just a bit on, got quarrelsome, and showed his teeth to the head waiter, who put himself under Ching Ching's protection and thus escaped annihilation.

Toasts were drunk. Ching Ching said he had never seen a place like Smockley. Everybody there was as a brother to him, and he hoped he would never be forgotten.

"Not likely!" shrieked the guests.

Ah! it was a night. The records of it will be handed down from father to son.

It was past midnight when the revellers went home, pleased and proud of the too brief hours they had spent with the man who was unique in their eyes, as in the rest of his admirers.

Everybody wanted a photograph of Sammy, and they all asked Bill Grunt to run down and spend the Christmas with them, while Ching Ching was implored to honour them with another visit.

At last the revel came to an end, as everything does in this moving world of ours.

The night passed, and morning came. With it a telegram, asking Ching Ching to go to town at once. He wired back that he would come by the twelve o'clock train.

He wished the precise time of his leaving not to be known, but it got abroad, and the scene at the station was not one likely to be forgotten.

All the Slapcrashers were there, Mr. Fossil Bone, Mrs. Grumps, Billy Pink, and a lot of the townsfolk.

So was Duffy.

He had been handed over to Mr. Bone pending certain inquiries into the treatment he had experienced at the hands of Mr. B. Rord Beans.

The High Art Academy was as good as broken up. Its head had disappeared, and Mrs. Beans had got into trouble through assaulting the bailiff with a poker.

The train rolled in, and Ching Ching embraced his son before the eyes of his admirers.

Then came a general leave-taking.

Sammy, Bill Grunt, Eddard, Posey, and Jack Cardigan—they all had to be parted from, and quickly, too.

In two minutes it was over, then the train rolled away, with the head of the Immortal One thrust from the window, and Posey's noble countenance just underneath it.

Above these was the dark hand of Sammy and the cocoanut fist of Bill Grunt waving handkerchiefs.

So they were borne away, and with the sense of a heavy loss the crowd dispersed.

"A strange man—a remarkable man," mused Mr. Fossil Bone, as he slowly sauntered homeward; "uneducated, but of limitless knowledge and unbounded mental resource and confidence, that enables him to hold his own against the world."

CHAPTER XXVIII.

GETTING READY FOR THE BREAK-UP—ARRANGEMENTS FOR THE HOLIDAYS—AN AVALANCHE.

AFTER the departure of Ching Ching and his chums there was a lull—Smockley became quiet to dulness, and there was very little doing.

But at the school the boys had a distraction in the form of the preparations for that desirable time known as "breaking-up."

Every boy knows what goes on at these times, and to go into details would be superfluous.

The expected day slowly drew near, and again there was rough weather at Smockley.

More snow, and plenty of it. "Much more than their share," as Mr. Fossil Bone put it, for there was very little in other parts of the country.

Duffy was now a pupil of the school, his uncle making no demur to the transition so long as there was no increase in the charges.

It is astonishing what a change good food and pleasant company made in the boy.

He was not a Solomon, and never would be one, but in a plodding way he got through some of his lessons, and was forgiven the rest.

He had not forgotten the tricks played upon him, or that memorable fight with Dick Cockles.

Sometimes he would suddenly take to chuckling in a low tone, and when he was asked what was the matter he would say—"I was thinking of the time when Young Ching painted me," or "I was laughing over the fight I had with Cockles," which showed that he had no malice in him.

Mr. B Rord Beans had disappeared, and his mother was also gone. She levanted one night, leaving the bailiff who was in the house locked up in a back room where he slept. He had to get out the next day by the window.

Mrs. Beans had left Smockley for good; but it does not follow that either she or her son will entirely disappear from our story.

One day, within about a week of breaking up, Dick Cockles asked Young Ching where he was going to spend his holidays.

"Mostly up in town with my dad," was the reply.

"Can't you stop at my house?" asked Dick. "My father has got a London house, and lives there now. Jem Stager is coming for a week at least, and I thought of asking Mrs. Grumps to let Billy Pink have a holiday. He's one of us, you know, although he does clean the boots."

"It's kind of you to think of Billy," said Young Ching, "but what will your father and mother say?"

"I've got a letter here that will answer you," Dick replied.

He drew a crabbed-fisted epistle out of his pocket, and after slowly conning over the first page, pointed to a line or two at the bottom.

Young Ching read—

"You may ask the whole school if you like, and they'll be right welcome, but make a point of having the young Chinese gentleman and Master Pink."

The last line set Young Ching grinning.

"It's all right, Dick," he observed, "you may book me. Dad is sure to be busy, and he won't want me at his heels. I've to go one evening with Billy to a place called Harmony Hall, but I fancy I can do pretty much as I like with the rest of the time."

So it was settled that Young Ching should stay with the Cockles family during a part of his holidays, at least, and Young Ching thought it rather a jolly arrangement than otherwise.

When Billy heard of it he got into such an excited condition that Mrs. Grumps had to release him from duty for a few hours, lest he should break or spoil all the knives and forks in the house.

"Go into the playground and compose yourself, William," she said.

Billy had no objection to going into the playground, and he had it all to himself for a time.

It was about a quarter to twelve, and the sun was shining so brightly that it was thawing the snow in spite of the keen air.

But the ground was not particularly sloshy, for it froze in the shade.

Billy spent the first quarter-of-an-hour in blissful contemplation of the good time coming. He was aroused from his day-dream by the voice of Dick Cockles.

"What cheer, Billy?"

"School over?" asked Billy.

"Yes, I'm first out. What are you doing here?"

Billy explained.

"And you really will be glad to go home with me?" said Dick.

"I can't tell you what I think," replied Billy. "It makes me feel as if it couldn't be true."

He put his hand on Dick's shoulder, and Dick put his hand on Billy's.

Thus they stood for a few moments, regarding each other with looks of deep affection.

"I never was so happy before," observed Billy.

"It's what some poet chap I read of would call 'the crowning moment of our lives,'" replied Dick.

And as he spoke a crown was indeed put upon them.

Owing to the thawing effects of the sun, the snow on the roof of the school-house suddenly slipped and came down with a rush.

The boys heard it coming, and, looking up, beheld what appeared like a white cloud descending upon them.

The idea of running certainly entered their heads, but neither attempted it, and down came the avalanche, flooring Billy and knocking Dick into a sitting position.

Both were fairly smothered, and Dick, as he struggled from under the snow, heard a roar of laughter, while the familiar voice of Young Ching cried out—

"At it again, are you? Couldn't you let the snow on the roof alone?"

Spluttering and gasping, Dick fought his way out of the snow, and Young Ching scraped away the heap that was on the top of Billy, and lifted him to his feet just as he was on the point of choking.

"Oh! you two—you two!" observed Jem Stager. "Ye are verily the children of misfortune. Methinks the Fates have some untimely end in store for thee."

"They go about asking to be killed," said Young Ching, serenely. "Look where they were standing. Just where the snow fell heaviest and thickest, of course!"

"It was like an earthquake, wasn't it?" observed Billy to Dick.

"Yes," replied Dick, gravely, "but worse. Oh! lor, what a lot of snow I've got down my back!"

"Go and put on some dry things," said Young Ching, and the companions in misfortune disappeared.

"If they don't get into some messes together during the holidays," observed Jem Stager, as he took Young Ching's arm, "I'm a Dutchman."

"You are not a Dutchman," replied Young Ching, "and into messes they will get. But I want to talk to you a bit about Warren Fane. All you fellows know there is some secret surrounds him."

"Rather," said Jem.

"I guessed what it was, or something near it, before I had been here many days," said Young Ching. "Can't you hit upon it?"

"I've sometimes thought he was a cut above us," replied Jem.

"That's it, Jem; he's a big swell, and for some reason he's hidden away here. What that reason is, I fancy we shall soon learn. He had some letters this morning, and after he had read them I heard him say to Biron—'I sha'n't be much longer with you, Tom.'"

"He has behaved like a brick to us, and I for one shall be sorry when he's gone," said Jem.

"All I can say of him is that he is as good a fellow as ever lived," replied Young Ching.

"And about as good a thing as you could say," returned Jem. "By-the-way, old fellow, we must not break up without another visit to the old Manor House."

"Another midnight feast?"

"We can have it earlier—say ten o'clock—and the expense need not fall on the shoulders of one only. Let us subscribe for it—every fellow contribute what he can afford."

Young Ching thought the idea a good one, but he had also a notion that it would be a chilly affair, unless they could have a good fire on the hearth of the old banqueting hall.

This notion he laid before the boys that evening in the schoolroom when the idea of the feast was brought forward for general discussion.

"As for sitting and freezing," said Tom Biron, "there would be no fun in that, but how is the wood to be got there?"

"It's in the house," replied Young Ching. "There is no end of odd stuff about the place. Some of the rotten floors won't be the worse for burning, and there are worm-eaten trestles and planks in the outhouses which we could cut up with a saw."

The discussion of ways and means went on, and after a while the following arrangements were decided on—

A good saw was to be bought, and a pound of tallow candles, for lighting the place and greasing the aforesaid saw, were to be at once conveyed to the place.

Half-a-dozen boys, as they could get away, were to go in the evening and take their turn at cutting up the old wood.

The food and drink were to be conveyed to the place at the time required by " good old Dossy Dodge " and his cousin the champion sweep.

The feast was to take place on the evening previous to their departure from school.

Young Ching selected the time, and gave a reason for it.

"It has always been the practice of Fossil Bone," he said, "never to punish or take notice of anything a boy may do within twenty-four hours of the breaking-up. I may say that we have never taken advantage of it, and I don't want to do so now, but in case of any little accident—well—you comprenny, dear boys."

They did comprehend, and approved of the arrangement, for all saw there was just a possibility of their being found out.

The last time they had a feast at the old Manor House they had a narrow escape, and it was just as well to provide for contingencies.

Of course, they had been many a time to the old place since, but their visits had, for the most part, been during their legitimate outings.

It was the fact of their going out so late that made it perilous.

They had nearly a fortnight in which to prepare, and a working committee of five was formed, with Young Ching for chairman.

They collected the funds, arranged the general expenditure, bought the saw and conveyed it to the Manor House, afterwards arranging the nightly parties of wood-cutters.

A lantern was provided to help the workers to journey across the loneliest part of their way in safety.

In short, nothing was omitted, as they thought, to make it a successful affair, and secure from interruption.

It was a jolly time, full of excitement and little bits of adventure, which gave food for many a jolly chat.

Dick Cockles, of course, got into ditches and other places calculated to bring him discomfort, and once he narrowly escaped being arrested by a Smockley policeman, whom he and Jem Stager ran against at midnight, when returning from their evening's work.

The policeman saw they were lads who had no business out at that hour, and thought he had got a couple of boys running away from home to deal with.

If he secured them he would certainly gain official honour, and possibly a reward.

Jem easily evaded the officer as he sprang out of a dark doorway, but the hand of the policeman knocked Dick's cap off, and in stooping to pick it up he was pounced upon.

Jem Stager acted as he always did, like a boy of resource, and charging the officer while he was in a stooping position, he bowled him over.

In falling the man let go of Dick, and like a scared rabbit released from a trap, he bolted off, nor paused to look back at Jem, who was trotting steadily behind him, until they reached the school-house garden.

Little incidents like this gave zest to the affair, and nothing very serious coming out of them, the final entertainment at the Manor House was so far unmarred.

In due time the evening came, and after a very light supper at eight o'clock, the boys, to the great wonderment and delight of Mrs. Grumps, expressed a desire to go to bed before the usual time.

" Which they are regular patterns," said the worthy old woman. " In course they wants to rest, so as to be ready for their journey to-morrow. Ah! it isn't offen you find old heads on young shoulders, but they ain't ordinary boys."

She had yet another source of delight in store for her. Billy Pink also asked leave to go to bed at nine instead of ten.

" It's like you, William, to follow a good example," she observed, " and I have hopes that you will do so all your days. Go to bed at once, like a good boy."

Which Billy did by walking straight out of the back door, to see that the playground and garden doors were in working order for exit and return.

CHAPTER XXIX.

THE FEAST AT THE MANOR HOUSE—A KNOCK AT THE DOOR—ABE BOTT THINKS HE IS AVENGED—THE BREAKING-UP.

IT was a bright starlight night, with a frosty air, as the boys, following their old tactics, made their way out of the town and across the intervening country to the old Manor House.

As the hour was comparatively early a few people were about, and to avoid all was next to impossible.

But nobody, as they believed, took any notice of them, and before the hour appointed had been announced by the cathedral clock they were all assembled in the banqueting hall.

On their arrival at the old Manor House they found the fire already lighted upon the hearth.

Dossy Dodge, or his cousin, had attended to this, and on either side there was a heap of logs ready for use when required.

On the banquet table were the packages of good things ordered for the occasion, only requiring arrangement.

This was the work of Jem Stager and Dan Mittens, the appointed stewards, and it was speedily performed.

There was a full supply of cakes, tarts, ham, beef, and tongue, with bottles of currant and ginger wine, lemonade and ginger beer having been voted too chilly for the occasion.

The old seats were there, and the boys sat down, with Young Ching and Warren Fane at either end, representing chairman and vice-chairman.

The fire on the hearth blazed gloriously, filling the banqueting hall with a mellow light, and the half-dozen candles on the board gave a fairly good supplementary illumination.

The suit of armour was in its old place, but it was very quiet now, there being no Young Ching inside it to lift the hair of the more timorous boys, as he had done on a previous occasion.

The boys had no plates or dishes, and the eatables were arranged on pieces of stiff cardboard, which did quite as well.

The wine had to be drunk out of mugs, footless glasses, and even egg-cups, anything, in short, each boy being his own provider in this respect.

But it lost none of its flavour through this primitive mode of drinking.

When the edge had been taken off the appetites created by the night air, Young Ching rose to his feet.

"Chums all," he said, "charge your glasses. I have a toast to propose."

The "glasses" were charged, and every eye was turned upon Young Ching, who stood in a graceful attitude, quite at his ease, and in every way a credit to his august father.

"Chums all," he repeated, "barring one, for a reason you will soon understand. I have a health to propose. We have one amongst us who, I have this day learnt, is about to leave us, never to return to the school, where I have during my brief stay enjoyed myself most scrumptiously."

"Hear—hear," cried Jem Stager, and there was a rattle of drinking cups upon the table.

"As a school," continued Young Ching, "it is far from perfect, of course, but it is not a bad one in its way. Anyhow, I have no doubt it is better than it was when that old ruffian Slapcrash was at the head of it."

"Rather, I should think so—not to be named in the same year with the old Slap-crashers," observed Jem Stager.

"Well, passing that over," continued Young Ching, "I will come to the subject of my toast. Need I eulogise him? Need I say one word as to his merits? Chums all—Warren Fane!"

The boys leaped with one accord to their feet, and there were cries of "Warren Fane!" as the lads toasted him in their innocent and harmless liquor.

The object of this demonstration sat quietly at the foot of the table until order was restored.

His face was rather pale, and there was a sad expression in his eyes as he rose to his feet.

He stood before the boys, a noble specimen of English youth, and during the few moments that intervened before he began his reply his dark eyes wandered from face to face, until he had given all a look that was not forgotten by many for a long time afterwards.

"Dear boys," he said, "I did not expect what has just taken place. But, believe me, I am grateful for it, and I thank you with all my heart. It was a surprise to me, and now, if you will have a few moments' patience, I will say a few words concerning myself."

He paused, and the boys were so still that the ticking of a watch that Tom Biron wore, Warren Fane's gift, could be heard.

IN HIS EXCITEMENT HE DASHED AGAINST SOME TUBS OF BUTTER AND BROUGHT THEM
DOWN LIKE THE WALLS OF JERICHO.

"I cannot tell you precisely who I am," Warren Fane continued, "nor is my name of any great importance just now. No doubt you will learn it ere long. If I had permission to tell you all I would, but what I can impart I now give to you."

He paused again, with his eyes resting on the table and a troubled look upon his face. After a palpable struggle with his emotions he looked up.

"I am," he said, "what the world calls of aristocratic birth; although I do not myself recognise anything aristocratic that is not noble or good. But let that pass. I am the heir to vast wealth and a great name, and a man has sworn that I shall never inherit either.

"I have no father," continued Warren Fane; "he died three years ago. He was a good and a brave man, but he did not escape making an enemy. Who does? His greatest enemy is the man who threatens to take my life.

"He did not openly threaten it," Warren Fane went on, with a gesture of scorn. "He knew the law would take notice of that—not he! But he hurled his threats in private at my dear devoted mother, who loves me as mothers always love an only child.

"But for her," he continued, with flashing eyes, "I would have defied this man or monster, who puts assassins on my track, and does it, I do not doubt, so that in case of my death at their hands he will go scot free. Alone! boy as I am, I would have proclaimed his infamy to the world, but with a gentle, loving, timorous mother, what could I do? At her bidding I have gone hither and thither under an assumed name, to light at last upon this place, where I have found such friends as I hope I shall have as—long as I live."

There was a sadness in his voice as he uttered these last words, as if he had a prophetic vision of his enemy prevailing.

Then he sat down, and the next moment Tom Biron was on his feet.

"Boys," he said, "one word. You have heard our dear chum's story as far as he has permission to tell it. I have nothing to add to it because I know no more than you, but I wish to say this, that if anything happens to him—"

Cries of "No—no—never—it can't be," interrupted him. When silence was restored he went on—

"Let us all hope and pray it will not be, but if his enemy, whoever he is, should prevail, I here vow that as far as my poor efforts go I will give my life to avenge him. The murderer shall not go scot free."

Then Young Ching sprang up, saying—

"His enemy shall not win the day if it is in my power, even at the cost of my life, to prevent him."

A scene of excitement followed, the boys springing to their feet, and one and all crying out that they would, each in his small way, stand by Warren Fane.

In heart the boys were all right, but what they could do physically when called upon remains to be seen.

The noise they made in their enthusiasm was subsiding, and Jem Stager had just risen to his feet when all were startled by a loud knocking at the door.

A look of alarm sprang into the faces of some of the younger boys, and they were leaving their seats in a panic when the voice of Young Ching was heard.

"Steady, lads," he said; "somebody has found us out, but if you keep cool all will be well." Here another knock was heard. "All right—we will attend to you in a moment. Chums, they are at the main door, which is some distance from our way out—keep cool! Douse the lights, pocket what is left, for consumption at home, and follow me."

Quietude was quickly restored, the candles were blown out, and as the fire had now sunk to a glowing mass, the hall was in semi-darkness.

On tiptoe, headed by Young Ching, the boys started for the postern door.

Rap—rap!

"Open the door there. We must come in. It is the police."

The boys heard the voice, and knew by its official tone that there was no shamming. It was the police, and their position was very serious.

"Now, boys," said Tom Biron, in a low tone, "all depends on your coolness. Unfortunately, the moon is up by this time, and if we are to get away safely we must be as wary as Indian scouts."

Young Ching softly opened the door and peeped out.

The moon was up, and by its light he could see four men at the great hall door.

Three were members of the police force, and the fourth was Abe Bott, the ex-champion sweep.

"It's Abe Bott that's got hold of our being here," whispered Young Ching. "He has brought the police on us."

"The hour of his revenge has come," said Jem Stager, "but shall he prevail? No—perish the thought!"

"Be quiet, Jem," interrupted Tom Biron. "The only chance—(knocking again)—the only chance we have is to slip out and keep close to the wall until we get round the end of the house—then make a run for it."

"That's the plan," assented Young Ching. "You lead the way. I'll stay behind and see all out. (Hammering again.) We must be smart. They will be coming round in this direction presently to find a way to get in."

Tom Biron did not stay to discuss the order of going, although he saw that Young Ching had taken up the post of honour, and therefore the position of the greatest danger.

He slipped out, and the rest followed one by one.

They went quietly on, with no appearance of alarm or haste, and were all outside but Young Ching and Jem Stager, when Abe Bott's voice was heard.

"There they go, sneaking out by the little door."

"Run for it now," said Young Ching; "hurry up there in front."

The other boys had taken the alarm, and there was a stampede homewards.

Young Ching looked back, and saw Abe Bott and the three police approaching at a heavy trot.

"Barring accidents," he thought, "we can outrun them ten yards in every hundred."

He started off, and Abe Bott, recognising the hatless head of Young Ching, uttered a shout—

"That's young pigtail!" he roared; "pinch him, if you let the rest go."

———

CHAPTER XXX.

THERE'S MANY A SLIP—THE BREAKING-UP—OFF
AND AWAY.

YOUNG CHING had allowed Jem Stager to get on ahead, but as the dramatic youth was hurrying up some of the least fleet of foot he could speedily be overtaken.

With a light step Young Ching ran down the old terrace of the Manor House, and as he turned the corner he saw a plank about ten feet long leaning against the wall.

Immediately it flashed upon him that this might be utilised with advantage.

Taking it in his hands, he waited for the approach of the pursuers.

He heard their heavy feet advancing, and just as Abe Bott, who was foremost, came within a few feet of the corner, Young Ching tossed the plank right in his path.

Bott had not time to pull up, nor did he possess sufficient agility to leap over the obstacle so suddenly thrust in his way.

He tripped over it and fell heavily—the Smockley policemen close behind piling themselves upon him with crushing effect.

Delighted with the success of this little manœuvre, Young Ching hurried off after his friends, who were well on towards the canal.

He could see them, a straggling body, each doing his level best to get back to the school without delay.

No mishap seemed to have befallen them, and as a matter of fact even Dick Cockles and Billy Pink escaped everything in the form of disaster.

As Tom Biron reached the bottom of South-street he heard the cathedral clock chiming half-past eleven.

It was late enough in all conscience, but not so late as he thought.

"I hope Fossil Bone is in bed," he said to Warren Fane, who was close behind him.

Perforce the boys on entering the town had to drop into a walk, so as not to attract the attention of the few worthies they were likely to meet on their way home from the White Hart and other places of social entertainment.

Nobody interfered with them, and eventually the foremost party reached the garden gate.

Tom Biron tried it.

It was fast.

"Bowled out this time," he said, "and done for."

"It can't be helped," replied Warren Fane; "after all it isn't a hanging matter."

The boys speedily gathered up behind, each in his turn dismayed by the intelligence of the fastened door.

Young Ching and Jem Stager were the last to arrive.

"Here, give me a leg up," observed Young Ching; "I'll get over the wall and let you in."

"Pray don't trouble to do that," a quiet voice interposed; "the front door is open."

It was Mr. Fossil Bone.

He had just emerged from the house, and

the light in the hall sent its rays into the street.

He stood in the line of light, and they could see that his face was unusually stern.

There was no help for it, the boys had to face the music, and in solemn silence they filed into the hall.

"Take off your boots, put on your slippers, and come up to the schoolroom," said Mr. Fossil Bone. "I will talk to you there."

He went up first, leaving them to pull off their boots, as directed. This they did, pulling very long faces at the same time.

Perhaps the only boys who were not particularly troubled were Young Ching and Warren Fane.

They led the way upstairs, where Mr. Fossil Bone was seated at his desk. A fire was burning in the grate.

"Take your usual places," he said. "Pink, you stand by my desk."

"He's going to have the first cut at me with a stick or something," thought Billy.

"Boys," continued Mr. Fossil Bone, in a tone both quiet and grave, "I was astonished and pained to-night when I learnt from the police that you had all gone out of the town. The man who called here did not know where you were gone, and I must now ask you to enlighten me on this point."

There was a moment's silence, and then Tom Biron arose.

"I will tell you the whole truth, sir," he said.

This he did, and as he proceeded it was clear to the boys who watched Mr. Fossil Bone closely that he was in a measure relieved.

But he still remained very grave.

Mr. Fossil Bone remarked, when Tom had told the story in well-chosen words—

"You have done wrong, very wrong, but it is not so bad as I thought. I feared you had got into queer company, as boys often did, I regret to say, in my time, when schools were rough, and the manners of the people coarser."

He paused and rested his eyes for a few moments on the fire, then he looked round again at the expectant faces lifted up to his.

"To-morrow," he said, "we break up, and it has ever been a rule of mine not to punish offenders within twenty-fours of their going. This is the only reason why you will escape punishment for what you have done. It must never occur again, remember—and now go to rest."

They could have cheered him, but they felt it would be out of place just then.

With commendable quietude they filed out of the room and went off to bed.

"It's a blessed thing we've got a man of feeling at the head of this school," said Jem Stager, as he proceeded to undress, "otherwise some of us would now be wriggling a bit."

"I knew we were safe," replied Young Ching, "but the Manor House business is all over, which is a pity."

"Don't jaw, boys," said Tom Biron; "to bed and to sleep, that is our best watchword to-night."

Ere they got to sleep they heard a ringing at the door, and guessed it was the police.

They wondered what Mr. Fossil Bone would say to them, and as others may be curious on that point, what took place may here be given.

It was the police, or one of them—the inspector—and he had come to report what the boys had done.

Mr. Fossil Bone listened quietly, and then observed—

"They have been guilty of trespass, I believe?"

"Yes, sir?"

"Whose property is it?"

"It is in Chancery, sir."

"Then report it to the Court of Chancery, and let it take proceedings. Here are five shillings towards the police fund. Good-night."

"Good-night, sir."

The inspector had a police fund of his own, into which the five shillings went, and no other officer ever heard a word about it.

Nor was there much more heard about the trespass the boys had undoubtedly been guilty of.

The school broke up next day, and the people of Smockley were too glad of a prospect of peace to make any bother about the affair. The Manor House was nobody's property, and nobody had a right to complain.

In all directions went the boys.

Tom Biron, Warren Fane, Young Ching, Billy Pink, Jem Stager, and Dick Cockles went to London together, to part at the terminus.

Young Ching and Billy were bound for Harmony Hall, there to spend the evening with the Great Ching Ching and certain of his chums.

On the morrow they were to meet Jem Stager and Dick Cockles and go to the home of the latter, a visit that was destined in more ways than one to be memorable.

Tom Biron and Warren Fane departed together in a hansom cab, neither stating where they were going, nor were they asked.

"It is no affair of ours," said Young Ching, "and we are sure to see or hear of them before the holidays are over."

So they were, but in a way far different from that which he anticipated.

CHAPTER XXXI.

THE VISIT TO DICK COCKLES—ARRIVAL AT THE SHOP—BUTTER DOWN AGAIN—THE COCKLES FAMILY.

YOUNG CHING and Billy Pink, after having spent the evening with the Immortal father of the former, slept at an hotel in the Strand, where everything was very comfortable, and, in Billy's eyes, magnificent.

Poor old Billy! It was indeed a great thing for him to be in London, with every comfort around him. No wonder he felt like one in a dream.

He slept in a big bed, that would have accommodated half-a-dozen of his size, and was awoke in the morning by a deferential waiter.

"If you please, sir," he said, "breakfast will be ready in half-an-hour. Shall I help you to dress?"

It was the first time in his life that Billy had been called "sir," and it fairly took his breath away.

As for an offer to be helped with his toilet he was rather disposed to resent it.

The last time he received such an offer it came from his mother, and was sarcastic—

"Are you going to get up, Billy, or shall I come and help dress you?"

That was the way she spoke, and it was a gentle hint to the too somnolent Billy that he had better get up. Help from her would have been open-handed.

Here was a waiter making the same offer, and evidently doing it seriously. Even as he spoke he began to arrange Billy's things upon a chair.

"I don't think I'll trouble you," said Billy.

"No trouble, sir," replied the waiter, as he turned Billy's trousers over the back of a chair.

This movement caused a lot of little items to shoot out of his pockets, among which marbles, brass buttons, and various bits of metal were prominent.

"Beg pardon, sir," observed the man. "I wasn't aware you had anything in 'em."

"I think I would rather dress myself," Billy said.

"Very well, sir," replied the waiter, and vanished in a twinkling.

Billy looked around him and felt that he had been transported to another world.

Everything in his eyes was on such a magnificent scale.

The water-jugs and basins alone were worth walking a dozen miles to see.

"And I owe it all to Young Ching—bless him!" thought Billy.

Having poured out some water with great care, so as not to spill any on the carpet, he performed his ablutions and dressed himself as fast as he could be expected to do under the circumstances.

When he arrived at the hotel the night before he was very tired and sleepy.

He saw very little of it, except as a sleepy boy does, through a sort of haze, but now it was all clear before him.

"It's like a fairy tale," he mused, as he buttoned on his collar. "What would my dad and mother and sisters say to it? They would fall right down on the flat of their backs and lay there until they were picked up again."

Having finished his dressing, he opened the door and looked out.

Yes, he just remembered coming along that landing, but where he was to go to now he could not tell.

While trying to solve this problem, the polite attendant came bounding up the stairs.

"Breakfast quite ready. I will show you the way, sir," he said.

Billy followed him down to a room below, where there were at least a dozen tables laid out in royal style, or Billy thought so.

Several people were scattered about partaking of breakfast, and seated by a roaring fire was Young Ching, coolly reading the morning paper.

"How did you sleep, Billy?" he asked, in the off-hand way of an old chum. "Waiter, will you serve breakfast now?"

The waiter, who had been looking at Young Ching with great deference, replied—"Yes sir, certainly sir," and disappeared.

But only for a moment, when he returned with a coffee-pot, and placed it on a table by the fire.

" Now, Billy," said Young Ching in an undertone, " just pull yourself together, and don't stare about you as if this were the Chamber of Horrors."

" All right, Ching," said Billy, " but I say —is—is—the Queen here?"

" Your grandmother is here—sit down," retorted Young Ching.

Billy got through his breakfast somehow, noting in the midst of his amazement that the waiter appeared to stand in awe of Young Ching.

The other visitors also regarded him with a wondering expression of face, but he was indifferent to it all.

He ate his breakfast like an old traveller, and through him Billy managed to get outside a good meal, but had he been alone he would have eaten very little.

" Dad won't be able to see us to-day," said Young Ching, after breakfast was over, " so we must amuse ourselves as well as we can until three o'clock."

" Yes," replied Billy; " but I am already amused. Did you ever—"

" No, I didn't," quickly interposed Young Ching, " and it would not have mattered if I did. Jem Stager will be here about three o'clock, and then we will go together to Dick Cockles' house."

" Do you know where it is, Ching?"

" I've got the address, and I'll soon find it. Now, Billy, what shall we do this morning to kill the time?"

He stood upon the hearth-rug, with his back to the fire and his hands behind his back —a petrifying figure to the waiters and some of the guests.

" I'll do anything you like," replied Billy.

" Waiter," said Young Ching, " is there anything going on just now?"

The waiter could not speak for a moment. He shuffled some of the dirty plates together and looked blankly at the speaker.

" Anything going on, waiter?"

" Yes sir—no sir—lots of things—Christmas season, sir—all in the paper, sir."

" Thank you," replied Young Ching. " Now, Billy, are you ready? We will go out and have a look round. Waiter, a hansom, please."

More delight to Billy—a ride in a hansom. Young Ching told the man to give them an hour's run round the West-end, and the man was taking them up Regent-street, when Young Ching said to Billy—

" You really must be more a man of the world. What would have become of us if I had funked that hotel business as you did?"

" It was all so new to me," pleaded Billy.

" So it may have been," returned Young Ching; " but you needn't let people see it. Those waiter fellows tried their familiar dodge on me at first, but I soon sat upon them—I asked for the manager."

" Who?" exclaimed Billy.

" The manager—the head of the place. ' I want to know,' I said, ' if I am to be attended upon or not, or if there is any doubt about my bill being paid.' That scared them. I also told them not to try any of their games on you, or I would soon let them know what o'clock it was."

" It was very kind of you, Ching," replied Billy. " I wondered what caused the fellow to be so kind. He made me feel as if I were a duke."

" They will charge duke's prices for you," said Young Ching, coolly, " and whoever you are they have a right to keep their place. Hang their cheek! ' Ah! going to stay here long?' said one to me. I got out that old eye-glass of mine, Billy, I fixed it in my eye, and I looked at him until he gradually went in like a snail into its shell. You must stand up for yourself, Billy, or the world will make mincemeat of you."

All this and much more did Young Ching impart to Billy Pink, for his education and edification.

How he profited by it his future career will tell.

They had a good long drive together, and then a walk.

When they got out of the cab the driver tried the game of imposition on Young Ching.

" My fare's ten bob, young 'un," he said.

" Your fare is half-a-crown, old 'un," replied Young Ching, " but as it is Christmas time there is three shillings for you. If you don't like to take that give me your number."

" You wasn't born yesterday," observed cabby.

He took the money and drove away.

No great adventure or anything very stirring happened to the boys before they got back to the hotel to dinner.

Billy naturally distinguished himself in a small way.

He got into people's way, and slipped up in Bond-street as he was crossing the road, narrowly escaping being made into pumpkin-squash by an omnibus.

Young Ching attracted a good deal of attention, and two or three smart errand-boys tried their little jokes on him.

One and all repented their folly.

"He's got a knuckle-duster on—he must have," muttered one, as he ambled off with his hand to his nose.

Young Ching had no knuckle-duster, but he had good knuckles and the knack of using them. That was all.

The boys found a message awaiting them. It was from Young Ching's august father. He had dictated it to an astonished waiter, who wrote it on a menu-card.

"Be melly while you can, dear boys."

There was also an envelope, which, on being opened, was found to contain a crisp five-pound note.

"I'll make a hole in this," said Young Ching. "Dick's got a lot of brothers and sisters, and a package of toys would not be amiss."

A visit to the Lowther Arcade after dinner quite settled Billy.

He had never heard of, never dreamt of, such a host of toys.

No wonder he tripped over a wooden horse and fell into a tray of small things, such as beads and infants' tea-services, causing havoc to the tune of three and ninepence, which Young Ching had to pay.

However, beyond this Billy did no damage worth mentioning, and at the appointed hour Jem Stager turned up at the hotel and was hailed with exuberant delight.

Jem's people were Londoners—they lived Islington way—and he was to spend a day or two of his holidays with Dick Cockles, and afterwards run to and fro.

"Dad swears by the hair of his forefathers," said Jem to Young Ching, "that if you don't pay us a visit he will come and take you by main force, and, as becomes a Stager, he is a valiant knight."

The precise spot of Dick Cockles' home we are not going to specify. It was not a day's walk from the Elephant and Castle, Newington Causeway, and that is all we can say.

The elder Cockles has quite as much business as he can do, and he doesn't want us to work up a connection for him.

The boys agreed to walk thither, as Jem knew every inch of the way, and their luggage was to come on by a porter. Also the parcel of toys for the juvenile Cockles.

Dick was on the look-out for his old chums, and saw them ere they reached the shop.

He plunged forward and shook hands with them all round, gasping with joy.

Then he ran back to the shop.

It was a quiet part of the day, and Dick's father was taking a look round his stock when Dick dashed in, crying—

"Here they come, father!"

In his excitement he bounced against a pile of butter-tubs, some empty and some full, with a lot of tins on the top, and he brought them down, like the walls of Jericho, with a crash.

Mr. Cockles, a man of vast proportions and a slow thinker, did not for the moment grasp what had happened.

He thought that the engine of his patent sausage-machine, in the cellar below, had blown up, and a wild cry burst from his lips.

Then catching sight of several youngsters in the shop laughingly helping his son out of the ruins, he got a faint idea of what had really occurred.

"Why ain't you more careful, Dick?" he said; "but it's like all you boys of genius, you can't be held in—that's right, gentlemen, pick him up—never mind the boxes, I'll send a man to look arter them. Come into the back parlour. Welcome and hearty are you all!"

Dick was got out from the wreck, not a little bewildered by his fall, and, rubbing his elbows and knees, he followed the rest behind the counter, and through the door opened by his father.

Mr. Cockles, breathing hard, as if he had also fallen, shook hands with them, and then rang a bell twice.

"That's the signal for Mrs. Cockles," he said.

Mrs. Cockles was obedient to the signal, and came hurrying in—a broad-faced, cheery woman, who kissed the three boys as if she had been their mother—and in a twinkling had some currant wine and biscuits on the table.

"Which you be quite wore out, and must want something."

In vain they assured her that they had no need of anything.

"You've got to have it," she observed.

"It is man's nature," added Mr. Cockles, "to be kep' up with wittles and drink."

Not being in a position to deny this well-known fact, they partook of a glass of wine

"BROAD BEANS, AS I LIVE!" EJACULATED YOUNG CHING.

and a biscuit, and were then invited upstairs to what was called the " company room."

"All the children are waiting for you," said Mrs. Cockles.

Then they went upstairs—all but Mr. Cockles, who returned to the shop.

There they all were.

One girl older than Dick, and all the rest of the boys and girls younger.

How many there were Young Ching did not count, but he was told that there were two sets of twins, and the family likeness between them was amazing.

Even the baby, fighting playfully in the arms of a nursemaid, was a small edition of Dick.

At first they were shy with the strange boys, but Billy Pink at once set to work to fraternise with them.

Young Ching and Jem Stager looked after the elder girls, and were soon on an amicable footing with them.

Billy, being a born lover of babies, must needs nurse the younger Cockles, and begin to dance with it.

Ere long he stumbled over a stool, and down he went with the baby, apparently rolling over it.

"Oh! dear, he's killed it," screamed Mrs. Cockles.

"No, ma'am," replied Billy, "the baby hasn't been touched."

And there it was, laughing and crowing like anything, in proof of what he said.

But Billy's task as a nurse came to an end.

What a noise they made—romping, laughing, and dancing—until Mr. Cockles sent up word that a bit of plaster had been shaken off the ceiling right into a newly-opened tub of prime Irish butter.

After that they were a little quieter, but not much.

Young Ching and Jem Stager acted as Brutus and Cassius, and the girls said it was lovely.

Jem really alarmed them when he drew out his pocket-knife and rapped out—

> " *There is my dagger,*
> *And here my naked breast; within, a heart*
> *Dearer than Plutus' mine, richer than gold:*
> *If that thou be'st a Roman, take it forth:*
> *Strike, as thou didst at Cæsar.*"

"Oh, don't!" cried Polly, the second girl, jumping up; "he doesn't mean it."

Then they all laughed, but Jem was pleased,

for Polly's anxiety was a tribute to his power of acting, and he liked her the better of the two.

"After tea," said Dick, "I'll bring out my stage and show you how to work the 'Maid and the Magpie.' Dad's bought it complete."

"I daresay we shall get some fun out of it," returned Young Ching, quietly; "better get Billy to help you."

"I'll do the best I can," said Billy.

"Then the success of the show is assured," observed Jem Stager.

"Of course you must cut in," growled Dick; "but it's all right. I'll talk to you when we are outside my dad's house."

"That's right, Dick," said Young Ching; "if Jem says another word to you I'll take him in hand."

Then Young Ching and Jem exchanged a wink, and tea was commenced.

CHAPTER XXXII.

A VERY PLEASANT EVENING.

TEA was laid in a room at the back part of the house, and it was, as Jem said, "a gorgeous banquet."

The Cockles family evidently lived well, for there were no signs to show that the table was anything unusual.

In sausages alone the variety to Billy Pink was quite bewildering.

"And you may eat 'em freely," said Mr. Cockles, who appeared at the table, "for they are all our own make. We know what is in 'em."

He was evidently a good-humoured man, and his faith in Dick's abilities and learning was wonderful.

To Young Ching, who sat next to him, he was continually putting questions about the progress his son made at Slapcrash School.

"Goes ahead like a house a-fire, I'll bet," he observed.

"Dick does his best," replied Young Ching.

"Up in his jography and can read any writing."

"Dick shines more as a reader than anything else."

"Not many like him in the school?"

"Not one."

"Ha—ha!" roared Mr. Cockles, "I knew it. Dick says he's a bit of a fool, but that's because he's a modest boy. Try a bit of that 'ere polony. Let me see, your father is a tamarind, isn't he?"

"A what?" exclaimed Young Ching.

"A tamarind—a Chinee potentator."

"Oh! a mandarin. Yes, he's as good as one."

"Dick said he was a tamarind—or I thought so. Maybe I didn't take notice as much as I ought. Don't be afraid of that polony. It's as mild as milk. Dick's at the top of his class, ain't he?"

"He's always there or thereabout," replied Young Ching, and Cockles senior roared again.

Young Ching was not going to undeceive the generous-hearted man.

What did it matter? Dick in due time would come into the sausage business, and the education he was getting was good enough for that or for most businesses.

Tea over, they again adjourned to the front room, some of the smaller fry being quietly taken off to bed.

Then Dick got out his stage, and he made Billy give him a hand in getting it ready.

Need we record the mess they made of it?

How they upset the lamps, knocked over the show, and finally set fire to it when the first scene was on?

No, that sort of thing was inevitable, and, faithful to their instincts, they carried it out.

Cockles senior, with two bangs of his big hands, put out the fire, but he squashed the show at the same time.

"It's a gimcrack thing, Dick," he said, "and I'll get you something more solid next time."

After that the girls went to the piano and played, while their father beat time.

Then Jem Stager let out that he sometimes sang at home, and he gave them a comic song which made them all roar.

After that Young Ching sang one of his father's Chinese ditties, amidst great enthusiasm, and Billy Pink obliged with his father's song, which was known as "The Farmer's Boy."

Dick was going to sing too, but having choked himself with a piece of apple, his father thought he ought to reserve his vocal efforts for another evening.

At supper time two or three neighbours dropped in. They all ate a lot but talked little, and for the most part could not keep their eyes off Young Ching.

It was just when a lull for a moment took place that one of them said to him—

"Born in China, young gentleman, I suppose?"

"No," replied Young Ching.

"His father is a bandoline," observed Cockles senior.

"Good gracious! what's that?" asked Mrs. Cockles.

"Mandarin," explained Young Ching.

"Ah! certainly," observed the guest, who had not the faintest idea of what was meant.

Altogether it was a very jolly evening, and it was arranged that on the morrow the boys should rest during the day and go to some theatre in the evening.

Mr. Cockles could not go, but Mrs. Cockles would arrange to accompany them, and they were to have seats in the upper boxes.

Drury Lane was the playhouse chosen.

"I'll send early for the tickets," Mr. Cockles said. "My man will be up that way about ten o'clock. There is nothing like a first night at a pantomime."

So the boys thought—the noise alone was worth the money.

Tired and happy, the boys went to bed, and if their surroundings were not quite so gorgeous as at the hotel, they were even more comfortable.

Mrs. Cockles, to Young Ching's great amusement, tucked them all in, and as the boys were obliged, owing to the size of the Cockles family, to occupy one large room, it made it all the merrier.

When she was gone they were quiet for awhile, all being disposed to sleep.

Suddenly Billy Pink asked—

"What is all that row in the street—is anybody being killed?"

"It's only the usual noise," replied Dick, sleepily.

"Oh! you get out!"

"It's a fact—ask Jem."

Jem said it was nothing unusual. The streets were never quiet in London.

"I'm blessed!" was all Billy could say.

Every hour brought him some new wonder to dwell upon, and while he was thinking of this he fell asleep.

———

CHAPTER XXXIII.

A FOGGY DAY—AT THE PLAY—DOGGING HIM
TO THE END.

WHEN the boys awoke in the morning they found it was still dark, but Dick, after carefully listening for a few seconds, said it was quite nine o'clock.

" It isn't light," said Billy.

" I reckon it's a fog," replied Dick.

Then he jumped out of bed and pulled the curtain aside.

" Yes : it's a fog—a whopper—black as ink !" Dick cried.

" It's a nice look-out for the play !" groaned Stager.

To Billy Pink a London " particular " was a novelty, and he could hardly believe that the day had really come.

But facts are things that cannot be denied.

It was half-past nine when they went down to breakfast, and all the others had got through their meal an hour before.

Mrs. Cockles was laying the table for them, and gave them a hearty " good-morning."

" We thought it better to let you sleep," she observed.

She made no reference to the fog, but Billy Pink had got it on the brain.

Sitting there, eating and drinking by gas-light, he could not quite make it out.

Two or three times he got up and had a look into the street.

He could see nothing except a faint glare of the gaslights about, but he could hear the slow traffic, with the warning cries of pedestrians and drivers.

Now and then a flickering light would move along, which Dick told him were links carried by boys, and if the fog held there would be a lot at the theatre that night.

After breakfast Mr. Cockles took the boys to see his famous chopping-machine, or rather machines.

There were a dozen of them, all kept going with a small two-horse power engine, the like of which, he firmly believed, was not to be found in the wide world.

It amused the boys for an hour, and then they went up to the shop, where three men were busy getting the things in order.

" The fog's lifting a bit," said Mr. Cockles, with a glance at the street.

It must have been lifting very little, for the people going by were no more than spectres— misty beings cautiously groping their way.

Billy Pink only went one step outside the shop, to get a look at the fog, when a man fell over him, knocking his head with some severity against the shop door-post.

" You little beast !" he hissed, aiming a blow at Billy, and then he vanished in the gloom.

" You boys had better keep indoors," said Mr. Cockles ; " to-night, if it gets no better, you will have to go in a cab, an hour early."

" I told you we should not stop at home," said Dick ; " we Londoners don't think much of a bit of fog."

" Is there such a thing as a whole one ?" asked Billy.

" Yes, and a whole one and a-half," replied Jem ; " this is almost a clear day."

As the hours went by the fog did clear a little, and by dinner-time you could see nearly ten yards from the door.

Afterwards it lifted more and more, until only an ordinary fog, such as country people can understand, filled the streets.

The tickets for the theatre had been got somehow, and at six o'clock a cab came to the door.

The boys, the two elder girls, and Mrs. Cockles were ready, and away they went, a very respectable cab-load.

" I call this jolly," said Billy Pink, who was squeezed like a sardine in a corner.

Young Ching and Jem sat with Billy, their backs to the horses. Mrs. Cockles had the two girls beside her, and Dick stood.

That is, he stood sometimes, for whenever the cab stopped, as it did about every fifty yards or so, he staggered and fell into his mother's lap, to be righted with an " Oh ! dear, Dick ! what are you doing ?"

At last the theatre was reached, and then the fog was nothing to speak of, but there were a lot of people in the street who had been unable to get into the pit or gallery.

Our party passed into the main entrance and so to their seats aloft, Billy Pink in a semi-dazed state, uttering not a word.

What has he ever conceived at all approaching the inside of a theatre—the orchestra, the seething pit, the roaring gallery !

He turned and looked at Young Ching in a helpless sort of maner, and got a reassuring nod by way of reply.

After some little trouble they found their seats, and then it was discovered that one of them was occupied by a stranger.

He was a man of foreign aspect, wearing a coat buttoned close up to his chin, and as the performance had not begun he was still wearing his hat—a dark soft felt one.

At first he did not seem disposed to obey the courteous attendant's request to give up his seat, but on looking round and seeing the party waiting, he rose with some precipitation and passed out.

As he went past them he turned his face away, but to Young Ching there was something familiar in the form of the man, and he looked closely at him.

" The very same !" he muttered.

" What's that ?" asked Jem Stager.

" I'll tell you when we sit down," replied Young Ching.

Mrs. Cockles was accommodated with a centre seat in front, the girls on either side of her.

The boys sat immediately behind, in a row.

Young Ching stood up for a moment and ran his eye round the upper boxes.

" What's up ?" asked Jem.

" You remember that foreign fellow who attacked Warren Fane ?" replied Young Ching.

" I heard of him, but I never set eyes on him."

" He's here to-night."

" Here ! Where ?"

" The fellow who passed out a few moments ago is the man."

" What an odd thing we should meet him here ?"

" Very, and rum things do happen in this world. I am beginning to find that out already."

Jem Stager looked rather troubled, but Polly turning to ask him to let her look at the programme, his thoughts were diverted in another direction.

They looked at it together, and so far as Jem was concerned the foreigner was forgotten.

Young Ching also ceased to bother about him, and talked to the eldest girl until the curtain rose upon the new and gorgeous pantomime.

Then the stage naturally engaged his attention, but he did not become entirely absorbed in it.

The face of the foreigner kept appearing before him in spite of himself.

He remembered it as he saw it at Smockley, with its dark malignant eyes—once seen never forgotten.

He had not seen those eyes that night, only the profile of the man, but that was enough, and somehow he fancied his grim presence there boded ill.

His gaze wandered from the stage round the house.

Nearly opposite them was an empty box close to the stage—the only one, as far as he could see, in the whole house.

" I wonder if anybody is coming to it ?" he muttered.

" Coming where ?" asked Jem.

" That box," replied Young Ching; " the empty one—why, there's somebody entering it now, Jem ; do you see who it is ?"

" That's Warren Fane in evening rig-out," whispered Jem. " What a manly fellow he looks !"

" And that handsome woman, with such beautiful jewels, must be his mother; but who is the third one ?—it's—"

" Tom Biron," the boys observed together.

CHAPTER XXXIV.

THE ATTACK ON WARREN FANE.

YOUNG CHING and Jem were speaking in a low tone, and the others were too absorbed in the spectacle upon the stage to heed what they said, which was just as well perhaps.

" Jem," whispered Young Ching, " it is just what I fancied—that foreign fellow isn't here for nothing."

" It must be chance."

" Not a bit of it."

" But this is quite a different part to where Warren sits. I don't know much about theatres, but I fancy you would have to go outside to get down there."

" Still, Jem—"

Young Ching paused, for at that moment his eyes caught sight of the foreigner on a seat near the upper boxes.

He had his eyes fixed on the stage, and was laughing with apparent heartiness at some of the fun going on.

The man's face was changed so much under this new emotion that Young Ching began to think he must be mistaken.

Anyway, he resolved to keep his eye on the foreigner during the play.

He did so for an hour, scarcely looking at the stage himself, but never once did he detect the man looking towards the box that held Warren Fane and his friends.

" I must be mistaken," he muttered, " and have been worrying myself about nothing."

Having come to this conclusion he settled himself down to enjoy the pantomime.

A few minutes later the eyes of the foreigner were fixed on the box below with a malignant stare.

Young Ching, glancing at the foreigner at intervals, and not seeing anything peculiar about his actions, gradually became absorbed in what was going on upon the stage.

As the curtain was about to descend he turned his eyes towards the place where the foreigner sat.

His seat was empty.

From there he glanced quickly at the box recently occupied by Warren Fane and his friends.

That was empty also.

In a moment Young Ching grasped the portent of the foreigner's leaving.

There was no time to say anything to his friends.

Had he stopped to do so they would in all probability have wanted to know this and that, and so much valuable time would have been wasted.

Young Ching felt he must act with decision.

Slipping out of his seat, he glided to the corridor and from thence to the staircase.

Looking down he saw a number of people leaving, among whom he recognised Warren Fane and his mother, as Young Ching assumed the handsomely-dressed lady to be.

Close behind was the foreigner.

"He means mischief," thought the son of the Immortal One, and with a rapid step he descended.

In the vestibule there was a bit of a crush, for quite a number of people seemed anxious to get away as soon as possible.

By the time Young Ching got to the bottom of the stairs there were a number of people between him and the foreigner.

Not being so tall as those immediately in front of him, Young Ching lost sight of the object of his pursuit.

But on reaching the outside he saw him again.

Young Ching's position on the top of the steps enabled him to observe what was going on.

A carriage with a beautiful pair of horses was standing near at hand—a footman held open the door, and a lady was settling into her seat.

Warren Fane was about to follow her.

Close behind her was the foreigner, and like a flash of light his arm rose in the air.

How he got there Young Ching never clearly knew, but he was of opinion that he must have flown.

Anyhow, it was but the work of a moment

before he was on the foreigner's back, holding him with a grasp that fairly choked him.

The blow he aimed at Warren Fane had, thanks to Young Ching, fallen short.

Warren Fane, on hearing the commotion, saw his Slapcrash chum struggling with a man who had dropped a knife.

The crowd was now pouring out from every door of the theatre, and the confusion was immense.

Strange to say, nobody seemed to know what was going on, those most keenly interested of course excepted.

Before Warren could help his old friend, the foreigner, a man of great strength, had wrested himself free from Young Ching's grasp, and darted up the street towards Covent Garden.

Just as he reached the top he ran full butt against a hansom cab, and was dashed with fearful violence to the ground.

Before the driver could pull up, one of the wheels passed over the fallen man, and a horrified crowd gathered round his apparently dead body.

Of this neither Young Ching nor his friends saw anything.

All they knew was that the foreigner had got away, and that but for Young Ching he would have taken Warren Fane's life.

"Come in here," said the lady. "You must ride home with us."

"I cannot, thank you," replied Young Ching. "I am here with friends, and they do not know where I am."

"Ching," said Warren, holding tightly to his hands, "how shall I thank you?"

"Don't say anything about it," replied Young Ching. "That's the way to thank me."

"Pass on—pass on!" cried a policeman; "make way with that carriage, please."

"Come and see us to-morrow," pleaded the lady. "Here is our address," slipping a card into his hand; "mind, you are not to disappoint us."

Young Ching promised he would come. He had rarely seen a more beautiful face, and had certainly never heard a more melodious voice, so if for no other reason than finding out who she was he would have gone.

A shake of the hand all round, including Tom Biron, who had sat in the carriage half-dazed by the rapidly-acted tragic drama, and the carriage was driven away.

Young Ching went to look for his friends,

but did not find it a very easy task to single them out in the crowd.

At last he caught sight of Mrs. Cockles' bonnet, a thing of superlative beauty, and made towards it.

Billy Pink, who looked very white and troubled, was the first to espy him.

"Here he is!" he shrieked, in a voice heard high above the noise of the crowd.

They crowded round, asking all sorts of questions, mostly in dumb-show.

He answered—

"I will tell you all about it when I get home."

So home they went in a four-wheeler, jolted and shaken together like so many beans in a bag.

Jem Stager took advantage of an extra jolt to kiss Polly, and did not get his ears boxed.

She did not even reprove him.

So he did it again, and was caught in the act by Mrs. Cockles.

"Bless the boy!" she said; "what a forrard young rascal it is. Polly, you must have given him some encouragement."

Polly did not say anything, and the matter dropped.

After all, the offence was not a very serious one.

Boys will be boys, and as for girls—we all know what they are—demure as kittens and just as playful.

Mr. Cockles was waiting up for them, with a good supper ready, and after partaking of it everybody went straight to bed.

Of course Dick Cockles and Billy Pink had an attack of nightmare, but that was in the natural order of things, and of no moment to anybody but themselves.

Young Ching was not asked anything more about the cause of his absence at the theatre. Everybody was too sleepy, so he said nothing.

Before going to bed he looked at the card which had been given him.

On it was printed, "Countess of Arrondale, 17, Belgrave-square."

"A countess!" thought Young Ching. "Well, it's a peg above me in one way, but I don't suppose there is anything to be afraid of—I shall not be eaten."

Then he got into bed and went straight away to sleep.

All the others had gone that way some time before him, and when Mrs. Cockles slipped in to see if they were comfortable Billy and Dick were snoring like young grampuses.

CHAPTER XXXV.

YOUNG CHING VISITS A COUNTESS—POOR OLD BEANS—BURNT TO THE GROUND.

ON the morrow there was no fog, and at breakfast Young Ching related his adventure of the previous evening.

It is no figure of speech when we state that the eyes of Cockles senior came right out of his head.

"And do you mean to say that my Dick's been to school with the son of a countess?" he asked.

"Fact," replied Young Ching.

"Well! I never!" exclaimed Cockles senior with a gasp. "I suppose he didn't show what he was, did he?"

"Yes, he did," replied Young Ching; "he showed himself to be a thorough good fellow."

"Hear—hear!" from Jem Stager.

Young Ching was going to Belgrave-square about noon, and the other boys said they would walk with him.

"Sha'n't all go in," said Jem Stager; "we don't want to flood them with the Slapcrash aristocracy."

Accordingly after breakfast they started, Young Ching and Jem refusing an offer made them by Mr. Cockles to have a carriage and pair.

The boys preferred walking, there was more fun in it, and the distance, by way of Westminster-bridge, was not very great.

They accomplished it under the hour, and leaving his chums at the entrance to the square, Young Ching walked across to a house which a policeman pointed out to him as the Countess of Arrondale's.

Young Ching rang, and a noble creature in plush, evidently prepared to receive his visitor, was on his best behaviour.

"My lady will see you in a minute, sir," he said, "and my lord is in the breakfast-room."

He ushered Young Ching into a splendid apartment on the ground floor, and there he found Warren Fane (we must stick to the old name for the present) and Tom Biron.

Need we say what a hearty welcome Young Ching got?

"I could not half thank you last night," said Warren, "nor shall I ever be able to repay you for your pluck in saving my life."

"If you say another word about it," replied Young Ching, "I'll run away."

"We have been up nearly all night," continued Warren Fane. "The fellow who tried to stab me is dying; he has made a con-

THE SLAPCRASH BOYS.

The Liveliest of School Stories.

MRS. COCKLES SEES A GHOST. "OH! WHAT A GASHLY THING."

No. 8.　　　　　　　　　　　　　　　　　　Price One Penny.

fession, and, if I am not mistaken, my old enemy is skedaddling out of the country by this time."

"Tell him all," suggested Tom Biron.

"Here is my story in brief," Warren Fane went on. "My father, the Earl of Arrondale, had a cousin, the Honourable Hugh Staniton, who was heir to the earldom after him. Our family name is Staniton, I may tell you.

"Years ago both fell in love with my dear mother, and my father, being the better man, won her. This was one cause of hatred on the part of Staniton, and no doubt led him to do a great deal he would otherwise have left undone.

"You know about my father's death.

"Well, after he was gone, Staniton had the audacity to propose to my mother. He was rejected, of course. He is a blackguard—a gambler, with a name as black as my boots, and is cut by all decent people. But he is a man to be feared as well as despised.

"He swore, as I told you, that I should never inherit the family title and estates, and he took a broken-down Italian—the Count Aviala—into his confidence.

"The count, as we have good reason to believe, was to have a large reward if he disposed of me. He tried to do so à la Italian brigand and failed, and he now lies dying, while Hugh Staniton, who I may say got a hint from us, is flying for his life. That's the whole of my story."

"You think all danger is over?" said Young Ching.

"I am certain of it," replied Warren Fane; "even my dear mother sees that, and is no longer nervous about me. Here she comes."

The door opened and the countess came in, looking brighter and more beautiful than before.

Young Ching thought he had never seen such a face and person.

She was still comparatively young, her age being about thirty-five, and she looked several years younger.

Her manner towards Young Ching was not effusive, but her deep gratitude was shown in a most unmistakable manner.

"We can never forget what you have done," she said, "if we live for a hundred years."

Young Ching was pressed to stay, but he said he could not. He would come another day, if he might.

"My dear fellow," replied Warren Fane, "choose your own time."

He frankly told the countess that he had arranged to spend that day with his old chums, and then, by a slip of the tongue, he let out that they were waiting for him round the corner.

"Why didn't you say so before?" observed Warren Fane. "Hang it, old fellow, what do you mean by letting some of my old friends stay out in the cold?"

He was off like an arrow from a bow, and in two minutes had them all inside.

Dick Cockles, as he came into the room, tripped over a tiger-skin rug, and Billy Pink fell upon him.

Barring that little *contretemps*, their entry was as it should be.

Nobody made fun of their fall, although Jem Stager had to struggle to keep his countenance, and cake and wine being sent for, everybody was soon happy and comfortable.

Billy Pink was a bit dazed by the countess.

She remembered him as the "well-behaved boy" whom she had seen at the old schoolhouse, and if she thought it odd that he should be with the others she did not say so.

Probably Warren had told her the history of Billy's devotion to Young Ching.

After a most delightful hour they took their leave, and were shown out by the mighty footman, on whose corns Dick Cockles trod with all the weight he had in his body.

The eyes of the footman blazed, but Warren Fane had accompanied the boys to the door, so the poor footman did not dare to retaliate.

It was cold coming out from the warm house, so on reaching the Green Park the boys broke into a trot, and at a smart pace went as far as Westminster.

They crossed the bridge, and turned into some of the bye-streets, not because it was the shorter way home, but because Jem wanted to go to a shop in the Borough.

On reaching a very quiet thoroughfare the notes of a flageolet fell upon their ears. It was being played in the most mournful manner by a man in the middle of the street, at the sight of whom all the boys stopped dead.

The man caught sight of them, and all the music seemed to trickle out of the end of the instrument in a sort of wail.

"Broad Beans, as I live!" ejaculated Young Ching.

"Yes, gentlemen," observed Mr. B. Rord Beans, with an assumption of his old dignity, "I am here on a philanthropic mission."

"What's that?" asked Young Ching.

"I am the agent of a society for the propagation of soothing music among the poor. We are of opinion that it is time that the barrel organ, with its braying noise and villainous jigs, was superseded by something more classic—more elevating. Here " (holding up his instrument) " is a thing of the soul."

He had taken hold of Billy Pink by the collar, and really, despite his faded attire, looked like the usher of old addressing his pupils.

"All my life," he went on, huskily, "I have been a teacher, but on my tree of knowledge the only fruit that has grown is crab-apples. Could any of you, dear boys, loan me a sixpence for a few days?"

"Wait a moment," said Young Ching.

He drew Jem Stager aside, and they whispered together.

Mr. B. Rord Beans continued to address Billy Pink and Dick Cockles, High Art Music being his theme, but he had his eye on the other two boys.

Presently Young Ching slipped a small paper parcel into his hand.

"We wish you better luck," Young Ching said.

"Boys," replied Mr. B. Rord Beans, in a voice choked with emotion, "I can only thank you. It would give me great pleasure to make you some faint return in the form of a high-class symphony on this noble instrument, but I feel I cannot do it. I am overcome."

"All right," observed Jem Stager; "keep your pecker up. Good-bye, Mr. Beans."

They all shook hands with him and hurried off.

At the bottom of the street they stopped and looked back.

Mr. B. Rord Beans was not playing—he was entering a public-house in the distance.

"High Art won't flourish there," said Jem, and with all speed they went home.

On entering the house by the private door, Young Ching heard a voice above that was sweetly familiar to his ears.

"Dad, as I'm a sinner!" he exclaimed. What can he be doing there?"

With three or four bounds he was at the top of the stairs and inside the sitting-room.

There indeed was Ching Ching, the Immortal One, seated by the fire, with Mr. Cockles facing him.

There were glasses on the mantelpiece, and both were partaking of liquid refreshment.

Of the state of pride and satisfaction Mr. Cockles was in we can say nothing, because words would not adequately describe them.

It is doubtful if Royalty would have so warmed and expanded him. He was a stout man at any time, but now he looked enormous.

"My dear papa," exclaimed Young Ching, "what an unexpected pleasure!"

"My sunny heir," replied Ching Ching, "I am here wif intelligents ob a startler natur. Slaplycrash Schooler am burn to de groun."

CHAPTER XXXVI.

CHING CHING AT THE HOUSE OF COCKLES—A STARTLING PROPOSAL—WILL IT BE CARRIED OUT?

THE other boys had come in, and they all heard the news.

For a few moments a dead silence reigned, then it was broken by a fearful howl from Billy Pink.

"What de marrer wif you, Biller?" asked Ching Ching, with some sternness.

"Poor Mary," howled Billy, "and poor Mrs. Grumps!"

"Dere noborry hurted," said Ching Ching. "Mary and Missers Grumpers was bof got out by de fire scraper. Missers Grumpers certly flattered a fireman by fallin' on him, but dat was all. Missa Fosser Boner got out by de front door, and he came to town wif intelligents ob de disasker."

"And he isn't going to have a school in Smockley any more," observed Mr. Cockles, in a deep, melancholy voice.

On hearing this Dick Cockles also set up a howl.

"What's the matter with you?" asked his father.

"No more Slapcrash School!" roared Dick. "Oh—oh—ow!"

"You wait until you know what's going to be done," said his father.

"Nuffin settlered juss yet," observed Ching Ching; "only reposals."

"To travel round the world," gasped Mr. Cockles.

"Sit down, boys," said Ching Ching, "and let us have a discusser. Member dis, I ony tink ob it dis mornin' an namer it to Missa Boner. My reposal am dis. Dat he take some ob you boys roun' de contlement ob Eulope, and get a peeper p'raps at oder quarterers ob de globe. Young Missa Handsomer Harry go wif you, an mebbe myself, fren Willum, an juss possable Eddard too, for wifout him dere would be no real harmony."

Ching Ching stopped, and the boys, acting on impulse, sprang to their feet and gave a loud hurrah.

Go round the world!

Travel and see the great places of which they had often read but never seen.

It was a glorious idea, and well worthy of the great mind that originated it.

"Member dis alser," said Ching Ching, as he made a cigarette with one dexterous twist of his finger and thumb, "dat it not to be all players. You got to do your lessers cordin to de country you in. Greekers in Greek—Russhers in Russia—Frenchers in France—and so only to de end. Dat bout de idee. Me and Sammy knock him out togedder."

"Splendid!" cried Dick Cockles.

"Splen—" half-echoed Jem Stager, and then stopped.

His face slowly lengthened, and an anxious look came into his eyes.

"The expense will be great," he said, "and my father is not a rich man."

"De termers," said Ching Ching, with an airy wave of his hand, "am de samer as before—any extras got to come out ob de Ching Ching funs. Dat nuff. Oh! tank you!"

Mr. Cockles had been holding a light for the Great Man until the spill was nearly burnt out.

Just as his big fingers were being singed, Ching Ching took it from him, gave it a flip into the air, caught the flame as it descended, on the point of his cigarette, gave one draw and it was aglow.

This dexterous feat drew forth a round of applause from the boys, but Mr. Cockles was too overcome to do anything but sit and gasp.

Then when Ching Ching, who had been standing up for a moment or two, drew his foot out of his slipper, used it as a hand to draw up his chair a little nearer, and sat down again after restoring his boot to its leather covering, Mr. Cockles felt he had got a settler.

It was altogether outside anything he had ever seen in connection with the human frame.

In the matter of novelty it was a crusher.

"I've been to circuses, Mister Tambourine Ching Ching," he said, "and all I can say is that they ain't in it with you. Them tricks with half-crowns you was a showing me just now—why—"

"Jess so—jess so," hastily interposed Ching Ching, as his son and heir cocked his eye at him curiously. "Dey disappear, but like the flowerers of springy time dey will comer gain."

"I sha'n't care if they don't," said Mr. Cockles; "lor', how well it was done—a flip of the finger and thumb and—"

"Jess so—jess so," again interposed Ching Ching; "it a simpler trick—easy nuff to get 'em way, and like de youngly man in de song, dey will be returners."

"Do it again," said Mr. Cockles. "I'll get another four half-crowns—"

"Not at present," replied Ching Ching; "meanwhile" (drawing up to him) "you hab de ole half-crowners up you sleebe"—here he laid hold of Mr. Cockles' arm and gave it a shake. "One," down came a half-crown; "two," down came another; "tree," down came a third; "de larst," and down came a fourth. "Affer all," continued Ching Ching, "it am a joker ob your own."

"Mine?" cried Mr. Cockles, "mine? Good 'eavens! I ain't got 'arf a trick in me! I tried once to draw a newspaper from under a pile of tumblers, and I chucked the glasses all over the room and broke a window."

"Perhaps, dear papa," said Young Ching, "you will do a few tricks to amuse us? Let them see how you can put your leg up your back and pick your pocket with your own foot."

Ching Ching never blushed, he never had anything to blush for, but when anything, as it occasionally happened, slightly disturbed him, his eyes closed until they could scarcely be seen.

Young Ching's suggestion led him to close them up quite tight, but only for a moment.

Why should the great man be disturbed?

Had any memory of the past been roused by the suggestion of his offspring?

What chord had been rudely touched?

"My sunny heir," he said, "dere am sum tings dat can be done in our early purley years dat am out ob placer in our primely age. De tricker dat you speak ob was a lily ting I do in my youf, but now—"

"Just once, dear papa," pleaded Young Ching. "I've heard Eddard Cutten say it is a masterpiece."

"Jess oncely den, and memby dat it for de larse timer," said Ching Ching; "scuse me if I slect dese orlaments on de mantly piecer for de speriment, Missa Cockler."

He utterly amazed Mr. Cockles by taking

the ornaments from off the mantelpiece, and by a curious backward movement of the leg he thrust them up his back and deposited them in a pocket he had there.

The boys watched the operation with the keenest interest. As for Mr. Cockles, he gave out a series of gasps very much like the sounds emitted by a small steam-tug careering on the river Thames.

At last the mantelpiece was cleared, and the trick was so far complete.

But at that moment Mrs. Cockles came in, and her motherly eyes went straight for the denuded mantelpiece.

"Save us!" she exclaimed; "where's the chimney shepherds and dogs, and the portrait of Uncle Joe, and the feather fans, and the crystal goblets you won in a raffle?"

"Steady, my love!" replied Mr. Cockles; "his highness the grandorin has got 'em up his back."

Then did Mrs. Cockles turn her eyes upon Ching Ching, who bowed with an airy grace, without so much as rattling one shepherd against another, and said—

"It's all right, lubly moder ob de gelius of de Slaplycrashers—it only a domesty tricker."

Then did he pacify the good woman by restoring one by one each thing to its place, without using a hand, except to make a fresh cigarette and smoke it while the performance was going on.

A breathless silence prevailed.

Cockles senior ceased to gasp. He was past it, and if the performance had been of another minute's duration something serious might have happened to him.

At last it was over, and Ching Ching sank back into his seat like a subsiding wave.

The boys, led off by Mrs. Cockles, applauded rapturously.

Mrs. Cockles was obliged to take down one of the feather fans and fan herself.

"It's made me quite hot," she observed, and she looked it.

"Dat am nuffin to what my fader hab done," said Ching Ching. "One ob dese days, Missa Cockler, I tell you sumfin bout him."

"Tip us a yarn—I mean, relate us an anecdote about him now, dear papa," interrupted Young Ching.

"My sunny heir," replied Ching Ching, looking at him steadily, "de word tipper am a ting dat relude to waiterers and such-like pussons in dere spear. Wif regar to an anec-

doter bout my fader, I gib it in due time and seaser. Mealwhile praps Missa Cockler blige de compary wif a song."

This proposition was so utterly unexpected that everybody may be said to have been taken aback except the proposer.

Songs in daylight are not quite the thing, and under no circumstances had Mr. Cockles ever been drawn into the harmonic circle.

Mrs. Cockles said as much with wifely haste, and Ching Ching graciously replied—

"It no marrer—on some oder occasser den."

He rose and said he must be going, but Mr. Cockles would not hear of it.

"But dere ole Sammy and fren Willum Grunter," said Ching Ching, "dey misser me at homer."

"Let me send for 'em," urged Mr. Cockles. Ching Ching demurred.

"I'll send a man in a cab to bring 'em here," said Mr. Cockles.

"De expenser," answered Ching Ching.

"Expense, when you are concerned!" cried Mr. Cockles; "blow it, says I!"

He was not to be denied, and accordingly a cab was dispatched for his old companions, while Mrs. Cockles went away to prepare dinner.

Ching Ching settled back into his seat again, and Mr. Cockles, having had a look at the shop to see that all was going on right, came back and settled down also.

"Never did I expect to have the honour of entertaining a banjorine," he said; "a real China banjorine."

"Mandarin, father," whispered Dick.

"Here, you go and play," replied Mr. Cockles. "I know what I'm talking about, and if I don't, here's a gentleman all the way from China who will put me right."

"Always suspect your eldys, fren Dick," observed Ching Ching.

"I like that way of putting it," said Mr. Cockles, warmly; "a boy who don't do right by his parents and such-like had better keep out of business, for he will never make any hand of it, if he lives to be as old as Merrythoser."

So the boys went away, and Ching Ching and Mr. Cockles enjoyed themselves in a manner that may easily be guessed at, until two o'clock, when Sammy and Bill Grunt arrived in a four-wheeled cab, with one of the shopmen sitting on the box with the driver.

Three boys were hanging on behind, and at least a dozen others were running beside the cab in a breathless condition.

"Hurrah!" cried Young Ching, looking out of the window; "we shall do now. What a day we are having, to be sure!"

CHAPTER XXXVII.

MR. COCKLES ENJOYS HIMSELF AND MRS. COCKLES GETS A SCARE — CHING CHING LECTURES ON THE DUTIES OF CHILDREN.

IT is doubtful if Mr. Cockles had for years been half so happy as he was the rest of that day and night.

He could himself only recall two occasions when he felt such a glow within him.

One was when Mrs. Cockles, then Miss Stickleton, said "Yes" when he asked her if she would marry him, and the other was when his son and heir, Dick, came into the world.

"Such an honour I never expected," he kept saying to Ching Ching, calling him "Bangerine" and other strange names.

Sammy also impressed Mr. Cockles as being the noblest specimen of the sable race he had ever set eyes on.

The Immortal One informed him that there was a great deal of mystery in connection with Sammy.

"Bless me!" exclaimed Mr. Cockles. "I should never have thought it. He's got such an open countenance."

"He got all dat," replied Ching Ching, "alser de intelligents ob a feelopeser."

"Never," exclaimed Mr. Cockles, without having the least idea of what a "feelopeser" might be.

"I tink I tell you sumfin," said Ching Ching a few moments later, "if you say nufin bout it. Can I make a confider ob you?"

"You may make anything you like of me," returned Mr. Cockles, "and I shall take it to be an honour."

"Well den," continued Ching Ching, "I make a confider ob you—you know de Sanwickly Islers?"

"The Sanwickly Islers," repeated Mr. Cockles, musingly; "well I've heard or seen something in that way—the—the—yes—I may say I knew 'em partly."

"And the Coddle Islers ob de Indy Ocean," pursued Ching Ching.

"I don't think I know them quite so well as tothers," replied Mr. Cockles.

"It nuff dat you know sumfin ob em," returned Ching Ching, sweetly. "Ob courser you know de contlenant ob Gibralty?"

"Oh! yes, quite well," replied Mr. Cockles.

"Well, den," observed Ching Ching, "you have more or less inflamation about de proplety dat Sammy come into one day."

"What! all that?" exclaimed Mr. Cockles, aghast.

"De lot," observed Ching Ching; "he born ob royal blood and am lireal descender from Mungry Park."

"I thought there was something superior about him," replied Mr. Cockles, wiping his heated brow; "and the other gentleman, the stout party with a look of the sea about him, what's he?"

The boys had gone out of the room, and Bill and Sammy were seated at the table enjoying their pipes, also some refreshment in tumblers.

Bill, who had been up a great part of the night looking for Eddard Cutten, was in a sleepy and rather owlish condition.

He did not present the appearance of being exactly a Solomon.

But appearances are deceitful, as we know.

Under the cover of a wooden countenance there has sometimes been found a brilliant genius.

"Fren Willum Grunter," said Ching Ching, sadly, "am not now what he was."

"Is that so?" replied Mr. Cockles.

"Yes," continued Ching Ching, sighing; "but dere was a timer when all de elemies ob dis isler trembler at de name ob Grunter, but lass, alas! ole agers hab brought him to dis passer."

"He don't look so old, neither," observed Mr. Cockles.

"I not be certer to a year or two," Ching Ching went on, "but Fren Willum Grunter am sumfin' ober eighter."

Mr. Cockles was so taken aback that he nearly slid out of his chair.

He looked at Bill, who had one eye closed, and then at Sammy, who was quietly listening to Ching Ching and trying to work out those mental problems which the talk of Ching Ching always presented to him.

"Well!" observed Mr. Cockles, "I can only say that the longer I live the more I learn. He seems a bit sleepy, your Mr. Grunt."

"Admiral Grunter," explained Ching Ching.

"Admiral, in course," returned Mr. Cockles; "what am I thinking on? He's gone off now."

"Let him sleeper," said Ching Ching; "ole

ajers hab needer of it. Perhaps he been tinking ob his moder. It allers hab dat defect on him."

"His mother's dead, in course, years ago."

"No, Missa Cockler, not dat I know ob. At dis momenter she may be alibe and ably to read small printers, tred a needle, and walk a miler fore breakfaster, like dem ricalous ole laders you read ob in de paperers when de Highly Courter ob Parlimink not sitting."

Mr. Cockles felt he could bear no more.

He had that day acquired sufficient mental food to last him for a month.

The subjects presented to him for reflection were of a nature that would keep his vivid imagination in full play for a lengthened period.

Happily a rest for his mind was at hand, for Bill just then began to snore.

Of course all conversation was put an end to, and the nasal sounds emitted by Bill Grunt fell on the ears of Mr. Cockles with the force of a hitherto undreamt-of power.

Suddenly Bill stopped and took two bars' rest.

Ching Ching utilised the time to make an observation.

"Beuriful," he observed; "jess like de church organer ob Sent Polls."

"I ain't got a wery good ear for music," replied Mr. Cockles, "so I—"

Bill started off again with increased force, producing such a row as even Ching Ching had not heard from him before.

But it did not startle or ruffle the great man.

His face was filled with a serene joy, and with his right hand he gracefully beat time to the music.

Sammy placidly smoked on, and Mr. Cockles, in a feeble way, made comparisons between Bill's snores and the other snores he had heard during his lifetime.

He had always believed he could do a bit himself in that way.

Mrs. Cockles also was no mean performer when duly provoked by a late supper.

Other people had snored in the hearing of Mr. Cockles, but they were all penny whistles to Bill.

In a nasal sense, Bill Grunt was a full brass band of forty instrument power.

A short sleep in the daytime served him, and in five minutes or so he woke up.

First he opened one eye, and, after the lapse of a few seconds, the other.

This was his usual way of returning from the land of dreams.

Seeing the eyes of Mr. Cockles fixed on him a little wildly, Bill apologised.

"I've had a quiet wink or two," he said, "and I hope you'll excuse it. Manners is manners everywhere."

"Eber de same," murmured Sammy.

"I must say, admiral," replied Mr. Cockles, "that you've got a power for snoring the like of which I never met with before."

Bill's mouth opened to reply, but his denial of the soft impeachment was never spoken, for a loud scream was heard in the next room.

"That's my Maria," said Mr. Cockles; "something's happened to one of the young 'uns—hupset something."

Another scream rent the air.

"Two of 'em gone wrong," continued Mr. Cockles, rising hastily; "bless my stars, what is it?"

He made all haste across the room, and, followed by the other three, penetrated into the next apartment.

There they found Mrs. Cockles seated on the floor staring wildly about her.

"What's the matter, love?" asked Mr. Cockles.

"I've seen a ghost," cried Mrs. Cockles, "with a big head and two legs. Oh! it was a gashly thing."

"There ain't no sich things as ghosts," said Mr. Cockles; "get up, Maria."

"I can't," she replied, "for I'm gone quite limp in my legs."

"I'd help you," replied Mr. Cockles, "but I'm rather short of breath, and took aback also, so—"

"Low me," interrupted Ching Ching, with the grace and gallantry of a prince.

Gently as a mother raises a fallen child he picked up the very substantial Mrs. Cockles and placed her in a chair.

Then he produced his fan and cooled her heated brow.

"Dere," he said, "you are berrer now."

"Oh! thank you, Mister Gambolin," she replied, gratefully; "I'm all right now, but it was a horrid thing—that ghost."

"Low me to get you dat ghose for spection," said Ching Ching.

He glided across the room to a screen, and with one movement closed all its folds.

Behind it were four boys, whose grins of delight suddenly changed to a preternatural solemnity of visage.

Near them was a huge mask, hideous enough to frighten a woman of stronger nerves than Mrs. Cockles possessed.

USING THE POLE LIKE A LANCE, YOUNG CHING CHARGED AT THE STRANGER.

The eyes of the adults were fixed sternly on the culprits.

Ching Ching's countenance was quite magisterial.

"Whar you get dis ting?" he asked.

"We have been out and bought it, dear papa," replied Young Ching.

"For what puppos?"

"We thought it would please the nurse and the little ones. Dick had it on and was footing it—I mean wending his way to the nursery—when Mrs. Cockles cropped up—I mean came into the room, and that's all, dear papa."

"And nuffy, too, my sunny heir," replied Ching Ching. "Dick Cocklers come forf."

Dick, his hair fairly on end with the knowledge of his infamy, stood forth.

"Behold your moder," said Ching Ching.

Dick beheld her with two eyes that stood out independently from his head.

"De firse ruler ob boy lifers," observed Ching Ching, "am to suspect dere palents. Wifout dat dere am nuffin for dem to hope for in dis worle—cept degraden infamy, a lot ob hard workers, and de leese possibler pay. In shortly—shamers, ruin, and a purly grabe."

"Hear—hear," softly murmured Mr. Cockles.

"Not to you lone, fren Dicker," continued Ching Ching, "do I redress dese worders"—here he looked slowly from one to the other at the rest of the boys, lingering an extra moment on his own promising offspring—"but to oney all. Suspect your palents. Do your dutifullers by dem. Be bedient. And when you get a lilly pocket-money to spare, never invess it in such tings as dese. Fren Dicker, be tankful dat your moder am libe at dis momenter, and not a silenk corpse. We will now leave you to your deflections."

He turned sorrowfully away, and returned to the place from whence he came.

There he sank into his chair quite overcome with emotion.

Mr. Cockles bent over him with friendly solicitude.

"Can I offer you anything, Mr. Trumbyrine?" he asked.

"A spicion of what we had afore," murmured Ching Ching.

While Mr. Cockles was mixing it he was surprised to see the face of Sammy all on the grin.

Bill Grunt's countenance expressed nothing more than usual, but he was refilling his pipe like a man who was enjoying himself.

"Dem boys reglar young debils," observed Sammy; "and may dey be eber the same and more so as dey grow older."

"Sammy!" exclaimed Ching Ching, springing up and grasping his hand, "I knew dat in dis hour ob doubters you stan by me. Eber a witless to de trufe—eber to de fore wif comflimations; and de sentlements dat fren Willum Grunter spress on de subjy are alser grattlefying. Missa Cockler, not too strongly, please!"

Mr. Cockles, greatly impressed by the apparently contradictory nature of the Immortal One's sentiments, had been pouring out the whisky with his eyes on the Great Man.

When the gentle suggestion about the strength of it was offered, he had filled up the glass to the brim with neat spirits.

With a gasping agony he emptied some of it back again, and some he spilt on the table-cloth. Then he took the kettle off the fire and did what else was required, like a man in a dream.

"He's too much for me," he thought, as he passed the decanter on to Bill; "altogether out of my line. A man wants to be eddicated up to his intellect, or it's apt to be confusing."

CHAPTER XXXVIII.

ONE MORE DAY OF ENJOYMENT—AN AERIAL FLIGHT—MR. FOSSIL BONE COMES OUT AS A PUGILIST

THE rest of the evening was spent in a most enjoyable manner.

There was nothing done or said to mar the serenity of the time, and to Mr. Cockles it was like a lengthened sojourn in fairyland.

Young Ching was on his best behaviour, and Dick, who had asked his mother to forgive him, and had received a kiss and half-a-crown by way of reward, was, like the Richard in English history, "himself again."

Of what the Immortal One did to make the time pass pleasantly we can say little more.

Desirous, as he always was, to add to the comfort and happiness of his fellow man, he exhibited a variety of tricks with cards, coins, pocket-knives, and sundry other things, that were simply a series of astounding exhibitions.

He asked Mr. Cockles to take a card out of a pack and told him what it was before he looked at it.

Then the card was put into Mrs. Cockles'

work-box, from whence it disappeared without any visible agency.

It was afterwards found in the crown of Bill Grunt's hat, which was on a chair in the corner.

Coins came and went from his hands at will —not singly, but in dozens and half-dozens.

He balanced and spun plates edgeways on the point of a fork, kept half-a-dozen eggs going in the air, and in sundry and divers ways so staggered both Mr. and Mrs. Cockles and charmed the rest that the whole thing was like a delightful dream.

Even Young Ching was deeply moved.

"As I'm a sinner," he said to Jem Stager, "the more I see of dad the more I'm flum-maxed."

To which Jem responded—

"By the sword of the Crusader he's a licker!"

The boys were sent to bed at ten, but it was twelve o'clock and past before a cab was sent for to convey the trio of chums away.

Mr. Cockles was filled with admiration, and he burned to do something to show his appre-ciation of his friends.

He desired to make them gifts.

Money, he knew, would be rejected. So he fell back upon his unrivalled stock-in-trade, and as they passed through the shop on their way out he pressed all sorts of sausages upon them.

"Just as a relish for breakfast," he said.

Ching Ching did not say nay, he only suggested that Bill Grunt should be the bearer of these offerings of friendship.

Bill complied, of course.

With two huge polonies in his pockets, and a large package of other varieties of the tooth-some articles, Bill started.

Mr. Cockles was no doubt getting a bit worn out with excitement, and the package was imperfectly tied up.

As soon as Bill got outside the string at one end came off, and about two yards of the ordinary sausages immediately fell out.

Ching Ching, who was in the highest spirits, put them round Bill's neck like an old-fashioned watch-chain, and hustled him into the cab.

As Bill was sitting down the rest of the string came off, and naturally the remainder of the sausages tumbled on the floor.

To pick them up of course took time, and while it was being done Ching Ching looked aloft.

At an upper window he saw by the light of a street lamp four youthful heads thrust out, and four grinning faces expressive of keen enjoyment looking down.

The moment Ching Ching looked up the heads vanished and the window was drawn down quietly.

When the last fond adieu had been indulged in with Mr. Cockles, the cab rolled away, and the Immortal One looking out saw four boys' faces flattened against the panes of that upper window.

"Natral," he murmured; "in dealering wif de young it am always best to member dat we had a youfull timer in days dat am goner."

Good old Ching Ching.

Thus spoke or thought the parental philoso-pher, who did not expect to find old heads on young shoulders.

It had been a most delightful day to the boys.

To Jem Stager and Dick Cockles the father of their chum had been in a great measure a revelation.

They had heard a deal about him, of course, and seen something of him, but never until that day had they really understood what a man he was.

"Dad," observed Young Ching, as he got into bed, "has as many sides as a prism. He can be grave or gay, as the humour takes him. He is the best of friends, but as a foe he is to be dreaded."

"Is he a foe to any man?" asked Jem.

"Not in himself," replied Young Ching; "but he will not put up with any nonsense, for he is perfectly aware that to keep the peace you must not be every man's tool. He's got a head, has dad—had he been educated—well, had he started fair, like some people, he would now have been—"

"Emperor of Pekin," said Billy Pink, "and such an Emperor as they never had before."

"Where is Pekin?" asked Dick.

"Don't you know that?" returned Billy Pink, in surprise.

"No, I don't."

"Well, then, it's the capital of the Con-tinent."

"Where is the Continent?" asked Dick.

"Oh! you can't expect me to know that," replied Billy. "I've not had so much school-ing as you; but wherever it is it isn't good enough for Ching's father. He's a—a—a—whacker."

Then Billy got into bed and rolled himself up in the clothes.

The other boys did the same, and they were soon fast asleep.

In the morning, about ten o'clock, Mr. Fossil Bone appeared at the house of Mr. Cockles.

He had come to take the boys out for the day, and they were right down glad to see him.

Mr. Fossil Bone had a short chat with Mr. Cockles about the proposed educational trip to the Continent.

"It's a good idea," he said, "but I would rather start with the boys alone. Ching Ching is a very excellent man, and in his way a good father, but I do not think he could help me."

"In my opinion," observed Mr. Cockles, firmly, "he could educate the boys better than anybody—meaning no offence to you, sir."

"None at all," replied Mr. Fossil Bone, smiling; "but his education would be quite a different thing to mine. My idea is to start first with the boys, and then Ching Ching and his friends can come on afterwards, say in a month or two, and meet us."

"Whatever you gentlemen arrange," returned Mr. Cockles, "I fall in with, mind that, and as for expense, that's nothing. The sausage trade never was brisker, and I've a pound or two in the bank to get along with."

Mr. Fossil Bone shortly afterwards started with the boys for the Crystal Palace, where one can certainly get a good shillingsworth of fun in the holiday time.

Neither Young Ching nor Billy had ever been there before, and to Billy it was another staggerer.

A great crowd was there. Billy was sure it was composed of half the people in the world at least, and the row alone was worth the money.

A pantomime by daylight is not an exhilarating spectacle, and compared to Drury-lane the Palace gorgeous spectacle was not thrilling. But they enjoyed it.

It was after the pantomime that both Dick and Billy were lost.

They got separated from the rest by the eddying of the crowd, and as no place to meet at had been arranged, the prospect of finding them again was rather remote.

"So foolish of me," said Mr. Fossil Bone, "not to settle on some spot for a rendezvous. I think we had better say that we will meet here by the orchestra, then I will take this side of the Palace and you boys the other.

Walk from end to end and look for your friends."

Young Ching and Jem Stager, who had felt just a little constrained when under the eye of their schoolmaster, set out in high glee together.

They were not in a very anxious state about either of the missing youngsters, as boys of their size are not generally stolen by gipsies, so they began their quest by skedaddling off to the grounds, where the swings and roundabouts were.

It was getting dark, but the naphtha-lamps were burning, and the swings were in full blast, nearly all being engaged.

"Shall we have a go?" asked Young Ching.

"Decidedly," replied Jem.

Both jumped into one that was just emptied and away they went, expertly working the ropes until they got as high as the swing would go.

It was exhilarating, their upward and downward flight, and they were enjoying themselves immensely when a loud cry, followed by a commotion, was heard on their right.

Young Ching, looking down, beheld a number of people rapidly congregating round a swing at the end of the row.

The swing itself was still going, but it was empty.

"Somebody has fallen out of the concern," said Young Ching.

Then it flashed upon both of them in a sort of inspiration who that somebody might be.

"Steady!" cried Young Ching. "Stop her!"

The man who ought to have attended to his cry had rushed into the thick of the mob to see what had happened. A little time elapsed, therefore, before the two boys could stop the boat.

Before it had fairly stopped they both jumped out and ran to the crowd, through which, with the corkscrew-like ingenuity of boys, they worked their way.

When they got into the centre their fears were confirmed.

There were Dick and Billy in the arms of two men, who were trying to restore them to consciousness, while a police-officer was examining their limbs.

"I don't think any bones are broken," he said, as Young Ching came on the scene.

"They are dead, anyway," returned one of the men holding the boys, "for they both pitched on their heads."

"Dead," said Young Ching, contemptuously; "not a bit of it! Here, Billy, wake up!"

He bawled into the ear of Billy, who opened his eyes with remarkable promptitude, and cried out—

"Is that you, Ching?"

"Yes, it's me," replied Ching. "What have you been doing?"

"I fell out," responded Billy, as he made an attempt to stand up.

By this time Dick had come round a bit, and when it was found that he also could stand, the interest and sympathy of the public sensibly lessened.

"Confound the young cubs," observed one man, disappointed that there was not a tragedy; "they are not hurt a bit."

The crowd melted so rapidly away that ere long there was not more than a dozen people standing gaping at the heroes of the sudden fall.

The men owning the swings went back to their posts, and Young Ching laid hold of Billy's arm, signalling to Jem to perform a like office for Dick.

"Come along you two," he said; "I never heard of anybody like you. How came you to fall?"

"When we were high up," replied Billy, "Dick pitched upon me head first, and we tumbled out together."

"Don't tell fibs, Billy," yelled Dick Cockles; "it was you who tumbled upon me."

"No it wasn't," replied Billy.

"Yes it was."

As each stuck to his version of the affair, doubtless honestly enough, the exact rights of the case could not be got at.

Young Ching cut short all wrangling over it.

"There's a pair of you," he observed.

"And so say all of us," sang Jem Stager.

"Sit down here a minute," said Young Ching, pausing beside one of the fountains, "and don't roll into the water, or I shall leave you to drown. Don't you know that you have broken Fossil Bone's heart?"

"No!" exclaimed Dick.

"If you haven't you've cracked it," chimed in Jem; "or never more may I wear the bright sword of the warrior—he's going about like a madman—searching for you. Come and let us find him, before he is driven to do something desperate."

When they came to a refreshment stall,

Young Ching gave the two perpetrators of the aerial flight a little wine, and they both felt and looked better after taking it.

But still the memory of their flight remained.

Every few seconds or so they carefully felt their heads, elbows, and knees, and looked wildly about them, as if not quite certain that it was all over.

But after partaking of the wine their symptoms of terror relaxed.

Young Ching was of opinion that Mr. Fossil Bone ought to be found without delay, and they went in search of him.

They found the heart-broken schoolmaster in the Alhambra Court, surveying the rich ornamental work wth serene delight.

Dick and Billy both expected some sort of ovation, such as rushing at them and folding them in his arms.

But he did not indulge in anything spasmodic, simply saying—

"So you have found them—I thought you would. And now we will go and have a cup of tea."

They had a cup of tea, and this had a further stimulating effect upon the two aerial performers. Then they went to see some tumbling and juggling, and a man who spun plates and balanced them on sticks pleased Dick immensely.

"I'll have a go at that sort of thing when I get home," he said; "it seems easy enough."

"Begin with some plates your mother has put away and won't want for a year or two," suggested Jem.

It was now time to go, and people were thronging towards the railway-station intent upon getting home.

A great many had been refreshing the inner man more than the inner man required, and this was especially marked in a person who had the appearance of a highly respectable cobbler dressed in his go-to-meeting clothes.

By some means he had lost his hat, and the instinct of self-preservation from cold had prompted him to tie up his head in a red cotton handkerchief.

Notwithstanding his serious loss he was in high spirits, and instead of walking was dancing his way down the boarded passage like a creature of air.

Unhappily he got in Billy's way, or Billy got in his, and they collided.

The wearer of the handkerchief, being at the moment of collision at an acute angle, went over on his back with a bang that was heard above the noise of the crowd.

One moment he was down, the next he was up, and the third he was going for Billy.

But a champion of the inoffensive boy was there to shield him.

"Was it Young Ching?"

For once—it was not.

It was Mr. Fossil Bone.

"My good man," he said, "you are in the wrong."

"What do you know about it?" demanded the man, with an animosity much at variance with his recent sportiveness.

"I saw the whole thing," replied Mr. Bone, "and if he was in the wrong he is but a child."

"I don't care what he is," returned the man. "I shall give him one for himself and teach him manners."

"Indeed, my friend, you will not."

The wearer of the handkerchief made a rush, but he was countered by Mr. Fossil Bone with the smartness of an expert in the noble art of self-defence.

To the undoubted amazement and great joy of Young Ching and Jem, they saw their quiet, easy-going tutor put up his hands like one who knew what he was about, and with a blow from the shoulder he put the cantankerous wearer of the handkerchief where he had been before—that is, on his back.

The second time, with amazing activity, he got upon his feet, but was knocked down again.

A third time he came to the scratch, only to receive three blows in rapid succession, when he fell to rise no more as a combatant.

"I throw up the sponge," he said, faintly; "you know too much for me."

"Boys," said Mr. Fossil Bone, placidly, "we will now proceed."

The people who had been stopped by the brief fray gave him a round of hand-clapping as he marched on with his beaming pupils.

"Jem," whispered Young Ching.

"Yes, old fellow," returned Jem.

"What did you think of that?"

"Prime."

"Up to Dick, eh?"

"Rather."

"That's the sort of man to go abroad with, to my way of thinking."

"But who would have thought he had it in him?" asked Jem.

"It is your quiet ones who come out strongest when they are wanted," replied Young Ching.

CHAPTER XXXIX.

ARRANGEMENTS FOR GOING ABROAD—TOM BIRON AND WARREN FANE MAKE A CALL.

WHATEVER the boys thought of it, Mr. Fossil Bone did not seem to trouble himself about the little affair.

He made no reference to it on the way home, nor during the time he spent with the Cockles family before going to his hotel.

As he was leaving he drew Jem Stager aside and said—

"I am going to-morrow to see your father, to hear what he says about the proposed trip abroad. You wish to go, I believe?"

"I should consider it the grandest thing that ever came my way," replied Jem.

"Very well," replied Mr. Fossil Bone. "I will do my best to induce your father and mother to fall in with my views. Good night."

After he was gone Mr. Cockles was told of Dick's accident, and for a few minutes his parental brow was clouded with anxiety.

"It might have been a serious job for you, Dick," he said. "Don't be too venturesome in future, and don't forget that you are the hope of the family."

"I won't, father," replied Dick, dutifully.

The boys were pretty well tired out and went early to bed, where Billy Pink, as became a boy of his vivid imagination, had dreams.

He was in a swing boat and fell out of it, but he never reached the ground.

All night long he floated between the swing and the earth, and no amount of effort on his part brought him to terra-firma.

It was worse than the original falling out.

But boys make light of dreams, and he awoke in the morning invigorated and refreshed.

Shortly after breakfast there came a telegram addressed to Cockles junior, and Mr. Cockles on receiving it could hardly believe his eyes.

"A telegram for my boy," he said. "Well, if he isn't getting on!"

He took it upstairs to where the boys were amusing themselves in various ways.

Mrs. Cockles and the entire family were also there.

"Dick," said Mr. Cockles, impressively, "here's something for you that I didn't get when I was a boy—nor your grandfather—nor his father—no, nor anybody else afore that unless it was kings and queens—a real tel—e—gram."

"For me?" queried Dick.

He took it wonderingly, opened it, and immediately his amiable countenance was suffused with joy.

"It is from Warren Fane," he said; "he and Tom Biron will call on us this afternoon, but if it isn't convenient we are to wire back."

"Isn't that the gentleman you said was an earl?" asked Mrs. Cockles.

"Yes," replied Dick.

The face of Mr. Cockles became bedewed with perspiration.

"An earl *here*?" he said; "why I thought they never came out of the swell places."

"You won't find Warren Fane different to others of his age, Mr. Cockles," observed Young Ching.

"But we ought to do something to receive him properly," said Mr. Cockles. "How about a brass band?"

"Don't think of it, father," exclaimed Dick.

"Well, a big card with the word 'Welcome' on it hung across the shop door."

"I assure you, Mr. Cockles," replied Young Ching, "that there is no need of anything of the sort."

"You know him better than I do," said Mr. Cockles, with a sigh, "but I should like him to be received properly, and not give him an idea that we are stingy."

"You receive him as you did us," replied Jem Stager, "and he won't complain."

Mr. Cockles was not quite satisfied.

He had hospitable instincts, and he wished to receive visitors in a manner befitting their station.

The honest sausage-maker was not a toady or a tuft hunter, but he thought that everybody was entitled to good treatment and civility.

He was a man who was willing to bestow favours, and in his way he was kind to everybody.

With regard to Warren Fane, he looked upon his coming, not as a compliment to himself, but to his boy.

On Dick lay the honour of it all.

Notwithstanding what he had heard, he seriously thought of getting all his men together to give the young earl a cheer when he arrived.

He had seen lots of titled people at election times and on great public occasions cheered, and he supposed it was the right thing to do.

But happily his amiable intentions were foiled.

About three o'clock two quiet-looking young gentlemen walked into the shop, and the foremost held out his hand to Mr. Cockles, who was behind the counter.

"How do you do, Mr. Cockles?" he said.

"Well, I'm middlin'," replied Mr. Cockles, giving his hand a wipe with his apron before accepting the hand of the other; "but you'll excuse me. I don't know who you are."

"Probably I am known to you as Warren Fane," was the rejoinder, "and this is Tom Biron."

"Well, I never!" said Mr. Cockles, with a gasp; "you to come in this way. Why, you ain't walked, have you?"

"Yes, we have," replied Warren Fane, "just for exercise."

Mr. Cockles shook hands with Tom, and with a fixed look in his eyes, common to him when he was a bit staggered, he opened the door that led to the upper rooms.

"Come this way," he said, "and excuse things that isn't exactly as they ought to be, but with a family you can't keep everything in apple-pie order. Hear 'em upstairs now."

There was, indeed, a lot of romping going on, and on arriving at the sitting-room Warren and Tom had the pleasure of seeing Young Ching and Jem having a game with the two elder girls, while Billy and Dick were engaged in a friendly wrestle to see who was the best man.

This point was left undecided by their falling together into the fender a moment later.

The clatter of the fireirons was deafening, while both were claiming the victory, ignoring the fact that their heads, copiously adorned with hair, were being singed and filling the room with an odour far from agreeable.

"At it, as usual!" cried Tom Biron.

The boys sprang up, and then there were hearty greetings all round. The girls were introduced, and Mrs. Cockles came in.

Warren, of course, gave himself no airs, and everybody was at home with him immediately.

When Mrs. Cockles asked him if he would stay to tea, he said he "should be delighted, and meant to ask himself if she had not asked him."

"And he's a earl. Friend of my Dick's!" thought Mrs. Cockles. "Well, if my father was to rise up from his grave he would think it was a dream."

YOUNG HANDSOME HARRY AND THE ANARCHISTS.—NOT DAUNTED BY THREATS.

Jem Stager was all right at first, but he soon looked gloomy.

Mary and Polly, girl-like, began to make eyes at the new-comers, and Jem did not like it.

"Look here," he said, "it's a shame. Warren ought to know better."

"Oh! dry up," replied Young Ching; "who cares. When they are gone we will cut the little flirts, and that will square matters."

"Not a bad idea," returned Jem.

So he bottled his wrath and looked pleasant, and the time passed merrily.

Mr. Cockles was busy in the shop until seven, and then he came upstairs and sat down by the fire.

The pride he felt fairly swelled him, as it had done when the Immortal One was beneath his roof.

"It's amazin'," he kept saying to himself; "what with tamborinds from China, and one thing and another, I'm regular floored."

He got his final flooring that night when Warren Fane, just before leaving, took out of his pocket a very handsome brooch—a new year's present from the countess, his mother, to Mrs. Cockles.

There was also a packet for Young Ching, which he was told to put in his pocket, but we can let the reader into the secret of what it was.

It was a watch, with the crest and monogram of the Arrondale heir set in brilliants.

A slight recognition, as the giver put it, of the gallant conduct of the recipient.

"Altogether," as Mr. Cockles said to his wife when the evening was over and they were alone, "it's a series of knock-downs, my love, and if you don't floor your sister Priscilla with that brooch she can stand up against anything."

Priscilla, it may be said in passing, was the wife of a thriving market-gardener, and a little given to show in the matter of dress.

The next day the boys went out and had a ride on a penny steamboat.

It was a cold day, the passengers were few, and a very blue-looking lot they were, but Billy enjoyed that ride.

He asked Jem if the sea "was more up-and-downy?" and Jem's answer was—

"Of a verity, friend Billy, thou art young indeed!"

The great thing was, of course, to see as much of London as possible, and Jem had a good idea of it.

Young Ching knew something of it, too, or walked about as if he did, which was much the same thing.

They went here and there, rode in omnibuses, tramcars, and had one ride in a hansom, all packed together, after which they finally decided to have a peep at Madame Tussaud's.

"Billy must see the Chamber of Horrors," said Young Ching.

There Billy became as a boy frozen. The waxwork was so life-like that he could not believe the figures to be dummies.

He got into people's way, apologised to the dumb kings and queens, and mistook living people for moving waxworks.

There was one reverend gentleman standing before the figure of a murderer in the Chamber of Horrors. He was very still—glancing with burning indignation at the well-portrayed figure of the notorious criminal.

Billy got right in front of him and stared hard at his fixed face.

"This is a licker," he exclaimed. "Who would think such an innocent-looking fellow as this could be a murderer? He looks more stupid than our parson at home, and folks used to say he was the biggest fool going."

The reverend gentleman, awaking from a dream of horror, and hearing a noise right under his nose, listened to Billy's remarks with some surprise.

He fixed his eyes on Billy just as Billy turned his towards his three grinning companions.

"Looks a bigger fool than our parson at home," Billy went on, "but mother used to say they were a poor lot anywhere."

"Boy!"

It was the outraged reverend gentleman who spoke, and his voice was like that of a man speaking through a trumpet.

Billy staggered back, and was stopped by the figure of Lefroy.

"Boy!" repeated the reverend gentleman, "I grieve to find in one so young—"

"I beg your pardon, sir," replied Billy, "but I didn't know as you were a moving figure."

This ingenuous remark naturally won the cake, and Billy's friends went off into a roar of laughter.

So did two or three casual spectators of the scene, and the reverend gentleman flushed to the roots of his hair.

"This is a premeditated insult—a planned

outrage," he cried, aiming a blow at Billy, who ducked and avoided it. "Where are the attendants? Where are the police?"

"All right," interposed Young Ching; "don't make a fuss about it. It was a natural mistake. You stood so still and looked so much like one of them that anybody might have done the same thing."

Taking hold of Billy's arm he marched off with him, and Jem and Dick followed, leaving the outraged reverend gentleman to glare about him rather helplessly.

After that Billy was very careful, and he was almost afraid to look at the figures. Even when he was sure of them being all right he spoke of them in whispers.

Dick did not do anything to distinguish himself, beyond falling down the stairs as they were coming out, taking an old gentleman with him in his fall.

Some slight verbal altercation took place, in which Dick was called "a young idiot," and the old gentleman was reminded that it was his own fault, as he had no right standing on the stairs gaping about him like a stuffed owl.

"I think I got the better of that," observed Dick, as they emerged into the street.

"You did, friend Dick," replied Jem Stager. "You pierced his hog armour there."

"Where now?" asked Young Ching.

Four such boys could not go through the streets without some notice being taken of them.

Dick and Billy made things lively by cannoning against passers-by, some of whom took offence thereat and aimed blows at them, or else used strong epithets bearing on their personal appearance and mental endowments.

And when they got into the main streets the attention of the public, especially the juvenile public, became more marked.

Young Ching appeared to be known to a great many of them, and they hailed him as friend and brother, to Billy's great amazement.

"Were you ever here before, Ching?" he asked.

"No," was the reply; "but the dad's known, and I bear just a suspicion of resemblance to him. Not that I shall ever come up to his standard," he added, with a sigh.

"I don't know about that," returned Jem; "he has his gifts and you have yours."

Young Ching shook his head in modest deprecation of Jem's statement. Like his father, the dear boy was modesty itself.

"We have had rather a slow day," Young Ching said, a few minutes later. "How I hate these things. What right has a barber to stick up a painted clothes prop more than any other tradesman?"

They were just outside a shaving shop, with the orthodox striped pole.

These poles are aggravating things, and invariably have a trying effect on a sensitive mind.

It was the quietest street they had been in yet, and the only observers of the party of four were two or three very small boys and a seedy-looking man, apparently "a little on."

"An example must be made of this hairdresser," said Young Ching. "Come out, will you?"

With a quick turn of his wrist he loosened the pole in its socket, and shouldering it, marched off, followed by his companions.

The small boys, aghast at the outrage, watched from a distance, but the man who had been following became aggressive.

"You've got no right to do that sort of thing," he said; "drop that pole, will you?"

Young Ching took no notice of him, but Jem Stager gave him a few words of friendly advice.

"You get along home," he said, "unless you want to be carried there on a stretcher and have your people weeping and wailing over your corpse in the lordly hall of your ancestors."

"I never had any ancestors," replied the man. "I am poor and broken, but I know what my rights are and other people's, too. That young—young—what is he?"

"Ambassador from Pekin," replied Jem, gravely.

Here the man lurched against Dick Cockles and Dick collided with Billy, all three foregathering in a heap up against a brick wall.

Young Ching looked around.

"What do you want?" he asked, addressing the stranger.

"I want you to act straight and fair," was the reply. "I am poor, but honest. You are rich—ambassador—from Pekin—I—"

Young Ching walked on, the man still following him.

"Always be just and true," the drunken stranger observed to Young Ching; "poverty is no crime, but dishonesty lowers a man below the beasts of the field. You had better give me that pole."

"Here it is," said Young Ching.

Using it like a lance he charged at the

stranger, and catching him fairly in the ribs, drove him with some force against an adjacent shop.

The man, breathless and not a little alarmed, sank into a heap on the pavement, and Young Ching tossed the pole beside him.

"Trot along, boys," he said; "here's a bobby coming, and it won't do to play Smockley pranks on policemen here."

The officer looked sternly at them as they passed, but they survived that and got to the corner of the street.

Then they halted and looked back.

A most gratifying sight met their gaze.

The man so poor and honest was in the grasp of the policeman, who held him with one hand and carried the pole in the other.

A discussion between them appeared to be going on.

The boys could not hear it, but they guessed at its nature.

It was soon over, and he who was not ashamed of poverty, but was proud of his honesty, was led away expostulating.

"What a moral there is in that," observed Young Ching. "The most dangerous thing going is to poke your nose into other people's business. A just punishment is sure to overtake you. Here, we won't go home to tea. Come along, and I'll stand treat."

CHAPTER XL.

PLANS FOR THE FUTURE.

YOUNG CHING led the way into a very respectable-looking coffee-shop, fitted up with the usual boxes, the majority of them having occupants.

He selected the one next to where a bald, fiery-looking old man was engaged in worrying a large plate of bread and butter and watercresses.

Having ordered some rashers and eggs for himself and friends, Young Ching stood up and looked into the next box.

He was just behind the bald-headed one, who was talking to himself loud enough for broken sentences to be heard.

"Now is the time—tea not ready—I'll live out—hang the day I was married—hang all women—"

Young Ching, after looking round to see if he was observed by anybody but his friends, and perceiving he was not, put his arm over the screen and with his fore-finger lightly tickled the bald cranium.

Up came the man's hand and smote the spot just as Young Ching drew his away.

"Hang the flies!" he muttered.

Then he went to work again, biting big semi-circles out of his bread and butter and hissing anathemas on his wife, with whom he had evidently quarrelled.

Young Ching after a little light conversation slowly rose again and repeated the tickling operation.

This time he was nearly caught.

The fist of the bald-headed one came up so smartly that barely a hair's breath was between the two hands.

"Hang the flies!" said the man. "What beastly places these coffee-shops are. Always swarming with flies. Another—oh! dash it—come—"

He put up both his hands, and by alternate slappings performed quite a tune upon his cranium.

This performance and the noise attending it naturally attracted the attention of the other occupants of the boxes.

They stood up to see what it meant, and at that moment the proprietor of the coffee-shop came along with the tray for the boys.

He also was fat, bald, and fiery.

"What's the matter?" he asked, as he put the tray down on the table.

"A noisy old gentleman in the next box," replied Young Ching. "He keeps on talking to himself, and smacking his head as if he were a mother performing on a naughty boy. We sha'n't enjoy our tea if this sort of thing goes on."

Young Ching spoke the last words a little louder than was necessary, and they were overheard by the occupant of the box.

Up popped his head.

"What's the matter with you?" he asked.

"That's not the question," replied the coffee-shop keeper. "What's the matter with you is what we want to know?"

"Flies is the matter with me!" was the fierce answer.

"Flies!" exclaimed the coffee-shop keeper, "in the middle of winter. What are you talking about? There's not a single fly in the place."

"I say there is—hundreds!"

"You talk bosh, sir."

"I say you are all flies—now then!"

"And I say you are a fool."

With wonderful rapidity were these sentiments exchanged; and then the bald-headed customer came out of his box.

"I say," he shouted, "that—as—I sat there—quietly—enjoying my—vittles—I had a swarm—of flies—about my head."

"Where are they now?" naturally demanded the indignant proprietor of the place.

"I'm not going to look for them," was the savage answer; "that is your duty. Catch 'em! squash 'em!"

"Have you finished your tea?" asked the proprietor.

"No, I hain't," was the answer; "and if I had—what then?"

"I shall be glad if you will get out of my shop."

"I shall stop as long as I like."

"No, you won't!"

"I will!"

This was not to be borne. The blood of the proprietor was roused, and he closed.

The struggle was brief.

They went through the swing doors together, and a moment later the proprietor came in again.

"Where's his hat?" he asked.

It appeared that it had fallen to the ground, and while he was stooping to pick it up the owner thereof suddenly reappeared.

He also had come for his hat, and seeing the proprietor in a stooping position, favourable for assault, he did there and then administer to him such a kick that the owner of the coffee-shop shot under the table clean out of sight.

Then he fled and left his hat behind him.

Two or three kindly-disposed persons helped the proprietor out, and he limped back to the place where he kept his stores, vowing deep and lasting vengeance on his foe.

"Another moral can be drawn from such an incident as this," said Young Ching, as he proceeded to help his guests to ham and eggs. "Never, dear boys, make a fuss about flies, and always be sure you are on the right tack before you get up a row. Now peg away. As the governor says—bless his old pigtail—' Let us be melly while we can.' "

And merry they were, as merry as boys can be when all things go right with them.

The ham and eggs vanished like smoke, and another dish had to be ordered, also another pot of tea and more bread and butter.

Both Billy and Dick were like a well-greased pair of African chiefs, white, of course, but quite as shiny.

"I do call this prime," said Billy. "What would father say to a tea like this?"

"He would not say much until he got through it," replied Young Ching, "then he would fall asleep."

"Yes!" said Billy, "that is a bit like father."

Young Ching paid for the tea, and asked the proprietor in tones of the most tender solicitation if he felt better.

The inquiry was not received in a proper spirit.

"I don't know how to answer you," was the reply, "but I tell you, young gentleman, that I've got my suspicions about you."

Then Young Ching put on an air of dignity.

"What do you mean?" he asked.

"I mean what I say, and no more," was the answer.

"You are a low fellah!" said Young Ching, suddenly assuming a masher's air, "and I withdraw my patronage from this shop for e-var—ta-ta, old man."

The proprietor was so overcome by the demeanour of Young Ching that the boys were laughing outside before he could offer anything in the way of retort.

Then he thought he would run after them and say or do something.

Next he thought he wouldn't.

And finally he decided that he had better let them alone.

"Anyway," he muttered, "I know the sort of flies that started the row."

The boys lost no time in getting back, for Mr. Cockles did not like them to be about after dark.

They passed through the shop, in which Mr. Cockles was not, and were going upstairs, when a familiar voice fell upon their ears.

It was that of a woman, and she was speaking thusly—

"No, never as long as I live will I desert Mr. Bone and the boys. I'll see to their washing and mending, be it by night or day, at home or in furrin parts, and I'll be a mother to my sweet boy, which his name is William Pink and no other."

"It's Mrs. Grumps!" exclaimed Billy.

And so it was.

The boys were glad to see her, and she gave them one and all a motherly embrace.

Evidently she had succeeded in making herself at home in the house of Cockles, for she had taken her bonnet off and put on a wondrous cap she had brought with her in case she stayed to tea.

She and Mrs. Cockles were already friends.

"I told Mr. Bone," said Mrs. Grumps, when they had got over their greetings, "that I wasn't afraid of no furriners, and no matter what he said, I meant to go with him to look after the boys' clothes and see that they come home right from the wash.

"'Things are very different abroad,' says he.

"'I don't mind that,' says I.

"'Furriners are a peppery lot,' says he.

"'I'll pepper them,' says I, 'just as I did when the barrel organ wouldn't move on when we had the boy ill at Bumpstead.' I just took that Italian organ man by the hair of his 'ed —having first knocked off his hat to get at it —and then I give it three hard knocks agin the lamppost—one for being there, another to let him know he wasn't to come again, and a third one for luck. When I lets go he flies off like smoke and was never seen no more.

Oh! it won't do to prevaricate with furriners, as I knows.

"Besides, I've another reason for going," said the old woman, with just a little trembling in her voice. "I've got a son at sea somewhere, and I hopes to meet him one of these days."

The next day Mr. Bone called, and they learnt from him that he had pretty well arranged everything for the speedy departure of the boys.

He was quite resigned to the prospect of Mrs. Grumps' company.

"She will be of great use," he said. "There are so many little things a man cannot look after, and I have no doubt we shall be very glad of her at times."

END OF PART II.

PART III.

CHAPTER I.

In a hut far up the Rhine, and close to the time-worn castle of Namedi, five men were assembled.

Evening was at hand, and the rays of the setting sun gilded the tops of many a rock and crag seen through the open door, while the shadows of the secluded hollows and vales were deepening into the dark lines of night.

Of the five men two appeared to be German, and the others had a Russian cast of countenance. All their faces had the deep-set bitter expression that one sees in men at war with society.

They were, in short, five conspirators—anarchists—who had came to this lone spot to arrange and perfect their nefarious designs.

Three squatted on the ground, while the other two leaned against the lintels of the door and gazed with heavy eyes on the scene before them, indifferent to its beauties.

One of the latter was a thick-bearded man, wearing the hair of his head long enough to cover his neck and ears.

His dress consisted of a rough tunic, loose breeches, and high boots.

They all, in fact, wore boots of the description that is worn by Russians more than any other nation, and their attire generally was that of the rough peasantry of Russia and Germany mixed—cosmopolitan garments—in harmony with their coarse features and burly forms.

They spoke English in a guttural tone, but with a fluency that would seem strange to any-one not acquainted with the fact that in both countries our tongue is studiously cultivated.

"Give us an idea," said he with the long hair. "How is it to be accomplished?"

"It is to you, Polowski, that we look," replied the man facing him; "you are our leader. Tell us what to do and it shall be done."

"Choose the king or prince who is to die first," said Polowski.

"What matters which it is? We hate them all, and the rich, too, for we live with our noses to the grindstone of poverty, and sweat all day and far into the night to get no more than a crust of dry bread and a drop of water. Otto Lurgan, speak!"

He turned to the three men crouched on the ground, all of whom had German faces. He who had been addressed as Otto Lurgan answered—

"There is nothing in my country worth powder and shot, because there are so many. One prince dies—another comes. The people care little. Let us strike at the people. Half a town blown down with dynamite would rouse them to our condition."

"Are we not of the people?" asked one of the men by his side.

"Spoken like Karl Steimetch," was the answer, given with a sneer. "No—we aim at being leaders, the true leaders of the people."

"Before we can do anything," said the other man on the ground, "we must have money."

"That was spoken like Schavaloff," observed Polowski; "what say you, Kranmitz?"

The Russian facing him laughed, not in a pleasant fashion, but in a subdued hyena-like way.

"Yes, money," cried Kranmitz, "and let us get it from some of the English who go prowling and prying about these old castles. We can capture and hold them to ransom."

This proposition was received in silence—presently broken by Karl Steimetch.

"Hold them—where?" he asked.

"In yonder castle," said Polowski, pointing to a pile of buildings on the right; "have you ever explored it?"

"Not I," was the answer, with a shrug.

"I have," said Polowski, "and a nice roomy castle it is, with hiding places enough for a hundred prisoners if we could capture them."

"And keep them. They must have food."

"There are flocks around, Otto, that will give them and us food. Now, listen, all of you."

Polowski lowered his voice and went on—

"I was in the village to-day and saw a prize arrive—a mere lad, but with high bearing and a look of money about him. He had a spectacled man with him whom he addressed

A DEED OF DARING—POLOWSKI IS TAKEN A TRIFLE ABACK.

as his tutor. I talked to that tutor and wormed a lot out of him."

"Good," said Karl.

"He told me that this boy with a high bearing is the son of Sir Henry Marsh, once known and still spoken of as Handsome Harry—a man noted for his daring. The son is so like him, and has so many of his sire's physical attributes and courage, that everybody calls him Young Handsome Harry."

"But we cannot go down to the village and capture the boy," observed Kranmitz.

"Peace!" exclaimed Polowski. "They are coming to the castle to-day to watch the sinking of the sun and the rising of the moon."

"Must we capture the tutor, too?" asked Schavaloff.

"He is worth nothing," replied Polowski, "for he is poor—he speaks timidly, and says his name is Frisby Whelks. More I ascertained," Polowski continued. "This Handsome Harry is to be followed by some young friends of his, also with a tutor, and therefore rich. Now, if we could bag the lot there would be thousands hanging to it. All we have to do is to be bold and secret."

"Design and we will execute," said Otto Lurgan, briefly.

Polowski was about to speak again when he saw two specks moving up the zigzag narrow path that led to the castle.

"Behold our prey!" he exclaimed. "Otto, Schavaloff, Kranmitz, you will be enough, for there is no fight in Frisby Whelks."

"What is to be done with the boy?" asked Otto.

"Take him to one of the outer buildings of the castle. I will join you there."

The men appointed to the work hurried off to intercept the two strangers.

All were armed, the weapons they carried being old shot guns and knives.

The latter were hidden from sight, while the former gave them the air of sportsmen.

In a quarter-of-an-hour they were close upon the two strangers, and could see that one was a tall, handsome youth, with an aristocratic appearance. The other was a little man, with weak eyes and a nervous air.

For the sake of the latter the former was constantly stopping to rest.

At length the three men, bearing down upon them with as casual an air as they could assume, heard the young fellow expostulating thus—

"Come, Whelks, if we don't get along we shall not reach the castle to-night."

"Oh! my poor legs," groaned Whelks. "I feel just as if all the sinews were being drawn out—what a boy you are to go climbing about in this way—a mountain goat wouldn't do it if it was not obliged to."

Young Handsome Harry, as we shall call him, for he had a right to the title both by birth and looks, laughed musically.

"Excuse me, Whelks, but you are a duffer," he said.

"I will excuse anything," replied Whelks, "if you would only keep on level ground—bless me—who are—are these—gentlemen?"

The anarchists were now close up to them, and suddenly brought their guns to bear upon the pair.

"Stand!" cried Otto, "or we fire."

Frisby Whelks made an effort to stand, but his legs gave way under him, and he sank into the position a tailor adopts when at work.

"Exc-c-cuse me," he said, "but I couldn't he-e-lp it."

Young Handsome Harry, with his hands in his trousers' pockets, looked quietly at the men.

"What do you fellows want?" he asked. "Money, I suppose?"

"Yes," said Otto.

"Then all I can say is," returned the brave youngster, "that you are barking up the wrong tree. We haven't brought our purses with us."

"Never mind," said Otto; "you must come with us. If you do not resist no harm will happen to you."

"Are your guns loaded?" calmly asked Harry.

"Yes."

"Then I should be a fool to resist. What do you want me to do?"

"Go with us to the castle and see our chief," Otto replied.

"Very well. I will see your chief," returned Harry. "He is a brigand, I suppose?"

"No."

"What is he then?"

"A political outcast," was Otto's answer. "Banned by the class you spring from."

"Oh! indeed," was the calm reply. "Well, let us proceed—it will soon be dark. Now, Whelks, up on your pins, or you will be left behind."

"He will not go with you," said Schavaloff. "I have a message for him to deliver."

Frisby Whelks got upon his feet, but he stood rocking to and fro as if the worse for drink.

"Go and arrange for two thousand pounds to be paid us, to ransom your young master," said Schavaloff. "Try no tricks, for we shall be on the watch, and the first sign of attempted rescue will be the signal for his death."

"Two thousand pounds!" exclaimed the tutor; "where am I to get it?"

"That is your business," replied Schavaloff. "You know better than we can tell you how to communicate with his friends. If you do not, ask him."

"Return to Anderbach," interposed Harry, "and wire from there. My father will order the sum to be paid by the bank in that place."

"That's business, young sir," said Otto, who was holding the youth by one arm while Kranmitz held the other. "There's your instructions, Mister Shakebones. Hasten away unless you want to be helped along with a charge of shot."

Frisby Whelks looked wildly at Harry, who exclaimed—

"Why don't you go? You can do nothing here."

"But I—I don't think it right to leave you," stammered the tutor.

"Tell me what good you can do by remaining," said Harry. "Go down to the village and there hire a conveyance to take you on to Anderbach. Say that I have fallen into the clutches of some ruffians who want money, and that I see no chance of doing anything but paying them first and hanging them afterwards."

"You speak boldly," observed Otto, bending his brows.

"Will soft words set me free?"

"No."

"Nor will hard ones kill me. You want money more than my life, so there's an end of the matter."

"A cool young sprig," muttered Otto. "Now you with the shaky knees—begone," he continued, in a louder tone. "Schavaloff, cover him with your gun, and if he is not out of sight in thirty seconds put a charge into him."

"Mercy on us!" exclaimed Frisby Whelks; "don't shoot."

Then he set off down the hillside, with his legs threatening every moment to give way under him, but he kept his perpendicular in a miraculous manner, until he turned a corner and disappeared.

"Now, young man," said Otto, "we will repair to the castle, and you shall see our chief."

CHAPTER II.

POLOWSKI AND YOUNG HANDSOME HARRY—A KNAVE DEFIED.

POLOWSKI was not far behind his subordinates—he was ascending the mountain as the terrified Frisby Whelks went down.

They met in a narrow gorge, and the tutor turned as if to flee back again, but his legs betrayed him and he sank upon his knees.

"What cheer, old friend?" cried Polowski, smacking him on the back; "don't you know me?"

"Oh! yes. I remember you now," replied Whelks, rising; "what a slippery road it is—one can hardly keep his feet."

The anarchist smiled grimly, and Frisby Whelks, like a man released from bondage, sped on his journey without uttering another word.

Polowski soon came in sight of the prisoner and his captors—walking briskly ahead.

Harry was held on either side by Otto and Kranmitz, and Schavaloff walked behind, ready to fire at him in case he attempted to escape.

"He is cool," muttered Polowski. "There is no fear in that tread."

Karl Steimetch now overtook Polowski, and they went up the winding path together.

The castle of Namedi was one of the finest on the Rhine, perhaps *the* finest in its palmy days.

Even now, when long deserted, and with wind and weather left to do what they willed, it still reared its towers proudly, and showed but few signs of decay.

But around it were evidences of more modern life, in the form of huts erected by herdsmen, who were sparsely scattered about the hills.

One of these huts was built close to the castle walls, between two large circular towers, and into this the anarchists took their prisoner.

The only things within that could possibly answer for furniture was a cask or two, and on one of these Polowski seated himself.

"Let me see the sprig of English nobility," he said; "face about, youngster."

Harry turned towards him and looked him bravely in the face.

"Your name?" said Polowski.

"Harry Marsh," was the reply.

"Age?"

"Sixteen."

"You look more."

"Never mind what I look—that is what I am."

The bold bearing of the youth irritated Polowski. Folding his arms he stared at him savagely.

"You are the son of an English aristocrat," he said.

"I am the son of an English gentleman," replied Harry. "I claim no more, and any man who behaves himself is a gentleman."

"I say," contradicted Polowski, folding his arms and growling out his words, "that you are an aristocrat—one of a race we have sworn to destroy."

"You have set yourself a stiffish task," retorted Harry. "But I understand you want to rob first and kill after. Oh! your black looks will not frighten me."

"Give me a gun," cried Polowski, leaping off the tub. "I'll blow his brains out."

"Hear reason!" returned Otto, seizing Polowski by the arm. "We want money, and must have it. Here is a chance of—"

"I'll kill him," hissed Polowski. "Shall this cub defy me—a man whom kings shall learn to tremble at?"

He was so infuriated by Harry's cool demeanour that he would have shot him had he not been prevented, and he was only pacified by a proposition from Otto.

"We differ," Otto said, "but let there be no quarrelling. I have a pack of cards. Let us choose one each. If mine is higher than yours we will keep him for ransom. If yours is highest you shall do as you please."

The other three men meanwhile were holding Harry in their grasp.

He felt it would be utterly useless to struggle for his life until the last moment.

If Otto won he would simply be held as a prisoner, but if Polowski was victorious the brave boy resolved to fight before they slew him.

Though outwardly cool he suffered—as even the bravest man or boy would have suffered at that awful moment.

What fate could be harder?

An hour before he was free, happy, and enjoying all the advantages of a pleasant tour—looking forward to joining Young Ching and the others, whom he knew to be somewhere in the neighbourhood.

Only a few hours ago he had hoped for many happy months, wandering here and there with the pupils of Slapcrash School.

And now he was in the hands of murderous ruffians, who staked his life on the drawing of a card.

Is it to be wondered at that he thought of the home he had left behind him, of his noble father, handsome mother, and younger brothers and sisters?

Who—in the terrible fix he was in—would not have done the same?

Otto brought out a pack of cards and shuffled them on the top of a tub.

"Cut," he said.

Polowski lifted about twenty cards, turned the lot over, and showed—a king.

A malevolent smile passed over his face.

"I shall get my way with the aristocratic cub," he muttered.

Otto looked vexed, but it was not for Harry's sake.

"It is a pity," he said, "for the ransom is of more importance to us than his life."

"Show your card," cried Polowski, eager to carry out his brutal desire.

Otto lifted about half-a-dozen cards and turned the undermost upwards.

Another king.

Harry's breath came thick and fast.

The excitement and suspense were dreadful.

When the second king appeared all the anarchists simultaneously uttered a shout.

Polowski dashed his cards down on the tub.

"Was there ever such luck?" he snarled.

Otto gathered the pack up and re-shuffled them.

"Cut again," he said.

"No. You first," growled Polowski.

Otto separated the pack and turned up a card.

It was only a three.

A sickening feeling came over Harry.

He leant forward and watched Polowski as he advanced with a triumphant air and divided the remaining cards.

Slowly he turned them over.

A two was at the bottom.

With a terrible imprecation he threw the cards upon the floor and stalked towards the door of the hut.

"Do what you like with the cub," he said, "but mind this—he must be held safe. I will see him to-morrow."

CHAPTER III.

MR. FRISBY WHELKS IN A WILD STATE — A LIVELY PARTY AT THE INN—THE MANTLE OF GLOOM.

FRISBY WHELKS had about four miles to walk before he reached the village of Namedi—a small collection of huts and houses, with an inn for the refreshment of inhabitants and the accommodation of travellers.

He got over that four miles of ground somehow—how he never knew—but it was quite dark when he reached the one street of the place, which was narrow and crooked.

The roads were ill-kept, and there were lots of holes for a man to stumble into, but the terrified tutor happily did not fall.

He reached the inn door and stopped to recover his breath.

Inside there were sounds of laughter, and many voices speaking in the dear old familiar English tongue.

Oh! how musical it sounded in his ears.

The bar was deserted, so he made his way to the big kitchen behind.

Once more he paused for breath.

He was in such an excited condition that he would be unable to tell his tale until he had partaken of some form of stimulant.

But knowing that time pressed he opened the door and peeped in.

A very cheerful scene was before him, for a tolerably good fire was blazing on the hearth.

Around it were gathered six persons—a man, a woman, and four boys.

The man had the unmistakable look of learning about him which somehow lays hold of all those who study, but he was also of a genial bearing, which is not always to be found in his class.

This was Mr. Fossil Bone, head-master of Slapcrash School.

The lady was a good-humoured personage of the model housekeeper sort.

Viewed as a matron of the old school she was a perfect picture.

This was Mrs. Grumps, also of Slapcrash School, travelling with the boys to see to those wants which did not come under the head of learning.

The four boys were respectively Young Ching, Jem Stager, Dick Cockles, and Billy Pink.

Mr. Frisby Whelks had an important communication to make, but he was utterly unable to deliver it.

He knew that these were the friends Young Handsome Harry had been seeking, but their appearance at the inn only added to his mental excitement.

They did not observe his arrival, and leaning against the doorpost struggling with his emotions, he became an involuntary listener to what was going forward.

"I am afraid, William," said Mr. Fossil Bone, "that I shall never make an entomologist of you."

"I don't think you will, sir," replied Billy, meekly; "I can't remember the hard names."

"He's got his gifts," broke in Mrs. Grumps, "but we must not expect him to understand everything. When I was a girl I never could make out the difference between orthology, entermeologer, tintacks, and fossidy."

Jem Stager was beginning to laugh when Young Ching gave him a dig in the ribs.

"Be quiet, can't you?" he said. "Billy isn't the only ignoramus. Dick, what are you thinking of?"

Dick Cockles, who had been looking into the fire in a dreamy sort of way, started and looked up with a smile upon his face.

"I was thinking of home," he said.

"Comparing the Cockles' home - made sausages with the bags of sawdust we had for dinner to-day," muttered Jem.

"What did you say?" asked Dick, with a slight tendency towards pugilism in his face.

"I was merely commenting on the many attractions of your home," replied Jem, politely.

"You said something about sausages," returned Dick.

"Now, boys," interposed Mr. Fossil Bone, "no quarrelling. It is my rule not to interfere with you out of study hours, but I must interfere when anything disagreeable arises. Stager, you owe Cockles an apology."

Jem Stager rose up with the air of a noble —a stage noble, we mean.

"Here is my apology—oh! trusty friend," he said to Dick. "Verily if I said aught to disturb thee take it as the utterance of a thoughtless loon and pass it by."

Dick was just going to reply when a groan was heard.

"What's that?" he cried, leaping up.

Every eye was turned towards the door, where Frisby Whelks presented a most ghastly and ghost-like appearance.

There was no light in the kitchen but that of the fire, which flickered about and added to his supernatural appearance.

"Mercy on us—a ghost!" exclaimed Mrs. Grumps.

"Nonsense," said Mr. Fossil Bone. "Steady, boys—it's a living person. Now, sir! Who are you? Advance and show yourself."

Frisby Whelks came forward a few paces,

then accidentally colliding with a chair he sank into it.

His limp attitude, the wildness of his eyes, his hat on one side—all led to one couclusion.

"Gracious goodness!" exclaimed Mrs. Grumps. "The man is in a beastly state of intossication."

Frisby Whelks disclaimed the idea of being under the influence of liquor with a motion of his hand.

"No," he said, hoarsely, "not that."

"Well, what is the matter with you?" asked Mr. Fossil Bone. "You have the dress of an English gentleman. Who are you?"

"Tutor," was the feeble answer.

"Whose tutor?"

"Harry Marsh's—son of Sir Henry—Young Handsome Harry."

Immediately there was a commotion among the boys, but Mr. Bone checked it with a word.

"Remain quiet!" he said. "Something is evidently wrong with this gentleman. Now, sir—compose yourself, and try to explain."

"Nothing matter with me—but Young Handsome Harry — brigands — thieves — murderers."

"Brigands!" exclaimed Mr. Bone. "Bosh!"

Frisby Whelks took off his hat and fanned himself.

"You may say 'bosh,'" he retorted, "but it's true all the same. Not ordinary brigands—Germans and Russians. Oh! he's dead by this time."

Then he began to shake all over, and Mr. Fossil Bone, feeling sure it was agitation and not drink that troubled him, took a glass off the table and handed it to him.

A draught of the liquor it contained had a reviving effect upon Frisby Whelks, and he was able after a few minutes to tell his story.

It naturally dismayed the listeners, and Young Ching was especially affected.

"I would like to shoot them," he said.

"But who are the villains?" asked Mr. Bone. "I thought all that sort of thing had come to an end—and I don't quite see what can be done to-night—but let us have the landlord in."

He went to the door and shouted for Monsieur Picard, and in response a cadaverous Frenchman appeared.

The story of Frisby Whelks was told briefly, and the Frenchman listened with a quiet smile on his face.

"It is not posseeble," he said, in reply. "Nothing of ze robbare or brigand am here."

"But he was with me this afternoon," cried Frisby Whelks, wildly. "Have we not been here two days?"

"Oh! yes, it is so!" Monsieur Picard replied.

"And did I not tell you that we were waiting for the friends who are here to-night?"

"You say so mooch, monsieur."

"And was he not taken away from me this afternoon?"

Monsieur Picard shrugged his shoulders.

"I do not deny it, monsieur," he replied.

"But you said it was impossible," observed Mr. Bone.

"Monsieur!" returned the Frenchman, "it is some choke."

"A joke."

"Ve haf some vild young men from England come here dat love de choke. It is enough. Zey play him now."

"It will be a serious sort of joke for them," observed Mr. Bone, "which they may possibly find out. What would you advise us to do?"

"Noting," Monsieur Picard replied. "Your friend vill come back in the morning as vell—betterer zan ever. He vill laugh and say he pass a merry night vith his friends."

After the Frenchman's reply, Mr. Bone looked at Frisby Whelks with a puzzled air.

"What do you say to that?" he asked.

"There was no joke about the fellows," replied Frisby Whelks, "and if they were disguised Englishmen it was the mos complete disguise I ever saw."

Mr. Bone did not know what to do.

He could see that Young Handsome Harry's tutor was the sort of man to be easily scared.

Harry might be in the joke. Boys play all sorts of tricks, as he very well knew.

"I hope nothing is wrong," he observed. "But if there is we can do naught to-night. There seems to be only one gendarme in the place, and he would be no good against the number of men you speak of."

"I ought to go on to Anderbach," said Frisby Whelks, "but I don't feel as if I can."

"Vy should you?" returned Monsieur Picard; "it can only be a choke."

"It may be," replied Frisby Whelks, "but to me it seemed serious enough. Give me something to eat. I have had an awful time of it."

The boys listened to all that had been said with grave faces.

Like their worthy friend—Mr. Fossil Bone—they knew not what to make of it.

Young Ching ought to have understood the joke if there was one. But he did not.

"In my opinion," he whispered to Jem Stager, "it is all true, and the Frenchman is in it."

"Why not say so?" asked Jem.

"Because it would be of no use. Nobody would believe me or you. We can make certain of it in the morning."

"How?"

"By going up to the castle to see. Anyway, it's no use worrying to-night, for we can do nothing. Harry's tutor—did you ever see such a shaker?—has been sent for the ransom, therefore they don't mean murder at present. As for us, we are not worth the catching, so I vote we go boldly to the place and see how much joke there is in the business."

"Suppose they take us, too?" said Jem.

"They will not do that," replied Young Ching.

In this respect he made a mistake. The anarchists had already laid their plans concerning him, and his going up to the castle would be equivalent to a mouse walking into a trap.

The merry party was turned into a gloomy one.

Despite the assurances of their host, they could not see any joke in what had transpired, and one and all longed for the morrow to come to set the matter at rest.

The old inn had ample sleeping accommodation in it, some of the rooms being very large, and containing two or more beds.

In one of the largest the boys were going to sleep together.

Good old Mrs. Grumps had seen that the sheets were well aired, and in so doing had made herself obnoxious to Madame Picard—a thin-faced and sour-looking Frenchwoman.

But Mrs. Grumps did not care.

"I've got my duty to do," she said, "and I will do it in spite of all French frogs, male or female."

Having seen the boys to bed, she went downstairs to the kitchen again, and found the schoolmaster and the usher before the fire.

"Mrs. Grumps," said Mr. Fossil Bone, "I have been talkng to Mr. Whelks, and we have come to the conclusion that this affair of Harry Marsh's is a serious matter."

"It's my opinion, too, sir," returned Mrs. Grumps. "I don't know the dear lad, but I am sure, from what I have heard, that he is a good boy."

"I have made up my mind not to rest until I have got some inkling of the truth," continued Mr. Fossil Bone. "Mr. Whelks"—here he looked pityingly at the usher—"seems a bit abroad, and don't quite know what to do."

"I am a poor nervous thing," said Frisby Whelks, "and when we started Sir Henry told me in his humorous fashion that his son would take care of me. Oh! dear, what shall I do if anything happens to him?"

"It's no use crying," replied Mr. Bone. "I will see what can be done to help you, and I think I had better go out alone to make a few inquiries about our host. I may frankly say that I do not care much for him."

"He and his wife are a pair," vaguely observed Mrs. Grumps, speaking with an intensity that showed she did not mean to be complimentary.

"At any rate," said Mr. Bone, rising, "I shall not take his word for what has transpired, so I will have a quiet look round, but will be back in an hour."

After he was gone Mrs. Grumps ordered supper for three, making herself better understood by signs than words.

"We don't want any kickshaws," she said, "but something solid—fit for English people to eat—chop or steak, or ham and eggs."

Monsieur Picard took the order, and politely said he "would please madame if it were poss-ee-ble."

The supper was ready, but Mr. Bone had not returned.

Mrs. Grumps began to get uneasy.

She went to the outer door and saw Monsieur Picard standing there smoking a cigar.

"Mr. Bone hasn't come back," she said.

"Madame," replied Monsieur Picard, with dry politeness, "it is not to be said to me zat I am his keepare? Oh! no. Monsieur Bone is a man for himself—alone. He want no advice—take no vord—he do just as he haf ze pleasure."

And the Frenchman laughed with a grating sound—that was not good to hear.

CHAPTER IV.

YOUNG HANDSOME HARRY IN CONFINEMENT—
THE CONSPIRATORS—DRINK IS A FRIEND FOR
ONCE IN A WHILE.

IT was about one o'clock in the morning—the night was fine and the sky studded with stars.

In a room in the basement of Namedi

THE SLAPCRASH BOYS.

The Liveliest of School Stories.

ON THE EDGE OF THE PRECIPICE—MRS. CRUMP IN A TERRIBLE PREDICAMENT.

No. 9.   Price One Penny

Castle, Young Handsome Harry slowly paced to and fro.

There was no furniture in the place to impede his movements, and through a heavily-barred window there came just sufficient light for him to see the extent of his prison-house.

How many lads of his age, no matter what their nationality might be, would not have quailed had they been in his undoubtedly dangerous position?

But this youngster—the offspring of as brave a man as ever drew sword—was outwardly calm.

Whatever should be the end of his adventure, and he knew it might be very serious, he was resolved to meet it.

If a tear sprang into his eye it was for those at home, who would miss him and mourn over his fate.

He could see that he had fallen into a nest of cruel fanatics, ready to charge all the misfortunes of their lives to their betters.

In an adjoining compartment he could hear his gaolers talking together.

They had been carousing until they had set their blood on fire, and he had to listen to their fervid denunciation of all living men.

After a time they began to quarrel among themselves.

"Why did you not let Polowski have his way?" said one.

"Because we have to make money out of the prisoner," was the reply.

At this the others laughed hoarsely.

"Before the money can reach us," said another, "we shall have a regiment of soldiers here. Are we not outcasts too bad even for rabid Geneva?"

To this the answer was—"Wait!"

The debate was waning at the time when Harry was pacing to and fro.

Into the voices of the men there had entered a thickness that spoke of the work of strong drink, and one of the band was already asleep and snoring.

"I wish they would all go to sleep," muttered the lad, "then I would see if there is a chance of getting away from here."

He halted by the door and tried it. It was heavy, and made no more movement to the pressure he put upon it than a rock would have done.

"Not that way," he muttered.

Then he looked up at the unglazed orifice that served as a window, and at the few stars it permitted him to see.

How bright and beautiful they looked.

"Brighter than I have ever thought them before," he sighed. "I wonder if anyone at home is awake and looking at them."

At this moment the voices in the room grew louder, and once more he heard references made to himself.

An additional voice was now there.

It was that of Polowski, who had returned.

"I can't rest," he was saying. "Revenge burns within me. I don't ask for the pleasure of killing him, but he shall be whipped!"

"Let him alone," replied Otto Lurgan.

Harry recognised the latter voice as that of the man who had practically saved him, and despite what he had suffered, he looked upon Otto as a friend.

"I forgive him!" the boy exclaimed, "but as for the rest—"

He stopped short, and with clasped hands wrestled with his feelings.

He felt that it was his duty on the verge of death to forgive his enemies, but he found it hard to do so.

"I cannot yet," he muttered, and a moan followed the admission.

He was generous and noble, like his father, but he was only mortal, and it is not always easy for us to practise all the virtues.

The noise of argument increased.

Polowski seemed determined to carry his point, and all but Otto were backing him up.

"Have I not," roared the anarchist leader, "suffered the knout? My back is one mass of scars, that I shall carry with me to my grave. What mercy was shown to me, and why should I show mercy to any living thing?"

"But this lad is not responsible for what you have suffered," urged Otto. "He belongs to a free people, who are not lashed like hounds if they open their mouths. Beside, is it wise and prudent? You forget we want money—we must have it—we—"

An imprecation burst from Polowski's lips.

"Curse your money," he said. "With me it's a second consideration. I want revenge—revenge!"

It was terrible to hear him.

There was an intensity in his voice that chilled the blood of the listener in spite of his natural courage.

"Unbar that door!" roared Polowski.

He was evidently maddened with drink, and the rest were little better. Otto alone spoke clearly.

"I will not unbar it," he said, "but you may

if you wish. Only understand this. If you torture the lad I wash my hands of the whole business."

"You are a cur!"

"You lie!"

Then followed the sounds of struggling men and voices burning with anger.

Suddenly a despairing cry was heard and somebody fell heavily.

"Kill him!" was the cry.

Harry stopped his ears. Not that the sounds which followed were so appalling in themselves, but too clearly could he guess the meaning of them.

The fallen man was being butchered.

It is a terrible word to use, but it is the only one that will in any sense fully describe the work that was going on.

Presently Polowski spoke again.

"Now," he said, "we will deal with the cub."

Harry dropped his hands from his ears and braced himself for a struggle.

"I will not die like a tame sheep," he muttered, "nor shall they beat me while I have the strength to resist."

He drew back opposite the door and prepared for the advent of his foes.

A bar was taken out of its socket and cast to the ground. Then the door was thrown open.

Before him stood Polowski with a heavy whip-handle in his grasp. Behind him were Schavaloff, Kramnitz, and Karl Steimetch, the latter with a pine torch in his hand.

Harry did not wait for them to come in.

The opening of the door revealed to him his one chance of freedom.

With the bound of a young lion he rushed at the men and shot through them like a stone from a catapult.

Sodden with drink, and unprepared for the onslaught, the conspirators yielded like wooden figures—two of them falling prone to the earth.

Before Harry was another open door, with two steps leading to the outer air.

In a moment he was through it and lighted upon a narrow bridge covering a moat.

"Catch him! Stop him!" he heard Polowski cry.

A splendid athlete, and a wonderful runner for his age, Harry dashed across the bridge and bounded down the narrow broken path.

The anarchists were not slow in following him, Polowski foremost.

He had a gun in his hand, and as he covered the flying figure he pulled the trigger.

Only a faint clicking sound followed.

"Curse it!" he cried, "the gun is not loaded."

In a frenzy of disappointment he dashed the weapon into the moat, and sped after his lost captive.

The others, only half-sobered, followed him at a slower pace.

As far as they were concerned Harry was safe.

Away down the hillside sped the boy, and after him came Polowski, like a sleuthhound.

The latter could run well also, and he sprinted at a pace one would not have expected from a man of his heavy build.

Harry did not look back. He knew that he had not a moment to spare.

There were no lights in the village, for there all the inhabitants were at rest.

But he knew the direction to take, and keeping his head cool he sped on.

He ran for dear life—for home—for friends—for everything.

Behind him he could hear the heavy feet of his foe, pounding the hard road, grinding the soil, and scattering the small stones as he came.

So keen are the faculties at such a time that he registered the gradation of sound made by Polowski with the nicety of a delicate sounding-board.

Now fainter, now clearer, came the footsteps behind him.

For hours he had not tasted food, and the fearful excitement had told upon him.

But he ran for his life.

Around his waist he wore a belt which he tightened a couple of holes.

Then squaring his shoulders he put a spurt on.

But Polowski was not to be shaken off.

Poacher, thief, rebel, anarchist—he had lived a hunted life, and was strong of limb and long of breath.

Down the winding path to a piece of comparatively level ground went pursuer and pursued.

"He is gaining," thought Harry.

It was a terrible thought, but it only served to nerve the boy to greater efforts.

He ran at a pace that amazed himself, and his feet seemed scarcely to touch the ground.

The footsteps behind him were losing their distinctness. But, oh! how slowly.

"Can I keep on like this to the village?" the boy thought.

The voice of nature replied, "No," but his strong heart answered "I will."

The way now lay between two piles of rocks —a short ravine wrapped in deep shadow.

Here huge stones made the ground difficult to traverse.

Running now was toil almost beyond human power.

"Stop!" cried Polowski, "or it will be the worse for you."

Harry did not waste breath in replying. He had none to spare, for the Russian was not fifty yards behind.

Harry's breath now came short and thick. His tongue began to loll out, and he knew his eyes were staring, for he could feel them slowly bulging out of their sockets.

Into the ravine he plunged.

Only the keenest of eyes could see the obstacles in his way, but happily he had the clear vision of youth and health.

Over one boulder he went with a leap that cost him a mighty effort.

Then along a few yards of shifting shingle, that made him slide and slip.

A crash!

What is that? Polowski down?

Yes. The ruffian had fallen with a violence that settled the question of pursuit. His gasps of fury were like the snorts of an angry beast.

Harry stopped for a moment and looked round.

He could dimly see a dark form rising from the ground.

"Saved!" gasped the boy, and for a moment he reeled with the sudden reaction that came over him.

Then giving his belt another pull, he staggered rather than walked on for a few yards, with his second wind coming to him.

He emerged from the ravine and was soon on another piece of level ground—a spread of turf as comforting to the eye and foot as a cricket-field.

It gave him fresh strength, but he knew it would be only fleeting, so he did not attempt to linger.

Beyond the grateful turf was the high road, with here and there a rude hut erected by the wayside.

Once there he would be safe.

It was bordered by a stone wall, over which he would have to climb.

He reached the wall and paused for a few moments before attempting to get over it, panting so loudly that the noise he made reminded him of the puffing of a distant railway engine.

He looked back and saw that he was not pursued.

Polowski was either unable or afraid to follow him.

With a grateful feeling no words can express, the boy clasped his hands and raised his eyes for a moment to the arch of stars above him.

Then he slowly climbed over the wall and dropped upon the road.

The moment he had done so he saw a man crouching near him.

In his hand was a rifle, which he levelled at the boy, and in a loud voice he bade him "Stand!"

The shock was so great that Harry reeled and fell.

CHAPTER V.

THE MISSING SCHOOLMASTER—A YOUTHFUL SEARCH-PARTY.

"WAKE up, Jem—it is six o'clock."

Jem Stager, a fairly good sleeper at any time, had passed a heavy night, and was not so easily roused.

A good shaking had to be added to the words, and then he opened his eyes.

"Hallo! Young Ching!" he yawned.

"Wake up, can't you?" was the answer. "Don't you know what we have to do?"

"I remember now," returned Jem, leaping out of bed.

Young Ching left him and went over to another big bed in the room, in which Billy Pink and Dick Cockles were still soundly sleeping.

With them Young Ching used little ceremony.

He simply pulled off the clothes and gave each a spank that effectually scattered their morning dreams.

"Here! what are you doing, Dick?" demanded Billy.

"What are *you* doing?" replied Dick.

"Nothing."

"You hit me."

"I didn't—you hit me, and if you think—oh!—it's Young Ching."

"Dress—the pair of you," said Young Ching, "while I run down and make inquiries."

He slipped out of the room, and the other three proceeded to dress with as much speed as they were capable of.

"I hope nothing serious has happened to Harry," he said.

"So do I," replied Billy Pink.

"But I must say I fear the worst," continued Jem, dolorously.

"'*For I have passed a miserable time,*
So full of ugly sights and ghastly visions,
That, as I am a Christian faithful man,
I would not pass another such a night
Were it to bring a world of happy dreams.'"

"What's that?" asked Billy Pink. "Long-fellow—the poet chap Mr. Bone speaks of?"

"No!" said Dick, "it's Doctor Watts."

"It's Shakespeare, you thickheads," interposed Jem. "Clarence said it in the Tower on the morning they pickled him in malmsey wine."

"You might be civil when you put us right," observed Dick.

"I really can't be civil at all times," replied Jem. "You Siamese Twins of Ignorance are much too trying."

"We didn't ask you to spout Shakespeare to us," said Billy.

"I know you didn't," replied Jem, suavely. "Neither of you are likely to ask for anything that will do you good, but you have got to partake of it in the form of forced mental nourishment, whether you like it or not."

"Oh! bless your what's-his-name nourishment!" growled Dick.

Jem was about to comment on the reprehensible indifference to mental food exhibited by Dick, when the door opened and Young Ching reappeared.

There was no mistaking his face—it meant something was wrong.

"I say, boys!" he exclaimed, "here's a go. Dear old Bone went out last night and hasn't come back. Mrs. Grumps is sitting by the kitchen fire weeping. She says we shall all be briganded."

"This is a bad job," said Jem, seriously.

Dick and Billy said nothing at first, but their expressive faces indicated several printed quires of apprehension.

"Oh! my," presently observed Dick.

"What now?" asked Jem Stager, gloomily.

"Suppose we are left to ourselves, with Mrs. Grumps to take care of."

"Horrible thought!" cried Jem.

"Come downstairs," exclaimed Young Ching. "Something's got to be done."

The boys filed out of the room and went down to the kitchen.

There they found Monsieur Picard, Frisby Whelks, and Mrs. Grumps.

The latter was in a fearful state of trepidation.

"I am sure he is dead," she was saying. "He was never a man to stop out all night, his habits being regular and orthycrocks at all times—"

"Madame," said the Frenchman, "you alarm yourself needlessly. Monsieur Bone is adding to ze jest."

Then, observing the boys, he bade them good-morning and moved away to let them come to the fire.

"It isn't cold," said Young Ching, "and we think of going for a walk."

"You won't go out without me," said Mrs. Grumps.

"Of course we expect you to go with us," replied Jem Stager, gravely.

Young Ching looked at him reproachfully, but the thing was done. Mrs. Grumps would have to accompany them.

"Will you come with us?" Young Ching said, addressing Frisby Whelks.

"Where are you going?" asked the tutor.

"To the castle you spoke of."

"Oh! dear no!"

Mrs. Grumps looked at him with matronly scorn.

"Do you call yourself a man?" she asked.

"I don't know that I call myself anything," he replied, rather sullenly.

"Quite right," said Mrs. Grumps, briskly; "you hain't got a right to."

Turning to the boys she said—

"I'm ready to start. If this gentleman is afraid we are not. Monswore Pickardle, or whatever your name may be," she added, addressing the Frenchman, "have the goodness to put us up a bottle of milk and a bag of biscuits."

"As you please, madame," replied the Frenchman; "and what time will you haf breakfast?"

Both Young Ching and Jem Stager detected a sarcastic tone in this inquiry, but they said nothing, merely exchanging a look full of meaning.

The Frenchman went out and speedily returned with a rush basket containing the articles she required.

"Madame," he said, "it may be better for you to stop here."

But Mrs. Grumps, when roused, was a very determined woman.

"You mind your own business, young man," she said, "and as for you," turning to Frisby Whelks, "if I had your heart do you know what I'd do?"

"No, I don't," replied Mr. Whelks.

"Why, I'd just get into a mousetrap and live there," she aswered. "Now, lads, keep with me."

And out she marched with the boys, like a pugnacious old hen with a lot of young chickens.

To confess the truth, Mrs. Grumps soon came to the conclusion that she had been rather hasty, and ere they had got out of the village she began to wonder if she were not doing wrong in risking the lives of the boys —that is, always supposing brigands were in the neighbourhood.

For herself she cared little. She was neither young, beautiful, nor rich, and thus felt she was brigand-proof.

But for them it was quite another thing.

"I think," she said, halting suddenly, "that you boys had better go back."

"So we will, Mrs. Grumps," replied Young Ching, "presently."

He broke into a trot and forged ahead, followed by all except Billy Pink, who was quickly collared by the old lady.

"No, William," she exclaimed. "Whatever happens you can't be spared. What's to become of your great futurity if the brigands kill you?"

"I should like to go on, ma'am," said Billy.

"No doubt you would like to go on," was Mrs. Grumps' reply to Billy Pink, "and risk your precious young life. Come back, you young rascals—come back."

"By-and-bye," replied Young Ching.

"How wrong of me to bring them out," muttered Mrs. Grumps, as she also broke into a trot, "but I was that 'ere aggravated by the moustarchied Frenchman I felt I could do anything. Besides which that precious Whelks tempted me to do something to make him blush for himself. Come back, you boys, I say."

But they were well ahead, and gradually increased their pace.

In the distance stood the castle of Namedi, a perfect landmark and guide to them.

"Come on," said Young Ching, between his teeth. "We will get a peep at the place, anyhow. If anything like a brigand shows himself we can skedaddle."

"All right," replied Jem Stager. "Shall the heart of Britons quail? Shall heroes in their efforts fail? Lead on, dear chum, to victory or death."

"Here comes Mrs. Grumps," said Dick Cockles. "She is putting a spurt on."

"Come back, you villains!" cried Mrs. Grumps, in an agony of fear. "I never meant it."

"We shall not be long," replied Young Ching. "Here, Jem, this looks like a short cut to the castle."

He turned aside to a gap in the roadside wall, jumped through it, and was promptly followed by Jem and Dick, the latter with a faint idea that he had a very fair prospect of meeting with an untimely end.

CHAPTER VI.

AN ANARCHIST CONFOUNDED—A RUN FOR LIFE —LOVELY WOMAN AT HER BEST.

IT would be difficult to say what Young Ching and his companions really intended to do.

They could hardly expect to be able to cope with men of the class described by Frisby Whelks, but perhaps they did not fully believe his story.

Young Ching, like his father, was a stranger to fear, and it is possible that he did not attempt to realise what odds might be brought against him.

One thing is certain.

The bare idea of Young Handsome Harry being in peril was sufficient to stimulate him to do almost anything.

It is true that the boys knew very little of each other personally, but their slight association had been sufficient to create a strong feeling of friendship between them.

In addition there was the tie between the two fathers.

Young Ching had heard so much of Sir Henry Marsh that he had learnt to look upon him as a hero—a model on whom to found himself.

"What will Sir Henry think if anything happens to Harry?" thought Young Ching.

It was characteristic of the son of the Immortal One that he did not think of his own peril.

He had never yet got into trouble without having found his way out again, and he did not see why there should be a break in the run of his good fortune.

So on went the boys, over the rugged ground, and behind them came Mrs. Grumps and Billy Pink, who was commanded, on pain of losing her affection for ever, not to leave her side.

She had to give up expostulating with those in front as soon as she reached the rough ground, but she still followed on.

The boys presently came to a bit of wood, of no great extent, but sufficient to conceal the castle for a time from view.

It was a collection of birch and other trees growing behind huge boulders, and the travelling was " very stiff."

Beyond the trees the land was open right up to the castle.

As the boys were about to emerge from the wood, Young Ching grasped Jem Stager by the arm.

" Hist !" he said.

Young Ching pointed ahead, and Jem and Dick saw a man about a hundred yards away seated on a large stone.

He was resting his arms upon his knees, and his back was towards them.

In appearance he corresponded with one of the men described by Frisby Whelks.

It was Polowski.

His fall had shaken him so much that he had been obliged to rest for an hour or so in the ravine before returning to the castle.

When he got there he found his late companions gone. Only one remained—the still form of Otto Lurgan.

Hastening away from the sight of his handiwork with such speed as he could muster up, Polowski had wandered about, uncertain which way to go.

" Jem," whispered Young Ching.

" Yes, old chum," replied Jem.

" Now's the time to make a name."

" What do you mean ?"

" Let us go and collar the fellow."

Jem stared, and so did Dick Cockles.

" Don't you think it can be done ?" asked Young Ching. " I am sure he is one of the ruffians Whelks spoke of, and all we have to do is to creep up behind, pull him over on his back, and hold him."

" Is that all ?" said Jem Stager, drily.

" Are you game to try it ?" asked Young Ching.

" But how long shall we have to hold him ?"

" Oh ! never mind that," replied Young Ching; " we can tie his arms and legs. If you are not game to do it say so."

" I am," whispered Jem.

" So am I," added Dick.

" I will lay hold of him by the collar," said Young Ching, " and as I pull him over each of you must get hold of a leg and cling to it like a wild cat. A man is pretty well helpless when he's seized that way."

Jem was not so sure about that, but whatever Young Ching did he was willing to join in, and, anyway, if the man was too much for them they could but run.

" Quiet, now," said Young Ching.

And forth they went on their daring mission.

When Mrs. Grumps emerged from the wood she saw her young charges well on their way towards the gloomily meditating Polowski, and amazement deprived her of the power of speaking aloud.

But she could think, and in her mind was the unuttered remark—

" There isn't anything in the world they won't try to do."

She and Billy went upon their trail, but ere they could overtake the trio Young Ching had made his attempt to capture Polowski.

It is no great disgrace to him or his companions that he failed.

His programme was carried out.

As soon as he got close up to the Russian, which he did unperceived, he laid hold of his coat-collar and pulled Polowski back with a sharp jerk.

At the same moment Dick and Jem darted to the front and got hold of his legs.

Polowski was a powerful man, and was not to be made captive by three daring striplings.

Throwing up his herculean legs, he fairly tossed Jem and Dick a couple of feet into the air, and then he made a clutch at Young Ching.

But that agile youth had already seen that the task he had undertaken was too great for him, and had let go.

Polowski sprang to his feet and felt in his belt for a knife.

" Ah ! would you ?" said Young Ching, picking up a large stone; " drop it and get away ! I don't like using this sort of thing, but I will if you come that."

Jem and Dick had likewise armed themselves with stones in self-defence, and were working their way round to Young Ching with their faces to the foe.

Polowski snarled at them like a wolf, but

BILLY PINK AND DICK COCKLES ASTONISH A WAITER.

there was a lot of the dog in him, and he was afraid of a stone.

"You are a nice lot," he growled; "but I've marked you, and some day I'll make you pipe another tune. At my name monarchs are learning to tremble."

"Your grandmother," replied Young Ching; "what next? Who are you?"

"Polowski the anarchist!" he cried. "I tell you—keep off, woman."

Mrs. Grumps had joined in the fray.

She had given Billy the rush basket to carry, and held in her grasp a good old family umbrella.

"You murderous villain!" she gasped. "Where's the young gentleman you've killed? Where's Mr. Bone?"

"If you come another step nearer," hissed Polowski, "you are a dead woman."

Mrs. Grumps took another step nearer—in fact, two—and aimed a blow at Polowski which he had to step back to avoid.

"At him, boys," cried Young Ching; "he's a cur."

He was right in his estimation of the ruffian's character.

Polowski did not wait for their onslaught, but turned and fled.

Mrs. Grumps leaned on her umbrella and looked proudly at the boys.

"Which," she said, "I've always said that you boys had no equals, and I'm ready to maintain it to my dying day."

"It's a good job that some of us have no equals," replied Jem, with a significant glance at Billy Pink. "If we had the world would burst with genius."

To this Billy Pink replied, serenely—

"We can't all be fools, you know," at which Young Ching chuckled, and gave Billy a smack on the back.

"Now what's next?" Young Ching said. "Shall we storm the castle and see if there are any more duffers like what's-his-name— Polowski, the king-slayer?"

"No," interposed Mrs. Grumps, determinedly barring the way. "I'm not going to let you risk your precious young lives any further. That sort of man is dangerous. If he can't get you fair he will do so foul."

By this remark Mrs. Grumps showed that she was gifted with an average amount of intuition.

Polowski was a dangerous man.

Where he hated he did so with the intensity of the inborn assassin.

Nothing less than the lives of his foes satisfied him.

Thereupon were Young Ching and his companions in greater danger than they apprehended.

The moment after Mrs. Grumps spoke another voice was heard, calling them from afar off.

At first they could not see who it was, but Young Ching recognised the familiar tone.

"That sounds like Mr. Bone," he said.

"And there he is," observed Jem Stager, pointing away to the left.

They all looked in the direction and saw that amiable teacher of the young violently gesticulating for them to descend.

CHAPTER VII.

A PARTY FORMED TO GO TO THE CASTLE— WHAT THEY DISCOVERED THERE.

THE appearance of Mr. Fossil Bone was so unexpected that none of the boys could at first make any response to his signals.

Young Ching was the first to return the schoolmaster's salute.

Holding up a hand by way of reply he said to the boys—

"He appears to want us to go down, and I suppose we must. Anyway, he is safe, and that is a comfort."

"I never felt more glad," said Mrs. Grumps, "for if anything had happened to that dear, kind-hearted man I believe I should have broken my heart."

They moved downward in a body, and Mr. Bone awaited their coming.

As the boys proceeded in his direction they saw a peasant's cottage, almost hidden by trees and rocks, and in front of it was a personage they had caught a glimpse of the day before.

It was the village gendarme.

"Boys," cried Mr. Bone, when they came within hail, "what have you been doing up there?"

An explanation was necessary, and Mrs. Grumps gave it.

"Which," she said, "they were bound on as daring a hexpedition as ever was, to resky that young gentleman, him as is spoken of as Young Handsome Harry, and to see what has happened to you."

"Boys," said Mr. Bone, with a very serious face, "I appreciate your intention and admire your daring, but you really must not risk your lives in this way. We are not in England now!"

"I don't think it matters much where they are," said Mrs. Grumps, glowing with pride; "you'll never change 'em."

By this time they were clambering over a wall which skirted the road.

Mr. Bone assisted Mrs. Grumps to get upon the other side, which she succeeded in doing by taking the top row of stone with her.

"You must be very quiet," said Mr. Bone, "for I have a patient here. It is Harry Marsh."

"A patient!" exclaimed the boys.

"He has suffered a shock," continued Mr. Bone. "Last night I started with the gendarme to see if there were any signs of living people at the castle. If so, we meant to get help and rescue our young friend, but either he has not been there at all or has succeeded in escaping."

"Is he wounded, sir?" Jem Stager asked, his mind at once turning to daring fights and broadsword combats.

"No," said Mr. Bone; "but he must have been in an exhausted condition when he got over the wall. We heard him approaching, and concluding that it was one of the band of ruffians spoken of by Mr. Whelks, crouched down behind the wall to capture him. The moment he got over this worthy fellow," pointing to the gendarme, "presented his rifle at him and bade him stand. He immediately reeled and fell."

"He must have been exhausted," said Young Ching, emphatically.

"For hours he has been delirious," resumed Mr. Bone, "and I have been watching over him. He is now in a quiet sleep. I am sorry my absence has given rise to any anxiety, but it never entered my head, for I have been so anxious about Harry Marsh. What a splendid fellow he is!"

"And couldn't Mister Moustarches have come?" asked Mrs. Grumps.

"I kept him here," said Mr. Bone, "fearing the place might be attacked, as the only occupier of the cottage is a feeble old woman. Stay here, boys—I will go in and see how he is."

The boys gathered in a group together, and Mrs. Grumps turned her attention to the gendarme.

He was a well-built fellow, with a full-blown moustache, and looked as if he could fight if need be.

"Do you speak English, sir?" asked Mrs. Grumps.

The gendarme shook his head.

He did not understand what was said to him, but the negative motion was as good an answer as could have been given.

"Poor thing!" exclaimed Mrs. Grumps, "but it's like them foreigners—not half of 'em are edicated."

Here she detected a smile on Jem Stager's face, and in her usual placid eye there came a temporary gleam of severity.

"Are you laughing at me, Mister Stager?" she asked.

When Mrs. Grumps "mistered" any of the boys they might reckon she had been offended.

"Laughing at you, Mrs. Grumps!" exclaimed Jem; "at you! Oh! how can you think so? By my faith as a knight and baron of the weald—of—somewhere, I would perish rather than do aught to annoy thee."

"You needn't have broke forth into poetry to say so," returned Mrs. Grumps, mollified, "and don't do it again. It isn't perlite. William would not have done it. He's too high bred."

Again did Jem struggle with a smile, and the face of Dick Cockles expanded into a grin.

Mrs. Grumps regarded them in turn with withering severity, and was about to reprove them when Mr. Bone reappeared.

"Young Ching," he said, "you may come in."

Young Ching responded with alacrity, and followed the schoolmaster into the cottage.

It was a poorly-furnished place, but very neat and clean.

On one side was a fire burning on the hearth, where an old woman was stirring some savoury soup simmering in a saucepan.

Opposite the fire was a humble couch, on which Harry was reclining.

He looked rather pale, but otherwise seemed pretty well.

"How are you, old fellow?" he said, holding out his hand to Young Ching. "I've had a bit of a shaking up, but I shall be all right as soon as I have had something to eat."

"You can tell us everything after you have had some breakfast," said Mr. Bone.

Young Ching shook hands with the invalid, and sat down on the side of the couch.

"We have had a strange yarn from Mr. Whelks," said Young Ching.

"He hasn't told you anything stranger than the truth," was the answer.

The soup was now ready.

As a nourishing compound it may have been very poor stuff, but Harry was glad of it, not having had anything to eat for fourteen hours.

He speedily disposed of the same, and then stood erect.

"I feel as if I have been well thrashed all over," he said, "but otherwise there is nothing the matter with me."

"You must have a carriage back to the inn," said Mr. Bone.

"Not a bit of it," replied the gallant young fellow. "I can walk. But what beats me now is my fainting away. It is true I had a rough time of it— Stay! I had forgotten one thing. There is a murdered man lying in the castle."

"A murdered man!" echoed Mr. Bone and Young Ching.

The old woman did not understand him, and therefore did not exhibit any emotion.

"Yes," cried Harry, "and I think something ought to be done to secure his murderers. I shall be happy to swear to the villains."

"How many are there?" asked Mr. Bone.

"Four."

"Then we must have help, so back to the village we must go."

"I am ready," said the hero of the night's adventures. "Give me an arm, Young Ching. Thanks, old boy. I will do as much for you if ever you get into my condition. Upon my word I never was half so stiff in my life before."

As he was going out of the cottage he took some money out of a pocket in the belt of his trousers and slipped it into the old woman's hand.

She looked at it and uttered a cry of delight.

Mr. Bone saw the action, and also caught a glimpse of the money.

"Gold!" he exclaimed. "Ah! I don't suppose the old woman has handled much of it in her lifetime. But how is it you were not robbed?"

"They took all they could find in my ordinary pockets," replied Harry, laughing, " but they never thought of the real bank."

Followed by broken words of gratitude from the old woman, they left the cottage, and outside Harry met with a hearty greeting.

Mrs. Grumps fairly perspired with admiration.

With the gendarme marching in front they started back, Harry gradually losing the stiff-ness of his limbs, so that when the inn came in sight his step was almost as elastic as ever.

On the way he heard all about Frisby Whelks, and the way he told his story. It made him laugh heartily.

"You must not be too hard on poor Whelks," he said, "for his parents were both jumpy people."

"Generously spoken," observed Mr. Bone.

The first person they saw on entering the inn was Picard, whose sallow complexion turned to a ghastly hue as his eyes fell on Harry.

He opened his mouth, apparently to say something congratulatory, but no sound came forth.

The eyes of Mr. Bone lighted up with sudden sternness.

"If you know anything of yonder nest of villains," he said, "you had better say so."

"Monsieur," pleaded Picard, "how shall it be for me to know?"

"We shall see," replied Mr. Bone. "Is breakfast ready?"

"Zere is enough to eat in ze house," was the sullen answer.

Mr. Bone, Harry, and the gendarme had a little private conversation together, and then the latter went away to get help to search the castle.

There was very little probability of finding the anarchists there, but they would see proofs of the horrible murder Harry had spoken of.

Shortly after he was gone Picard, disguised as a peasant, surreptitiously left the inn by the back way.

The morning's work had given all our friends a good appetite, and despite the serious nature of recent events they were very jolly.

Frisby Whelks was the quietest of the party, but Harry tried to put him at his ease.

"I don't blame you," he said, "for you simply can't help it. After fainting away I don't feel as if I could lecture anybody on the score of courage."

"It was not fear you felt," said Mr. Bone.

"What was it then?"

"You were worn out, and at the moment when you thought you were free the gendarme and his rifle gave you such a shock of disappointment that it was too much for human nature to stand up against."

"Yes, that seems to be about it," said Harry, thoughtfully. "It was really the bitterest disappointment I ever experienced, but it is all over. I will take another egg and some toast."

The gendarme secured the services of a dozen strong fellows armed with a variety of weapons, from an old musket to a scythe.

They formed a valiant body, and set forth upon their expedition with a martial air.

"They won't capture anybody," said Harry.

The boys wanted to go and see what happened, but Mr. Bone and Mrs. Grumps set their faces against it.

The latter was especially emphatic.

"Once is enough to risk your young lives," she said, "but for all that it makes me proud of you. I shouldn't be surprised if one day William became a general, for I have read that the French used to say every private carried his bacon in his knapsack."

"Baton, my dear madam," explained Frisby Whelks.

"And may I ask, young man, what's the difference?" demanded Mrs. Grumps.

"Oh! there's a lot of difference," he feebly replied. "Bacon is one thing, and a marshal's baton is another."

"And you're another," retorted Mrs. Grumps, "so there's an end of that argument."

Frisby Whelks prudently allowed it to be the end of the matter, and walked into the village.

The boys were already there sauntering up and down.

"You have had a narrow escape, Harry," observed Young Ching.

"Yes," was the answer.

"And what beats me," said Jem Stager, "is the folly and madness of these men. Their scheme of brigandage seems to me to be most hopeless."

"Desperate men will do desperate things," replied Harry.

"It's our first real adventure," said Young Ching, "although we have had some fun on the way. How did you find us out?"

"I got information of your route before I started," replied Harry. "The fact is, as soon as I heard you had gone, I said to my dear old dad—'I must go.' 'Very well,' he said, 'a little travelling won't harm you, but you must have a tutor.' Time pressed, and Whelks was the best we could get."

"A duffer," observed Young Ching.

"Undoubtedly," replied Harry, "but as my dear dad said, I could take care of myself, and all I wanted was the appearance of not being alone. Heard from home since you left?"

"Once," said Young Ching, with a grin. "Poor old— But that will keep. Here— what's the row now?"

Some distance up the street a huge dog was barking fiercely at Dick Cockles, who had mounted a wooden fence and was yelling at the brute.

Billy Pink was engaged in harassing the enemy with stones.

"The bite of that dog would be dangerous," said Harry. "Let us go and drive the brute away."

Accompanied by Young Ching and Jem Stager, he bore down upon the spot, and they were just in time to prevent serious mischief.

Billy Pink as a thrower of stones was not so good as he used to be.

The life he had been leading lately had cut him off from the old boyish pursuit of pelting every bird he saw perched on a post or hedge.

His right hand, therefore, had lost its cunning, and in aiming at the dog he hit Dick, who received a stone as big as an orange just above the belt, which turned him right over, and he fell on the other side of the fence.

The dog was bounding after him, but not quite clearing the fence he floundered about for a moment on the top.

That moment saved Dick from a worrying.

Harry and Young Ching seized the dog and dragged it back into the road. Then the former gave it a kick that sent it away howling.

The next moment Dick was seen scrambling back again.

"Let me get at him," he yelled.

"Are you mad?" said Jem Stager, collaring him. "Don't you attempt to follow the dog. He will eat you."

"I am not speaking of the dog," replied Dick, with a laugh. "It's Billy I mean."

"What do you want to get at him for?"

"To punch his head. Didn't he hit me with a stone?"

"Suppose he did," said Young Ching. "He saved your life by knocking you over just as the dog sprang up. Where's your gratitude?"

Dick suddenly became calmer.

"I didn't look at it in that sense," he said.

"No, of course you didn't," returned Jem. "If I were Billy I would cut you dead."

"Oh! it's all right," returned Billy.

"The fact is," said Jem, "nobody is to blame—not even the dog."

"He flew at me as I was passing," urged Dick.

"What of that?" calmly asked Jem.

"What of that? Why, everything," roared Dick. "How would you like it?"

"You have asked me a peculiar question, Dick," observed Jem Stager.

"I don't see it."

"I do," said Jem. "Look at the bearings of the case. Here you are, the son of an eminent purveyor of toothsome bags of mystery. Never mind what is in them. The dog evidently suspected something, and in revenge for the injuries inflicted on the canine race generally, he—"

"Oh! you've always got some absurd joke to make," grunted Dick. "Come on, Billy—let's go and see if we can get any sweets in this blessed place."

And away they went with their arms affectionately linked—drawn to each other on the principle of natural selection.

"One of these days, Jem," said Young Ching, "Dick will have a go at you."

Jem laughed.

"All right," he replied, "I won't hurt him."

They were sauntering back when a shouting behind caused them to turn.

The gendarme and his friends were advancing through the village.

"No prisoners," observed Young Ching.

"But they are excited," said Harry. "Let us hear what they have to say."

They had a lot to say, and as they all talked together it was difficult to make out their words, but the substance of their utterances was as follows.

They had been to the castle and found strong evidence of murder having been committed, as described by Harry.

But the body of Otto Lurgan was not there.

"It had been dragged away," said the gendarme, "and we traced it a hundred yards down the hill, where we found something that Monsieur Picard must answer for. It is a letter to one Polowski, telling him of the English guests at his inn. He has described them to the brigands and must be arrested."

———

CHAPTER VIII.

DEPARTURE FROM THE VILLAGE—FOES IN HIDING —MRS. GRUMPS HAS A SHOCK TO HER NERVES.

PICARD, as we know, had left the inn disguised, and his wife professed to be in utter ignorance of his movements.

"He is not here," she said, "and that is enough. Let him go where he likes—it is nothing to me."

The gendarme was not astonished at these sentiments, as it was well known throughout the village that Picard and his wife did not live happily together.

"We will look for him elsewhere," he said.

The gendarme had already communicated with the authorities at Anderbach, and before evening arrived there came to the village half-a-dozen of his mounted *confrères*, all very fierce and terrible, and bent on capturing "those murdering brigands."

They virtually took possession of the inn, and showed a marked disposition to make merry before commencing business.

Indeed, they made merry all that evening, and did not go in search of the anarchists until the following morning.

Of course, it was then "all U. P.," as Young Ching said, and they might as well have looked for the man in the moon.

Two days later our friends left the village, where they had enjoyed themselves passing well, and left a few slight records of their liveliness behind them.

Mr. Fossil Bone was going to Basle, in the north of Switzerland, where there is very beautiful scenery not overrun by tourists.

There he expected to spend a short time among the chain of minor mountains that run through its southern part, and after that he intended to scale the Alps.

It was to be a tour on foot, save so far as Mrs. Grumps was concerned.

That estimable lady being rather heavily built, and not so young as she was thirty years before, a mule had been bought for her.

He was an obstinate brute, with occasional bursts of humour. When at his best he would amble along like a camel, but he required what the boys called "stimulants."

Between Mrs. Grumps and this mule no love was lost.

She was indignant at the beast's obstinacy, and he bitterly resented her being so heavy.

The name of this interesting animal was Julius Cæsar, but he was generally spoken of as Julius or Juley. To the boys he was a source of unmitigated delight.

Had he carried Mrs. Grumps in an amiable manner, they would scarcely have been interested in him, but as he required their constant attention, they found him a source of joy.

The start from the inn was a brilliant scene.

All the village turned out, as if it had been a public holiday.

There was Julius Cæsar ready to proceed, but unwilling to let Mrs. Grumps get upon his back, and wriggling here and there to avoid her.

Young Ching and Jem Stager held his head, and the other boys looked after his flanks, touching him up with sticks as he shifted about.

Mr. Whelks, anxious to make peace, volunteered to assist Mrs. Grumps into her seat, and it was about as stiff a job as he had ever undertaken.

He clasped that lady in his arms and raised her a few inches, then, as Julius slipped away, he staggered forward and nearly fell with his burden.

This performance was repeated two or three times, the villagers crying—"Hi—hi!" and the boys bursting with laughter.

"That will do, young man," said Mrs. Grumps, pushing the tutor away. "You are a poor, helpless creature. It's a good job I'm not your mother."

At last, with the assistance of Mr. Bone, she was got upon the brute's back, and then without warning Julius broke into a trot.

Young Ching and Jem, accustomed to his little manœuvres, slipped aside, but the youths of the village were knocked over to the number of half-a-dozen, amidst the screams of their parents and friends.

Harry trotted on one side of the head of the mule and Billy Pink on the other, while Jem Stager and Young Ching kept just clear of his heels.

Dick Cockles and the two men were behind, and the inhabitants, including dogs and other live stock, brought up the rear.

On the outskirts of the village was a deserted house which had the reputation of being haunted.

Once upon a time it had been a smithy, but the last man to wield a hammer there was found beside his forge brutally murdered.

It was never known who did it, but the crime sufficed to establish a ghost in the place, and nobody afterwards would live there or even go near if they could help themselves.

It was now shut up, but was not, as the people supposed, untenanted.

Through sundry cracks in the old wooden shutters of the forge five pairs of eyes glared upon our friends as they went by.

The four remaining anarchists and Picard were concealed there.

Polowski ground his teeth as he looked at Harry swinging along at the mule's head—as fine a specimen of athletic youth as ever was seen.

"There he goes," said the anarchist. "Well-dressed and happy—and what are we? But I will settle with this fine bird one day. He is on the wing now, but by-and-bye I will bring him down."

"Death to the rich," hissed the others in chorus.

Our friends, unconscious of the lurking foe, went on their way, the villagers rapidly tailing off.

Soon Julius Cæsar subsided into a walk, and so gave everybody a chance of regaining their breath.

Mrs. Grumps had been terribly shaken, but she tried to make the best of it, and smiled as she panted.

"Which it is a beast," she said, "but thank Heaven we are none of us doomed to ride on such pigs for ever and ever."

Mr. Bone had a map of the country with him, which he consulted every now and then.

When they had passed the castle of Namedi a distance of two miles or so, he directed them to take a turning to the left.

Ahead of them was a jagged line of tremendous hills, which to the uninitiated were veritable mountains.

"We have to cross them before night, boys," said Mr. Bone, "for that part of the route is inclined to be dangerous. I beseech all of you if there is any danger not to be up to your pranks."

Of course they all said they would be patterns of good behaviour, and on they went up a steep road, with here and there a herdsman's hut.

For the most part they appeared to be deserted, but occasionally they came upon a sad-eyed man, wretchedly clad, eating black bread and very odorous cheese.

"It is so strong," said Jem Stager, "that I wonder it doesn't blow their heads off."

Harry could not pass any of these poor creatures without a gift of some sort.

As he handed them a few coins their eyes would expand and they would stare at him as if he was a visitor from another world.

Just before noon the travellers stopped to rest on a plateau that commanded a view of the country they had passed through.

The forefeet of Julius were hobbled, not without protest on his part, and he was allowed to roam around.

THE TWO DAUNTLESS BOYS FACE THE WOULD-BE ASSASSIN.

A leathern trunk was opened by Mr. Bone, disclosing sundry eatables and drinkables, neatly packed by Mrs. Grumps.

What appetites they had, and how they laughed and chatted. The sense of freedom they felt was delightful.

"It really is jolly," said Young Ching.

Even Frisby Whelks became almost frisky.

He made strenuous efforts to let off jokes, and got on very well for a time, because nobody took any notice of him until he chose Mrs. Grumps as a theme.

"The ancient Julius Cæsar," he observed, "bore the burden of State, and the modern Julius Cæsar staggers under the burden of fair woman."

"Young man," said Mrs. Grumps, "do you mean to say that I give the beast the staggers?"

"No—not exactly that," replied Mr. Whelks, beginning to curl up.

"Then what do you mean?"

"I don't mean anything in particular."

"Young man," said Mrs. Grumps, "will you oblige me by looking at William Pink?"

The tutor nearly collapsed as he did so, for he saw that Billy had his mouth full of something, and was vigorously masticating it, thereby giving to his jaws an appearance remarkably like those of a crocodile.

"Are you looking?" asked Mrs. Grumps.

"I am," was the response.

"And you ought to keep looking if you want to know how to behave yourself," said Mrs. Grumps. "He is a boy, and you are supposed to be a man, but you ain't worthy to black his boots."

Then the tutor subsided into nothingness, and Mrs. Grumps went on with her luncheon.

Nobody else took part in this conversation, and to outward appearance nobody listened to it, but a glance full of meaning passed between Mr. Bone and Harry.

Luncheon over, Julius Cæsar was captured, and Harry, without apparent effort, assisted Mrs. Grumps to remount.

"And beautifully done it was," she said. "Young man, did you see that?"

The young man was Frisby Whelks and he did see it, wearily signifying as much by a slight bow.

As soon as the remnants of the meal were packed up they started again.

The road they had to take was pretty clear, but it was narrow, and became more rugged as they journeyed onward.

From an artistic point of view it was lovely, but it was very lonely.

As they were jogging along, Harry occasionally looked back, and by the merest chance he espied some moving figures about a mile behind them.

Had they been ordinary pedestrians he would have taken no further notice of them, but their movements were suspicious.

They seemed to be dodging about.

And moreover they were five in number.

"I wonder if they are the Black Bandits of the Rhine," he thought.

This was the name the boys had given to Polowski and his friends, and it was appropriate enough, for no blacker band of ruffians ever walked the earth.

Harry was not certain it was his recent acquaintances, and not desiring to create an alarm which might be a false one, he said nothing about what he had seen.

Quietly Harry looked back every few minutes for the next half-hour or so.

He did not catch sight of the men every time, but he saw them two or three times more.

Then they suddenly vanished, and did not reappear.

Supposing they were strangers, there was nothing in their disappearance to wonder at.

The country was very rugged, with roads leading in various directions, and here and there was a cottage or a hut, to one of which they might have gone.

For nearly an hour Harry continued to take occasional glances to the rear, but he saw no more of the men.

Then he concluded that they were harmless wayfarers, and dismissed the matter from his mind.

By-and-bye they came to a spur of a great hill, around which the path curved, with a precipice on the left fully two hundred feet deep.

"Now, boys," said Mr. Bone, "steady does it, and walk in Indian file. There is no danger if you proceed quietly."

It was really their first lesson in mountaineering, and although the precipice was nothing compared to what they were to become familiar with by-and-bye, it was quite enough to try their nerves.

A fall of two hundred feet is as good as two thousand, so far as killing one is concerned.

Harry thought nothing of it, and to give confidence to the rest he went on before, with a step as sure and fearless as that of a mountain goat.

Arriving at a projection he turned to look back, and saw something that fairly curdled his blood with terror.

Julius Cæsar had bolted away from the party behind, and was coming along the ledge at a full gallop.

Mrs. Grumps was on the brute's back, sticking there like a limpet, but any moment might bring destruction to animal and rider.

The slightest slip on the part of Julius would pitch him over the precipice and Mrs. Grumps with him.

Harry's position was not an enviable one either. If Julius Cæsar did not stop in his mad career he might hurl him over.

In a moment the resolution of the gallant youth was taken.

Planting himself firmly on his feet, he awaited the rush of the beast, calling out as he did so—

"Hold on as tightly as you can, Mrs. Grumps."

She did not hear him.

Wild terror had brought about a species of mental collapse, and his quick eye could see that the grasp she had of the mane of Julius was relaxing.

"Merciful Heavens!" he exclaimed, "she will be killed. Stand still, brute!"

Harry and the mule had met, and his hands grasped the reins close on either side of his head.

For a moment Julius Cæsar seemed as if he would resist, but the iron grasp upon his jaws told him he had met his master, and he yielded.

At the same moment Mrs. Grumps yielded too.

She lost her seat, but happily slid off behind.

Julius, relieved of his burden, began to kick.

"Heave ahead, you beggar!" cried Harry, hauling at the reins. "Don't move, Mrs. Grumps, or your brains will be kicked out."

The boys were coming on at a run in pursuit, farther back still was Mr. Bone, and last of all Frisby Whelks.

Mr. Bone was shouting to the boys.

"Take care—mind you don't fall—steady—not two together—oh! Heavens! that is horrible."

From out of the group of scurrying boys there suddenly shot a dark object right over the precipice.

The schoolmaster stood still, and it seemed to him as if his very heart had ceased to beat.

The boys had also stopped and thrown themselves down upon their stomachs, with their heads over the precipice, their keen eyes looking into the depths below.

CHAPTER IX.

JULIUS CÆSAR GETS TOO MUCH FOR WHELKS AND IS ALLOWED TO RUN WILD—THE STEAMBOAT ON THE RHINE.

IT is no figure of speech when we declare that for a moment or two Mr. Fossil Bone's life came to a standstill.

As for Frisby Whelks, when he saw the heavy object fall over the precipice he shut his eyes, gave one gasp, and sat down heavily upon the ground.

"Boys," said Mr. Bone, huskily, "who is missing?"

"I told him not to swing it," replied Jem Stager, "but he would do it. It's just like Billy, and now it's gone."

"It—it?" said Mr. Bone.

"Yes, sir, the bag with the rest of the provisions."

Mr. Bone burst into a roar of laughter, so loud that the rocks reverberated with the sound, and Mrs. Grumps, who had been considerably shaken by her fall, was restored to full consciousness.

Opening her eyes she looked round and exclaimed—

"Goodness me! what's the matter now? Was it thunder?"

Nobody answered her, for Young Harry had gone on ahead with Julius Cæsar, and the boys behind were staring at Mr. Bone, whose laughter—the outcome of a sudden revulsion of feeling—bordered on the hysterical.

"Don't mind me, boys," he said, as soon as he could speak. "The fact is, I thought it was one of you who had fallen over, but when I found it was only the bag, I—ha-ha-ha! Well! it is just what you might expect from Pink."

"I don't see where the laugh comes in," grumbled Jem Stager to Young Ching. "Our tea was in that bag."

"Now, boys," said Mr. Bone, "let me come in front. I see Mrs. Grumps has need of assistance. Follow me one by one, and do be careful. Don't get peeping over the precipice after that bag, or you may follow it."

He assisted Mrs. Grumps to rise, and that

estimable lady having given herself a shake to see if any bones were broken, and finding none were injured to that extent, she declared herself ready to go on.

"But I shall walk and not ride," she said. "Never will I get on the back of that brute again, if I die with fatigue forty times a day."

"You want a little brandy and water after that tumble," returned Mr. Bone, "but I am sorry to say that Pink has dropped the bag into the valley below."

"I slipped, sir," said Billy, dolorously, "and thought I was going over myself."

"Any other boy," returned Mrs. Grumps, "would have gone. It's a marvel, William, that you are here now. I don't want any brandy."

Mr. Bone saw that some little alteration would have to be made in the programme. It would be impossible for Mrs. Grumps to keep on afoot.

The spirit was willing, but the flesh was heavy, and an early breakdown was inevitable.

As soon as they got on to better ground he stopped to consult his map, and found he could get to a town where the Rhine steamer called, by bearing off five miles to the eastward.

Thither he resolved to go.

"Can you walk five miles, Mrs. Grumps?" asked Mr. Bone.

"Fifty," she answered.

"Very well," replied the schoolmaster. "Then somebody else can ride the mule."

Harry was still leading the brute, who had ~aved in, and was bearing itself in a very commendable manner.

"Get up, Harry!" shouted Young Ching. "Mrs. Grumps doesn't want the mule any more."

"All right," replied Harry, and with a bound he was astride the beast's back.

Julius Cæsar put back his ears and seemed as if about to try some of his tricks, but he changed his mind and ambled forward as gently as a goat.

But Harry did not want to ride, and he was soon off again.

"Some of you fellows have a turn," he said.

"Mr. Whelks looks tired," observed Young Ching, with a sly wink at Jem.

Mr. Whelks looked more than that—he had the appearance of a man on the borders of a collapse.

Fatigue and the shock he had recently received combined to utterly unnerve him. In his heart he felt he should like to ride.

"Get up, Whelks," said Mr. Bone.

"Do you think he is really quiet?" asked the tutor. "I am no horseman, having ridden only once in my life, and then I fell off."

"All you have to do is to sit straight and hold on tight with your knees," said Harry.

After a few more inquiries, to which he received reassuring answers, Mr. Whelks was induced to get into the saddle.

Young Ching and Jem Stager gave him a leg up, that as near as a toucher landed him upon his head on the other side.

"Really," he said, "this is comfortable, and the motion is very easy."

"Sit up, man," said Mrs. Grumps. "Who ever see sich a figger?"

Mr. Whelks was not picturesque it is true, for the way he bent his head forward and curled up his legs behind gave him the appearance of a crudely-formed letter S.

Harry led the mule, and the rest trudged behind, Mrs. Grumps displaying unexpected walking powers.

As soon as they had got round the spur of the hill they saw the spire of a church in the distance.

"That's where we stop to-night," said Mr. Bone, "but we have a long way to go. These level plains are so deceptive."

He called it a level plain, but it was hardly that.

The ground was broken up in various places, and here and there were piles of rock and patches of wood.

Mr. Whelks was enjoying himself on the mule.

He was getting used to the saddle, and every now and then he lifted his head up so that he almost sat upright.

When he did so Mrs. Grumps encouraged him with some such remark as—

"That's right, try and look like a man if you ain't one."

Young Ching and Jem Stager also stimulated him with kind criticisms.

Walking a little way in the rear of Julius Cæsar, but clear of the reach of his heels in case he kicked out, they entered into conversation, presumably for their own edification, but really intended for Mr. Whelks' ear.

"Mrs. Grumps may say what she likes," said Young Ching, "but he can ride."

"I never saw anyone with a better knee-grip," returned Jem Stager.

"Look at him now—who does he remind you of?"

"Why, that colonel of Hussars who used to ride about at Smockley."

"The colonel was a little taller, but he did not sit so well."

"I wonder he allows Harry to lead the mule."

"He will alter that directly."

Mr. Whelks felt flattered, for the boys were apparently conversing together, and he was not supposed to hear. He felt that it would look better if he did ride on alone.

The question was, dare he?

Julius Cæsar showed no tendency to vice, and was going along steadily. Yes, he would try it.

"I don't think I need trouble you, Harry," he said. "You may let his head go."

"It is no trouble," replied Harry, looking back, "and I don't think he is—" Then catching Young Ching's eye, he added— "Just as you like, you know."

"Oh! I can manage him," said Frisby Whelks, confidently.

Harry let go, and Julius Cæsar, without a moment's pause, bounded in the air, causing Mr. Whelks to rise quite a foot out of the saddle.

The mule and man came down together, the latter dropping into his seat with a jerk that threatened to dislocate every bone in his body.

"Oh!" he gasped.

"Hold on!" shouted Harry.

"Secure the beast's head!" cried Mr. Bone, seriously alarmed for the safety of his brother instructor.

"I'll do it, sir!" said Billy Pink.

"And I'll help you!" shouted Dick Cockles.

As they rushed at him Julius Cæsar whipped round and let out his heels, but kicked short. Frisby Whelks fell forward and grasped the mule round the neck.

"Whoop!" exclaimed Young Ching. "Come out of the way, Billy."

"Bless the boy!" said Mrs. Grumps. "Why will he always do these brave deeds, a-risking his vallyble life. Get out, you beast!"

She hurled her umbrella at Julius Cæsar with such good aim that it struck him like a dart—ferule foremost—about the neighbourhood of the tail, and away he went with a snort.

Frisby Whelks clung to him as drowning men cling to a plank in the sea, and was borne away at a furious pace.

They could see his legs and body rise up and down as he was jerked about by the bounding action of the beast.

Naturally the boys gave chase, but Mr. Bone stayed behind with Mrs. Grumps.

"We can do nothing," he said. "He is sure to be thrown, but I trust he won't be hurt."

"I hope he'll get some sense knocked into him," replied Mrs. Grumps. "I haven't any patience with such a creature."

Which was perfectly true. Patient generally, she lost all that valuable commodity when Whelks was the subject of her thoughts.

The road wound about a bit a furlong further on, through a patch of fir-wood, and Julius Cæsar reached the spot before the boys were half-way there.

At this point Julius Cæsar kicked up his heels, no doubt in derision of his pursuers, and Frisby Whelks was hoisted so high that he looked as if he meant to stand on his head on the animal's neck.

"Hang it," said Harry, "this is getting above a joke. Cockles, pick up his hat. I'll hurry on."

Harry forged ahead with Young Ching, the pair running at a smart pace—Jem Stager was next, a little behind, but not far in the rear.

The boys sped round the bend and came in sight of Frisby Whelks lying at full length in the road, with his arms and legs spread-eagled.

Julius Cæsar had vanished.

"I hope it's nothing serious," said Harry.

They ran towards the fallen man and raised him into a sitting position.

No signs of injury were visible, but he did not appear to have the least idea of where he was.

"Come where the moonbeams linger," he said, faintly, "close to the fairy dell. Has there been a public riot? Who shot me out of a catapult?"

"Come, Whelks," replied Harry, shaking him gently, "pull yourself together. You are not hurt."

"I was born on a February night when the clock was striking twelve. It was the twenty-ninth, being leap year. I've been leaping ever since," muttered Whelks.

He closed his eyes, and after a minute or so opened them again. Then he seemed better.

"Where's the mule?" he said, looking about him. "Bless me, he's skedaddled."

Dick and Billy now arrived, the former bearing Frisby Whelks' hat, which Young

Ching took from him and put on the tutor's head hind part before.

Then Mrs. Grumps and Mr. Bone appeared upon the scene.

The former did not sympathise with the equestrian, but fell upon him at once.

"Young man," she said, " never venture to get on the back of anything but a rocking-horse. What do you mean by skeering sensible people out of their wits?"

"I've been scared myself," replied Whelks, slowly rising.

The boys gave him a good brushing, and then they all trudged on, looking about them for the missing Julius Cæsar.

But no sign of the restive beast could they see. He had vanished as utterly as if the earth had opened and swallowed him up.

"It is money lost," said Mr. Bone, "but good riddance to the brute. Mrs. Grumps, can I offer you an arm? You seem to be getting tired."

"Tired!" returned Mrs. Grumps, protestingly, "not a bit of it. I could go all over the Grumping Hills and up Monk Blank without so much as stopping for breath."

And in proof of this assertion she set forward with a stride that would have made a champion walker envious.

"She can't keep on at that rate," thought Mr. Bone.

And the sequel proved his judgment had a good foundation.

CHAPTER X.

ON BOARD THE STEAMER—THE BLACK BAND— TOO BRIGHT TO LAST.

THREE days have passed, and the scene changes to the deck of a steamer going up the Rhine to Basle.

It is a glorious day, warm for the time of year, and the hour being noon the sun is at its brightest and warmest.

So warm are its rays that an awning has been stretched aft, under which the elder passengers have seated themselves.

Not so the boys.

They must roam about and see what is to be seen, peeping into the engine-room, talking to the steward, and in a general way making themselves felt, after the manner of boys.

Young Ching, Jem Stager, and Handsome Harry have wandered forward, where there are a number of peasant passengers bound for the vineyards.

They seem to be a lazy, sullen lot, talking little to each other, and staring wearily at the strangers, Young Ching coming in for more than his share of attention.

Billy Pink and Dick Cockles are hanging over the side of the boat, gazing into the ruffled stream below.

By one impulse Young Ching and Jem Stager acted together. Young Ching gave Billy a good hearty smack on the most prominent part of his person, and Jem Stager honoured Dick with a similar attention.

Then, quick as lightning, they dived down behind some empty boxes, and Harry, with his hands in his pockets, became absorbed in the smoke emitted by the funnel.

"Look here, Dick," said Billy, "I won't stand it."

"That's cheek," replied Dick, "when I saw you do it."

" Do what?"

"Why, lay into me. A joke's a joke, but you hit hard— Oh! you two beggars!"

"Such incidents as these," said Jem Stager, as he and Young Ching rose up, "illustrate the misleading nature of circumstantial evidence. Now, if we had kept concealed, you would each have been certain that you had been assaulted by the other, previous experience being of no use to—"

Dick muttered something about some people being uncommonly clever, and giving Billy a nudge they walked away.

"Let's go and see how Mrs. Grumps is getting on," he said. "She's down below."

"I'll come too," cried Jem.

"You keep away," replied Dick. "Hurry, Billy."

They dashed across to the companion, and Dick shot down with the whirr one sometimes hears in a house of business when a specially active assistant flies downstairs.

Billy followed, and Jem crying " Tally ho! gone away!" pursued.

Half-way down the stairs Jem was suddenly pulled up by a crash, a scream, and an outburst of agonised broken English.

Dick in his hurried flight did not see a waiter with some cups of coffee on a tray about to ascend the stairs, and as he came down like an avalanche the waiter had no time to get out of his way.

Down went the waiter, and down upon him came Dick.

Billy, not to be outdone by his friend,

planted himself upon the summit and added to the dismay and agony of the waiter.

"Vat dis?" he cried. "Why is for you to keel me?"

Most of the passengers were on deck, but there were two or three in the cabin, among whom was Mrs. Grumps, who rose up from her seat and exclaimed—

"I never did see sich people as these foreign waiters. If they can't kill people outright they does their best to scald 'em to death."

Jem Stager, laughing in a quiet way, hurried down to the assistance of his friends and dragged them off the waiter, who was just beginning to kick and claw, for he had got some of the coffee on his shirt front and the heat of it was telling upon him.

"Bring them boys here," said Mrs. Grumps, "and let me see what's been done to 'em. Oh! you villain!"

She shook her umbrella, which she seemed to be using as a walking-stick, at the waiter, who showed by his face that he was afraid of her.

"Madame," he said, apologetically, "it is the boys zat come on top. If I knock zem down, zen I am to blame."

"Don't talk to me," replied Mrs. Grumps. "But go away and put a dickey on, so that you may look decent. I hope you are not hurt, William?"

"No, ma'am," replied Billy Pink.

"Or you, Richard?"

"I've some of the coffee over my legs," answered Dick, "but I don't mind it."

"That's right. Bear and forbear," said Mrs. Grumps.

"How are you to-day, Mrs. Grumps?" inquired Jem. "Can you walk any better?"

"I cannot, young man," replied Mrs. Grumps, who appeared for some reason to look coldly on Jem, "and I don't suppose that you will die of grief on that account."

"I am sorry your feet have swollen so," said Jem, humbly.

Mrs. Grumps sniffed sarcastically, and resumed her seat with the slow action of a sufferer from gout.

But it was not gout she was troubled with— it was the result of the bit of walking she did on the day when Julius Cæsar disappeared.

She broke down before they got to their destination and had to be left by the roadside until a conveyance could be sent for her. The next morning found her in bed with a pair of feet swollen to the size of boxing-gloves.

Jem had got into trouble by being too anxious in his inquiries after her "poor feet." She suspected him of poking fun at her, and it is just possible her suspicions were well-grounded.

Leaving the cabin he returned to the deck, where he found Young Ching and Harry in close conversation.

"I tell you I am right," Young Ching was saying. "I feel sure I am not mistaken."

"What's up?" asked Jem.

"Ching says the Black Band are on board," replied Young Harry.

"And I am right," said Young Ching. "They are up in the bow of the steamer, two of them disguised as women. They pretended to be asleep when I went forward, and covered their faces, but I'll swear to Polowski."

"Do you think they are following us?" asked Jem Stager.

"Yes—if they are here at all," replied Harry. "But I should like to make sure."

"Go forward and look at them."

"All right. Wait for me."

Jem and Young Ching sat down, and Harry, putting on the air of a casual stroller, walked forward.

"What will you do if it is that lot?" asked Jem.

"Oh! tell Bone, and leave him to do as he pleases," replied Young Ching. "What was that row down below just now?"

Jem told him, and Young Ching smiled a gentle smile.

"Billy and Dick all over," he said; "and poor old Mrs. Grumps! I'm afraid she won't walk again in a hurry."

"It's a pity she came," muttered Jem.

Harry now reappeared, walking a pace or two further on, and lying down on a seat facing them.

"There's none of the Black Bandits there now," he said. "I've had a look at every face, and I don't see any of my old friends."

"Gone below," replied Young Ching.

"If they have we must let them remain there. We have no right in the fore cabin. There's the bell for dinner."

"Stop a moment," said Jem Stager; "there's a fine old castle coming into view. Doesn't it remind you—"

"No, it doesn't," replied Young Ching. "I'm too hungry to be reminded of anything but dinner."

"Julius Cæsar was a sentimental cuss to you," grunted Jem. "I'll stop—no I won't.

THE SLAPCRASH BOYS.

The Liveliest of School Stories.

THE DOOR WAS BEING FORCED BY THE MURDEROUS BAND OUTSIDE.

No. 10.

Price One Penny.

I'll come down and eat a double share to spite you."

An hour afterwards the fine old town of Basle hove in sight.

Dinner was over, and everybody was on deck, including Mrs. Grumps, who had been assisted up the stairs by her many friends.

Even Jem Stager had helped by stimulating Dick Cockles, who was pushing behind.

The form of stimulation he used had a head and a point to it, and is an article in common use.

Dick did not say anything at the time, being breathless with his exertions, but he held in reserve a few choice linguistic shots for Jem, to be fired at a more convenient season.

The scene from the deck was the most beautiful the boys had seen.

For a time Young Ching and Harry forgot all about the bandits of the Rhine, as they termed the five villains they had just cause to dread.

Nor did they think of them again until the steamer was moored to the landing-stage at Basle, and the fore-cabin passengers were crowding ashore.

Most of the peasant passengers were booked for the town, intending to seek work in its outlying districts, where the vine is much cultivated.

The better class of passengers for Basle naturally waited until the first rush was over, many of them having a considerable amount of luggage.

Our friends had very little.

Mr. Bone had arranged for them to travel with what they stood up in, with a change of linen extra. The clothes as they were worn out could be replaced at some convenient halting-place.

This plan had the advantage of leaving them almost as free in their movements as birds of the air, and naturally lessened the bother of travelling.

The boys were standing a little way from the gangway, watching the peasants going ashore with their bundles and bags.

Suddenly Young Ching grasped Harry by the arm.

"There they go," he said, pointing to the crowd.

Harry followed the direction of his finger, and saw three men and two women just stepping on shore.

They had no luggage, but were closely muffled up, in a manner that was unusual considering the warmth of the weather.

None of the men wore the dress in which Harry had known them at the castle of Namedi, but he had little difficulty in making out Polowski, Karl Steimetch, and Schavaloff. The two supposed women might be Picard and Kranmitz.

"You are right, Young Ching," he said, "and the beggars have been skulking. They must have feared being bowled out."

"What shall we do, old fellow?" queried Young Ching.

"Nothing. There is no use in making other people uncomfortable. We can keep our eyes open, and if we catch them prowling about we can speak to Bone. But they may be here, like the rest of these people, in search of work."

"Do you think they care for work?" asked Young Ching.

"No—but they have to do it unless they rob or starve," answered Harry. "They have failed at the robbing business, and naturally turn to something less to their taste to live."

"That's what you say but not what you think," returned Young Ching.

The five men—for those who seemed to be women were men—disappeared in the moving life ashore, and a few moments later Mr. Bone called his little flock together.

Mrs. Grumps had to be taken care of, and despite her protestations that she was able to walk as well as anybody, Mr. Bone insisted on her being carried ashore.

Two of the steamboat men were engaged, and having made a chair with their hands, they carried the dear old lady to land.

"To think that I should be made a Cherry Ripe of at my time of life," she said, "and by foreigners, too. I never shall forget it. Oh! you two muffs—do you want to shoot me into the water?"

"If madame vill not do ze wriggle," replied one of the men, "ve vill carry her like a babe."

Presently they got her ashore and into a carriage without accident, and the rest followed.

CHAPTER XI.

A NIGHT AT THE INN—VOICES BEHIND THE PARTITION—HARRY AND YOUNG CHING OVERHEAR A PLOT.

HAVING given up his ticket and rewarded the perspiring carriers, Mr. Bone consulted a small book he had in his pocket, and gave the driver directions to proceed to the Old Tabard Inn.

"It is under English management, I am told," he said. "Drive slowly, my. man, and we will follow on foot."

"Milord would do better at another hotel," suggested the driver, in a most insinuating tone.

"Milord will go where he pleases," replied Mr. Bone. "So get along."

The man gathered up his rope reins and gave his raw-boned horse a touch with the whip, accompanied by a "hi-hi-you."

Then a lot of little boys who had gathered round shouted—"Hi—hi! milady," as a compliment to Mrs. Grumps, which caused her to look down upon them with majestic pity.

Away they went with the little boys following, until Young Ching, lagging behind, suddenly produced a pea-shooter from his pocket, popped a handful of peas into his mouth, and favoured the youthful Basleites with a raking fire.

They fell back howling with wrath and derision, but taking good care not to come within shooting distance again.

"I used it once before at Calais," Young Ching said, as he returned the pea-shooter to his pocket, "the same day I posted a letter to—never mind who."

"Is it a secret?" asked Harry, smiling.

"Not exactly."

"Then I may make a guess who the letter was for. Something in the way of a joke, was it not?"

"What does it matter?" answered Young Ching. "I won't say anything about it as it may have missed fire. We shall hear to-day, perhaps, as there ought to be letters waiting for us at the Post-office."

The vehicle, a curious cross between a phaeton and a waggonette, rumbled through a number of streets thronged with picturesque people and quaint houses, both looking as if they would be improved by the application of a little soap and water, and at length stopped in front of a gabled house at the corner of a thoroughfare as narrow as one of the famous Rows at Yarmouth.

Over the door there swung an old signboard, but what had been on it was obliterated by wind and rain.

The windows had a scrubby look, and two or three uncanny-looking loafers hung about the door.

"This is hardly what I expected," said Mr. Bone; "but we won't judge by the exterior.

I had a good reference from a friend of mine who stopped here two years ago."

"Not a bad place," observed Young Ching, "to get robbed and murdered in."

Mr. Bone may have heard him but he made no reply, and after another look up and down the house he went in, bidding the rest wait until he could find out what sort of accommodation was to be had.

The interior of the inn was better than the outside. In arrangement it was decidedly English.

First there was a bar, with a good-looking girl behind it, and on the right a room marked "public."

A bar-parlour was visible also, and a passage led the way to a staircase—a solid bit of work, with broad, carpeted steps.

"Can I have private rooms here?" Mr. Fossil Bone inquired.

The barmaid looked at him closely for a moment before replying.

"I don't know, sir," she said, in good English, "but I will see."

She touched a bell and a man emerged from the bar-parlour. In appearance he was so much like Picard that Mr. Bone at first thought it was that very person.

But after all there was nothing strange in that. Foreigners to the English eye do resemble each other strongly, and was there not a placard hanging in the bar bearing the inscription—

"Tabard Inn, by M. Foulon. English spoke."

M. Foulon was at first not sure that he could receive so many guests, for his house was full. Yet stay—ah! yes! there was a room to eat in, and three or four rooms with beds.

So Mr. Bone went back to his party, and bidding the boys go in, helped Mrs. Grumps to alight.

That wretched Mr. Whelks had a hand in the job, and of course bungled it.

Getting out of the carriage Mrs. Grumps bore rather heavily on him, when he slipped, and she would have fallen but for Mr. Bone.

"Oh! get away—do," said Mrs. Grumps to the dismayed tutor. "There isn't any more stammerer in you than there is in a willow rod."

M. Foulon was ready to receive madame, and also a big woman dressed as a chambermaid, who assisted Mrs. Grumps upstairs to a sitting-room overlooking the street.

The furniture in it was good enough

did not seem too clean. Nor had the room the appearance of having been recently occupied.

As for the multitude of guests, none were visible just then, but possibly it was the hour for them to be abroad.

"Now, boys," said Mr. Bone, "sit down and we will have some tea. Whelks, ring the bell and order it."

"For goodness' sake!" interposed Mrs. Grumps, "don't give that poor creature anything to do. He will be sure to muddle it. William, will you ring the bell?"

Billy Pink, being thus adjured, crossed the room and laid hold of the bell-pull hanging by the side of the fireplace.

He gave it a smartish tug and down it came—without ringing the bell.

"I knew it, sir," said Billy, "as soon as I touched it."

"Of course you did," observed Mrs. Grumps, encouragingly, "which that poor Whelks wouldn't have done."

Mr. Whelks did not say anything, but he looked a great deal. Much as he respected Mrs. Grumps, it would be wise of her not to go too far. That was what he thought.

"Young Ching," said Mr. Bone, "go down and order tea. Ask them to let us have some ham and eggs and fruit."

"I'll go with you," observed Harry to Young Ching.

Mr. Bone did not interfere with this arrangement, and the two friends left the room together.

As they closed the door Young Ching looked at his companion and said—

"Strange crib this. What do you think of it?"

"I think," replied Harry, "that Bone has made a mistake. It's not what he expected."

"Such a dingy hole," said Young Ching.

They were going downstairs when they met M. Foulon coming up, bearing a tray with bottles of wine and packets of tobacco upon it.

To him they gave the order, and told him of the broken bell-rope.

"Oh! yes," he said, "it was old. No matter—to-morrow it will be repaired. You shall have your tea directly."

He passed down a corridor, and they stood watching him until he got to the far end.

There he opened a door and the sound of half-a-dozen voices floated out.

But in a moment he had entered and the door was closed.

"Did you notice anything peculiar?" said Harry.

"No," replied Young Ching. "To me it sounded like a lot of young fellows drinking and talking together."

Presently they returned to the sitting-room, where they found Mrs. Grumps with her bonnet and mantle off, prepared to preside at the tea-table.

The other boys had gathered at one of the windows, watching the passers-by in the street.

"Rum lot of people here," said Jem Stager. "Like dim shadows of a bygone age they float before my vision. Look at that old Jew there. Did you ever see anything more like Dick, or Dick as he would be if the sausage trade failed and he had to embark in the old clothes business?"

"More like you, Mister Clever," growled Dick. "Isn't it, Billy?"

"I thought it was Jem's father," replied Billy, with one of his slow grins.

"You had better let them alone, Jem," observed Harry. "Their combined forces appear too much for you."

"First of all they must get force from somewhere to combine with," replied Jem, scornfully. "Do you happen to know what the phrenologist once said about Dick's head?"

"No phrenologist ever said anything about it," returned Dick.

"I knew you would say that," replied Jem; "but as I happened to be there I ought to know what took place. He laid hold of Dick's head this way"—Jem took Dick's head between his hands—"then he put a finger to Dick's chin"—Jem extended his finger to Dick's chin—"and raising his eyes he said—Oh! you little beast!"

Jem let go of Dick's head and thrust his right hand under his left arm. Dick had given him a bit of a bite.

"That's a strange thing for a phrenologist to say," said Young Ching.

"He didn't say it," returned Jem, curtly. "Look here, Dick, if you do that sort of thing again I'll knock your head off."

"You let my head alone then," retorted Dick. "Who are you to go a-feeling about for bumps? Look after your own."

"You'll have a job to find 'em," added Billy.

"Dick is the little beggar Doctor Watts

had in his eye when he wrote 'Let dogs delight to bark and bite,'" said Jem. "It wouldn't have mattered if he had an ordinary mouth, but it's a regular mincing-machine."

After all Jem was not much hurt. It was the shock that made him a little bitter for the moment, and tea appearing he was soon all right again.

He had got off a decent joke about Dick's jaws, and that was consoling.

Mrs. Grumps presided with her usual grace, and not the least charm of her bearing was the way in which she treated Frisby Whelks.

Evidently she considered him to be in need of all the care of a little boy.

"There's your tea," she said. "Don't ask for any more sugar because it isn't good for you, and don't eat and drink at the same time, or you will choke."

"Pardon me, madam," said Frisby Whelks, "but these instructions are usually confined to the very young."

"And how old may you be?" asked Mrs. Grumps.

"Thirty-three," was the answer.

"Then I look upon those thirty-three years as having been wasted," said Mrs. Grumps; "there's nothing to show for the labour of 'em."

Mr. Bone tried to create a diversion, but he failed, and Mrs. Grumps was proceeding to further verbally maul the tutor when Billy Pink, who had not followed one part of the good lady's instructions, choked while drinking his tea.

But he did not choke like an ordinary boy.

He choked quietly.

That is, he felt the fit coming on and tried to stop it, with the most alarming results.

His cheeks distended, his eyes came out of his head, and his whole appearance bordered on the horrible.

Young Ching was the first to notice it, and guessed what was the matter.

"Go out," he whispered, "and have a good cough on the landing."

Dick Cockles, facing Billy, at that moment looked at his dear friend. He was in the act of drinking, and he also choked, just as he might have yawned or sneezed—in sympathy.

Likewise did he endeavour to ward off the explosion, with similar results.

Jem and Harry now tumbled to what was going on, and although they naturally felt for the sufferers, it was impossible to take a very serious view of the matter.

"Put your heads under the table," said Jem.

"Hey! what's this?" exclaimed Mr. Bone.

"Save us!" cried the alarmed Mrs. Grumps, also "spotting" the sufferers. "What are them dear boys took with?"

Billy Pink had heard Jem's bit of advice, and it occurred to his brilliant mind that the best thing he could do was to act upon it.

So down he dived under the table, and Dick followed him.

There they vented their agony, and the way they coughed was very startling.

Mr. Bone got up and peered under the table, so did Frisby Whelks.

The latter happened to be near Mrs. Grumps, from whom he received a sudden push.

"Don't stand staring there," she said, "but go and help the dear boys."

"Oh! hang the boys," muttered Whelks, as he fell upon his hands and knees.

But his assistance was not required, for Billy and Dick had a knack of getting over the small ills of life, and in a few moments they reappeared in a flushed condition.

"Bless them boys," said Mrs. Grumps, looking sternly at Frisby Whelks, who was resuming his seat; "they don't make a fuss about nothing, like some people."

Frisby Whelks snorted and bit viciously at his bread and butter, but he maintained silence, which was the better course perhaps.

After tea Mr. Bone and his brother tutor went out to make a few purchases.

The boys were destined to stay at home and amuse themselves quietly, which they did by performing a few gymnastic feats with the chairs and tables, to the great edification of Mrs. Grumps.

Harry could stand "close feet" and clear an ordinary chair at a single bound, with a neatness that brought him well-earned applause.

Young Ching very nearly did it, his heels just scraping the top of the chair.

Jem thought he would "have a go" at it another day, but Dick Cockles' spirit brooked no delay.

"I've got to jump over that chair or die," he said.

So at it he went, and instead of clearing it the chair and Dick became very much mixed up on the floor.

After this they had feats of strength, but what they did we will not attempt to record.

Each in his way astonished Mrs. Grumps, who fairly perspired with admiration.

"And well may your father be a famous man," she said to Harry, "for a son like you would be the making of anyone."

"That's one way of putting it," observed Jem Stager; "but what's the use of argifying with the dear old girl?"

The two men returned shortly after eight o'clock, and after a glass of light wine and a biscuit the boys were despatched to bed.

Four bedrooms had been prepared, and the boys were divided.

Jem Stager had to sleep in an apartment with Dick and Billy, whilst Young Ching and Harry had a double-bedded room to themselves.

Theirs was a low-ceilinged room, with portraits painted on the panels, which were for the most part dimmed and almost obliterated by Time.

The two beds were placed side by side, and the boys lost no time in tumbling in.

"A pretty quiet place this," said Harry. "I haven't seen any crowd of visitors yet."

"Somebody is talking in the next room," observed Young Ching, sleepily.

"That is where that drinking lot are," replied Harry. "They seem to be still at it. I wonder who they are? Here's a crack in the panel."

"Have a look at them."

"I'm trying to," said Harry, kneeling up in bed, and fixing his eye close to the narrowest of cracks. "But there is nothing to be seen. Perhaps I can hear something?"

He glued his ear to the woodwork, and Young Ching, who was very sleepy, was dozing off when he heard a sharp exclamation from his companion.

In a moment he was wide awake again.

Like his father, he had the power of collecting his faculties at a moment's notice.

"What is it?" he asked.

"Hush! not a word!" replied Harry, in a thrilling whisper; "wait until I speak to you again."

Young Ching could hear the murmuring of voices in the next room, but he could not distinguish the words.

A few minutes elapsed and he was dozing off again, when a movement on the part of his companion aroused him.

Harry had settled down in his bed again.

"Ching," he said, "you had better go to sleep."

"I can see you have heard something," Young Ching replied. "Tell me what it is."

"Nothing particular—it will keep until the morning."

"No it won't, and I can see it is something you don't want me to know. Don't be afraid. I shall sleep all the better if my curiosity is satisfied."

"Very well, then," said Harry, "I will tell you. It is Polowski and that lot in the next room, and they are planning robbery and perhaps murder."

CHAPTER XII.

MR. BONE DOES NOT KNOW WHAT TO THINK—A MORNING STROLL AND A STRANGE MEETING.

"HARRY," said Young Ching, "are you sure you have not been dreaming?"

"My dear fellow," replied Harry, "am I a dreamer? Unless I have been deceived in the most wonderful manner it was Polowski's voice I heard."

"Isn't it strange that they should be here?" asked Young Ching, softly.

"At first it seems so," replied Harry; "but did you not notice that Foulon and Picard are like two brothers? In my opinion they are brothers, and that is the way the presence of the Black Bandits is accounted for."

"Who are they going to kill?"

"I will tell you all in the morning," said Harry. "To-morrow night is fixed for the job. Did you bolt the door?"

"Yes."

"Then let us go to sleep. I'm tired out, and I am sure you must be so too."

It is not every boy who would have slept under the circumstances, but our young friends were soon in what is called "the land of unconsciousness."

They slept until a knock at the door aroused them.

It was morning and daylight was streaming through the window. Young Ching leaped out of bed, unbolted the door, and saw Billy Pink ready dressed.

"We are all waiting for you," said Billy.

"Don't stop for us," replied Young Ching; "we will follow on."

"But I don't know which way we are going," said Billy.

"Never mind that," returned Young Ching; "we'll find you."

Billy went away, and what message he gave to Mr. Bone is uncertain, but the rest of the

party—less Mrs. Grumps, who was still in bed
—were seen crossing the street a minute later
and making for the high country which could
be seen above the houses.

The two friends soon dressed and hurried
out of their bedroom. The door of the next
room was open, and they peeped in.

There were the usual signs following a
public-house evening—ashes of tobacco,
empty pots and glasses, and an overturned
chair or two, but that was all.

"It is no use lingering," said Harry. "What
are you looking at?"

Young Ching had hung back a bit, and was
peering under a small table in the corner.

"There's a package under that table," he
said.

Listening for a moment and finding all was
still they crossed the room and had a look at
the parcel.

It was about a foot square, very heavy, and
appeared to be a box covered with canvas.

So closely was the wrapper stitched that
they could not get the faintest glimpse of the
interior, and after two or three futile efforts
they put it down and went out.

In the corridor they met the landlord.

"Good morning, gentlemen," he said.
"You haf risen early, but not early enough for
your friends."

"We could not get any sleep last night,"
replied Harry. "There was a merry party
next door."

"Ah!" said Foulon, "Turks are merry men
always."

"Turks?" queried Harry.

"It is so," replied Foulon; "travellers from
Con-stan-ti-no-ple."

He drawled out the last word as if loth to
get to the end of it. Young Ching looked at
him keenly and softly whistled.

"Where you go?" asked Foulon of Harry.

"Up to the hills for a walk," was the reply.

"Ze Turks go zat way. It may be for you
to meet dem," said Foulon.

"Thanks," replied Harry, drily. "I should
like to."

"Turks be hanged," he said to Young Ching
as they emerged into the street. "They were
no more Turks than I am. By-the-way, we
might meet somebody on the hills. Let us
buy a couple of sticks."

Many of the shops were open, and at one
devoted to all sorts of fancy goods they found
what they wanted.

Armed with a couple of stout sticks they
made for the open country.

A walk of ten minutes or so brought them
to the outskirts of the town, and before them
lay a country pretty well barren of trees, but
with vineyards, houses, and quaint Swiss huts
dotted about.

The roads were for the most part without
walls or hedges, and as yet scarcely anybody
seemed to be at work.

"I don't see our people," said Young Ching.

"I don't see anybody," replied Harry; "but
it doesn't matter. Let us make for the hut on
the hill yonder and then we may catch a
glimpse of them."

They were hurrying in that direction when
they saw a man in the distance, about half
a mile away.

He was approaching at an angle that would
by-and-by bring them together, provided they
kept straight on.

"Ching," said Harry, "don't you see anything peculiar in that fellow?"

"He's got a rum sort of dress on," replied
Young Ching. "Why—it's a Turk's dress."

"One of last night's party," returned Harry.
"If we go round by that knoll we may get a
good look at him without being seen."

The knoll was a jutting rock, about a
hundred yards away from the rock they were
originally making for.

They could get at it quickly by crossing a
rugged piece of ground, and if they were
careful they might escape observation.

The manœuvre was successfully accomplished, and they got to the hiding-place without being observed by the individual
approaching.

He was a smooth-faced man clad in a
Turkish dress.

His face was far from being a pleasant one,
having the look of a man with a sour temper.

One can see a score such faces in a crowd
at a time of political agitation, when the idler
and the evil-disposed surge to the front.

"Here he comes," said Harry. "He's going
up to the hut. I've got an idea that I know
his figure, Ching."

"Yes, old fellow?"

"It's Polowski!"

"Nonsense!" said Young Ching; "he had a
beard."

"He has cut it off," said Harry. "I am
going to make sure whether it is him or not.
We two ought not to be afraid of him."

"I am not," said Young Ching. "Go for
him!"

"I am only going to ask him a question,"
replied Harry.

THE LAST WE SAW OF THEM WAS THEIR FEET—THEY WENT FAIRLY OVER, HEAD FIRST.

Harry and Young Ching came out of their hiding-place, and the former cried out—

"Pardon me, sir, but can you tell me the time?"

The man faced about, and sure enough it was Polowski.

Not all the shaving in the world would take away the evil glint of his eyes or the repulsive outline of his coarse features.

Naturally he recognised the boys instantly.

With a snarl that was uncommonly like the growl of a wolf, he thrust his hand into his pocket and drew out a knife.

"Why do you follow me?" he hissed.

"Nobody follows you," replied Harry; "it is you who follow us. Oh! you may scowl. We are not afraid of you, Polowski, and I can tell you one thing—we are going to make this country too hot to hold you."

"If any of our friends are near," said Young Ching, "I'll bring them up. He looks ugly."

He put his hands to his mouth and sent forth an Australian "cooey" that echoed about the hills like the music of a cornopean.

It was immediately answered some distance away.

"Jem Stager," said Young Ching. "All right—at him, Harry!"

"Keep off, you fiends!" cried Polowski, brandishing his knife. "Do you hear—I'll be the death of you."

They both fell upon him with their sticks, and gave him several smartish blows.

He warded them off from his head with his arms, giving vent to bitter invectives.

Then he suddenly rushed at Harry and aimed a blow at his heart. Harry stepped quickly aside and dealt him a crack on the head that made him reel.

In another moment Polowski would have fallen in for a second blow, and probably been captured, but Young Ching gave a note of alarm.

From out of the hut above four men were emerging in hot haste.

Their dress was similar to that of Polowski, and that they were his friends Young Ching was certain, although he had no time to make sure.

"Clear out!" he cried. "This way."

He leaped past Polowski, giving him a crack on the hand that held the knife, and with Harry by his side sped off in the direction of Jem Stager's answering cry.

It was really the only thing to do, for what could two boys do against five men?

They were not followed.

Polowski, from motives which can be easily guessed, hurried up to his friends and spoke a few words to them, gesticulating fiercely.

Meanwhile Harry and Young Ching had come in sight of their friends botanising.

Mr. Bone was gathering small plants and herbs from the hillside, and explaining their nature to Jem Stager and the other boys.

Mr. Frisby Whelks was seated on a stone reading a book.

"Steady, boys," cried Mr. Bone; "you will break your necks."

"It is no time to be steady," replied Harry; "we have been running for our lives. The Black Bandits are round the brow of the hill."

"Is this a jest?" asked Mr. Bone.

"No," replied Young Ching, "it's true. We are strong enough now. Let us go back and capture them."

"For mercy's sake," observed Frisby Whelks, rising hurriedly, "let us get along home."

"One moment," said Mr. Bone. "We won't hurry over it, although I think it advisable to retreat. Have you any weapons, Whelks?"

"I—I—I've a penknife," stammered Frisby Whelks.

"A toothpick," muttered Jem Stager.

"Boys," continued Mr. Bone, "happily I am armed. I have thought it necessary to be so since our adventure at Namedi. In my hand "—producing a revolver—"I hold six lives. It is not my desire to take any, so let us return to the hotel. You go first, and I will bring up the rear."

"Fall in," commanded Jem Stager, with the air of a drill-sergeant.

"Stager," said Mr. Bone, "it is hardly the time for joking. We are at least two miles from the town, and there is no help near. If these monsters have the courage to attack us we should be almost at their mercy."

"And here they are!" said Young Ching.

The five men were coming slowly round the hill looking for them. Espying the party they uttered a yell.

Mr. Bone, revolver in hand, planted himself in rear of the boys.

"Go slowly down the hill," he said, "and I will keep my face to the foe. As far as I can see they have no firearms."

"Oh! dear, we are all dead men," groaned Whelks, as he pulled out a penknife about three inches long, immediately dropping it to the ground.

"Don't stop to pick that up," said Jem Stager, giving him a push, "but trot along!"

"D—o—o—n't be rude," gasped Whelks. "Oh! dear—Harry—I—never thought of this when I left my home to travel."

"Don't give way," said Harry, kindly. "Keep on your legs, for we shall not be able to carry you."

The unhappy tutor was limp about the knees, and could scarcely stand. It was really pitiable to see him.

"Lay hold of him, Young Ching," said Harry. "Come, Whelks, pull yourself together."

"Farewell, my country," gasped Frisby Whelks; "land of my birth, adieu."

Mr. Bone, with a determined expression of face, frequently turned towards the foe.

The Black Bandits did not like his looks, and kept out of pistol-shot, knowing that he would assuredly shoot any one of their number who dared to attack the boys.

Mr. Bone felt like a lion protecting its young.

The retreating party soon came to more broken ground, and here they were at a disadvantage, for the Black Bandits could skulk behind the rocks and make themselves dangerous.

The ruffians saw their advantage and widened out, Polowski giving directions in a language unintelligible to the boys.

But Mr. Bone understood him. He spoke in Russian, and this is what he said—

"Bring them down with stones. Bowl over that tall fellow and the young Chinaman."

The heart of the schoolmaster grew sick within him.

He had no fear on his own account, but he knew that if one or more of the boys were put *hors de combat* most serious results must ensue.

Either that boy or boys must be left behind or the whole party become practically at the mercy of the foe.

The Black Bandits were soon popping in and out between the rocks, seeking any point of vantage for their cowardly designs.

CHAPTER XIII.

THE FIGHT WITH THE ANARCHISTS — UNDER SHELTER—FRISBY WHELKS IS MADE USEFUL AGAINST HIS WILL.

Of course our friends could have run for it—Whelks excepted—but with the tutor so limp and helpless they were in a sense handicapped.

Suddenly Mr. Bone made up his mind what ought to be done.

"You boys run," he said. "Leave Whelks with me. I can hold out until you fetch the gendarmes from the town."

"Oh! don't leave me," cried Whelks, clinging to Harry. "You are so brave, these fellows are afraid of you, I—"

"Silence!" said Mr. Bone, sternly. "I tell you—ha! they have begun."

A stone whizzed by, narrowly escaping Young Ching's head.

The thrower was Steimetch, who popped up about thirty yards away.

But ere he could drop down again a very smart bit of work was put in by Billy Pink.

Billy was the first to see Steimetch get up, being the nearest to him, and with his old throwing instinct in the ascendant he sent his stone at the ruffian as true as David of old did at Goliath.

The result was that Steimetch had hardly cast his stone when he received Billy's between the eyes and fell back with a howl.

"Bravo! Billy," cried Dick.

"I must say well done, too," said Mr. Bone. "We cannot do anything better than meet these ruffians with their own weapons. Look out, there!"

Several stones came whizzing by, and one struck Harry in the chest.

The blow must have been a heavy one, but he never so much as flinched.

"Thank you, friend Polowski," he said. "I will remember that."

Mr. Bone was about to issue another command when a stone struck him on the temple, and he fell senseless to the ground.

A yell from Polowski announced its success.

Leaping up, he called on his friends to follow, and dashed down upon the boys.

Never in their lives had they been in greater peril, but thanks to the promptitude of one of their number, the anarchist was foiled in his intention.

Young Ching snatched the revolver from the hand of the insensible schoolmaster and fired at Polowski.

He took no particular aim, there was no time for that, but the bullet found its billet.

Polowski pulled up short, uttered a howl of pain, and clapped a hand to his cheek.

Whatever the nature of his injury it sufficed to stop the others, and caused them to take refuge behind the rocks again.

Polowski also lost no time in getting under cover.

"Bravo, Ching!" cried Jem Stager; "by the seven pipers that played before Moses thy aim was true, and if it had been a little truer yon parlous knave would have paid the penalty of his many crimes."

"The same old Jem," muttered Young Ching.

Handsome Harry was kneeling beside Mr. Bone, who showed signs of recovering, and in a few moments he opened his eyes. He immediately grasped what had happened, and a faint smile overspread his face.

"I thought I was made of sterner stuff," he said. "Thank you, I am pretty right again now."

His head was bleeding, and he bound it up with Harry's assistance.

"Give me that weapon," he said to Young Ching. "Now, boys, retreat slowly while I cover you."

They began a retrograde movement, Frisby Whelks keeping close to his pupil in the most ludicrous manner, "like a young chicken sticking to a hen," as Jem afterwards said.

Dick, Billy, Jem, and Mr. Bone formed one party, there being a slight gap between them and Harry, Young Ching, and Whelks.

Ere long the stones began to fly again, and soon happened one of those accidents which often take place in warfare of all descriptions, petty and otherwise.

A stone struck the revolver and fairly shattered the lock, rendering it useless.

"We must run now," said Mr. Bone, bitterly.

They started off, but Harry was detained by Frisby Whelks, who clung to his arm.

"Don't do that," said the boy.

"Oh! save me," gasped the wretched tutor.

Young Ching could have got away with the others, but he was not going to desert his friend.

The anarchists had found out what was the matter, and had risen in a body.

With yells they dashed after Mr. Bone and his companions, overlooking the other three for a moment.

But this movement cut off the trio from the flying party.

"Up the hill!" said Harry. "It is our only chance. Make for the hut, Ching!"

They could see it peeping over the rocks above, and it was indeed their only refuge.

Frisby Whelks, now that they were obliged to go the wrong way, was suddenly endowed with the strength he ought to have had before.

Like a sprint runner he went up the hill.

Ere he had gone far the Black Bandits espied him, and turned back in pursuit of what seemed to be their surer prey.

It was a race for life, or a chance of life.

The hut might give them security for a time, but for how long?

"On!" cried Harry. "Go ahead, Whelks! If you drop now we shall leave you."

Frisby Whelks did not drop.

His little boots and gaiters flew over the ground, and he was the first to reach the hut, into which he plunged and fell full length upon the floor.

The boys followed and closed the door.

It had but one bolt, which Young Ching quickly shot, and then looked round for something to barricade the door with.

A table, two or three chairs, and a box was all the furniture, and these they hastily piled against the door.

Frisby Whelks, still at full length upon the floor, kept groaning.

"If you don't get up," said Harry, "I'll knock you on the head."

"Oh! dear, it's horrible. We are all as good as dead," gasped Whelks.

Bang!

The anarchists had arrived, and in a body threw themselves against the door.

It resisted the first onslaught.

"Open," cried Polowski, "or we will make you suffer for it."

"Don't answer them," said Harry.

"Not me," replied Young Ching.

"If we open the door," said Frisby Whelks, trembling, "perhaps they wouldn't hurt us."

"The moment they get in here," replied Harry, "say your prayers, for it will be all over with you."

"Oh! lor!" gasped Frisby Whelks.

He was just getting up, but on receiving this dire intelligence he flopped down again.

The boys still had their sticks, and Harry picking up another one from the floor, thrust it into the tutor's hand.

"When the worst comes," he said, "fight for your life."

"Yes—s-s-s," stammered Whelks, waggling the weapon about in a helpless way.

After the first rush at the door there was a few moments' quietude, and then they went for it again.

The door shook, but no more.

"It may hold out," said Harry. "In an hour we shall have help."

"An hour," observed Young Ching, drily; "that's a long time."

"It is, old boy," was the response, "but after my escape from the Castle of Namedi I shall not despair."

"Nor I," said Young Ching.

"No-o-o-o-r I," quavered Frisby Whelks, waving his stick. "Where is the be-est place to hit a man?"

"Wherever you can," replied Young Ching, curtly.

Bang!

A third rush and the door bent a little.

Then several huge stones were dashed against it, and the noise frightened Whelks so much that he jumped at each blow.

"Oh! dear," he said, "they are getting quite angry. Per-r-r-haps we had be-e-tter open the door."

They did not answer him.

The boys were estimating how long they would be able to hold out, and neither of them believed the door would stand anything like an hour.

But all they could do was to remain passive until it was broken down, and then fight for their lives.

As for parleying with the foe or capitulating, they knew it would be akin to madness.

"Polowski's the leader," said Young Ching; "when they get in we ought to make for him."

"Yes," replied Harry; "lame him. Never mind his head, for that is too thick to hurt. Hit him across the knees."

"I wish my father were here," sighed Young Ching.

"And mine," said Harry. "I reckon there would be a sudden evaporation of that lot outside."

The anarchists gave up pushing the door for awhile, and rained stones upon it, keeping up a continuous fusilade.

The noise inside was deafening.

But although the door was none of the strongest it withstood the assault for some time —an hour it seemed to the boys, but it is doubtful if half that time had elapsed.

Suddenly there was a snap.

The bolt had yielded.

But the door did not open more than an inch or so, the furniture still keeping it in its place.

The question of its entirely yielding though was now only a matter of minutes.

"Ready, Ching?" said Harry; "remember what I said. Hit him across the knees and drop him."

"What about the other four?" asked Young Ching, grimly.

"Do the best you can," was the answer.

Polowski had got hold of the door and was shaking it violently.

The furniture was beginning to yield, and it would be futile to endeavour to hold it together. Therefore the boys did nothing but stand ready for the onslaught.

Behind them was Frisby Whelks groaning and moaning, and holding his stick up as if it had been a lighted candle, surely as poor a picture of manhood as one would care to see.

An inspiration came to Young Ching.

Why should he stand there and quietly allow the door to be shaken down?

There were Polowski's knuckles and why should they not be cracked?

He leaped forward and cracked them.

And it was more of a smash than a crack.

Polowski fell back with the cry of a wounded beast, and the boys rushing up jammed the furniture together and reclosed the door.

"Well done, Young Ching," said Harry.

"If you have hurt him much," said Frisby Whelks, "he will be very angry."

"Oh! bother you for a fool," said Young Ching. "Don't talk rubbish. Why don't you make yourself useful? Push here."

"I can't do much," said Whelks, as he laid himself against the little pile.

Young Ching looked at his friend, and acting on an inspiration each laid hold of a leg of the tutor and hoisted him on to the top of the barricade.

"Every pound is a help," said Young Ching.

Whelks fell into an inverted chair, and became wedged knees and nose together. He was too much astonished to remonstrate, or to do anything but gasp and stare wildly about him.

Both the boys burst into laughter, and it was as merry a sound as ever was heard.

"Keep where you are, Whelks," said Harry; "you are useful for once in a way."

Bang—bang!

The battering of the door had begun again, and stones were also hurled against the wooden shutter of a small window.

Suddenly the sounds of assault ceased.

A shout was heard, followed by the firing of a rifle. Then the scampering of feet, and afterwards a voice outside calling upon the boys.

"Mr. Bone," cried Young Ching; "hurrah!"

With the impetuosity of the moment he began to tear away the barricade, and Harry gave him ready help.

In their excitement they forgot Whelks, and he was brought down with a run. The door was pushed open and Mr. Bone came in.

"My dear boys," he cried, "I am indeed rejoiced. Just in time—just in time."

"It's all right, thank you," said Young Ching. "But how is it you are back so soon?"

"We met the gendarmes coming up," was the reply. "They were coming on duty at a fair held a few miles from here. The villains! —the scoundrels! But where is Whelks?"

"Here!" replied a feeble voice.

"Where?" asked Mr. Bone.

They all looked round, and at first could see nothing of Whelks, but a slight quivering of the furniture betrayed his whereabouts. He was under it.

"A splendid hiding-place," said Mr. Bone, as he pulled the table and chairs off the tutor, "but really you need not have taken the trouble to stow yourself away. It is friends who are here, not foes."

"I assure you, my dear sir—" began Whelks.

"Do not assure me anything," said Mr. Bone.

"But really I was not—"

"Never mind if you were—all's well that ends well. But come, boys—let us get down to the hotel—outside there is something not fit for your young eyes—a dead man. Picard has paid the penalty of his crimes—one of the gendarmes shot him dead—the rest, I am sorry to say, have got away."

They went out of the hut, and there, indeed, was Picard lying on his back with his face lighted up by the morning sun, but still in death.

He had been shot in the forehead, as a small round hole attested.

Four gendarmes stood by him, looking at the still face with some signs of curiosity, but no more.

"He has the look of Foulon," said one; "they might be brothers."

"They are brothers," said Harry to Mr. Bone. "I have a story to tell you. These men arranged last night to rob the Chateau Napoleon. Is there such a place here?"

The gendarme said there was, and that it belonged to an old French nobleman, who had ever been a royalist, and would not live in France while it was a republic.

Then it came out that this nobleman had always been a bitter foe to men of the Polowski class, and more than once his life had been threatened.

"I judged it was to be no common robbery from what they said," returned Harry. "Polowski was for leaving not one inmate alive."

"Why did you not tell me before?" asked Mr. Bone, gravely.

"I have not had an opportunity," was the reply.

"Well! neither the robbery nor murder will come off now," said Mr. Bone; "therefore we will go and get some breakfast. I am sure you must need it." Then to the gendarmes— "I will see you anon, gentlemen. You will find me at the Old Tabard Inn."

The gendarmes saluted, and Mr. Bone hastened down to the inn, where Jem, Dick, and Billy had already arrived in safety.

CHAPTER XIV.

THE FAIR AT LAROCHE—ALL THE FUN OF IT—
BILLY AND DICK ON THE SAME OLD TRAIL.

"WHICH I do say," said Mrs. Grumps, with emphasis, "that if you are a man you will never meet them boys anywhere without taking your hat off."

She addressed Frisby Whelks, who was partaking of breakfast with all the gusto of a hungry man.

He looked at Mrs. Grumps in a malevolent way, but he did not make an immediate reply.

At this laxity of manners she promptly took offence.

"What have you got to say for yourself?" she continued.

"Really, madam," he replied, "I don't know that I have anything to say except—that—that —really I don't know what to say."

"Of course you don't," returned Mrs. Grumps, scornfully. "You don't know what to say or do. I feel as if I could box his ears."

Then somebody chuckled at the table, and Young Ching said—

"Don't, Billy—always respect your seniors."

"I've done nothing," replied Billy. "I was thinking of what your father would have said if—"

"And ands were pots and pans," interposed Young Ching; "that will do, Billy. The little tragedy didn't come off, so we won't say anything more about it."

"Boys," observed Mr. Bone, "notwithstanding what has happened to-day, I do not see why we should be mournful. How would you like to go to the fair? They are, I believe, exceedingly amusing in this country."

What were the boys likely to say? Go, of course, and the sooner the better.

"We shall not stop here," continued Mr. Bone, "as no doubt the host will get into trouble over his recent guests. I am sorry we came. It seems that the inn has changed hands, and is a different place to what it was when my friends put up here. As soon as I have arranged for a place to sleep in to-night, we will hire a carriage and be off."

"Good old Bone," said Jem Stager, in what he thought was an undertone, but a quiet look from the schoolmaster showed that he had been overheard.

For once Jem felt as if he would like to get into something small and hide away for an hour or two.

Not a word was said—the look was sufficient —it is so with some people.

One man may bellow and roar for a month and nobody will take any notice of him, while a quiet glance from the eyes of another suffices to shrivel up an offender.

It was now eleven o'clock, and the fair began at one. A carriage could get there in an hour, so there was plenty of time.

Mrs. Grumps decided to go.

"I can sit in the carriage and look on," she said, "and this young man had better remain with me, or he may get into mischief."

"This young man" was Frisby Whelks, whose dismay was plainly written on his face.

But he dare not rebel, and nobody had a word to say on his behalf, for all felt that his recent exhibition of cowardice entitled him to some punishment.

Rooms were got for the party at an adjacent hotel, but the hiring of the carriage was not such an easy matter.

Everybody that was anybody at Basle was going to the fair, and all who could afford to ride intended doing so.

The consequence was that every carriage worthy of the name was engaged.

But at last a sort of waggonette and a pair of animals that were supposed to be horses brought up at the hotel door.

In front of the vehicle there was a seat for the driver and two other persons. The body behind would accommodate a dozen other people.

"There is plenty of room," said Mr. Bone,

"but the question is—will the thing hold together?"

It was indeed a question, for the age of the structure must have been very great.

Paint had long been a stranger to it, and the wheels wobbled and squeaked.

The driver, an old man who matched the vehicle in outward appearance, was confident it would go anywhere and do anything.

"I take him up ze hill," he said, "then I run him down ze hill, then I give him jomps in big holes, and behold! he is stronger zan evare."

"Well, you know all about it, I daresay," replied Mr. Bone. "Now, Mrs. Grumps, I think you had better sit forward on the left, as the strongest wheel appears to be there. Who goes on the box?"

Dick and Billy promptly volunteered for the perch, and were allowed to elevate themselves.

Mr. Bone and Frisby Whelks took seats facing Mrs. Grumps, while Jem, Young Ching, and Harry sat at the door end.

"I am not given to prophetic utterances," said Jem Stager, as he sat down, "but as I am a living boy I do aver that we shall have a glorious burst up ere we return."

"Who cares?" replied Young Ching; "it will all be in the fun of the fair."

People were wending their way to the scene.

Everybody seemed to know our boys' driver, who was hailed by the name of Pierre, and in their native tongue they bandied jokes at his expense.

He was asked who had brought him and his vehicle back from the grave, and who had lent him two ghosts for horses. These questions were evidently meant as a reflection on the turn-out.

Mr. Bone, Frisby Whelks, and all the boys but Dick and Billy, understood what was said, but happily Mrs. Grumps did not.

"They seem to be such nice people," she said, "and so kind to the poor old man."

Pierre had borne the badinage quietly, but he suffered, and held in reserve a lot of pepper for somebody by-and-by.

You may chaff a man about his horses if they are good ones, but if they happen to be bad ones it is an unpardonable outrage.

The old waggonette rattled along the road until the village of Laroche hove in sight.

It was a good-sized cluster of houses at the foot of the hills, and around it meandered a small stream, one of the tributaries of the mighty Rhine.

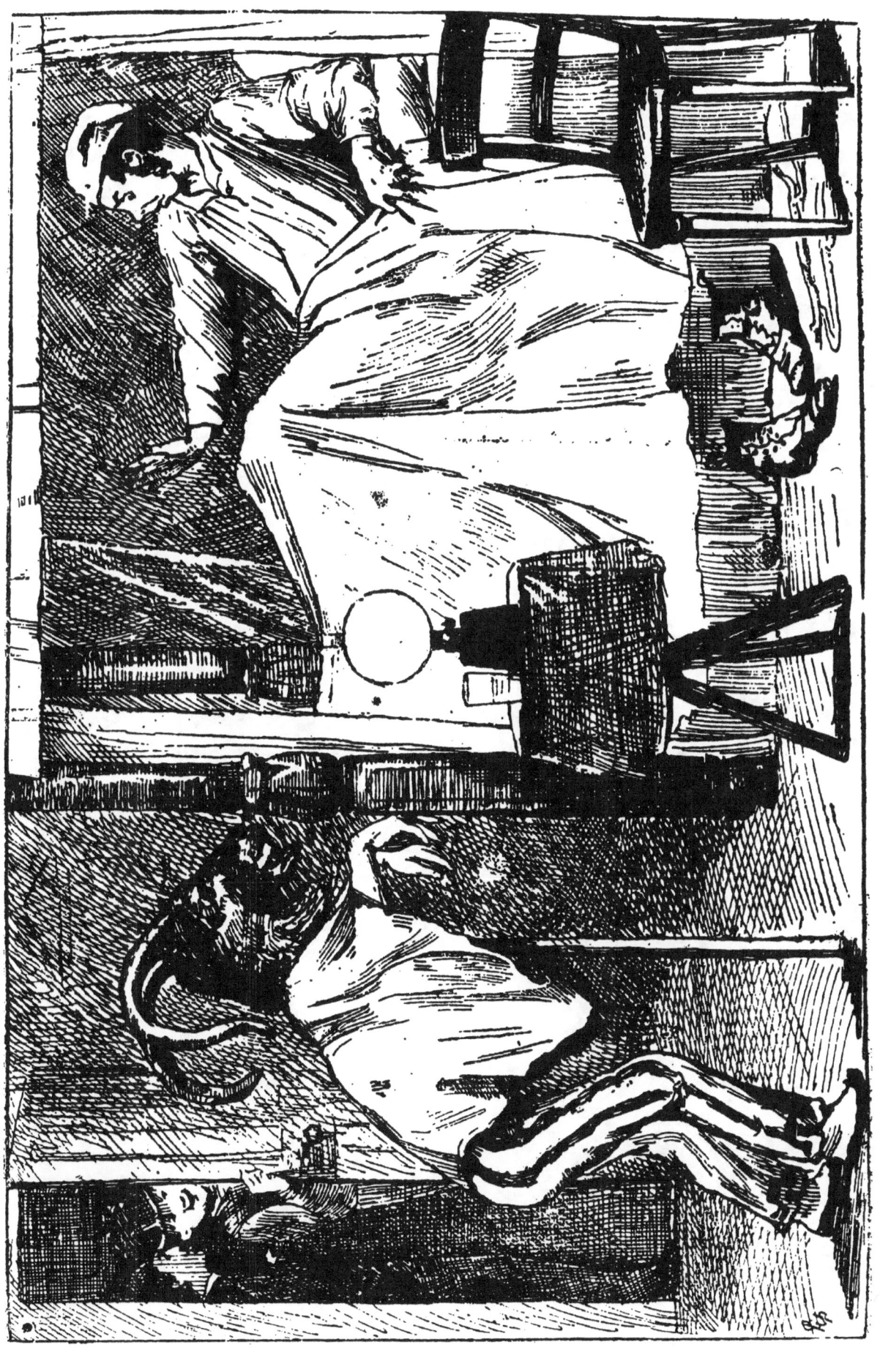

" IS THIS THE NIGHT-MARE, OR GOAT-MARE, OR WHAT IS IT?"

The fair was held in a meadow between the village and the river.

Already the showmen were at work, banging drums and making all sorts of discordant music, enough to curdle the blood of any lover of melody.

Pierre woke up his horses with a few expert touches of the whip, and shouting "Hi-hi—you!" dashed up to the outskirts of the booths at the fearful pace of nearly six miles an hour.

As a final touch to this performance he pulled up smartly, so smartly indeed that neither Billy nor Dick were quite prepared for the stoppage, and shot off their seats together.

Dick went head first on to the back of the near side horse, and rolled to the ground, firmly convinced that the whole world had suddenly been riven asunder.

Billy Pink kept his perpendicular, and dropped upon the other horse in the position of a rider.

The shock was sufficient to jerk all speech out of him, and to mix up his mighty mind, but he kept his seat.

Mrs. Grumps, rising up hastily to see what had become of her young genius, saw him sitting like the statue of King Charles upon his horse at Charing Cross.

"That boy is a horse-tamer," she said, "and he can do anything with the equaline speechers."

As she spoke Billy's wits partly came back to him, and without a word or sign he rolled off the horse and fell upon his back.

By that time Young Ching and Jem Stager had got round to render assistance.

They picked him up and put him on his feet.

"What cheer, Billy," cried Jem Stager.

"You let him alone," said Mrs. Grumps, wrathfully. "It is odd that you couldn't let him get off that horse without interfering."

"All right, ma'am," said Jem. "Of course you didn't fall—did you, Billy dear?"

"I got off," replied Billy, with the evasiveness of a gifted mind.

Harry had gone to Dick's assistance, and as he was fast recovering from the shock there was no occasion for any delay.

"Now, boys," said Mr. Bone, "go and amuse yourselves, but keep out of mischief and be back here at three o'clock for something to eat. I will have it ready for you."

The boys disappeared down a double row of booths, and Frisby Whelks was gently lowering himself out of the carriage when Mrs. Grumps seized him by the collar.

"No, young man," she said, "I dursn't let you go. As your mother is not here I must take care of you."

"Really," said Frisby Whelks, looking at Mr. Bone, "this is going too far."

But Mr. Bone did not seem to hear him—he was engaged in lighting a cigar, and as soon as he got it aglow he sauntered off.

"I must appeal to you, madam," said Frisby Whelks, "to be more considerate to my feelings."

"You haven't any," replied Mrs. Grumps, "at least, not of the right sort. Sit down and don't be troublesome."

"You talk to me as if I were a boy," said Whelks.

"Bless you, I don't," replied Mrs. Grumps. "You are not a boy—I wish you were—then you wouldn't always be in such trouble—you are nothing, young man—absolutely nothing."

"Nothing or otherwise," said Frisby Whelks, "I am not going to be sat upon in this way."

"Who's a sitting on you?"

"You are, madam, and I'm going to the fair."

He bolted for the door of the carriage, and Mrs. Grumps made a grab at his coat tails. She secured both—one held and the other did not.

The right one came off about a foot from the bottom, and Mrs. Grumps in her astonishment let go the other.

Free at last, Frisby Whelks bounded off in his mutilated attire and hurried into the thick of the fair.

CHAPTER XV.

A MERRY ANDREW HAS SOME OF THE FUN TAKEN OUT OF HIM—CATASTROPHE AT A PEEP SHOW.

THE fair still holds its own in many places abroad, and at Laroche there was a vast collection of shows of all sorts and sizes.

The shows were arranged in an oblong square, and the space between them was being rapidly filled up by peasants pouring in from the country around, all in holiday attire, and looking very picturesque, if not quite so pretty as we see them represented in pictures.

There were lots of girls, of course there always are, and many a pair of eyes were turned on Handsome Harry as he sauntered by the side of Young Ching.

The son of the Immortal One also came in for some attention, and Jem Stager attracted several demure glances towards himself by smiling sweetly on the youngest and prettiest girls.

Neither Billy Pink nor Dick Cockles cared for flirtation, and when a fat little miss grinned at Dick he made a face at her.

To his profound astonishment the girl promptly boxed his ears.

"Here, drop it, will you," he said; "what are you laying into me for nothing for?"

The girl made a face at him, and half-a-dozen peasants began jabbering and laughing at the scene.

Dick could not hit the girl back again, so after glaring at her like a young basilisk he moved away, with Billy by his side.

"Hallo!" said Dick, "where's the others?"

"Gone forward," replied Billy.

"Let 'em go," said Dick; "you and I can get on best by ourselves."

They sauntered on a bit and stopped before a show where a Merry Andrew was appealing to the crowd, pointing to a picture representing a man fish dressed in his Sunday clothes and walking in a park on his tail.

"That ought to be good," said Dick; "let us go in."

"All right," replied Billy.

Both ascended the platform, and after Billy had fallen over the big drum they got to the pay place.

Dick put down half-a-franc, and the old woman who sat there swept it into the till.

"Any change?" asked Dick.

The woman stared at him and said something he did not understand.

"Sixpence is too much!" exclaimed Dick; "all shows at home are a penny."

The woman said something to the Merry Andrew, who came to her side, and she pointed at the boys.

"Vat you vant?" he asked.

"My change," said Dick. "I put down six-pence—or the blessed thing you call a six-pence here."

"Ah! yes," said the man, serenely; "it is for von to go in, and if your friend pay he shall go in too."

Dick knew that he was being imposed upon, and he said nothing of the sort would do.

"Don't pay, Billy, but tumble inside."

Billy plunged through the curtains and Dick followed. Just inside was a flight of descending seats, down which they rolled.

About half-a-dozen people had gone in before them, and one—a lank peasant—happened to be in their line of descent.

He was partaking of a sandwich, and was in the act of biting a semi-circle out of it when Billy pounced against his back and shot him forward.

Dick Cockles rolled after them, and the whole three foregathered on the ground together.

The Merry Andrew, breathing all sorts of threats, followed and laid hold of the two friends.

He was a strong man, and tucking one under each arm, the Merry Andrew carried them up again.

They kicked and punched him like two valiant young Britons, but he paid little heed to their blows.

On arriving outside again he was received with a yell of delight from the crowd, and he thought it a good opportunity to make capital out of the situation.

"Behold, messieurs," he said, "two sons of Albion—"

"Let go, will you?" cried Dick, "or it will be the worse for you."

"Be quiet, you little pigs," said the Merry Andrew, facetiously.

But help was at hand.

Harry and the other boys came bounding up the steps, and the former laid hold of a huge frill collar the clown was wearing.

"What are you doing, you beggar?" he said. "Let the boys go. What's the row here?"

"More little pigs," said the clown, making a face at the crowd.

Harry did not hesitate about what to do.

He jerked the Merry Andrew forward, and the collar yielded.

With a howl of rage the fellow dropped the boys and made a grab at Harry.

Dick and Billy lost no time in getting off the platform, and Young Ching stopped all pursuit by hitting the Merry Andrew between the eyes with one of his own drumsticks.

Jem had got the other, and dealt him a blow on the side of the head.

"Now vanish—vamoose," cried Young Ching. "Don't stop to fight, Harry. He's too much for you."

It was prudent advice, and all the boys skedaddled, while the crowd roared with delight.

It was the funniest thing they had seen outside a show that day.

The woman who took the money, after sitting still and staring awhile in surprise, got up to help the infuriated Merry Andrew, but she only received abuse for her kindness.

She retorted, and the delighted spectators were treated to a choice collection of verbal rockets and blue lights.

But self-interest soon calmed them both.

The Merry Andrew looked about for his collar, and finding it was gone, went into the show to put on another, while the woman would have beaten the drum if she could have found the sticks.

But they had been taken away as trophies of war.

"Where are those little sinners?" asked Harry, as he made his way through the crowd.

"Gone off," replied Jem Stager, "to fresh fields and pastures new."

"I wonder what the row was about," observed Harry.

"It doesn't matter," replied Young Ching. "Only what might have been expected from them. I say, Jem, these drumsticks may come in handy."

As he spoke he hit a fat man in the back with his, and shot forward half-a-dozen paces.

The fat man turned round and stared hard at a person who was gaping about him, overcome with the wonders of the fair.

"You hit me, friend," he said, and by way of return he gave him a violent dig in the ribs and walked on.

Meanwhile the two companions in misfortune had put half-a-dozen shows between them and the scene of their recent exploits before they halted.

This time it was a small peep show that attracted their attention.

It was a circular one, about six feet in diameter, and the spectators when looking through the glasses had their backs to the people.

They were partly shielded from observation by a canvas screen, placed at a sufficient distance from the show to enable them to walk round when erect.

But when in the stooping position necessary to enjoy the views there was a partial outline of their bodies on the canvas.

Only one person was inside at that moment, and it proved to be Frisby Whelks.

He was standing by the entrance waiting for additional sight-seers before gazing at the wonders of the show.

Frisby Whelks was in want of companionship, and he hailed the boys with joy.

"Come in," he said, "I'll pay for both of you."

That was a proposal worth accepting, and the two boys passed in.

Frisby Whelks paid for them, and the showman bade them walk slowly round from glass to glass.

Now it so happened that Young Ching had seen Frisby Whelks hailing the two chums, and of course he and his companions bore down upon the peep-show.

No admission was to be obtained, for the showman had closed and fastened the curtains, and in an incomprehensible jargon was explaining the views as his visitors passed round.

From the brief description we have given of the show it will be seen that the movements of the sight-seers were observable from without.

This was especially the case with Frisby Whelks, who was represented outside by a globe-like protuberance of the canvas.

It was an opportunity which could not be allowed to pass, especially by two boys who each had a drumstick in his possession.

"Both together," said Young Ching.

"Don't!" whispered Harry, laughing; "he'll smash the show."

"What matters?" returned Young Ching; "we will see that no harm comes to the boys. Now, Jem, there is no need to run. Strike home and tuck your drumstick under your jacket."

"I'll 'strike as thou didst at Cæsar,'" replied Jem, tragically.

Harry, with a smile on his face and his hands in his pockets, awaited the catastrophe.

The bulge in the canvas slowly shifted as Frisby Whelks worked his way round while the showman was explaining the views.

What we give is a translation, as the showman spoke in his native tongue.

"Behold! it is an earthquake of Lisbon you look on. It was fine—the sun shone—all was gay. In a moment—no cry—no warning—the earth rocked—the ground opened—the houses fell—the—"

Bang!

Crash!

The deed was done.

Frisby Whelks had been smitten, and plunging forward he rammed his head into the spy-hole.

It was a frail structure, and required no effort to get inside it, so there he was with the framework of the earthquake spy-glass round his neck.

He had been much interested in the description of the earthquake, and for a moment or two he thought a real one had come to pass.

Nor was his astonishment less than that of the showman, who in wild terror dashed against the outside canvas, and the whole affair came to the ground.

Frisby Whelks, with his coat minus one tail, and invisible as far as his head was concerned, stood revealed.

Immediately there was a great uproar.

A cry 'for gendarmes was raised, and one happening to be near he came to the front.

Frisby Whelks had not recovered his wits sufficiently to stir.

The showman, with much gesticulation, proceeded to explain.

"See—he put his head in. I show him the earthquake of Lisbon—I tell him the earth rock—he is moved—he thrusts his head forward—so—and behold he is fixed. Take him away to prison. Let him pay."

The gendarme laid hold of Frisby Whelks by the waist and drew him back.

Around his neck he had a wooden frame, part of the wrecked show.

Not a word did he say in his defence, for he had not a syllable left in him.

But the gendarme happened to be one of those who had been a witness of the death of Picard, and he remembered Frisby Whelks.

"Be at rest," he said to the showman. "He is English—a gentleman. You will be paid— I will take him to his friends. Behold! you have my word—my word of honour."

Then he led the still bewildered tutor away, and the showman proceeded to repair his show as well as he could.

But one part of it would never be exhibited more. The earthquake of Lisbon had been utterly ruined. It had been reduced to fragments by the head of Whelks, and would never charm the eye of the public again.

CHAPTER XVI.

DINNER AND A RIDE HOME—JUST WHAT MIGHT HAVE BEEN EXPECTED.

"I WONDER where those boys are?" said Mrs. Grumps, as she stood up in the carriage and looked about her.

It was luncheon time, and Mr. Fossil Bone was helping Pierre to unpack a large hamper and display its toothsome contents upon a cloth spread on the ground.

"Like all boys," said Mr. Bone, "they forget the flight of time when they are enjoying themselves."

"And that Whelks!" continued Mrs. Grumps. "Where is that poor creetur?"

"I daresay he is about," replied Mr. Bone, carelessly.

As he gave this answer his eye twinkled, and it is within the bounds of possibility that he knew something of the little mishap which had befallen Harry's tutor.

Pierre was much interested in the luncheon. Not only did his mouth water, but his eyes also watered with longing for his share of the good things.

"You Engliese eat good," he said. "Oh! it is a great thing to be of your country."

"We do something else besides eat to make us what we are," replied Mr. Bone.

As he spoke Harry and Jem Stager walked up to the waggonette.

"Where are the rest of the boys?" asked Mr. Bone.

"Young Ching is looking for Pink and Cockles," replied Jem Stager.

"And may I ask," inquired Mrs. Grumps, looking indignantly at Jem, "why that boy William is lost?"

"He and Dick have been lost a dozen times this morning," replied Jem, hurriedly.

"By your running away from 'em, I suppose, Mister Stager?"

"Nobody ran away from them, Mrs. Grumps. They are always losing themselves."

"Oh! don't talk to me," said Mrs. Grumps. "I know what they are, and what you can be when you try. It's shameful how you neglect them."

"All right," muttered Jem, under his breath; "if you get anything into your old head it can't be hammered out."

Mrs. Grumps was about to say a little more, when Young Ching appeared, rather in a hurry.

His face had a flurried look, and Mr. Bone saw that something was wrong.

"Where are those boys—the other two?" he said.

"Will you come to the waxwork show, sir?" asked Young Ching. "The people there won't let them come out."

"Why not?"

"Somebody's put a piece of stick in the works of one of the moving figures," said Young Ching. "It is a model of Washington declaring the independence of America. When they set it going both legs came off, and Washington is smashed."

"But why do they detain my boys?" asked Mr. Bone.

"They say that Billy Pink did it, and also that Dick Cockles put a piece of treacle toffy into the big musical-box they keep going inside. It is in a fearful mess, and the waxwork man went mad. He threw a three-legged stool at Dick and knocked Napoleon's head off."

"Oh! the villain!" exclaimed Mrs. Grumps.

"It seems a strange thing that you boys cannot go anywhere without getting into trouble," said Mr. Bone. "Is the show at the lower end of the fair?"

"Yes," replied Young Ching.

"I'll go and see about it," said Mr. Bone. "You need not come. Stop here and take care of Mrs. Grumps."

As soon as he was gone Jem Stager turned to Young Ching and said, in a low tone—

"I told you that you were going too far."

"It is so difficult to stop when you once begin," replied Young Ching; "and wasn't it aggravating to see those hideous figures jerking their heads and arms up and down as if they had the jumps?"

"We needn't have stopped, you know," returned Jem. "But as I am a knightly man I thought I should have burst when I saw that man trying to fish the toffy out of the musical-box."

"Well jammed in, wasn't it?" said Young Ching, with glee.

Handsome Harry was talking to Mrs. Grumps. He was explaining to her what had become of Frisby Whelks.

Frisby had damaged a show and been locked up by a gendarme, who was looking about for Mr. Bone, was the substance of his story.

"I never had such a troublesome boy in my charge," said Mrs. Grumps. "Really his mother ought to have come with him."

Harry could hardly keep his countenance, for it tickled him to find that Mrs. Grumps looked upon his tutor as a boy.

It was nearly half-an-hour before Mr. Bone returned, and he brought all the missing ones with him.

Dick and Billy looked as if they had suffered shipwreck, and had had a hairbreadth escape of their lives.

Dick glared at Young Ching, and turning to Jem Stager he said—

"You think yourself mighty clever, don't you?"

"Yes," replied Jem.

"For all that," said Dick, "Mr. Bone intends to charge for the broken waxworks in your bill, so put that in your pipe and smoke it."

"Now, boys, if you want anything to eat, sit down," interrupted Mr. Bone.

They did want something to eat, and fell to.

Pierre was fed also. He sat on the box and ate pie enough for five, inflating himself perceptibly. Mrs. Grumps also did pretty well for an invalid.

But she could not quite let Frisby Whelks alone.

She did not say anything to him, but whenever he looked up at her, as he did every ten seconds, she shook her head at him as much as to say—

"Oh! you naughty boy."

CHAPTER XVII.

THE END OF A HAPPY DAY—MESSAGE FROM THE BLACK BANDITS—ONCE MORE UPON THE MOUNTAINS.

MR. FRISBY WHELKS bore it as well as he could, but it took all the flavour out of his pie, and he failed to make a satisfactory meal.

After it was over the boys wanted to go into the fair again, but Mr. Bone stopped them.

"No," he said; "you have had about five pounds' worth of fun to-day, and that is enough. We will get along home."

"It is the way of some people," said Mrs. Grumps, looking hard at Frisby Whelks, "to go and do things that stop other people from enjoying themselves."

"I do wish you would leave me alone," replied the exasperated Frisby Whelks. "I am not a boy."

The meal was now over, and Pierre went to get his horses, which he had carefully hobbled and turned loose upon the banks of the river.

They saw him coming, and at once became skittish, neighing and prancing about like kangaroos troubled with rheumatism.

He made a dart at their heads, and one of them reared up and fell sideways into the river.

Fortunately it was not very deep, and the brute was got out.

As it had been turned loose with the greater part of its ragged harness on, it was in a bedraggled condition, and presented a very forlorn appearance.

But there was no help for it. No other animal could be got, and it was harnessed with the other to the carriage, looking like a half-drowned rat.

The pleasure seekers took their seats, and the conveyance started.

"How this thing wobbles," said Mrs. Grumps.

"It is the make of the thing," replied Mr. Bone. "If you look at it closely you will see it is like a wasp, weak about the waist."

The "waist," as Mr. Bone termed it, was that part of the vehicle between the body of the carriage and the box seat.

Pierre had had a good dinner, with more wine than he usually got at a sitting, and he was a little excited.

He was also very angry with the horse that had fallen into the river, and gave it a pretty good allowance of whip-cord.

At first it had no effect, but presently they came to a long, downward slope, and both horses broke into a trot.

"You had better go quietly," said Mr. Bone to Pierre.

"And why?" asked Pierre. "Behold I make dem go! Hi—hi!—you—you! Vorwarts!"

The horses had nothing to pull, and they were obliged to gallop to the bottom or fall down by the way.

The pace they went must have astonished themselves. Pierre was astounded and elated.

"Hi—hi!—you," he shrieked. "Vorwarts! Houp-la!"

The mongrel vehicle began to sway in a most dangerous manner, and to bump over stones with a violence that threatened its complete dislocation.

Mr. Bone stood up and expostulated with Pierre, who tried to work the old brake, but it snapped like a carrot.

Billy and Dick put an arm round each other, and with their disengaged hands clung to the seat.

The boys at the back began to grow hilarious.

"This is travelling," said Young Ching. "Whoop!"

The vehicle had gone over a big stone, its hind part rising a foot into the air and coming down with a crash.

"We shall have an accident," said Mr. Bone, angrily. "Pull up your horses, man."

"I must get to ze head of dem to do it," replied Pierre. "Houp-la! proceed."

"Mind this," said Mrs. Grumps, shaking her umbrella at Frisby Whelks, "if any of these precious boys are hurt you shall suffer for it."

He scarcely heeded the threat, his mind being occupied with the terror of the situation.

The vehicle had now gathered a momentum that drove the wretched brutes forward with an irresistible pressure. On—on—down the slope.

Peasants coming up stopped and stared, and a few turned to run after the vehicle and cry "Hi—hi!"

Presently they were nearing the bottom, and hope came into the heart of the watchful Mr. Bone.

Possibly they might escape without an accident.

But hope is often a gay deceiver.

They were within twenty yards of the termination of the hill, beyond which was a nice level bit of travelling, when the vehicle was suddenly jerked into the air and came down with a smash.

"Hold tight," cried Mr. Bone.

There was need to hold tight, especially on the part of those in front, for the mongrel vehicle had broken in two at the "waist," and the fore part was whisked away by the now half-maddened horses.

Mr. Bone had one moment's glimpse of its flight, with Billy, Dick, and Pierre clinging together and shouting for help.

Then he was occupied by the ruin about him, for the back part of the vehicle had collapsed like a house of cards, and those lately seated therein lay among a chaos of rotten boards, broken wheels, and musty cushions.

Frisby Whelks, in addition, had Mrs. Grumps on the top of him, madly floundering about like a stranded whale.

The first out of the ruin was Young Ching, then came Handsome Harry, and together they lifted up Mrs. Grumps and stood her on her feet.

"I hope you are not hurt," said Harry.

"I'm as near murdered as makes no odds," cried Mrs. Grumps. "Let me get at him."

"Him" was Frisby Whelks, whom Jem Stager was dragging out of the ruin by the heels.

Mr. Bone had freed himself and was taking a hurried look round.

"No great damage done," he said. "Remain here, you boys, and take care of Mrs.

THE SLAPCRASH BOYS.

The Liveliest of School Stories.

FRISBY WHELKS UPON THE MOUNTAINS—WHO UPSET THE MILK?

No. 11.   Price One Penny.

Grumps. I must go and see what has become of the others."

Off he went, and Jem Stager having got Frisby Whelks clear, propped him up in a sitting position.

He was gasping and groaning in the most horrible manner.

"Don't go on in that way, you hypocrite," said Mrs. Grumps. "I know the vally of it, for you and that Frenchy old man on the box arranged it between you. But mark you this, Mr. Vicious—if either of them dear boys as have been flowed away with is killed, I'll go into the witness-box and have you hanged right away."

Frisby Whelks smiled a sickly smile, and turning round exhibited his mutilated coat. Mrs. Grumps fell upon him again, in what we really consider an unjustifiable manner.

"You go about in rags," she said. "A nice example to set the boys."

"Why!" he exclaimed, "you did it yourself."

"Did what?" asked Mrs. Grumps.

"Tore my coat tail off."

The amazement in the face of the dear old lady was something prodigious.

It was also comical, and Jem Stager began to laugh.

Upon him Mrs. Grumps turned like a benevolent tigress.

"Mister Stager," she said, "it is not the first time you have laughed at your elders and betters, but I hope as how it will be the last. Do you think Willum Pink would have done it?"

"No," replied Jem. "He doesn't often see a joke."

"And may I ask where the joke is when a man comes into the presence of ladies with one coat-tail short?" inquired Mrs. Grumps.

"Why—the—the—joke"—Jem hesitated a moment, and then a bright idea came to help him—"the joke is in his coat-tail, I suppose."

Handsome Harry laughed at this, and Mrs. Grumps' face expanded into a smile.

"You was always a lively boy," she said, "and I 'spose it's your nature. But as for that creetur"—shaking her umbrella at Frisby Whelks—"his conduct is most unmanly."

"I can't stand any more of it," exclaimed the goaded Whelks. "I can't see why this dead set is always made against me, and I—"

He was interrupted by the voice of Mr. Fossil Bone, who was calling to them from the turn of the road.

"Leave the bits of that old rattletrap in the road and come here," said the schoolmaster.

They set forward in a body, Frisby Whelks hanging a little in the rear.

Harry and Young Ching helped Mrs. Grumps along arm in arm.

In this way they rejoined the schoolmaster, and from where he was standing they saw that the front of the waggonette had not travelled far.

The harness, about as rotten as it could be, had given way, and the horses had gone on alone.

Near the overturned fragments Billy, Dick, and Pierre were sitting in the road, the two boys looking a bit dazed, and the driver holding his head with both hands.

"Providentially no bones have been broken," said Mr. Bone. "We had better go to that cottage yonder until we can procure a vehicle to convey us back to Basle."

The cottage was one of the better sort of peasant residences, and as it was only two hundred yards or so further on, they were soon there.

It belonged to a small farmer in the neighbourhood, but all the family except a very deaf old woman had gone to the fair.

Pierre acted as interpreter, for the old woman spoke a jargon that was difficult for any but a native to understand, and he having succeeded in making her comprehend what was required, she invited them in.

She set before them wooden bowls filled with milk, and some rye bread, the best form of refreshment at her command.

It was better than nothing, and out of courtesy they all partook of it.

"Now," said Mr. Bone to Pierre, "what about a conveyance back to Basle?"

"Milord," replied Pierre, "they will all be at ze fair."

"To the fair, then, you must go to hire one."

"Milord, I vill, but it may take so long to get it."

"Get it, short or long," replied Mr. Bone. "We have to get back somehow, and this lady cannot walk so far."

"I will be back in two hours," said Pierre, who made himself a cigarette and lighted it as he went on his way—rather groggy, perhaps, on his legs after his recent accident, but on the whole decidedly debonnaire.

Two hours to wait.

It was a long time for five boys, afflicted with the natural restlessness of their age, so Mr. Bone told them they might go outside and have a run about the hills behind the house.

"But don't go far away," he said. "Be within hail."

Of course they promised, and glad of the liberty accorded them they went forth.

Mr. Bone lit a cigar, and seated in an old rocking-chair he talked to Frisby Whelks.

Mrs. Grumps and the deaf old woman both dozed off in their respective chairs.

Half-an-hour or so had passed when a sharp knock was heard at the door.

It did not disturb the two women, but the men were a little startled by its suddenness.

"See who it is, Whelks," said Mr. Bone.

Frisby Whelks rose and went to the door.

With great care he opened it an inch or two and peered out.

"I don't see anybody," he quavered.

"Open the door, man!" said Mr. Bone, impatiently. "There are no tigers or wolves hereabouts."

Frisby Whelks drew back the door and thrust his head out.

After a look up and down the road he confirmed his first report.

"I don't see a creature about," he said.

Mr. Bone got up and joined him at the door.

It was perfectly true—nobody was to be seen.

"Very odd," muttered Mr. Bone. "It must have been a runaway knock of one of the boys."

He was about to return to his seat when he espied a small piece of folded paper lying on the ground.

Stooping down he saw scrawled upon it in pencil these words—

"To the Englishmen and boys."

With a wondering face he raised it from the ground and slowly unfolded it.

Inside were words of deep portent.

"*Death to those who stand in the path and check the course of the anarchist and his vengeance. Not one of you—man or boy—shall ever return home ALIVE.*"

The missive was in every way startling, but Mr. Bone did not show its nature by his face.

Without a word, and quite coolly, he stepped into the roadway and scanned the country round.

In the far distance, towards the fair, he saw a few stragglers wending their way thither, but no other wayfarers were in sight.

At the back of the cottage was rugged country, an extension of the line of hills near Basle.

There were narrow paths up the hills, tempting to boys who are fond of climbing, and by one of these the five boys must have gone, for they were nowhere in sight.

"I wish I had kept them with me," Mr. Bone muttered.

"What is that bit of paper?" asked Frisby Whelks.

"Nothing particular," was the answer. "By-the-way, I wonder where those boys are gone. I cannot see them."

"Back to the fair, perhaps."

"I can hardly think that."

There was a grain of comfort in the suggestion, but it was not wholly satisfactory.

Mr. Fossil Bone was a kindly man, but like all good and true people, he did not allow anyone to take liberties with him.

"No," he said, after a pause, "they are gone over the hills, and somebody ought to go and call them back."

"I would gladly go," said Frisby Whelks, "but the shock of that vehicle breaking up—"

"I will go myself," interposed Mr. Bone, half-angrily; "pray do not offer weak excuses when you do not wish to do a thing. I leave the women in your charge—close and bar the door until I come back."

"Can-a-a-not I come with you?"

"And leave two helpless women alone? No, sir—they will want a protector, perhaps, and you are better than none."

So saying he gave Frisby Whelks a push on one side and closed the door.

After waiting a moment to hear the bolt drawn Mr. Bone made his way to the back of the cottage.

There was a farmyard behind, through which he passed, and next it was a grassy slope. Beyond that the hills.

"If I could only tell which path to take," he muttered.

But that was no easy matter.

Half-a-dozen at least were offered for his acceptance, all widely diverging and spreading out in various directions.

The situation was trying.

"I must get to high ground and have a look about me," he muttered.

He was a very active man for his years, and quickly scaled one of the hills near him.

Gaining the summit, the view he had was a very extensive one.

On his right was Laroche, the noise of the fair floating up to him.

On the left lay Basle, the intervening country being dotted with cottages, while here and there stood a mill.

At first he could see nothing of the boys, and a deadly fear was taking hold of him when he saw Young Ching come hurriedly round the shoulder of the next hill.

He was followed by two more, whom Mr. Bone made out to be Harry and Jem Stager.

But that was all.

These three came hurrying along the slope as if for dear life, and Mr. Bone expected each moment to see them pursued by some foe.

But there was nobody in their rear.

The mystery of their hurried descent was thus made apparent. Something had happened to Billy Pink and Dick Cockles.

What was it?

With visions of bloodthirsty anarchists in his eyes, and fearing the worst, Mr. Bone hurried down to meet them.

CHAPTER XVIII.

ANOTHER TERRIBLE CALAMITY—THE WAY THEY DID IT—AND THE ONLY WAY TO GET OUT OF IT.

Now Mr. Bone and the boys were approaching each other by two paths ending in a small valley.

He was seen long before half the descent had been accomplished, and by leaving the path and taking to the rougher country the boys soon joined him.

It was evident that there was real cause for alarm, as all the lads, despite their recent exertions, looked pale.

"What calamity have you to tell me of?" Mr. Bone asked.

"Billy and Dick have fallen over a precipice," replied Young Ching.

"How did that happen, and what right had you near a precipice?" asked Mr. Bone.

"We only went up to have a look at the fair in the distance," replied Jem Stager.

Mr. Bone, despite his natural self-command, wrung his hands and moaned.

"We told them not to go too near the edge," said Young Ching, "but they kept daring each other, until at last Dick slipped and laid hold of Billy. Then over they went together."

"The last we saw of them," interposed Handsome Harry, "was their feet. They went over head first."

"Terrible—terrible!" exclaimed Mr. Bone. "Come and show me where this awful thing happened. Oh! what an ending to our happy excursion."

"I wish I could have held them back," remarked Harry, "but they were both so pig-headed."

"Boys like Pink and Cockles require keepers," said Mr. Bone. "Stop a moment—we won't go up the hill. That would be waste of time. Let us go to where the remains of the poor lads will be found. What a story to take home to their friends."

Jem Stager took out his handkerchief and wiped his eyes. He was, as might have been expected, deeply affected.

Young Ching also had a hard job to keep back his tears, while Harry bit his underlip as he walked on beside Mr. Bone.

"If we make our way round the hill," Harry said, "we shall come to the foot of the precipice."

"What height is it?" asked Mr. Bone, with a groan.

"Quite a hundred feet."

Mr. Bone groaned again as he observed—

"Men and animals have fallen from great heights and escaped. Sir Charles Young and his two brothers went down two thousand feet, and only one was killed. But they alighted on a bed of snow. There can be no hope for these lads. You say they went clean over?"

"Clean, sir."

"No scraping against the sides?"

"Nothing but the thud of their fall. We all heard that."

"And no cry followed?"

"Not a sound, sir."

"Did you look over to see where they had fallen?"

"We were too much shaken for that," said Young Ching.

"I went as near as I dare," interposed Harry, "and looked over, but I could see nothing."

They worked their way round the base of the hill, and very rough travelling it was. Half-an-hour elapsed before they reached the desired spot.

"They ought to be here," said Harry, pointing to the broken ground at the bottom of a cliff as near perpendicular as could well be.

"We shall find their remains wedged between the rocks," observed Mr. Bone.

The boys began their dismal search, with eyes that could see very little, simply because they were dimmed with tears.

The voice of Mr. Bone was also affected.

Occasionally they looked up, but all overhead was blurred. Their task in every way was a painful one.

"It was sinful of me," said Mr. Bone, "to trust you boys about this country, where there are so many dangers. I shall never forgive myself."

"Poor old Billy—the most faithful of friends," murmured Young Ching.

"I wish I had never said an unkind word about the sausage trade," moaned Jem. "Ah! here is one of them—no—it is only poor Dick's cap."

It was undoubtedly Dick's cap, but where was poor Dick?

They must have fallen pretty close together, but there were no signs of the boys' remains.

"This is very odd," said Mr. Bone. "Are you sure they fell over?"

"I saw them go," replied Young Ching. "They kept daring each other, and when Dick—or was it Billy—I don't know which—got near the edge, he seemed to turn giddy and fall forward—and then—"

Young Ching was stopped by an appealing voice that came from somewhere overhead.

He fairly staggered backward, and they all looked up.

Three parts of the way up the precipice there was a shelf of rock, over which two faces were peering.

Not the slightest doubt could be entertained as to who they belonged to.

"Oh! Mr. Bone—it makes us so sick and giddy here. Can't you come and help us?"

"Cockles!" gasped Mr. Bone. "Is it indeed you?"

"Yes, sir."

"And Pink with you?"

"It's me, sir," replied Billy. "We fell down and can't get up again."

"Don't try," said Mr. Bone, hurriedly. "Keep still until I can devise some means to help you. Boys, we may save them yet, but their situation is one of extreme peril. Night will be here soon, and darkness would be their destruction. Stager, you get back to the path above, then lie down and talk to them. Harry and Ching, come with me back to the farm to get ropes and other things we may want."

Talking in this way, and trembling in spite of his great efforts to preserve his composure, Mr. Bone hurried towards the farm, with the boys in close attendance upon him.

Jem Stager lost no time in getting to the scene of the disaster, and lying down on the pit of his stomach he peeped over.

About fifteen feet below, Billy Pink and Dick Cockles were sitting on a ledge of rock.

Jem Stager proceeded to comfort them.

"I say, you two chuckle heads," he cried; "a nice mess you made of falling over, didn't you?"

"We couldn't help it," replied Billy, with a piteous upward glance.

"Not help it," retorted Jem, scornfully; "anyway, you could have let us know that you hadn't gone all the way down. Why didn't you shout out and say you were not dead?"

"I couldn't," replied Billy.

"Why not?"

"I fell sitting."

"So did I," said Dick.

"Well, don't try to fall the rest of the way," returned Jem, "although I don't exactly see how you are to be got up again."

"Oh! don't say that," cried Dick.

"I do. But don't be alarmed, for you shall be regularly fed, and Bone has gone down to buy some waterproof bedding. You will be very comfortable there—when you get used to it."

"Oh! my poor father," groaned Dick.

"Your father can come and see you now and again," replied Jem, "so can your mother, and if your brothers and sisters are good they can come, too. So you won't be so lonely after all."

Comforting as these words undoubtedly were, they did not have a very livening effect.

Both Dick and Billy groaned aloud.

"Stop that awful row," said Jem; "if you had been killed outright you might have made a fuss about it. A nice job it has been for us, piping our eyes when you were not dead. I call you a pair of humbugs."

"It's worse for us," pleaded Billy.

"No it isn't," said Jem; "people will pity you, but they won't pity us. You'll be one of the sights of the place, and thousands will come to see you. They will feed you with buns, and all sorts of good things, just as they do the bears at the zoological."

"You are an ass!—you always were," exclaimed Dick, with sudden exasperation.

"What did you say?"

"I said you were an ass," repeated Dick.

"Mean and cowardly I call it," said Jem. "You are cheeky because you know I can't get at you. It's just like you, Dick—as soon as you are safely out of reach you begin to slang your best friends."

"You're no friend," retorted Billy, "to come chaffing us when any minute we might be dashed into bits."

"No fear of your breaking," said Jem. "A boy of your solidity could fall from the moon without smashing."

"Why don't you go away?" demanded Dick.

"Because I was told off to comfort you," replied Jem.

"Oh—oh!" exclaimed Billy.

"What's the matter now?" asked Jem.

"This bit of rock is giving away—oh! dear!"

"Dick—Billy!" cried Jem, "I'm sorry I chaffed you. I didn't mean it—indeed, I didn't! Are you really falling? Oh! do forgive me! I'm awfully sorry!"

CHAPTER XIX.

SOLD AGAIN—THE RESCUE—MR. FOSSIL BONE MAKES A RESOLVE AND KEEPS IT.

JEM was truly repentant. It was not the first time he had chaffed Dick and Billy, but he was resolved that it should be the last.

And really it seemed as if it would be the last, for Dick and Billy kept on yelling that the rock was slipping downwards, until Jem fairly burst out crying.

Then they stopped, and Jem listened for the sound of their falling.

But instead of that he heard a sort of chuckling, which gradually assumed the form of suppressed laughter. Jem pricked up his ears.

Yes—they were laughing, and laughing at him without a doubt. The idea was rather exasperating.

Jem could take a joke at times, but he was a better hand at giving one. Anyway, he did not care to be laughed at by boys whom he considered to be his inferiors in an intellectual sense.

"What's the matter with you down there?" he asked.

"We are enjoying ourselves," replied Dick Cockles. "Oh! I'm so sorry—I'll never do such a thing again—ha-ha-ha!"

Billy joined in, and the rocks rang with their laughter.

Jem stood up with his hands in his pockets, softly whistling.

In a few moments a smile began to dawn on his face. It gathered strength and expanded into a grin.

"Sold," he said, "and serve me right, but I didn't think they had so much grit. If they

can laugh down there they've got backbone. I say, you two—I confess I'm sold—are you all right?"

"Rather," said Dick, "and we feel we shall be all right, eh! Billy?"

"I should think so, Dick," was the chuckling answer.

Jem sat down near the edge of the cliff and chatted with them until he heard voices in the distance.

It was the rescue party, augmented by Pierre and the driver of a vehicle he had brought back from the fair.

They had brought two stout poles, sundry ropes, and a pulley. Frisby Whelks was the only absentee.

Mr. Bone directed the arrangements for the rescue.

The two poles were lashed together, and the pulley fixed. The stoutest rope of all was chosen for hoisting, and at the end of it a large loop was made. This was for the boys to sit in.

Higher up a smaller one was made, for them to put an arm through and hold on.

As it was necessary for somebody to descend and see that the two unfortunates were properly fixed, Young Ching volunteered for the duty. He was lighter in build than Handsome Harry, and was therefore the better fitted for the task.

The rescue was accomplished without any serious hitch.

Young Ching descended and put Billy into the noose, bidding him keep his eyes shut until he felt himself safe on the ground above.

Then he gave the word, and Billy Pink was carefully raised to safety.

Dick was the next, and last of all Young Ching, who put his foot into the noose, and holding on with one hand, was hauled up to Mr. Bone, who grasped him by the tunic and helped him to safety.

"You *must* run a needless risk, Ching," said the schoolmaster.

"I did not think it one," was the answer.

Pierre and his brother coachman shouldered the poles and led the way down the hill.

Pierre seemed to take the loss of his horses lightly, but this was afterwards accounted for by his confessing that they would indubitably return to their stables, or failing to do so they would be driven there, as nobody in Basle would give them shelter.

Nor did he groan over the loss of his vehicle, and this was also explained.

A friend of his bet him five francs that he

would never get to the fair with it, and of course he had won. Not only had he reached the fair, but he had got half-way back ere the calamity came about.

Frisby Whelks was found in charge of the vehicle hired to take them home, and Mrs. Grumps was in charge of Frisby Whelks.

The unhappy tutor had had a very trying time of it.

If the horse was at all restless, Mrs. Grumps called out to him—Frisby Whelks, not the horse—"Whoa there! stand still," and she was thus adjuring him when the rescuers and rescued appeared.

"I shall be driven to do something desperate to that old woman," thought Whelks.

Mr. Bone was anxious to get back. Night at hand and the letter dropped near the door, when conjoined, were not nice things to think of.

The vehicle was a roomy one, the horse in the shafts a powerful animal, and the road being slightly on the decline all the way, the whole party could ride back in it.

On reaching the gates of Basle, Mr. Bone got out with the boys, and sent Mrs. Grumps forward in charge of Frisby Whelks, much to the tutor's disgust.

Mr. Bone was very thoughtful.

He was debating in his mind whether it would be better to go home or not.

When he started with the boys he had not anticipated the adventures we have related, with the dangerous associations which had been involuntarily formed.

It would never do to go home with the loss of a single youngster. He would much rather lose his own life.

Going back was not at all to his taste. Query—what should he do?

To get out of the neighbourhood of Polowski and his associates was the first thing.

In what country were they least likely to be found?

"I'll take the boys to Spain," he murmured, as they turned into their hotel. "It is a land of beauty and romance, and the tales about brigands are, of course, all humbug. There are no such things nowadays. A swift run through Switzerland, then across south-eastern France, and we shall be there."

Over supper Mr. Bone confided his newly-formed plans to his young charges, and he frankly gave them his reason for diverging from his original course.

"We must act with regard to the Black Bandits," he said, "as some people do when they come upon a nest of hornets—get out of their way. Therefore I shall select the most unfrequented roads."

Who would not have been delighted with the notion of travelling in this fashion—away from the general route of tourists?

The bare mention of it sufficed to raise the spirits of the boys, already sufficiently volatile.

Frisby Whelks approved, and recovered a part of his lost nerve. He even talked defiantly of the Black Bandits now that he felt that he was likely to get clear away from them, and told stories of how other similar villains had been circumvented, captured, and punished by brave men.

Mrs. Grumps, prior to this, had gone to bed tired out.

Frisby Whelks also had had enough of it, and after his supper he betook himself to rest also.

Notwithstanding his newly-acquired courage he could not go to rest without a light, and having made friends with the chambermaid he was furnished with a lamp to burn as a night light.

Worn and weary with the events of the day he fell asleep.

How long he had slept he did not know, but in after days he calculated that it was something under an hour, when he was roused by the opening of the door.

It had no bolt, or he would have fastened it ere he went to rest.

Horror on horrors—what is this?

An enormous goat was slowly insinuating itself into the room.

He judged it was enormous from the fact that its head was almost as high in the air as that of a man, and it was bleating in the most pathetic manner—

"Ba! ba! black band—have you any wool?"

Mr. Whelks heard the words distinctly, and the way his hair stood upright showed that he had as much wool as is ordinarily allotted to man.

As if by some invisible agency he was drawn into a sitting position, and at the same time he felt as if his eyes were being drawn out of his head.

"Ba—ba! bold Whelks—keep yourself cool."

He again heard the words distinctly—more distinctly than before, and the thought that it might possibly be an attack of nightmare came to his momentary relief.

But only for a moment.

He remembered that he had seen the stuffed head of a mountain ram in the passage, and had remarked to himself on the wonderful intelligence of its glass eyes.

Was it possible that the ghosts of goats, like human beings, were permitted to return and scare good honest people?

Frisby Whelks believed in ghosts.

His grandfather knew of several—he had the old man's word for it—his father had looked upon two, and Frisby, as a boy, had almost seen one.

Could it be that the ghost of a goat had come to him in this strange land and determined to haunt him?

Had he been fully awake he might not have entertained the idea, but now he was badly frightened.

"Ba! ba—Whelks—ba! ba—black band—ba—"

Then the head of that goat suddenly rose up in the air, shot over the foot of the bed, and descended upon him.

He fell back gasping, clasping the uncanny thing in his arms.

In a frenzy he fought with it, struggled for dear life, and finally fell out of bed with the thing in his arms.

Then, as in a vision, he saw a pair of striped trousers whisk through the doorway, and outside arose suppressed sounds of merriment that suddenly stilled his fears.

He knew by inspiration all about the goat's head.

Looking at it, he saw that it was fixed to a broom-handle, so putting that and the striped trousers together, the dark secret of the dreadful adventure was revealed.

"Young Ching," he gasped, and rising to his feet he ran to the door.

It closed as he drew near it, and half-a-dozen moments were wasted in fumbling with the lock ere he could open it again.

When he succeeded he bounced into the passage and came face to face with the chambermaid, who uttered a scream of horror.

She was an ancient dame, but Frisby Whelks, in a moderate allowance of night garments, naturally astounded and alarmed her.

After a hideous yell she pounced upon Frisby, boxed both his ears so that he saw a regular milky way of stars, and pushed him back into his room.

"Hang the wench," muttered Whelks, "and confound all womankind. As for boys—they are the invention of the evil one."

Burning with wrath, he banged the door, put a chair against it, and got into bed again.

Relieved to the extent that he had seen nothing supernatural, he curled himself up, and after a time sank once more into repose.

CHAPTER XX.

THE BLACK BANDITS IN COUNCIL — A DARK DEED DECIDED ON—THE LISTENER AT THE DOOR—A WARNING.

IT is fourteen days later, and the scene is in a house in one of the poorest parts of Geneva. Gathered together in a back room are four men busy with the making of bombs.

These men are the Black Bandits of the Rhine. They have obtained work through Polowski, who has kept secret the name of his employers, but for that none of his companions care. Money is plentiful.

They have eaten and drunken, and are in their way merry.

Steimetch, Schavaloff, and Kranmitz are engaged in filling egg-shaped bombs, just the size for a man to hold concealed in his hand.

"Steady, you fool!" said Polowski to Schavaloff, as a bomb slipped, and he only just caught it as it fell. "These things have a knack of exploding when roughly handled."

He took it away from Schavaloff, who looked up at him with a sullen glare.

"Just like you," he muttered; "nobody can do anything but yourself."

"You are an ignorant ass," returned Polowski. "Into your head the nature of these explosives will never be driven until an opening is made with a pickaxe. These bombs when dropped or thrown will explode. And what follows, idiot?"

"I shall know," replied Schavaloff, "when I have the chance to throw one."

"You shall have the chance," returned Polowski, "to-morrow. Some old friends of ours have arrived here to-night—to-morrow, I learn, they turn their faces to the frontier. Can you guess who they are?"

"We have so many friends," observed Kranmitz, with a grin; "all men are our friends."

"A curse upon the whole world," cried Steimetch, raising his right hand. "It is made up of tyrants and fools. Men who trample on others, and those who voluntarily put their heads under the oppressors' feet."

"That will do," observed Polowski, quietly; "it is neither the time nor place for spouting. Business is on the board. The friends I allude to are those English lads with their keepers."

"Ah!" exclaimed Steimetch.

"To one of their keepers we owe the attentions bestowed upon us by the police here," Polowski went on. "He has written a description of us, and sent it round to all the places he could think of. Before leaving Basle he had the description printed, and he sows the bills like seed wherever he goes."

"How do you know all this?" asked Schavaloff.

"They are staying at the Hotel d'Italia," replied Polowski, "and is not Luigi, the chief *garçon*, our friend?"

"So," ejaculated Steimetch, in a guttaral tone.

"Luigi hears and sees," said Polowski; "he also reads. He has keys that fit the locks of trunks—he looks for information everywhere. By chance he finds a reference to us—he tells me of it—describes who is with him—and I learn that our old enemies are here."

"Perhaps they are dogging us," suggested Steimetch.

"No," replied Polowski. "Luigi heard them talking. They travel through the by-ways, and have only come to Geneva to get things they need—clothing or something in that way. To-morrow they depart with a guide."

"That guide must be got at in some way."

"The guide has already been got at," said Polowski, triumphantly. "Luigi has done it. He will take them through the solitary Ravine Napoleon. It is seven miles from here, and but little used. A man armed with these," touching one of the bombs, "and lying on the rocks above, holds the lives of all in his grasp. Schavaloff, you are the man for the work. Will you experiment with the bombs?"

"It's a secret place—you are sure," replied Schavaloff.

"A desert at the early hour they will pass through. They start at sunrise. You will go an hour before them and choose your hiding-place."

"They are pretty toys," said Schavaloff, as he took up one of the dreadful weapons. "Yes, I will annihilate the cubs and their keepers."

He gloried in his task. It was just the sort of thing he could enjoy—revenge and personal safety combined.

It was strange how these men had learnt to hate our young friends. By a process of reasoning they had made them out to be the original aggressors, and attributed all the misfortunes of the band to their malign influence.

With Polowski this hatred is easily explained. He could not forgive anyone being better off than himself. All who owned anything in the shape of property—as he assumed every well-dressed person did—were his foes.

"It is settled then," he said, "so put aside your work to-night, boys, and let us go and drink. You need not thirst now."

They gathered up the bombs in course of manufacture and placed them in an oaken chest under a bench by the window.

It was secured by means of a padlock and the key given to Polowski.

While all this was going on a man was kneeling on the floor outside the room, with his ear glued to the keyhole.

He had been there for some time, and had never once shifted his position nor attempted to change the sense of hearing to that of sight.

As the click of the lock of the chest reached his ear he glided to the end of the passage and got into a cupboard, shutting himself in.

The Black Bandits emerged from their room, Polowski locking the door, and they went away talking and laughing.

The man in the cupboard did not stir for fully five minutes after their departure.

Opening the door an inch or so he listened intently. The house was quite still save for the whirr of a pin-grinder, whose workshop was in the attic.

With a cat-like step the spy approached the door of the anarchists' room, and with a scarcely perceptible sound he inserted a key in the lock.

A turn of the wrist and the workshop was open to him.

He did not hesitate now, but with a few swift movements accomplished his object, which was to get at the contents of the chest.

The new-comer must have been a bold man, for, regardless of the explosive nature of the things about him, he lighted a wax-taper, and by its imperfect light selected a completed bomb from a dozen at the bottom of the chest.

Then he closed the lid, re-secured the box, and glided out, leaving all as he had found it, save the bomb which he had appropriated.

"Those who live by the sword shall perish by the sword," he muttered, as he went away.

Let us go now to the Hotel d'Italia, where Mr. Bone and Frisby Whelks are talking together on the first-floor balcony of that well-kept hotel.

They overlook the street, and watch the passers-by with the interest of men who wish to see what is to be seen.

Mr. Bone is smoking a cigar, and Frisby Whelks is doing his best to get through a cigarette without shuddering.

The boys and Mrs. Grumps are in bed.

"A beautiful city, beautifully situated," observed Mr. Bone, "but notoriously the home of the foulest ruffians on earth."

"I wish we had not come here," replied Whelks. "I felt the creeps as I entered the place."

"You have been subject to the creeps; more or less, ever since I have known you. It is a pity that man should plot against man, and yet I do not even wonder at it when I think of the lot of the truly helpless poor. Understand, I do not class Polowski with these. I—"

He stopped short. Something white came fluttering over the balcony and fell at his feet.

The next moment he was peering into the street.

Many people were passing to and fro, but not one had his face turned upward. It was impossible to tell who had tossed the missive on to the balcony.

"I suppose I had better look at it," said Mr. Bone, as he stooped and picked it up. "Whelks—try and be a man. Don't shake so."

"I—I—can't help it," replied Mr. Whelks. "Those mur-r-r-derers are everywhere."

"This may not be from them," said Mr. Bone, as he stepped through the open window into the room.

He turned up the gas, and by its light unfolded a paper and read the following warning—

"*Do not go through the Ravine Napoleon to-morrow morning, and in any case defer your journey until noon. Trust and believe in me.*—A FRIEND."

Mr. Bone read it twice over, and then handed it to Frisby Whelks.

"You see," he observed, "there is nothing to be alarmed at. It is only a letter from a friend."

"How can you tell that?" groaned Whelks. "Perhaps it is a dodge to keep us here to slaughter us!"

"There is something in your idea," returned Mr. Bone, "but not much. The Ravine Napoleon is a more convenient place than the streets of Geneva for any foul work. But I think I will go round to the police-office—it is not far."

Mr. Bone took up his hat and departed.

Frisby Whelks turned down the gas and went back to the balcony, seating himself in the dark.

He did not attempt to smoke another cigarette, but sat there watching the people below, until he saw a face turned up towards him.

Once seen it was hardly possible to forget it, especially when it was aflame with drink and evil passion, as it was now.

It was the face of Polowski.

He did not see Whelks, who had shrunk into the smallest possible compass, but was apparently looking for someone overhead.

A window was raised above and a voice was heard.

Half-a-dozen words, incomprehensible to Frisby Whelks, were exchanged, and the window was closed again.

But the tutor, despite his fear, knew the voice.

It was that of Luigi, the head waiter at the hotel—a dark-eyed, sombre-looking man—who made a great impression on that most impressionable man, Frisby Whelks.

Ten minutes later Mr. Bone came back as quietly as he had gone away.

"It's all right," he said. "This is a letter from a friend."

Then Frisby Whelks told him what he had seen and heard, and how he felt sure that Luigi was in league with the anarchists.

"Very likely," replied Mr. Bone; "half the people here are conspirators."

Frisby Whelks went to bed, and after another cigar Mr. Bone followed him.

As he was going upstairs he met Luigi coming down. His first intention was to pass him, but he suddenly changed his mind.

"A word with you," he said.

"Your servant, monsieur," replied Luigi.

The conversation was carried on in French. We give a literal translation.

"You are one of the chief servants here," said Mr. Bone. "Have you a good place?"

"Most excellent, monsieur."

"Why do you risk it by leaguing yourself with murderers?"

Luigi's face flushed and then paled to a ghostly hue.

"Is monsieur of the police?" he asked.

"No," returned Mr. Bone, "but I know something about you and your friend, Polowski."

"He is no friend of mine," returned Luigi. "Polowski got me to join a society years ago. He say it is harmless, but, lo! I am expected to do murder. I decline and fly. He find me here and he say—'Do as I tell you or you die.' Monsieur, I was obliged."

"To do what?"

"It is death to tell."

"Nonsense," replied Mr. Bone. "Tell me everything. If you do so I will spare you. If not I will go for the police."

It was a bold threat, for he had no real grounds to call in the police, but it answered.

Luigi, under a promise of his name not being dragged into the matter, revealed the fact of his connection with Polowski.

He had imparted to him the route the party would take, and a little while ago Polowski had come by appointment to learn if any change in the plans had been made.

"I told him no," said Luigi.

"You do not know what Polowski purposes to do?" Mr. Bone inquired, anxiously.

"No, monsieur—I am not in his secrets," returned Luigi. "I am only the unwilling tool."

It was a mystery both ways—the intentions of Polowski and the missive giving warning of coming evil.

Who was this mysterious correspondent? Rack his brains as he might, Mr. Bone could not get at any idea concerning him.

He dismissed Luigi and went upstairs.

Before he went to rest he visited the boys as they lay asleep. They were all in calm repose, except Billy Pink, whose head was hanging over the side of the bed, at the imminent risk of bringing his young life to an end through an attack of apoplexy.

Having righted him, Mr. Bone went back to the corridor and looked over the balcony.

It was a well staircase, and he could see all the way downstairs.

On the next landing Luigi was seated on a chair, holding his head between his hands.

His attitude was that of a man troubled by remorse.

"I need not fear him," muttered Mr. Bone, as he went to bed.

In the morning the boys were astir early, as they expected to start soon after dawn.

To their disappointment they were told that they would not leave until noon, and meanwhile they must keep to the hotel.

Mr. Bone was their informant, and his manner implied that he was not to be trifled with. There was to be no going out on the quiet, "just to look about the town."

"Something is up," said Young Ching.

"I'll get it out of Whelks," replied Harry.

Frisby Whelks was in a most pitiable condition.

The fact of breakfast being on the table seemed to have little interest for him, which was a very unusual thing, for he had an appetite in great disproportion to his physique.

Mrs. Grumps, having been told there was no hurry to get up, was having breakfast in bed.

Harry was not long in getting at the facts. The temporary absence of Mr. Bone immediately after breakfast gave him the opportunity he wanted.

"Now, Whelks," he said, "what's the row?"

The boys all gathered round the tutor, who sighed heavily and looked piteously at them.

"Out with it," said Harry.

"I can't tell you exactly what it is," replied Whelks, "but some of us will not get away from here alive."

Then he groaned and rolled his eyes, looking as dismal as if an executioner were awaiting him.

By degrees they got from him all he knew, and if the boys were a little disquieted it was only natural.

"I wish my dad was here," said Young Ching; "he would make these Black Bandits look blue. What a cowardly tribe they must be, dodging about after a lot of boys."

"But who is the writer of the warning note?" asked Jem. "Do you think your father is—"

"No—no," replied Young Ching, hastily; "he can't write English, you know, and if he wrote Chinese you would not be able to read it."

"How long have we to stop here?" queried Jem.

"We start at eleven," replied Mr. Whelks; "the guide will be here by that time."

"And we go by the ravine?"

"Mr. Bone says so, but I think it rash. We ought to travel by another route."

And then Frisby Whelks groaned again. He would have liked a journey to the moon by way of a change. It might be rather solitary up there, but it would be safer than where he was.

BILLY PINK AND DICK COCKLES IN A VERY BAD WAY.

Things were very dull until ten o'clock, when dear old Mrs. Grumps showed up, and forthwith fell upon her favourite prey—the ever-offending Frisby.

This kept things lively until eleven o'clock, when Mr. Bone announced all ready for a start.

"I suppose you have told the boys," he said to Mr. Whelks. "But it doesn't matter, for I don't think there is any peril to be apprehended. Polowski is arrested, and two of his companions have fled North, so I think the band is broken up."

This was good news and cheered the spirits of all.

At the door stood a number of mules to carry the party and what little luggage they had.

For Mrs. Grumps there was a shaggy pony, as since her experience of Julius Cæsar she looked on all mules as poison.

They went away joyously, with a guide at their head—a cheery young Swiss, who sang as he moved forward.

The boys sang, too, and a merrier party never rode out of the city of watches and foul conspirators, as Geneva has been termed.

. Away round the lake to an open country lying between great hills, and so on to the ravine named after that mighty tyrant, Napoleon.

It was a narrow gorge, and at the head of it was a gendarme on horseback.

He checked the party with upraised hand.

"Messieurs of age may advance," he said, "but for the young, no. It is not for boys to look upon. The thing is too sad—too terrible."

CHAPTER XXI.

THE HAND OF A STRANGE AVENGER—A RUN ACROSS THE GREEN WITH SOME LIVELY RESULTS.

MR. BONE went forward and exchanged a few words with the gendarme, both speaking in an undertone. Turning to Frisby Whelks, the schoolmaster said—

"I think in this case you may be included among the boys, and had better not advance until directed."

"And proud he ought to be to be classed as one of 'em, if only for a few minutes," said Mrs. Grumps, with an admiring glance at her young friends.

The curiosity of the boys was aroused, and they craned their necks with the hope of getting a glimpse into the ravine.

But as it abruptly bent to the right a few yards away, there was nothing of interest to be seen.

Mr. Bone, after cautioning the boys not to be disobedient, but to remain there until he returned, went forward on foot with the gendarme.

The guide took possession of his mule meanwhile, and Handsome Harry gallantly watched over the pony on which was perched the portly person of Mrs. Grumps.

All the animals seemed to share in the curiosity and excitement of the hour.

Hitherto they had been as placable as sheep, but they now began to move about restlessly, the mule which Frisby Whelks bestrode being the most excited of them all.

"Whoa! will you," he cried, as it curvetted this way and that. "Gently there, good boy!"

Young Ching was just behind the animal, and he gave it a quiet dig with a stick he carried. Up went its haunches, and Frisby Whelks fell upon its neck.

"I don't think I ever saw such a man to throw himself about," said Mrs. Grumps. "Sit up do, you creetur."

Jem Stager was now in a favourable position to do as Young Ching had done, and as he was not the boy to lose an opportunity of making himself useful, he administered dig the second to the mule.

This time it reared, and Frisby Whelks uttered a wild cry of despair.

At the same moment the mules of Billy and Dick began to kick in the most violent manner.

Billy kept his seat like a centaur. He had had a lot of experience at home in riding, it being the practice of the boys of his district to take surreptitious rides on donkeys put out to grass upon the common.

Dick was not so well up in the saddle, and he was shot upon the neck of his brute, where he sat and held on to its ears with the pertinacity of a true-born Briton.

"That man is always breeding the Riot Act," said Mrs. Grumps, with a dim idea of a certain legal proceeding generally introduced at times of excessive civic commotion.

"Can I help it!" hissed Frisby Whelks. "Do I want to be hustled this way and that—"

Then up went the heels of his mule, and away he sped over its head, with his arms and legs spread out like the wings of a bat.

He fell just in front of Mrs. Grumps' pony,

startling it. But Harry had hold of the bridle, and soon steadied the animal.

The wrath of Mrs. Grumps was so great that she would indubitably have descended from her steed and administered umbrella chastisement upon the prostrate tutor but for the reappearance of Mr. Bone.

The gravity of his face showed that something serious had happened, and every available eye was turned upon him.

We say available eye, because those in the head of Frisby Whelks were not available for anything just then, his fall having created a sort of fiery cascade that hid all things from view.

"Boys," said Mr. Bone, "we must remain here a few minutes. A very terrible thing has happened, and I do not know whether I ought to tell you or not."

Of course they all said they would like to know, and the guide being relieved of the charge of Mr. Bone's mule, speedily brought the others to order by a few words and a liberal allowance of stick.

Frisby Whelks got up and struggled again into the saddle.

"Once at home," he muttered, "I'll never come to this blessed country again!"

By the direction of Mr. Bone the whole party drew a little aside from the mouth of the ravine.

"This morning," he said, "a terrible tragedy has been enacted in the ravine. A wretched man has been literally blown to pieces by the explosion of a bomb. Fearful as his fate was, I am inclined to think that he merited it."

He paused to struggle with an emotion that nearly overpowered him.

A hush was upon all around him.

"I hear them coming," he continued. "Boys, turn your faces the other way. You will not? Well, it is natural, I suppose, but I trust they have— Yes—it is covered."

From out of the ravine there came four gendarmes, carrying a roughly constructed bier, on which lay something that was suggestive of the human form.

It was covered with pieces of coarse sacking, and as they walked slowly along the wind lifted a corner of it, disclosing a man's hand.

A shudder passed through the boys, and the colour fled from their cheeks, for not only was it the hand of a dead man, but it was dismembered from the body.

"I told you not to look," said Mr. Bone.

"Now we will ride on. I will finish my story when we have passed through the ravine."

"Oh! tell us now, sir," exclaimed Young Ching.

"My lad," replied Mr. Bone, "I am no lover of sensational horrors, and I would rather you had never known anything of what has happened here this morning, but as you have had a glimpse of the results, I suppose I must tell you all. Yonder goes the shattered remains of Schavaloff, one of the anarchists who attempted to take the life of Handsome Harry in the castle of Namedi."

Now they were interested indeed, and it may be said of the eyes of Dick and Billy that they had seldom stood so far out of their heads.

"We have the story clear," continued Mr. Bone, "because Schavaloff's self-appointed avenger left a brief record of it beside the remains. It is written in French, and I have made a brief translation of it for you. The original paper the gendarmes retain."

Mr. Bone took out his pocket-book and read this short but solemn record of Schavaloff's end—

"*The man Schavaloff came here this morning to destroy the English party with a bomb. I, the avenger, watched him take up his position, and from a rock above hurled another bomb close beside him. What it did you will see. It is enough. So die all men who are deliberate shedders of blood. THOSE WHO LIVE BY THE SWORD SHALL PERISH BY THE SWORD.*"

"I need not point out to you what a narrow escape we have had," said Mr. Bone, as he closed the book. "One of these infernal machines bursting in our midst would have dealt out destruction to all around. You are lads of courage or I should not have told you. Be humbly thankful for your escape. Do not forget it to-night ere you go to sleep. I need say no more. We will now go on."

They were all silent as the cavalcade moved forward.

No sound was heard save the patter of the feet of the mules as they trotted into the ravine.

It was not a very extensive one, nor were the sides so high as those found in mountain rifts in other parts. But it was dull and gloomy enough in all conscience.

Mr. Bone and the guide rode on first, and presently they came to the spot where the awful tragedy of the morning had been enacted.

There was no need to point it out, nor did Mr. Bone linger for that purpose.

Neither were the boys desirous of stopping to gratify any morbid craving.

They saw enough as they passed to think about for many a day to come.

There was the ledge of rock—about twenty feet up—on which Schavaloff had lain in ambush. It was blackened and split, as if struck by a thunderbolt, and bespattered by the life blood of the would-be murderer.

But where was the mysterious avenger?

Who was it that was in the secret of the anarchists' plans, and had made himself the protector of the boys?

It was no one connected with them.

Young Ching knew that if his father were near he would have looked after his safety, but he would not have adopted such means to destroy the murderer.

They did not speak more than a word or two until they were in the open country again, with a flood of sunshine making all things around them bright and beautiful.

Then their tongues were loosened, and after the first thankful expressions they tried to elucidate the mystery of the unknown avenger.

But they could make nothing out of it.

"There is a nice stretch of grass ahead," said Mr. Bone, "so you boys can gallop forward if you like, only do not go too far away."

"Why not have a race?" observed Jem. "Perhaps Mr. Whelks will join us?"

"No thank you," replied Frisby Whelks, "I'd rather not."

"I will go forward," said Mr. Bone, "and make myself a winning-post, so get into a row, and when I hold up my hand start. The guide will take care of Mrs. Grumps."

"Never mind me," observed Mrs. Grumps; "my dear four-legged creature is good enough, and Mister Guide looks as if he wanted to race with the others."

That was a fact, so Mr. Bone laughingly assented. Then he rode across the open piece of grass, and pulled up about two furlongs ahead.

Of course his object was to distract the minds of the boys from the serious events of the morning, and success crowned his efforts.

All got into a pretty straight line, with the grinning guide on their right, and immediately Mr. Bone raised his hand off started the mules

Frisby Whelks sat astride his mule beside Mrs. Grumps, whose pony was as quiet as a lamb.

"Why don't you go with 'em?" scornfully asked Mrs. Grumps.

"I—I'd rather not."

"I'd rather you would," she answered, and without any more argument she smote his mule with her umbrella.

It bounded forward and tore away in pursuit of the rest, the hapless Whelks bouncing up and down and swaying to and fro in a most alarming manner.

Meanwhile the boys raced on, and weight soon began to tell.

Harry was a good rider, having been used to the saddle since the day he could sit upright in one, and he handled his steed in a masterly manner.

Young Ching and Jem Stager, both rather light in their seats, rode recklessly, shouting and urging on their mules with their sticks and heels.

Dick Cockles and Billy Pink, the lightest of all, sat quietly, holding on like grim death, and keeping well to the front, owing to the advantage they had in weight.

All together, bar the guide, they raced across the grass, Dick and Billy forging slowly in front, until they were within twenty yards of home.

Then they must needs cannon and bowl each other over.

Jem Stager's mule, immediately behind, stopped short, and caused its rider to describe a parabola.

Young Ching and Harry were thus alone left in the race, which now became a contest between skill and dash.

It was not until they were within a yard of Mr. Bone that the race was won.

Then Young Ching, at the risk of being pitched on his head, threw himself forward, as he had once seen a famous jockey do at the end of a race, snatching the victory from Harry's grasp.

"Well done," cried Harry, laughing.

Behind, last but not least, comes Frisby Whelks.

His mule, with tail in air, flies over the ground, and not only comes up to the winning post in good style, with its wild-eyed rider praying for safety, but dashes against Mr. Bone and bowls him over, gallant steed and all.

Frisby Whelks sees all created things turn

upside down, and presently something hits him in the back.

Then once more night is on him and he is among the stars.

But notwithstanding these calamities nobody is seriously hurt.

They all get up in turn, and bewail or laugh over their tumbles, according to their dispositions.

And after a little shaking up and brushing down they go gaily on their way.

CHAPTER XXII.

ON THE MOUNTAIN—FRISBY WHELKS AND THE GOAT.

ANOTHER change of scene. After a long and rather trying journey the party reached Zermatt, where Mr. Bone proposed to rest for a week.

There was need of it, for Mrs. Grumps had collapsed again, and Frisby Whelks had given signs of utter prostration.

In addition to the need of rest, the valley is an historical place, and one of the most majestically picturesque spots in the world.

There the Matterhorn raises its imposing head, and thousands of crags, precipices, crevices, and mighty glaciers lie around.

It is a giant fairy land—awe inspiring and overpowering in its wild beauty.

"It will do the boys good to remain here for a week," said Mr. Bone.

An hotel was hardly the place for them, so he got lodgings at what was called "a farm house," but the farming is of a peculiar kind.

There is any quantity of ice and snow, but little earth.

Every available spot is cultivated like a garden, and peasants may be seen during the day digging and planting out curious shelf-like projections along the side of the hills.

There is food enough for goats but not for cows. So goats are plentiful, as Frisby Whelks soon found out.

It is a curious fact in natural history that certain animals object to a certain class of men.

The goats objected to Whelks, and were very much down on him.

Every Billy goat considered it its bounden duty to butt him, and the Nanny goats derisively bleated at him as he went by.

The hostess of the house where they were staying also objected to Whelks, but only

expressed it in snorts and the most broken of broken English.

"You—no—good," she said; "no goat like you—so—ah! yah!"

Of course the boys wanted to risk their necks by going with a party scaling the mountains, and equally of course Mr. Bone objected to it.

"I must not forget that I am responsible for your safety," he said.

Although he forbade them to go, he was bent on going himself, and he privately joined a party that was about to endeavour to make an ascent of the Matterhorn.

The only intimation he gave of it was to Frisby Whelks one evening—it was the third after their arrival—that he should be away on the morrow.

"I start at sunrise on a little excursion with some friends," he said, "and I shall be away all day. You must keep an eye on the boys until I return."

"I will do my best," replied Whelks, feebly, "but you know what they are."

"They are pretty well sure to keep together," said Mr. Bone; "where they go you must go also."

"I will do what I can," drearily answered Whelks.

At breakfast the next morning the boys missed their friend, and found Whelks presiding at the table.

They had a sitting-room that looked on the valley, where a number of people were walking about—more than usual.

Outside the hotel several telescopes were being used by eager sight-seers.

Harry, who had read books about Switzerland, said they were looking at a party scaling one of the mountains.

"And I expect Mr. Bone is gone with them," he added, with a keen look at his tutor.

"Mr. Bone will not be back till night," replied Whelks.

The boys exchanged glances of intelligence. A whole day to themselves, or practically so. It was a delightful thing.

Frisby Whelks saw the glances and interpreted them.

"You are not to go far away," he said, "and I am not to lose sight of you."

"We can't be shut up all day," replied Harry.

"Wouldn't Mrs. Grumps like you to keep her company?" suggested Young Ching, in a manner that would have done credit to his insinuating father.

Frisby Whelks looked indignantly at him, but not making a very great impression, he contented himself with saying—

"I shall accompany you wherever you go."

Mrs. Grumps was "keeping her bed," but she had her resting-place close to an upper window, where she could hear what was going on outside.

After breakfast the boys sauntered out and Whelks followed them.

They went to a shed a little higher up the hill, where a lot of goats usually came to be milked.

Their hostess, a buxom Swiss woman of forty, was busy "robbing little kids of their nutriment," as Jem Stager termed it.

In other words she was milking the Nanny goats.

The boys stood watching the woman, who smiled at them and said—

"Morning—good—so—hope—well you are."

"We are in a state of overpowering salubriousness," Jem Stager replied.

"Why don't you answer the woman in a respectable manner?" asked Dick Cockles.

"You mind your own business, my gentle offspring of a mystery-maker," returned Jem. "By-the-way, what a novelty and advertisement it would make for your dad. Goat sausages straight from Switzerland every day! Brought on the backs of camels through the desert of Saraha, so as to have them fresh!"

All laughed except Dick and Frisby Whelks.

The latter was holding a bit aloof, with his eye on a Billy goat whose demeanour was very threatening.

The beast was cavorting around with skips and jumps, now and then stopping to butt an imaginary foe.

"I know what would be a novelty to you," said Dick to Jem.

"What's that?" inquired the imperturbable youth.

"Letting people alone," replied Dick. "I wish somebody would make *you* into sausages."

"You need not air your cannibal yearnings here," returned Jem, "and I thought you drew the line at cats, but—ah! would you?"

Dick had suddenly assumed a threatening demeanour, and probably led away by a bad example, he butted Jem and fairly bowled him over.

Billy Pink roared with delight, and Young Ching and Harry laughed their loudest.

Jem had a fine sense of the ludicrous, and it was not in his heart to be angry with Dick.

"'Twere well done and done quickly," he said, as he got upon his feet. "Thou art a promising kid, my knight of the polony."

"I did you that time," chuckled Dick.

"That you did," chorussed Billy.

"Come into the shed and see your brethren, Billy," said Jem.

Their hostess was going in, and all the boys followed her, Frisby Whelks remaining outside.

There were several Billies and a score of Nanny goats, with their young, in little stalls inside, and the boys watched the Swiss woman as she put muzzles on some of the larger kids, to regulate their allowance of milk, and so get some for herself.

She had about half-completed this task when a cry for help was heard outside.

"Whelks," said Young Ching, calmly.

"Same old goat trick," observed Jem Stager.

The Swiss woman hurried out, and the boys sauntered to the door.

There they saw the wretched Whelks in the grasp of the woman, and an old Billy goat charging at him furiously.

Close by was a pail of milk upset, and a few yards further away a kid was skipping joyously, as if in derision of the tutor.

"You—do—him—kick," said the Swiss woman, shaking Frisby Whelks to and fro. "You make a sound of him like drom—ah! so —vat for—who you to do it?"

"I've done nothing, absolutely nothing," cried Whelks, "but this brute—oh! his horns have penetrated my flesh. I shall not be able to sit. Madam, I implore you to be more considerate. Now he's done it."

The sound of rending cloth was heard, and Frisby Whelks clapped a hand behind him. The Billy goat, satisfied with his felonious work, skipped away to the kid, and the pair disappeared in a series of bounds down the mountain side.

"Who the milk pay?" asked the Swiss woman.

"I kicked at the goat and didn't see the pail," replied Frisby Whelks.

"You no eye—you no noting," was the answer, as she gave him a final shake and let him go.

Released, Frisby Whelks retreated backward to a rock and sat down.

The boys watched his movements and saw that a very serious calamity had happened to him. Nevertheless they grinned, and barely succeeded in stifling their laughter.

"Have you boys any pins about you?" asked the tutor.

"What's the matter, sir?" asked Jem.

"Not much," was the reply. "One of my garments is torn."

The boys had no pins about them, save one about a third of an inch in length, which Billy Pink had in his jacket.

"I am going indoors for a few minutes," Whelks said; "wait here until I return."

They did not answer him, as it was not their intention to wait.

As soon as he was in the house Young Ching said—

"Where away, boys? I vote we go down and have a look through those telescopes."

"Lovely!" ejaculated Jem Stager, and away they went pell-mell.

Frisby Whelks heard them from the house, and appeared in the doorway with a needle and cotton in his hand.

"Do you hear me?" he asked.

They did hear him, but just then suffered from a very convenient deafness.

Away down the rugged road they ran and presently came to the chief hotel.

About a score of people, mostly English and Americans, were lounging about, but nobody was at the telescopes.

The fact was the scaling party were for the present out of sight, and would not re-appear until a certain point was reached.

Hence the apparent indifference of the people.

There were two men in charge of the telescopes, and they had three each to look after. One of them was a smiling old man, whose face was perpetually on the grin.

"Young gentlemens," he said, "haf peep?"

Of course they would.

Harry offered to stand treat, and each fixed his eye at a glass. Dick Cockles and Billy Pink were, as usual, not far away from each other.

"I don't see anybody," observed Billy.

"I can see Bone," replied Dick, who was not deficient in imagination.

"You can't do anything of the sort," replied Jem. "There's nobody in sight—is there, mounseer?"

"Mounseer" was the grinning old man, and with a slight extension of smile he replied—

"Not so, sar, but dey soon come. It is for patience."

"I don't care what he says," said Dick. "I can see two people."

"Two grandmothers," replied Jem, leaving his telescope. "We can see nothing but ice and snow, but perhaps you have got hold of a double-developing forty-horse-power telescope. Let me have a look through it."

"Keep to your own," said Dick.

"That's unreasonable," replied Jem, as he gently put his arm around Dick. "Are you coming away, or must I assist you?"

"Give him a punch, Billy," said Dick.

Billy, ever faithful and true, like dear old Sammy, promptly took his eye away from his telescope and advanced towards Jem with a threatening air.

"Why don't you fellows keep quiet?" asked Harry.

"I want to look through Dick's telescope," replied Jem, "and I'm going to do it."

"No you won't," returned Dick. "Give him one, Billy."

"If ze gentlemans haf quarrels," said the smiling old man, "ve may haf breaks of ze telescopes."

"Get away, Billy," cried Jem. "I'll give you something if you come near me."

As he spoke he dodged a blow aimed at him by Billy, and jerked Dick round.

Dick, who had doggedly kept his eye on the telescope, felt himself going and grasped the stand.

The smiling old man uttered a loud cry and dashed forward.

But he was too late to save the telescope.

With a metallic crash, mingled with shouts, Jem and Dick and the telescope went over together.

"You've done it now, you duffers," said Young Ching, as he put his hands into his pockets and looked calmly down upon the fallen ones.

"Ah—ah!" groaned the old smiler, "it is too mooch—too mooch. And it is ze best of ze glasses."

"I won't pay anything," cried Dick Cockles, struggling to his feet, "and I can't if I would. All my pocket-money is gone."

"Billy Pink did it," said Jem Stager, sitting up. "My eye! what a smash."

A smash it was.

Each leg of the stand had parted from the other, and the telescope was knocked clean out of time.

Sundry bits of glass, most fatal sign of all, were strewn about. The wreck was pretty well complete.

The visitors hanging about did not say anything, but sounds of half-suppressed laughter were heard.

"All this comes of Whelks not looking after you," said Young Ching. "Here he comes, with his Sunday breeks on, so let us hear what he has to say for himself. All right, monsieur," to the old smiler, who was groaning bitterly, "you will be paid."

"You will get its value," added Jem Stager, "even if you have to take it out in sausages. The honour of the house of Cockles has passed into a proverb."

"Oh! you be blowed!" yelled Dick.

CHAPTER XXIII.

YOUNG CHING AND THE MERRY SWISS BOY—
ARRIVAL OF THE DILIGENCE AND AN ADDITION
TO THE PARTY.

"I DON'T know how it is, Cockles," said Mr. Bone, "but you always seem to be in some sort of trouble."

It was evening, and the worthy schoolmaster had come back safe, but stiff and sore with climbing the mountain.

Incidentally as he came along home he heard of the smashed telescope, and that Harry had offered to pay for it.

Dick Cockles made no reply. He was not a boy to peach or to make a martyr of himself, even when he had a right to do so.

The boys were all there, so was Frisby Whelks, likewise Mrs. Grumps.

"It was as much my fault as anybody's," said Jem Stager. "I wanted to look through Dick's telescope and he objected."

"Why?" asked Mr. Bone.

Dick grinned.

"I said I could see you, sir, but I was only joking," he replied, "for all the time you were out of sight."

"Pink had something to do with the catastrophe," observed Frisby Whelks. "I saw them all on the ground together."

"Did you," interposed Mrs. Grumps, with a sneer. "You've got hyes for hevil, young man, but can never see any good with 'em."

"Well!" said Mr. Bone, "the telescope must be paid for. And you boys must be careful. The expenses of this trip are double what I expected, and I shall have a bad time with your parents on my return. Now let us have some tea."

The telescope threatened to be a very expensive affair. First of all the owner of it wanted fifty pounds, then he came down to forty, afterwards he demanded thirty, then twenty, but finally took three pounds ten, and seemed to be tolerably well satisfied.

During the rest of their stay at Zermatt the old telescope man never saw the boys without grinning in such a way that Jem Stager told him at last not to make an ass of himself.

There was another man, it will be remembered, who had telescopes there, and he seemed to be anxious to also have an accidental benefit.

As the boys went by he would call out—

"Haf look—good peep—no charge. All free if you no smash."

But the boys were not to be tempted, having received strict orders not to have anything more to do with the telescopes.

Being also prohibited from going up the mountains, time soon began to hang rather heavily with them, and Young Ching in particular was anxious for something to do.

He had a fight with a Swiss lad, half-a-head taller than himself, who took it into his head to chaff the party in the most excruciating English.

"You Englese," he said, "all go bout—haf keeper—all Englese boy—crack head—fight you—licks."

They took no notice of him for a time, but as he had a knack of cropping up at all times and in all places, especially when least expected, it presently began to be a bit of a nuisance.

"Somebody had better fight him," said Young Ching, "and if you don't mind it I'll be the man."

They all said it was about as good a thing as could be done, and they were not kept waiting long.

Within an hour, as they were exploring a sort of gulch with the faint idea of discovering gold, the Swiss boy suddenly appeared.

"All Englese boy—" he began, and then stopped short.

The entrance to the gulch was only a few feet wide, and Harry and Jem Stager having slipped past him, his retreat was cut off.

He turned a ghastly leaden colour.

"No—kill—me," he said, with trembling lip.

"I'm going to give you something for your cheek," replied Young Ching. "Can you fight?"

He gave an illustration of his meaning by raising his clenched hands and sparring for a moment.

"No fight—all," said the Swiss boy.

"No—me—me," replied Young Ching, "nobody else will touch you."

"Sure—is it so—fair?"

"Yes—come on."

The Swiss was sensibly relieved, and thought he had an easy job with Young Ching, being much the bigger boy.

Fighting in a fair way was not in his line, and the moment Young Ching signified that he was ready the merry Swiss boy ran at him —clawing, biting, and kicking.

"Don't let him get hold of you, Ching!" cried Harry.

"Not if I can help it," was the answer.

It is unnecessary to record the details of the fight in full, although it was short enough.

In five minutes all was over, and the merry Swiss boy was led by Jem Stager into the open valley.

His two eyes had been reduced to the merest peep-holes, and it was more than likely that they would entirely close up ere he got home.

"All you've got to do," said Jem, "is to follow your nose, and when you fall down get up again."

"Oh! I no see—no see," moaned the crushed Swiss joker.

"Nosey," observed Jem; "nothing of the sort—eyes see—icey—chilly business—now mind how you walk."

"What's the fellow made of?" said Young Ching, contemptuously. "I hardly hit him before he began to blow like a whale."

"He has a lot of blubber about him," observed Dick Cockles.

"Here—come—you stop that," interposed Jem; "it isn't in your line. Puns and envelopes of mystery will never mix."

The diligence was due, and all the boys went to see the old-fashioned vehicle come rumbling in, swaying to and fro, to the manifest terror of sundry passengers on the roof.

The driver wore a hat bedecked with ribbons, but he handled the reins like a man, and brought his half-dozen horses expertly to a standstill outside the hotel.

Only one Englishman had come by it, and he was a masher of mashers. But he was very young, which was a good thing, for that gave him, in the ordinary course of nature, plenty of time for improvement.

He had a back seat, and instead of getting down by the wheel like a man, waited for the women's ladder to be brought.

"Well! did you ever?" exclaimed Young Ching.

"I know that fellow," said Harry. "We went to school together, and he was the champion all-round victim. How are you, Filberts?"

The masher was half-way down the ladder, and the appearance of his old friend acted on him like a galvanic shock.

He started, turned round, and fell.

Harry caught him neatly, and put him on his feet as if he had been a little boy.

"Steady, Filberts," he said; "or one of these days you will meet with an accident."

Filberts fumbled about his waistcoat, got hold of his eyeglass, and fairly screwed it into his right optic.

"By Jove!" he exclaimed, "it's Harry Marsh! How are you?—oh! don't."

Harry had grasped his hand and given it a squeeze that made him blink. Oscar Filberts was not made of very muscular matter.

"Allow me to introduce you to my friends," said Harry.

"Delighted—sure," replied Filberts.

The necessary formula was gone through, and the masher shook hands with them all.

"Awfully delighted," he said, "for I thought I should be here alone."

"We go away to-morrow," said Harry.

"Nevar!" exclaimed Filberts, in dismay.

"Fact, and unless you have something particular to do here, you had better go with us."

"I'll go, by Jove!" was the answer; "anywhere but back to Paris. I've run away from my ma."

The boys burst into laughter. They could not help it, but of course they tried to stop themselves.

Oscar Filbert took it very good-naturedly.

"You fellaws may laugh," he said, "but I had to be deuced clevar to get away from ma. Now, about my traps. I haven't much, for when a man runs away from his—"

"The less luggage the better," observed Harry. "Don't have it put into the hotel. We will help you with it up to our crib."

"My dear Harry," replied Filberts, "you were always a good fellaw. I'm regular done over with joy at meeting you, by Jove!"

Young Ching did not appear to view the addition to their party in the light of an acquisition, nor did Jem Stager, and their faces lengthened a bit.

Harry noticed it, and winked at them as Billy and Dick, always volunteers when there was hard work to do, laid hold of Filberts' leather bag and started off with it.

"It's awfully kind of you, deah boys," he / said. "I would do it myself, but I've no muscle."

"Filberts is a very good fellow," said Harry, as he dropped behind with Jem and Young Ching. "What he is the foolish training of his mother has made him. She used to come every day to the school to see him, and even now he has had to run away from her."

"What is his age?" asked Jem.

"Twenty—much older than we are," replied Harry, "but quite a boy. You will learn to like him."

Filberts admired the strength of Billy and Dick, and dilated on it all the way to the farmhouse, where they put down the bag without showing signs of having turned a hair.

"Amazing strength," he said. "I daresay you could almost lift it alone."

Billy Pink, who was a sturdy youngster, whipped up the bag and held it over his head. Filberts beamed with admiration.

"I would give a hundred pounds to be able to do that, by Jove!" he said.

Harry went into the house, where, as he expected, he found Mr. Bone. He had been resting since his ascent of the mountain, and was reclining in an easy-chair when Harry entered the room.

A conversation ensued, and the gist of it was that Harry wanted his old school chum to be entered as one of the party, to which Mr. Bone demurred.

"I really find that I have enough to manage as it is," he said.

"I'll manage poor Filberts," replied Harry; "he is very tractable. Unless he is looked after some knave will get hold of him and fleece him. His mother is immensely wealthy, and she gives him anything he asks for. I daresay he has a lot of money about him now."

Finally Oscar Filberts was sent for, and he pleaded so earnestly to become one of the party that Mr. Bone assented.

"Have you any money about you?" asked the schoolmaster.

"A little," replied Filberts.

"Let me have it to take care of," said Mr. Bone.

The "little" proved to be over two hundred pounds in notes, and a good handful of gold.

"Goodness me!" said Mr. Bone; "what were you going to do with this?"

"Spend some and give the rest away," replied Filberts.

"I see that you will be better with us," said Mr. Bone. "Give me your mother's address, and I will write to her to ease her mind, by assuring her that you are safe."

"Say that Harry Marsh is with me," replied Filberts. "She'll know it's all right then."

Mr. Bone wrote a letter to Mrs. Filberts, telling her where they were going, and asking her to write or wire to the post-office at Andulia, in Spain.

He promised to keep her posted up with the movements of her promising son.

Great was the delight of Filberts when he heard that he was to join the party, and in his joy he would have given away bank-notes all round if Mr. Bone had not previously taken possession of them.

Failing this, he asked Billy Pink and Dick Cockles to accept a diamond ring and his watch and chain, as a slight acknowledgment of the services they had recently performed for him.

Of course they declined to take either.

"Any boy at home would have carried it for threepence," said Billy.

"Would they now?" exclaimed Filberts, admiringly. "I never should have thought it. But some people are strong. I wish I was."

Poor Filberts. He was a weed of a young fellow, but there was no vice in him.

He was a masher in dress, but in nothing else. His heart was as simple and guileless as that of a child.

Frisby Whelks was out for a walk while these things were being settled, and when he came back he was a bit troubled on learning that an addition had been made to the party.

But two minutes' talk relieved him.

"He won't be much trouble," the tutor said, "for he's as soft as wax, and I think I can make him obey me whatever the others may do."

CHAPTER XXIV.

IN SPAIN—THE TOWN OF ANDULIA—BILLY AND DICK IN TROUBLE AGAIN.

ANDULIA is to be found in the northern part of Spain, but it requires looking for, as it is not put down on every map.

Spain is a neglected country in this respect, and taking the civilised world through, few places are so little known.

A picturesque spot is Andulia. Nature has tried all she could to make it beautiful, and man has done little to mar it.

The town is small, solidly built, and in an

architectural sense harmonises with the country around.

It was evening when the jingling bells of a small train of mules announced the arrival of strangers, and the sound brought the scanty population to the doors of their houses in the main street, through which the cavalcade was travelling.

It was our old friends, safe and sound, bar Mrs. Grumps, who was still a sufferer in her feet, and not capable of enjoying the trip as she wished.

A guide escorted them. He was a leary-looking young Spaniard, who ogled the girls as he passed, occasionally kissing his hand to a Spanish maiden.

He said his name was Cararra.

Mr. Bone had picked him up twenty miles away from the town.

His English was very good for a Spaniard, and he had shown quite a friendly anxiety for the safety of the party.

In confidence he assured Mr. Bone that there were brigands about, but he need not fear them, as they only went in for rich prizes —such as noblemen.

"They rob seldom," he said, "but they like a good thing when they can get it."

Somehow he had got into his head that Mrs. Grumps was very rich, and that Billy Pink was her son, and nobody took the trouble to put him right, because it did not seem to be a matter of any consequence.

As things turned out it proved to be a very serious mistake indeed.

Cararra led the way to the best cabaret in the town, judging by its exterior, and they rode into a yard at the back, where there was stabling for a score mules, but only one attendant, a sour-visaged old Spaniard, who keenly inspected the visitors one by one.

Cararra whispered a few words to him, and his eyes brightened as he turned them upon Mrs. Grumps.

The luggage was taken off the back of a pack mule and conveyed into the inn. Then Cararra ushered the guests into a room on the ground floor.

There a suave landlord awaited them, and dinner was ordered by Mr. Bone. That done he proceeded to settle with Cararra.

The guide did not attempt any extortion, at which Mr. Bone marvelled, his experience of these gentry being that they generally asked for three times as much as they were entitled to, and fought their way back to a legitimate price with the resolution of soldiers of the old guard.

Cararra, as we have said, did nothing of the sort. He took a fair remuneration for his services and went away singing.

The travellers, old and young, were pretty well tired out, and after dinner somnolent signs set in, especially in Dick and Billy, who kept dozing and falling off their chairs until Mr. Bone trotted them off to bed.

Oscar Filberts was in the same condition, and a general move was soon made to their respective places of rest.

The rooms were very old, and furnished simply and quaintly. But the boys had no longing to observe their surroundings. They tumbled into bed and slept immediately.

They were all up in the morning at a comparatively early hour, long before the servants had opened their eyes.

Filberts would have lain in bed, but Young Ching threatened him with a cold sponge, and he tumbled out, knowing that his friend would keep his word.

Oscar was no doubt a tremendous fool in some things, and in a muscular sense a child, but his heart was sound, and the boys all liked him, as Harry said they would.

He was very free with his money, but that was not taken into account, and they had to check him in his lavish expenditure, usually made for the benefit of others.

Strange to say he thought more of Billy Pink and Dick Cockles than of Young Ching and Jem Stager.

He got it into his head that they were lads endowed with prodigious strength—phenomenal muscular heroes, and he would often feel their arms, uttering ejaculations of admiration, and finishing off with a sigh of envy.

All this Dick and Billy naturally took with complacency, and rewarded him by treating him as a boy and a brother.

Billy told him in confidence to remember that in case of a row he (Billy) would stand by him, and Dick assured him he would see he was not imposed upon by bigger boys than himself.

As Filberts was quite a head taller than Dick, this promise may be looked upon as a bold one.

The boys amused themselves by looking over the stables and the many curious outbuildings attached to the inn.

After that they strolled into the town.

It was a small place, about the size of an ordinary country market town in England.

THE SLAPCRASH BOYS.

The Liveliest of School Stories.

FRISBY WHELKS GONE A LITTLE BIT WRONG AGAIN.

No. 12.

Price One Penny.

There was one main street, with courts and alleys on either side of it.

A good many people were about, for Spaniards work only in the morning and evening when they work at all. The mid-day is given up to lounging and the siesta.

They are an indolent race, prone to love-making and smoking.

The twang of the guitar is heard at all hours of the day and the greater part of the night.

Early as it was, a man was playing in the main street, and round him had gathered a laughing group of women and girls.

The arrival of the boys drew the eyes of the Spanish girls upon them, Harry coming in for more than his share of glances.

Young Ching's cool air also seemed to have a fascination for them, and they whispered to each other behind their hands—

"Is it not some great man's son?"

One of the girls spoke to Harry in Spanish.

"You are English," she said.

"Yes," he replied, in the same language.

"You come to live here?"

"No, we shall be going in a few days."

"Oh! why not stay—learn the guitar and sing to us? It would be so nice."

Harry laughed and turned away. The girl glided up to him and took his arm.

"You will stay?" she said.

"I think not," replied Harry, gently endeavouring to release himself. "You must not do this sort of thing, for your own sake. What will your friends think of you?"

"Oh! it is nothing," she said. "See, your friend is taken prisoner."

It was Young Ching she referred to.

A dark-eyed girl had followed the example of the other and taken his arm. He looked at her in serene surprise.

"Do you understand English?" he asked.

A shake of the head was the reply.

"That's all right," said Young Ching, "especially as I have only about a thimbleful of Spanish to deal out to you. Jem, secure a girl. Filberts, Dick, Billy, take to yourselves a Spanish beauty. We will have a procession through the town."

"That won't do," said Harry.

"Yes it will," coolly answered Young Ching; "anything for fun. Hook on, you dark-eyed senoritas."

The girl understood what he meant, especially as he supplemented his words with a little expressive action, and there was a laughing rush made upon the boys.

Jem Stager was disgusted.

"I call this foolery," he said. "All right, fair maid, you needn't grab me so tightly. Hang it, we shall have all the town after us."

Filberts had got two girls, one on each side, and well pleased he seemed to be with their company.

Dick and Billy were blushing up to peony standard.

The procession was formed and they were about to start when an unexpected obstacle appeared in the form of half a score Spanish lads, about sixteen or seventeen years of age.

They planted themselves in front of our friends, uttering wild cries, the offspring of jealousy. Two or three drew knives and flourished them in the air.

"This looks well," said Jem Stager. "By my faith, we shall have to break a lance for these young maidens."

"Get out of the way, you fellows," said Harry. "Ching, there's going to be a row."

"All right," replied Young Ching.

And a row there was. The young Spaniards made a sudden rush upon our friends, and immediately the whole street was in an uproar.

Women and girls screamed, and the hoarse voices of men were heard.

Dick and Billy, true to their promises to Filberts, made an effort to protect him, but both were suddenly seized from behind and dragged into a side street.

Then, to their terror, a sack was thrown over their heads, and they were carried off by men, who held them unmercifully tight in their strong arms.

Presently they felt that they were ascending a hill, for their bearers walked very slowly, and panted as they struggled on.

Billy Pink thought of home and friends, and if his young heart failed him a little it was only what might be looked for.

He knew the secret of his strange seizure. He had been captured by brigands!

As for Dick, if not in an actual state of collapse, he was so limp that he could offer no resistance.

He also had a shrewd idea of what had happened to him.

Suddenly the boys were put upon their feet, and the bags or sacks drawn off their heads.

Dick sank into a sitting position on a stone, and Billy dropped upon his knees.

Before them was a group of armed men—brigands, without a doubt.

"Ha! my young friends," exclaimed the foremost, "you have forgotten me."

The voice was familiar.

His apparel was different, and of a richer material than before, but it was Cararra, the guide.

Just for a moment the light of hope flashed upon the boys as they recognised him, but it speedily died away.

"I have you," he said. "You are my prisoners, and ten thousand pounds each must be paid or I will kill you. Rise and come with me to my castle. There you shall write a letter to your friends, telling them to get the money at once. If not I will cut off your fingers and toes and afterwards destroy you."

CHAPTER XXV.

THE MISSING BOYS—SEARCH FOR THEM—FRISBY WHELKS IN ANOTHER SORT OF QUAGMIRE.

THE row in the street was brought to a somewhat abrupt termination by the appearance of two gendarmes armed with stout canes.

Without any preliminary nonsense, or even a mild "Move on!" such as we have at home, they proceeded to deal out to the youthful natives a series of blows, trusting entirely to chance as to where their hard knocks fell.

The English lads they did not touch, and the girls also escaped unharmed, thanks to their skill in dodging the officers of the law.

Of course the intended procession came to an end, and with the exception of Oscar Filberts, they escaped without injury.

Several retreating Spaniards had swept over Filberts, and left him on the ground in a breathless condition.

Jem Stager helped him up.

"By the crescent and the sword," said Jem, "but thou foughtest right gallantly."

"Did I hit anyone?" asked Filberts, with sudden alacrity.

"Did you hit anyone?" exclaimed Jem. "Did you? Here, where's that Spanish cub with the two fearful black eyes? Ah! he's gone. His friends must have led him away. He won't see much for a week. Did you hit anyone? All I can hope is, Filberts, that you will never, even in sport, hit me."

Filberts had a vague idea that he might have hit somebody by accident, for he distinctly remembered his arms and legs flying wildly about ere he fell.

"Where's Billy and Dick?" asked Young Ching, looking up and down the street.

Nobody had seen them go, and Harry suggested that through being scared they might have run back to the inn.

To the inn they accordingly went, but learned that the boys had not returned. Jem Stager was very wrath.

"They've got into another mess," he said, "and we shall have a day's fun spoilt by looking for them."

At this moment Frisby Whelks appeared at the door of the inn and bade them good morning.

"Not all up I see," he said, glancing at their diminished numbers.

They told him that there had been a bit of a row in the street, and Billy and Dick had been spirited away somehow.

"Perhaps they ran into the country," Young Ching observed.

Mr. Bone was not up, and they were all exceedingly anxious to find the missing boys before he appeared.

If they did not do so there would be very little liberty that day for any of them.

"Go to our room, Filberts," said Harry. "We shall get along better without you."

"Are there brigands here?" asked Filberts.

"I was only joking," replied Jem.

"Many a true word is spoken in jest," said Harry. "We have no time to spare, so come along."

Off they went, taking Frisby Whelks with them, and as it was hardly worth while looking about the streets for the boys, they bore away into the country, through a lane that led to the back of the town.

Beyond were the hills up which the missing boys had been carried by Cararra and his men.

Towards them the boys went, bent on getting to some point of vantage from which they could scan the country round.

Young Ching walked by the side of Harry —a little ahead of the rest. After a quick glance back he asked, in a low tone, if he really thought there was any fear of brigands.

"I think it very likely," said Harry. "My father has often said that most Spaniards are brigands at heart, while my dear mother agrees with him, and you know what she is."

"Yes, Spanish born, so she ought to know. But suppose they have taken— Look out! here's a green pond—look at the duck-weed. Doesn't it remind you of dear old home?"

The pond cropped up in their path so suddenly that they scarcely noticed it until they were almost into it.

With a quick movement they turned aside, and Jem Stager followed, but Frisby Whelks walked straight into it.

"Help — murder — I'm drowning!" he shrieked.

There were only a few inches of water, so drowning was out of the question, but there was lots of mud, and he stood a very fair chance of being smothered.

In his bewilderment and terror he tried to get out the wrong way, and went further in.

"Come back—where are you going, Whelks?" cried Harry. "You'll be lost—it's a regular quicksand."

"Quick mud," muttered Jem Stager.

Frisby Whelks worked his way along by pulling his feet out of the mud, but he was sinking deeper and deeper every moment.

Already he was up to his knees.

"Help—help!" he screamed.

"Keep quiet," cried Harry, "or you will be a gone coon."

Going in to his aid was not to be thought of, for it would only have placed the boys in the same fix, without in the least helping Whelks.

Young Ching glanced about him and saw a pole lying a short distance away.

"That's the thing," he said, and darted off to get it.

Without that pole Frisby Whelks would indubitably have ended his career there and then, for he was sinking slowly but surely into the dreadful mass of mud and water.

The origin of it appeared to be a spring, which kept the light soil around in a state not unlike batter-pudding.

The pole saved Whelks.

He was given one end of it, and the boys tugged manfully at the other end until he was landed, muddy and breathless, on solid ground.

But he had left his boots behind him, and was in a pitiable plight.

Any further efforts on his part to find the lost boys were not to be thought of.

"I suppose we had better all go back," said Harry. "I don't see any signs of them around. Stay here a moment, though. I'll get up that tree yonder and have a look about."

The tree in question was a species of poplar, tall and sparely branched. He swarmed up it with the greatest ease, and went so high that his weight sensibly bent the top of it.

"How terribly rash he is," cried Frisby Whelks. "He'll fall—oh!"

But Harry was not going to fall—he was only leaning forward to get a clearer view of something or somebody far away over the hills.

As a matter of fact he had a glimpse of the brigands climbing up the hillside with their two captives, but they were too far off for him to clearly define who or what they were.

He came down the tree hand-over hand, and told the others that he had seen a number of men carrying what appeared to be two bundles up a path, but he did not think they had cause to be interested in their movements.

So far their quest was ended, and they went back to the inn with the faint hope of finding the two unfortunate friends safe under its roof.

But they only found Mr. Bone, who had just interviewed Filberts, and had got the truth out of him as easily as a cork is drawn from a bottle.

"I really am not sorry," he said, "that our Continental wanderings are drawing to a close, for I have been subject to an unbroken series of anxieties on account of one or the other of you ever since we started. Remain here while I go into the town and make a few inquiries."

When he was gone breakfast was laid by a dark-eyed Spanish maiden, who seemed disposed to enter into friendly conversation with the boys, but as she did not know a word of English she was not entirely successful.

Frisby Whelks, too, was averse to frivolous social intercourse with foreign maidens, and kept a stern eye upon them, which Young Ching compared to a blunt gimlet.

Mr. Bone came back looking very quiet and rather pale. He sat down and said—

"It will be useless to wait for them. We had better have our breakfast, and if they are not back by the time we have finished we must go and look for them."

Luckily Mrs. Grumps had not risen. It was her rule now to have breakfast in bed, travelling having put twenty years on her, she very often observed.

It was not quite so bad as that, but there was no doubt that travelling had been a little too much for the dear old lady.

Breakfast was a silent meal, and mine host saved considerably by the general lack of appetite.

Of course neither Dick nor Billy returned, and whither they had gone was an unsolvable mystery.

Mr. Bone sent for the host, a plausible Spaniard with a strong odour of garlic hovering about him, and they had a long talk together.

But nothing came of it.

Mine host knew nothing of the boys and could suggest very little.

"Boys were troublesome," he said. "They come and go at will. I have some, and they are a pain to me. They are rebellious, but I say—'Go and do as you please. Be hanged! I care not.'"

"But these boys are not mine," replied Mr. Bone, "and I cannot dispense with them in that way. Now to the point. Tell me what you think has become of them."

Mine host shrugged his shoulders.

"I should not like to say," he said.

They were both, by-the-way, speaking in the Spanish tongue.

"Have you—be honest with me—such things as brigands hereabouts?" asked Mr. Bone.

"Senor," replied mine host, gravely, "we Spaniards have nothing to lose, and when by ourselves brigands have nothing to do. But say that a rich foreigner comes among us, there is a change, perhaps. It may be that a brigand will arise to meet the occasion."

"That is, a man who is ordinarily an honest citizen, at a pinch, becomes a brigand."

"That is so, senor."

"And do you think that has happened now?"

"It may be."

"You do not know?"

"Senor, I am an innkeeper, and have my business to attend to."

Mr. Bone had considerable doubts about the fellow, for he had a shifty eye, but what could he say to him?

There was not the shadow of a proof of his culpability, nor, indeed, that anything serious had happened to the missing boys.

From the host to the gendarmes went the anxious schoolmaster, to learn much the same thing from them.

It was possible that it might have entered into the hearts of some of the people to turn brigands, but they could not tell. Should it be so Mr. Bone would learn by-and-by.

"How?" he asked.

"Senor, the brigand asks for ransom," was the answer.

It was terribly trying, but it had to be borne, and the only thing Mr. Bone could do was to hire half-a-dozen men to scour the country.

On his return to the inn he found Mrs. Grumps had appeared and had learnt that the boys were missing, but, contrary to his expectations, she was not at all ruffled.

"Young Cockles," she said, "have got

William with him, and that dear boy will see him safe out of trouble."

One of the men employed to scour the country was the sour-visaged ostler, who was called Lara.

He was the first to start and absolutely the last to return.

The others brought no tidings of the boys, but Lara set all doubts of their fate at rest.

"Senor," he said to Mr. Bone, to whom he went immediately on his return, "I have been up the hills, and I met a man whom you know—Cararra. He told me of the little senors."

"Yes," replied Mr. Bone, "and what did he tell you?"

"That they were held by his band—"

"Whose band?"

"Cararra's, senor. He is a great man at times. Yesterday a guide—to-day a brigand chief. To-morrow I know not what."

"Go on," said Mr. Bone. "He has taken my boys. I know now. What sum does he ask?"

"Ten thousand pounds a head," Lara replied.

"Nonsense! rubbish!" exclaimed Mr. Bone. "I have not two hundred pounds with me."

"He gives you seven days, senor, to get the money."

"I tell you, man, that it's impossible," replied Mr. Bone; "what does he think we are?"

"He knows you are English," said Lara, "and that you travel, and are therefore rich."

"Can you take a message from me to him?" asked Mr. Bone.

"It is risky," replied Lara, doubtfully, "especially if it is not what Cararra expects. He is passionate and remorseless. He strikes quick and sure."

"You can go, I know," said Mr. Bone. "Tell him this—that I am but a schoolmaster, travelling with pupils, and that I am not rich. One of the boys they have captured is the son of a peasant. He has nothing. The other is a tradesman's son and has little. I will give him twenty pounds if he will send back the boys—no more, because I have it not."

"Twenty pounds!" exclaimed Lara. "Cararra will laugh. He will throw stones at me."

"Go to him as I say," replied Mr. Bone. "I feel sure that nothing will happen to you. You shall be paid for your services."

This interview took place in the presence of the boys and Mrs. Grumps, but as the Spanish language was used, what was said had to be translated to the majority.

Mrs. Grumps was not at all astonished at the brigand's ridiculous demand.

"He knows the vally of my William!" she said. "Bless the boy. He's got the look of sperioty about him."

They could not smile at her, as they would have done at another time, for their hearts were heavy.

Now that they knew the missing ones had been captured by brigands they felt it was a serious business.

The danger lay in the ignorance of the brigand chief.

He had got it into his head that his captives were the sons of enormously rich people, and would probably stick to the idea.

He might also decline to abate the amount demanded for ransom.

In that case what would happen?

Would he begin a series of cruelties such as the boys had read of?

It was terrible to think of. And they all felt so helpless.

Away in this remote part of Spain, without the means of quick communication with their friends, without any real aid from the authorities, it seemed impossible to do anything to save the hapless boys.

All sorts of suggestions were made and abandoned as impracticable.

Handsome Harry volunteered to see the brigand and promise him a large sum if he would give him time to communicate with his father.

"He would give a thousand pounds if I asked him," said Harry.

"But the villain demands twenty thousand," replied Mr. Bone. "Besides, if you went near him he might capture you and demand ten thousand more. No, we are helpless, and it seems to me that nothing but a chapter of accidents will aid us."

"Perhaps they may be able to get away," suggested Young Ching.

Mr. Bone shook his head.

"They are not boys of resource," he said, dolefully.

Lara came back at nightfall with the intelligence that Cararra had threatened to shoot him if ever he dare come near him with such an insulting message again.

"He demands another five thousand for your jest, senor," Lara said, "and gives you a day less to get it in. Cararra will wait the

time he names, and if the ransom is not there he will send another sort of message to you."

Mr. Bone did not ask what class of message this was to be. He understood clearly what it meant.

So did Young Ching and Harry.

It was a distressful evening, and the whole party sat moodily in the room.

Filberts had not spoken a word for an hour, when suddenly he burst out with the startling announcement—

"My ma will pay the money."

"Your mother!" exclaimed Mr. Bone; "why should she do so?"

"Say it's me the brigands have got hold of," said Filberts; "she will do it then—or—or—"

He stopped a moment and looked about him with quivering eyelids and a trembling lip.

"I am a cowardly creature," he went on, "but I don't mind doing the proper thing if I can. Let me go to the brigand and say—' I'm rich, and if you keep me my ma will pay you anything you ask for ransom. She won't mind —it wouldn't be missed.'"

Mr. Bone rose and took him by the hand.

"I heard somebody say a day or two ago that you were a fool. Heaven send us a few more such fools to leaven this wise and heartless world."

"It isn't much," said Filberts; "I've got the money, you know."

"But it would not do," replied Mr. Bone. "It can't be done. Nevertheless, whatever happens, your generous offer will not be forgotten. Now, boys, go to bed and try to forget this trouble in sleep."

After they had said good night to their elders the boys departed.

Harry took the arm of Filberts and walked with him upstairs.

"I always thought you were a good fellow," he said, "but I never dreamed you were a hero."

"Me a hero!" exclaimed Filberts, incredulously.

"Yes, for you have done a thing to-night that would put many men to shame. It made me feel small, I can tell you, for I never so much as thought of it."

"I don't see anything in it," replied Filberts. "You are joking with me."

"Joking! Hear him, boys!" said Harry.

"Oh! yes, hear him," replied Young Ching. "He made me feel small, too. But I forgive him. Here, all of you come in our room and let us have a talk together."

"You talk and I'll listen," said Filberts.

'A hero—me a hero? It's nonsense. When a fellow's got the money and another fellow wants it, or a brigand fellow wants it to give up other fellows, I—"

He stopped short, for they were now in the bedroom occupied by Young Ching and Harry, and the latter gently pushed him into a chair.

"Sit there, Filberts," he said, "and don't try to reason out that which is too great to be reasoned upon. Now, Ching, what is to be done?" •

"I hardly know," was the answer.

"The money that blackguard demands can't be paid, so only one thing remains."

"And that is—"

"To try and rescue them."

"I'm on," said Young Ching. "You and I will go, and we would set off at once if we knew which way to take."

"I can guess it pretty well," replied Harry, "for I saw the beggars going up that path last night, taking the two youngsters like lambs to be slaughtered. We have to find out where that path leads to. It's a moonlight night, and that is in our favour."

"But suppose they get hold of you?" queried Jem.

"That we have to risk," replied Harry. "I don't see anything else to be done. Bone doesn't know what to do. He is a good fellow, but not at all cut out for romantic work, and he has not had the training that makes the adventurer. Ching and I both have the blood of adventurous men in our veins, and when it is stirred within us we have just got to go and do something, if only for the love of the thing."

"That's so," agreed Young Ching. "Now, Jem, you and Filberts go to bed, and bar the door, to prevent anyone coming in to look after us. Harry and I can drop out of the window and get away without any trouble. Don't worry about us—we shall be all right."

CHAPTER XXVI.

THE YOUNG ADVENTURERS ON THE MOUNTAINS —A SENTINEL ON DUTY—THE GATE OF THE CASTLE REACHED.

HARRY had a clear idea of the point to be arrived at, but an inevitable ignorance of the country led him to be careful in choosing his way.

In mountainous districts you may suddenly come across a chasm that will necessitate going miles round to get to the other side.

Travellers, in endeavouring to negotiate a short cut, have often been taken in and done for by these little freaks of nature.

As soon as the boys were clear of the town they bore away to the left, wisely keeping to defined paths so long as they led anywhere near the desired direction.

When about a mile had been traversed Young Ching saw a piece of rope lying in the roadway, evidently dropped by some passing cart.

"This may be useful, Harry," he said, as he picked it up.

"You can never tell," Harry answered.

It was a wonderful night, so far as clearness and quietude were concerned.

The only sounds that broke the stillness were the faint tinklings of the everlasting guitars coming from the town.

Midway in the heavens was a broad-faced full moon, smiling benignantly on all created things.

"I wonder if there is such a thing as a man in the moon!" said Young Ching, looking up at the brilliant orb of night.

"If there is I pity the poor beggar," replied Harry. "I should think it's about twenty times more desolate than the Great Desert. Hark! what is that?"

They both stopped and listened.

High up on the right there were sounds of laughter—faint, but sufficiently defined to be distinguishable.

"That is where we want to get," said Harry.

They went on a little way, and then struck into a path that turned up the mountain.

It was narrow and not too clearly defined, and evidently was not troubled with a superfluity of traffic.

"Now I think we are right," said Young Ching.

One of the towers of the castle of Andulia was peeping over the spur of the mountain, but it was not distinct.

"It looks like it," returned Harry, "and if it is, that's the place to look for our friends."

"Harry, you know I am not funky," said Young Ching, softly, as they walked along briskly, "but suppose they get hold of us, what will be the end of it?"

"Can't say," replied Harry; "but my idea is that the only thought we ought to have about it is the way to get Dick and Billy out of the fix. Never think you can't do it—if you do you are a gone coon."

"I have often wondered if my dear old dad has any sense of danger," observed Young Ching; "and nothing seems to ruffle him except one thing."

"What is that?"

"He can't stand seeing youngsters ill-treated, but fires up at once when anything of that kind is going on, and when he does get excited those who have offended him have to clear out. I was out with him one evening in the country, when we came across a big hulking tramp unmercifully beating a little boy with a stick. Dad uttered a peculiar hiss and went for him. I thought he would have killed the fellow, and he fairly made a rag of him."

"Good old Chingy," murmured Harry.

"Then he told the fellow, who was the father of the boy, that he would look him up shortly if he continued to ill-treat his son, and the fellow believed it. With his lips quivering he vowed he would never lay a hand on him again."

"What did your father do—kick him?"

"Oh! no—he simply rained blows on him. You could not follow them they were so quick. It was a treat."

And Young Ching, overcome by the memory of that festive occasion, stopped to chuckle.

They were now in a position to get a fair view of the castle, and by the direction the path took it was pretty certain that it led up to it.

The sounds of laughter had increased, but soon ceased altogether.

"Very quiet now," said Harry; "they are sure to have a sentry on the watch."

Keeping in the shadow as much as possible the boys crept on. If they exchanged a word it was in the faintest of whispers.

Slowly the castle unfolded itself to their view, and displayed its magnificent proportions against the starry sky.

It had at least half a score of towers of varied dimensions, and a massive gateway flanked by two high walls, in which there was here and there a break, recording the work of time.

The castle was a glorious spectacle lit up by the rays of the moon. It seemed to dominate the country and say—"Behold! I am monarch of all around me."

The young adventurers stopped within two hundred yards of it, in the shadow of an overhanging rock, to survey the imposing structure, and judge how they ought to proceed to gain an entrance into its interior.

Between them and the castle there was a broad patch of moonlight. Anyone watching from the walls could not fail to see them if they attempted to traverse it.

One of the great gates hung upon a single hinge, and so far matters were in their favour, but the dreaded sentinel was there.

He was walking slowly to and fro on the summit of one of the walls referred to.

On his shoulder he carried an old-fashioned musket, and they could see the glitter of some weapon in his sash.

"That fellow would be sure to see us," said Young Ching.

"Yes," replied Harry, "but in an hour the moon will be behind the mountain, and then the castle will be in shadow. We must wait."

It was a long hour, but the young watchers showed no signs of restlessness.

The necessity of keeping still was indisputable, and they stood like statues awaiting the time when they might risk a move.

Slowly the moon went on its course, and at last the shadow of the mountain began to fall upon the open space the boys must traverse to reach the castle.

It crept onward without the movement being actually visible to the eye, until it reached the broken gate.

Up the wall, until the sentinel was in shadow, and only the tops of the towers were illuminated by the silvery light.

"Shall we go forward now?" asked Young Ching.

"Yes," was the answer, "but make no sound."

Harry stooped down and took off his shoes. Young Ching followed his example.

With feet only protected by their socks they started along the stony road.

Slowly the sentry paced to and fro.

Slowly the boys glided on.

Higher rose the silvery light, until only the tops of the towers reflected the rays of the moon.

The sentinel, weary of his vigil, sought to lighten the time by singing a song.

It was reassuring to the boys. He did not so much as suspect their presence.

At the end of one of his walks the sentry paused, and they heard the faint ring of the butt of his musket as he dropped it softly on the flooring of the wall.

Harry and Young Ching glided on inch by inch, not daring to look up, lest their faces should betray them.

The song ceased, and the last gleam of light

died away from the summits of the towers as the young adventurers reached the gate and stopped to exchange a glance of exultation. Speak they dared not.

The sentry paced to and fro. They could hear his footfall upon the battlements of the castle, and for many minutes neither moved.

Discovery meant failure or worse.

If captured by the brigands they might expect little mercy, for any attempt at rescue would only arouse their utmost resentment.

———

CHAPTER XXVII.

WITHIN THE CASTLE—WHERE ARE THE PRISONERS?—A USE FOR A PIECE OF ROPE—WHAT ABOUT RANSOM NOW?

YOUNG CHING felt as if he had a tropical heat around him, so warmly ran his blood in that hour of excitement.

Harry's face was flushed and his eyes glittering.

The inherited love of adventure was deeply stirred within them both.

Inside the gateway was a courtyard, and there, even in the dark, the ruinous work of time was apparent.

Possibly man had had something to do with the shattered walls, but time had done its share.

On one side of the courtyard were the remnants of a chapel, little more than broken walls, but on the other side the ruin was not so pronounced.

The roofs of the buildings remained, and there, if anywhere, the brigands and their captives were to be found.

That they were there neither of the young adventurers for a moment doubted.

The sentry on the wall was an index to the whole position, but it had yet to be discovered where Billy and Dick were confined.

The doors of the buildings in the courtyard were, with one exception, closed and fast.

The boys went carefully round and proved that much. The one exception was a door which had rotted partly away and fallen from its hinges.

They passed through this doorway and found themselves in a covered chamber, but it was too dark for them to thoroughly examine it.

At one end of it they found another door, which opened to the touch, and revealed nothing but the pitchy blackness of a sort of cell.

Harry had some matches with him, and after a look outside he struck one and examined the place.

The cellar was about seven feet wide and ten deep, once a prison without a doubt, for the staples and chains that long ago held some hapless creature fast were still fixed on the walls.

"Close the door," said Harry; "it is a horrible place."

They went back to the entrance of the chamber and sat down, somewhat depressed by the conviction that they could do no more just then.

On the castle walls the sentry was again singing.

"What a melancholy tune!" said Young Ching.

"We should not bother about it if we were not as we are," observed Harry. "I don't see that we can do anything but put up with the singer and watch for what may turn up."

"Will anything turn up to-night?"

"I don't think so."

"Then we stand a good chance of being here until to-morrow!"

"Yes, and all to-morrow, perhaps. It will try us, of course, for we are not likely to get anything to eat or drink. But it is for our chums' sake."

"All right as far as that goes," replied Young Ching; "but what a state they will be in down yonder."

"We cannot relieve them," was all Harry said.

They sat listening and watching, but the dark hours brought nothing to help them.

The castle was so vast that any attempt to explore it was out of the question, especially as the doors they most desired to pass were fast.

Patiently they waited until dawn.

Oh! how long it was in coming, but at last the night slowly melted away and the stars disappeared.

On the mountain tops the light of the blessed sun shed its rays, and in a little while daylight was in the valleys.

The sentry came down from his post, and the boys saw him slowly approaching.

To their astonishment they discovered that it was Cararra himself.

Why he should take sentry duty was not quite clear, unless he had been looking for the return of Lara, with an offer of the payment of the ransom demanded.

He went slowly by in a meditative mood, with a weary and somewhat dejected air.

Young Ching during the night had formed the piece of rope into a sort of lasso, but he had made the running noose in the middle.

A daring idea came into his head.

No other brigands were about. Cararra was alone.

What if they captured him?

There was no time to think of probable results. Capturing him would be going a long way towards the end they desired.

He held up the rope and with half-a-dozen whispered words made Harry understand what he proposed to do.

The answer was only one soft word—"Yes."

It was all conceived and carried out in a brief space of time, so brief that it could be counted by seconds.

With noiseless steps they slipped out, and Young Ching gliding behind the thoughtful Cararra, slipped the noose over his head.

Holding one end he stepped quickly back, and handing Harry the other, they drew it tight.

Cararra dropped his gun and stood for a moment quite still, wondering what it was that enfolded him in its snake-like embrace.

Young Ching gave his end of the rope to his friend, and springing forward took possession of the gun.

"Stir a step or utter a word," he said, "and I will shoot you dead."

He looked as if he meant it, and the brigand, who was at heart a cur, turned livid.

"Go on," said Young Ching, pointing the gun towards their recent retreat. "Go in there—not a word."

Cararra obeyed, licking his lips, which had suddenly become hot and dry.

There was light enough now to see into the interior of the inner cell itself, and there they compelled Cararra to go.

"You will not kill me?" he said, in a whining tone.

"Yes, we will," replied Harry, "unless you do exactly as we tell you. Stand there—cover him, Ching—if he makes a movement shoot him down."

Young Ching kept the musket at the present, pointed directly at the brigand's head, so that he had the opportunity of looking into the barrel if he desired.

But he shifted his eyes about, and looked like what he was—cowed and beaten.

As for the boys, they were strung up to a pitch of excitement that was almost as hard as pain to bear. Harry's hands shook as he put some of the ancient iron shackles about the brigand.

The fastenings were too rusty to act, but by linking the chains together, and tying them with the ends of the rope close behind his back, he made the brigand secure.

"Now," he said, "you are our prisoner, and you must ransom your life—you have five minutes to do it in."

"Alas," groaned Cararra, "I am poor."

"Where are our friends?" demanded Young Ching; "quick, I have my finger on the trigger, and if you are slow in answering I may pull it."

"Your friends," said Cararra, "are in the first cell at the end of the courtyard. The door opens with a spring which I alone have the secret of."

"Tell me how it works!" exclaimed Harry.

"I alone can work it," replied the brigand.

"Shoot him, Ching," said Harry, with a wink behind the brigand's back.

"Stop," cried Cararra, in terror. "I—I— think there is a key in my pocket that will open the door—I—"

"Silence," interposed Harry, as he began to search him.

The key was speedily found.

"Stand by him, Ching," continued Harry, "while I go and see if he has lied. If I am not back in ten minutes shoot him and get back as quick as you can."

"I have made a mistake—stay," groaned Cararra. "It is the second door."

"I thought you were lying," observed Harry, "but you are speaking the truth now. Watch him, Ching."

In a fever of excitement—a great contrast to the coolness he had exhibited during the long watch of the night—Harry darted off, while Young Ching, steadying the musket, took careful aim at the dismayed brigand.

"I am a dead shot," Young Ching said, "so don't so much as move a finger."

"Have a care," groaned the brigand; "the lock is old, and the gun sometimes goes off from the slightest touch of the trigger."

"That is your look out," returned Young Ching, coolly; "you should keep better weapons. Call yourself a brigand, bungling about with an old thing like this."

Young Ching felt bound to talk, he was so elated, and he went on chaffing until he heard the sound of feet outside and somebody sobbing aloud.

CHAPTER XXVIII.

THE RESCUE—RETURN TO THE INN—MRS. GRUMPS KNEW IT WOULD BE SO.

YOUNG CHING was not left long in doubt as to the cause of these tearful demonstrations. They emanated from Dick Cockles and Billy Pink.

The fact is the boys were more upset by their unexpected release than they had been by their capture.

After their first feelings of terror they behaved in the most creditable manner, and were quite composed, externally at least.

Neither had an idea of ever seeing their friends again, and they felt sure that they were doomed to die.

It was a terrible thought, but they rose to the occasion.

"Let us act just as if Young Ching and the others were looking on," said Billy.

"I'll try to," replied Dick, "and if ever my father hears I died like a true Briton he will be proud of me."

With this spirit in them they had passed the night. Then came the appearance of Handsome Harry.

If he had been a supernatural visitor his arrival could not have astonished them more.

"Come along," he said; "there is no time to lose."

Then the reaction set in.

Young Ching went out to meet them and Billy fell upon his neck.

"I never expected to see you again," he sobbed.

"And you won't see me for long if you make that noise," replied Young Ching; "we shall have all the hornets out of their nest to see what is the matter. Harry, go on with them. I'll follow you in a moment."

Harry took each by an arm and hurried them off. Young Ching went back to the depressed Cararra.

"Look here, you blackguard," he said, "I've got orders to kill you. So prepare to be finished off."

Then Cararra began to weep and beg for his life. All he had done was but a jest, he solemnly declared. He was willing to swear it as hard as Young Ching liked.

"Just so," said Young Ching, "and we are going to kill you in jest."

"Mercy," groaned Cararra; "it is not for myself I beg. I haf an aged father dependent on me. Oh! it is so—"

"An aged grandmother," interrupted Young Ching. "Oh! what a cur you are. Call yourself a brigand. Why! you are not even a decent area sneak. I don't know that you are worth shooting."

"I am sure I am not," replied Cararra. "It is a dog I am—a cur."

"Well, I'll just go and hear what my friends say," said Young Ching; "perhaps they will let you off, although mind you I'm not disposed to do it. Don't make that row, and keep quiet until I come back."

"I am dumb—dumb," moaned Cararra.

Young Ching went out, closed the door behind him, and in a few seconds was outside the castle.

A glance down the mountain side showed him his friends making all speed towards the town, although they occasionally looked back to see if he were coming.

Waving his arm for them to go on, he shouldered the brigand's gun and coolly started at an ordinary pace on the track of his friends.

The released boys with their gallant young rescuers were neither pursued nor molested, and the rescue expedition was successful beyond the most sanguine hopes of its originators.

They reached the inn without making any noise, and a handful of small stones thrown at the window brought Jem Stager to it.

He was dressed, and evidently had not been asleep all night.

In one sense the night had not yet passed, for it was barely five o'clock, and nobody else in the inn was stirring.

Jem was quite overcome at the sight of the missing lambs restored to the fold, but he did not burst into tears.

He had no great stock of the "salt drops of sorrow," and did not display them except on very special occasions, to be counted on the fingers of one hand.

Filberts was also awake, and he helped Jem to haul in the returned ones, the bed sheets being used for that purpose.

When they were all in the room congratulations were exchanged, and Filberts wanted to give Billy and Dick all the money he had, but of course they would take none of it.

"We want an hour's sleep," said Harry, "so off with your boots and lie down. At breakfast we can turn up just as if nothing had happened."

An hour later Mr. Bone had risen, in a very unhappy frame of mind. He came quietly to

THE BRIGAND STOOD QUITE STILL, WONDERING WHAT IT WAS THAT ENFOLDED HIM IN ITS SNAKE-LIKE EMBRACE.

the boys' bedrooms and found them all fast asleep.

On seeing Billy and Dick he was a bit staggered, but the fact that none of the boys were undressed, and were simply lying on the outside of the beds, let him to a certain extent into the secret.

"Brave boys," he muttered. "I ought to be proud of them, and I am, but we must have no more of this—homeward we start this day."

He was very thankful, for the rescue of the boys seemed miraculous in his eyes, and he knew that he could not hope for it to be always thus.

Something serious might happen in the end, so he would make the best of his way to England.

He hovered about the outside of the inn until the house was stirring.

Lara was busy in the inn yard washing an old-fashioned carriage, occasionally glancing furtively at the schoolmaster.

The news of the defeat of the brigands' project had not yet reached him.

By-and-by Frisby Whelks came out, looking as if he had suffered from a nightmare for a week right away. He had been dreaming of brigands and the atrocities generally associated with those gentry.

Mr. Bone did not say anything about the rescue of the boys, nor did he even mention them.

Frisby Whelks dare not make any inquiries. He feared the worst.

The host came out to say that breakfast was ready and "milady" waiting.

"Milady" was Mrs. Grumps, and she was seated at the head of the table in an unruffled condition.

The boys had not appeared.

"Whelks," said Mr. Bone, "go and tell them breakfast is ready."

Whelks departed and got his staggerer when he met them coming in a body down the corridor, Billy and Dick leading the way.

He stared at them in a wild-eyed manner, very painful to look upon.

"It is not their ghosts, Whelks," said Harry; "they are real flesh and blood."

"Oh! dear! how did it happen?" asked Whelks. "Have you really been with the brigands?"

"Rather," replied Dick; "but we've got the right sort of friends to see we did not stop with them."

The boys passed on, and Frisby Whelks, with his hand to his brow, fell into the rear. Things all round were getting decidedly too much for him.

Boys captured by brigands one day and back again the next was certainly a phenomenal thing. He never felt more puzzled in his life.

Mrs. Grumps was very glad to see the two boys walk in, but she was not astonished—not she.

"I knew you would be ekal to getting away from 'em," she said. "I once saw a brigand on the stage, and a meaner or more miserable crittur I don't remember."

Mr. Bone received the boys just as if they had never been away, gave them good-morning, and made a remark on the beauty of the day.

This was a bit of a staggerer for the boys, but Mr. Bone liked to have a quiet little joke now and then.

Presently he said—it was when breakfast was nearly over—

"Boys, I am glad to see you all together again, but I may honestly say I hardly hoped for it. A very brave thing has been done, marvellous when your ages are considered"—here he looked at the two heroes of the rescue—"and I am happy to find that in spite of all the nonsense talked about the decadence of our country the old spirit lives still. Look where you may, to whatever part of our United Kingdom—to England, Ireland, Scotland, or Wales—there are daily evidences of the pluck and daring that has ever been the characteristic of our people."

He paused and looked at Frisby Whelks for a moment, as if wondering whether he could include him. All he could do was to take a kindly view of that gentleman's nerves.

"It is useless and unjust," he continued, "to reproach those who are not endowed with physical bravery. A man cannot give himself a stout heart. It must be born in him. But when he has it let him be proud of it. Courage is a gift invaluable. Now, boys, go and pack your things. We start in two hours."

He had learnt enough of Andulia to know that it would be useless to endeavour to punish the author of the outrage. There was very little law and order in the place.

The best thing he could do was to get away and leave Cararra to suffer from the sting of disappointment. He was resolved, however, to stand no nonsense.

When he chose to be resolute the schoolmaster was a very determined man.

So, without saying anything to the boys, he armed himself with two revolvers of six chambers each, which he had been carrying in his bag against possible contingencies.

After breakfast he sent for Lara, who had not seen the boys or heard of their return.

He came with an expectant face into the presence of the schoolmaster, who received him alone.

"Lara," said Mr. Bone, "you have been the go-between of Cararra in this matter."

"To my sorrow, senor," replied Lara, hypocritically.

"I have nothing to do with your sorrow," returned Mr. Bone. "All I desire of you is to take a message to your friend."

"My friend, senor?"

"Yes! I like to say what I think when talking to men of your stamp. Go to Cararra and tell him that I am leaving here, and that if he dares to follow us I shall make it my business to shoot him dead. You understand?"

"I do, senor," said Lara, dismayed, "but pardon—the young gentlemen—who were captured—"

"They have returned," carelessly replied Mr. Bone. "Now get you gone, and see that your message is delivered without delay. You may also take it to yourself. Any nonsense on your part will lead to your prompt punishment."

Lara was utterly dumbfounded—he had not another word to say, but went out of the room with a well-whipped air upon him.

In the passage he paused a moment to try and collect his thoughts.

"Got away," he muttered; "what has Cararra been doing?—the fool—the dolt—but I always said he would make a poor brigand—he is only fit to play at it."

Mr. Bone was busy with maps and papers, making out the route he would take—it was to be the shortest, for he felt that he had been long enough abroad, and it was high time he was back in the old country.

The journey to Lisbon must be abandoned—it would take too long, and probably be very uninteresting.

As for Spain, Mr. Bone had had enough of it, with its dirt and discomfort and treacherous guides.

Back through France would be best, calling on Mrs. Filberts, in Paris, to ease her mind about her son. Letters had been sent to her, but nothing could be so reassuring as the sight of him.

Mr. Bone had taken to Filberts—with all his weakness there was grit in him.

He could never be very brave or very strong, because he had been coddled from his infancy, but he was a thorough good fellow.

Mine host was glad the boys had returned, and the gendarmes of the village also called to offer their congratulations and see what they could get to drink.

All were dismayed at the decision of Mr. Bone to go away at once.

He was assured that Cararra would be captured and hanged, and Mr. Bone smilingly said he would gladly return to view the execution of that malefactor if they sent him word when it was to be.

A great many other people in Andulia were troubled.

They looked upon the arrival of the party of strangers as a harvest which would amply repay gathering in, and now there was to be no harvest at all.

And who was to blame? they asked.

Why, that fool Cararra, and that aged ass Lara.

The aged ass was threatened with the stick when he returned from the castle, whither it was known he was gone.

Failure in this case, as in that of others, had brought contumely on the authors of the scheme.

Success would have made heroes of them.

Thus it will be seen that Spanish life is in this respect very much like it is elsewhere.

Mr. Bone was not to be moved.

At the time he named all was ready for departure.

Lara being away and the landlord sulky he and the boys saddled the mules and brought them to the door.

Frisby Whelks was boots for the nonce, and brought down the luggage.

Around the departing people a considerable throng gathered.

There were a lot of girls in it, and they were very bitter against Cararra.

"But for him," they said, "we might have had English lovers who by-and-by would have married us. We should have been rich and lived happily."

The Spanish boys, however, were jubilant, and made no concealment of their joy.

"The English braggarts are going," they said. "They are afraid of us."

"They are worth a hundred of you," replied the Spanish girls. "Go and strike one if you dare."

This the Spanish whelps did not attempt to do, but they became very bold with their tongues, and used offensive epithets.

Finding no notice was taken of this they grew bolder, and crept up nearer and nearer while the luggage was being strapped on the mules.

At last one of the foremost got near Young Ching, and in the midst of a derisive criticism of the boys generally he received a back-hander that laid him fairly in the dust.

His companions scattered, and the girls screamed with delight.

But the men and women looked gloomy.

"Take no further notice of them, Ching," said Mr. Bone; "they are not worth it."

There was prudence in the counsel, because any mob is dangerous, especially when it feels that it has the upper hand in point of numbers.

The women, however, were on the side of the boys, and the general feminine opinion seemed to be that the representative of young Spain had been rightly floored.

All ready now.

Mrs. Grumps was helped into the saddle, Mr. Bone seeing that she had a quiet mule.

Harry took charge of the pack-mule in addition to riding his own.

The others mounted, Frisby Whelks with the feeling that he was going to a fearful end, and with the usual jingling of bells they rode away, leaving Andulia to mourn its loss and curse the folly of Cararra.

CHAPTER XXIX.

GAY PARIS—POLOWSKI AGAIN—THE AVENGER.

IT was a fortnight later, and the scene Paris. All our friends had arrived there in safety, and for two days had been enjoying themselves thoroughly.

Oscar Filberts had seen his mother, and she had wept tears of joy over him. She also gave him a lot of money.

He was allowed to keep all the tears, but Harry insisted on being banker, and took possession of Oscar's money.

"You literally throw it away," said Harry.

Mr. Bone had secured apartments for them in a street near one of the Boulevards, and it was decided that they should live in true Paris fashion, partaking of their meals at the cafes and only sleeping at home.

It was intended that they should stay one week in the gay city and then go on to old England.

Slapcrash school had been rebuilt. It was quite finished, and all it required now was a little airing, so as to fit it for occupation.

Mrs. Filberts was a very kind woman, and lived only for her son. She took kindly to Mr. Bone, seeing in him just the man her son needed to guide him, and when she proposed that the schoolmaster should take Oscar to England with him, nobody was surprised.

"Of course he is too big for school," Mrs. Filberts said, "but he can live with you, and you can try to make him something more like a man of the world."

"I don't know that I would not rather see him as he is," replied Mr. Bone. "But a little experience won't hurt him. In the quiet old town he will make just the sort of friends he is in need of."

Billy Pink and Dick had been in Paris before, on their way out, but their stay was a short one. Now they were to have a whole week in fairyland.

The weather being fine, the boys virtually lived in the open air. They had their meals just within the cafe, and afterwards came and sat outside while Mr. Bone smoked a cigar.

Mrs. Grumps did not think much of Paris.

"I don't call 'em men, but dancing-masters," she said, in allusion to the lively manners of Frenchmen. "Their legs, eyes, and shoulders are always going."

Frisby Whelks would have enjoyed himself if he had been let alone, but the estimable Mrs. Grumps thought it better to have him constantly under her wing.

The boys could go about as they pleased, like men, but Frisby was treated as a boy.

All his expostulations were met with the same answer.

"You are a poor creature, and must be looked after, so don't talk nonsense, but sit still."

And there he sat outside the cafe by the side of his self-elected guardian hour after hour, while the boys and Mr. Bone wandered about seeing what there was to be seen, enjoying themselves in a delightful way.

One evening the boys had been to look at the Eiffel tower, then on the point of completion, and were returning to their particular cafe to partake of tea prior to going to a theatre, when Young Ching saw a man sauntering on the other side whom he thought he knew.

He was dressed as a French peasant—a

close-cropped, evil-looking fellow, with a stubbly beard upon his face.

"Who is that fellow, Harry?" he asked.

Harry looked in the direction indicated and involuntarily started as he recognised who it was.

"That's Polowski," he said; "he is growing his beard again."

"So it is," returned Young Ching. "I wonder whether he has seen us?"

"I should say not," replied Harry, "and there is nothing strange in his being here. Paris is one of the homes of the conspirator and political assassin."

"Shall we see where he is going?"

"If you like."

"What mean these secret councils?" asked Jem Stager, who was walking behind arm-in-arm with the gratified Filberts, who looked upon Jem as a great authority upon poets, painters, and all things appertaining to the high arts.

Harry told him in a few words, and asked him to see the others back to the cafe.

"We shall not be long," Harry said.

"I think I should let the beggar slide," replied Jem.

"Yes, when he slides into a prison," observed Harry. "A wretch like that is no better than a wild beast let loose upon the people."

There was no time for further discussion, for although Polowski was walking slowly he was getting away, and they must go at once upon his trail or lose him.

So, with a final word to Jem, they crossed the road and followed Polowski.

His movements were those of a man who had come a little too early to an appointment and did not care to hang about one spot.

At least that was the view the boys took of it, for they kept a wary eye on his movements in case he retraced his steps.

It was well they did so, for about a hundred yards further on he suddenly faced about and walked rapidly back.

Quick as lightning the boys slipped under a tree, and the growing shadows of night favoured them.

Polowski went by without so much as casting a glance at where they stood.

The boys were about to renew their work of following when two other men came hurrying up.

Harry instantly recognised both.

"Steinmetch and Kranmitz," he said; "all that remains of that precious band. I say,

Ching, we must find out where they are lodging and bag all together. Come on."

They left their hiding-place and followed the two men, who presently turned into a side street, where the traffic was comparatively quiet.

There they overtook Polowski, who turned round and gave each a hand.

"Welcome, my brethren," he said; "you have kept your tryst."

"The accursed police are so inquisitive," growled Kranmitz. "England would have been safer for us."

"I don't know," said Polowski; "they have a way there of making men like us uncomfortable. But come, my brethren, we must to the place I have provided for you and work. Do not forget that tyrants still live."

The boys, who had come cautiously round the corner and stood within the shadow of a house, saw the trio hurry away, and debated for a moment on the advisability of following them.

"They are going to what we should call the slums at home," Harry said. "A rough lot is to be found there."

"Will they take any notice of us?"

"They might of you—that is what I am thinking of."

Young Ching passed his hand over his head and smiled.

"I suppose I am a little out of the common," he said.

"Ching," observed Harry, "you must leave me to finish this business. Go to the cafe and tell Mr. Bone I shall be back in less than an hour. Now don't argue, there's a dear fellow."

"I think you are right," replied Young Ching, "and I am certain that we need not be anxious about you. I'll back you against half the Frenchmen we have seen here."

Harry waved his hand and darted off.

The trio of conspirators also had disappeared, when with a sigh he wended his way back towards the cafe.

"I'd like to be in it," he muttered, "but Harry is right. I might attract attention."

He found his friends outside the cafe they had used since their arrival.

Tea and sundry eatables had been put upon the table, and they were about to begin.

"Where's Harry?" asked Mr. Bone, who had been apprised by the others that Young Ching and Harry were tracking Polowski.

"He will be here directly, sir," replied Young Ching.

"I shall never know any peace until I get you all safe home," the schoolmaster said. "I think you ought to have left that fellow alone."

"We wanted to find out where he is staying."

"The police would have done that."

"I don't believe in the French police," replied Young Ching.

"Nor do I," replied Mrs. Grumps, " although I've seen none since I've been over here, unless you call them gendarmy chaps police?"

"Yes; they are the French police," replied Mr. Bone.

" Then I pities the people as lets themselves be locked up by sich like," said Mrs. Grumps. 'A more whipper-snappish lot I never set eyes on, and I am sure William is a match for any one of 'em."

Billy Pink tried to look as if he had not heard the compliment, but signally failed.

Slowly a blush overspread his countenance.

"Of course he is," observed Dick Cockles; ' he was a match for one to-day."

"How?" asked Mr. Bone.

"Oh! it doesn't matter, sir," replied Billy.

"Yes it does," replied Mr. Bone; "so tell me how Pink became a match for a gendarme."

Then it came out that early in the morning Billy and Dick were strolling along, arm in arm, deeply engaged in a confab of some sort, when they ran against a meditating gendarme whom they did not see.

He awoke out of his day-dream and boxed Billy's ears, whereupon Billy promptly gave the gendarme a kick on the shins and dropped him.

"He fell all of a heap, sir," said Dick, "with such a clatter as never was, and squalled like several cats."

"What did you do?" asked the schoolmaster.

"Ran away."

"Just as well you did, for if you had been arrested you would have found kicking a gendarme's shins no joke."

"Would they have sent us to prison, sir?" asked Billy, with his eyes bulging slowly out.

"Undoubtedly," replied Mr. Bone.

"Will they do so now, sir?"

"If they catch you."

Billy looked at Dick, who slipped his hand under the table.

A grip was exchanged, and it meant this—

"We will go to prison and even to the scaffold together."

Firm and faithful to each other were they.

Not quite half-an-hour had elapsed when Harry suddenly joined the group.

He came so quietly that no one saw him until he dropped into a chair beside Mr. Bone.

It needed only half a glance to show that something had shaken him up considerably.

Mr. Bone noticed it, but as Harry did not volunteer any information on the subject he made no inquiries.

All Harry wanted was a cup of tea and a biscuit.

"You boys may walk up and down a bit," said Mr. Bone, "but don't go far away. Ching, if you are tired you may remain."

Young Ching did not say he was tired, but implied he was by keeping his seat.

Mrs. Grumps thought she would like to promenade with the boys.

"Give me an arm, Mister Whelks," she said, "and see if you can bear yourself like a man for once."

If Mrs. Grumps had known what was in Mr. Bone's heart she could not have done better. By her taking it into her head to promenade she left him with only the two boys, whom he wished to speak to.

"Now, Harry," he said, "you have discovered something. What is it?"

"I have to-night either seen a dead man returned to life or his ghost," replied Harry.

"Who was it?"

"Otto Lurgan—one of the band," said Harry.

"The one who was your friend?"

"He certainly befriended me, for without him I should not be here now."

"But you saw him dead," interposed Young Ching.

"Yes," returned Harry, "but he could not have been dead, for I have seen him to-night. I left him but a little while ago."

"Did you speak to him?" asked Mr. Bone.

"No, for I had no opportunity. I traced the three of whom Ching has told you—"

" He has not," replied Mr. Bone.

"I will tell you now, then. Polowski, Steimetch, and Kranmitz are in Paris. We followed them for awhile and then I took up the trail alone, tracing them to a low street in the St. Antoine quarter."

"You were wrong to go there."

"Having got so far I did not care to turn back. Nobody took any notice of me."

"But they might have done so, and in that case you stood a very good chance of being robbed and murdered."

"Well, Mr. Bone, I have come out of it all right. I traced them to a house where the door stood, open. They entered and I was about to follow—"

"Harry!"

"Only a little way in, sir, and after all I did not enter, so no harm has been done. I was about to do so when I saw a man cross the street and draw towards me. I at once popped into the next doorway to find out what he was going to do. The light of a lamp fell upon his face and I saw it was Otto Lurgan."

"You may have made a mistake."

"His features are stamped upon my memory, and he was not changed, save that he looked more like an avenging spirit than a man."

"That is it," said Mr. Bone, dropping his hand somewhat heavily on the table. "He is an avenging spirit. Do you remember that ghastly affair in the ravine near Basle, but it is a foolish question—of course you do. It was the hand of Otto Lurgan that hurled that bomb. He may be on a similar errand of vengeance to-night. Did he enter the house?"

"He did, with a step so quiet that I could not hear it, and that left my mind in doubt as to whether it was a man or a spirit I had seen. I could not remain, for a sudden terror seized me. I felt as if I must go, and something like 'Get away—get away,' sounded quite distinctly in my ears. Hark! what is that?"

Some men were coming down the Boulevard, talking loudly and gesticulating violently. Everybody they passed stopped to listen and some followed.

Mr. Bone caught the import of what they were saying. Roughly translated it may be read as follows—

"An explosion first—then a fire—supposed to be making bombs—three dead and one dying—police there—great discoveries—if the fire is got out—"

"Harry," said Mr. Bone, "show me the way you went. I think we shall see the end of the Black Bandits to-night—three dead and one dying—that means the avenger has suffered also. Ching, I leave you guardian of the rest."

"Hang it," muttered Young Ching, "I would rather have gone, but of course somebody must be left to look after the children."

Mr. Bone and Harry slipped away unobserved, the latter leading.

With a perfect recollection of the route he had come home by, Harry never faltered or halted to look about him.

Once out of the bright Boulevards there was but a poor light to guide them, until in turning a corner they came in sight of the famous quarter of St. Antoine.

There, indeed, all was bright, but not from the usual street illumination. It arose from a fire that was raging in one of the narrow streets.

"That's about the spot," said Harry.

"I am right then," muttered Mr. Bone. "Otto, the avenger, has completed his work. I do not like assassination in any form, but if ever it was justified it is in this case."

Two turnings more brought them in sight of the fire.

It was a double conflagration, with a gap between, and what that gap had been a heap of fallen bricks and timber in the middle of the road explained.

The house which the conspirators entered had been blown down.

A crowd had gathered, but it was kept moving by the gendarmes, who used very little ceremony. They pushed first and the word to pass on followed.

Near the fire groups of people were eagerly discussing the nature of the disaster, and Mr. Bone listened to the conversation of two excited Frenchmen, who seemed to know all about it.

"It was sure to be so," observed one; "so much that is dangerous in the hands of inexperience. Fulminating powder and dynamite are not things to play with."

"No," replied the other. "They were making bombs for the tyrants, and the bombs have proved tyrants to them."

CHAPTER XXX.

THE AUTHOR OF THE DEED—HIS CONFESSION—LAST HOURS IN PARIS—HOMEWARD BOUND.

MR. BONE was satisfied save on one point. Who was the man yet alive, and where was he lying?

A few inquiries cleared up this matter, and with a guide he was soon on the way to a hospital kept by some good nuns, who had devoted their lives to the sacred duty of relieving the sufferings of others.

Harry accompanied him, and together they entered what appeared to be a private house. but was in reality a well-known hospital.

There a nun received them, and in answer to Mr. Bone's inquiries, ushered them into the room of the Lady Superior.

From her they could obtain no clue to the name of the wounded man, but the description she gave of him answered for Otto Lurgan.

Nobody could be allowed to see him. He was insensible, and under the care of two doctors.

Two gendarmes watched beside him, and their orders were to permit no strangers to come near him.

There was nothing to be surprised at in this.

The nature of the catastrophe had alarmed the authorities, and it was only their duty to act as they had done.

"Whether it was an accident or not," said Mr. Bone, as they left the hospital, "will never, perhaps, be arrived at, but we who know so much concerning the band of miserable fanatics may form our own conclusions, and they will not be far wrong."

On their return they found those they had left behind in a state of suppressed excitement.

Mrs. Grumps was seated near one of the tables, holding Frisby Whelks by the collar, to the overpowering amazement of several of her French neighbours, and Filberts sat on the other side of her, under parole not to move without special permission.

Ranged in front of her were three boys— Jem Stager, with a dry expression of face, being seated between Dick and Billy. Young Ching stood by looking serenely on.

It seemed that the absence of Mr. Bone and his companion had been discovered almost immediately after their departure, and Mrs. Grumps had got it into her head that kidnappers of the brigand type were abroad.

She therefore ordered the rest to keep within sight, and sat down to spend the time in watching the passers-by until the missing ones escaped and returned.

"As I knew you would do, sir," she said to Mr. Bone, when she had explained matters, "and right glad am I to think that you have overcome the villains."

"I assure you, Mrs. Grumps," M. Bone replied, "that we have been in no danger. We have not been captured by anybody."

"Oh! you may tell me that," she observed, "but I knows the ways of all of you, and you are not likely to make a song of being captured by foreign thieves. How I hates the sight of 'em, with their shruggings and moustachers."

As she was not to be moved from the ground she had taken up, they wisely let her have her way, and Mr. Bone, after having had some coffee, despatched everybody but himself to bed.

"He's going to have a bit of a spree," said Jem Stager, bitterly.

"Not he," replied Harry. "He's not such a fool as to squander his money on the gimcrack fun of Paris."

Mr. Bone was bent on more serious business, and that night did not go to bed until very late.

Nobody heard him come in, but his weary air at breakfast betrayed that he had been keeping late hours.

And presently he said—

"Boys, I saw the last of the Black Bandits die at three o'clock this morning. It was Otto Lurgan, who had been nearly murdered at Namedi Castle by his old friends, but survived to be society's avenger on these remorseless men.

"It was not until his life was given up by the doctor," he continued, "that my patient wait at the hospital was rewarded. I told my story—our story—to the Lady Superior, and she transmitted it to the doctor and gendarmes in charge, so I was allowed to see him after all. He was sensible when I was admitted, but I did not recognise him, not having set eyes on the man before.

"He spoke English pretty well, and addressed me by my name. 'I am glad you are here. It is right you should be,' he said; 'for you can tell the boys that I have been your friend.'

"'I can believe that,' I replied.

"'They left me for dead at the castle,' he went on, 'but I was only nearly so. Despite my wounds I managed to recover consciousness after they had tossed me into the dry moat. I crawled down to a cottage where there was on old peasant woman, to whom you had been very kind, and she nursed me until I was well again 'for the sake of the handsome boy,' she said."

Harry could not help feeling that he was alluded to, simply because it was he who had given the old woman the money.

"So you see," said Mr. Bone, in continuation, "a little deed of kindness is like sowing seed. It is sure to grow into some after benefit for those who are the authors of it.

"Otto Lurgan set himself a double task—to

protect us and to destroy the would-be destroyers of society. Wherever we went there was he—hovering about us as a protector, and as Polowski also haunted us with another object, his dual task was comparatively easy.

"That he saved the lives of many or all of us is not to be denied, and although there was no positive danger to us in this place, it is possible that by his daring he has saved us from peril even here. Had Polowski seen us he would not have rested until he had satiated his malevolence by doing us some injury.

"Lurgan had lost sight of him for some days, and it was while watching over us that he saw him again and tracked him to his lair, where he was making preparations for one of his attempts upon the lives of those whose sole offence was that they were better off than himself.

"I need not preach to you on the folly and the madness of these men. They work nobody's destruction so surely as their own.

"Nor do I defend Otto Lurgan in all he has done. His way of punishing the conspirators was very un-English, but he acted according to the light within him, and not without a certain amount of heroism.

"He resolved that he and his old fellow-conspirators should die together.

"Boldly he went into the room where they were at work, and deliberately brought about the explosion which wrecked the house. A tap with the hammer on some loose fulminating powder lying on the table did it, and all but himself were killed outright.

"We have now done with these men and their pitiful story. The Black Bandits in a measure have marred the pleasure of our trip, but the evil they would have done has been frustrated, and all our lives have been spared. Let us think of that in a spirit of thankfulness."

Mr. Bone ceased speaking, and the boys, who had listened to him gravely enough, were silent for awhile.

It was Young Ching who first spoke.

"Perhaps it is a good thing we did not know all," he said, "or we might not have been quite so jolly as we were."

"In faith, no," muttered Jem Stager, "but it is an old story—vice faileth and virtue is triumphant. I think I will one day write a play about it."

"And a pretty mess you will make of it," muttered Dick Cockles, just loud enough for him to hear.

Jem felt in his pocket for something he had

there. In a moment or two he fished out an eye-glass, and after an effort succeeded in getting it fixed in his eye.

Through the dirt encrusted upon it he regarded Dick with quiet scorn.

But he said nothing.

The look he gave Dick, in his opinion, sufficed.

Despite the element of tragedy in the news they had heard, all the boys felt a sense of relief, for there was not one who had not thought occasionally of the Black Bandits, and always with a sense of insecurity.

Otto Lurgan had done good service, but for all that they felt, as Mr. Bone did, that he was not exactly a hero of the British pattern. Still, they did not judge him.

He had died with his old associates and there they left the matter.

There we must also leave it and go on with our story, now drawing to a close.

Letters arrived that day for all.

There was quite a bundle of them obtained from the post-office.

Young Ching had some, dictated by his father, which afforded him a vast amount of pleasure, and there were passages in them that set him roaring with laughter.

It may be taken as a fact that a certain old man named Eddard, whose lot in life was not altogether a happy one, had something to do with his merriment.

Billy Pink was jubilant. There was a letter from his mother and sisters, and messages from his father.

Billy read a lot about his old friends the geese. In a general way they were thriving, although a great number were deceased, having died violent deaths and been sent to market in due course.

All his friends were well, although his father was "failing a bit in his hearing," which is an infirmity all rustics getting into years look forward to.

One of his sisters was going to be married to a thriving young dealer, who was proud of being engaged to the sister of the "celebrated traveller, Billy Pink."

Dick's letters were quite a little library.

Not only had his father written one like a short three-volume novel, but his mother had penned another, that was as long as the deed of Magna Charta.

Likewise had his brothers and sisters indited epistles of varied length, according their several abilities.

They were all of a comforting natur

Business was looking up. Two of the small ones had had the measles, but got right again wonderfully quick, and all the rest were as well as well could be.

Harry and Jem Stager also received letters, and throughout the whole of the communications there ran a note of "welcome home," like a thread of gold woven into a garment.

It seemed to the boys as they read their letters that they were too distant from those they loved.

While far away they thought nothing of distance, but now that they were within a few hours of the old country they began to long to be there.

The letters killed all the pleasure that Paris could give them, and they did not want any more of it.

"Can we go home to-night, sir?" asked Billy, unconsciously acting the part of spokesman.

"No," was the reply, with a smile, "but we will take the early train in the morning, and if all is well we shall get home by about tea-time. I will wire to your friends."

This he did, and then the home-sickness abated a little, but not much.

In the afternoon answering wires came back from all, even Billy's friends, and when he tried to picture his father sending off a telegraphic message he utterly failed to do so.

The fact is, Billy's father being, as many of our readers know, a simple rustic, he had never taken kindly to the telegraph wire.

It was too quick for him, and just a wee bit uncanny. He had often been heard to say that evil would come to England for taking up with it.

And now here he was wiring to his son across the sea.

"*Coming to London with mother to meet you.*"

That was another great thing. And Billy had to think a lot before he could get at the bottom of it.

"I know what's o'clock," he cried at last. "Ching, your father is going to pay for everything."

"What matters who pays?" replied Young Ching.

"I wouldn't be a Frenchman for anything," said Billy, a little later on. "Fancy having to stop here all our lives."

Billy said this aloud as he and Dick were walking up and down, arm-in-arm.

A Frenchman heard them and stopped.

"Ah! you poor leetle Englese boy," he said. "You know not Paris or you would not talk so. It is de moder of nations. Queen of all things."

"That I'm sure she isn't," replied Dick Cockles, shortly. "She isn't Queen of England, and never will be."

"Ah! you not understand," observed the Frenchman, shrugging his shoulders; "it is not zat sort of queen I speak of. No. Paris is—"

"Oh! Paris be bothered," interrupted Dick; "go away."

"You Englese haf no manners," returned the Frenchman.

"We've got manners enough not to talk to people we don't know," replied Dick, "'specially when we feel he ain't wanted. If you don't go away we'll knock your hat off, won't we, Billy?"

"In a minute," was the ready response.

The Frenchman, who was a very small man, flushed and drew himself up.

He had something very withering or threatening on his lips, but it was checked by Harry, who, seeing what was the matter, sauntered up.

"Anything wrong?" he asked, quietly.

"This Frenchy keeps bothering us," replied Dick; "he says Paris is the grandmother of England."

"I say noting of ze sort," yelled the Frenchman. "You pity us zat vant no pity. I merely say zat you vas—Vell, I forget vat. But it is enough. I say no more. Good of ze day to you."

He did not quite like the look of Harry, and so brought the interview to a close.

As he swung himself round with a sarcastic bow he bounced against Filberts, who had also arrived on the scene.

Oscar had long sighed for an opportunity to distinguish himself.

It offered itself now, and with a promptitude that staggered the Frenchman, Filberts hit out with a circular motion, and struck him on the crown of his hat.

Down it came over his eyes, and a push from Harry shot him in a doorway.

There they left him struggling for freedom, and breathing vengeance against all things British.

"Come away, you young buccaneers," said Harry, as he took Dick and Billy each by an arm and hurried them round a corner.

"Surely you don't want to be locked up and left behind!"

"No," said Billy; "shall we run?"

"We need not do that," replied Harry, "but we will go indoors until that Froggy has got out of his hat and gone away."

CHAPTER XXXI.

HOME AGAIN!

HOME again! How sweet it is after travel to be able to look upon our native land once more.

The boys had seen many strange things and gone through wonderful adventures, but their eyes had never been more gladdened than they were by the sight of the cliffs of Old England.

They landed at Dover, Frisby Whelks and Oscar Filberts having taken the sea-sickness of the whole party upon themselves during the passage.

Mrs. Grumps did not suffer, but she sat on deck very grim and silent during the short journey across the Channel.

On landing she said—"Now I feels as if I was really clear o' them furriners," at the same time heaving a deep sigh of inexpressible relief.

There was no rest until they got home. They were expected at Cannon-street about five o'clock, and they knew there would be lots of friends to meet them.

Harry's father would be there, Ching Ching, Sammy, Bill Grunt, and others.

Dick Cockles was expecting his father, and Billy Pink also expected his.

What a meeting it would be!

"Ching," said Harry, "I am glad to get home again, but I feel one thing."

"What is that?" asked Young Ching.

"That I shall not rest there."

"That is something like what I feel," observed Young Ching, musingly. "Our two fathers had a good fling, and when we are old enough I hope we shall have the same one day."

"I have an idea of suggesting something," said Harry; "but I won't do it now."

"How fresh and beautiful everything looks in the old country!" Jem Stager observed.

"There is nothing like it, boys," replied Mr. Bone. "Go where you will you cannot match it."

Frisby Whelks was of the same opinion, but on other grounds.

He felt safer on English soil than anywhere.

In due time the train rattled into the station, and before one of the boys could pop their heads out the door opened and Ching Ching appeared.

"Welcome, my sunny heir," he cried, and folded the precious lad in his arms.

"Harry, my boy, I'm glad to see you," rang out the rich voice of *the* Handsome Harry.

"Dick—come to your father."

"Billy, how you've growed."

"Jem, travel has improved you."

Such were the greetings of the several parents, and then Bill and Sammy and two or three other friends came forward. What a hand-shaking there was.

Eddard was not there, or the enthusiasm and joy of the hour would have melted him.

"Dinner waiting in the hotel," was the word passed.

All were ready for it, and the luggage having been put in the cloak-room, they were escorted to one of the private rooms in the hotel.

Pink senior and Mr. Cockles were a little out of their element, but they buckled to in the most wonderful manner, and ate a dinner of seven courses as if they had been used to it every day of their lives!

There was quite a little babel of voices, so much was there to talk about.

Wine passed round—the younger boys drinking it with water, and the elders taking just enough to make them merry.

All the boys were going to their friends for a week, and then the Slapcrashers would journey to the newly-built school.

Billy Pink had a fine prospect before him—that of petrifying the stay-at-homes of his native village.

What yarns he would tell, if he could only think of them.

Jem Stager had his select circle to stagger, and meanwhile he edified his father, who was with the party, with anecdotes of the Black Bandits of the Rhine.

Mr. Stager was a sharp business man, who knew something of the world, but he was duly impressed, and Jem was satisfied.

After dinner a lot of friends dropped in, and the men smoked and chatted until nine o'clock.

Then came the breaking up.

Once more hands met, kind greetings were exchanged, and cabs were called.

Frisby Whelks went down to Smockley with Mr. Bone and Mrs. Grumps, and Oscar Filberts stayed in town with Young Ching.

Harry and his father departed for their country home.

Billy Pink took train for his native place, and all went their several ways.

The boys being no longer abroad we must leave them. By-and-by we may find them all together again.

THE END.